READER'S DIGEST
SELECT EDITIONS

READER'S DIGEST
SELECT EDITIONS

The condensations in this volume
are published with the consent of the authors
and the publishers © 2008 Reader's Digest.

www.readersdigest.co.uk

The Reader's Digest Association Limited
11 Westferry Circus Canary Wharf London E14 4HE

Printed in Germany
ISBN 978 0 276 44290 2

**SELECTED AND CONDENSED
BY READER'S DIGEST**

THE READER'S DIGEST ASSOCIATION LIMITED, LONDON

CONTENTS

W hat would you do if a stranger walked up to you in a bar and told you all the details of a murder? That's what happens to Tim Wallace, the hero of this brand-new thriller from the USA. When the man's story turns out to be true, Tim is put in a no-win situation. He's already a suspect in his wife's death but the police are now convinced he's a killer. Tension mounts as he tries to prove his innocence, and it's guaranteed you won't be able to put the book down until the very last page.

A n Irish village in the 1960s: an idyllic place in which to train as a fledgling GP, especially under the wing of larger-than-life Dr Fingal O'Reilly, who offers wise advice for every problem—medical or otherwise—and a bottle of whiskey just to help things along. Barry Laverty, the young GP introduced to SE readers in *An Irish Country Doctor*, returns in further adventures involving Dr O'Reilly, his housekeeper, Mrs Kincaid, and all the colourful folk of Ballybucklebo.

Patrick Taylor

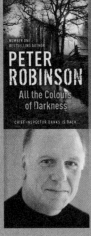

ALL THE COLOURS OF DARKNESS

PETER ROBINSON

291

Peter Robinson is now very definitely one of Britain's crime-writing elite. Part of the reason is his engaging detective, Alan Banks, star of *In a Dry Season* and *The Summer That Never Was*. And DI Banks is back, this time to investigate two deaths that occur on the same day in Eastvale, North Yorkshire: a body hanging in a bluebell wood, and a vicious attack at a wealthy man's mansion. Establishing a connection will take Banks into the shadowy, ruthless world of the secret services.

Tom Hanks is planning a film of this remarkable, true story of a high-flying advertising executive whose life was transformed when he became a barista. Fifty-three-year-old Michael Gates Gill lost his prestigious job, his marriage and his health. At rock bottom, he dropped into his local Starbucks for a coffee. They happened to be hiring, and a woman called Crystal encouraged Gill to join. To his amazement, he found a happiness and fulfilment in his new life that he had never felt in twenty-five years at the top.

HOW STARBUCKS SAVED MY LIFE

MICHAEL GATES GILL

461

DON'T TELL A SOUL

DAVID ROSENFELT

Innocence can be a hard thing to prove,
when you're guilty.
And, just occasionally, much harder to
prove, even when you're innocent.
As Tim Wallace is about to discover . . .

PROLOGUE

Friends have asked me why I'm telling this story, and for a long time I had no intention of doing so. For one thing, it has already been told so many times. Television has covered it endlessly, newspapers and magazines have made it a staple on their covers, and the inexhaustible blogosphere has grown exhausted in the rehashing.

Everyone remembers where they were the day it all went down. It is seared into the public consciousness, and nothing I write can change that. Nor would I want it to. But I have something new to tell, information that citizens can perhaps benefit from hearing. I was there; I had a front-row seat.

After having told my story for months to every imaginable branch of the federal government, they have mysteriously insisted that I maintain a public silence. This I will not do. I will tell it as it happened, and I hope the picture I paint will be as unbiased as possible. It will be daunting for me, or painful, or cathartic, or a great relief. Probably all of the above.

So why am I telling the story? I guess I just feel you should know the truth.

ONE

'It's the little things that change your life, Timothy Wallace.'

Whenever Tim Wallace's mother, Carol, had something important to tell him, she ended it with 'Timothy Wallace'. She always called him Tim, but when she was imparting some special wisdom it was 'Timothy', as if his formal name would lend it some additional credibility and significance.

She was a small woman, but she would put on her most solemn face and stare at him; the sadness in her eyes would make Tim want to look away.

'The little things can change your life, Timothy Wallace.'

What she was really talking about was fate, and how fate was dictated by moments you could neither expect nor control. She followed it with the story he had heard so many times. If her friend Donna hadn't taken a bus downtown that day, Donna wouldn't have met Charlie, the man she eventually married. Then Charlie could never have fixed Carol up with Kenny Wallace. And Carol and Kenny would never have had their son, Tim. And Kenny couldn't have abandoned them when Tim was only six months old.

So Donna's deciding to take the bus that day was the 'little thing' that changed Carol's life for the worse, but in turn literally gave life to Tim.

That was what was strange about the 'little things' that changed your life. They could be good or bad, and sometimes you didn't know right away.

For Tim, and especially for Maggie, the 'little thing' was the hat.

IT WAS AN IMPORTANT, even symbolic, moment for both of them.

Tim and Maggie had been married for almost five months, and while Tim had sworn 'for better or for worse, in sickness and in health', that hadn't as yet included his boat. His pride and joy. His sanctuary.

He had owned the modest thirty-foot motorboat for six years, having bought it for himself on his twenty-fourth birthday. It was his place to decompress, to read, to be alone, to think, to get away from whatever might be bothering him, or to focus and reflect on what was good.

Tim's close friends, Danny and Will, had been out on the boat with him a few times, but never a woman. Not even Maggie. Not until that day.

The fact that this milestone didn't happen for the first four months after their marriage was more a function of the calendar than anything else. It isn't until early May that things start warming up on Long Island Sound, which is where Tim kept the boat. He was waiting for a decent day, and while the weather forecast for this one wasn't perfect, it would have to do.

'Why don't you keep it docked down there?' Maggie had asked on more than one occasion, pointing down at the Hudson River from the window of their twenty-third-floor apartment in Fort Lee, New Jersey.

Fort Lee wraps round the New Jersey side of the George Washington

Bridge, and its real estate is wildly valued for its proximity to, and view of, New York City. Tim and Maggie lived in Sunset Towers, as prestigious an address as Fort Lee possesses, and used that vantage point to make full use of the theatre, restaurants and energy that New York provided.

They were just leaving their apartment when Maggie unveiled the hat. He assumed it was a hat, because it was sitting on her head, but it looked like a manhole cover on steroids, with a brim so large that the 3rd Infantry could find shade under it.

'What the hell is that?' he asked, when she put it on. He knew that sounded a little harsh, so he added, 'Honey.'

'My new hat,' she said, turning slightly to show it off in its full glory. 'They only had one left.'

'So other people beat you to that?'

She nodded. 'Isn't it great?'

'And your plan is to carry that round on your head all day?'

'I'm sensing that you don't like it.'

'No, I like it,' he said, smiling. 'It's just that it's among the ugliest things I've ever seen.'

She nodded. 'That's good: I was afraid you'd want to borrow it.'

The drive out to the pier, with no traffic, was about forty-five minutes. Of course, there had never yet been a day in New York without traffic, and on this particular day it took an hour and fifteen minutes. During the ride in Tim's convertible, he suggested Maggie hold the hat in her lap. Were it to blow out into the open road, he opined, it could take out a tractor trailer.

So Maggie's hair blew in the wind, and she was characteristically unconcerned about it. Maggie had dark, curly hair, and in Tim's view it would look good even if she put her head through a car wash. In fact, he always thought she looked best when she got out of the shower, when her hair was wet and unbrushed. Of course, she was also naked then, which may have helped.

Halfway into the ride, Maggie reached out, took his hand and squeezed it. 'Did you tell Danny and Will you were taking me on the boat today?'

He shook his head. 'No, I didn't tell anyone. I figured I'd surprise people after the fact.'

Once they arrived at the pier, Maggie was so anxious to see the boat that she kept walking ahead of Tim. There were hundreds of boats lined up, moored perpendicular to the pier, and she had no idea which one it was.

She therefore had to keep waiting for him to catch up, and since he was carrying lunch and other supplies, he wasn't moving that quickly.

But when she happened upon it, she recognised it instantly. He hadn't told her that he had renamed the boat *The Magster*, his nickname for her.

She stood there, in her extraordinary hat, staring at the inscription on the hull. Finally, still looking at the name and not Tim, she said, 'You think I'm going to cry? Well, I'm not. I love it, and I love you, but I'm not going to cry.'

'I wouldn't expect you to,' he said. Maggie had a thing about crying; she wanted to save it for the 'really important stuff'. Which was fine with him.

As soon as they got on the boat, Maggie made it clear that she wasn't there as a passenger. She wanted to know how it all worked, and insisted on doing everything from starting the motor to steering out into the Sound. She seemed to relish the entire experience, and even called out, 'Ahoy!' to a nearby boat as they navigated out on the water.

After the first hour they just relaxed out there, drifting with the motor off, and reading the Sunday *New York Times*. Not long after, the wind started to pick up, and Tim knew there was a chance the day would have to be cut short. He suggested they have lunch, and Maggie got up to prepare it.

Tim was the type that could happily eat his dinner standing next to the refrigerator, but to Maggie each meal was an event. It always amazed him; he had a constant struggle with his weight, stuffing 180 pounds onto his five-foot-eleven frame, while the five-foot-seven Maggie wouldn't weigh 120 pounds if she were carrying a barbell.

Within five minutes the small table was set with a dazzling array of dishes, each in its own special serving piece. No plastic containers for Maggie. She had even brought champagne to toast the substantial federal contract that Tim's construction company had recently won.

She looked at the table with satisfaction. 'What do you think?'

'I think it should be enough,' Tim said. 'Actually, if a navy destroyer floats by, we can invite the crew to lunch.'

'What about them?' Maggie asked, pointing to a large boat about 500 yards away. She waved in their direction, but there didn't seem to be anyone out on deck. Tim had seen it periodically during the morning. It was a boat he was familiar with, a ninety-foot Oceanfast 360, retail price close to $2.5 million. He had a dream of owning a boat like that, albeit not painted an ugly green with a white stripe, as this one was.

'Anybody who'd paint a boat like that such an ugly colour doesn't deserve lunch,' he said. 'Besides, they're rich enough to buy their own. Let's eat.'

Eat they did, and after Tim had consumed enough food to sink *The Magster* from his weight, Maggie asked, 'You want some dessert?'

'I can't,' he said. 'I do not have a single cubic inch of internal space left.'

'That's a shame. I made crème brûlée.'

'Unless I use my emergency space,' he allowed. 'That's always an option.'

She nodded her understanding. 'If this isn't an emergency, what is?'

Maggie got up and walked over to the cooler to get the dessert, but as she leaned over, a gust of wind blew the hat off her head and over the side.

'Damn!' she yelled, as she just missed catching it.

'Don't worry,' Tim said, looking at the huge hat floating on the water. 'A freighter will find it and tow it back to shore. All we can do is wish it well.'

'Tim, it's right over there.' She pointed to the hat, which was already almost thirty yards away.

He tried to put on his most incredulous look. 'You mean you want me to go out there . . . to get that ridiculous hat?'

'Of course I do. Come on, Tim, it's drifting away.'

'Maggie . . .' he said, wondering how he was going to get out of this. He looked up at the gathering clouds for inspiration. 'It's going to rain soon.'

She nodded. 'Don't worry, you'll be wet from getting the hat anyway.' Then she came in with the clincher. 'I'll give you my undying love.'

He muttered, 'I thought I already had that.' This was not a battle he was going to win, so he walked over to start the engine. The hat was moving away from them, taunting him, and he would at least pull the boat as close as he could before jumping in. The water was getting slightly choppy.

Tim restarted the engine, and was not happy that it made a strange noise. He made a mental note to get it checked once they got back to the pier. He pulled the boat about ten yards from the hat, and prepared to go in to get it.

'Put on your life jacket,' Maggie said.

'What for? I can swim like a fish.'

'Tim, please put it on.'

He sighed, and put on the bright orange jacket, fastening it under her watchful eye. He jumped into the water, which sent a cold chill through him, and swam with powerful strokes towards the hat, already several yards further away. In the distance Tim could see the Oceanfast 360, and hoped that the people on board did not see him. This hat retrieval was embarrassing, and not his finest moment on the high seas.

When Tim finally reached the hat, he put it on his head and turned back towards the boat so Maggie could see him wearing it. 'What do you think?'

Maggie wasn't looking at him; she was standing near the side of the boat, looking at the motor. 'Tim,' she called out, 'I think there's something . . . Tim, there's something wrong with the motor!'

'TURN IT OFF!' he yelled. 'TURN IT OFF!'

'It's smoking!'

'MAGGIE! TURN—'

The next thing he saw was a flash of white, so quick it barely registered. And then nothing.

TWO

*I*t went west.

That was the entire message that was in the handwritten note slipped to Roger Blair in the prison mess hall during dinner. He was seated at a long table, twelve seats on each side, and he looked around at the other inmates seated with him. No one seemed to be interested, which was not surprising. In this place, it took all available energy to worry about yourself.

It went west. That's all it said, but Roger needed no further explanation. He realised immediately that it meant something had gone terribly wrong. It also meant something else that Roger understood very well.

He was going to die.

It was the kind of death sentence against which there was no appeal. There was nowhere to go for help, no stay of execution that could be granted. Going to the prison authorities would, if anything, hasten his demise.

The only remaining questions were when and how. Roger hoped it would be soon; days spent waiting to die were days not really worth living. The 'how' was almost certain to be a sharp blade in the back, or across his neck, or maybe a garrotte. Whatever technique was chosen, it would be different from the state's; there would be no lethal injection, no offered 'last meal'.

For the rest of the day he looked around warily, waiting for them to make their move, even though he was not sure he wanted to see them coming. For the first time in a long while, Roger thought about his wife, and felt the urge to talk to her. But she had stopped coming to see him a while back, and his attempts to find her had turned up nothing. With the end approaching, he wasn't feeling resentful towards her; he just wanted to say goodbye.

Nothing happened the entire afternoon, which was not a great surprise. These things were better done in darkness. As always, lights went out at ten o'clock, leaving Roger lying on his bed, alone and awake. He listened for an approach, but it was not forthcoming, and he drifted off to sleep.

The cell was seven by ten, and at this hour was completely dark. Roger did not know what time it was when he heard the cell door rattle slightly. The lock kept him in, but he harboured no illusions that it could keep them out.

Within moments Roger could sense that his executioner was inside. 'Took you long enough,' he said.

If the intruder was surprised, his voice did not betray it. 'It's time.'

'Yeah,' Roger said. There was no fight in his voice, nor was there any resistance planned. They would keep coming at him. Might as well get it over with now. 'You even know why you're doing this?' he asked.

He heard a slight laugh of surprise. 'Yeah. For money.'

There was a click and a small beam of light appeared out of the intruder's hand. Roger could still not see his face, and he didn't want to.

'I don't mean that,' Roger said. 'I mean—'

The blade swept across his neck, ending his sentence and his life.

A life that had long ago gone west.

FROM THE MOMENT he heard the facts, Detective Jonathon Novack realised exactly what he had. It was a cold-blooded murder, and he knew who'd done it. He knew it in his gut, and he could count the times his gut was wrong on very few fingers.

There is a bunch of things that homicide cops in urban areas do not have, at least not in Novack's experience. They don't have long weekends off, they don't have secure, happy marriages, and they don't have coincidences in their work. And in this instance, for Novack's gut to be wrong, this would have to be the mother of all coincidences.

Novack had long ago learned to strip away all the bullshit and focus on the facts, and in this case the facts were clear. Tim Wallace had taken his wife, Maggie, out on his boat, a boat he had been out on, without incident, at least a hundred times. While drifting on Long Island Sound, he turned on the motor, and decided to swim to retrieve a hat his wife had lost overboard. At that very moment, the motor blew up, obliterating the boat and his wife.

Quite a coincidence.

And a slam-dunk, no-doubt murder if ever there was one.

Except it didn't turn out quite that way, and if there was ever a more frustrating case, Novack couldn't remember it.

The coastguard had been on the scene of the explosion within minutes, and they found Wallace floating, held up by his life jacket, in a state of what the doctors called convulsive shock. That lasted ten days, long enough to miss his wife's funeral, or more accurately her service, since the body was never recovered. When he finally regained full consciousness and coherency, he claimed not to remember anything after seeing the flash of white.

Unfortunately, experts determined that the blast could conceivably have been an accident, based on a defect in a similar motor that caused an explosion a week earlier off the coast of Florida.

That was followed by a surprising willingness on the part of Wallace to take a lie-detector test, and his just as surprising refusal to hire a lawyer. He passed the test with flying colours, and while that is not admissible in court, it certainly had an effect on both Novack's boss and the district attorney.

And Novack could find no evidence of problems in the marriage. They had met eighteen months before, had had a whirlwind courtship, and no one would say anything other than that they seemed completely in love.

The media jumped on the case, immediately joining Novack in the suspicion, almost the certainty, that Wallace had engineered his wife's death. But as day one became month one, the pundits ran out of unsubstantiated charges, and there were no revelations to add any fuel to the fire.

The simple fact was that Novack had uncovered nothing. And while his gut didn't require any evidence, his bosses, the courts and every other part of the justice system did. It was enough to make him nauseous.

But not enough to make him stop. This case would never get cold, not in Novack's mind. He would work on it whenever he could, probing it from every angle, until he put away the son of a bitch who literally blew his young wife out of the water.

DECEMBER 31 held no special significance for Tim Wallace. It was simply another day to be in pain over the loss of Maggie, a sorrow that was not about to be affected by the fact that it happened to be New Year's Eve.

The aching had not lessened in the months since that awful day out on the water. And if truth be told, Tim didn't really want it to lessen. Maggie was dead, blown to bits while he went swimming for a hat, and the knowledge of that was supposed to hurt. He wanted it to hurt.

He also wanted to work; work represented an impersonal world, a place he could be without feeling Maggie's constant presence, or, more accurately, lack of presence. And here he caught a break: Wallace Industries, the small construction company that he had begun six years prior, was thriving, and they had more work than they could handle.

Soon after 9/11, Tim was among the first to predict a boom in security construction. Many buildings, especially those owned by the government, were in need of reinforcement and specially constructed concrete perimeters. They simply had not been built in the expectation that they would someday be bombed, or that a plane might be flown into them.

Tim was shrewd enough to declare his company to be expert in this area, and it did not take long for him to start receiving very healthy contracts. The federal government had money to spend, and Wallace Industries was one of the places they spent it. The company was nearly finished with its part of a massive complex in downtown Newark, called the Federal Center, a project costing in excess of $3 billion. It would be a model of its type, with each building possessing state-of-the-art security, and was planned as the forerunner for similar projects countrywide. They were virtually federal cities within cities, it being easier to provide security for one large complex than for buildings spread out in different locations.

Almost two years ago, Tim had brought in Danny McCabe as his partner. They had met when first starting out at a large construction company, and had become firm friends. Danny was hard-working and talented, a problem-solver in a business that had round-the-clock problems. He also brought a crucial contact to the company: his uncle, Fred Collinsworth, senior United States senator from New Jersey, and the ranking member on the Senate Appropriations Committee. Uncle Fred had proved invaluable in steering federal work to his nephew's company, most notably the Newark project.

Granting the project to Wallace Industries was not strictly nepotism.

Many smaller construction companies were given substantial contracts, a move that earned the senator the enmity of the Franklin Group, a huge multinational corporation that was used to getting these kinds of gigantic government contracts, and its chairman, Byron Carthon.

But Collinsworth was unconcerned with the Franklin Group. He knew that when the contracts were granted to many smaller companies for similar Federal Center complexes around the country, he would immediately have a huge base of political and financial support, a situation that could help propel a politician, if he were ambitious, to the highest of national offices. And Collinsworth was nothing if not ambitious.

Danny and Tim's other very close friend, Will Clampett, worked for them as an independent contractor handling the computer issues so vital to modern construction. Danny and Will frequently attempted to draw Tim back into the social world. They felt it would be better for him to get out more, take his mind off things, even if he had no interest in dating.

Tim's efficient thirty-one-year-old assistant, Meredith Tunney, shared this feeling and joined in the gentle persuading, but Tim remained firm. He would not do anything until he was ready, and 'ready' seemed light-years away.

Meredith had been a godsend for Tim and the company. Hired just two months before Maggie's death, she had kept Tim's life in order ever since, paying his bills, making all his appointments and reservations. This enabled him to keep his life only on the brink of chaos, without crossing the line.

Danny, Will and Meredith were all plainly worried that New Year's Eve would be a particularly difficult night for Tim, despite his protestations that he'd be fine. Meredith spent the day with him in his Englewood office, wondering how she could broach the subject of his plans for the evening. She was going out with friends, and by three thirty in the afternoon she wanted to take off to get ready, so she took a deep breath and plunged ahead.

He was at his desk doing some paperwork when she walked in and said, 'So, Tim, what have you got going on for tonight?'

He didn't even look up. 'A couple of parties, then into the city to watch the New Year ball drop at midnight, then probably clubbing until morning.'

She frowned. 'Come on, really. You're not going out?'

He finally looked up. 'No, this year I think I'm going to go in,' he said. 'Everybody else will be "out", so I'll have "in" all to myself. Pizza, half pepperoni, and a DVD of *Godfather I* and *II*.'

She shook her head sadly and looked at her watch. 'Well, I've gotta go get ready; anything you need before I leave?'

'Can you track Danny down? I need to talk to him.'

'He went home an hour ago, Tim.' Then, pointedly, 'It's New Year's Eve; he has plans. Plans that I'm sure he would love to include you in.'

Meredith got nowhere with that and left, while Tim spent a couple more hours doing work. He stopped for a take-out pizza on his way home.

His apartment felt as barren and unwelcome as always, except for the soothing presence of Kiley, his golden retriever. It was obvious that Kiley missed Maggie terribly, but she seemed to try to compensate by providing comfort for Tim.

Danny and Will had suggested repeatedly that Tim move out of this apartment, as a way of putting the memories behind him. He hadn't done, partially out of a vague feeling that it would be disrespectful to Maggie, as if he were moving on without her. He realised that he was living in the past, but the past seemed a hell of a lot better than the present. As far as the future . . . well, he didn't want to go there . . .

Kiley and Tim shared the pizza, though she only liked the crusts. There was very little on television, so he followed his original plan and popped in the *Godfather* DVD. On his large plasma screen, it looked at least as good as it had ever looked in any cinema.

At close to nine o'clock, as Tim was making his nightly decision as to whether to fall asleep on the couch or trudge into the bedroom, the doorbell rang. Kiley looked at him from her vantage point on the recliner chair, as puzzled and annoyed by the intrusion as he was.

'This can't be good,' he said, and she seemed to nod in agreement.

Tim opened the door, and Danny and Will came barging in.

'Happy goddamn New Year,' said Danny. 'Let's go.'

'Go where?' he asked, though he knew exactly where they meant.

'Oh, I don't know . . .' Will said, 'maybe the same place we go every New Year's Eve. Duuuuuhhhh.'

Will and Danny were demonstrating the feigned upbeat attitude they had maintained around Tim since shortly after Maggie's death. They were fully aware that their friend was in agony, and instinctively felt that if they were in an obvious good mood around Tim, it would brighten him up as well. The fact that it hadn't worked for all these months somehow never led them to a conclusion that their strategy was ineffective. It simply hadn't worked yet.

Tim knew that Will was talking about a bar in nearby Teaneck called the Purple Rose. It was a comfortable place, and they never considered going anywhere else. But Tim had not been back to the Rose since Maggie died, and had no plans to change that any time soon.

'It's not going to happen, guys,' he said.

'Tim, here's the deal,' Danny said. 'You're my partner and my friend, and even though you're a complete pain in the ass, I love you. But tonight you walk into the Rose under your own power, or you get carried in under ours.'

'Try and understand this,' Tim said. 'I don't want to go. It doesn't feel right, not yet, and I don't want to do it.'

Danny nodded. 'We know that, Tim. And we know how hard it is. But you're not getting there on your own, so tonight we're giving you a push.'

'Guys, I appreciate this, OK? You think it will make me feel better, but it won't. It really won't.'

Will had nudged himself into the recliner chair with Kiley, and was petting her head. 'Maybe you're right,' he said. 'And if you're miserable, you bail out. Besides, everybody will be so drunk they won't know you're there.'

'And the French fries,' Danny added. 'Remember the French fries?'

The Purple Rose had the world's greatest French fries, thin and crisp. 'I remember,' Tim said. 'And someday in the future I will have them again.'

'Tonight,' said Danny. 'Tonight is the night.'

'Tim,' Will said, 'it's time to put it out there. Maggie would want you to do this. She would want you to go out and have some fun.'

Tim would ordinarily have rejected that out of hand, but for some reason, this time he thought about it. He knew that what Will said was true: Maggie would want him to go out with the guys. So maybe now was the time . . .

He finally nodded. 'OK . . . you're right. I'll go.'

Danny put his arm on Tim's shoulder. 'This is great. And by the way, since this is your coming-out party . . . you're buying.'

THE PURPLE ROSE apparently never got the memo that everything had changed since Maggie's death.

At least, that's the way it struck Tim. He found it somehow jarring that the place was the same as always: sawdust on the floor, wooden tables carved with every possible initial, a wood-burning fireplace in the centre, vintage Wurlitzer jukebox and at least thirty televisions, usually showing sports. Of course, on New Year's Eve the televisions were tuned to the Times Square festivities, and on a human-per-square-foot basis the place was every bit as crowded as the streets on which the famous ball would drop.

Tim, Danny and Will had their own reserved table, in deference to their years as loyal patrons. They ordered food and beer; then Danny and Will headed off to try their luck with the countless single women milling about.

Tim was at the table for less than a minute when he realised that he simply was not ready for this. Feeling angry with himself for giving in, he sat and watched everyone else celebrate having made it through another year.

Danny and Will occasionally came by to check on him, and he told them without enthusiasm that he was fine. He looked at his watch repeatedly. There was just a half-hour till midnight, but it was going to feel like for ever.

'Hi. Happy New Year.'

Tim looked up and saw an attractive woman standing right in front of him, a pleasant smile revealing perhaps the whitest teeth Tim had ever seen.

'Mind if I sit down?' she asked, but did so without waiting for an answer.

'Which one of them sent you over?' he asked.

She smiled again, and pointed back into the crowd. 'The drunk one in the blue shirt; I think his name is Danny. He said you needed cheering up.'

'Trust me, it's not a job you want to tackle.'

'What's wrong?' she asked with apparent sincerity.

'I'm sorry. I've never been one for opening up to strangers in bars.'

'I'm not a stranger,' she pointed out, holding out her hand. 'I'm Janice.'

Tim shook her hand. 'Hello, Janice. I'm Tim.'

'Nice to meet you, Tim. So will you tell me what's wrong?'

'My wife died,' Tim said, and immediately regretted it.

'Oh God, I'm sorry,' Janice said. 'That must be so hard for you.'

'It was harder on her.' Tim stood up. 'Excuse me for a second, will you?'

He left the table and headed towards the back of the bar. He wasn't sure where he was going; he just had a need to get away from Janice and her sincerity and her white teeth.

There was a phone booth back near the rest rooms, and Tim got in it and closed the door. He leaned his head forward, against the phone, and took deep breaths to try to get control of himself. He felt like he was losing it.

Tim had no idea how long he was in there, though he didn't hear anyone outside yelling 'Happy New Year!' yet. Slowly he got himself together. The phone booth seemed to have a soothing effect on him.

'You making a call?'

He looked up and saw a heavyset guy with his face pressed close to the glass, fogging it with his breath, signalling his desire to use the phone. Tim opened the door and let the intruder take his place. Then he headed back into the main room. Will was standing near the bar, his left arm round a woman and his right arm round a beer.

Tim made his way over to him. 'I'm going to take off, Will.'

Will looked at his watch. 'It's five to. Just give it ten minutes, OK? Start the New Year with friends.'

Tim felt wiped out, too much so even to argue. 'OK. I'll be at the bar.'

He found a place at the end of the bar to wait out the time, alone in a room full of people. Unfortunately, this solitude lasted less than a minute before a man came over to him. He was probably forty, tall and good-looking, with one of those square jaws that projected authority. He wore a suit, with his tie loosened at the neck, as if he had just got off from work and stopped by for a drink. Except in this case it was many drinks, because the man was clearly very drunk. As he held out his hand to say hello, Tim thought that if he didn't take it the man could conceivably fall over.

'Hey, how's it goin'? Name's Jeff. Jeff Cashman.'

Tim made his response as unenthusiastic as possible. 'Tim,' he said.

Cashman was in no condition to detect subtlety. 'Good to meet ya, Timmy. Happy goddamn New Year.'

'You too.'

Tim hoped that Cashman would move on to meet other new friends, but instead he leaned in towards Tim. 'You a good guy?'

Tim looked up at the closest television as if he couldn't hear him. They seemed to be ready to drop the ball on the freezing Times Square crowd. Unfortunately, when Tim looked back, Cashman was still there.

'Hey, Timmy,' he said again, 'you a good guy?'

Tim nodded with resignation. 'Yeah.'

'Can you keep a secret? A really big one?'

'No . . . I think you should tell someone else.'

'No, I wanna tell you. I wanna tell someone this year.' He looked at his watch, exaggeratedly. 'So I gotta hurry.'

'Look, Jeff, I'm not the guy you—'

Cashman interrupted him. 'You know where Kinnelon is?'

When Tim didn't answer, he took it as a sign that he couldn't be heard over the din. He shouted, 'Kinnelon! You know where it is?'

Tim was well aware that Kinnelon was a town in northwest Jersey, about thirty miles from where they were standing. 'Yes, but—'

'I murdered somebody there. A girl called Sheila . . . three months ago.'

'That's not funny,' Tim said.

Cashman nodded. 'No, it's not funny,' he said. Then he paused. 'Well, it's sorta funny. Before I killed her, I cut off her middle finger. Then I buried her behind the swing set at this little park they have on Maple Avenue.'

Cashman had finally accomplished what no one else had been able to. He had cut through Tim's funk. 'What the hell's the matter with you?' he asked.

All Cashman did was laugh. 'Nothing. Not any more. I actually feel much better now. Now it's your problem.'

Suddenly the entire place was counting down, and the televisions confirmed that the glittering ball was descending. 'TEN . . . NINE . . . EIGHT . . . SEVEN . . . SIX . . . FIVE . . . FOUR . . . THREE . . . TWO . . . ONE . . . HAPPY NEW YEAR!' Everybody in the place started screaming and hugging and kissing each other. Everybody except Cashman and Tim.

Cashman finally got up to leave. He put his finger to his mouth. 'This is our secret, OK, Timmy?' he asked. 'Don't tell a soul.'

He laughed again as he walked away, but it was a silent laugh, drowned out by the noise of all the normal people having fun.

'TRUST ME, I freaked him out . . . totally freaked him out,' said the man who twenty minutes before had pretended to be Jeff Cashman.

His employer for the evening laughed. 'But he believed you?'

'Damn straight. You should have seen his face.'

'I wish I had. Was he scared? Or annoyed?'

They stood talking at a rest stop near exit 156 on the Garden State Parkway. 'Cashman' could see there was someone in the passenger seat of the employer's car. It looked like a woman, but in the dark it was hard to tell for sure. Other than that they were alone, because at that hour, with the temperature just 15°F, nobody else seemed inclined to stop to rest.

Cashman wrapped his arms round himself to ward off the cold. 'Scared . . .

freaked out. I don't know what you have planned for him, but this part worked.'

'That's great. Nice work.'

'Yeah. So if you'll give me my money . . .'

'In the trunk.'

'What do you mean? Cash? You could have given me a cheque.'

'Sorry, I'm not being clear,' the employer said, seemingly amused by the misunderstanding. 'There is no money. I want you to get in the trunk. Now.'

'What are you talking about?' Cashman asked.

The man's voice took on a harder edge. 'That time I was clear, but you're being difficult. I want you to get in the trunk.'

'Come on, what's going on here?' asked Cashman, unable to keep the fear from creeping into his voice. 'Quit joking around.'

'In the time you've known me, have I ever joked around?' Not waiting for an answer, he continued, in a matter-of-fact tone of voice, 'Now, I want to kill you while you're in the trunk. Otherwise I have to do it out here, and then lift you in. That shouldn't be so hard for you to understand.'

'Cashman' panicked and turned to run. He made it about a foot and a half before a powerful hand grabbed him from behind.

The last thing he heard was the snapping of his own neck.

ONCE THE BODY was wrapped in plastic and put in the trunk, the man took out his cellphone. He would have preferred to make the call from the warmth of the car, but he didn't want the woman to hear what he had to say.

He dialled the number he had been given, fully aware that the man who answered could at that moment be anywhere in the world.

'Talk to me,' was how the phone was answered.

'Our friend did what he was supposed to do. The message has been delivered.'

'Good. And where is our friend now?'

'We won't be hearing from him again.'

'You are as good as advertised. Maintain your high standard.'

Click.

The man put away his cellphone and smiled to himself. It wouldn't be long before he too was rich enough to be anywhere in the world, doing anything he wanted. Not long at all.

IF THE NIGHT OUT was meant to ease Tim's entry back into the world, it didn't quite go according to plan. It was a completely uncomfortable experience, capped off by an encounter with a raving lunatic. At least, Tim hoped he was a raving lunatic, because the alternative was that he was a brutal killer. He didn't look like a killer, but then Tim had never actually met one.

Tim had turned his phone ringer off when he got home, and in the morning he saw the message light flashing. He showered, dressed and had breakfast before reluctantly pressing the button.

It was Will, saying, 'Hey, Tim, I hope last night wasn't too painful. Danny and I are going down to the Rose to watch the Bowl games. How 'bout meeting us down there? Just beer, burgers and football, I promise.'

Spending New Year's Day watching the games was another tradition that Danny, Will and Tim observed religiously, and Maggie had been there last year as well. But Tim had no desire to go back to the Purple Rose, at least not this decade. If he was going to watch any football, it would be at home.

Tim took a few minutes to Google the terms 'Sheila', 'murder', 'missing person' and 'Kinnelon' in various combinations, and came up empty. This was probably more reassuring to him than it should have been; like many other people, Tim had come to believe that if something wasn't on Google it didn't exist. Having performed that cursory investigation, he turned off the computer, put Kiley in the car and drove to the dog park.

Dog parks, a creative invention of the late twentieth century, are large enclosed areas in which dogs run and play together, off leash. Their owners stand off to the side and talk primarily about their dogs. Occasionally tennis balls are thrown, creating a frenzy. Maggie and Tim used to come here every Sunday, and it was one of the few things they did together that he continued. It just didn't seem fair to deprive Kiley of enjoyment and exercise.

When Maggie was there, she did most of the socialising with the other humans, and Tim became the designated tennis-ball-thrower. There were a few people he spoke to regularly, one of whom was Eden Alexander, a woman two years younger than him.

As always, Eden was there when Tim and Kiley arrived. She wore a Mets cap with a blonde ponytail pushing through the opening in the back, and greeted them with her ever-present smile. Tim had a tendency to think that people who were relentlessly upbeat were probably not all that bright, but Maggie told him once that Eden had a Ph.D. in art history from Stanford.

Kiley's tail started wagging the moment she saw Eden's German shepherd, Travis—a certain indicator of affection. Human smiles and apparent warmth can be insincere, but Kiley's tail-wag could be taken to the bank.

When Eden saw Tim, she separated from the group of women she was standing with. 'What are you doing here?' she asked. 'Isn't this New Year's, male, sit on the couch, drink beer and watch football day?'

He snapped his fingers. 'Damn, I completely forgot.'

She laughed. 'There might be hope for you yet.'

Eden had been helpful to Tim in the weeks after Maggie's death. She came by his apartment occasionally, just to say hello and ask if he needed anything. He was almost obsessive in not letting friends help in any way, yet he'd let Eden take Kiley to the park a few times. She was there without being intrusive, and Tim quickly learned that was a talent not to be taken lightly.

Since Tim had been coming to the dog park without Maggie, he hadn't felt particularly comfortable. He was aware that his reluctance to socialise came off as more aloof and unfriendly without Maggie's amiability as cover.

'Really cold today, huh?' he asked.

Eden did a double take. 'Wait a minute. Was that . . . was that chitchat?'

'I'm making conversation. It's a New Year's resolution.'

'No, that wasn't conversation,' she said. 'That was chitchat. And since I've never heard you chitchat before, there must be something going on.'

'Nothing's going on.'

She didn't believe him. 'Come on, you can talk to Auntie Eden.'

For some reason, he did feel able to talk to her. 'Something weird happened last night,' he said. 'Actually, a step beyond weird.'

'You mean besides my date?'

'I went to the Purple Rose with some friends . . .'

She nodded her approval. 'Good. Did you have fun?'

He shook his head. 'Not even a little . . . but I didn't expect to. What was a surprise happened just before midnight. Some guy I never met before told me he committed a murder three months ago.'

'Oh my God!' she said loudly, and a few of the women looked over. Eden smiled at them and lowered her voice. 'Just like that?'

Tim nodded. 'Just like that. He asked if I could keep a secret, then told me about it. Like he was getting it off his chest and onto mine.'

'Was he drunk?' she asked.

'Very.'

'Then maybe it was the alcohol talking.'

'I hope so.'

'Did he tell you who the victim was?'

'He said her name was Sheila, and that he killed her in Kinnelon. I'll spare you the gruesome details.'

Eden thought about it for a few moments. This was not an area in which she had any expertise. 'You think he could have been telling the truth?'

Tim shrugged. 'I doubt it, but obviously I can't be sure. I Googled it, but didn't find anything.'

'Are you going to go to the police?' she asked. 'Just in case?'

'I don't know; it's probably just a drunk in a bar spouting bullshit. I was thinking I could check a little more on my own. Maybe drive out there.'

'Today?'

'I guess so. I haven't really thought it through.'

She seemed dubious. 'You're going to go try and dig up a body?'

'You think I'm nuts?' he asked.

She smiled. 'Pretty much; just be careful. Hey, why don't you leave Kiley with me? She'll have a great time with Travis.'

It was a good idea, and Tim accepted the offer. They arranged to meet back at the dog park at four o'clock; then Tim went looking for a body.

THREE

Kinnelon is an affluent residential community in the most rustic part of New Jersey. Particularly beautiful in winter, it borders the state's ski resorts. As a teenager, Tim used to ski at Great Gorge, twenty minutes down the road. He figured he'd just drive along Maple Avenue looking for a park with a swing set, and maybe a headstone that said HERE LIES SHEILA. MURDERED BY CASHMAN. That was pretty much the extent of his plan.

The route took him through the centre of Kinnelon, which was very quiet because of the holiday. He saw two cars parked in front of the small town hall, and decided to park there, though he expected it to be closed.

He was surprised to find the front door open. A woman in her mid-seventies was sitting at the general information desk.

Tim walked over to her. 'Hello,' he said. 'Happy New Year.'

She nodded slightly.

'I was wondering,' Tim continued, 'if you had any information on missing persons in this area within the last six months, actually in Kinnelon itself.'

She looked at him as if he were insane. 'We don't keep records like that here, young man. That would be a police matter.'

'Of course. I understand that. I'm not asking for official information, but are *you* aware of a young woman who might be missing, or a recent murder?'

She huffed, as though he had insulted her. 'I should say not.'

Tim smiled pleasantly and left, actually feeling that even while being rebuffed he had learned something. He got back in his car and drove slowly along Maple Avenue. After only about four blocks, he saw the park.

It took up a full block. Tim drove round it to the side where the swings were set up. The entire park was snow-covered, and it was cold enough that the snow barely showed indentations when he stepped on it.

There were five kids, bundled up in ski jackets, playing on the swing set. Four women stood nearby, talking to each other while casting wary glances at Tim. He smiled and gave them a little wave. They neither smiled nor waved back. When Tim walked behind the swing set, the women all walked closer in a protective, synchronised manoeuvre.

'I dropped something around here,' he said lamely.

Actually, there was no need for him to be there at all. He was hardly going to take a pick and shovel out of his car and dig up the whole area.

He stared at the ground for a minute or so, then got in his car and headed home, thankful that no one he knew had witnessed his investigation.

When he reached the dog park, Eden was waiting for him. 'So?' she asked. 'Was there a murder or wasn't there?'

Tim proceeded to tell her the events of the day.

'So what do your instincts tell you?' she asked, after he had finished.

'That a drunken asshole sent me on a wild-goose chase.'

'You don't think you should at least tell the police?'

He knew he should do that, but didn't want to. 'If I thought there really was a Sheila . . . but there's no evidence that Cashman was telling the truth.'

'Except that there is a park with a swing set on Maple Avenue in Kinnelon.'

She was right, of course. While Cashman's identifying a real place proved nothing, it did add at least something to his credibility.

Tim felt a need to defend his reluctance to bring the story to the police. 'My recent experience with law enforcement was not the most pleasant.'

Eden knew at least some of his dealings with the police after Maggie's death, and their clear suspicion of him, so she didn't press the issue. 'You'll make the right decision,' she said, then smiled. 'Or maybe you won't.'

LEAVING FOR WORK in the morning, Tim was only five feet from the front door when he saw it, stapled eye-level to a telephone pole. It was a missing-persons flier, with a picture of a young woman, identified as Sheila Blair. It said that she had been missing for three months, and was last seen in the Kinnelon area. Anyone with information was to contact the state police.

It had to be Cashman's Sheila, Tim knew. There are no coincidences that enormous. He took down the flier and put it in his briefcase.

Danny had beaten him in to work, and Tim brought him up to date on his weird conversation with Cashman, and his fruitless trip out to Kinnelon.

'So you think it was bullshit?' Danny asked.

'I did until this morning. Then I found this.' Tim took out the flier. 'It was tacked to a telephone pole in front of my apartment.'

'That's her?' Danny asked.

'It sure fits. He didn't give me her last name, but the first name, and the time, and Kinnelon . . . How could it not be her?'

'You've got to talk to the cops about this,' Danny said.

Tim nodded. 'I know; I'm dreading it.'

'It doesn't have to be Novack. There are other cops in the world.'

'Yeah,' Tim said. Danny knew all about Novack, the cop with the relentless certainty that Tim was Maggie's murderer. In the months since, Novack had called occasionally, to ask about some innocuous detail of that awful day. It was his way of telling Tim that he was still on the case.

'You want me to go with you?' Danny asked.

Tim shook his head. 'No . . . I'm just going to go and get it over with.'

He decided to avoid any chance of dealing with Novack by going to the local Fort Lee police precinct, a nondescript building in the centre of town.

Tim approached the desk sergeant and told him that he had information about a possible murder. He was immediately whisked in to see Detective

Joanie Patrick, an attractive, petite woman of about thirty. Tim told her the story pretty much as he had told it to Eden and Danny, concluding with the flier. She was quiet and mostly expressionless throughout, though Tim detected a lip curl of disapproval when he mentioned going out to Kinnelon.

When he finished, she asked, 'Could you identify Jeff Cashman if you saw him again?'

He nodded. 'Definitely.'

'But you never met him before?'

'If I did, I certainly don't remember it.'

'Your wife never mentioned him?'

The question was like a punch in the gut. She knew who Tim was, and she was already considering the possibility that this new situation was somehow related to Maggie's death.

'No, my wife never mentioned him,' Tim said coldly. 'Are we finished?'

Detective Patrick let him go after finding out how to reach him if she had further questions.

'What are you going to do about this?' Tim asked.

'We'll contact you if we need you,' she said dismissively.

She was clearly not going to tell him anything, and the truth was that Tim didn't really want to hear about it anyway. He had done what he was supposed to do. He had told the authorities about it, and now it was their problem. Cashman had got it off his chest, and now Tim had as well.

THE VAN was a three-year-old Chevy Caravan, chosen because it looked exactly like tens of thousands of others on the road every day.

The drive up from Florida had so far taken three days. Ricardo Vasquez had been instructed not to exceed sixty-five miles per hour, and to obey every traffic law to the letter. On the New Jersey Turnpike, sixty-five seemed like walking. Ricardo stayed in the right-hand lane and watched the world whiz by him. That's OK, he thought. He would take the money he'd get for this trip and buy a Porsche, and then they could eat his dust.

Until then he would be very careful. Only Lucia had any idea where he was, and she wasn't smart enough to know what he was doing. She wouldn't tell anybody anyway; she knew what he would do to her if she did.

Ricardo had been on the road since seven o'clock, and hadn't had breakfast before he left. As it was approaching eleven, he was starving. Until now, he had followed his instructions—to get all his meals at fast-food places along the highway and eat them in the car—but he was getting sick of it. He wasn't looking for anything fancy, just some blueberry pancakes, with sides of bacon and hash browns. He got off the highway near a town called Cedar Grove, and within five minutes he had found a perfect place.

Ricardo didn't bother to look around when he got out of the van. Even if he had, he would not have noticed the grey MPV that had been following him since he entered New Jersey. Ricardo did not know about it, just as he didn't know about the GPS transponder on the bottom of the Chevy, which made following at a safe distance easy.

Ricardo did make sure that the van was locked before going inside. This seemed like a sleepy little town, but he imagined its citizens would wake up pretty quickly if they learned that there were barrels of illegal drugs worth many millions of dollars sitting outside Grandma Patty's Pancake House.

Patty proved to be a disappointment. The portions were large, but tasteless and greasy. The blueberries were not even mixed in the pancakes, as he liked them, but dumped on top. Ricardo would have complained, but he was not about to draw attention to himself. He even left a tip.

Annoyed that he had wasted time, Ricardo got back in the van and pulled out onto the road. He did so quickly, without really looking, without seeing the teenage boy stepping onto the pedestrian crossing with his five-year-old brother.

He felt the thud before he realised what had happened, and watched in horror as the little boy was thrown off the fender onto the verge. The teenager seemed unhurt. He ran to his brother, lying dazed in the grass.

Ricardo had only a moment to decide what to do. To stop and get out was to invite disaster. To take off was his only chance. Even if someone had witnessed the accident, it would be OK. The van had fake Florida plates, and he would just steal new ones at the next rest stop.

Within a minute of making the decision, it was obvious that it was not turning out well. He heard the siren before he saw the police car in his rearview mirror. The van was not about to outrun it, especially in its loaded-down condition, but Ricardo was sure he was a better driver than any small-town cop. He did not head back for the turnpike; that would draw in the state police and choppers. Instead he wanted to make it through the town and out onto the back roads.

He was nearing eighty miles an hour when he reached into the glove compartment and took out the .44 Magnum. The siren seemed to be getting louder; then Ricardo realised that an additional police car was coming at him from a different direction. They were closing on him in a sort of pincer movement. Ricardo flew down the streets, his senses keenly tuned.

Suddenly, as the cars were closing in, he saw his chance. It was a narrow alley, and his pursuers didn't have the advantageous angle that he did. Ricardo hit the brakes and took the turn on two wheels. Smiling at the realisation that the only people in a position to appreciate the manoeuvre were the cops left behind by it, Ricardo headed back towards the turnpike.

The first bullet ripped through the base of his neck and severed his spinal column. He was dead by the time the second bullet tore through the back of the van. The resulting explosion was powerful enough to level half a city block, and blow out windows in a paper factory three blocks away.

The real plan, of which Ricardo had been unaware, was that he wouldn't make it to New York alive anyway; the chase merely hastened his demise by less than an hour. And, as was clear from the size of the explosion, what he was carrying in the van wasn't drugs at all.

FOR JONATHON NOVACK, the phone call was the best Christmas present he had ever had. It was too soon to know how Tim Wallace's trip to the Fort Lee police fitted into his wife's murder, but it had to be connected. And somehow Novack was going to use it to nail Tim's ass to the wall.

Novack was at his ex-wife's house in Fair Lawn when he got the call from Detective Patrick. Cindy had divorced him three years ago, but in some bizarre way the divorce hadn't taken. Even though Novack had moved out, he still came round every chance he could.

Cindy had initially viewed this as a significant problem. For one thing, potential suitors were less likely to visit knowing that her six-foot-three detective ex-husband was on guard. Over time, however, she had got used to the arrangement. Novack, as she and everybody else referred to him, could still be a major pain in the ass, but he was more attentive, and as he had his own apartment she could more easily throw him out of the house than when he lived there. Cindy had finished her master's in speech therapy, got a job in the local school system and started an after-school private practice. She was now making more money than he was. Even the sex, while never a problem between them, had got better since their split. So all in all, the divorce had done quite a bit for their marriage.

Within thirty seconds of getting the news about Tim, Novack was in the car and on the way to pick up his partner, Detective James Anders. Anders had been partnered with Novack for only four months, and hadn't been involved with the Wallace case. But he had heard about it; Novack saw to that.

The two of them immediately went to Tim's office, and since Meredith said he was out to lunch, they decided to wait for Tim to arrive.

Tim didn't seem at all surprised to see them. 'That was quick,' he said.

'You were expecting us?' Novack asked.

'Yeah, you could say that.'

Novack introduced Anders, and Tim brought them both back to his office.

'So tell us all about this Cashman guy,' Novack said.

It was a story Tim was getting tired of telling, but he went through it one more time. Neither Novack nor Anders interrupted.

'And you're sure you never met him before?' Novack asked when Tim had finished.

'As sure as I can be. And I haven't seen him since that night.'

'So he comes up to a perfect stranger and confesses to a murder. Any idea why he would do that?' Novack asked.

'He said it was his way of getting it off his chest. He said that now it's my problem, which I'm starting to believe is the truth.'

'Tell me about the flier,' he said. 'Where did you find it?'

'I told you . . . on a telephone pole in front of my apartment.'

'Right,' Novack said. 'Have you seen others, or just that one?'

'Just that one. Look—'

'Didn't you see any of the fliers in Kinnelon when you were there?'

'No, but—'

'So somebody in Kinnelon goes missing; they wait three months, print one flier, and post it thirty miles away in front of your apartment?'

'I don't know. Maybe Cashman posted the one I saw. Why don't you catch the slime ball and ask him?'

'You seem nervous,' Novack said.

'I'm not nervous; I'm annoyed. I did what I was supposed to do and reported this. You can do with it whatever you want.'

'And we appreciate your cooperation,' Novack lied. 'Right now I'd like you to come with us. You don't have to, but it would be helpful if you did.'

'Where to?' Tim asked.

'Kinnelon. To look for Sheila.'

'What do you need me for? I've told you everything I know.'

Novack shrugged. 'Maybe you'll think of something else when we're there.'

The drive out to Kinnelon was an uncomfortable one for Tim. He sat in the back, while Anders drove with Novack in the passenger seat. They didn't ask him for directions, just drove directly to the park. Tim couldn't see how he could be of any real value to them. He assumed that they were hoping he'd somehow trip up and reveal himself to be a murderer.

The park looked nothing like it had the last time Tim was there. There were six police cars, fifteen officers and some digging equipment. Novack told Tim to stay nearby, and he and Anders headed for the officer in charge.

The temperature was in the mid-teens, and the Kinnelon police sergeant was clearly not happy to be there. 'I'm Conway,' he said. 'You're late.'

'That's because we drove all the way here from civilisation,' Novack said. He motioned towards the activity behind the swing set. 'Find anything?'

Sergeant Conway shook his head. 'No, but then there's nothing to find. Nobody's reported this woman missing—no one's even heard of her. And there's not a damn flier within fifty miles.'

They started walking towards the swings, and Tim followed along.

'Is this the only swing set round here?' Anders asked.

Conway nodded. 'It is, but we can dig up the entire town if you'd like.'

'You think we shouldn't have called you?' Novack asked.

Conway shrugged. 'We're small-town; we don't think. We just keep our shovels ready and start digging when and where you big-city guys tell us.'

Novack nodded. 'And don't think we don't appreciate it.'

They all stood off to the side, about twenty feet from where the digging was going on, trying to keep warm. After about thirty minutes, none of them had any feeling in their extremities.

'Sergeant . . . over here,' one of the diggers called, his voice urgent.

Conway, Novack, Anders and Tim hobbled over on frozen feet. When they got there, one of the officers pointed down into the ditch.

It was the skeletal remains of a hand, pointing up out of the frozen ground, the middle finger missing.

'Holy shit,' said Novack.

THE DISCOVERY of the body immediately turned the park into a crime scene.

Anders led Tim away and into the back of the car, where he was forced to wait almost two hours by himself. Anders left the car running and the heat on, but Tim didn't get to see what was going on, or hear what was said.

Novack and Anders finally returned to the car, and began the drive back. They weren't saying anything to each other, and certainly not to Tim.

'Did you learn anything?' Tim asked.

Novack nodded. 'Sure did. Every day is a learning experience.'

Back at the station house, Novack brought Tim to the office of Sergeant Robert Taveras, the sketch artist for the department. The small office was set up like an artist's studio, with the sergeant's chair facing an easel.

Taveras had an easy-going way about him, and went to some lengths to get Tim to remain calm. 'I want you to tell me everything you remember about Cashman's face, but don't try too hard . . . don't push it. Just relax and remember him naturally, as you would anyone else.'

Tim had always been very visual and attentive to detail; he had trained as an architect before moving into construction. He directed Taveras confidently, and a likeness of Cashman immediately started to take shape.

'Have you done this before?' Taveras asked, impressed.

Tim shook his head. 'First time. Square off the chin just a little.'

Taveras did as he was told. 'Like that?'

'Almost,' Tim said. 'Can I show you?'

Taveras gave him the pencil, and Tim made a slight adjustment to the chin before handing it back. 'That's it, except the cheeks were a little fuller.'

Taveras worked on the cheeks, then stepped back so Tim could get a head-on look. As far as Tim was concerned, he was looking at Jeff Cashman.

'That's him.'

'You sure?' Taveras asked.

Tim nodded. 'It gives me the creeps just to look at him.'

Taveras sprayed the canvas to prevent it from smearing, then picked up the phone and called Novack, who came right in.

'We need more witnesses like this guy,' Taveras told him.

Novack looked at the drawing. 'So that's your Jeff Cashman?'

Tim didn't like Novack's use of the word 'your'. It implied that Cashman was Tim's creation. 'That's Jeff Cashman,' he said.

Novack turned to Taveras. 'OK, let's get it copied.'

'Will do.'

'Can I go home now?' Tim asked Novack. 'Do you need me any more?'

'Are you planning any trips?'

The question annoyed Tim. 'What if I was?'

'Then I would tell you to change your plans,' Novack said.

'Why?'

'Why? Because we just dug a woman out of the ground. She was killed and probably tortured. And if I decide it'll help me catch the scumbag who did it by talking to you, I don't want to have to go looking for you.'

'I'm not planning any trips.'

'It's refreshing to meet such a concerned citizen. You're free to go.'

ONCE TIM HAD LEFT, a copy of the Cashman drawing in hand, Novack went into Anders's office to rehash the events of the day while things were still fresh, or as fresh as they could be at ten o'clock, after a very long day.

'He killed her,' Novack said. 'And now he's rubbing our noses in it.'

'Why would he do that?' Anders asked.

'How the hell do I know? Maybe he's a sicko.' The truth was that the recent events didn't fit with Novack's view of Wallace, which was not of a serial killer, but of a guy who for whatever reason killed his wife.

Anders got up and grabbed his jacket.

'Where are you going?' Novack asked.

'Home. Just in case my girlfriend still lives there. You going to Cindy's?'

Novack shook his head. 'Nah . . . it's Tuesday. Lately she doesn't want me to come over on Tuesday. I'm not sure why.'

'Maybe she has a normal, emotionally stable, non-degenerate guy come over on Tuesdays. Just for a change of pace.'

Novack shook his head again. 'Nah . . . last Tuesday I hid out in the bushes by her house, just to make sure.'

TIM MADE A QUICK STOP at home to walk Kiley before heading back out. His destination was the Purple Rose, a place he hadn't planned to frequent again for a long time. But this was no time to sit back and wait.

Danny and Will were at their regular table when he arrived; it would have been a news event if they weren't. But Tim's first stop was the bar, to talk to Frank Lester, the bartender. A smallish man in his late fifties, Frank always had a calm smile on his face, no matter how chaotic the bar got.

'Hey, Tim, good to see you. We miss you round here.'

'Thanks, Frank . . . I was here New Year's Eve.'

'You were? I didn't see you. Wild night, huh?'

'Yeah . . . I was the one hanging from the chandelier.' Tim reached into his jacket for the drawing of Cashman. 'Were you here all night?'

Frank nodded. 'Until around three in the morning.' He motioned towards the table where Danny and Will sat. 'I put your drunken friends in a cab.'

Tim put the picture on the bar. 'Did you see this guy that night?'

Frank stared at Cashman's face. 'It's possible . . . He looks a little familiar. But I couldn't be sure. You want to leave it here and I'll ask other people?'

'No, that's OK. Thanks.' Tim started to walk away.

'Hey, Tim?' Frank said, and Tim stopped and turned. 'It's really good to have you back here, buddy.'

Tim nodded his thanks and continued on to see Danny and Will, and their surprise and delight at his arrival was obvious. They made a big show of bringing over another chair for Tim, and positioned it in the centre, thereby affording him the best view of the televisions.

'What happened with Novack?' Danny asked when Tim was settled.

He told them about the trip to Kinnelon and the discovery of Sheila's body.

'No shit?' Will asked, amazed. 'She was where Cashman said she'd be?'

Tim nodded. 'Yeah. With a middle finger missing.' He took out the drawing of Cashman. 'You guys recognise him?'

Neither Danny nor Will recognised the picture, but both admitted that they were drunk that night.

'Do they know who this Sheila was?' Will asked.

Tim shrugged. 'I don't think so, but Novack's not exactly confiding in me. He doesn't believe a word I say.'

'Cops aren't supposed to believe people,' Will said.

'I feel like I owe Sheila more than this,' Tim said. 'Hey, what about the women you guys were with? Maybe they'll recognise the picture.'

'Tim, it was New Year's Eve, remember? Alcohol . . . ?'

'So I was the only one in the place who was sober that night?'

Will raised his glass. 'Pretty soon you'll be the only one sober tonight.'

'It's subject-changing time,' Danny said. 'Did you catch the news today?'

'No. Why?'

'Some guy crashed his car after a police chase down in South Jersey. It exploded. Took out windows three blocks away. They think it was Cintron 421 . . . at least a hundred pounds.'

'Jesus . . . Did you find out any of the particulars?'

The partners constructed buildings that could withstand significant explosives, and Cintron 421 was about as significant as you could get without a mushroom cloud.

'Not yet, but I called my uncle. If we're lucky, he'll call me back.'

'Let me know what you hear,' Tim said.

Danny got up and headed for the bathroom, and Will said, 'Hey, Tim, I'm sorry about the other night. We were just trying to get you to have some fun, and now you've got all this aggravation—'

'Not your fault, Will. You couldn't have known.'

'Yeah, but I'm sorry about it, you know?'

Will, while outwardly the gruffest of the three friends, actually possessed the most sensitivity, though he took pains to hide it, professing to be rigidly self-ruled by logic. A genius with computers, Will designed the programs that governed such things as temperature control, ventilation and alarm systems in Wallace Industries buildings.

Danny returned, and Tim said his goodbyes and went straight home. When he got there, the phone was ringing.

'You get it,' he said to Kiley. 'It's probably Novack.'

But Kiley was not inclined to answer the phone, so Tim did. 'Hello?'

'You told them, Timmy.'

The voice was filtered through a computer, and therefore not recognisable, but Tim knew very well what the words meant. 'Cashman?'

'I trusted you. It was our secret.'

'You murdered her.'

'Right . . . just like I said. But you shouldn't have told them, Timmy. It was our secret. I'm very disappointed in you.'

'You're right, I'm sorry,' Tim said. 'Why don't we meet somewhere . . . tomorrow . . . so we can talk about it?'

'Oh, we'll definitely meet again. Pleasant dreams, Timmy.'

Click.

FOUR

'If Cashman lived within two hundred miles of here or Kinnelon, he changed his name,' Novack said, as he paced round the office of his boss, Captain Mark Donovan. He and Anders were there to bring Donovan up to date on events so far, and what they had learned about them.

Donovan represented everything that Novack would have expected not to like in a cop. The son of a former commissioner, he had been groomed from day one to move smoothly to the top of the department, and everyone who wore a badge knew that this precinct-captain position was just another check mark on a résumé. But Donovan was quite open about his political ambitions, and agreeably deferential to cops. He gave respect and in turn received it, even from the normally disrespectful Novack.

'Jeff Cashman doesn't seem like that unusual a name,' Donovan said.

Novack nodded. 'There are seventeen in the area; none of them's our boy.'

'What about the victim?'

'Just as dry,' Anders said. 'If her name really was Sheila Blair, nobody's reported her missing. It's possible that Cashman just made the name up.'

'DNA?' asked Donovan.

Anders nodded. 'Running it now.'

'You want to go public with the Cashman sketch?' asked Novack.

Donovan thought about this for a moment. 'No . . . I don't want to let him know we're looking for him yet.'

'That's if he exists,' said Novack.

Donovan's face registered his surprise. 'You think Wallace is lying?'

'Damn straight. I think Cashman is Santa Claus and the Tooth Fairy,' Novack said, and Donovan saw Anders grimace slightly. 'Look, you're Cashman,' Novack continued. 'You commit a murder months ago, you get away with it, then you give it up to some stranger in a bar? Does that make sense?'

Donovan turned to Anders. 'You don't agree?'

Anders shook his head. 'I look at it a different way. You're Wallace. You commit a murder, get away with it, then you go to the police with a made-up story about some guy confessing in a bar? That make any more sense?'

'Maybe Wallace was feeling guilty, couldn't stand it, and had to let somebody know where she was,' Novack said. 'So he makes up this story.'

'The same could be true of Cashman,' Anders said. 'But if I'm Wallace, I know you've been after my ass for months. So if my conscience makes me tell the cops about Sheila, I make an anonymous phone call.'

'Not if Wallace wanted to fuck with my mind,' said Novack.

'Come on, you're the one who's obsessed here. Not him.'

Despite his respect for Novack's instincts, Donovan knew that Novack was overboard in his unrelenting focus on Wallace. But he decided to jump in for the moment on Novack's side. 'The flier is a significant piece here.'

Novack nodded vigorously. 'That's right; the only flier gets posted outside Wallace's apartment. And only Wallace's prints are on it. It says to notify the state police, but we know nothing about Sheila. We can't find anybody who's even heard of her. Wallace printed and hung the flier himself.'

'Maybe Cashman did it, but he's setting up Wallace,' Anders suggested. 'Maybe he has a grudge against him.'

Before Novack could respond, Donovan's intercom buzzed. He answered it, listened briefly, then hung up. 'Wallace is here to see you,' he told Novack.

Anders was surprised. 'He's here again?'

Novack turned to his partner and grinned. 'Sicko.'

Tim was waiting in Novack's office when he and Anders got back. 'Well, good morning. Glad you stopped by,' Novack said.

Tim was clearly not in the mood for chitchat. 'I'm in a hurry to get to work, but there's something I had to tell you.'

'You want some coffee?' Anders asked.

'No. He called me.'

'Who called you?' Novack asked.

'Cashman. His voice was filtered through a computer, but it had to be him. He knew that I told you about him, and about Sheila.'

'How did he know that?' Anders asked.

'He didn't say, but he was angry.'

Anders again, 'Did he threaten you?'

'Not exactly. He said he was disappointed in me, that we'd meet again, and he told me to have pleasant dreams.'

'The animal,' Novack said, shaking his head in mock horror.

'Hey, this isn't funny, you know. We're talking about a murderer here.'

'That's for sure. We're definitely talking about a murderer.'

The veiled reference to Novack's suspicions did not escape Tim. 'You think I'm making this up? Maybe you think I killed Sheila?'

Novack was not about to back down. 'I'm still working on what I think, so for now I'll tell you what I know. You've been involved with the violent deaths of two women in less than a year. That's unusual. You can go out on the street and check out a thousand people . . . fifty thousand . . . and none will have that track record. Two murder cases for one innocent citizen is a lot.'

'My wife's death was not a "case". It was an accident.'

'Well . . . I have my doubts about that,' said Novack, with a slight smile.

'I know what happened,' Tim snapped. 'I was the only person there.'

Anders seized at that. 'Which is why you're the only person who can answer questions about it.'

'Check his notes,' Tim said, indicating Novack. 'I answered every stupid question he had ten times. I even answered them when I was hooked up to a lie detector. Look, am I being held here? I have work to do. Can I leave now?'

'This time you can leave,' Novack said.

Tim stood up and moved to the door, then turned. 'There's a maniac out there. He kills women and cuts off their fingers. I don't know why he drew me into this, but you might want to stop wasting your time and find out.'

TIM'S NEXT FEW DAYS were 'Cashman-free', which is to say that he heard nothing from either Cashman or Novack. Tim enjoyed the respite, and was able mostly to block it from his mind as he went about his business.

Tim usually spent the bulk of his time in his office, leaving Danny to supervise most of the work at the Federal Center site, but events lately were preventing him from doing that. They were in crunch time, with the building scheduled to be opened in just four weeks with a gala reception. A number of decisions had to be made, and made quickly.

As it came together, the Federal Center was an immensely impressive project, which would bring in a huge amount of money and jobs to the state. Tim and Danny's company had a significant stake in the success of the complex. If things went according to plan and budget, they could naturally expect a substantial amount of work when the complexes went national.

The car explosion in South Jersey had no direct effect on Tim's work, but it had a psychological effect. After two days the story had succumbed to the ever-changing news cycles and the lack of new information, so the media moved on. But for people in the know, it was scary as hell.

Federal authorities had identified the ill-fated driver of the car as Ricardo Vasquez, but had so far failed to connect him to any terrorist cells. If media reports were to be believed, they also had no idea where he got the explosives, where he was taking them or what triggered the detonation. This lack of knowledge sent spasms of insecurity throughout the security industry.

The truth was that the buildings under construction could conceivably handle the amount of explosives Vasquez had been transporting. The construction mandate was to build a structure that could withstand a powerful explosion from outside, perhaps a car bomb, with relatively minor damage. If the blast took place inside the building, the essential task was to contain it. The centre's unique security feature was its 'lockdown' capability. In the event of a perceived danger from outside, the building openings could be encased with reinforced steel doors, creating a virtually impregnable barrier.

Before he left the site, Tim went into the computer room, where he knew Will would be working. It was an extraordinary place. Two entire walls were covered with computer equipment and monitors. Will was hunched over a keyboard as though he were playing an instrument.

'Damn,' Tim said, 'it looks like you could control the world from here.'

Will looked over and smiled. 'Probably. But right now I'd rather be out in the world and let somebody else do the controlling.'

'Having a rough time?'

Will shrugged. 'Just the usual. It'll be ready.'

Once Tim got in the car, Meredith called him to say that Eden Alexander had called, and wanted to take him and Kiley to dinner.

'You have her number?' Tim asked.

Meredith gave it to him, then asked, 'And who might she be?'

'I didn't tell you?' Tim asked. 'I got married yesterday during lunch.'

She ignored the sarcasm. 'Are you going to have dinner with her?'

'Bye, Meredith. Take the rest of the day off.'

Tim would have expected to be dismissive of the idea of having dinner with her. Instead his reaction was mixed, somewhat unsure.

Eden sounded surprised to hear from him. When he asked why, she said, 'I didn't even think your assistant would give you the message.'

'Meredith? Why?'

'Have you noticed she's rather protective of you? She was pumping me for so much information . . . Captured terrorists have been questioned less.'

He laughed. 'Sorry. She considers me rather helpless out in the real world.'

Eden suggested that they go to a local restaurant called the Firepit, since it allowed dogs. The idea held some appeal for Tim, but he hesitated.

Eden picked up on it. 'Tim, relax. I'm not inviting you to a weekend in the Poconos in a heart-shaped tub. It's not even a date.'

'It's not that. I—'

'I'll tell you what; we can be at different tables, with a wall between us,' she said. 'And you can sit in a soundproof booth, under a cone of silence.'

'That might work,' he said.

'I just thought it would be nice, for us and for the dogs, and I wanted to hear where things stand with the police and that poor woman in Kinnelon.'

'Sounds good,' Tim said, surprised to be hearing the words come out of his own mouth. 'I'll get Kiley and meet you there in an hour?'

'Great,' she said, and hung up.

Eden and Travis were waiting for Tim and Kiley when they arrived, and she had already secured two water dishes placed beneath the table.

'Sorry we're late,' Tim said, as Kiley and Travis sniffed their hellos.

'You're not late. I'm chronically early.'

'Why?' he asked.

'I'm not sure; I always assumed it was my not wanting to miss anything.'

Tim smiled. 'Did I miss anything?'

'Not so far.'

Tim ordered a burger, while Eden opted for a vegetable dish, and they both had a beer.

Once they were settled in, Tim recounted to her the phone call from Cashman, as well as his unpleasant encounters with Novack.

'What is his problem?' Eden asked. 'You did exactly what you're supposed to do. Would he rather people didn't report these things?'

'He thinks I killed Maggie,' Tim blurted out.

'That's outrageous,' she said. 'How can that be?'

'He always has. Now I'm sure he thinks I killed Sheila as well.'

'So what are you doing about it?'

Tim shrugged. 'There's nothing I can do, and nothing I need to do. He couldn't find any evidence before, and he won't find any now. There's nothing to find. The only consolation in all this is that it drives him crazy.'

'You think only guilty people get charged with crimes and go to jail?'

'I don't really think about it much at all.'

'I think you should get yourself a lawyer,' she said. 'This guy scares me.'

'You think Novack is more dangerous to me than Cashman?'

'Probably, but maybe get a bodyguard too. After you get a lawyer.'

'You know anyone?' Tim asked. The only lawyers he had ever dealt with were corporate types, and he couldn't picture them in a room with Novack.

'Matter of fact I do. My brother's a criminal attorney. Nick Alexander.'

'Nick Alexander is your brother? The guy who defended Billy Scarborough?' Scarborough was the CEO of an energy trading company caught up in fraud scandals and charged with what seemed like a thousand counts of fiscal crimes. Nick Alexander got him acquitted of every count.

'That's him. He's had some big cases, and he's on television all the time. He can attract attention to how unfairly you're being treated.'

'The last thing I want is media attention,' Tim said, not mentioning the danger such attention posed to his business. 'So what do you do for a living?'

She laughed. 'You have a driving curiosity about me?'

'What do you mean?'

'I mean we were talking about something that made you uncomfortable, and suddenly you asked the first question about me that you've ever asked.'

He nodded. 'Guilty as charged. I'm afraid I've been a little self-centred this decade. But I really want to know what you do.'

'I'm a professor of art history at Montclair State,' she said.

'Really? So am I. I'm surprised I haven't run into you on campus.'

They lingered after coffee, talking normal, non-Cashman talk, and decided to leave only when Kiley and Travis made it clear they were getting bored.

'I enjoyed this. Thank you,' Tim said.

'So I was right not to tell you about my biological clock?' she asked.

'You didn't have to. I heard it ticking.'

NOVACK COULD FEEL the frustration setting in already. Everything was coming up empty, much as it had when Wallace killed his wife.

Cashman was nowhere to be found, but that was to be expected. As far as Novack was concerned, Cashman didn't exist. He was created by Tim as part of the game. The fact that Tim was playing this game came as a surprise to Novack. He'd had Tim pegged as a common-or-garden wife killer; this elevated him to a higher plane of evil.

'Are you OK, John?' Cindy asked, as she looked at him sitting at the kitchen table. She was preparing his favourite dish, chicken parmigiana.

Lost in his own thoughts, he didn't answer.

'John? Earth to John, come in, please.'

'What? I'm sorry . . . what?'

'Are you all right? You seem tense and distracted.'

'Why do you say that?'

'Well, you're grinding your teeth and your hands are curled into fists.'

He looked at his whitened fingers. 'It's just something at work.'

'You're kidding!' Cindy exclaimed in mock surprise. 'I thought you were upset that the ballet left town.'

'Wallace killed another woman,' he said, knowing she would remember the investigation into Maggie's death. 'He's rubbing my nose in it.'

Cindy's instinct was to walk over and put her arm round him. But she knew he hated to be touched when he was stressed. 'Who did he kill?' she asked.

'We haven't been able to identify her. But Wallace led us to the body.'

'But if he knew where the body was, doesn't that—?'

Novack interrupted her with a shake of the head, and told her about Cashman and the alleged conversation on New Year's Eve.

'It couldn't have happened that way?' she asked.

He just stared at her, a frown on his face, and she smiled.

'You'll get him this time.'

He nodded. 'Yeah, we will. Hey, you want to go get something to eat?'

She smiled. 'I'm making dinner, John. That's what I've been doing, in the kitchen where you are currently sitting, for the last half-hour.'

'I knew that,' he lied. 'It smells delicious.'

RICARDO VASQUEZ had become a hell of a lot more important in death than he had been in life. He had not been carrying just any old explosives; this was stuff that the US military used in Afghanistan. No one knew where Vasquez had been heading with his cargo, but there is no Afghanistan exit on the New Jersey Turnpike.

FBI Special Agent Carl White, assigned to Homeland Security, was in charge of finding out all there was to know about Vasquez. It was an assignment for which he was uniquely qualified, having worked undercover with Miami PD for three years before joining the bureau. Smart, instinctive and comparatively fearless, he knew the area Vasquez was from; he could navigate through it with ease and get whatever information was to be found.

Carl was assigned four agents to work directly for him, and was promised whatever other manpower he needed. They spent the four days after the explosion turning Ricardo Vasquez's life upside-down. They came up empty.

Ricardo was simply a small-time punk, with plenty of connections to other punks, but none to terrorists. He just wasn't bright enough to have been a strategist in any plot. And any terrorist who entrusted Ricardo to transport such a cargo couldn't have been very smart either.

But he'd had the explosives, and he was taking them somewhere. Those facts could not be challenged, yet Carl had no explanation for them.

DIFFERENT PEOPLE RELAX in different ways, and the best way for Tim was to play racketball. It required tremendous energy and concentration, and enabled Tim's competitive nature to kick into high gear.

He and Danny had a regular game on Saturday mornings, something Tim looked forward to. Danny was nearly as good as Tim, and though he didn't often win, the matches were almost always close. They kept a standing eight o'clock reservation for court four at the Englewood Racket Club. If they got there early the court was always empty, so they could just start playing.

This was the first time they had played since Cashman entered Tim's life, and he made a conscious effort to go all out. After one particularly gruelling point, Danny stopped playing and started laughing.

'What's the matter?' Tim asked.

'Did we bet on the game and you forgot to tell me?'

'What do you mean?'

'You're like a maniac today,' Danny said. 'Relax or you'll have a heart attack. You're an old man.'

'I'm a week older than you,' Tim said. Then he smiled. 'Although this has been a long week.'

Their normal routine was to play the best of three games. This time Tim won the first two games in record time.

'You want to play another one?' he asked.

'You haven't humiliated me enough?'

'Not even close.'

Danny pointed his racket at Tim. 'You just made a big mistake, pal. You pissed me off.'

Danny played the next game with considerably more intensity, but his reward was merely to lose by a slightly closer score.

'One more?' Tim asked.

Out of breath and drenched in sweat, Danny shook his head. '*No más.*'

They had just turned to leave when Tim noticed something in the clear fibreglass compartment recessed in the back wall, where players usually put money or other valuables while they played. Tim and Danny never used it, because they kept their things in the locker room.

'What's that in there?' Tim asked, pointing. 'It looks like a jewellery box.'

They both walked towards it, and Danny opened the door and took out the box, which had a Tiffany insignia.

'You planning on proposing to me?' he asked. 'You buy me a ring?'

'See if there's anything in it,' Tim said.

Danny opened the box and looked inside. His face took on a puzzled expression, then a look of pure shock. Suddenly he started to scream.

'What the—?' Tim stopped as the open box dropped from Danny's hand.

The jewellery box struck the floor and its contents fell out. It was not a ring, but a ring could have fitted on it.

It was a severed human finger.

Within ten seconds, at least half the people in the club came running to see what had prompted Danny's awful scream. As each person saw the finger, the screams became a chorus, which brought everyone else over to join in. By the time the police arrived, at least thirty people had entered the court area, though nobody touched the finger or the box. While the court was cordoned off, Tim and Danny were brought to the manager's office, and Detective Stan Mullins of the Englewood police came in to question them.

All too aware of how this was going to play out, Tim asked, 'How about if we wait until Novack gets here, so we can do this once?'

'Who's Novack?' Mullins asked.

'He's with the state police. He'll be taking over this case from you.'

Mullins's annoyance was obvious. 'Nobody is taking this case from me,' he said, then turned to Danny. 'We'll start with you. Tell me what happened.'

A shaken Danny said, 'Well, we finished our game, and—'

Danny was interrupted by Mullins's cellphone ringing, which he answered. 'Mullins.' After a pause, he said, 'That's bullshit. You . . . Yeah. But it's still bullshit.' Mullins hung up, and without another word walked to the door.

'I'll give Novack your regards,' Tim said, without drawing a response.

It was another twenty minutes before Novack and Anders arrived. Tim and Danny were separated for the questioning, and surprisingly Novack chose to question Danny, leaving Anders to deal with Tim. Anders made him repeat the story over and over, but even so Tim was finished first. Danny was finally brought back to the office after two hours of questioning.

Once they were in the car, he said, 'Tim, Novack's trying to pin it on you.'

Tim nodded. 'What did he say?'

'All he wanted to know was stuff like, were you ever alone on the court, did you carry anything in with you that could have concealed the jewellery box, that kind of thing. He was hoping I'd nail you.'

'You didn't have to. Cashman is doing it for him.'

'Tim, this is moving way past weird. You're dealing with a serious sicko. 'You think he came after you . . . maybe followed you to the bar that night? Or were you just in the wrong place at the wrong time?'

'He came after me; he knows too much about me to have put this all together on the fly. He may even have killed Sheila just to pin it on me.'

'You can't just sit back and let this happen to you.'

Tim nodded. 'I'm not going to. I'm going to get a lawyer.'

Danny was quiet for a moment, then said, 'Hey, Tim, I think that's a good idea, but be careful. We don't need publicity about this, you know?'

'I know.'

'I mean, my uncle is way out there on a limb for us, but he'll saw it off if he has to. You remember how he reacted last time.'

Tim remembered it well; Senator Collinsworth had been upset at the public suspicion of Tim following Maggie's death. Danny had calmed him down, and Tim's exoneration defused the situation, but it was a close call.

'I'm not hiring a press agent, Danny. I'm hiring a lawyer.'

Danny pulled into the circular driveway in front of Tim's apartment. 'You know anybody that handles that kind of stuff?'

Tim was surprised to see Eden, standing in front of the building. He pointed to her. 'No, but she does.'

'Who is she?' Danny asked. 'You got a life you've been keeping from me?'

Tim didn't answer, just got out of the car and went over to Eden. 'What are you doing here?'

'I heard about what happened at the racketball club,' she said. 'I thought you might need some help.'

'How did you hear about it?' he asked.

'Are you kidding? It's the top story on the news.'

'With my name attached?' he asked, cringing.

'No, but when I heard about the . . . finger . . . I made the connection.'

Tim nodded. 'Come on up.'

As they went into the building, Tim looked back and noticed that Danny hadn't driven away. He was just parked there, staring at them.

When they got upstairs, Tim briefly told Eden what had happened. 'I need you to call your brother for me, if you feel comfortable with that,' he said.

She nodded, went to the phone and set up an appointment for Tim at ten o'clock Monday morning. Then she wrote out the firm's name and address.

Tim looked at the paper. 'He works for Hammond, Simmons and Carcher?' It was one of New Jersey's largest and most prestigious firms.

'Yes, they brought him in to start a criminal-law division last year. They paid him a fortune, but it may not be the greatest fit.'

'Why not?'

'You'll understand when you meet him.'

WHEN ANDERS CAME into Novack's office, he had that look on his face. It said that Anders had something important to tell Novack. There was no telling whether it was positive or negative, just that it was important.

'Tell me something good,' Novack said.

Anders held up a thin folder. 'We got a DNA hit . . . We ID'd Sheila.'

It was all Novack could do not to jump out of his chair. 'Who was she?'

Anders opened the folder and looked down. 'Her name was Carol Sheila Blair. She lived in Carson, Wyoming, but would often go away for months at a time. Apparently that's why nobody even considered her missing.'

'Why was she in the DNA registry?' Novack asked.

'She had an armed-robbery conviction, part of a husband-and-wife team that held up a bank. Though "armed" is an understatement. He threatened to detonate a bomb if they didn't cough up the cash. She was waiting in the car, and they got away. Local cops made the collar three days later.'

'So she served time?'

'No . . .' Anders flipped through the pages. 'Just probation. She and her husband, a guy named Roger Blair, copped a plea. She walked, and he got three years. This was eight months ago.'

'That's all they got for robbing a bank and threatening to blow it up?'

'Looks like it. Not exactly frontier justice, huh?'

'So the husband is still in prison?'

'No. He had his throat slit a couple of months after he went in.'

Novack smiled. 'Saddle up, pardner. We're heading out west.'

'You think Donovan will spring for two plane trips?' Anders asked. 'Sheila was from Wyoming and killed in Kinnelon. We're not exactly swimming in jurisdiction here.'

'Are you kidding?' Novack asked, standing up. 'Wait here; I'll be right back. When I get finished with him, he'll throw in tickets to the rodeo.'

While Novack went off to talk to Captain Donovan, Anders did more than just wait for his partner. He called Keith Rivers, Senator Collinsworth's right-hand man, to tell him about this new development in Wyoming.

Collinsworth and Rivers had tentacles that reached everywhere, and they'd had no trouble getting to Anders, offering him substantial considerations for any information about the investigation. Anders had hesitated at first, but finally came to the rationalisation that much of the information would be harmless, and that he would judge it on a case-by-case basis.

The Wyoming information was an easy call to make, and Anders shared it with Rivers before Novack came back with the news that Donovan had approved the trip. They were going to Wyoming.

HAMMOND, SIMMONS AND CARCHER had their own four-storey building off Route 17 in Ridgewood, a dazzling mixture of glass and chrome that projected modern wealth and confidence. The receptionist in the lobby looked like she came with the building, perfectly put together and a model of efficiency. She juggled four calls while Tim was at her desk, yet within three minutes she had ushered him into Nick Alexander's office.

It was hard to believe that Nick's office was in the same building. It was a mess, papers strewn everywhere, sports memorabilia hanging at awkward angles on the wall, empty soda cans and chewed Popsicle sticks on the tables. With all of the reflections from the chrome and mirrors, the room felt like a carnival maze constructed out of trash.

Nick looked at home in sneakers and jeans, with a shirt half tucked into his trousers. 'Hey, come on in,' he said after they shook hands. 'Just move that stuff off the chair and sit down.'

'OK . . .' Tim said hesitantly. 'Thanks for seeing me at such short notice.'

'No problem . . . any friend of Eden's . . . Hey, you want something to drink? I've got Diet Pepsi and Yoo-Hoo.'

'No, thanks.'

'It's hot in here, huh? They turn the heat up in these buildings so high I lose five pounds a day. And you can't open the windows. You believe that?'

Tim nodded. 'A lot of buildings, you—'

Nick interrupted. 'I know; it drives me crazy. My old office, I had the windows open all the time. Even in the winter. You could smell the food from the Chinese restaurant next door starting at ten in the morning.'

'So,' said Tim, 'I'm here because—'

'The police, notably Detective Novack, think you murdered two people.' Nick twisted the top off a bottle of Yoo-Hoo and handed it to Tim.

'How did you know that?' Tim asked. 'Did Eden tell you?'

'No. I asked around a bit. Believe me, it's not a major secret.'

'With all due respect, I haven't hired you yet.'

Nick smiled. 'With just as much respect, I haven't accepted you as a client yet. You can be sure I didn't reveal to anyone that I had a professional interest in this case. In fact, I gotta tell you, at this point I don't.'

Tim nodded. 'Sorry.'

'No problem. Tell me your story, leaving nothing out.'

Tim spent the next half-hour doing just that. It was a story he had by then told frequently, but Nick's occasional probing questions brought out a fresh perspective. Tim realised that Nick was a lot smarter than he'd first thought.

'Is that everything?' Nick asked when Tim had finished.

'I think so.'

'Now tell me about your wife.'

'What about her? She has nothing to do with this.'

Nick shook his head. 'Of course she does. Her death is the reason Novack is after you. And Novack is the guy I'd be defending you against, at least initially, so I have to know what he knows and what he thinks he knows.'

The logic of this couldn't be disputed. 'Of course, you're right. It just bugs me when people talk about Maggie's death as if it were a murder case.'

'I don't blame you.'

Tim related the events of that awful day as best he could remember them, as well as his dealings with Novack afterwards. 'Finally, I let them give me a lie-detector test, and never heard from them again. The talking heads in the media stopped jabbering about it as well.'

Nick laughed. 'I was one of those talking heads; somehow I've got on the list of defence attorneys that they call.'

Tim smiled. 'I never watched the coverage. What did you say?'

'I don't remember, and it doesn't matter; I knew absolutely nothing about it. That never gets in the way; I just jabber about the presumption of innocence and mention that there are holes in the prosecution's case.'

'Were there?'

Nick shrugged. 'Must have been, or by now you'd be showering with guys named Bubba. Have you told me everything?'

'I think so. But I do have a question for you. What are you doing here?'

'What do you mean?'

'Well, you just don't seem to fit in this place. It's not your personality.'

Nick grinned. 'About eight months ago, the geniuses here decided to get into criminal law, maybe because most of their corporate clients are crooks. They wanted to hire the best. For some reason they thought that was me, so they threw a shitload of money at me and gave me autonomy.'

Tim laughed. 'Obviously you're exempt from the dress code as well. Every other guy in the place is wearing a suit.'

'Hey, I dress up pretty nice when I have to go to court. Which is one place we don't want you to wind up.'

'So you'll take the case?'

Nick thought for a few moments. Finally, he said, 'I'll draw up an agreement between us; among other things, it will detail the fee structure. You have money? Because somebody's got to pay for all this chrome.'

'It's not a problem.'

'OK. Take the document with you and think about it. If you sign it, I'm your lawyer.'

'You're my lawyer,' Tim said.

Nick raised his bottle of Yoo-Hoo in a toast. 'Cheers.'

FIVE

Carson, Wyoming, was everything Anders and Novack expected, and less. Forty-five hundred citizens were spread out over an area as large as Manhattan. Around half were involved in farming, half worked at the state prison at Lampley, twenty miles away, so Carson's economy was simultaneously at the mercy of the weather and the state crime rate.

The two detectives arrived at four in the afternoon, tired and frozen. The outside temperature gauge on their rental car showed $8°$ F, which felt generous. Their hotel was a dive out near the highway. It had fourteen tractor trailers in the dirt parking lot, though there were only twelve rooms. They dropped their bags in their tiny room and left, arriving at five o'clock prompt at the police station, a two-room building that had them longing for the spacious luxury of the hotel. The entire police force was there: a receptionist, a deputy and the chief himself, Matthew Drew.

Chief Drew was not what Novack had expected. An experienced police officer, he had spent eleven years in Reno PD. Born in Carson, he came back to care for his dying mother seventeen years ago, and had never left.

'This is a nice, quiet place to live,' Drew said after the hellos. 'But I guess you guys have come to change that?'

Novack smiled. 'Nah . . . we're just working the job. One of the perks is that we get to visit nice, quiet places like this.'

He had sent information ahead, including the sketch of Cashman.

'I showed the sketch around,' Drew said. 'Nobody here has seen that guy.'

'What can you tell us about the victim?' Novack asked.

'Born and raised here; a little wild by our standards but no real problems. She got bored and left to go to LA when she was nineteen.'

'To be a movie star?'

Drew smiled. 'A cocktail waitress. We set our sights low round here.'

'When did she come back?' Anders asked.

'About two years ago. She brought a boyfriend with her.'

'Roger Blair?'

Drew nodded. 'I think he was originally from back East. They lived in a trailer, about five miles out on the road. Pretty much kept to themselves. He was a mechanic, but he made most of his money blowing stuff up.'

'What does that mean?'

'He was an explosives expert; learned it in the army. Give him a glass of water and a tube of hair gel, and he could incinerate South Dakota.'

'He made that into a business?' Novack asked.

'You'd be surprised how much use there is for explosives. Irrigation, clearing land, demolition . . . He seemed to do OK for himself. She was his assistant.' Drew smiled. 'You should have seen them; it was like he was a chef and she brought him the ingredients.'

'How come he and his wife got off so easy?' Novack asked. 'What the hell is armed robbery out here, a misdemeanour?'

Drew shrugged. 'Yeah, I was pretty pissed off at that myself. Judge said it was a first offence, nobody got hurt . . . bullshit like that. He may have been pressured, but I don't have a clue where it could have come from.'

'What did the wife do when Blair went inside?'

'I don't know, but she wasn't doing it here. And nobody's seen her since.'

They spent the better part of another hour asking Drew questions, but he had no information that got them any closer to Sheila's killer.

'Do you know the warden at Lampley?' Novack asked.

'Sure. Name's Luther Marshall . . . I know him real well.'

'Any chance you could get him to meet with us?'

Drew called out to his receptionist. 'Hey, Bryna, they want to know if I could get Luther to meet with them.'

She laughed. 'That depends. You guys like beer?'

'On occasion,' Novack said.

'You guys like buying beer?' Bryna asked.

'Less so . . . Why?'

'Luther and I are having a few tonight,' Drew said. 'If you bring your big-city wallets, you can come along.'

DANNY'S DRIVE to Montclair took about forty-five minutes, but his preference would have been forty-five days. He had been summoned to meet his uncle, back for a few weeks while the Senate was on recess.

The invitation came in the form of a phone call from Collinsworth's chief of staff, Keith Rivers. That in itself was fairly ominous. When the senator had good news to share, he picked up the phone himself. When it was bad, Rivers would make the call. There was no third choice; the senator wouldn't be inviting him over unless he had some message to impart. And the invitation was for six o'clock, and for a drink, not dinner—this was going to be quick.

The only positive was that the senator's third wife, Elaine, whom Danny considered a pompous pain in the ass, was in Chicago at a fund-raising dinner for one of the charities she spent her time pretending to be interested in.

When he was brought into Collinsworth's spacious study, Danny was not surprised to see Rivers standing unobtrusively off to the side. Rivers was over six feet and 220 pounds, but he knew how to blend into the background.

Danny started with, 'Uncle Fred, it's great to see you.'

Collinsworth was sitting behind his desk, sipping from a glass of white wine. 'Danny, my boy, this is nice . . . you and I communicating like this.'

'I always enjoy talking with you, Uncle Fred.'

'That's good, because I'm easy to chat with, aren't I?'

Danny nodded. 'Very easy.'

'Then why the hell didn't you mention to me that the police are after your psycho partner for another murder?'

'He didn't do it. He—'

'Oh, so you only figured I would care if he actually got convicted? You were waiting for the jury to come in before telling me?'

'I'm sorry, but this time it's really ridiculous. There was a murder, but he knows who did it. The guy confessed to him.'

The senator waved this off. 'I heard the whole bullshit story. The police don't believe it, and I don't blame them.'

Danny cringed. 'Uncle Fred, they don't have anything on Tim, because there's nothing to have.' This was going to be painful; the senator was said to be pondering a run for the White House, and anything that stood even a remote chance of derailing him was going to be dealt with severely.

Collinsworth turned to Rivers. 'I wish I didn't have a weakness for family,' he said. Then, to Danny, 'Did you know they identified the victim?'

Danny's silence indicated that he didn't.

'Novack and his partner are out in Carson, Wyoming, following up on it,' the senator said. 'Does that sound like cops who are floundering around?'

'I swear this will blow over. There's no way Tim could kill anyone.'

'Right now he's in the process of killing your career.'

THEY SHOULDN'T HAVE AGREED to buy the beer. That's the first thing that went through Novack's mind when he and Anders met Warden Luther Marshall. They were at a bar called the Big Barn. Luther was sitting with Drew, and there were already four empty beer bottles on the table. The warden stood up to shake hands, slowly unfolding his six-foot-eight, 290-pound frame. It was unlikely, thought Novack, that there needed to be guards working at Luther's prison. Not even steel bars or cell doors would be necessary. No prisoner would dare piss Luther off by trying to escape.

But Luther proved to be an affable sort, and he and Drew were good guys to drink with, so much so that by the time they got round to talking about why the East Coast detectives were there, Luther had enough beer in him to flood an average-sized basement.

In fact, it was Luther himself who finally brought it up. 'So I hear you guys want to know something about Roger Blair?'

Novack nodded. 'Whatever you can tell us.'

'Not much; he pretty much stayed to himself while he was inside.'

'Did his wife come to visit him?' Anders asked.

'A couple of times early on, then nothing. Nobody else came either.'

'What about phone calls? In or out.'

'Hard to know,' Luther said. 'Nothing on the prison phone, but they get cellphones in there, so there's no sure way to keep track.'

'Any idea why he was killed? Or who killed him?'

'No, but it was a contract job, that's for sure. Chances are, the guy who did it didn't even know who was paying him, or why.'

'Sounds like a nice place you've got there,' Novack said.

'It's a real pleasure to go to work each day,' Luther said. 'Warms my heart.'

Anders took out Cashman's picture. 'You ever see this guy?' he asked.

Luther looked at it intently for a few moments, then shook his head. 'Looks sort of familiar, but . . . no. Don't think so.'

Novack took Tim's picture out of his folder. 'What about him?'

Luther looked at it and said, 'No, can't say as I have.'

Novack starting putting Tim's photo back in the folder when Drew grabbed it and put it back on the table. 'I know that guy.'

'How?' a stunned Novack asked.

'He was here in Carson. Last year.'

Novack looked at Anders and smiled. 'Small world, huh?'

As soon as Danny told him the news, Tim called Nick Alexander. 'I think we have a problem,' he said. 'Novack is out in Carson, Wyoming. They found out who the victim is; that's where she's from.'

'How did you find this out?'

Tim hesitated. 'I'd rather not say.'

'I probably should have explained this more clearly,' Nick said. 'It doesn't matter what you'd rather say or not say. What's important is that you tell me everything, or this is not going to work. Once I hear it, then I'm the one who can't talk about it, or I'd be violating my oath of confidentiality.'

'OK. My partner Danny's uncle is Senator Collinsworth. He told Danny about it, and Danny told me.'

'How did Collinsworth get the information?'

'I don't know. But he has ways of finding out pretty much everything.'

'Why was he interested?'

'He's been helpful in getting our company some major work on the Federal Center in Newark. If it turned out he was getting the work for a murderer, that wouldn't look great for him. Especially if he runs for president.'

'OK, let's back up for a minute. You said that Novack's being in Wyoming was a problem. Why do you see it that way?'

'Carson is a small town about three hours from Laramie. I was there last year. This just seems like another thing that can't be a coincidence.'

'What were you doing there?'

'There's a stone quarry about twenty minutes outside of Carson. We'd got word that some of our competitors were getting materials from there . . . better quality at a lower price. We have to check these things out.'

'Do you usually check them out yourself?'

'Not often. Maggie had died a couple of months earlier, and Novack was still on my case, so I thought it might be good to get away for a few days.'

'Was it worth the trip?' Nick asked.

'No, there was nothing special about the stone or the price. And then my car was vandalised; I was stuck there for a day while it was being fixed.'

'So people in the town would remember you?'

'Somebody might. I filed a police report. God, this is unbelievable. Why are they doing this to me?'

Nick wondered the same thing. 'What happened in Carson?' he asked.

'I mostly stayed in the hotel,' Tim said, 'and when the car was ready the next day I left. As far as I know, they never caught whoever vandalised it.'

'And you don't remember seeing anyone in Carson who looked like the woman on the flier outside your apartment?'

Tim shook his head. 'You think we should be worried about this?'

'Generally I find the best approach is to be worried about everything.'

NOVACK AND ANDERS were back in Chief Drew's office at 9 a.m. They wanted to question Drew's receptionist, Bryna Keller, who according to Drew had dealt with Tim Wallace when he was in Carson the previous year.

'Let me guess,' Bryna said when she arrived at 9.15 and saw Drew, Anders and Novack staring at her. 'You couldn't figure out how to make coffee.'

'True,' Drew said. 'But it can wait. These gentlemen need to talk to you.'

'What about?'

Anders handed her the picture of Tim. 'Him.'

Bryna looked at the picture with no sign of recognition. 'Who is he?' Then she brightened. 'Wait a minute . . . that's the guy who was here last year.'

Novack was delighted. 'Why was he here?' he asked.

'He was on some kind of a business trip . . . but I don't remember what his business was. He came in here because his car broke down, and Roger said it was vandalised. Something was poured into the gas tank, I think . . .'

'Roger Blair?' asked Novack.

'Right,' Bryna said, surprised. 'It was before he was jailed. You knew him?'

Novack shook his head. 'What's important is whether Wallace knew him.'

'Well, he serviced his car.'

'So you can place them together? You saw them in the same room?'

'Yes. In fact, it was this very room.'

'WE'VE GOT ENOUGH, CAPTAIN. We've got more than enough.'

Novack and Anders had gone directly from the airport to the precinct to meet Captain Donovan. Novack was hoping for a positive reaction to his request to arrest Wallace, but wasn't getting it.

'You've got logic,' said Donovan. 'You've got Wallace's story about Cashman, his knowing where Sheila was buried, his showing up with the flier, his having been in Carson. But there's no tangible evidence.'

'What about the finger?' Novack asked.

'You haven't got anyone who saw him plant it. There's no way McDermott would think you've got enough to take this to a jury.' He was talking about Lee McDermott, the district attorney who would ultimately decide whether to bring the case to trial, and who was widely known for his caution. Donovan turned to Anders, who had been largely silent. 'What do you think?'

'I think we need to get him off the street, Captain. Things are starting to break our way, and we'll come up with more. But as the pressure mounts on him, I don't want to give him a chance to do something stupid.'

Surprised at Anders's about-face, Donovan briefly reconsidered his decision, then said, 'No. Get me something else and we take it to McDermott.'

Novack was not about to let it drop. 'Something else? Wallace gave us the body; then he gave us the missing finger. If you go to my house and find somebody's head in my freezer, you can arrest me.'

'Arresting you is something I would look forward to,' Donovan said. 'Now get the hell out of here and nail the bastard.'

THE NEW JERSEY state crime lab was state-of-the-art, and it owed a good deal of its fine reputation to Dr Robin Miller, who ran the DNA department. Dr Miller ran her tests without prejudice or interest in the outcome, like a good scientist should. Her job was simply to determine the facts. Her administrative assistant, Stephen Cowlings, was left to prioritise the samples and deal with the law-enforcement agencies that submitted them.

The finger found at the racketball court was in fact tested before samples that had come in earlier. Novack's people had put in an urgent request, but that was becoming standard procedure, and Cowlings had a more personal reason for rushing this particular one through.

Dr Miller had first determined the type of preservative used to keep the finger in such pristine shape. She then achieved a DNA type, which was run through the lab's data base to see if a match could be made. Running the sample through the larger FBI data base could take up to three weeks.

Cowlings was out to lunch when the results were sent to his office, and it was the first thing he looked at when he got back. Reading it with delight, he knew that the police needed this information right away, but he also knew that somebody else needed it first.

Somebody who would pay for it.

'WE NEED TO TALK. Immediately.'

Nick Alexander's words sent waves of panic through Tim's gut. This could not be good news. 'Why? What's the matter?'

'Not over the phone.'

'You want to come here, to my office? Or should I come there?'

'Where do you live?' Nick asked, and when Tim told him, he said, 'I'll meet you at your apartment in twenty minutes.'

Tim left the office hastily just as Meredith came into the hallway.

'Tim? Are you all right?' she asked.

'I'm fine. Something came up that I have to deal with.'

'When should I tell people you'll be back?'

'I'll call you,' Tim said, and walked away.

When he arrived at his apartment building, Nick was in the lobby. They rode up in the elevator and entered the apartment without saying a word.

Tim was beyond worried. 'Please tell me what's going on,' he said.

'I just learned the results of the DNA tests on the finger,' Nick said.

'From Novack?' Tim asked.

'No, I have someone on my payroll at the state lab; it comes in handy.'

'What did the tests show?'

Nick didn't pull the punch. 'It was your wife's finger.'

WITHIN FIVE MINUTES of getting the news of the DNA match, Captain Donovan had agreed to Novack's request to arrest Tim. Less than an hour later, DA McDermott had signed on, and a half-hour after that they had secured a signed arrest warrant, and a warrant to search Tim's office and home.

Undercover officers were sent to confirm that Tim was at his office. Novack and Anders were to lead a group of six officers into the building, and all exits and stairwells were to be guarded. They went over every detail, utilising a diagram of the building.

When they presented the plan to Donovan, he looked at it from every angle. 'It works for me,' he said finally. 'Just don't screw it up.'

'It'll go down perfectly,' Novack said, smiling.

At that moment a call came in. Tim was not in fact at his office. An undercover officer, pretending to be a potential client, had been told by Meredith that she expected him back shortly.

The decision was made to wait until Tim returned, then move in.

IT WAS UNLIKELY that any news could have devastated Tim as completely as the news that the finger was a match to Maggie. When Nick said it, he sank to his knees, swamped by his feelings. 'It can't be,' he said. 'It just can't be.'

'I'm sorry, but it's a fact,' Nick said. 'The chance of these things being wrong is one in billions.'

'Maggie died in the explosion. I was there.'

'But you didn't actually see it. You said you saw a flash of white, and then you lost consciousness.'

'Are you saying she survived, and then she was tortured?' Tim's words came out as a plaintive plea, as if begging Nick for another explanation.

'I'm not saying anything,' Nick said. 'What I'm—'

'If that is her finger, and her body wasn't lost at sea, could she be alive?'

This time Nick's response was firmer. 'You need to listen to me, Tim. You are going to be arrested; there is no doubt about that.'

'What?' Tim heard the words, but had trouble understanding them.

'You're going to be arrested. So it's best to turn yourself in. That way we'll avoid some of the press coverage.'

'When . . . when do you want to do this?'

'Soon. In an hour. So pack a bag, get someone to take care of your dog . . . whatever else you need to do round here. Once you're ready, I'll call Novack and offer to bring you in; I'll be back here in an hour.'

Tim nodded. 'OK.'

Nick left, and Tim was alone with his agony. It was a good half-hour before he could think clearly. When his phone rang, he considered not answering it; then he checked the caller ID and saw that it was his office.

'Hello?' he said.

It was Meredith, and she sounded scared. 'Tim, there are police all over the building. They think I don't know who they are, but I'm not stupid.'

'It's OK, Meredith.' He didn't want to take the time to console her.

'No, it's not OK. Tim, I overheard two of them talking. One said he hoped you'd try something, that he'd love to take a shot at you. Then the other one talked about what would happen to you in prison.'

'Just stay in the office, Meredith. I have to go.'

Meredith's call had further shaken him, if that were possible. He knew nothing about his enemy, or how they had done this to him and Maggie. But one thing was obvious: they had won. It was planned and orchestrated to perfection, and when he was taken into custody he would never come back.

The worst pain of all was that he was the only person who could avenge Maggie, who could bring her justice, and he had no idea how to do that.

He was positive of only one thing. He had to run.

LUCIA ANGELOS had no idea that two cameras and three agents were watching her every move. No one had been around when she arrived at Ricardo Vasquez's apartment and let herself in with a key.

In watching Lucia search the apartment meticulously for over two hours, FBI Agent Carl White showed remarkable patience. There was no chance she would find anything; forensics had long ago turned the place upside-down. But Carl had got nowhere in figuring out what Vasquez was doing with the Cintron 421, and his instincts told him that Lucia would change all that. Finally, he sent the agents in to frighten her into talking.

Six agents burst into the apartment, guns drawn and screaming at Lucia to hit the floor. She did so, then started yelling that she had done nothing wrong. Carl had the agents cuff her and read her her rights, though in truth she hadn't done anything to warrant arrest. They drove her downtown to Miami PD, took her possessions and cellphone, then let her stew in the holding cell for four hours before bringing her into an interrogation room.

'What were you looking for?' Carl asked, the moment he walked in.

'My stuff,' she said.

'What kind of stuff?'

'Just stuff; clothes and things. A pair of shoes. Stuff, you know?'

'You keep your clothes and shoes inside the mattress?'

'Jewellery . . . I hide stuff in there,' she said.

'Let me see it,' he said.

'See what?'

'The jewellery "stuff" that was in the mattress—let me see it.'

She shrugged. 'It wasn't there. Must have been stolen.'

Carl pulled up a chair next to her and leaned in close. 'Here's the thing, Lucia,' he said softly. 'You think this is no big deal, that you'll jerk me around for a while and then I'll let you go. But this is the biggest deal you'll ever be involved in. A much bigger deal than you can handle. Whatever Ricardo was doing, it was a threat to this country. And if you don't help me,

DON'T TELL A SOUL | 63

I am going to bury you so far down that you will never come up for air.'

'I didn't do nothing wrong.'

'Then it's a shame that the next time you see your little Carmela she'll have three grown kids and grey hair. You understand what I'm saying?'

Lucia understood very well. She was afraid of them, but not as afraid as she was of the man who'd sent her to the apartment. 'Does my mother know about this?' she asked, since her mother was caring for the little girl.

Carl looked at his watch. 'The agents will be at her house in twenty minutes. Is she afraid of guns?'

Even if Lucia hadn't been told to give in, she would have done so at that point anyway. 'I was looking for money.'

Carl gave a slight nod of approval. 'Which money might that be?'

'Ricardo said he was being paid a lot of money, and he'd buy me stuff with it when he came back. It was promised to me, and since he ain't around to use it, I went looking for it.' When Carl didn't look convinced, she added, 'I earned it, you know? I took enough shit from him.'

'Who was paying him?'

'I don't know his name, but Ricardo was scared of him, I can tell you that. Every time he talked to him on the phone, he got all nervous.'

'You were there when they talked?'

'A couple of times. He talked soft, and I pretended like I was asleep.'

Every call from the apartment phone and Ricardo's cellphone had been checked, turning up nothing suspicious. 'What phone did he use?'

'A cellphone. He thought they wouldn't be able to connect him to it.'

'We checked all the calls he made,' Carl said. It was time for him to appear sympathetic. 'Lucia, you didn't start all this; you just got caught up in it. We don't want you; we want what you know.'

She nodded. 'OK. Ricardo didn't use his cellphone. He used mine. The one your people took from me.'

TIM HAD TO TAKE deep breaths and tell himself not to panic. He didn't want to make any stupid mistakes. He had to think and act deliberately, even though he was operating in an area in which he had absolutely no experience.

His estimation was that he'd have at least a five-hour head start. When Nick realised that Tim had left, it was unlikely that he'd immediately notify Novack. Surely he'd give Tim time in the hope that he would come back.

But Tim would not be back.

Logic told him that running was foolish and self-destructive, but it was no match for his gut feeling that it was his only chance.

He filled two suitcases with clothes and put them in his car. He also took what he had come to think of as 'the file'. He had never opened it, and had thought he never would, but it could be crucial to his current situation.

Tim went back in to get Kiley and write a note to Nick, which he left in an envelope on the door. It said that he needed a little time to think, and anything Nick could do to arrange that would be much appreciated. Tim regretted deceiving him, but he had no real choice.

Just before he left, he went to the top of his bedroom closet and opened a box he kept there. The box contained a handgun, which Tim had got after Maggie's death, when the media uproar resulted in his receiving a number of death threats. He hadn't touched it since, but thought he should take it, though he recognised that it might prove more dangerous than helpful.

With Kiley in the back seat, Tim drove to his bank. He knew that once he was considered a fugitive, his funds would be cut off. Tim had $21,000 in his current account, which he withdrew. He also took the maximum cash advances off his credit cards, smiling and telling the curious assistant manager that he was headed for Vegas. As he left the bank with almost $35,000, half the bank employees were staring at him. Tim knew that the police would soon be talking to every one of them.

The next issue was Kiley. Much as he wanted to, he couldn't take her with him. He briefly considered asking Danny or Will to care for her, but decided that Eden would be a better choice. He trusted her to be responsible, and to provide Kiley with a loving, permanent home if that was how this all turned out. He was not yet technically a fugitive, so she could say with some truth that she was simply doing a favour for a friend.

Tim headed for Eden's house, hoping she was home.

Not only was Eden home, she saw him through the window and came out to the porch to greet him. Seeing the look on his face, she said, 'What is it?'

As she led him inside, he said, 'I was hoping you could take care of Kiley. I'm going to go away for a while.'

'Where are you going?' she asked.

'I'm not sure. Will you watch her?'

'Of course I'll watch her. But please tell me what's going on.'

'The finger . . . the finger in the box . . . it was Maggie's.'

Eden put her hand to her mouth. 'Oh my God. No . . .'

'They're planning to arrest me, but if they take me in, I'll never get out.'

'How could they know it was—?'

'The DNA test. According to Nick, there's no doubt about it.'

'But how could that be?'

'I don't know. If it's really her finger, then I don't see how she could have died in the explosion. But that raises other possibilities that are terrible.'

'Oh, Tim, I'm so sorry.'

'Thank you. And I appreciate your doing this more than you know. If they find out, just tell them that I asked you to watch my dog, which you've done before. You had no way of knowing I was running from the police.'

'But where are you running to?'

'I honestly don't know. Someplace out of the way, where I can think.'

'Stay here. They'd have no reason to look here. Nobody except Nick even knows we're friends.'

Tim's answer was firm. 'No. Thank you, but no. Eden, you could go to jail. I cannot involve you in this any more than I already have.'

'I'm not talking about you staying here permanently. Just until we can figure out your next step. And I can help. You'll need someone to help.'

He knew she was right. He had to learn who was behind this nightmare, and what they had to gain from it, because he couldn't hide for ever. As a fugitive, alone, it seemed an impossible ask.

He nodded. 'Just for tonight. One way or the other I leave here tomorrow.'

EVEN BEFORE HE SAW the note, Nick knew intuitively that Tim had run.

It was understandable, but ill advised. Tim was not Osama Bin Laden preparing to hide out in the mountains. He was a businessman from New Jersey, and Nick figured his only outdoor survival experience was sitting in the upper deck at Giants Stadium for a December game against the Redskins.

Fortunately, Nick had decided not to call Novack until he had Tim in hand, ready to turn himself in. Since neither Tim nor Nick had officially been notified that there was an arrest warrant issued, Tim's not being available would not immediately lead to his being classified as a fugitive. But that was a short-term respite, and Tim would eventually be taken into custody. If he tried to contact Nick in the meantime, he wouldn't like what he heard.

Nick drove back to his office, then called Eden at her house.

After several rings, she picked up. 'Hello?'

'It's Nick. Has Tim contacted you?'

'No. Why?'

'Eden, if you talk to him, tell him to call me. Tell him it's not too late, but pretty soon it will be. Do you understand?'

'Yes.'

With that one-word answer, he knew that Eden had in fact seen Tim, and might even be with him at that very moment. She didn't question Nick about his cryptic message, which meant she already knew the answers.

'Eden, stay away from this. Don't make the worst mistake of your life.'

'Thanks, big brother.'

'I mean it. You can wind up in prison.' He could have added 'or worse'. The fact was, based on the evidence Nick was aware of, Tim was very possibly a killer of women, and an unusually sick one at that.

It was the job of a defence attorney to provide the accused with the best possible representation, so that a jury could fairly decide guilt or innocence. Nick normally spent no time wondering whether his clients had committed the crime of which they were accused. But this was different. It was personal. If Tim was guilty, Eden was in more danger than she could handle.

Nick got off the phone feeling more afraid and less in control than at any time he could remember. His client was perched on the edge of a cliff, and his sister was out there with him. And it was a long way down.

SIX

'I know where you can stay,' Eden said. 'Why didn't I think of it before?' They were sitting in her den, petting the dogs as they talked. It could have been a perfectly normal scene. But for the last hour they had been discussing what might be the best steps for Tim to take to maximise his chances of surviving. It was a conversation punctuated by lengthy, periodic silences, as each tried to grapple with Tim's predicament.

'Where?' he asked.

'There's a house in Lincoln Park; it's fairly isolated . . . set in the woods. The school owns it; we use it for visiting professors, graduate exchange students, that kind of thing.' She stood up to get her address book.

'And it's empty now?' Tim asked.

She nodded. 'For at least the next six weeks. A colleague of mine has been living there, but he's on sabbatical.'

'If I'm found there, it will be obvious to the police that you arranged it.'

'No, I could have told you about it long ago. Look, it's the perfect situation; anyone who lives nearby would be used to seeing different people in the house at different times. There's even a car there you could use.'

'That's good, because I can't just hole up in there; I'd have to come and go. Somehow I've got to figure out who has done this to me, and I'm not going to be able to call suspects in to be interviewed.'

She looked dubious. 'You have any experience at things like this?'

He shook his head. 'Of course not.'

They lapsed into another silence, broken by her saying, 'I can help.'

'You're already doing much too much.'

'I can help you check things out, talk to people.'

He couldn't help but smile. 'You have any experience with this?'

'About the same as you.'

He shook his head. 'You're too far out on a limb already. The more you do, the more jeopardy you're in. I'll bet Nick told you that when he called.'

'He did. But I'll be careful. You need help, and I seem to be your only chance. Now, we can debate it some more, or we can make concrete plans.'

They made plans, figuring out everything from how they would contact each other to how they would reduce the chance of his being identified.

By the time Tim went to sleep, he had closely cropped light brown hair, drugstore, non-prescription glasses and a plan to grow a moustache and goatee. Even without the facial hair, the difference was dramatic.

Eden came up behind him. 'Your own mother wouldn't recognise you.'

He nodded. 'Yeah, but Novack's not my mother.'

AT THAT VERY MOMENT, Novack was in Tim's apartment, directing a thorough search of the place. So far it had turned up nothing of obvious value, though forensics were still busy doing their thing. Novack was by this time all but certain that Tim was on the run; there were no suitcases to be found, and even the toiletries had been removed from the bathroom.

Novack called Nick at home. 'I'm at your client's apartment, counsellor.'

'Let me speak to him,' Nick said.

'That would be difficult. He's not here.'

'Then what the hell are you doing there?'

'Looking for your client, and exercising a lawful search warrant.'

'I'm coming over. I don't want you stealing any towels.'

'Bring Wallace with you, so I can arrest him.'

'On what charge?'

'The murder of Margaret Wallace.'

McDermott had decided to charge Wallace only with his wife's murder, not Sheila's. They had much more evidence, circumstantial and otherwise, in Maggie's case, and they could hold the other charge in reserve.

THE MEDIA WERE ENLISTED in the hunt for Tim at 6 a.m. Novack held a hastily arranged news conference on the steps in front of the state police headquarters. The temperature outside was 16°F, and the reporters were shivering and huddled together to ward off the cold. Novack strode to the microphone wearing just his sports jacket.

Like most police at such conferences, Novack adopted the attitude that he was there reluctantly. He treated the reporters' questions as unwanted intrusions, and the questioners as if they were there to defeat the cause of justice.

'Timothy Wallace is wanted for questioning as a person of interest in the investigation of the murder of Margaret Wallace. We're asking the public to call a hot-line number if they have any information as to his whereabouts.'

Since many of the reporters had covered the investigation after Maggie's death, this piece of news prompted a barrage of questions.

'Why now? Is there new evidence in the case?'

'I can't discuss any of the evidence in an ongoing investigation,' Novack said. 'You people know that by now.'

'Is there a warrant out for his arrest?'

'We are not prepared to discuss the warrant at this time.'

'Is he on the run? Is that why you need the public's help in finding him?'

'We have no information as to his whereabouts. When we find him, we'll know why we couldn't find him.'

Novack showed Tim's picture and passed out copies, and announced the number to call with information. He agreed to answer one or two more questions, incorrectly implying that he had answered the previous ones.

'Do you consider him armed and dangerous?'

'I would advise people not to find out; if you see him, call the number and let the police handle it. Thank you very much.' With that, Novack headed back to the comfort of the headquarters building.

THE POLICE HUNT for Tim was the lead story on every station's morning newscast. By this time, Tim was in the Lincoln Park house that Eden had told him about. He had been busy in the preceding hours. He had rented a prepaid cellphone at an all-night electronics store, using a fake name, and putting down $500 in cash on it. He had also taken licence plates off a car at a shopping mall, and put them on his own car. The theft of the plates was the first actual crime he was aware of ever committing in his life.

Tim had called Danny from a payphone early in the morning. 'What's the matter?' Danny had asked, once he got himself awake.

'They're trying to arrest me for Maggie's death.'

'What? This is bullshit; you took a goddamn lie-detector test, and—'

'It was her finger. At the racketball club, it was her finger.' The thought was so horrifying he found it jarring each time he had to verbalise it.

'Oh, no . . . Tim . . . How the hell could that be?'

'I don't know, but I have to find out.'

'Where are you now?'

'On the way to Pennsylvania, to a motel outside of Philly.' Tim wasn't sure whether he told the lie because he didn't want to put Danny in the position of having to conceal something from the police, or because he wasn't sure he could trust anyone, not even his partner and best friend.

'Tim, if the cops are after you . . . are you sure this is a good idea?'

'No, but it's the only one I've got.'

'So how can I help?'

'Pay my lawyer for me when he comes to you. We can take it out of the company, and—'

'No problem, Tim. I'll give him whatever's necessary. What else can I do?'

'Nothing. You need to stay as far away from this as possible.'

'What the hell are you going to do?'

'Figure this out.'

'I'M SORRY I did that to you,' Tim said as soon as Nick picked up the phone. He was worried about Nick's reaction; he needed him as an ally.

'You didn't do it to me,' Nick said. 'You did it to you.'

'I just didn't feel like I had a choice.'

'You had a choice, Tim. You made the wrong one,' Nick said bluntly. 'You felt the pressure and you threw up a goddamn air ball.'

Tim felt both annoyed and scared. 'Where do we go from here?'

'I'm under a legal obligation to advise you that you're committing a felony by evading arrest, and to advise you to surrender to the proper authorities immediately.'

'And if I don't?'

'Then you don't. You're calling the shots here, at least for now.'

'Will you continue to help me?'

'Of course I'll help you; I'm your lawyer.'

'Thank you,' said Tim. 'You don't know how much I appreciate that.'

'Before you say anything else, I do not want you to tell me where you are. If you do, I'm obligated to reveal it to the police.'

'OK. What am I allowed to tell you?'

'Any ideas you have that might help your situation . . . anything you want me to follow through on. Things like that.'

'I've been trying to think who would be doing this to me, and why,' Tim said. 'The only thing I have to go on is that Cashman is involved in this.'

'But you don't know who he is. Or why he targeted you.'

'No. But I saw him; I spoke to him. And you have his picture.'

Nick saw where he was going with this and jumped on it. 'The media will eat it up. I've probably had fifty calls already looking for information from our side; when they get the sketch of Cashman, they'll go crazy.'

'Somebody has to know him. Should we offer a reward?'

'You have access to money?'

'Just contact my partner, Danny McCabe. He'll front the money from the company for this and for your fees.' He paused. 'Is he allowed to do that?'

'Sure. Everybody's entitled to an expensive defence. I'll get right on it.'

'Can I keep calling you?' Tim asked. 'I mean, would they tap your phone?'

Nick had thought of this and discounted it. 'No way, at least not now. The chance that they'd risk destroying their own case by breaking attorney–client privilege would scare them off. Maybe later when they get desperate.'

'Listen, Nick . . .'

'What?'

'I've been trying to look at this a little bit from your point of view. You don't know me, and you probably think I'm guilty. But—'

'You're not going to tell me you're innocent, are you?'

'Actually, I was.'

'Save your breath. Believe it or not, for the moment it's irrelevant. You have a TV where you are?'

'Yes.'

'Then start watching it,' Nick said, 'because your lawyer's good-looking face is going to be everywhere.'

'THIS IS CARL WHITE, special agent with the FBI, from the Miami office,' Captain Donovan said.

'Good to meet you,' Anders said, shaking White's hand.

'What's going on?' asked Novack, aware that this wasn't a social visit.

'Agent White is interested in our investigation of Tim Wallace.'

'Why is that?' Novack asked.

'Remember the car that exploded near the turnpike?' Carl asked. 'Its driver called Wallace's office from Florida twice in the ten days before his death.'

'Any idea why?' Anders asked.

'Not yet.'

'It doesn't make sense,' Novack said. 'I don't see Wallace as a terrorist blowing up buildings. He does his killing up close and personal.'

'But I understand his wife was killed in an explosion?'

Novack nodded. 'She was. And we've also connected him to a now deceased explosives expert in Carson, Wyoming.'

'How did he become deceased?' White asked.

'He had his throat slit in prison. And we believe his wife was Wallace's second victim.'

White was clearly surprised to hear this. 'Wallace had two victims?'

'At a minimum,' Novack said.

'I've agreed with Agent White that we will share all relevant information from both his and our investigations,' said Donovan.

'With who determining relevance?' Novack asked.

A hard edge crept into Donovan's voice. 'That will be determined jointly.'

'Hey, I'm not looking to step on your toes,' White said. 'We all want to get Wallace off the street and find out what the hell is going on. The resources of the bureau might even be helpful to you.'

Novack thought about that for a few moments, then stood and shook White's hand. 'They might at that,' he said.

'THIS IS THE MAN we're looking for. He goes by the name of Jeff Cashman, but that's probably an alias.' As Nick said this, he held up the sketch of Cashman so that Larry King's audience could get a good look at it.

It was Nick's fifth television appearance of the day, and he was sitting in a studio on West 54th Street in Manhattan, from where he had done all five interviews. He had not actually met a single interviewer.

'And why are you looking for him?' Larry asked.

'Unlike the police, I do not intend to talk publicly about the evidence, but it would be very fair to say that Mr Cashman is a person of interest.'

'Is he of interest to the police as well?' King asked.

'He should be,' Nick said, frowning disdainfully. 'They've known about him for weeks, yet they've refused to release this sketch publicly and put out a request for information. If anyone has ever seen this man or knows who he is, please call me at 201-525-3176. We are offering a reward of twenty-five thousand dollars for information that leads to our finding him. Do not approach him; we consider him to be armed and very dangerous.'

'Your client, Timothy Wallace, has a warrant out for his arrest. Do you know where he is?'

'I don't have the slightest idea,' said Nick. 'And I'm very worried for his safety. Dangerous people have targeted him, and he's justifiably frightened.'

'So you've spoken to him?'

'That is not a question I would answer whatever the facts were. It starts to get into the area of attorney–client privilege. I just can't go there, Larry.'

King tried to press him for more information, but Nick was a master at answering evasively. He left satisfied that he had accomplished his main goals. He'd got Cashman's face in front of the public and had also conveyed to that public that there was another side to the story.

For Tim, sitting in a strange house watching Nick on TV was totally surreal. Hearing himself talked about in a predicament that was at the same time bewildering and overwhelmingly frightening was almost too much to bear.

He turned off the television and got into the strange bed. He had never felt so alone. He missed Maggie more than ever, and now feared for her in death as much as he ever had in life. What had she endured? How much had she suffered? How could he have left her so unprotected?

With Maggie gone, there was no one he could fully trust. Someone with an intimate knowledge of him was conspiring against him. How else could his life have been so thoroughly destroyed? Someone had known which boat was his and when he would be on it. They'd known where he would go on New Year's Eve, and where he lived. They knew he'd been in Wyoming, and where and when he played racketball.

It was disconcerting to Tim that the only person he could think of who fitted that bill was Danny.

But what would Danny have to gain? Could it somehow have to do with the business? Perhaps Danny was stealing money, or using the company for illicit purposes? But why go to such lengths? Why kill Sheila?

Tim simply could not imagine the Danny he knew doing any of this. But he could not comprehend anyone doing it, and someone obviously was. It pained Tim to consider it, but Danny had to be at the top of the list of suspects.

A list that at the moment included only one name.

LUCIA ANGELOS was glad it was over. She'd done as she was told, the FBI was gone and she'd even got some money out of it in the process.

It was time for her to take that money and start living, which was what she told her sister Maria on one of their endless phone calls. 'I'm going to move to New York and get a job.'

'You always say that,' Maria said, 'but you never do it.'

'This time I will,' vowed Lucia. 'There's nothing to keep me here. In New York at least I have you.'

'But I have Orlando.' Maria was referring to her husband, with whom she did not have a marriage made in heaven.

'So you can leave him, and we'll move in together.'

Maria laughed. 'Of course. We'll go to Park Avenue and have servants.'

Lucia was not familiar with Park Avenue, and she was about to ask about it when there was a knock on her door. 'Hold on a sec . . .' She put the phone down and went to answer it.

She opened the door and saw the man she hoped never to see again.

'Hello, Lucia, nice to see you. You're looking well.'

'I did what you wanted. I told the FBI everything you said.'

'I know you did. I'm just here to make things clean and neat.'

He moved towards her, and as he did she looked directly into his eyes. Suddenly she knew exactly why Ricardo had been so afraid of this man.

But by then it was too late.

BY TEN O'CLOCK in the morning, over a thousand tips had come in to Nick's hot line. This was far more than the firm's investigative arm was equipped to handle, and it was likely that many more could not even get through. The hope was that anyone with legitimate information would be persistent.

While the tips were being screened to eliminate the obvious fakes, Nick could only passively wait for something to develop, and passive waiting was never his speciality. He wanted to know all the evidence the prosecution had against Tim, but they had no obligation to turn anything over until Tim was in custody and arraigned. Still, Nick had his sources within the department, and he worked them vigorously for information.

EDEN ALEXANDER, who hadn't watched more than ten hours of television in the previous year, sat glued to the set. She cringed every time CNN broke in with a 'breaking news' banner. None of them had anything to do with Tim.

She and Tim had agreed that, even though she knew his new cellphone number, if they had to communicate it would be through email. She had opened a new email address on Yahoo with the screen name 'Kileysfriend', and checked it repeatedly. Tim had not yet sent her any messages.

Eden was not taking Kiley and Travis for walks, instead using the yard behind her house. She tried to be alert, to see if she were being watched, and so far had not detected anything. But she had little confidence that this meant much; for all she knew they could be tracking her every move.

IT IS A TRUISM in Washington that some of the most powerful people in government are complete unknowns to the public at large. One such person was Gregory Campbell, who had come to Washington from his home in Boise, Idaho, as part of the congressional page programme. He never left, attending Georgetown University and then immediately securing a job as a low-level minority staffer on the House Appropriations Committee.

For twenty-five years, Campbell made no effort to shed his cloak of public anonymity. Working fourteen-hour days, he became a crucial cog in the workings of government. He advanced to the position of lead minority staffer on the Senate Appropriations Committee, which is where he came under the wing of Senator Fred Collinsworth.

If one had to come under a wing, that was about as good as it could get. The senator, with his myriad contacts and influence in the financial world, gradually and secretly made Campbell a very rich man. There was no outright bribery, just the occasional prescient stock tip, or a fortuitous land purchase in an area that would soon be adjacent to new highways. Eventually Collinsworth arranged for him to move to the executive branch, specifically the General Services Administration, where he could be even more influential in steering large contracts to places the senator wanted them steered.

As soon as Gregory got the call that he was to meet with Keith Rivers, he knew that Collinsworth had a problem. Rivers was always the senator's chosen problem-solver, and he was as good a solver as Gregory had ever encountered.

They met at a restaurant in northern Virginia, though they could have dined anywhere in Washington and not attracted attention.

Soon after they sat down, the waiter came over and asked, 'Would you care for something to drink? Or would you like to hear our specials?'

'No,' said Rivers.

'I'll give you a few moments,' the waiter mumbled, and beat a hasty retreat.

Once he was gone, Rivers asked, 'Have you heard about the man wanted for murder in New Jersey?'

Gregory was not a watcher of television, nor did he read crime stories in the newspaper. 'I don't think so . . .'

'Daniel McCabe's partner is currently a fugitive.'

Gregory remembered that Collinsworth had dealt with this potential embarrassment once before. 'Is that the guy whose wife died on the boat?'

Rivers nodded. 'It is. There have been a number of developments in the case; you should familiarise yourself with the media coverage.'

'I will,' Gregory said, now fully aware of the purpose of the dinner.

Never a master of subtlety, Rivers insisted on stating it explicitly. 'It can never become public knowledge that the senator had anything to do with the awarding of the contract to that company. He didn't even know about it until long after the fact.'

Gregory nodded in solemn agreement. 'Of course.'

'The grand strategy of awarding the contracts to small-business people was his; then he left the details to people like yourself. He doesn't micro-manage; he lets people do their jobs.'

'Absolutely. That's one of his greatest strengths.'

'Enjoy your dinner.'

Rivers got up and left the restaurant without eating. Gregory wasn't sure that he had ever seen him eat, or that the senator even allowed it.

Gregory signalled for the waiter to come over. He wanted to hear the specials, and he sure as hell needed a drink.

AFTER HIS MOMENT of clarity regarding Danny, Tim had reversed himself and decided that it wasn't possible. He knew Danny too well to believe him capable of all this. Putting it to the back of his mind, he took a deep breath, and opened 'the file'.

The file included newspaper stories about Maggie's death and the subsequent investigation, the coroner's report, the coastguard report and all the other official documents that Tim had been sent after he had been cleared of the murder. He had never wanted to read any of it, but he had requested that Meredith prepare a file, and now he felt he had to go through it in the hope that he might learn something relevant.

It was beyond painful, and the worst part was the lack of humanity that Maggie was granted. In the cold type of the documents she was an object, without her smile, her personality, her dreams. Page after page was about Maggie, yet they had nothing to do with who she was.

The newspaper articles about that day out on the boat that had been written while Tim was still in hospital were basically speculation, albeit informed by the coastguard information office. But, as Tim realised with a jolt, even he may not have had full knowledge of what took place. If it was Maggie's finger that was found at the racketball club, then it was entirely likely that she had not died in that explosion. It destroyed the only consolation he had held on to, that her death was instantaneous and painless.

Tim found himself consumed by doubt. Had he not seen what he thought he saw? He forced himself to read the articles dispassionately, logically.

The story presented was a simple one: Tim had apparently left the boat to go into the water, and while Maggie was alone, the motor caught fire and blew up. A private plane travelling overhead saw the fire—five to ten minutes after the explosion, to judge from the size of the blaze—and called in the emergency. When the coastguard cutter arrived, small pieces of the boat were still floating and could be retrieved, but Maggie's body was presumed to have been blown apart and washed away. Tim was found floating unconscious, alone, held up by his life jacket. No other boats were in the area.

The coastguard report presented basically the same story, and Tim moved on to the police reports.

Suddenly, the realisation hit him between the eyes. No other boats? There was an Oceanfast not far in the distance when he went into the water for the hat. He and Maggie had both admired it. And it was certainly close enough to see the explosion. How could the people on that boat not have reported it?

Tim tried to answer that question for himself. Perhaps they were asleep, or they didn't want to be involved, or they were out there for a reason, nothing to do with the explosion, that they didn't want anyone to know about.

But none of those answers rang true. They had to have witnessed, or at least heard, the explosion. In such a situation they would surely have tried to help.

Unless they were out there watching Tim's boat.

And waiting for it to blow up.

ANDERS AND NOVACK went into Captain Donovan's office completely unprepared for what he had to say.

'There's a tip that came in from a guy who claims to know Jeff Cashman. I want you to check it out.'

Novack was immediately sceptical. 'Why is he coming to us? Why isn't he going after the reward?'

'Because he must want something else more than money,' Donovan said. 'My guess is he's looking for a "get out of jail free" card.'

'He's inside?' Anders asked in surprise.

'Captain, we're pretty busy on this, and—'

Donovan interrupted. 'He said Cashman was his cell mate, and that Cashman is not his real name.'

'What's his real name?' Novack asked, annoyed at this waste of time.

'I don't know. You'll have to ask this guy that when you talk to him.'

'Isn't there somebody else you can put on this?'

Donovan shook his head. 'Not on something this important.'

'Important?' Anders said. 'What makes a prison informant so important?'

'There's something you haven't told us yet?' Novack asked.

Donovan nodded. 'There is. According to this guy, they were cell mates at Lampley Prison, just outside of Carson, Wyoming.'

DESPITE NICK'S stated assurance that his phone would not be tapped, Tim was reluctant to contact him too often. But this time was worth the risk.

Nick's secretary answered the phone, and Tim asked to speak with him, telling her that it was Jerry Koosman calling. A huge Mets fan, Nick had suggested using the name of the former Mets left-handed pitcher as a signal.

'Talk to me,' Nick said immediately, not wanting the call to last too long.

'I read through the reports for the day Maggie died. There's no mention of another boat nearby. I saw one, but the people on board apparently never reported the explosion. The fire was called in by a pilot flying over.'

'So?'

'So people out on the water take care of each other; it's like a private fraternity. There would have to be a damn good reason for not reporting it.'

'Did you mention it when they questioned you back then?'

'I don't think so. I guess I just assumed the people on the boat had been the ones to report it. I never made the connection until now.'

'Anything distinctive about the boat?' Nick asked wearily. 'Maybe a skull and crossbones and a sign that said "Really Bad Guys On Board"?'

'Not quite,' Tim said. 'But it was an Oceanfast 360, worth over two million. Maggie and I were admiring it that day; we even joked about it.'

'How many of them would there be around here?'

'No way for me to know. But this one was painted an ugly green, like army khakis used to be. It also had two white stripes all the way round. It would be the only one of its kind, if it hasn't been repainted.'

'Then let's find out who owns it,' Nick said. 'Let's take one of our investigators off the bullshit hunt for Cashman and put him on this.'

'So nothing is happening on Cashman?'

'Only that every crackpot east of Maui is trying to get the reward.'

'He's out there, Nick,' Tim said. 'I'm not making him up.'

'OK. I'm on this boat thing,' Nick assured him. 'We'll get you out of this.'

'How?' Tim asked.

'We'll think of something.'

SITTING AT A CORNER TABLE at Spumoni's, a fashionable, overpriced DC restaurant, Jimmy Lee Curry was waiting for Susan Moreno to show up, buy him lunch and slip him an important story. When he was studying for his master's in journalism, he'd had instilled in him the need to be unbiased, ethical and relentless. But at this stage of his life, Jimmy Lee figured, the 'relentless' trait was overrated.

There were maybe a dozen journalists big enough to limit the extent of their investigative efforts to picking up their phone, and Jimmy Lee was one of them. People who had news to spread called him, and if he found it interesting enough, he wrote a column on it, and people fawned all over him.

Susan Moreno was in her mid-thirties, a tall, strikingly beautiful woman. In fact, she was just about the best-looking shark Jimmy Lee had ever met. The top assistant to Walter Evans, the superstar junior senator from Ohio, Susan had a reputation as his enforcer. When Senator Evans wanted something to happen, he sent Susan Moreno to make it happen. She performed the same function for Evans that Keith Rivers did for Senator Collinsworth.

Susan always waited until coffee was ordered before delivering her message, and this time was no exception. 'Have you heard about Tim Wallace, the guy in New Jersey who the police are after for killing his wife?'

'Of course.'

'His company's doing construction work on the Federal Center complex in Newark. They've been handling the security aspects of the buildings.'

'Why is that important?'

'Because he got the work through Senator Collinsworth.'

'Really? What is Collinsworth's connection to Wallace?'

'Wallace's partner is Collinsworth's nephew,' she said.

This was only moderately interesting to Jimmy Lee. 'I assume there's more to this? Something that more directly benefits your boss?'

She smiled. 'Pending our negotiations; we have to agree on the terms.'

'Which are?'

'You write this story, then in two weeks, the day after the Federal Center opens, you write the follow-up piece.'

He nodded; here it comes. 'And that includes . . . ?'

'Remember the explosion on the Jersey Turnpike a while back? The driver of the van that blew up had called Wallace a few times in the week before he died.' She waited for this to sink in, then added, 'So what we have here is Collinsworth getting major security construction work for someone who in turn is dealing with a guy with a truckload of Cintron 421.'

The question of what Susan's boss would gain from this story was now amply answered. Evans and Collinsworth were bitter rivals, especially since Collinsworth got the nod as head of the Senate Appropriations Committee, leaving Evans a disgruntled number two. They were also expected to play out their rivalry in the presidential election just two years away.

Jimmy Lee smiled. 'Now you're talking.'

Susan took a leisurely sip of coffee, then put the cup down and returned the smile. 'So, Jimmy Lee, you think this might be a decent story?'

'Do I need a second source on this?'

Susan shook her head. 'This is rock solid.'

'Why wait the two weeks for the second piece?' he asked.

She leaned forward, lowering her voice. 'It's just been decided that the dignitaries the night of the opening will include the President of the United States. Now security will be tripled because of this, so there's no danger. But your story will say that President Markham just spent the evening in a building built by Senator Collinsworth's mad bomber.'

'Why don't you stay and get the bill?' asked Jimmy Lee, standing up. 'I've got a story to write.'

'YOU HAVE NO IDEA where he is?' Danny asked.

'Of course not,' said Meredith. 'You think he would tell me and not you?'

'I don't think he would tell anybody. But that's not what I mean. I mean, can you figure out where he might be? You run his life, for Christ's sake.'

'Not this part of it,' she said. 'This part scares the hell out of me.'

'He's going to be fine. He didn't do anything wrong and he'll be fine.'

'Is it having any effect on the business?' she asked.

'Probably. The FBI has been down at the site, and Homeland Security have been all over the place, although they might have done that anyway.'

'Any chance they're going to cancel the opening?'

'Zero. Too many big shots are going to be there.'

'Have the police talked to you?' she asked.

'Twice, the FBI once. I told them I don't know where he is, and that he'd never do anything like they're saying.'

Meredith nodded; she had pretty much said the same thing to the same people. Of course, if she knew where Tim was, she would never tell the police anyway. She was not sure she could say the same for Danny.

'There was this woman I saw him with recently. Tall, blonde hair . . . You have any idea who she is?' Danny asked.

'No,' Meredith lied. 'He never mentioned anyone.' She neglected to say that Eden Alexander had called to invite Tim to dinner.

Eden Alexander. That was a name she was not about to share with Danny.

SEVEN

Georgie Silvers had no illusions about the opportunity that had presented itself. You don't spend twenty-two years in prison without knowing what you can get away with. What he had to say might get him special considerations, but there was no way it would let him walk.

He wasn't sure he even wanted to walk. He'd adjusted to life in this New Jersey state prison. Besides, if he got out, he'd wind up back here anyway.

These cops didn't even seem that interested in him, which was no great surprise. They hadn't been the ones to go public with the guy's picture.

Novack put the sketch on the table. 'So you know this man?'

Georgie nodded. 'Yeah. I was on the inside with him up at Lampley.'

'What's his name?' Anders asked.

Georgie laughed. 'Come on, you guys know that ain't the way this works.'

'You want something in return for the name?' Novack asked. 'What can we do for you? Maybe a villa in the Caribbean? A suite at Caesar's Palace?'

'I'm a reasonable guy,' Georgie said. 'You want the name, we can make a deal. I could have gone to that lawyer and collected the reward, but I'm trying to be a good citizen.' The truth was, he had little use for the money inside, and no family outside. The cops could do much more for him.

'Your country salutes you,' said Novack. 'What do you want?'

'A job in the library. Right now I'm in the kitchen, sweating my ass off.'

'You think we're here from the employment agency? We don't assign the jobs here, Georgie,' said Anders.

'No, but you can convince the people who do. And in July, when they do the prisoner reassignments, I want to go to Milford.' Milford Federal Prison was a minimum-security facility, not a place where repeat breaking-and-entering offenders like Georgie Silvers would wind up.

'Milford?' asked Novack, making no attempt to conceal his amusement. 'You want to go there? Run for Congress and take a bribe.'

'I'll tell you what; if this guy turns out to be somebody important, then try and get me to Milford. Is that fair? Meanwhile, get me the library job.'

Novack thought for a moment. 'OK . . . deal. Now what's his name?'

'Billy Zimmerman. We used to call him Dollar Bill, 'cause he was in for forging cheques.'

Novack and Anders made eye contact at the possibility that 'Dollar Bill' renamed himself 'Cashman'. It rang slightly too true for comfort.

'And he looked like this?' Anders asked, pointing at the sketch.

'Nah, not too much. A bunch of stuff's different. But I can tell it's him.'

'How?'

'That's what he said he'd look like, if he had to go into hiding. You know?'

'No, we don't know,' Novack said, annoyed. 'Why don't you tell us?'

'His girlfriend was a make-up artist, for one of those Broadway shows that goes on the road, I think. She—'

'What was her name?'

'Denise. I don't know her last name. She was working upstate in Buffalo at the time on that show about the French guys. It was a musical.'

'*Les Mis?*' It was the only Broadway show Novack had seen in ten years.

'Yeah, that was it. Anyway, she taught Billy how to do the make-up, but they arrested him in bed in the middle of the night. He said if he ever escaped, or if the cops were after him, he was going to change his appearance. He even had his girlfriend draw a picture of what he could look like.'

Novack pointed to the sketch. 'And that's it?'

Georgie nodded. 'That's it.'

THE MAN who had killed Jeff Cashman didn't much care for his latest assignment. Following someone was tedious work, the kind that dumb cops were invented to do. And following Eden Alexander was way beneath him; the only thing worse than leading her boring life was watching her lead it.

It also made no sense at all. If they wanted to know where Wallace was, the way to go about it was not to wait for this broad to lead them to him. The way to do it was to grab her and start inflicting some pain and fear.

The worst part was when she went to school to teach whatever it was she taught. He didn't want to follow her on campus; he'd look too out of place. Instead he parked near the front gate and waited the five or six hours it took for her to come out. Still, he wouldn't have to do this for more than two weeks. If she hadn't led him to Wallace by then, he would simply grab her and extract the information. It gave him something to look forward to.

After that he would make his own move. Instructing him to kill Cashman and the broad in Florida was a mistake his employers would come to regret. It led him to believe they probably had the same fate planned for him.

They thought of themselves as a force that could not be stopped. But no matter how much money and power they had, when it came to both brains and deadly force, they would soon find out that they were not in his league.

EDEN ALEXANDER had never seen the car or the man behind the wheel before. It was a grey MPV parked at the end of her street, and the man was blond, early thirties and so large that the car seemed filled to capacity.

She knew she was being watched, and that he was watching her.

Eden went to her own car, and drove to her job at the university. She waved to the guard at the gate as he let her in. She did not see the MPV behind her at any point, but she would have bet a week's pay it was there.

With an hour before her class, Eden went straight to the faculty room. She was relieved to see Andy Miller, a colleague and friend, having coffee.

'Andy, I need a favour,' she said.

'Shoot.'

'I'd like you to walk out past the main gate. If a grey MPV is near there, I want you to get the licence-plate number. Don't make it obvious that you're looking; don't write down the number, or anything like that.'

'What's going on?' he asked.

'I'm sorry, but I can't say.'

His concern was obvious. 'You OK, Eden?'

She smiled. 'I'm fine. Really.'

He stood up. 'OK. Grey MPV, get the plate number. I'm on the case.'

Andy left, and came back ten minutes later. 'WKT-535,' he said.

'Was there anybody in the car?' she asked.

He nodded. 'Big guy . . . blond hair. I didn't look too closely.'

She forced a smile. 'Great, Andy. Thanks, I really appreciate it.'

'Is there anything else I can do?'

'No, thanks.'

'And you're sure there's nothing wrong?'

'Really, Andy, everything is fine,' she lied, fighting panic.

That had to be a police officer in that car, and he would only be following her if he thought she might lead him to Tim.

Which meant they were both in big trouble.

HE WATCHED the geeky guy pretend not to stare at his licence plate, and immediately knew that the woman had made him do it.

It almost made him laugh out loud; clearly he had been so annoyed at having to waste time following her that he had been careless.

The fleeting, pleasant thought of putting a bullet through the geek's head flashed by him, but he knew that would only complicate things.

He would instead stop following the woman for a couple of days, no big loss since she wasn't leading him anywhere. Then he'd start back up, and if he was lucky she'd spot him again. If that happened he'd grab her, and she'd be only too willing to tell him everything she knew.

It would be a hell of a lot more fun that way.

TIM WAS GOING CRAZY just sitting around the house, and by now his grown-in facial hair had made him confident he wouldn't be recognised by a media-alerted citizen. So he decided he would make his first foray into the outside world by going to the library. He wasn't in need of reading material; he had neglected to bring his laptop with him, so he wanted to use the library computer to contact Eden.

Just walking out of the door of the house was an uncomfortable experience for Tim. He knew the police were not out there waiting for him, but he still looked around warily, and continued doing so even after he pulled away.

The Lincoln Park library was surprisingly large, and even at this early hour had close to fifteen people in it. Relieved to discover that he did not need a library card to use the computers, he signed in, using a fake name.

Tim logged on to the Hotmail address that Eden had created for him, and was surprised to see that he had seven emails waiting. Six were spam, but one was from 'Kileysfriend'. He opened the email and read:

I'm being followed. I don't know who it is, but I'm afraid it's the police. I have the licence number of the car. What should I do?

Tim was stunned. He wanted to get up and pace, to relieve some of the pent-up anxiety, but he couldn't do anything that might attract attention.
He typed a return email:

Tell Nick what you think and give him the plate number. Not over the phone.

He pressed 'send' and waited for a reply, knowing it could take a long time if she were not at home. Less than a minute later, her reply appeared:

I will; I'll write back after I do and tell you what he said. Are you OK?

He wrote back:

Yes. If you get into danger, tell the truth about where I am. This is not your problem.

Her reply:

I'll be careful.

That wasn't good enough for him, so he wrote:

I'm worried about you. Please don't take any unnecessary chances.

Her reply:

Same to you, buddy.

It made Tim smile, something he would have thought impossible under the circumstances. He wished he could be with her, to spend a normal day, but that really *was* impossible under the circumstances.

DENISE WAGNER'S career was not exactly taking off. She was no longer working on theatrical road shows; the fact that her drinking caused her to miss an average of three shows a week had made her less than sought after.

Denise was now in the ignominious position of working for her sister, who managed a large beauty salon in Manhasset, Long Island. Denise was a make-up consultant, and her function was to teach customers of Salon 37 how to apply their make-up in order to enhance their appearance. She didn't have the greatest attitude for the job, but she needed the work.

This was the first beauty salon Novack had ever been in. It was a frightening sight, women camped under enormous machines, and others sporting a head full of tinfoil. This was not the place to be in a lightning storm.

Novack asked the receptionist where he might find Denise Wagner. The woman pointed towards the back, but said that Denise was busy.

'Aren't we all?' asked Novack, not waiting for an answer.

Denise was applying eye shadow to a customer when she saw Novack coming. He noticed the flash of fear in her eyes, followed by resignation. This woman knew why he was here.

'Denise Wagner?' Novack asked, taking out his shield to show her.

'Yes.'

'I'm Detective Novack,' he said, before turning to the customer. 'I think she's done as much as she can for you.'

The customer was rendered momentarily speechless. Denise more gently suggested that she go have her hair worked on, and they could conclude the make-up later. The customer obliged.

'This is about Billy,' Denise said, a statement, not a question.

'Yes.'

'I saw his picture on television.'

'Did you contact anyone about it?' Novack asked.

She shook her head. 'No. I haven't seen him in over a year; I never want to see him again. He's out of my life.'

'But you're sure it was him?'

She nodded. 'I'm sure.'

'Do you know where he is?'

'No.'

'What can you tell me about him?' Novack asked. 'Any relatives, home town, previous jobs . . .'

'I'm sorry, but I really don't know anything. I met him in a bar when I lived out west. At first he seemed really nice. Then he started beating me, and I wanted to leave, but he wouldn't let me. We were together less than three months before he went to jail on some kind of parole violation.'

'And you showed him how to make himself look different?'

She nodded, an anxious look on her face. 'He made me show him.'

Novack questioned her for fifteen minutes, but got few details that might lead him to Billy Zimmerman, the man Tim Wallace knew as Cashman.

This was disconcerting to Novack. He had been positive that Cashman did not exist, and he had been wrong. What else had he been wrong about?

SUCH WAS THE EXTENT of Nick's connections with the police department and prosecutor's office that he knew about Billy Zimmerman three hours after Novack did. It was the first piece of good news the defence had got. Nick didn't expect Novack to do anything with it; he was out to nail Tim to the wall. But Cashman's existence confirmed a piece of Tim's story. That brought the total of confirmed pieces to just one. But for now it would have to do.

Nick was uneasy over the phone call he'd received from Eden a few minutes earlier. She'd sounded scared, and said she needed to talk to him in person. When she arrived, she looked even more worried than she'd sounded.

'I'm being followed, Nick. I'm sure of it.'

'Do you know who it is?'

'No, but I got a look at him; it's a big guy with blond hair. He's driving a grey MPV, and I have his licence-plate number.' She handed it to Nick.

He walked over to the window and looked down at the street, though from that height it was difficult to see much. 'Did he follow you here?'

'I didn't see him, but I didn't want to be too obvious in looking round. Do you think it's the police, thinking I might lead them to Tim?'

'I doubt it. They usually travel in pairs. And the MPV doesn't fit.' Then he said pointedly, 'Why would anyone think you might lead them to Tim?'

'I don't know, Nick. I haven't mentioned Tim to anyone but you. And I don't walk his dog out on the street.'

'Have you had any contact with him?'

She hesitated for a moment before admitting, 'We've emailed.'

'Shit.'

'Is that your considered legal opinion?' she asked.

'Eden, have I mentioned that you are digging a hole for yourself that you may not be able to climb out of?'

'Yes, repeatedly. Now, will you try and find out who is following me?'

He nodded with resignation. 'Yes.'

'Thank you, big brother.'

'SO CASHMAN IS REAL?' Captain Donovan said. 'I thought you said he was bullshit . . . someone Wallace made up.'

Novack could have responded defensively, but he didn't. 'That's what I thought, but I'm not so sure any more.'

'So where the hell does this leave us?' Donovan asked.

'In exactly the same place we were before. There's absolutely no evidence or reason to make us believe that Cashman set Wallace up on this.'

'But Cashman is real.'

Novack nodded. 'Right, and it's possible he was involved in this. Maybe he helped Wallace in some way, and Wallace turned on him. But Cashman sure as hell wasn't out on the water with Maggie Wallace; her husband was. And it was her finger at the racketball club.'

Donovan seemed far from convinced. 'I don't like this. We're acting like we know what's going on, and we don't know shit.'

'When we find Wallace, it will fall into place,' Novack said, without fully believing it.

'When might that be? I've got the brass coming down on me about this.'

Anders had been letting Novack take the heat, but now he felt he should say something. 'It'll be soon.'

'You a fortuneteller, or have you seen something I haven't?'

'This is not a guy at home on the streets,' Anders said. 'He's holed up somewhere, but eventually he'll have to come out, and when he does, he won't last twenty-four hours.'

Unconvinced, Donovan turned back to Novack. 'We're starting to look stupid for not being able to catch Wallace. But it's nowhere near as stupid as we're going to look if he's not our man, if Cashman set this up.'

'There's nothing to worry about,' Novack said.

'Then why the hell am I worried?'

To SAY the Passaic River was not as polluted as it once was is to damn it with faint praise. The truth is, a lot of effort over the years had taken what was once not much more than an above-ground sewer and turned it into an acceptably clean waterway. There were even a few stretches where people went to fish. One such place was the Morlot Avenue Bridge between Paterson and Fair Lawn, and that was where Jason Durant took his eleven-year-old son, Robbie, early on Saturday morning.

They stood on the bridge, dropped the bait in the water, and leaned forward so as not to be too close to the cars passing behind them.

After an hour of nothing happening, Robbie said, 'Doesn't seem like our day, huh?'

Jason looked at his watch, which read seven thirty. 'It's early.'

'You think the fish are still asleep?'

'Could be. But they'll wake up hungry, and that's when we'll get 'em.'

After another forty-five minutes, Robbie figured the fish must have forgotten to set their alarm. 'I don't know if the fish are hungry, but I am.'

'Might as well go get the food.' They had parked the car about a hundred yards away, near the river bank. 'Wait here . . . Call me if you get a bite.'

Jason walked towards the edge of the bridge, occasionally glancing back at his son. Reaching the car, he took out the cooler of food that his wife had prepared. As he hurried to get back to Robbie, he slipped on a stretch of mud. The cooler fell from his hands, and tumbled down to the river's edge.

Balancing himself so as not to slip, Jason made it down to the edge of the river. He reached the cooler, which had not gone into the water because it was wedged up against something.

A human arm.

Jason screamed, loud enough that if there were really any fish still asleep, their day had officially begun.

NICK WAS STARTING TO FEEL slightly better about the case. It was a vague feeling, not brought about by any particular good news, but simply because some news was at least starting to flow in.

There were six Oceanfast 360s in the New York area, and he had the preliminary investigative report that listed the owners of the boats, then and now, some of which were corporations and some individuals. None of the names meant anything to him.

Within an hour of his receiving the list, Tim called. Nick could hear the frustration in his voice as he asked if there was anything new to report, and he was glad that he could answer in the affirmative.

'The police know who Cashman is. His real name is Billy Zimmerman, and he was in prison in Lampley.'

'That's great! Do they know where he is now?'

'Apparently not, though that could be changing at any time.'

'So we wait?' Tim asked.

'No, our people are all over it. But the cops have more resources and easier entry. Meanwhile, I've got the list of boats in this area.' He read out the names of the boats, as well as the owning people and companies.

'I've never heard of any of them,' an obviously disappointed Tim said.

'Can you find out where the boats are? I can check them out.'

'What good will that do?'

'I've seen the boat; I'm pretty sure I'll recognise it if I see it again.'

'You want to take that chance?' Nick asked.

'I look different. And I won't do anything to call attention to myself.'

'If you're wrong, and you encounter the police, do not resist arrest. They consider you armed and dangerous.'

'I am armed, but I'm not dangerous.'

'You have a gun?' Nick asked, his surprise evident.

'Yes,' Tim said, then added defensively, 'There are murderers after me. I'm not going to use it against the police. It's not even loaded yet.'

'Don't bring it with you when you check out the boats,' Nick said.

'I won't. I'm afraid of it.'

CARL WHITE received the information first, reflecting his higher status as a federal agent. It was another jagged piece of a puzzle that didn't seem to fit anywhere. He had his assistant call Novack to tell him that there was some significant news and ask him to come right over.

When Novack and Anders were ushered in, White didn't spend any time on small talk. 'On Saturday morning, a resident of Fair Lawn found the arm of a white male while fishing in the Passaic River. Divers located the rest of the body, and DNA testing was done.'

Novack had to suppress an instant annoyance that White obviously had been made privy to evidence of a local crime before he had. 'And?'

'And it was determined to be Billy Zimmerman, aka Jeff Cashman.'

'Do we know when he died?' asked Novack.

'Too soon to tell,' White said. 'Autopsy is being done today.'

'You could have told us this over the phone,' said Anders.

White nodded. 'But then I wouldn't have been able to pick your brains.'

'About what?' asked Anders.

'The Federal Center opens next weekend with a big dinner.'

'We've known that for a while,' Novack said.

'Did you know the President of the United States is going to be there?'

'No,' said Novack. 'Lately he hasn't been checking in with me when he's making up his schedule.'

The comment annoyed White. 'So you don't see this as your problem?'

'I gotta be honest, I don't even see it as *your* problem. Because I don't see Wallace as a terrorist. I see him as an asshole who kills women for fun.'

'So Billy Zimmerman was a woman that Wallace killed for fun?'

'I don't know where Zimmerman fits in,' Novack admitted. 'But if Wallace was going to blow up the Federal Center, he wouldn't have walked in and told us the story about Cashman and Sheila.'

'Unless he was an asshole who also kills presidents for fun. By the way, we questioned the girlfriend of the guy blown up on the turnpike.'

Novack nodded. 'Yeah. We saw the interview report.'

'But you didn't know that an agent later went back to her apartment to ask her a few more questions. She was gone, but all her clothes and things were still there. She had been talking to her sister on the phone, got up to answer the door, and hasn't been heard from since.'

'So she's dead,' Novack reasoned.

'I wouldn't want to be her life insurer, that's for sure,' White said.

'There's no way Wallace went down there; it would be far too risky,' Novack said. 'He's in hiding.'

'And I don't see how he could have known about her in the first place,' White said. 'So it was somebody else. Which means it looks like you've got more going on here than you think.'

Novack had known that ever since learning that Cashman was not a creation of Tim's imagination. 'Yes, it does,' he said.

BOTH DANNY AND WILL found it more than a little weird to be at the Purple Rose. They had only gone there twice since Tim's disappearance, to try and restore normality to their lives rather than in hope that they might have fun.

The two friends agreed in advance not to talk about Tim's situation, but that resolution broke down before the first beers arrived.

'I just wish there was a way to help him,' Danny said. 'If I knew where he was, I could get him money, or something.'

'It said in the paper that he cleaned out his bank account,' Will said.

'Yeah, I know. He must be scared shitless.'

'He should be. The cops are acting like he's Al Capone. They've questioned me three times.'

'I'm one ahead of you,' Danny said. 'You speak to the FBI agent? White?'

'Yeah. He had a million questions about the buildings.' He shook his head in amazement. 'Like Tim's gonna show up with an army and attack it.'

'The security down there is unbelievable,' Danny said.

'I know . . . I've been going through it every day. I spent five hours last week teaching the computer set-up to a government guy. You know who's coming to the opening?'

'Not really . . . just what I read. A bunch of congressmen, my uncle . . .'

'He giving you grief about Tim?'

Danny nodded. 'Every hour on the hour. He has Rivers call me. Like there's something I can do about it.'

'If one of us finds out where Tim is, we tell the other, OK?' Will said. 'And we figure out a way to help him.'

Danny held out his hand and Will took it. 'It's a deal.'

EIGHT

According to Nick's list, the Oceanfast 360s were spread out through the metropolitan area. Three were at different piers on Long Island Sound, one was on the Hudson River, north of the city, and the remaining two were docked at other locations in New Jersey. Tim knew some of the locations; they were upscale, high-end piers that charged exorbitant fees. This made sense; you wouldn't leave a boat like that in some dump.

Tim understood the risks involved in checking out the boats himself, especially as he was casually familiar with many people in the boating community. In winter many of the boats would be in dry dock, and not many owners would be around. But with fewer people, Tim would stand out.

Though the Jersey piers were significantly closer, Tim decided to check out those on Long Island first. Two of the boats were said to be on the North Shore and one on the South Shore. Since the North was on Long Island Sound, where Tim's boat was that fateful day, he decided to head there first.

Even the drive there was an intense experience. Tim was sure that every-one in each car was staring at him; when a driver alongside him took out his cellphone, it took all his self-control not to pull off and turn round. He was glad he had used the car at the house, and not his own.

His first stop was at Mill Neck, a place that Tim had considered using when he got his boat, but decided against because it felt too crowded. He parked as close as he could to the pier, and left the car unlocked. He pulled his ski cap low on his head and bundled his coat slightly upward as if trying to ward off the cold, which left only a small amount of his face exposed.

There were at least four hundred boats in the dock area, but only a few people around. There was a fence round the entire property, but three gates were open. Tim tried to make it appear that he knew where he was going, as if he had his own boat there and that was his destination. The boats were set up in aisles, and Tim figured that walking quickly he could weave in and out and see all of them within five minutes.

Tim walked down the first aisle, didn't see the Oceanfast, and turned to walk back up the second aisle.

'Hey, can I help you?' The words sent a wave of panic through Tim that he attempted to conceal as he turned to answer a short, stocky man, mid-fifties, who seemed to be an attendant at the pier.

Tim smiled, trying to catch his breath. 'Nah, just looking around. I'm gonna buy a boat, and I'm trying to get some ideas.'

'This ain't a showroom, pal.'

Tim laughed. 'I know . . . but I heard there was an Oceanfast 360 here, and I wanted to get a look at it.'

'You know what those things cost?'

'Pretty dear, from what I hear. Me and a couple of friends, we're thinking of going in on it together.'

The attendant thought about that for a moment, then finally shrugged and pointed. 'Third aisle, near that end. But don't try and board it.'

Tim nodded. 'Gotcha. Thanks.'

Tim walked away, shaking from the encounter. He could feel the sweat under his clothes. He knew he'd have to get himself under control; if he reacted this way to a non-incident, he'd probably die of stress in a close call.

He wasn't halfway down the aisle when he saw the Oceanfast 360, and he instantly felt a wave of disappointment. The boat was made in two basic lengths, and this was the smaller version, the seventy-footer. While it was an extraordinary vessel, it was not the one Tim was looking for.

Tim put his head down and walked briskly back to the car. There was nothing else to do but go on to the next one.

THE LICENCE PLATE on the car following Eden was stolen. It had been the property of an eighty-one-year-old woman in Cherry Hill, New Jersey, who hadn't used her car in two years, and hadn't even noticed the plate was missing.

Nick called Eden to tell her what he had learned, but she sounded less worried than she had been.

'I haven't seen him in a couple of days, Nick. He probably got bored.'

'Or maybe he's just being more careful.'

'Is it the police?' she asked.

'Not unless they're into stealing licence plates.'

'So who is it?'

'I have no idea, Eden. And maybe he won't be back. But if you see him again, call me immediately. And only go to very public places. When you're home, make sure the doors and windows are locked and the alarm is on.'

'Will do, big brother.'

TIM KNEW it was the same boat the moment he saw it. Not just the colour, but the stripe design. It was one of at least a hundred boats at the pier in Southold, but it was the only one surrounded by its own fence, a silent statement that it was more expensive and more important than the others.

Tim could just make out the last three letters of the name on the hull: *e-a-s*. Since he couldn't approach more closely, there was no way to determine the boat's serial number. So he just stood there, staring at the boat and letting the memory of that day on the water once again roll over him. This boat, and the people on it, had been out there with him. At the very least they did nothing to help; at worst they were the cause of Maggie's death.

'Not bad, huh?'

Tim turned and saw a young woman dressed in work coveralls under a ski jacket and holding a sander; she was obviously there working on a boat. She had a welcoming smile on her face.

Tim gave the Oceanfast another quick glance. 'Beautiful, though I might go with a different colour.'

She laughed. 'That's for sure. Have you ever been on one?'

'In a showroom once. That's the closest I'll ever come. Is it yours?'

Another laugh. 'Afraid not. Mine's over there. You could fit mine in one of the bedrooms on this one.'

'Do you know who owns it?'

'Nah . . . I tried to talk to a guy on it the other day, but he blew me off.'

'People come on this time of year?'

She nodded. 'Yeah, but he wasn't one of the owners; he was there doing work. The owners are definitely big shots. A lot of Washington types have been on it, even some senators and congressmen.'

'Is that right? Which ones, do you know?' He smiled, not wanting to appear too anxious. 'I'm sort of a political junkie.'

She thought for a moment. 'Well, I know Senator Collinsworth was on it at least once, 'cause I recognised him. But I'm sure there were others.'

The news instantly re-established Tim's suspicions about Danny. 'Wow,' he said. 'When was Collinsworth on?'

'Last summer. I saw a whole bunch of people in tuxedos as they were sailing out. Can you imagine putting on formal clothes to go out on a boat?'

'Hard to believe,' he agreed.

Tim gently tried to coax more information out of her, but she didn't seem to have any. He extricated himself from the conversation, and she wished him a good day and went back to her work.

JIMMY LEE'S STORY didn't set the world on fire, but that didn't concern him in the least. People interested in politics read the column and noted that Senator Collinsworth had apparently engaged in nepotism in arranging for his nephew to get federal contracting work. The fact that the nephew's partner, Tim Wallace, was wanted for murder made it more delicious for Collinsworth's political enemies, but had no real effect on the public.

But Jimmy Lee knew that when he published the second part of his story, revealing that Wallace had had multiple contacts with the man transporting all those explosives, the reaction would be far greater. Especially since the President would have spent the previous evening in the building the fugitive helped build. Jimmy Lee had no problem with sitting back and waiting for that pay-off. He knew that timing was everything.

For Senator Collinsworth, the story was potentially a major problem. With his plan of spreading the contracting work for future Federal Centers to many small businesses, he would be able to build a network of beholden contributors that could fill his campaign war chest to overflowing. If the story about Wallace shone an unfavourable light on Collinsworth's involvement and jeopardised the future, it would be an unmitigated disaster.

Collinsworth did what he could to minimise the danger. He had Keith Rivers plant a competing story, which said that while Collinsworth had had the grand idea for these complexes, he stayed out of choosing contractors. Gregory Campbell, at the General Services Administration, was quoted, affirming that Collinsworth was not involved in the awarding of contracts.

One call Collinsworth did not bother making was to Danny, the nephew at the centre of all this. There was nothing to be gained from that; Danny would be smart enough to know that the days of his uncle getting him work were officially over. He might as well disappear along with his murdering partner, because as far as Uncle Fred was concerned, he no longer existed.

THE FIRST CALL Tim made when he got back to the house was to Nick. He was not in his office, but when Tim said that 'Jerry Koosman' was calling, his assistant told Tim to call him at home.

Before Tim could say why he was calling, Nick mentioned the story about Collinsworth that had broken that day. It was of little consequence to Tim; the last thing on his mind at the moment was future business prospects.

'I've got more interesting news about Collinsworth,' he said.

'Oh?'

'I found the boat that was out on the water that day; it's the one docked at Southold. And someone I met told me that Collinsworth has been out on it.'

Nick checked his paperwork. 'That one's owned by a company called Bennington, Inc. I'll have them checked out. In the meantime, I've got something else to tell you, which you are very definitely not going to like.'

Tim braced himself. 'What is it?'

'There's an FBI agent up here from Florida, assigned to this case.'

'FBI? Why? And why Florida?'

'Remember the car that blew up on the Jersey Turnpike?'

'Of course. It was carrying Cintron 421. Danny and I were worried.'

'Well, now you've got a bigger reason to worry about it. The driver of that car apparently called your office a few times in the week before the explosion. They think he talked to you.'

Tim exploded. 'Jesus Christ! Now they think I'm a terrorist?'

'So you know nothing about it?'

'Of course not. I—' Tim paused for a few moments.

'What's going on?' Nick asked. 'You still there?'

Tim's voice was suddenly excited. 'It all fits! Damn . . . it all fits!'

'Enlighten me,' Nick said.

Tim went on to explain his suspicions about Danny. 'This guy may have called our office, but he didn't talk to me. He must have talked to Danny.'

'What would Danny have to gain by all this?'

'It has to involve the business. He must want me out of the way. I don't know why but I'll figure it out. First, he tried to have me killed, and then—'

'Tried to have you killed?' Nick asked.

'I was the only person who knew Maggie was going out on the boat that day. I never even told Danny. That explosion was meant to kill me, not her.'

'Then how did her finger wind up at the racketball court?'

A few moments of silence from Tim, and then, 'Shit. I don't know; I just don't know. There are a lot of pieces we don't have, but every one we do have involves Danny. And Collinsworth has to be involved as well.'

'You somewhere safe?' Nick asked. 'Without telling me where . . .'

'I'm somewhere safe.'

'Then sit tight and call me tomorrow. I'll be in court on another case until about noon; call after that.'

'Have you got any idea what you're going to do?'

'To tell you the truth, I think it might be time to talk to Novack.'

CINDY COULD TELL that something was bothering Novack. This didn't qualify as a particularly stunning insight; something had been bothering him pretty much every day for as long as she had known him, always to do with work. On this particular night, though, he seemed more troubled than usual, and she decided to try and talk to him about it. She did so as they were sitting in the dining room after a dinner during which he had hardly said anything. He was drinking coffee, and she was clearing the table.

'Is it the Wallace case?' she asked.

'What?' he asked, obviously distracted.

'Is it the Wallace case?'

'Is what the Wallace case?'

'Whatever it is that has you so upset.'

'I tried to hide it.'

She smiled. 'Good job.'

'It's the Wallace case,' he confirmed. 'I don't like where it's going.'

'I saw the story today about the senator getting him the contract. Was that a problem for you?'

'I couldn't care less about that. It's just political bullshit.'

'Then what's wrong? Is it the fact that you haven't found Wallace yet?'

'That ain't helping, but there's something else. The FBI think he's a terrorist; they've tied him to that car that exploded on the turnpike.'

'A terrorist?' she asked, surprised. 'Are they right?'

He shook his head. 'No way. It just doesn't ring true.'

'But you still think he killed his wife?'

He half whirled to face her. 'He killed his wife. No doubt about it . . . none. And he killed that woman in Kinnelon.'

She was surprised by his reaction. 'OK, OK . . . don't take it out on me. What about that guy Cashman? Did Wallace kill him too?'

Novack thought about that for a moment. 'I don't know. I don't know where the hell he fits in. There's too much about this case I don't know.'

'And that bothers you,' she said.

He smiled. 'No shit, Sherlock.'

'I think we should go into the bedroom and make love,' she said.

He shrugged. 'Might as well . . . nothing else to do,' he said, then ducked as she threw the expected dish towel at him.

EDEN SENSED that the grey MPV was back even before she saw it. She was in the supermarket, and as she walked towards the front of the store, she looked into the parking lot. There it was, parked in a space near the back.

She thought she had been rid of him, and now was upset that she hadn't asked Nick to provide protection for her. Leaving her cart in the corner of the store, Eden went into the rest room and called Nick's office from her cellphone. His assistant said that he was in court and couldn't be reached.

Eden then went to a payphone and called Tim's cellphone. They had decided to communicate only through email, but this was enough of an emergency to take a chance. Tim picked up after the fourth ring.

'Hello?' He sounded scared.

'Tim, it's me, Eden. I'm sorry to call you—'

'It's OK,' he said. 'What is it?'

'I'm being followed again.'

'By the same guy?'

'I didn't see him, but it's the same car. I'm sure of it. I thought I was finished with him. What do you think I should do?'

'Have you called Nick?'

'I tried. He's in court.'

There was a pause. 'I think you should get into your car and drive to the police station and tell them what's going on. Tell them you have my dog, and that the guy following you must have something to do with me.'

'Are you sure? If they know about me, it might help them get to you.'

There was a longer pause. 'Where are you now?' he asked.

She told him she was at the grocery store, and that the man following her was at the outskirts of the parking lot.

'OK. Stay where you are for about fifteen minutes, then get back in your car and drive to the Paramus Park Mall,' he said. 'It won't be crowded; it's too early. Park in the rear parking lot, and go into any store over there.'

'Then what?'

'Stay inside for at least a half-hour, then get back in your car. The guy won't be following you. Call Nick and tell him what happened when you get home.'

'What are you going to do?'

'I'm going to start taking my life back.'

Eden was not happy about following Tim's instructions. She wasn't concerned for her own safety; Paramus Park was a very public place, and she would be in little danger there. But she was extremely worried about what Tim had in mind. If he was right that the man would no longer be out there when she returned to her car, then it would have to mean that Tim had intervened.

She had the feeling that kind of intervention was not Tim's speciality.

But she had no real option other than to do as he requested; it was Tim's life that was at stake, and he had to do whatever he could to save it. So she headed for the mall, hoping the MPV was behind her.

TIM HAD little more confidence in his ability to handle this than Eden. But he couldn't elude the police for ever, and if he didn't create something positive, he felt that his prospects for exoneration were nil. So he too headed for Paramus Park. And he brought his gun.

He got to the parking lot before Eden, and positioned himself in a place where he would be able to see her drive in. Almost ten minutes later, she got there, and parked towards the front of the rear lot.

There were cars parked at the very rear of the lot, bordering the woods. Tim had worked at the mall during one college summer break, and remembered that employees of all the stores were told to park in this area, so as not to take the closer spots from customers. Tim assumed that the driver of the grey MPV would park among these cars, to stay a safe distance from Eden, yet not stand out. He'd have to, for Tim's plan to have a chance of success.

He did.

Once the MPV was settled in, and it was clear the driver was staying put, Tim waited five minutes, then drove up and parked two rows behind. He walked up the aisle between cars towards the passenger side of the MPV. When he saw the driver look up, Tim felt a wave of fear, but by then the die had been cast. Pulling the gun from his pocket with his right hand, he yanked the passenger door open with his left. Fortunately, it wasn't locked.

The large blond man in the driver's seat whirled towards Tim and started reaching for his inside jacket pocket, but stopped when he saw Tim, who was pointing the gun at him with two hands and screaming, 'DON'T MOVE! DON'T FUCKING MOVE!'

The man seemed unruffled, but partially raised his hands, palms upward, and said, 'No problem, pal. Whatever you say.'

Tim got into the car and closed the door, keeping the gun pointed at the driver. He spoke in a firm, calm voice that surprised even himself. 'Reach into your jacket pocket slowly, take out your gun and place it on the seat. Make sure it stays pointed at yourself. If at any time it isn't, I'll shoot you.'

The man did as he was told.

Tim pulled the gun closer, but did not pick it up. 'OK. Drive,' he said.

'Where to?'

'Drive,' Tim repeated, and the man shrugged and pulled out of the lot.

Tim directed him up Route 17, getting off at Route 202 and heading towards Rockland County. The ride took almost twenty minutes, and Tim's arms ached from holding up the gun. Feeling an almost surreal sense of alertness, he directed the man to turn right down a long dirt road, to an area where Tim and his friends had hiked a number of years ago. Finally he had him pull over, in what could be described as the middle of nowhere.

'OK, turn the car off but leave the key in the ignition,' Tim said, and his order was followed. 'Now put your hands on the dashboard, palms down.'

Again the order was followed, though the man did not seem at all afraid.

'I'm going to get out and walk round the car. If you move your hands, I will shoot you in the head.' Tim opened the passenger door and walked round the front of the car, pointing the gun at his captive throughout. When he reached the driver's door, he opened it. 'Get out and stand over there with your hands clasped behind your head,' he said.

The man got out slowly and did as he was told.

'Why are you following that woman?' Tim asked.

'I wanted her to lead me to you.'

'Why?'

'So I could kill you.'

'Why do you want to kill me?'

'None of your fucking business.'

'Who are you?'

The man seemed to make a judgment. 'Look, I'm getting tired of this. I'm leaving, and the only way you're going to stop me is to shoot me. And I would be real surprised if you had the balls for that.'

'Try me,' Tim said, desperately hoping that he wouldn't.

The man took a half-step forward, causing Tim to tense and seem ready to shoot. When he didn't, the man smiled and took another step forward.

So Tim shot him.

He wasn't even sure he did it intentionally; fear may have caused him to squeeze the trigger inadvertently. The shot went off to the right, grazing the man's left shoulder.

The man reached for his arm, and put his hand on a small but growing spot of blood. The look of rage on his face made Tim's blood run cold.

Then the man smiled. 'You think things have been bad lately? They just got ten times worse. You will long for the way you felt yesterday.' With that he did an about-face, slowly walking away from Tim towards the woods.

Tim waited until the man was a couple of hundred feet away, then got back into the car on the driver's side. He was profoundly shaken by the encounter, but satisfied. He had met the enemy, and he hadn't been killed.

On the way back to the mall, Tim called Nick. He told him as concisely as he could what had happened, then said, 'Go to Paramus Park; there'll be a grey MPV parked near the back of the rear parking lot. It will have a gun on the front seat, which will have the fingerprints of the driver. In fact, both of our fingerprints will be all over the car.'

'Where is Eden?' Nick asked.

Tim was just pulling into Paramus Park, and was relieved to see that Eden's car was gone. 'I assume she's home; can we get someone to protect her?'

'Yes. Now get out of there quickly; in a little while that place is going to be crawling with cops, one of whom will probably be Novack.'

'You think that's wise?'

'Tim, ultimately we are going to have to deal with them. We've got to let them know there are other bad guys in the picture.'

NINE

Nick knew exactly what it meant when he got an 8 a.m. call from Novack, asking him to come down for a meeting as soon as possible. It meant that they had hit pay dirt on the fingerprint, and that Novack wanted to know everything Nick knew.

Nick had been cryptic the day before, telling Novack about the grey MPV with the gun on the seat, and mentioning that it had a direct relevance to the Wallace case. The police had descended on the place, according to an associate that Nick sent over there, but Nick stayed away.

Novack and Anders were waiting for Nick when he arrived, and he was ushered right in. 'You want coffee or something?' Anders asked.

'I'll have a vanilla triple-shot latte. And a sesame bagel. Toasted.'

Novack said to Anders, 'You know, we should spend every morning with an asshole attorney. It would make us appreciate the rest of the day.'

'I'll have black coffee,' said Nick.

Novack looked at the pot. 'We've got light brown.' He poured Nick a cup and handed it to him. 'So . . . tell me where the car with the gun came from.'

Nick smiled. 'So . . . tell me that Jeff Cashman is really Billy Zimmerman.'

'Was,' said Novack. 'He's dead. His body was fished out of the Passaic River a few days ago.'

Nick was surprised, but took the news in his stride. 'I suppose you think Tim came out of hiding to do that? You think he runs a murder factory?'

Novack smiled. 'Let's just say he's a person of interest.'

'OK,' Nick said. 'Moving on . . . whose prints were on the gun?'

Novack exchanged a glance with Anders, then turned to Nick. 'I'll tell you what. You tell us what you know, and we'll tell you what we know.'

Nick nodded. 'That works, until it butts up against client confidentiality.'

'Fair enough. You start,' said Novack.

'OK. My sister is a friend of Tim Wallace's. He left his dog with her before he ran off. She discovered that someone was following her in recent days, maybe thinking she'd lead him to Wallace. Which she could not do.'

'Because she hasn't the slightest idea where he is,' Novack said drily.

'Right. And did I mention she's on my staff, working on this case?' Nick had told Eden he was 'hiring' her, at a dollar a month, so that she could hide behind client confidentiality as well.

'What a surprise,' Anders said. 'Keep going.'

'I received a phone call saying that the car was there, with the gun on the seat. I have a description of the man as well.'

'A call from who?'

'Sorry,' Nick said. 'But I can tell you that the man was slightly injured in the encounter; a bullet grazed his left arm. Anyway, that's what I know. I believe it's your turn. Who was the driver?'

'His name is Richie Patrick. He's thirty-one years old, born in Bloomington, Indiana. He was wanted in three states for three different murders.'

'A hit man?'

Novack shook his head. 'That's too limiting. He's available for hire to do pretty much anything, but murder is his speciality.'

'You said he "was wanted",' said Nick.

Novack nodded. 'Right. Patrick was identified as killed in a plane crash eighteen months ago in Minnesota.'

'Well, he's apparently made a comeback.'

Anders seemed uncomfortable. 'We done here?' he asked.

'Not quite. There's something else I think I should tell you guys.'

'We're all ears,' said Novack.

'There was a boat out on the water that day, not far from Wallace's boat, when the explosion happened. The people on board never reported it, and they left the scene before the coastguard arrived.' He proceeded to talk in more detail about the Oceanfast 360, and how Tim and Maggie had seen it repeatedly during the day, including moments before the explosion.

'Why should we care about this?' asked Novack.

'Because I now know which boat it was, where it is located, what company owns it, and most importantly, who has been on it in the past.'

'Who might that be?'

'Senator Fred Collinsworth.'

IT SEEMED AS IF there were more dogs than people at the Federal Center in Newark. Every square inch of the building was being sniffed and examined, over and over again. The computers that controlled the building's lockdown system, which could close it up into a literally airtight, virtually impregnable fortress, and the ventilation system that provided oxygen to the people inside, were checked and rechecked. Will was again called in to provide a detailed description of the system he had helped design, repeating a meeting he had two weeks prior, albeit with a different Homeland Security computer expert.

This one was an attractive woman, who came into the computer room at the Federal Center building with a no-nonsense attitude. She asked that he show her everything about the system, leaving nothing out.

Will was slightly annoyed to be having to go through this again. 'Don't you guys ever talk to each other down there?' he asked.

'What does that mean?'

'I went through this with one of your colleagues two weeks ago.'

She shrugged. Inefficiency in the bureaucracy was not exactly a news event, and she had her job to do. 'So you should have it off pat by now.'

When they were finished, the woman made it clear to Will that he would not be on the scene on the big night. She and other government operators would be running the system from the computer room. He was to provide them with all applicable passwords and codes, which he did. It wasn't that they didn't trust Will; it was simply that they didn't trust anyone.

The outside of the building was scrutinised just as thoroughly. There was simply no way a vehicle could get close enough to damage the building, even if it were loaded with Cintron 421. The air space over the entire area would be off-limits, with fighter planes enforcing that restriction. Additional security would be fanned out into the surrounding neighbourhoods.

Everything was deemed by the Secret Service to be as it should be. The word was communicated to an anxious White House that all was secure, and that there was no reason to reconsider the President's attendance.

'WE SHOULD GO to Donovan with this,' Novack said. They had learned that the Oceanfast in question was registered to a holding company of indeterminable ownership. However, the listed name on the documents, a requirement for a boat licence, was Keith Rivers, Collinsworth's right-hand man.

'Why?' asked Anders.

'This is way past what we thought. And I'm not sure Wallace is behind it.'

'You've got to be kidding. You've been after this guy for months.'

Novack had been slowly moving towards this position for a while, and he was aware that he was moving more towards Anders's original point of view. 'I was positive he killed his wife; I didn't know why he did it. But he's not a terrorist, he didn't hop on down to Florida last week to kill that woman, he didn't create Zimmerman out of thin air, and I doubt that he killed him. He also didn't tie that boat to Collinsworth.'

Anders, playing devil's advocate, focused on the last point. 'He could have known who owned that boat. Maybe Collinsworth's nephew told him, and he made up the story that it was out there the day he killed his wife.'

Novack wasn't convinced. 'The finger doesn't fit in either. Why would he have saved the finger and planted it? He'd have known we'd nail him on it.'

'Sicko, remember?'

'I don't think so, not any more.'

'Come on, Novack. You saying some mysterious bad guys kill his wife, then wait almost a year to—'

'But that's the point. If he didn't do it, then the wife probably wasn't the target. It was her first time on the boat. What if *he* was supposed to die?'

'Then why not kill him now? Why go through all this stuff?'

Novack shrugged. 'Beats me; I'm just a dumb cop.' He looked at his watch and stood up. 'And I'm outta here.'

'Where you going?'

'I've got that departmental physical I've been putting off for three months. Call Donovan and set up a meeting for first thing in the morning.'

'What do you want him to do?'

'Offer to pull back the arrest warrant on Wallace, maybe as a way to get him to come in. I think there might be more to gain by hearing what he has to say than arresting him.'

'Donovan will think you're nuts.'

Novack shrugged. 'It won't be the first time.'

FOR SENATOR COLLINSWORTH, the worst was apparently over. Jimmy Lee Curry's story had run about his connection to Tim's company, and the damage appeared to have been minor. In a poll Collinsworth had commissioned on the subject, eighty-one per cent of Americans were not even aware of it.

The best news of all was a phone call Detective Anders had made to Keith Rivers, informing him of recent developments, which were so significant that Novack actually had strong doubts about Tim's guilt.

Collinsworth would have Rivers contact Danny and tell him the news about Novack's serious doubts, which might even lead to Tim's coming out of hiding, if Danny knew how to contact him.

The senator could now focus on the weekend's opening of the Federal Center. As the home state senator and a man directly responsible for the project, Collinsworth was going to make the welcoming speech. With the President in attendance, every major media outlet in the country would be there. Collinsworth would not let the moment go to waste. He had three writers working on the speech, which was to focus on the project's concept as a way to defeat terrorism and protect Americans. It also had to demonstrate Collinsworth's gravitas, and capacity to handle higher office.

It would be a moment for which he would be ready.

'I NEED TO SPEAK to Novack,' were the first words Cindy heard when she picked up the phone.

'I'm sorry, but he's not here,' she said.

'It's very important I see him right away. It's a matter of life and death.'

'Who is this?' she asked.

'Tim Wallace. Can you please give him a message for me?'

The name sent a shock wave through her, and it never entered her mind to be worried by the fact that he knew her number. 'Yes, I will,' she said, knowing that Novack was due to come over at any time.

'Please tell him to meet me at Squires Delicatessen in Fort Lee. Tell him to take a seat at a booth in the back. I'll be in five minutes after he arrives.'

'He'll want to know what this is about.'

'It's about me giving him information that will blow this case wide open, then turning myself in after I do.'

'I'll tell him,' she said. 'But I'm not sure how long it will take.'

'I'll wait. But make sure he comes; he's the only one I'll tell this to.'

Click. The call was disconnected, but Cindy continued to stare at the phone, only stopping when she heard the front door open.

Novack came into the room, and saw the look on her face. 'What's wrong?'

'Tim Wallace just called. He wants to see you right away.' She described the conversation in as much detail as she could remember.

'Did he say I needed to come alone?' he asked.

'No, but he said you were the only person he'd tell the information to.'

'Did you use that phone?' he asked, pointing to the phone on the desk.

'Yes.'

'Don't use it again. Make any calls you need to make on your cell.'

Novack took out his own cellphone and called Anders. He quickly described what had happened, and within three minutes they had a plan to place officers strategically on the blocks surrounding the deli, as well as two plain-clothes officers in the deli, posing as customers. Novack would delay leaving for another fifteen minutes to give Anders time to set it up.

'Are you sure you should go?' Cindy asked when he got off the phone. 'You said yourself he's a murderer.'

'Maybe,' Novack said. 'But we'll have cops everywhere. We can play by his rules for now.'

The fifteen minutes spent waiting to leave were among the longest Novack had ever endured. Wallace might change his mind. And Novack was suspicious of his motives; if he had crucial information to impart, he could have done so over the phone, or through his lawyer. Novack briefly considered calling Nick Alexander, but if Wallace was doing something contrary to his own best interests, Novack didn't want Nick talking him out of it.

He went upstairs to wash his face and change his clothes. When it was time to leave, he called Anders to confirm that everything was ready. Satisfied that it was, he went back downstairs. Then something hit him.

'Did he say how he got this number, or why he thought I'd be here?'

Cindy shook her head. 'No.'

'Make sure the windows and doors are locked. Don't open it for anybody. If I want to get in, I'll call you first.'

'You really think he might come here?'

'No, just covering every base.'

She hugged him and he left the house. He was halfway to his car when he heard her calling from behind.

'Call me as soon as it's over,' she said through the half-open door.

He turned to tell her that he'd do exactly that, and the turn of his body caused the bullet to miss his heart and hit him below the right shoulder. The bulletproof vest he was wearing did not provide full protection from the 'cop-killer' bullet, and he was blown back five feet from the impact.

He heard Cindy scream and saw her rush towards him. He wanted to yell at her to go back, but he couldn't form the words, and she reached him, crying and holding his head in her hands, sobbing his name.

TIM WAS WATCHING CNN when he found out that he'd shot Novack.

It started out as an alert, with a 'breaking news' banner. It said that Novack was shot in front of his house, and identified him as the lead detective in the Tim Wallace murder case. Within five minutes, coverage became wall-to-wall. There was open speculation that Tim was responsible, followed by a vaguely worded statement from the state police public-relations office that seemed to confirm that Tim had been the shooter. There was no word on Novack's condition, only that he was still alive.

Tim watched as if disembodied, and even wondered if there was another Tim Wallace, an alter ego, that had set out to destroy the world.

None of it made sense to him. Somebody had done this deliberately, but why? Tim was already a fugitive, widely believed by the police and public to be a murderer. What did this accomplish, except ratcheting up the pressure?

And why Novack? If people were set on destroying Tim, then Novack was their ally. He was the commander of the anti-Tim forces.

Tim called Nick at home and got the machine. He didn't leave a message, but called his cellphone. He was relieved when he heard, 'Alexander here.'

'Nick, what the hell is going on?'

There was a pause, and Nick's voice got much lower. 'Somebody shot Novack; they think it was you.'

'Why?'

'Did you call him tonight?' Nick asked.

'Novack? Of course not. Are they saying I did?'

'Somebody called saying it was you, and asking Novack to meet you somewhere. When he walked out of the house, he was shot.'

'I swear it wasn't me. Can't they trace the call or something?'

'I'm trying to find out more now, but they're saying very little.'

Tim was watching on television while talking, and suddenly there was a panning shot of the street, and Tim saw Nick on camera. 'You're there . . . I can see you on TV now.'

'Are they showing my good side? Listen, I gotta go . . . Call me later.' With that he disconnected the call.

NOVACK REGAINED CONSCIOUSNESS within minutes of arriving at the hospital. He had lost a lot of blood and was given a massive transfusion. It took a few hours to stabilise him sufficiently for him to be relatively clear-headed.

At that moment, he was the only person in the police department, and one of the few in America, who did not believe he was shot by Tim Wallace.

His reasoning was simple. Wallace had called Cindy before Novack got home, and the message was for Novack to leave immediately for the meeting. He had to have been already in position at the house, waiting for Novack to leave, so he could shoot him. But he could have shot Novack in the back, on the way into the house. There was no reason to wait for him to come back out; he couldn't even have been sure that Novack would take the bait.

And Novack finally, instinctively, knew one other thing with certainty. Not only was Wallace not the shooter, he was not a murderer at all.

SENATOR WALTER EVANS could feign outrage with the best of them, and when he took to the Senate floor the next morning, he was in rare form. Evans was only a freshman senator, but his youthfulness and charisma had vaulted him into the group of politicians considered potential presidential timber. The chamber was mostly empty, but with the cameras rolling, he could be sure that his words would reverberate on cable news.

Evans never mentioned Senator Collinsworth by name, yet there was no doubt that he was taking direct aim at him. He acted as if saddened that he had to address the issue at all, and in the process implicitly criticise a member of his own party. Evans railed against the 'old way of doing business', which wasn't good enough in 'this era of terror'. He took full advantage of Jimmy Lee Curry's revelation that Collinsworth had essentially put a murderer on the government payroll, knowing that the press would fill in the blanks.

Susan Moreno watched the speech from the comfort of her office and enjoyed it immensely. She thought her boss was doing a great job, avoiding specifics to make a very specific point, drawing attention to himself at the expense of Collinsworth, and she readied herself for the calls asking for Evans's appearance on the various Sunday talk shows.

She couldn't help smiling over the knowledge that her counterpart on Collinsworth's staff, Keith Rivers, must be furious and seeking revenge.

It was just one of the things she couldn't have been more wrong about.

THERE WAS A STEADY STREAM of visitors to Novack's hospital room over the next twenty-four hours. Fellow detectives came by to show their support for a downed colleague, and were delighted to find that Novack was doing well.

Anders was there frequently, as was Captain Donovan, though neither had anything positive to report on the hunt for Tim. Novack expressed to both of them his feeling that Tim had not been the one who spoke to Cindy on the phone, or who had shot Novack as he left the house.

'He'd have shot me on the way in,' Novack told them.

'Maybe he wasn't ready to shoot,' Anders said. 'Maybe you surprised him by showing up before he could get a good line of fire.'

'I can prove it wasn't him.'

'Then go right ahead,' said Donovan.

Novack turned to Anders. 'Cindy's out in the hall. Ask her to come in.'

Anders went out to get Cindy, who had been at the hospital since the shooting, except when she ran a crucial errand for Novack.

'Tell these guys what you did this morning.'

Cindy nodded. 'I went home and listened to some recordings in your Wallace case file.' Novack had kept a file on the case at home. It included copies of the taped recordings of interviews conducted with Wallace.

Donovan turned to Novack. 'You realise you just broke about ten departmental rules by having her do that.'

'Oops. Am I bad!' said Novack. Then to Cindy, 'Tell them.'

'It wasn't Wallace on the phone,' Cindy said. 'Not even close.'

'How can you be sure of that?' Donovan asked.

'Captain, she's a speech therapist.'

'I can go into speech patterns and accents, if you want,' Cindy said. 'But there's no doubt. The person who called that night was a Midwesterner; maybe Michigan, maybe Indiana. He's also older than Wallace.'

'Richie Patrick,' Donovan said, since the hit man whose fingerprints were all over the car was from Bloomington, Indiana.

Novack nodded. 'That's what I think. I also talked to Kelly in forensics; they think the shooter was in the alley across the street. It was no easy shot. There's no evidence that Wallace had any real experience with guns.'

'Have we been wrong on this guy all along?' Donovan asked.

'You weren't. I was.'

The most worried man in the room was Anders. He believed it possible that the reason Novack was shot was because he was starting to believe in Tim's innocence, and the shooter did not want his new view to prevail.

But Anders was most likely the only person that Novack had at that point confided in, and Anders had not kept that information confidential.

He had told it to Keith Rivers, which was the same as telling it to Senator Collinsworth.

It HAD BEEN A WHILE since Eden had heard from Tim, and she was going crazy. The media had already tried and convicted him of the Novack shooting. Nick had assured her that Tim had had nothing to do with it, and admitted sharing her feeling that he was innocent of all the other charges as well. It was comforting to her, and she could use all the comfort she could get.

Eden hadn't been going out much, if at all, out of concern that Richie Patrick might reappear. She hadn't seen him since that day at Paramus Park, and it was quite likely that he was deterred by the police officer Novack had assigned to sit in a squad car in front of her house.

But while Eden felt fairly secure personally, she was in constant fear for Tim, and she checked her email every few minutes, hoping that he would contact her. She would not call him, since once Nick told the police about her friendship with Tim, there was a possibility her phone could be tapped.

It was almost dinnertime when Eden received the email. It read:

I hate to ask you this, but I need you to tell Danny that I have to see him. Don't call; they might be monitoring his phone and/or yours. Tell him I need his help, and that he should meet me tomorrow morning at ten o'clock, where we used to play touch football. He'll know what that means. Thanks, and be careful.

Eden had no hesitation about doing what Tim asked, but there was a practical problem. She emailed him back, asking him where Danny lived. She waited for an hour, but there was no response. She knew at that point that she wouldn't be getting one, since the library would be closed by then.

Eden had no way to get Danny's address online or through the phone book; she didn't even know his last name. She had two choices. One was to go to the company office in the morning, and hope that Danny came in early rather than going straight to the site. The other alternative was to go to the Purple Rose. Tim had told her that he and his friends used to hang out there, and if Danny wasn't there, maybe somebody else would know how to contact him.

The police officer out front did not seem to be involved in the investigation; he was simply providing protection for her. Eden went out and told him that she was leaving to have a drink with a friend. He nodded without showing much interest and said that he would follow her. She got in her car and drove to the Purple Rose, hoping he wouldn't follow her inside. The officer just pulled into the parking lot behind her and waited in his car.

The Purple Rose was fairly crowded, and Eden went to the bartender for help. 'Excuse me, is Danny here? He's a friend of Tim Wallace's.'

'Danny? Yeah, I think he's . . .' The bartender's eyes scanned the room. 'He's right over there with Will.' He pointed to a table. 'In the blue shirt.'

'Thanks,' Eden said, and headed for the table. She didn't know Will, and couldn't convey the message to Danny in front of anyone else.

As Eden approached, she and Danny made eye contact, and he noticeably tensed. He stood up, and she said, 'Danny?'

'Yes.'

'I need to speak to you about something. In private.'

He waited a beat. 'Sure . . . of course.' He turned to Will. 'Can you give us a couple of minutes?'

It took Will a moment to register that he was being asked to leave. 'Yeah . . . no problem.' He got up and walked towards the back of the restaurant.

'Have a seat,' Danny said. 'I'm sorry, what's your name?'

'That doesn't matter. I have a message for you from Tim.'

'How is he?'

'He's fine. He wants you to meet him tomorrow morning at ten o'clock.' Danny looked around to make sure no one would hear them. 'Where?'

'At the place where you used to play touch football. He wants you to come alone, without telling anyone else about it.'

'Why does he want to meet with me?'

'I don't know.'

'Can I reach him tonight? Maybe he wants me to bring money, or—'

She cut him off. 'I've already told you everything I know.'

Eden turned to leave, and saw Will watching them with obvious curiosity as he walked back towards the front of the place. She left the restaurant relieved that she had been able to do what Tim asked. She called Nick to tell him what had transpired, thinking that Tim would be fine with her doing so.

Nick wasn't in, so she left a cryptic message on his machine, not mentioning the place where Tim and Danny were to meet.

Eden signalled to the officer as she was approaching her car, and he nodded and pulled out behind her. When they finished the fifteen-minute ride, she parked in front of her house, and he pulled in behind her. She walked over to him and spoke through the window.

'Can I get you anything? Coffee? Maybe something to eat?'

He smiled. 'No, thanks. I have a trunk full of doughnuts. Besides, someone takes over my shift in an hour.'

She smiled back. 'I wish someone could take over my shift. Good night.'

'Good night.'

RICHIE PATRICK was waiting for Eden when she entered her house. He sat calmly on the couch, petting Travis with one hand and holding a handgun in the other. 'If you scream, it will be the last sound you ever make,' he said.

She couldn't catch her breath. All she could think about was how she might alert the police officer outside. 'What do you want?'

He laughed. 'More than you've got, but you'll have to do for now.'

'The house is surrounded by police.'

'You mean that clown in the black-and-white outside?' She didn't say anything, so he continued. 'Where's your boyfriend . . . Wallace?'

'I have no idea.'

He smiled. 'Sure you do. But we've got time for that later. Let's go.'

'Where?'

'I'll tell you what, let's make some ground rules. You do exactly what I say, and you don't ask me another . . . single . . . fucking . . . question.'

The sudden intensity with which he spoke was chilling to her. She didn't respond, and his amiable smile returned.

'Good. Now let's go.'

He took her by the arm and led her out through the back door. They were gone by the time her protector finished his first doughnut.

TEN

Nick got Eden's phone message around ten o'clock, having just got back from dinner out. He returned the call, but there was no answer. He assumed she was still out after her meeting with Danny, but wasn't worried, because she'd mentioned that she was letting the police officer follow her. He left a message for her to call him back, and went to bed.

Nick woke up briefly at four in the morning, and reflected on the fact that Eden had not called him back. He assumed she'd got home late and didn't want to wake him. He certainly wasn't worried enough to call her at this hour. So he went back to sleep.

THE MEETING was at the same location in Rockland County where Tim had taken Richie Patrick. He chose it because there was only one entrance in by car, a long, winding road that Tim could observe from the hills above. He was in position well in advance.

At 9.55, Tim saw Danny's car start up the winding road. He saw no other cars, and there didn't seem to be anyone in the car with Danny.

The car stopped on the field where they had played touch football all those years before. Danny got out of the car and looked around. He kept glancing back towards the road, and whirled in surprise when he heard the words yelled from up above him. 'Start walking up the hill!'

Danny looked up, shielding his eyes against the sun's glare. 'Tim?'

'Start walking up the hill!'

Danny walked up the only path that would take him there. Tim kept his eyes on the car and the road, but saw no sign of anyone else. He let Danny get three-quarters of the way up before starting down to meet him.

Still pretty much blinded by the sun, Danny asked, 'Tim, is that you?'

'It's me.'

Danny again shielded the sun with his hand, which was how he saw that Tim was pointing a gun at him. 'What's that for? What's going on?'

'We need to talk, Danny.'

'So let's talk. Why do you have a gun? Is that thing real?'

'Why are you doing this to me, Danny?'

'Doing what?' Danny said, his voice cracking. 'Come on, it's just me here.'

'You set me up from the beginning. You killed Maggie.'

'No, no—'

'Danny, tell me the truth, or I'm going to kill you right here.'

'Tim, I swear I don't know what you're talking about. Please—'

'I'm talking about you knowing I'd be on the boat that day, about you knowing I was in Wyoming, about you being there at the racketball club.'

'Of course I knew. We're partners. You always know where I am too.'

'Danny, I'm not trying to figure out if you did it. I just want to know why.'

'Tim, I swear—'

'There was another boat out there the day Maggie died. I found it. You know who's been out on that boat? Your uncle.'

Danny seemed unable to process all of this. 'My uncle?'

'Right. The boat's owned by a dummy corporation, but Keith Rivers signed for the licence. Were you there that day, Danny? Waiting for the explosion?'

'Yours is the only boat I've ever been on, Tim. I swear it.'

'What does your uncle get out of ruining my life, Danny? What do you get out of it?'

'Please think about this, Tim. We're friends. Why would I do this to you? Why would my uncle do it? It's making him look bad.'

Tim walked towards him, until he was about ten feet away. He was pointing the gun with two hands. 'Danny, you're going to tell me the truth by the time I count to three, or I'm going to shoot you.

'One . . . two . . .'

Danny was so confused, so frightened, that he did not even have the capacity to make up a story. 'Tim, I have told you the truth,' he finally said, and braced himself. 'Please . . . there's nothing else I can say.'

Tim didn't shoot; instead, he lowered the gun. 'Danny, I need help.'

EDEN HAD NO IDEA where she was. Patrick had tied her hands, placed a gag over her mouth and a blindfold over her eyes, then put her in the back of what seemed to be a van. She tried to figure out how far they drove, but it was impossible. Instead she spent the time trying to get her fear under control.

When they arrived at their destination, he led her out of the van and over what seemed like a wooden footbridge. He took her down some stairs and into a room, then cuffed her to what felt like radiator pipes. They were uncomfortably hot. He took off the gag but left the blindfold on.

'This is gonna be your home for a while,' he said. 'Depending on your behaviour, it could be the last one you'll ever have.'

She didn't answer him.

'I'll be back tomorrow. No one can hear you anyway, but there's an intercom system which has a microphone recording any sound in the room. If I find that you've screamed, or even spoken in any way, I will cut open your throat and rip out your larynx with my bare hands. Understand?'

She nodded.

'Good. I'll see you tomorrow, and you'll tell me where your friend is.'

He left, and she willed herself not to cry. The microphones would pick it up, and she didn't want to give him the satisfaction.

NICK TRIED EDEN three times between seven and eight in the morning, then went to her house. He saw the officer parked in front of her house, identified himself, and asked him where Eden was.

'She's inside,' he said.

Nick could hear the dogs barking inside. 'She's not answering her phone.'

'Maybe she's asleep.'

'With that barking going on? Come on.'

The officer got out of the car and followed Nick to the front door. They rang the bell a few times and pounded on the door, but there was no response other than an increase in the level of barking. The officer broke a small window in the front door and reached in, unlocking it.

Eden's bed was still made, and it did not appear that the dogs had been fed. Nick knew that there was no benign explanation for this.

She was in desperate trouble. If she was still alive.

DANNY AND TIM talked for almost three hours, trying to figure out how Tim's life had been taken away from him, and how to get it back.

Much of the conversation was Tim filling in Danny on what he had learned, about the Oceanfast, about Collinsworth, about Carson, Wyoming, about Ricardo Vasquez calling their office and about Richie Patrick. He was hoping it might trigger a thought in Danny's mind, something that would somehow clear up what was a bewildering picture. It did not.

Danny's reaction was primarily astonishment, especially about his uncle's possible involvement. 'It doesn't compute,' he said. 'Your situation only makes him look bad for steering us the business.'

'He's got an angle we haven't figured out,' Tim said. 'This somehow gets him what he wants.'

'He's got more money than he could ever spend, so that can't be it. What he really wants is to be president, but how can this help him get there?'

Tim had no answer for that. 'There has to be another shoe that's going to drop. I'm being made the fall guy for something that hasn't happened yet.'

'Maybe about the Federal Center?' Danny asked. 'The opening is Saturday night; the damn President is going to be there. The FBI has talked to me twice, the Secret Service once. Maybe that's where the Cintron 421 was going.'

'Well, it's not going to get there now,' Tim said. 'That place will be swimming with security; nothing is getting near there.'

'But that guy called our office?'

Tim nodded. 'Yeah, I thought he was calling you. He must have been pretending to be somebody else, a salesman or something, so my number would show up on his phone record. The bastards have covered every base.'

'I hope you don't mind my bringing this up,' Danny said, 'but what I don't understand is how that could have been Maggie's finger. I mean, you saw the explosion, right? It knocked you out, didn't it?'

'All I remember was a flash of white. I assumed it was an explosion, and I believed them when they said Maggie's body was never found.'

'But they were sure? I mean, the DNA tests . . .'

'That's what they said. When it matches, it's one in billions that it could be wrong. And the labs aren't police labs, so . . .' Tim's voice trailed off.

'What is it?' Danny asked.

Something didn't make sense. Tim was still silent, trying to focus on it.

'Tim?'

He had it. 'Danny, I just thought of something; I've got to go.'

'OK; can I help?'

'I don't think so, but if you can, I'll get in touch with you.'

They walked to Tim's car, so he could drive Danny back to where he left his. As soon as they got in the car, Tim turned the radio on to the local news, and it was the first story they heard. A woman named Eden Alexander was kidnapped, and it was believed to be tied to the Tim Wallace case.

THE CEREMONY that would officially open the Federal Center was forty-eight hours away. Everything had been gone over countless times, and the place was in total lockdown mode, yet things were being checked and rechecked. The US Marshal's Office and Secret Service were running what amounted to a dress rehearsal. Employees of those agencies, as well as staffers from both the White House and various senators' offices, were there to recreate the next evening exactly as it would take place.

The evening was to be fairly simple. There would be a cocktail party, lasting ninety minutes. The President would arrive fifteen minutes prior to the end of the party, then join the assembled dignitaries as they moved into a large room, where dinner would be served and speeches would be given.

The room was chosen because of the uniqueness of its security. In the event of danger, a computer would lock it down, closing impregnable metal doors, in effect creating a hermetically sealed fortress that would be resistant to all but the most powerful explosives. The same computer would simultaneously start an emergency ventilation system, utilising oxygen tanks in the building's basement. There was a total of twelve tanks; each could supply enough air for a crowd this size to breathe for three hours.

The system was planned for use in future Federal Centers. Buildings would no longer have to be evacuated in an emergency, an often panic-filled process that could itself result in injuries and deaths. Instead a safe haven would be created within the structure itself.

Before dinner, short speeches would be given by Newark Congresswoman Nancy Fellows, Senator Evans and Senator Collinsworth. As his remarks concluded, Collinsworth was to introduce the President, for a speech that his aides promised would be 'short and to the point'. Once dinner was finished, the president and his entourage would leave the room, no doubt to sustained applause, then clear the building before the other guests departed.

Carl White spent virtually all of his time on the scene. His investigation into Ricardo Vasquez had run cold, but his instincts told him that Wallace's connection to the case meant it was tied to the Federal Center.

White was becoming a pain in the ass to Secret Service Captain Steven Radford, the man in charge of security for the evening. Radford had twenty-eight years on the job, and was not about to take anything for granted. He listened respectfully to White and tolerated his constant presence. The moment of truth was close, and Radford knew he had things under control.

Tim was devastated by what he had heard. It had to be Richie Patrick. He had told Eden that if she got into trouble, she should give up his location, and he hoped she had done so. But he knew that if she had seen Patrick and could identify him, he would not have the compassion to let her live.

Tim's focus shifted. He'd spent weeks thinking only about how to extricate himself from this situation; now his main concern was Eden. It was a new kind of agony. The plain truth was that if it were not for him, this evil would not have entered her life. Now he had to find a way out for both of them.

Tim checked into the Village Motel in downtown Hackensack. It was the kind of establishment that did most of its room renting by the hour, but it was clean, and the desk clerk did not require ID or a credit card.

He called Nick, who was distraught, blaming himself for not doing more to protect his sister. Unfortunately, he had little more to offer about Eden's situation. No demands for a ransom or anything else had been made.

After leaving Kiley and Travis with his assistant, Nick had been to see Novack, who was chafing to get out of the hospital.

'For what it's worth, I think he's done a one-eighty on you,' Nick said.

'What does that mean?' Tim asked.

'He wouldn't say so directly, but I've got a hunch he thinks you're innocent, that you've been set up for something all along. Too bad he can't convince his captain and the district attorney.'

'Will he see me? I mean talk to me . . . face to face . . . without arresting me? There are things he knows about that day, about Maggie, that I need to know. I think together we might have a chance to figure this out.'

Nick thought about it. 'He might do it,' he said. 'I could talk to him.'

'Can we trust him?' Tim asked.

'If he gives his word, we can take it to the bank.'

'Then talk to him,' Tim said. 'And please hurry.'

Patrick arrived at 7 a.m., though Eden had no way of knowing what time it was. He untied her, but kept her blindfold on. Then he grabbed her by the arm and told her he was taking her to the bathroom.

'If I find out you took the blindfold off, I will take a candle and burn out your eyes,' he said, matter-of-factly.

She heard a door closing, and sensed that she was in the bathroom by herself. She felt for the toilet, and for the sink, and did what she had to do.

A few minutes later, the door opened and Patrick led her out. He sat her in a chair and said, 'Here,' putting a box of what she discovered were crackers in her hand. She wasn't hungry, but ate a few, and he gave her some water.

She sat there, not knowing if he had left. Her fear was palpable, and her hatred. Given the opportunity, she knew she'd kill him without hesitation.

'There's a table in front of you,' he said. 'Put your hands on it, palms down.'

She did as she was told.

'I'm going to ask you a question. If you answer it correctly the first time, we're fine. Every time I have to ask it again, I'll cut off one of your fingers.'

She started to sob and shake, momentarily gripped in a fear beyond anything she could ever have imagined.

'Ready?' he said. 'Where is Tim Wallace hiding?'

Eden had known she would be asked that, and even felt relief that it was the question she expected. Tim had told her that if she found herself in danger, she should reveal what she knew. She would have done so anyway; this kind of fear was not something she was equipped to deal with.

SHE TOLD HIM where the house was, and answered a few specific questions about how to get there. Patrick could tell she was telling the truth.

'OK, you can take your hands off the table,' he said, when they were finished. He debated whether to kill her then, but decided he didn't have the time. It wasn't the killing itself; that would take only a few seconds. But there would be some cleaning up involved if he did it then, so he decided to wait until afterwards, when the clean-up would not be necessary. Besides, if things went wrong there might be a need for bargaining chips, and Eden alive was therefore worth more than Eden dead.

Patrick took her back downstairs, tied and gagged her, and left her in darkness. Then he drove immediately to the house in Lincoln Park that Eden had told him about. He no longer expected Tim to be there; once Eden's kidnapping was reported in the press, it would have been a clear signal for Tim to find another place to hide. But Patrick had other things to do, other plans to make. His employers would be unhappy about it, because having Tim in their custody was vital to their plan. But that would soon be the least of their problems. Things were going to go very wrong for them, were going to spiral out of their control, and for them it would be too late.

It would be much too late.

NICK AND NOVACK quickly negotiated the details of the meeting with Tim. The location was to be Tim's motel, which was structured so patrons could park in front of their rooms. Novack and Nick didn't have to enter a lobby where they might be recognised.

They pulled up in Nick's car, and after determining that there was no one around, parked and quickly went into Tim's dingy room.

Tim was standing on the other side of the room when they walked in. Nick closed the door behind them, and Novack and Tim just stared at each other. Both were so used to hating the other that it seemed to take them time to digest that they were there for a common purpose.

'Nice place you've got here,' said Novack.

Tim nodded. 'Yeah. I appreciate your coming. We don't have much time.'

'Before what?' Novack asked.

'First of all, I'm innocent; I haven't done the things you thought I did. But I suspect you know that now, or you wouldn't be here.'

'Keep going . . .'

'Nobody would go to all this trouble just to ruin my life. I don't have those kinds of enemies. I didn't know Richie Patrick until the day I shot him.'

'So why you?' Novack asked.

'It has to be about something much bigger. Look, no one could have known Maggie would be on the boat that day. I was the one meant to be blown up. They were there watching on the Oceanfast, probably ready to finish the job. But the sun was behind us; they'd have been looking into it, and it would have been hard to see. I doubt they realised I was in the water, still alive.'

Nick spoke for the first time. 'So why haven't they killed you since?'

'Because they figured out a better way for them. I was going to be killed to get me out of the way so they could do something criminal; I must have somehow been in their way without my knowing it.'

'So instead of getting rid of you so they could do it,' Novack said, 'they decided to do it and blame you for it.'

'Right. And in some way they dissected my life, manipulated me like I was a goddamn puppet, and set me up as public enemy number one.'

'Who knows you that well?'

'That's why you're here,' Tim said. 'You're going to tell me that answer.'

'Good luck,' Novack said, obviously sceptical.

'You said it was Maggie's finger at the club that day. How did you know?'

'We ran a DNA test. It came back conclusive.'

'Matched against Maggie's DNA?'

Novack nodded. 'Of course.'

'Where did you get it?'

'We've had it since we opened the investigation into her death.'

'But where did you get it? Maggie's body was lost at sea. And it's not like she was a convicted felon, somebody whose DNA would be on file.'

Novack slowly nodded his head. 'Shit. I don't know.'

He took out his cellphone and dialled a number. When it was answered, he said, 'Sam, about the Wallace case. Right . . . I need you to get the file. I want to know who collected the DNA, and how we got it. I'll wait.' Novack put his hand over the receiver. 'Sam's our forensics guy,' he said.

Novack held the phone to his ear for almost ten minutes. Everyone in the room was silent, waiting for the answer.

'I'm here,' Novack said, as Sam came back on the line. 'What did you come up with?' Another pause; then he said, 'You're sure? . . . OK, thanks.'

Novack hung up the phone. 'Sam collected the DNA himself. He checked the file, but he remembered it anyway. He said it was because she was hot.'

'Who?'

'Your assistant, Meredith Tunney. You were in hospital, and she took Sam to your house and gave him what we assumed was your wife's toothbrush. He got the DNA off that.'

'Of course; God, why didn't I see it? She ran my life. She scheduled our racketball games; she knew when I'd be on the boat. She knew everything.'

'How long has she worked for you?' Nick asked.

'Since a couple of months before Maggie died.' He sat down, trying to digest it all. His dominant feeling was relief that Maggie really had died instantly and painlessly on the boat. After a while, he said, 'I just realised something. I'm not sure, but I think Meredith may have been the one who told me about the stone quarry near Carson. That's what brought me there.'

'Where they were waiting for you.'

'Right. Once Maggie died, they figured I'd have more value to them as someone to set up. But if it wasn't Maggie's DNA, and Maggie's finger, and it wasn't Sheila Blair's, whose was it?'

Novack shook his head. 'We'll probably never know. They could have killed yet another woman just for that purpose. Killing doesn't seem to be something they're particularly hesitant to do.' He was immediately sorry he had said that, since Eden was still missing. So he added, 'Now that we know how they got to you, we need to figure out why.'

Tim nodded. 'It has to be about the business, and about Collinsworth.'

Novack shook his head. 'We're looking at a bunch of murders, an exploding car, a kidnapping. That would be pretty dirty, even for a US senator.'

'It's the Federal Center,' Tim said. 'Something must be planned for that, and I'd bet it's tomorrow night.'

'But now that attention's been called to it, security will be maxed out.'

'Meredith was in a position to give out our passes to get on the site during the construction. She could have got her people in there.'

'But why plan something and do all this to alert their opposition?'

'Because they're not worried about their opposition. They don't think they can be stopped.'

'IT'S MEREDITH. I need to talk to you about Tim.'

'Have you spoken to him?' Will asked. 'Do you know where he is?'

'I don't want to talk about it on the phone, but it's very, very important. I couldn't reach Danny, and I need to talk about it with someone right away.'

'OK . . . sure,' he said. 'Should I come to the office?'

'No . . . I'll come to you.' Will was in Ridgewood, so they made arrangements to meet in front of a small park on Ridgewood Avenue.

Will had been waiting ten minutes when he saw her pull up. She reached across and opened the door for him. As soon as he got in, she pulled off.

'What's going on with Tim?' Will asked.

She smiled. 'Not much. What's going on with you?'

Her answer confused him. 'You said you had to talk to me about Tim.'

'If I were you, I'd be more worried about yourself.'

'What? Why?'

'Well, at least Tim doesn't have a gun pointed at the back of his head.'

Will turned and saw a familiar-looking man pointing a gun at him from about six inches away. 'Hey! What the hell is going on here?'

The man smiled. 'Well, I would say you've got a bit of a problem.'

Will realised where he had seen him before. 'You're the guy from Homeland Security, the guy I took through the building's computer system.'

The man smiled again. 'And you have no idea how much I appreciated it.'

NOVACK LEFT TIM in the hotel room with instructions to stay put. He was still officially a dangerous fugitive, and Novack didn't want him getting shot by some cop looking to make a name for himself. Novack did make the concession that he would attempt to keep Nick informed of developments.

He called Anders and Donovan, and told them what he had learned, leaving out the fact that he'd met Tim in person. Novack then picked up Anders and they went to the offices of Wallace Industries, with four other officers.

Meredith was not there, but Danny was in his office. He told them that Meredith had not been in all day, and had not called to explain why.

'Where does she live?' Novack asked.

'I'll get it for you.' Danny got up to look in the filing cabinet. He located the file and gave Novack an address in Leonia. 'Any chance you'll tell me what's going on?' he said.

'Zero,' said Novack. 'If she calls in, do not tell her we were here.' He knew, however, that Meredith wouldn't be calling.

The subsequent raid on her house failed to apprehend her, mainly because she didn't have a house. The address she had on file was a vacant lot.

DONOVAN TOOK ON the job of communicating events to Carl White. Danny provided Novack with a photograph of Meredith, taken at a company outing, which they supplied to White, who turned it over to the Secret Service.

Facial-recognition monitors were posted at twenty-one locations surrounding the Federal Center, and the pictures of Patrick, Meredith and Tim were added to the existing terrorist data bank. If any of them came within five blocks of the location, the authorities would know about it in a split second.

Steven Radford, the Secret Service agent in charge, was not unduly worried by the account he heard from White. The fact that there were dangerous people who might be intent on killing the President and other high-level people was no surprise; such people are out there in droves. No matter what might be attempted, Radford felt confident that the location was secure.

EDEN HEARD THEM UPSTAIRS: a woman and two men, and one of the men was Patrick. She couldn't make out what they were saying.

Their arrival came at a particularly inopportune time. She was making ever so slight progress on loosening the rope tying her hands to the metal bar. The decision she faced was whether to keep working on it. If Patrick came downstairs quietly and caught her, he would do something horrible.

But Eden was by nature a realist. When Patrick had accomplished whatever he was planning, he was going to do something horrible anyway.

So she continued working on the ropes.

IT WOULD HAVE BEEN no surprise to anyone to know that Keith Rivers was giving the senator crucial advice. What would have rocked Washington was that the advice was given not to Senator Collinsworth, but to Senator Evans.

The conversation was over the phone; the men could not risk being seen together. Rivers was making sure that Evans knew every detail of what was to take place, and understood exactly what he was supposed to do. Evans was not as bright as Collinsworth, and Rivers's confidence in him was low.

'Are you sure you've memorised it?' Rivers asked. 'The timing's crucial.'

'I've got it. Just make sure our friends know what they're doing. You know what this means for all of us.'

'Yes, I do.'

'When was the last time you spoke to your boss?'

Rivers knew he was not talking about Collinsworth. 'Last night.'

'Is he in Washington?'

'No,' Rivers said. 'He's out of the country.'

'Maybe I should speak with him,' Evans said.

'He's not reachable until well after this is over.'

'Fine,' said Evans, but what he was thinking was that when this was over, he would talk to whomever he wanted, whenever he wanted.

Then even Rivers's boss could kiss his ass.

'THE FRUSTRATING THING about money is that it's impossible to own all of it,' Byron Carthon said, then waited for the laughter to subside. He enjoyed the sound of it, even though he knew it was not merited by the joke itself, but rather by the fact that he owned his audience, lock, stock and barrel.

There were seventy people in the audience: the top thirty-five employees of the Franklin Group and their spouses. They had come from Franklin subsidiaries all over the world to this outing, on the cruise ship *Serenity*, as it sailed the South Pacific. The purpose of the gathering, according to Byron, was to relax, talk and strategise about the company's future growth. His goal was to grow his company over the next ten years at a greater rate than the previous ten. That would be a tall order, as Franklin's growth had been mete-oric. Originally based in America, its tentacles had spread round the globe, and it was now the world's leading construction, mining, and oil and gas company. Ironically, its only blemish at that moment was its US operations.

Franklin had come out on the short end of what Byron Carthon consid-ered petty American politics. Certain politicians had used the company as a whipping boy, and government contracts had become less frequent and lucrative than in the past. Franklin's international operations had more than made up for that, but it was not good enough for Byron. The US market was still the most important, and Franklin would once again reign supreme.

What Byron did not tell his guests, what he would not tell anyone, was that the real reason for being on the ship was simply to be on the ship. It was the perfect place for him to be when his plan was finally executed.

And it was totally his plan, though history would never record it as such. It would leave Byron Carthon wealthy beyond even his imagination, and in control of everything, including the next president of the United States.

'You all have the agenda,' Byron said near the end of his remarks. 'There are no meetings scheduled until Monday. So take the weekend to relax and rejuvenate. For the next two days the world will go on without us.'

He neglected to mention that, after tonight, the world would never be quite the same.

TIM HAD the awful sensation that he was being dragged slowly towards the edge of a cliff, a process that would result in his plunging off the cliff in about two hours. That was when the Federal Center gala event was to start.

He was going insane cooped up in that motel room, but he couldn't figure out where to go. The Federal Center would be the most heavily guarded place in the country. How could it be so secure, yet so vulnerable? Something had to be accomplished from the inside. Yet everyone, from the highest dignitary down, would have to go through security screeners to get in.

Unless . . . unless it was an inside job controlled from the outside.

Tim grabbed the phone and called Danny on his cell. He was relieved when his friend picked up. 'Danny, it's me.'

'Tim, are you OK?'

'Where is Will? I've got to talk to him.'

'I wish I knew. I've been trying to reach him since yesterday. I've tried everywhere. Home, cell, even his new girlfriend. I don't understand it.'

In that instant, Tim's fears were confirmed. Will would never leave without letting Danny know where he could be reached in an emergency. To do so the day of the big opening was inconceivable.

'Danny, keep trying to find him. If you reach him, call me immediately.' He gave Danny his cellphone number; there was no hiding any more.

Tim hung up and called Nick. 'Nick, it's the computer.'

'What are you talking about?'

'Will Clampett did the computer security work at the Federal Center. He's been missing now for twenty-four hours and can't be reached.'

'So you think he's on the other side?'

'I doubt it. But whoever might want to control the computers could do so through him. And Meredith would know that. The computers can be operated from a remote location. Nick, that building has got to be shut down now.'

As soon as Nick got off the phone, he called Novack and told him what Tim had said. Novack called Danny and asked him to locate a picture of Will as soon as possible. Then he called Carl White, who at that moment was in the Federal Center itself. The guests had not yet started to arrive, but they would do soon. Novack quickly filled him in on what he knew.

'They could be making their move through the building computer somehow,' Novack said when he was finished.

'I don't see how,' White said. 'Secret Service techs are running the thing. I was in the room with them a little while ago. Everything seemed fine.'

'At least alert them to the possibility that something might happen. And make sure that room is secure.'

White was not used to taking orders from local detectives, but this was not the time to stand on ceremony, since Novack was right. 'Will do,' he said. 'And call me if you learn anything else.'

'If something happens,' Novack said, 'I'm afraid you'll know before me.'

THE PRESIDENT of the United States is the elephant in every room he is ever in. That's a given. But he is also the elephant in every room he is planning to enter. This was obvious to everyone at the cocktail party at the Federal Center. The President was not due to arrive until fifteen minutes before dinner began, but everyone in the room was already jockeying for position.

This little dance was complicated by the rivalries in the room, most notably the one between Senators Collinsworth and Evans. They and their chief staffers were determined to stay apart from each other, yet equally determined to be near the arriving President. It made for interesting theatre, a sort of senatorial Kabuki dance.

If Evans had ever been more nervous in his life, he couldn't remember when. He would have considered backing out, if such an option were available to him. It wasn't. So he made small talk with people of lesser political stature than him, a category that included pretty much everyone in the room, except for Collinsworth. And he avoided eye contact with Keith Rivers, the only other person in the room who knew what he knew.

CARL WHITE was getting nowhere with Radford. The Secret Service captain had listened patiently to White for two weeks, but this was showtime, and he had no time for wild theories. The computers were firmly in the hands of men with top security clearances, men whom Radford trusted completely. Besides, he saw no way that computer hackers, even in the highly unlikely event that they were successful, could be any more than an annoyance.

So Radford was too circumspect to say it straight out, but he implied that Carl should have an hors d'oeuvre and leave the Secret Service to do their job.

RICHIE PATRICK thought it was damn nice of CNN to act as his accomplice. There was one pool camera that would cover the speeches at the dinner, and CNN would be among those to show it on the air.

The timing had to be just right to provide maximum effect, and Richie, who would otherwise have no idea what was going on in that building, could just turn on the television and be perfectly well informed.

Once he triggered the event, then his computer monitors would tell him all he needed to know. But for now, CNN would do just fine.

TIM WOULD BE watching television as well, but he was watching with a feeling of helplessness and foreboding. He knew in his gut that something was going to happen, something awful, and it would involve the computers.

Soon he would understand what they were doing, and how they were blaming him for it.

Of course, by then it would be too late.

ELEVEN

resident Markham arrived promptly fifteen minutes before the end of the cocktail party. His every movement was perfectly coordinated by his staff. He managed to talk to and have pictures taken with everyone he was supposed to during that time. Markham was a master at this, and made personal comments that made each person feel good.

The President separately spent a little extra time with Senators Evans and Collinsworth. He knew both senators had ambitions to succeed him, and had been holding out the carrot of his future support to each of them. The truth was, he considered Collinsworth a pompous ass, and thought Evans overly aggressive and not very bright. He had told his wife that if he thought one of them might someday move into the White House, he'd burn it down first.

The guests moved into the main hall. It lacked the elegance that the evening called for, but no expense had been spared. The tables were set ornately, and the flowers alone cost more than any five of the waiters earned in a year.

After all, the nation was watching.

'I'VE BEEN in this business a long time,' Senator Collinsworth began. 'And I've learned that you have to dream big and then compromise. Nothing happens exactly as you hope; everyone has their own interests and agendas that have to be taken into consideration. All you can do is your best, and hope that the end result includes as much of your original vision as possible.

'But tonight is very, very different. This glorious Federal Center is exactly how I and others envisioned it just two short years ago. It is the perfect model for other Federal Centers all over this great country, and will come to symbolise the strength and ingenuity we have, and the security we are entitled to. In short, this Federal Center is truly a dream come true.'

Collinsworth went on for another seven minutes, claiming full credit for the Center while trying to appear gracious and modest. He managed to pull it off, to all those who did not know that he didn't have a gracious or modest bone in his body. There were few people in the room who fell into that category, but Collinsworth was playing to the viewing audience at home.

'And now it is my pleasure to introduce to you the man who ultimately made this all possible. Without his leadership, all the dreams in the world wouldn't have been enough. Ladies and gentlemen, please welcome the President of the United States, Christopher Markham.'

The crowd rose in a standing ovation. They had no idea that Richie Patrick had just typed in a code and pressed a button on his computer that effectively gave him control over their lives.

At first, almost nobody in the hall realised what was happening. The noise of the standing ovation, and the fact that everyone was facing the dais, watching the President make his way to the podium, prevented people from noticing what was going on behind them.

Large reinforced steel doors were closing in from both sides, and reinforced steel panels were moving over the windows, but since it was night-time, the lighting in the room didn't change. Few of the guests realised that what had happened was out of the ordinary. Carl White was one of those who did, and he immediately started looking for Captain Radford. But Radford was in an outer hallway, checking perimeter security. The closing doors locked him out, with no way back in.

White ran to the computer room, where there was no uncertainty about whether something was wrong. The room was in chaos, as the computer operators realised they no longer had any control over the systems.

Their monitors had gone dark for about two minutes, after which a typed message appeared. White arrived in the room just in time to read it.

This building is under my control. No one can get in or out, and those inside will live or die depending on their actions and the actions of those that speak for them.

Specifically, oxygen tank number three contains one fiftieth of one ounce of thallium. It is enough to kill every single person in the building a hundred times over. By simply pressing a button, I can instantly release it into the air supply.

This computer has been programmed to treat any interruption of power, from any source, as an enemy attack. It will similarly regard any attempt to enter the room or breach the barricades. The response will be immediate and deadly; in a matter of seconds all present will be inhaling thallium.

There is to be no contact between those inside and outside my building. You will have my non-negotiable demand in five minutes. I can see through every camera in the room, so be assured that I am watching.

Timothy Wallace

The message was sent to every mainstream media outlet in the country, and Captain Radford himself read it on one of the media monitors outside the building. He knew all too well that the steel barriers rendered the building virtually impregnable to outside attack, creating a safe haven within.

A safe haven that had become a prison, and possibly a tomb.

'HOW AM I DOING?' Patrick asked Will, who had watched in horror from the chair where he was tied, as events unfolded.

'How did you get thallium into that tank?' he asked. Will knew thallium to be a radium poison that, ingested even in minute quantities, caused a death that was slow and very, very unpleasant.

Patrick smiled. 'When you have a pass to get in, you can do anything.'

Will looked at Meredith, who smiled, obviously not having any second thoughts about her role in this operation. 'So how's he doing?' she asked.

Will turned back to Patrick. 'They'll figure out a way to take back control.'

'You know something?' Patrick said. 'They just might. But not in twenty minutes, and that's all they have.'

TIM WALLACE was not watching television. He had left his motel room long before. He still did not know what was going to take place, but he thought he had finally figured out where it was going to happen.

There was obviously no way for Tim to be sure he was right. The people controlling the building could be anywhere. But when they accomplished what they were setting out to do, they would want to disappear, without leaving a paper or electronic trail. And the woman at the Southold marina had said that people had been on the Oceanfast 360 doing work, and that they had blown her off when she tried to be friendly.

The boat was in the water, and there would be nothing to stop it from sailing away, silently and anonymously.

Tim tried to reach Nick, but had to leave a message telling him where he was going and why. He himself had no idea what he would do when he got there, especially when he realised that in his haste he'd forgotten to bring his handgun.

He was still at least twenty minutes away from the pier, and would spend that time listening to hyperventilating radio newscasters tell the world that he, Tim Wallace, was holding the President of the United States hostage.

INSIDE THE BUILDING, the guests were slowly learning what was going on. The Secret Service agents in the room were at an uncharacteristic loss as to how to proceed. The protocol was to take the President to a safe haven, where they would wait out whatever threat was out there. But they had nowhere to take him. So they shepherded him to a corner of the room and hovered round him like human shields, though their bodies would be useless against an airborne poison.

When Senator Collinsworth was informed what was happening, he saw his political life flash before his eyes. He knew that even if this turned out well, with no injuries and Wallace's capture, it would be the biggest story since 9/11. And its focus would be on Collinsworth, for providing a terrorist-murderer with the opportunity of a lifetime.

Meanwhile, Senator Evans kept taking deep breaths and staring up at a window, fifteen feet up at the east side of the room.

THE LATE-NIGHT PIANO PLAYER in the ship's main bar was better than Byron Carthon expected. He was doing a medley of Broadway songs, and Byron was a sucker for show music. The man was moderately talented, but not quite deserving of the $100 bill that Byron placed in his tip jar.

Byron had brought a bunch of his executives to the bar. Usually early to bed, he chose to stay up late. He ordered another round of drinks and requested a rendition of 'If I Were a Rich Man' from *Fiddler on the Roof*. The idea of Byron Carthon yearning to be a rich man drew a laugh from the others in his party, and Byron laughed along with them. It was obvious he didn't have a care in the world.

THE NEXT SET of instructions came exactly on time, as promised:

> You will immediately wire $5 billion to the Bank of Zurich, account number 327-548-6999873-24. Inform the bank that the US Government insists that they follow the instructions I have sent them. All transactions must be accomplished within the next fifteen minutes, or I will release the thallium into the building.

FRANTIC CONFERENCE CALLS were conducted among the vice-president, the attorney general, the director of Homeland Security, the chairman of the Joint Chiefs of Staff and the directors of the Secret Service, FBI and CIA.

The first thing to be determined was whether the threat was credible. The chairman of the Joint Chiefs and the CIA director both reported that their respective biological warfare experts had confirmed that the thallium could easily have gone undetected in those heavy tanks. The quantity necessary to be deadly would have made detection almost impossible, especially since no one would have been specifically looking for thallium.

Entering the building by force was quickly rejected as impractical. The building was incredibly well fortified, and explosives powerful enough to penetrate it might well kill or injure the hostages.

The question of the money was the easiest. Despite President Markham's many pronouncements over the years that the United States would never negotiate with terrorists, the decision was made to pay the money. If they could get out of this for $5 billion, they would feel they got off cheap.

JIMMY LEE CURRY stared at the television with horror and disbelief. Like the rest of the mesmerised viewing public, he couldn't be quite sure what was going on. But he was certain that life as he knew it was over.

Jimmy Lee had filed the story about Tim Wallace's terrorist connections, and it was slated to run in the online edition of his newspaper within the hour. The story might or not be pulled, since events had overtaken it. But even if it never ran, it would be a focal point of the investigations that would dominate the country in the coming weeks. Jimmy Lee knew he would be seen as the man who could have stopped all of this from happening. And if people died on this night, if the President of the United States died on this night, Jimmy Lee would go down in history as an unwitting executioner.

So as Jimmy Lee sat at home watching, he did not feel sorry for the people in that building facing death. He envied them.

SENATOR EVANS knew that his moment had come. He glanced over and made eye contact with Keith Rivers. He thought that Rivers nodded ever so slightly, but it didn't matter either way. It was time to act.

Evans looked up again towards the window at the side of the room. He could not see the place where the steel covering was not fully closed, but he knew it was there. This time he pretended to see something.

'Look at that,' he said to no one in particular, but loudly enough that at least half a dozen people near him could hear.

'What?' someone asked, but Evans did not respond. He was already up and walking towards the window, as if intent on whatever he had seen.

'Give me a hand with that table,' he said to those nearby, and they helped him drag it over to a position under the window.

Evans then pulled over a chair, which he put up on the table. He got up onto the chair, from where he could barely reach the ledge under the large window with his arms outstretched. Pulling himself up was a bit of a strain, but he had practised this many times. He would reach the window, then drop back down and secure a piece of metal or tool, which he would take back up. Then he would insert it into the opening he found, prise the panels open, and with the help of rescuers outside, bring everybody to safety.

He made it up there, but all he saw was steel. No opening. No way out.

He understood instantly that he had been betrayed. He also understood that he and everyone else in that room were going to die.

RICHIE PATRICK had been watching Evans's every move on his computer monitors, laughing in gleeful anticipation. Now he knew exactly what was going through Evans's mind. He had no sympathy for him, because Evans was stupid. He should have realised that in an operation of this magnitude, Patrick could not afford to leave anyone alive.

They were all going to die . . . Evans, Rivers, Eden, Will, Tim and even Meredith. She still thought they would marry and sail off into the sunset, but she was in for a rather rude, and deadly, awakening.

He would even kill Carthon, though that would be a little more difficult, and much more dangerous. But he would do it, no matter what. Because the truth, as Patrick knew it, was that you have to kill to stay alive.

It was the cost of doing business.

TIM ARRIVED AT THE PIER and parked on the opposite end, where he could not be seen from the Oceanfast yacht. He realised as he got out of the car that it might well have already gone out to sea. If it had, that would be game, set and match, and there would be nothing for Tim to do.

He ran towards where the yacht had been and was relieved to find it still docked there. He then cautiously made his way to it, trying to avoid being seen by anyone on the boat who might be watching, but he did not detect any movement or activity inside. Quietly he walked onto the boat.

For the first time he could hear someone talking. He edged along a corridor, past a kitchen and two bedrooms, towards the side where the sounds were coming from. He reached a room that seemed to be a kind of den, and peered in through the partially open door. Inside he could see Patrick sitting in front of an elaborate computer set-up, and Will and Meredith across the room on a couch. Will seemed to have his arms bound behind him.

Tim backed away, trying to figure out how to get Patrick away from the computer and out of the room. He went into the kitchen, where he picked up a knife and a large coffee mug. He then went out into the hall and positioned himself along the corridor in an adjacent bedroom.

Then he held out the coffee mug and dropped it on the floor.

But it wasn't Patrick who came to check out the noise. It was Meredith. Tim let her walk by, trying to figure out what to do.

He made his decision while she was on the way back. He waited until she was at the doorway before coming out just behind her and punching her as hard as he could in the right temple. The idea of hitting a woman, something that would have previously seemed inconceivable to him, didn't bother him at all. This was a person who had helped to kill Maggie.

Tim caught the unconscious Meredith before she reached the floor.

PATRICK DIDN'T WAIT for her return. As Will watched in horror, he pressed the code numbers that would release the thallium-tainted oxygen. Only then did he go to find out what was keeping Meredith.

In the Federal Center, the poisonous air slowly made its way into the room, as colourless and odourless as it was deadly.

BY THE TIME Patrick came down the hall, Tim had pulled Meredith's unconscious body into the bedroom. He heard Patrick coming, and as he walked by, jumped out at him and swung the kitchen knife.

He slashed Patrick in the area between the shoulder and the neck. Blood started gushing, and Patrick staggered a few feet and fell. Tim saw him go down, and started to move quickly towards the computer room.

The bullet hit him in the upper back and sent him sprawling. He fell to the ground and rolled over, an agonising pain shooting through him. He looked back and saw Patrick raising his gun to fire again.

He also saw Eden come up behind Patrick and smash him over the head with a heavy wooden lamp. It crushed his skull, killing him instantly.

Eden ran to Tim, who was conscious and alert, but covered in blood. 'Untie Will,' he said, and she hesitated a moment before rushing off to do so.

Once untied, Will went straight to the computer and shut off oxygen tank three, at the same time opening the doors and windows of the building. The guests, not even aware that they had been exposed to the thallium in varying degrees, rushed out of the room and fled the building.

Eden went back to where Tim was lying. He was unmoving, apparently unconscious. She heard a noise and looked up to see Novack running towards them, handgun drawn.

'It's over,' she said. 'But Tim . . .'

Novack went to Tim's side and saw that his eyes were closed. He felt for a pulse, as Tim opened his eyes and looked up at him.

'I'm gonna live,' Tim said.

'Damn . . . I can't catch a break,' Novack said, and then smiled.

He took off his jacket and wrapped it round Tim's back and shoulder to stem the flow of blood. 'You owe me for this jacket.'

EPILOGUE

If there's one thing I do not have to educate the public about, it is the devastating effect of thallium. Thirty-one people in that room that night have since died, cruelly chosen by fate according to their unwitting proximity to air vents.

Included in the fatalities were Senator Collinsworth and Keith Rivers, while Senator Evans has suffered but survived, though he surely will live out his days in prison. Among the lucky ones were President Markham and Carl White, both of whom were far from vents and quick to get to fresh air when the doors opened.

Evans and Meredith have provided much of the details of the conspiracy, though they will receive no benefit from the courts or public opinion for doing so. The crime was too heinous and too public for deals to be made.

Byron Carthon is living in Venezuela, for the moment successfully fighting extradition. There is speculation that if the Venezuelan government refuses to send him back to face the US legal system, Special Service commandos will be dispatched to render a more immediate form of justice.

Tim Wallace suffered substantial injuries on the boat that day, but physical therapy has got him back to almost full strength. He has been called a hero by various government agencies, and will soon be awarded the Congressional Medal, the highest honour a civilian can receive. He has not gone public with his thoughts about his experience, preferring to get on with his life.

Amazingly, there are those, conditioned by earlier media reports and current conspiracy theorists, who still believe Tim to have been a participant, even a leader, in the criminal operation. Those in the know are very public and very loud in correcting this absurd allegation, and Detective John Novack has probably been the most vocal of all in defending Tim's role.

Tim and I are spending a great deal of time with each other. We try to live our lives privately, but that's mostly impossible with the media following us everywhere. But we still go to the dog park every Sunday. I socialise and Tim throws the tennis balls, though not as far as he used to because of his injury.

We're planning on moving in together next month. Kiley and Travis seem very much in favour of it; their tails wag whenever the subject is mentioned.

Tim is upbeat and looking forward to the new life we are starting together.

The nightmare is officially over.

DAVID ROSENFELT

Born: March 31, 1949, New Jersey
Current home: Southern California
Website: www.davidrosenfelt.com

RD: You worked as president of marketing for Tri-Star Pictures for many years. How did you get into the movie business?

DR: I took the route that I would recommend to everyone. My uncle, who was the head of United Artists, hired me.

What was it like, and do you miss it?

DR: It was clearly an exciting place to be, as each movie offers a unique marketing opportunity. I can't think of any other product that can achieve such great success or devastating failure, literally overnight. Movies open on a Friday, and by Saturday you know whether they're a triumph or a disaster. I miss it sometimes, but being an author is a much better lifestyle.

RD: How long have you been writing novels, and what first inspired you?

DR: I started in 2002. I was writing television movies, and I wanted to create a court-room drama. The studios weren't making them at the time, so I decided to try my idea as a novel, *Open and Shut*, which introduced lawyer Andy Carpenter.

RD: For readers who haven't yet read your legal mysteries, what kind of guy is Andy?

DR: Andy is smart and resourceful, leaning towards the flamboyant in the courtroom, and has a killer's instinct when it comes to cross-examination. I'm not a lawyer myself, but Andy and I are alike in a lot of ways. We're both physical cowards, very logical and sarcastic, we love sports, and neither of us understands women.

RD: Are you tempted to try genres other than thrillers and mysteries?

DR: I wish there was a market for comic novels . . . that would be my favourite genre. Comedies are a staple of the movie business, but few and far between in fiction. Generally, comedy in novels is an offshoot of another genre.

RD: You describe yourself as 'a novelist with thirty-seven dogs'. Can you tell us about that and what it is about dogs that you love so much?

DR: My wife and I rescue dogs, and we've set up a sanctuary for them at our home. The numbers fluctuate between twenty-five and thirty-eight. Right now, we have twenty-seven. There isn't enough space to describe why I love them.

RD: Is that because you had a lot of dogs at home when you were a child?

DR: No, but we always had one.

RD: Where did you grow up, and how does it compare to where you live now?

DR: I grew up in New Jersey, and for me it was the best place in the world. Now I live with my family just south of Los Angeles. It's not my favourite location, mainly because it's relentlessly hot and sunny there. I prefer real weather—thunderstorms and snow, etc.

RD: How many dogs have you rescued, in total, over the years?

DR: The number of unwanted pets in Southern California is horrifying. We've rescued more than 4,000 dogs.

RD: What happens to the animals that you can't take in yourself?

DR: They're abandoned in animal shelters and very likely to be put down. Instead of leaving them to this fate, we try to find great homes for them.

RD: Why did you focus on golden retrievers?

DR: When we met, my wife had a golden named Tara, and she was beyond extraordinary. Her death was the catalyst that pushed us into dog rescue, and now about sixty per cent of our rescues are goldens. They are loving, intelligent and patient, and possess more dignity than any other living thing on the planet.

RD: On your website you express gratitude that neither of your children has inherited your 'eccentricities'. Are you willing to share those publicly?

DR: I just have a peculiar, often bizarre, view of the world. It often comes out in my novels, especially the Andy Carpenter books. I guess I just see things somewhat differently to most people. I'm highly sceptical, absurdly logical, and I see humour in things when it probably isn't there.

RD: Which has been most challenging and/or rewarding role of your life— being a movie mogul, a dad, a dog-rescuer or an author?

DR: That's a tough one, and I should point out that I was never a mogul. Being a dad and dog-rescuer were easily the two most rewarding. I've been blessed with great kids, so dog-rescuer is probably the toughest. You see a lot of things you wish you didn't have to see.

RD: And, if your family had to pick just three adjectives to describe you, what would they be?

DR: Self-deprecating, and that would preclude my mentioning the other two.

An Irish
Country Village
Patrick Taylor

At the end of his first year in Dr Fingal O'Reilly's country practice, Barry Laverty is a firm admirer of his eccentric but wise mentor, and cock-a-hoop about his progress along the road to becoming a fully fledged country GP. Still, with some tricksy and hard-to-please patients around, young Dr Laverty is about to learn the hard way that it's foolish to count one's chickens before they are hatched . . .

1

Barry Laverty—Dr Barry Laverty—heard the clattering of a frying pan on a stove and smelt bacon frying. Mrs 'Kinky' Kincaid, Dr O'Reilly's housekeeper, had breakfast on, and Barry realised he was ravenous.

Feet thumped down the stairs and a deep voice said, ''Morning, Kinky.'

''Morning yourself, Doctor dear.'

'Young Laverty up yet?' Despite the fact that half the village of Ballybucklebo, County Down, Northern Ireland, had been partying in his back garden for much of the night, Dr Fingal Flahertie O'Reilly, Laverty's senior colleague, was up and doing.

'I heard him moving about, so.'

Barry's head was a little woozy, but he smiled as he left his small attic bedroom. He found the Cork woman's habit of tacking 'so' to the ends of most of her sentences endearing and less grating than the 'so it is' or 'so I will' added for emphasis by the folks from his native province of Ulster.

In the bathroom he washed the sleep from his blue eyes, which in the shaving mirror blinked at him from an oval face under fair hair, a cowlick sticking up from the crown.

He finished dressing and went downstairs to the dining room, passing as he did the ground-floor parlour that Dr O'Reilly used as his surgery. He paused to glimpse inside the now familiar room.

'Don't stand there with both legs the same length,' growled O'Reilly from the dining room opposite. 'Come on in and let Kinky feed us.'

'Coming.' Barry went into the dining room, blinking in the August sunlight streaming in through the bay windows.

''Morning, Barry.' O'Reilly, wearing a collarless striped shirt and red braces to hold up his tweed trousers, sat at the end of the mahogany table.

''Morning, Fingal.' Barry sat and poured himself a cup of tea. 'Grand day.'

'I could agree,' said O'Reilly, 'if I didn't have a bit of a strong weakness.' He yawned. The big man's craggy face with its cauliflower ears and listing-to-port nose broke into a grin. 'It's what we used to call "a self-inflicted injury" when I was in the navy. It was quite the party yesterday.'

Barry laughed and wondered how many pints of Guinness his mentor had sunk the previous night. He still wasn't sure if the man's magnanimous offer had been the Guinness talking or whether O'Reilly was serious. When he'd first woken he'd thought he might've dreamed the whole thing.

'Fingal,' Barry said, putting down his cup. 'You were serious, weren't you, about offering me a full-time assistantship for one year and then a partnership in your practice?'

O'Reilly's cup stopped halfway to his lips. Pallor appeared at the tip of his florid nose—a sure sign that fires smouldering beneath his crust were about to break through the surface.

'Was I what?' O'Reilly slammed his cup into his saucer. '*Was I what?*' he roared. 'Why the hell would you think I wasn't serious?'

'Well . . .' Barry struggled desperately to find diplomatic words. 'You . . . that is, we . . . we'd had a fair bit to drink.'

O'Reilly cocked his head to one side, stared at Barry—and began to laugh, great throaty rumbles.

Barry looked expectantly into O'Reilly's face. His nose tip had returned to its usual florid state. The laugh lines at the corners of the big man's brown eyes had deepened.

'Yes, Dr Laverty, I was serious. I'd like you to stay.'

'Thank you.'

'Don't thank me. Thank yourself. I'd not have made you the offer if I didn't think you were fitting in here in Ballybucklebo, and if the customers hadn't taken a shine to you. You just keep it up.'

O'Reilly stood and walked round the table. He stretched out his right hand.

Barry rose and accepted O'Reilly's handshake. 'Thanks, Fingal,' he said. 'Thanks a lot and I will try to—'

'I'm sure you will,' said O'Reilly, 'but all this serious conversation has me famished. Where the hell's Kinky?'

Barry heard a noise behind him and turned to see Mrs Kincaid standing in the doorway.

'You're ready now for your breakfast, are you, Doctors?' she said, setting a tray on the sideboard, lifting plates and putting one before O'Reilly and one in front of Barry. 'I didn't want to interrupt. I know you're discussing important things, so.' Her eyes twinkled and she winked at Barry. 'But you get carried away sometimes, don't you, Dr O'Reilly dear? I hear that kind of thing is very bad for the blood pressure.'

'Get away with you, Kinky.' O'Reilly was grinning at her, but with the kind of look a small boy might give his mother when he knew he'd been caught out in some peccadillo.

Barry turned his attention to his breakfast. On his plate two rashers of Belfast bacon kept an egg company. Half a fried tomato perched on a crisp triangle of soda farl. A pork sausage, two rings of black pudding and one of white topped off the repast. If professional reasons weren't enough to keep him here, Mrs Kincaid's cooking tipped the scales.

'Thanks, Kinky,' he said.

'Thanks, Kinky,' said O'Reilly, tucking a linen napkin into his shirt-neck. 'Once I get this into me, I'll be a new man.'

As Barry sliced his bacon he heard the front doorbell, Kinky's footsteps and a man's voice. Kinky reappeared in the dining room. 'It's Archibald Auchinleck, the milkman.'

'On a Sunday morning?' O'Reilly growled, ripping the napkin from his throat. 'Between you making breakfast late with your questions and the patients interrupting it,' he said, eyeing Barry, 'I'll die of starvation.' He stood and left the room.

'I'll pop this back in the oven. Keep it warm, so.' Mrs Kincaid lifted O'Reilly's plate.

Suddenly a roar shattered the morning.

'Do you know what bloody day it is, Archibald Auchinleck, you pathetic, primitive primate? *Do you?*' O'Reilly's shout made Barry's teacup rattle.

Barry couldn't hear the milkman's reply.

'Sunday. Well done. Pure genius. Not Monday. Not Friday. *Sunday.* Now what does it say in the good book in Genesis, chapter two, verse two, about the seventh day?'

Muted mumbling came from across the hall.

O'Reilly continued his rant. 'It says, and please correct me if I'm wrong, "And on the seventh day God ended His work . . . and He rested." And what did He do?'

Barry could just make out the reply: 'And He rested, sir.'

'Yes, He rested. Now, tell me, what possessed you to come to annoy me today, Sunday, with a simple backache you've had for bloody *weeks*?'

Never, never, never let the patients get the upper hand. It was O'Reilly's first law of practice.

O'Reilly's voice dropped in volume. 'All right, Archie. I know you only get Sundays off from your milk round. It's probably all the stooping and bending to deliver the bottles that's giving you gyp, and having a boy in the British Army must be a worry. I'll see what I can do for you.'

That was O'Reilly in a nutshell, Barry thought. A tendency to erupt like a grumbling volcano, wedded to an encyclopedic knowledge of his patients and a sense of obligation to them that made the oath of Hippocrates sound as trite as a Christmas-cracker motto.

Barry stood and looked out through the bow window. It was a beautiful day and O'Reilly had said he could have today off. He intended to enjoy his freedom to the full. Tomorrow would mark the start of his assistantship to Dr Fingal Flahertie O'Reilly.

A GRUMBLING O'REILLY was back in the dining room finishing his reheated breakfast. Archie Auchinleck had left clutching a prescription.

Kinky adjusted her Sunday-best hat before leaving to attend morning service in the Presbyterian church across the road from O'Reilly's house.

'Enjoy yourself, Kinky,' Barry said. 'You deserve a little entertainment after cooking such a champion breakfast as that.'

'Entertainment, is it?' said Kinky, drawing herself up, but then she sighed. 'You young people. You think everything should be like those Beatles nowadays. Sometimes I think they must believe they're more popular than Jesus himself. It's a disgrace, so.' She readjusted her hat and swept out of the door.

Barry hoped he hadn't offended her, but any woman who could stay on as housekeeper with Dr O'Reilly since shortly after the Second World War would be hard to offend. Nevertheless, a wise man would do well to keep her on his side.

He'd not be spending the day exactly as he'd hoped. He had plans, but they didn't include Patricia Spence, the shining girl he'd met by chance last month on a train journey to Belfast. The twenty-one-year-old civil-engineering student who had burst into his cosmos as brightly as a super-nova. The young woman who was so committed to her studies she'd told him ten days ago she wasn't ready to fall in love. He hadn't seen her since then, but yesterday afternoon she'd miraculously shown up unannounced at the Galvins' going-away party. She'd cooked him dinner last night in her flat. Today Patricia was off visiting her parents in Newry, south of Belfast. She had promised to phone him soon.

It was a beautiful day, he thought, so why not get out and enjoy it? He hadn't had time for a walk in weeks.

He stuck his head into the dining room. 'I'm nipping out for a while, Fingal.'

'You're what? Half an hour ago you said you knew you'd have to satisfy me that you were worth taking on as a partner. The practice isn't a Butlins Holiday Camp.'

Barry took a deep breath. 'Do you not want me to go?'

He saw O'Reilly shake his head. 'I didn't mean to spoil your day off. I was just thinking about Archie Auchinleck.'

'With the sore back?'

'That's what he says.'

Barry was interested in spite of himself. 'Then what is it?'

'His boy.' O'Reilly looked up from the plate. 'He's only got the one, and he joined the British Army.'

Barry remembered seeing something on television about some British troops with a United Nations peacekeeping force. 'He's not in Cyprus, is he?'

O'Reilly nodded. ''Fraid so. And the Turks or the Greeks have been shooting at them. Archie's worried sick.' O'Reilly rose. 'I shouldn't have yelled at him. There's not a bloody thing us doctors can do until his boy gets back home. It's frustrating as hell.'

And, Barry thought, you get angry when you get frustrated.

'Go on with you, then. Make the most of your time.'

'Thanks, Fingal.'

Barry let himself out through the front door and started to walk along Ballybucklebo's Main Street.

The August sun had climbed over the crest of the Ballybucklebo Hills. The steeple of the church opposite cast a shadow over the yew trees and headstones in the little churchyard. Barry watched people hurrying along Main Street towards the church, men in black suits, women in summer frocks, hats and white gloves, children neat and clean. Barry recognised some of the worshippers. Julie MacAteer, the young woman from County Antrim who'd moved here recently, smiled at him, her long blonde hair swinging under a little straw hat.

''Morning, Doctor.'

''Morning, Julie.'

Maggie MacCorkle, who'd first presented with a complaint of headaches—two inches above the crown of her head—wore an outlandish hat. Every day she put different flowers in the hatband. Two maroon antirrhinums today.

''Morning, Dr Laverty.'

''Morning, Maggie. And how are you today?'

'I've a toty, wee headache,' she said, motioning to a spot exactly two inches above her head. 'But it's nothing for you to worry about, Doctor.'

'And Sonny?' he said. Sonny was in the Bangor Convalescent Home recovering from a bout of pneumonia.

Maggie grinned her toothless grin. 'The old goat's on the mend now, thanks, Doctor. I'll be getting him home any day.' Both in their sixties, Sonny and Maggie were to be married soon.

'I'm pleased to hear it. Give him my regards.'

'I will.'

'And say hello to the General.' General Sir Bernard Law Montgomery, Maggie's one-eyed, tattered-eared cat, enjoyed a good scrap and bore the scars to prove it.

Barry smiled. Knowing about these people and having them greet him as a friend warmed him as much as the morning sun. He strolled on.

Blackbirds were singing in the churchyard yews. The birds' songs had to compete with the faint pealing of church bells coming from the steeple of the Catholic chapel at the other end of Main Street.

Barry saw a couple approaching. The man, black-suited and bowler-hatted, was short and rotund. He stamped along, accompanied by an equally dumpy woman wearing a floral dress. He was scowling. 'Flo, get a move on.'

Councillor Bertie Bishop and his wife, Florence, the wealthiest couple in Ballybucklebo. Barry hadn't met Mrs Bishop before, but as he knew from his dealings with the councillor, Bishop was the most grasping, conniving weasel in the Six Counties.

''Morning, Councillor. 'Morning, Mrs Bishop.'

Barry was rewarded with a ''Morning, Doctor' from the missus and a growl from the councillor. Well, he thought, Councillor Bishop had good reasons for disliking his medical advisers. Until last week he might have thought he was the craftiest man in the village. He wasn't the first man to underestimate how wily O'Reilly could be.

Barry turned the corner and passed between whitewashed rows of single-storey cottages on either side of Main Street. Some were thatched, some had slate roofs, and the little buildings, one attached to the other, jostled together like a group of neighbours lining the road to await a parade.

He reached the crossroads in the middle of the village, where the permanent maypole leaned companionably beside Ballybucklebo's only traffic light, and crossed the street. The breeze that bore the scent of salty seaweed from Belfast Lough made the sign of the public house, the Black Swan, known to the locals as the Mucky Duck, sway.

As he walked under the single-arch railway bridge, he heard the Bangor-bound train rattling overhead. He'd ridden that train daily from his home to Queen's University in Belfast when he was a student.

Barry started to climb a low dune that separated Shore Road from the foreshore. He picked up a pebble and chucked it across a narrow beach into the water of the lough.

He didn't need to worry about sectarian strife here. O'Reilly had assured Barry of that and offered evidence. Seamus Galvin, a Catholic, was the pipe major of the Ballybucklebo Highlanders Pipe Band. Barry had seen the band in the recent Twelfth of July Orange Parade, and neither Seamus nor the Orange lodges had seemed to object. The local Catholic priest and the Presbyterian minister played golf together every Monday. O'Reilly was giving him the opportunity to settle here where the Orange and the Green simply didn't seem to matter.

He lengthened his stride and followed the crest of the dunes, sorry that Patricia wasn't with him to stroll among the marram grasses and clumps of sand seawort. He decided he'd walk for an hour, then head back to

O'Reilly's for lunch. No, he corrected himself. He'd have to start thinking of the grey stone house at Number 1 Main Street as his house too. In a year, DR BARRY LAVERTY, PHYSICIAN AND SURGEON would, he hoped, be inscribed on another brass plaque beside the front door.

This *was* his home. He was going to hear from Patricia soon and, most important, Barry had decided the direction his career should take.

He heard a mewling overhead, stopped, and looked up to see gulls soaring down the wind, wings outstretched. Now that he was committed to an assistantship, he looked forward to stretching his own professional wings.

Perhaps, he thought, half an hour more would be enough before he headed back, because he was really looking forward to his lunch and the prospect of a lazy afternoon. Unless, of course, as was often the way here, something unexpected cropped up.

2

Barry sat in O'Reilly's upstairs lounge, another of Kinky's fine meals in his stomach. He'd almost finished the *Sunday Times* cryptic crossword. He wondered when O'Reilly would be back. The pair of them had almost collided as Barry came in through the front door and O'Reilly rushed out, muttering about 'bad pennies turning up again'.

Barry wondered who the problem patient could be, then turned back to his puzzle. His concentration was not helped by Lady Macbeth, O'Reilly's pure white cat, who, perched in Barry's lap, kept dabbing with one paw at the end of his pencil.

The front doorbell rang. Barry heard Kinky answer the door, and from downstairs came the sounds of her voice and a child's sobs. Barry shoved a complaining cat to the floor, rose and headed downstairs.

Kinky met him in the hall. 'It's little Colin Brown and his mammy. The wee dote's cut his hand, so I've put them in the surgery to wait for himself to come back. I told them you were on your day off.'

The unexpected had happened. 'I'll see to them,' he said, knowing that was precisely what O'Reilly would have done, and headed for the surgery.

Mrs Brown knelt in front of O'Reilly's old roll-top desk, trying to comfort her six-year-old son. Barry recognised the little boy, Colin. Yesterday he'd been at the Galvins' farewell party in O'Reilly's garden, playing happily and howling with laughter. Today his howls were accompanied by tears. His right hand was wrapped in a bloodstained tea towel.

Barry knelt beside the mother. 'What happened?'

'I'm not sure,' she said. 'The poor wee lad came running in from the tool-shed bleeding all over the place, so I wrapped his hand,' she nodded at the tea towel, 'and brung him right here, so I did.'

'All right,' said Barry. 'Can I have a look-see, Colin?'

The little boy cocked his head to one side and held his wounded hand close to his chest. 'No.'

Mrs Brown moved closer. 'Come on, Colin. The nice doctor's going to make it better, so he is. He's not going to hurt you.'

Barry wished her remark could be true, but, judging by the amount of blood on the towel, the cut was going to need stitches.

Colin held his hand to his mother. 'It's sore,' the boy whimpered.

Mrs Brown made gentle shushing noises and slowly unwrapped the tea towel. 'Go on,' she said, 'show it to the nice doctor man.'

Colin held his hand palm up to Barry. He could see little but blood. He said, 'I'll have to give it a clean.' He stood and moved across the room to stand beside the examining couch. 'I'm going to ask your mammy to bring you over here. OK, Colin?'

Mrs Brown led the lad over and lifted him onto the couch. At least, Barry thought, the wee fellow has stopped crying. He pushed an instrument trolley beside the table. A presterilised pack lay to one side of the green-towelled top.

'Can you put your hand on there, Colin?' He waited until the boy stretched out his arm. 'Good boy.'

Barry opened the pack. Inside, a sterile hand towel, a pair of rubber gloves and some cotton wool lay beside a roll of instruments. He was going to have to wash the wound with disinfectant, but shuddered to think of how the solution would sting and burn—unless . . . yes. It might work.

'I'm just going to wash my hands,' he said, moving to the sink.

Barry heard footsteps behind his back and turned to see O'Reilly watching. He gave Barry a reassuring nod. 'You carry on.'

Barry finished scrubbing. He was disappointed to have O'Reilly here, supervising. Still, he was going to need some assistance. If nothing else, Barry's being here, working, should show O'Reilly that young Dr Laverty was well aware that he wasn't at one of Butlins Holiday Camps.

Barry dried his hands and slipped on the rubber gloves. 'Now,' he said, removing some cotton wool and a pair of forceps from the pack. 'Let's get this cleaned.' He grasped the cotton wool in the forceps, soaked it in saline solution and gently sponged the palm of the boy's hand. It was going to need stitches. The wound, two inches long, ran diagonally across the palm from the web between the thumb and first finger towards the boy's wrist.

Barry turned to O'Reilly. 'I need a hand.' Barry made a rapid motion with his right wrist, showing O'Reilly in dumb play the action that would be needed to place a suture.

O'Reilly nodded. 'Local?'

'Please.'

Barry stood so his body blocked Colin's view of the hypodermic. He drew back the plunger, drawing air into the barrel.

'Here,' said O'Reilly. He held a bottle of Xylocaine in one hand, inverted the bottle and waited as Barry thrust the needle through the rubber cap and injected air. The pressure forced the local anaesthetic out of the bottle and into the syringe. Barry set the hypodermic on the sterile towel.

He held out a small metal cup. 'Could you pour a bit of local in there?' This was the technique that moments earlier he had hoped might work.

He saw O'Reilly's brows knit as he poured. He'd bet the older man hadn't seen this trick. Barry had learned it a year before from a senior registrar in the Casualty Department. He lifted the cup, turned and poured a trickle of the solution directly into the wound.

Colin whimpered, but his mother had taken a firm grip on the boy's arm.

'I'll be damned,' said O'Reilly. 'I wonder why we didn't think of that. I suppose the local's absorbed directly?'

'Aye, and the wee one won't feel the Dettol or the . . .' Barry mouthed the word 'needle'.

'Do you know,' O'Reilly remarked, turning to Mrs Brown, 'it's a grand day for Ballybucklebo since Dr Laverty came.'

Barry felt himself blush. 'Now, Colin,' he said, 'I'm going to paint the cut brown.'

Barry used forceps to soak a cotton-wool ball in Dettol, then dabbed.

Dettol usually burned like the blazes. Not a squeak. The local was working. He swabbed the cut liberally with antiseptic.

'Now, Colin, your mammy's going to keep holding on.' Barry dropped the forceps on the table and lifted the syringe. 'You may feel me pushing a bit, Colin.' Barry drove the needle in at one end of the wound and steadily advanced its tip until it was close to the other end. Then he slowly withdrew it, squeezing on the plunger as he did. He pulled out the needle. Now for the other side.

'Right,' he said when he'd finished. 'I'll give that a minute or two to work.'

'You all right, Colin?' Barry asked.

'Yes, sir.' He'd stopped crying.

Barry smiled at the boy's mother and was gratified when she smiled back. 'Right,' he said again, loading a curved needle, to which was attached a black silk suture, into the jaws of a needle holder.

In less than five minutes Barry had placed four neat stitches, and the wound was shut. 'Finished.' He smiled at Colin.

'I never felt nothin',' the wee lad said, eyes wide as he stared at his hand. 'Wait 'til I tell Jimmy Hanrahan and them others at Sunday School this afternoon that I got stitches.'

Barry could hear the pride in the boy's voice and knew how his injury was going to put up his stock with the other boys.

'Thanks very much indeed, Dr Laverty, sir; and you on your day off too.' Mrs Brown tutted. 'We don't want to keep you.'

Barry smiled. 'Not so fast. I have to dress it.' He rummaged for a box of Elastoplast adhesive strips, and stuck one over the wound. 'Bring him back on Friday to have the stitches out.'

'Friday? Right enough, we'll be here, won't we, Colin?'

'Yes, Mammy.'

'Say thank you to the nice doctor, Colin.'

'Thank you, Dr Laverty,' the boy piped. 'Do you know what? When I grow up, I'm going to be a doctor too.'

'Away on with you,' Barry said, grinning from ear to ear, knowing it wasn't only the thirty-five pounds a week O'Reilly paid him that made him want to stay in Ballybucklebo.

As soon as Mrs Brown and Colin left, Barry got on with tidying up.

'Leave the rest for Kinky,' O'Reilly said. 'I need a word with you, Barry.'

Barry felt a sinking feeling in his stomach. 'What about?'

'The emergency I'd to go to.'

Had it been someone Barry had seen recently? Had he made a mistake? Before he had time to ask, he heard O'Reilly's growl.

'What the hell are you doing here, Donal Donnelly, and how did you get in without ringing the doorbell?'

Barry turned to see Donal Donnelly, a gangly youth with a shock of carrot-red hair and buckteeth, filling the surgery door frame. Barry knew that he was the betrothed of Julie MacAteer. Julie was pregnant, and Donal, the father-to-be, was soon going to make an honest woman of her. Pregnancy out of wedlock was more than frowned upon in some circles in rural Ulster in 1964.

Donal swallowed. 'I'm sorry, Doctor. I just came to ask a wee question. I slipped in when Mrs Brown was going out.'

'Well, you can bloody well slip out again. I've not had my lunch, and I've important things to discuss with Dr Laverty.'

'I'm not sick, sir,' Donal squeaked. 'I've come about a racehorse. I could make a few bob for Julie and the baby.'

O'Reilly halted. 'A horse? Which horse?'

'Arkle, sir,' Donal whispered.

Barry knew Donal had a racing greyhound called Bluebird—O'Reilly had won £400 betting on her—but what did Donal have to do with a racehorse?

'Arkle? Away off and feel your head, Donal. You might be able to rig a race with a dog, but you'll have as much chance of getting near Himself as you would trying to whistle and chew meat.'

'Excuse me,' Barry said. 'Who's Himself?'

O'Reilly laughed. 'Arkle's a steeplechaser, the best animal ever to come out of Ireland. He's so well known that we just refer to him as Himself.'

Now Barry understood. 'Isn't that the horse that won the Cheltenham Gold Cup on Paddy's Day this year?'

'Aye,' said Donal, 'and the Irish Grand National.'

Donal sidled into the surgery and shut the door behind him. 'I've a wee notion how to make a few quid with Arkle, so I have.'

Barry watched Donal rummage in his trouser pocket. He produced a silver coin. 'See that there, sir?' He handed it to O'Reilly. 'That's a half-crown from the Republic, so it is.'

Barry knew the coins well. One side bore the image of a harp; the reverse showed the horse known as the Irish hunter.

'I reckon when I go to the races I could sell them to the English punters for a pound a piece, so I could.'

O'Reilly laughed again. 'How in the blazes could you do that? Why would anyone pay twenty shillings for something that's only worth two shillings and sixpence?' O'Reilly demanded.

'Because, sir, the writing on the coins is in Irish. An Englishman wouldn't be able to read that, but he would see the horse. I'd tell them the coins were specially coined Arkle medallions. I've a pal at the Ulster Bank. He can get me fresh minted ones straight from the Bank of Ireland.'

Barry watched O'Reilly's sides shake. 'Oh dear,' he finally gasped. 'That's ingenious.'

'Aye. But what I don't know, and that's what I want to ask . . . Do you think it would be legal, sir?'

Barry asked, 'Why are you asking us, Donal?'

Donal shuffled his feet. 'You're the only ones I can trust to keep it a secret. You know what gossip's like here, sir.'

Barry did indeed.

'So, like I asked, would it be legal?'

O'Reilly shook his head. 'Probably not, Donal . . .'

'Oh.' Donal's shoulders sagged.

'. . . but I'm damned if I know what you could be charged with if you got caught.'

Donal straightened up and Barry watched as a hint of a smile played on his lips. How could O'Reilly be so utterly irresponsible? He was as good as encouraging Donal to commit fraud.

'Fingal,' Barry said, 'are you sure it's a good idea?'

'No,' said O'Reilly, 'but I wish I'd thought of it.' He turned to Donal. 'Dr Laverty's right, Donal. I can't encourage you to go ahead.' O'Reilly's left eyelid drooped in a wink.

'Thanks very much, sir,' Donal said, smiling.

'Off you trot,' said O'Reilly, 'and close the door after you.'

As Donal left, O'Reilly smiled, a little sadly, Barry thought.

'Right, Barry. I still need to have that word with you.' The edge had returned to O'Reilly's voice. 'I've been out to see a former patient of ours.

His wife phoned in a panic. She couldn't get hold of her own doctor.'

Barry took a deep breath. 'The Fotheringhams?'

'I'm afraid so.'

Major and Mrs Fotheringham were a pair of ageing Anglo-Irish gentry whose hypochondria had caused O'Reilly many a late-night emergency call. Barry vividly remembered going alone to see the man when he was complaining of a stiff neck. He had been in a hurry, assumed the stiffness was another of Major Fotheringham's imagined ailments, and had rushed the examination. He had failed to diagnose that Major Fotheringham was bleeding into his brain from a ruptured, thin-walled artery. The mistake had almost cost the man his life. No wonder the major and his wife had transferred to the care of another doctor.

'I suppose poor Mrs Fotheringham was having another one of her attacks of the vapours.'

'No,' said O'Reilly, 'she wasn't. She phoned to say she couldn't wake the major up.' O'Reilly paused. 'When I got there, he was dead.'

'He was *dead*?'

'Yes. I'm sorry. I think the pair of us need to have a chat about this . . . about what it's going to mean for you going on working here with me. You heard what Donal said about how rumours spread here.'

Barry couldn't tell from O'Reilly's voice what that meant. Was he going to withdraw his offer? He hung his head and waited.

'Come on,' said O'Reilly. 'You could probably use a drink. I could, so let's go up to the lounge.' He turned and left.

Barry followed, feeling like a pupil who has been summoned to the headmaster's study for a caning.

'HERE.' O'REILLY HANDED Barry a glass that, judging by the peaty smell, contained Irish whiskey. 'Park yourself.'

Barry took the glass and sat on the edge of an armchair in the upstairs lounge. Through the window he could see over the roofs to Belfast Lough. He sighed when he realised how much he was going to miss Ballybucklebo.

O'Reilly shooed the white cat from his usual chair and sat. '*Slàinte.*' He took a pull on his drink.

Barry hunched forward, nursing his glass between both hands, and waited. O'Reilly fumbled for his pipe. Barry recognised that this was the older man's way of playing for time before he said something difficult.

O'Reilly exhaled a cloud of blue smoke and said, 'So? What are we going to do about this?'

Barry set his glass on the coffee table. 'I'm sorry.'

'Aye, no doubt. But "'sorry" won't butter any parsnips.'

Just get it over with, Barry thought. Tell me you've changed your mind about the offer. 'It's my fault. If I'd sent the major to hospital sooner—'

'What's done's done,' O'Reilly said. 'There's no profit ploughing the same furrow twice.' He stood. 'I told you when it happened there was no point blaming yourself.' He moved closer and dropped a hand on Barry's shoulder.

'But—'

'No bloody "buts". In the first place, anyone could have missed the diagnosis, particularly in a man with the major's history of screaming for intensive care every time he had a runny nose. In the second, aneurysms hardly ever bleed again once they've been treated, unless the neurosurgeon made a bollocks of the surgery.'

'I don't think that's very likely.'

'Anyway, something else could have killed the man.'

'I doubt it,' Barry said. 'How often does one patient have two lethal diseases at the same time?'

'True,' said O'Reilly, looking Barry straight in the eye. 'But we won't know that until after the post-mortem.'

'Post-mortem?' Barry frowned. 'Why a post-mortem?'

'There'll have to be one.' O'Reilly's gaze never wavered. 'I couldn't sign a death certificate. I hadn't seen the man as a patient recently enough. You know the rules.'

Barry did, but given the major's recent history of brain surgery, certainly the government department responsible for registering births and deaths would have had no trouble accepting O'Reilly's word if he had chosen to write 'aneurysm of a cerebral artery'. Was there a remote chance the statutory coroner's autopsy would turn up something to exonerate Barry? Not that it mattered. The damage was done, and not only to the Fotheringham family. If Barry stayed, O'Reilly's practice could lose patients—a lot of patients—once the word was out in the village. He took a deep breath and said levelly, 'Dr O'Reilly, perhaps . . . perhaps it's not such a good idea for me to stay here. Perhaps I should look elsewhere?'

O'Reilly took another drink. 'Do you really want to leave?'

'Do I have any choice?' Barry glanced at his mentor and saw that his face was puce, his nose tip turning pallid, as he roared, '*Of course you have a bloody choice, Laverty.* And we agreed, it's Fingal, not Dr O'Reilly.'

'You mean you'd keep me on?'

'Only if you want to stay.' Colour was returning to O'Reilly's nose.

Barry hesitated. He knew it was only a matter of time before tongues started to wag, before people who had been prepared to forgive him his youth and obvious lack of experience would refuse to see him. 'Well, I—'

'Good,' said O'Reilly. 'That's settled then.' He smiled at Barry. 'You'll stay. We'll wait for the post-mortem results; they could take a couple of weeks, and even if it was the bloody aneurysm, two weeks'll give you time to get your feet back under you.'

Barry swallowed the lump in his throat. 'That's very generous of you, Fingal.'

'Nothing generous about it. I'd be an eejit to let a man go who can put in stitches for wee Colin Brown the way you just did. Medicine's changed since I graduated. Strange as it may seem, maybe, just maybe, I might learn a thing or two from you.' O'Reilly handed Barry his glass and raised his own. '*Slàinte.*'

'*Slàinte mHath*, Fingal.' Barry sipped his neat whiskey.

'Right. Now that's decided, we need a plan of attack.'

The 'we' pleased Barry.

'Come here,' said O'Reilly, heading for the door.

Barry followed him to the landing, where O'Reilly stood staring at a photograph of a dazzle-painted dreadnought. 'Do you know what ship that is?'

'HMS *Warspite*. You and my dad served on her in the war.'

'Right,' said O'Reilly. 'She was launched in 1913. Took a powerful battering at the Battle of Jutland in the Kaiser's war, but . . .' He jabbed Barry with his pipe stem. 'But she came back.'

'Fingal, I'm not a battleship.'

'No, but when I told you the major was dead, it hit you like a twelve-inch shell. You should have seen your face. You're wounded, but if you're half the man I think you are, Barry Laverty, you'll get over it, just like my old *Warspite*. When she was refitted, she came back as Admiral Cunningham's flagship in the Mediterranean in the Second World War. She was the most successful battleship in the British navy.' O'Reilly let go of a blast of tobacco smoke. 'You're going to need a bit of repair work to get your confidence in yourself back. It'll take time.'

'I know.'

'And we'll have to get the customers back to trusting you.'

'How?'

'Pianissimo, pianissimo,' O'Reilly said. 'Very, very softly. And damn it, I'd planned to let you off the leash a bit.' O'Reilly turned back to the lounge. 'It's not very efficient having the pair of us working together all the time.' He planted himself back in his armchair.

Barry followed.

'I'd hoped that now you know your way around, I'd be able to run the surgery while you were making home visits and vice versa.'

'I'd been expecting it,' Barry said, thinking of the free-flying gulls he'd seen that morning.

'Huh,' said O'Reilly, 'you shouldn't buy a dog and bark yourself, but I don't see we've any choice.'

'So you will keep an eye on me?'

'If we stick together and the patients see that *I* trust you, it'll work wonders. You wait and see.'

3

'Salt-mine time for the pair of us,' said O'Reilly, rising.

Monday's breakfast was over. Barry had eaten little. Despite O'Reilly's reassurances the day before, he was nervous.

O'Reilly strode out of the dining-room door. 'Come on.'

Barry straightened his tie and followed him into the surgery.

O'Reilly had taken his customary place in the swivel chair, pulled out his half-moon glasses and stuck them on the bridge of his nose. So, Barry thought, it was clear who was going to be in charge. Well, it was what they'd agreed on yesterday.

'Nip along, Barry . . .'

'I know, and see who's first.' He'd been anticipating working medically, not as a glorified receptionist. He opened the waiting-room door. Every seat was taken. He recognised most of the patients. Julie MacAteer smiled at him. Usually there would be a chorus of 'Good morning, Dr Laverty', but apart from Julie's voice there was silence.

He swallowed. 'Good morning,' he said. 'Who's first?'

A man he did not recognise stood. 'Is himself in?'

'Of course.'

'Right, then. I'm your man.' The questioner was dressed in jodhpurs, a collarless shirt and an old black waistcoat. He was tiny—Barry reckoned about four foot nine—and had bow legs. He held one hand over his left eye.

'Come with me, please, Mr . . .?'

The patient did not give his name and did not remove his cap.

So that's the way it's going to be, Barry thought. I'll bet the cap comes off the minute he sees O'Reilly.

'Good morning, Dr O'Reilly, sir,' the man said, clutching his cap in his right hand.

'Morning, Fergus Finnegan. Sit down on a chair.'

Barry hoisted himself onto the edge of the examining table.

'Mr Finnegan here's a jockey,' O'Reilly remarked. Then he asked, 'And what can we do for you today, Fergus?'

Barry heard the 'we' again, just like last night.

'My eye feels like it's full of the sand on Ballyholme beach.'

'Did you hurt it? Get anything in it?'

'No, sir.'

'Right,' said O'Reilly. 'Let's have a look.'

Finnegan said, 'I can't look at the light. It hurts.'

Barry listened. The man's symptoms suggested inflammation of the conjunctiva, the thin membrane that covers the front of the eyeball.

O'Reilly peered through his half-moons at the eye, sat back and said to Barry, 'Take a look at this, Dr Laverty.'

Barry stood beside O'Reilly. Finnegan's eye was flaming red. All the small blood vessels stood out. The inside edges of the eyelids were swollen and scarlet. The eyeball looked dry.

'What do you reckon?' O'Reilly asked.

'Acute bacterial conjunctivitis.'

'It is *not*. It's pinkeye, so it is.' Finnegan stared at Barry. 'Acute conjunctivitis, my aunt Fanny Jane. What do *you* think it is, sir?'

'I don't think,' said O'Reilly. 'I don't have to. You're right, Fergus, but Dr
Laverty's right on the money too.'

'Makes a change,' Finnegan muttered.

Barry clenched his teeth. He glanced at O'Reilly, who peered at Barry
over his spectacles.

'Remember the *Warspite*,' said O'Reilly quietly.

Barry took a deep breath. 'There's a germ in your eye, Mr Finnegan. It's
infected.'

'Are you absolutely certain?'

Barry said calmly, 'No, Mr Finnegan. Nothing's absolutely certain in
medicine, but . . . you're a horsy man?'

'Aye.'

'I'd give a hundred to one on that I'm right.'

Finnegan whistled. 'I'd not like to bet against them odds, so I wouldn't.'

'Nor,' said O'Reilly, 'would I. Have you not heard how smart Dr Laverty
is, Fergus?'

'I heard different,' the man muttered.

'Did you now?' O'Reilly said calmly. 'There's a thing. And do you
believe everything you hear? Would you believe it if I told you there was a
plague of frogs in Ballybucklebo last night?'

Finnegan bowed his head. 'No, Doctor.'

'I'm glad to hear that. Treatment, Dr Laverty?'

'Penicillin ointment every two hours for the infection, dark glasses so the
light won't hurt, and'—Barry remembered how country patients put great
faith in potions—'one per cent yellow mercuric oxide ointment.' He knew it
was only a weak antiseptic. It was the penicillin that would clear up the
infection. 'The last stuff's called golden eye ointment,' he said. 'I'll write
you a script.'

O'Reilly said, with a tiny wink to Barry, 'And speaking of horses, never
mind Dr Laverty's hundred to one on; I'll give you ten to one the eye'll be
better by Friday.'

'Ten to one? For a pound?' Finnegan scratched his chin and said, 'I'm
your man, Doctor.' He held out his hand and O'Reilly shook it to seal the bet.

Barry handed the man the prescription. 'Take that round to the chemist.'

'Come back on Friday,' O'Reilly said. 'And, Fergus, don't forget the pound note. Now just let yourself out and close the door behind you.'

When the door was closed, O'Reilly grinned. 'You done good, son, particularly with the golden ointment.'

'Thanks, Fingal,' Barry said. 'And thanks for the support. But if all the patients are going to treat me like that, do you not think I was right last night? About leaving?'

'I don't know,' O'Reilly said, 'but you'd better be right about the penicillin. If he's got one of those new penicillin-resistant bugs, I'll be out ten quid on Friday. Now be a good lad—'

'And nip along and see who's next.' Barry left and walked to the waiting room. What was the point of staying if all the patients were going to treat him with suspicion? 'Next, please,' he said.

'That's me, Dr Laverty.' Julie MacAteer rose.

'Good morning, Julie.' At least Julie still trusts me, he thought. He led her along the hall. 'How's Donal?'

'He's up to something. He was full of himself when he came home.'

The Arkle caper, Barry thought.

'But he's very busy too, Doctor. He's on the roofing job at Sonny's old place. I don't think Councillor Bishop's too happy.'

Barry stood aside to let her precede him into the surgery.

O'Reilly rose. 'Did I hear you say Bertie Bishop's not happy? What a pity.' He chuckled. 'I don't know what got into the councillor to agree to fix Sonny's roof for free . . .'

The hell you don't, Barry thought. We blackmailed the councillor into doing it and into settling £500 on Julie when she left her job as the Bishops' housemaid. No wonder he growled at me yesterday.

'. . . but sure it's a fine Christian thing he's doing. It might even be ready when Sonny gets out of the convalescent home, I hear.'

Julie smiled. 'You know me and Donal are getting married?' She dropped a hand to her tummy. 'Have to actually.'

'And that's why you're here?' O'Reilly asked.

'The last time I came in you gave me the laboratory forms to take to Bangor this afternoon, so I thought I'd kill two birds and come in for my first checkup before I go down there. My last period was ten weeks ago, on May 23rd. I brought a sample.' She handed O'Reilly a small bottle. 'I'd like

Dr Laverty to examine me,' she said. 'He was very kind when I first came in.'

Barry smiled at her. He pulled a screen in front of the couch. 'Nip in there, Julie,' he said. 'Lift up your dress and take off your pants. There's a sheet to pull over yourself. I'll be in in a minute.'

When he went behind the screen, Julie lay with her lower abdomen and legs partly hidden under the sheet. He quickly ran through the routine pre-natal questions, then he put on a pair of rubber gloves.

He could feel the uterus, tilted forward and enlarged. It seemed to be about the right size for ten weeks. Was the organ softer than it should be? He wasn't sure, but there was no point worrying Julie unnecessarily.

He pulled the sheet up to cover her. 'Everything looks fine, Julie. You'll be due on February the 13th.'

'If I'm a day late it'll be St Valentine's Day.' She sat up. 'Thank you, Doctor. It's my first and I suppose all women get a bit antsy about it.' She put a hand on his arm. 'Will you deliver the baby?'

Barry smiled. 'If you like,' he said. Then he thought, If I'm still here.

She lowered her voice. 'Don't you pay no heed to what some of the folks are saying.'

'Thanks, Julie. Now, get yourself dressed.'

Julie came out from behind the screen.

'I'd like to see you in a month.' He'd deliberately not said, 'We'd like to see you.' He glanced at O'Reilly, who said nothing.

'I'll be running along,' she said. 'See you in a month, Dr Laverty and . . .' She hesitated. 'Donal and me hope to see you both at the wedding.'

'We'll be there,' said O'Reilly. 'Give our best to Donal.'

In the dining room, O'Reilly shoved his empty plate aside. 'All right,' he said. 'Let's see what Kinky has for us on a Monday afternoon.' He picked up a piece of paper on which Mrs Kincaid had written a list of patients who had requested home visits. 'Just one,' he said. 'Myrtle MacVeigh. She says her kidneys are acting up again, but Kinky doesn't think it's too serious.'

'Then why didn't she come to the surgery and save us a trip?'

O'Reilly laughed. 'You'll see.' He stood up. 'And anyway, she lives out near Sonny's place. Do you fancy dropping by to see how the work on his roof's coming along? Make sure Councillor Bishop's kept his word?'

'Why not? Is your car in the garage or out in front?'

'The garage.'

Barry glanced down at his corduroy trousers and wondered how they would fare when he crossed the back garden to O'Reilly's garage. Every time O'Reilly's black Labrador, Arthur Guinness, spotted Barry, he'd make a beeline for him and wrap Barry's leg in a fond embrace, usually to the ruination of his trousers.

'Get your coat. It's raining out,' said O'Reilly, striding past the table.

Barry nipped into the surgery and picked up his black bag. Then he grabbed his raincoat. The moment he set foot in the garden he saw Arthur Guinness charging across the lawn, tail going nineteen to the dozen.

O'Reilly stuck two fingers in his mouth and whistled.

Arthur skidded to O'Reilly's side at the back door, halted on the wet grass, slammed his backside on the ground and stared up at O'Reilly.

'Back in your kennel and keep dry, you buck eejit.'

The dog obeyed. Barry's trousers were safe.

'Come on,' said O'Reilly to Barry, turning up the collar of his raincoat. 'We're getting soaked ourselves.' He crossed the lane and opened the garage door. 'Hang on. I'll get the car out.'

Barry waited as the engine of the old, long-bonneted Rover caught and the car was reversed into the lane. He climbed into the passenger seat and was immediately thrust backwards like an astronaut in an acceleration sledge as O'Reilly took off.

The car bounced over potholes and listed as the doctor took the bends in the road. Barry distracted himself by staring out of the window. Across a narrow strip of dune grass lay a shingle beach. Beyond, the battleship-grey waters of Belfast Lough were sullen under curtains of drizzle.

O'Reilly slowed, indicated a right turn, and started to drive inland. Accelerating, he took a shallow curve with the wheels of the car well over the centre line. He narrowly missed a cyclist stolidly pedalling in the same direction. Barry glanced back in time to see the unfortunate rider hurl himself and his bicycle into the ditch. He recognised Donal Donnelly.

'You nearly hit Donal, Fingal.'

'I never pay any attention to cyclists. They know my car. They get out of the way.'

Which, Barry thought, was true enough. He glanced behind again to see Donal clamber out of the ditch and remount.

'Good Lord,' he said. The bicycle, which he recalled had been black and covered in rust patches, had been transformed 'Donal's painted his bike. It looks like a wheeled version of Joseph's coat of many colours.'

'Sounds like Donal.' O'Reilly turned left onto a farm lane, then stopped in a farmyard. 'We're here.'

Barry grabbed his bag, heaved himself out of the car and walked to the farmhouse, a two-storey, grey stone building with brown trim on the frames of its sash windows.

O'Reilly knocked on the door. It was opened by a child of about four.

'Ma. The doctor's here.'

O'Reilly tousled the girl's hair and said, 'How are you, Lucy?'

'Ma's sick again,' she said. 'Come on in.'

Barry followed O'Reilly into the kitchen. A turf-fired Aga range radiated a pleasant warmth and the scent of burning peat. Children's toys were littered around a tiled floor. A baby was crying somewhere in the house.

'She's in here,' Lucy said, opening a door for O'Reilly. It led to a ground-floor bedroom where thrown-back bedclothes lay on a double bed.

Barry went in. Three identical cots, two of them occupied by sleeping babies, were ranked along one wall. No wonder O'Reilly had said he would understand why Myrtle MacVeigh couldn't come to the surgery. She had four kids, three of them about six months old.

'Thanks for coming, Dr O'Reilly,' she said. She was sitting in an armchair. 'The ould trouble's back again.'

It was after two o'clock, but she still wore slippers and a pink dressing gown half open over a flannel nightie. She was giving a bottle to a baby. He could see a sheen of sweat on her brow.

'Myrtle had a postpartum urinary infection after the triplets were born. I thought we'd got it cleared up,' O'Reilly said.

'Who's he?' she asked, nodding in Barry's direction.

'Myrtle, this is Dr Laverty, my assistant.'

'Aye,' she said. 'I've heard all about him, so I have.'

O'Reilly made no comment. Instead he asked, 'What seems to be the trouble?'

'It's my kiddleys, so it is.' She sounded certain.

'It probably is,' O'Reilly said. 'Would you like to tell me how they're bothering you?' He dropped a hand to her wrist.

'It come on the night before last. I took the shivers something fierce. I feel dead rotten and . . .' She spoke directly into O'Reilly's ear.

'Mmm,' said O'Reilly, 'dysuria and frequency.'

He was letting Barry know that the patient was experiencing a burning pain every time she urinated and was passing water very often.

O'Reilly leaned over Myrtle, and Barry saw him put a hand in the small of the patient's back. 'That sore?'

She gasped.

It was probable that her kidneys were affected as well as her bladder.

'Your pulse is a bit quick too.' O'Reilly stood up. 'What do you reckon, Dr Laverty? *I* think Myrtle's right.'

So O'Reilly wasn't going to pretend he was seeking Barry's advice. Barry had to agree with his colleague's diagnosis. 'Kidney infection,' he said.

O'Reilly produced two bottles. 'I think a bit of this sodium citrate and sodium bicarbonate will help. And these are sulphamethizole.'

'Is them the same ones you give me last time?'

O'Reilly nodded.

'Great,' she said. 'They done me a power of good.'

Not as well as they might have if, as seemed probable, the infection had recurred. Barry hesitated, then said, 'I've some nitrofurantoin with me. In my bag.' He waited to see how O'Reilly would respond to the unasked-for suggestion to use a more modern antibiotic.

'Have you? Then give them here.'

Barry handed the bottle to O'Reilly.

'I want them sulphur-what-do-you-me-callums Dr O'Reilly said,' Myrtle insisted.

Barry bit his tongue.

'No,' said O'Reilly levelly. 'Sulphas are old-fashioned. It's a good thing Dr Laverty's here. He's up on all the new stuff.'

'I like the old stuff,' Myrtle said, taking the bottle from the baby's mouth.

'Yes,' said O'Reilly, 'like your granny's cure that you tried which didn't work. You do like the pair of us say and you'll be right as rain in no time.'

She managed a weak smile. 'I'll need to be with my lot. It's a good thing wee Peter's out with his da today.'

Good God, Barry thought, the poor woman has *five* children. It was a miracle she was coping at all.

'Right,' said O'Reilly. 'I'll have a word with the district nurse. I'll ask her to pop round and give you a hand 'til you're on your feet.'

'Thank you, sir.' She stood and laid the baby in the empty cot. 'I hope you're right about them nighties-fer-aunties, young man,' she said, looking directly at Barry for the first time.

'He is,' O'Reilly said. 'I promise.' He gave her instructions about how the medication was to be taken, then continued, 'One of us will pop round tomorrow, but please give Mrs Kincaid a ring if you need us sooner.'

'I will, Doctor,' she said, 'and I hope it'll be yourself that comes, so I do.'

'We'll see,' O'Reilly said. 'Now we'd better be running along. We'll let ourselves out.'

Barry said nothing until the Rover was jolting back down the lane. 'It doesn't look as if anyone's going to take me seriously.'

'Rubbish. Just keep on doing your job as best you can.'

'I hope you're right.' Barry sighed.

'I am,' said O'Reilly, turning left onto the tarmacadamed road.

As far as Barry could tell, not much had been happening to Sonny's place. Ivy straggled up the walls of the roofless house. The front garden was overgrown and cluttered with old cars and a yellow caravan.

Ever since Sonny had taken ill, been admitted to the Royal Victoria and subsequently discharged to a convalescent home in Bangor, Maggie MacCorkle had adopted Sonny's five dogs. They usually lived in the caravan while Sonny slept in his car, because his house had been roofless since a dispute years ago about the installation of new slates.

Councillor Bishop's building firm had been engaged to repair the roof and had removed the slates. Bishop's sudden demand at that point for payment in advance, contrary to the way things were usually done, had riled Sonny and he'd refused to pay. According to O'Reilly, Bishop had told Sonny he could bloody well whistle if he thought the job would be finished without the cash, and Sonny had suggested that Bishop do something physiologically impossible.

There matters had stood until O'Reilly, with Barry's help, had accused Bishop of being the father of Julie MacAteer's unborn child, said he could prove it, and threatened to let the word slip out. This had proved sufficient coercion for Bishop to agree to rebuild the roof—at no cost to Sonny.

Unfortunately, Donal Donnelly had come forward, confessed his sins and asked Julie to marry him, leaving O'Reilly with no hold over Bishop. Since then he and Barry had been worried that Bishop might renege on his promise.

Barry stood beside O'Reilly. The rain had stopped. The land smelt fresh, and wisps of vapour drifted from the tarmac as the sun warmed it. He could see that scaffolding had been erected at the nearest gable end, and ladders ran from the ground to the highest level of the spidery structure of rusty iron tubing. A man stood on the upper platform.

'So, what do you think's going on, Fingal?'

O'Reilly pushed a black-painted iron gate in the low blackthorn hedge. 'Bertie Bishop's keeping his word.' They walked through the gate and up the path. O'Reilly stared at the man on the roof. 'If I'm not mistaken, that's Seamus Galvin up there.' He shook his head. 'I suppose he's trying to get a few more quid together before he and Maureen head off to the States.'

They halted at the foot of the scaffolding.

'Is it yourself up there, Seamus Galvin?' O'Reilly roared.

The man peered over the edge of the platform. 'It is, Dr O'Reilly, sir. Hang on. I'll be right down.'

Galvin came down the ladder and jumped off. ''Afternoon, Doctors.'

'And how's the job coming?' O'Reilly enquired.

'It's a bugger, Dr O'Reilly,' Seamus said. 'The roof beams is rotten. Every one of them'll have to be torn out and replaced, so they will. It's going to cost Mr Bishop a right wheen of money.'

'What a crying shame,' said O'Reilly, smiling broadly.

'How long,' Barry asked, 'will the job take?'

'Hard to say, sir. We'd get it done a damn sight quicker if Donal Donnelly didn't keep going home for his lunch.'

'Donal? We passed him on our way here,' Barry said. 'Seamus, do you happen to know what Donal's done to his bike?'

Seamus laughed. 'Indeed I do, sir. He decided it needed painting before he gets married. There was a clatter of half-used pots of paint lying about his place. He says it's art.'

'Art?' Barry laughed.

'Aye. He says he's seen a picture in a magazine by a Yankee fellah.' Seamus scratched his head. 'Haddock. Jason Haddock.'

'Could you mean Jackson Pollock?' Barry enquired gently.

'The very man himself. Donal thinks it's the greatest thing since sliced bread. Here he comes, sir. See for yourself.'

Barry turned and watched Donal Donnelly wheeling his gaudy machine along the path. It did look like something painted by Jackson Pollock.

'Was it lunch you were having, Donal, or did you stay for your supper too?' Seamus yelled.

'Away off and chase yourself, Seamus.' Donal propped the bike against the gable end. 'Good day, Doctor.'

'Good day yourself, Donal.'

Is he not going to greet me? Barry was wondering, when Donal remarked, 'And you too, Dr Laverty.'

'Are you coming to work, or are you just going to stand there flapping your jaw?' Seamus demanded.

'Coming.' Donal put one foot on the bottom rung, then asked O'Reilly, 'Will I be seeing the pair of you at the races?'

'Indeed,' said O'Reilly.

Donal lowered his voice. 'My pal at the bank'll have a brave wheen of Irish half-crowns for me by Friday.' He started to climb. 'Thanks to the both of you, then. It's a great comfort to a fellah to have the likes of you two fine doctors in Ballybucklebo, so it is.'

'Away on with you, Donal,' Barry said, but his step was lighter as he and O'Reilly began to walk to the Rover.

'Right,' said O'Reilly. 'Let's get home. Maybe we can both put our feet up for a while.'

'That would be grand,' said Barry. He felt something tugging at his leg. Stopping, he found that a thick, thorny briar had snagged the left leg of his corduroys. He tugged hard and felt the material rip. Blast! Ballybucklebo was well on the way to becoming the last resting place for every pair of trousers he owned. He trotted to the gate and got into the Rover.

'It seems to me,' O'Reilly said, staring at the old house, 'that God is in his heaven and all is right with the world. Bertie Bishop's doing the job for Sonny, Seamus and Donal are both at work, and you'—he leaned closer to Barry—'seem a damn sight more cheerful than you were at breakfast.' He started the engine. 'But,' he said, 'one of us had better be on call tonight.'

Barry waited, hoping that O'Reilly would want the night off.

'It had better be me,' O'Reilly remarked, driving off as if he were intent not so much on breaking the sound barrier as shattering it beyond any hope of repair. He winked at Barry. 'And if you're not working maybe you could nip over to the Kinnegar and see that Miss Spence.'

Barry was damned if he could decide whether O'Reilly had volunteered to work because he was hesitant to leave his assistant unsupervised, or whether it was a measure of the man's innate generosity that he was willing to give Barry time to spend with Patricia. He'd phone her as soon as he got back to Number 1 Main Street to see if she would be free tonight.

4

'Come in.' Patricia met Barry at the door of Number 9 the Esplanade, then led him upstairs to Flat 4, where she unlocked the door and held it open for him. 'I am sorry about yesterday,' she said. 'I didn't get away from Newry 'til all hours. I should've phoned you.'

'It's all right.' Barry kissed her chastely on the cheek. 'I've been a tad busy myself. I'm glad you're able to spare me an hour.'

When he'd phoned earlier, she'd been pleased to hear from him, but had made it clear that this was very much a working day and evening for a civil-engineering undergraduate taking extra summer courses.

'Sit down, Barry. Sorry the place is a bit cluttered.' She lifted a pile of textbooks from her sofa and stacked them on her small dining table to keep company with ring binders and loose sheets of paper.

He parked himself on the sofa. 'Looks like you've been busy,' he said. He pointed at the drawing table in one corner of the room. 'Tools of the trade?'

'Yes.' She came and sat beside him. 'We're learning about stresses on bridge supports. We have to be able to read structural plans.'

'You remember Jack Mills? You met him on Saturday at O'Reilly's hooley?'

'The junior surgical registrar? The one with the blonde?'

Barry laughed. 'That's Jack, all right. Anyway, when he and I shared digs, we had one of the tools of our trade, an articulated skeleton, hanging in our room. We called him Billy Bones.'

'Like the pirate in *Treasure Island*?'

'The very lad. Mind you, being Jack, he had the poor thing dressed in ladies' underwear.'

'And I'll bet,' she said, 'every piece was from one of his conquests.'

'How did you know that?'

'I watched him with the blonde.' She took his hand. 'He seemed like a decent enough chap but I'm not sure I'd want to go out with him.'

'He's my best friend, but I'm damn *sure* I'd not want you to. I'd be too jealous.' The thought of Patricia with anyone else made his stomach tighten.

She squeezed his hand. 'Not many men I know would admit to being jealous,' she said. 'I like that . . . now your Jack—I'll bet you he believes buying a girl a cheap dinner is the price of admission to her bed.'

Barry frowned. 'Now that's not fair.'

'It is. Most men are like that. But you're not, and it's another thing I like about you. I feel safe with you.'

Barry was sure he was blushing. 'I'm a regular Prince Charming,' he said, to cover his confusion. He smiled. 'It's because I'm much too sensitive.'

'Sensitive?'

'Yes. Absolutely. A good slap in the face brings me out in red welts.'

She laughed, a throaty chuckle. 'You think I'd slap your face?'

'No. I think you're probably a judo black belt who'd tear my arm off and beat me to death with the soggy end.'

'Barry!' She bent forward and kissed him. 'I'd do no such thing.'

'I'm glad to hear it,' he said, seeing how lovely she looked even in old jeans and a baggy sweater. Her black hair was highlighted by the setting sun's soft light. He held her to him, breathing in the subtle scent of her. He moved back, put his hands on her shoulders and looked into her eyes, sloe black, slightly tilted, set above Slavic cheekbones. 'You are very lovely,' he said.

'Thank you.' She put her head on his shoulder. 'And thank you for coming over tonight.'

'I thought I was interrupting your studies.'

'You are, but sometimes I need to be interrupted. Sometimes'—she swallowed—'I think I've got myself in out of my depth.'

Barry stroked her hair. 'You're not the only one,' he said. Even now, thoughts about his uncertain future kept intruding. 'I'm feeling a bit that way right now about the practice.'

'Why?'

He hesitated, not wanting to burden her with his troubles. Then he said, 'O'Reilly's offered me a partnership in a year.'

'That's wonderful.' She kissed him. 'I'm so pleased. If it's what you want.'

'I'm pretty sure it is. I could settle in Ballybucklebo, but I'm in a bit of bother.'

'What?'

'A bit of loss of confidence in me by the patients.' He could see the sympathy in her eyes. 'O'Reilly reckons I can work my way through it. I feel . . . I feel like I'm sitting my final exams all over again.'

She stood and crossed her arms. 'That's why *I'm* worried. I've one coming up next week.'

'An exam? You'll murder it, I know.' Barry scratched his chin. 'I thought examinations were held in June.'

'They are. This is a special one. For a scholarship.' She bunched her fists. 'And I *have* to win it.'

He didn't know what to say. 'But if you don't win, it's not the same as one of your professional exams, is it? I mean . . . it wouldn't really set you back at all?'

'No. It wouldn't.' He detected a note in her voice that sounded defeated. 'Not me personally.'

'Then who?' Barry frowned. 'I think,' he said, 'that if it's upsetting you, perhaps you should withdraw.'

'I can't.'

'Why not?'

'Because I'm a woman.' She stood squarely in front of him. 'I told you how difficult it was for me to get into a professional school . . .'

'I remember.'

'Half the other students, aye, and some of the faculty too can't wait for me to trip up.' She crossed the room to the window, her gait awkward as a result of childhood polio, turned and faced him. 'If I do, they can smirk and say "I told you so" and then it'll be even harder for girls to get in. I have to win for them, not just me. Do you not see that?'

'I suppose,' he said, 'but I don't like to see you getting yourself upset.' He stood and crossed to where she stood, then looked her straight in the eye. 'Listen. I still haven't got to know you very well, but I do know some things.' He'd learned the technique in a psychology course. When someone is discouraged, build on their known strengths. 'You had polio . . .'

He heard her gasp. He knew how she hated to have attention drawn to her handicap, but he ploughed on. 'You haven't let it slow you down one bit . . .'

Her face was expressionless.

'You did get into the Faculty of Engineering . . .'

'I suppose . . .' She sounded hesitant.

'How many in your class are going to sit the scholarship exam?'

'Ten, and I'm the only woman.'

'You should be proud of yourself for that alone. You may not succeed . . .'

'That's what I'm scared of.' Her eyes were moist.

'. . . but you'll have to carry on. I've had to.'

'I don't understand.'

'It's the lack of confidence I mentioned. Two weeks ago I muffed a diagnosis. The patient nearly died but the neurosurgeons fixed him; at least I thought they'd fixed him.'

'But they hadn't?'

'I don't know. O'Reilly went to see him yesterday. The man was dead.'

'Barry.' Her hand covered her mouth. 'No. I didn't know.'

'Of course not. I hadn't told you.' And I'd no intention of telling her, he thought, except it seemed the right thing to do if it could help her. 'I didn't want you to think you were the only one who could fail at something.'

He felt her arms go round him as she held up her face to be kissed, and he hugged her and kissed her and then held her at arm's length.

'Thank you,' she said, 'for telling me. It does help when you're serious about important things.'

'Yes, I can be,' he said quietly, looking into her face. He knew they each had come within a whisper of saying, 'I love you,' but he'd not rush her.

'Look,' he said, 'you have to be getting on with your studies, and I have to be running along.'

'I suppose so,' she said. 'I'm not sure I want you to go.'

He'd sell his soul to be able to stay, but . . .

'I don't either,' he said, 'but I want to be able to boast that my girl has won a civil-engineering scholarship at Queen's.'

She made no demur at his calling her 'my girl'. But she let his hand go and took a deep breath. 'It's not to Queen's, Barry. It's to Cambridge.'

O'REILLY WAS in the upstairs lounge, sitting in an armchair with his back to the door, a large glass of Irish whiskey clutched in his right paw. He was listening to the crashing chords coming from the gramophone. Lady Macbeth lay curled up on his lap.

''Evening, Fingal,' Barry said to the back of O'Reilly's head.

'Pom-pom-pom-pom-pom-pom,' O'Reilly boomed, waving his left hand in time with the beat.

Barry stood in front of the chair. ''Evening, Fingal.'

O'Reilly grinned at Barry and said, 'Be a good lad and switch the thing off. I'm heavily encatted'—he indicated the sleeping kitten—'and I don't want to disturb Her Ladyship.'

Barry switched off the machine.

'Grand stuff, old Ludwig van B,' O'Reilly said. 'Help yourself to a sherry.'

Barry went to the sideboard, poured himself a small glass of sherry, then sat down in the chair opposite O'Reilly.

'You're home early,' O'Reilly said. 'How's your Patricia?'

Barry sighed. 'She's fine but—'

'But what?'

'She's trying to win a scholarship to Cambridge.' It was, Barry knew, something in which he should take great pride, but if she won it, she'd be there in England—and he'd be here.

'Is that a fact? Good for her.'

Barry sipped his sherry. 'I'm not so sure,' he said, wondering if he should leave O'Reilly and try to find an assistantship in Cambridgeshire or apply for a specialist training position in Addenbrooke's teaching hospital.

'Why ever not?'

'She'd be going next term.' He looked into O'Reilly's face. 'I'll miss her, Fingal.' He'd more than miss her. He was terrified that he would lose her.

'I know how you feel,' O'Reilly said. He stood, decanting Lady Macbeth to the carpet, and walked over to stare out of the bay windows. 'I'd to leave a girl once. A lot of the men in the services did.'

Barry said nothing. Mrs Kincaid had sworn him to secrecy when she'd confided in him about O'Reilly's loss during the war.

'My dad was away for five years,' Barry said.

'He came back to your mum, didn't he?'

'Yes.' Barry had been five when a strange, gruff-voiced, bearded man in a naval uniform had burst through the front door of the house in Victoria Road, Bangor.

O'Reilly said softly, 'There was nobody here for me.'

Mrs Kincaid had explained to Barry how the love of Dr O'Reilly's life, a young nurse, had been killed by a bomb when the Luftwaffe had raided Belfast in 1941.

'I'll mebbe tell you about it one day.' O'Reilly turned to face Barry and said, very deliberately, 'I know you've been having second thoughts about staying here.'

'Well . . .'

'And now you're wondering about looking for a post in Cambridge?'

How the hell did O'Reilly know he was? He seemed able to peer directly into Barry's mind.

O'Reilly walked back from the window. 'I'd not be the one to stand in your way.'

'That's very generous of you, Fingal. I've seen how much help you need with the practice.'

'Not at all,' he said. 'I know you're in love with the girl . . .'

Barry felt himself blush. That was the kind of sentiment Ulstermen kept to themselves, and yet O'Reilly hadn't hesitated to come right out with it. 'Well, I—'

'Did you ever see *South Pacific*?'

'Yes.'

O'Reilly sang gently in a deep baritone. '"Once you have found her, never let her go." Take my advice on that, son.'

'Thanks, Fingal.'

'Of course,' said O'Reilly, 'you're the one who'll have to decide.'

'Decide what?'

'If you're going *from* or going *to*. Yesterday you talked about leaving because you felt you weren't going to succeed here. That would be going *from*. Tonight you have a notion to follow the girl you love. That would be going *to*.'

O'Reilly was absolutely right. 'I'd need to think on that.'

'Do, because if you go *from* you'll always wonder if you could have made it here. But then if you don't go *to*, you could end up regretting it for the rest of your life.'

5

'Oh Lord,' O'Reilly groaned, peeping through the crack as he held the waiting-room door ajar. 'Not him. Not on a Tuesday.'

Barry couldn't see past O'Reilly. 'Who, Fingal?'

'The all-high mucky-muck of Ballybucklebo.'

Barry smiled. 'Would that be Councillor Bishop?'

'In the flesh,' said O'Reilly, just before he opened the door.

Barry heard the chorus of 'Good morning, Dr O'Reilly,' and O'Reilly asking, 'Right, who's first?'

'Who the hell else would it be, O'Reilly?' Barry recognised the councillor's voice. 'Me and the missus have waited long enough, so we have.'

'It's not *quite* nine yet,' O'Reilly remarked. 'But I'm sure your time is precious. Do come along.'

Barry went into the surgery and set up the examining couch. O'Reilly took his seat in the swivel chair. Fingal's nose tip was pallid, reflecting like the upper tenth of an iceberg the dangers lurking beneath the surface.

Councillor Bishop strode in, much, Barry thought, as it is given to a man of five foot four and a good fourteen stone to stride. The councillor wore his customary black suit. He sat on one of the wooden chairs, tucked his thumbs under the lapels of his jacket and snarled, 'Would you get a move on, Flo?'

'Coming, dear.' Florence was probably in her early forties but looked ten years older. Her hair was short, and a peculiar red that could only have been achieved by the liberal use of henna. Her floral dress must have been tailored by a company specialising in bell tents.

'And what seems to be the trouble?' asked O'Reilly civilly.

'There's nothing wrong with me, so there's not. She's just not up to much. I want you to fix her, O'Reilly.' He seemed to be unaware of his wife's presence. 'And don't waste your time asking her what's wrong. She can't hardly get a sentence out of her. She can't finish a job about the house.'

'Sorry, dear . . .'

'And since that Julie MacAteer, the wee tramp, quit, we've no maid, and there's no one but Flo to do the work.'

'Sorry, dear . . .'

'Come the end of the day she gets as weak as water.'

Barry frowned. Weakness, inability to finish a task, or a sentence. Damn it, those symptoms were common in a rare neurological disorder, but he couldn't remember which one.

'I'm sorry to hear that, Florence,' O'Reilly said gently.

'She's been like that for six months. Never mind your sympathy. Do something.' Bishop pulled out his fob watch, flipped open the lid and scowled at the dial.

'I think,' O'Reilly said, rising, 'we'd better take a look at you, Florence.'

O'Reilly helped Mrs Bishop to stand and guided her to the examination couch. Barry watched him carry out a rapid, yet thorough, examination.

He glanced at Barry and gave an almost imperceptible shrug, as if to say, 'Buggered if I know.'

Weakness, inability to finish a task or a sentence, no obvious physical findings? Barry screwed his eyes shut. Sometimes when he did, a remembered page of a textbook would appear. He vaguely saw something about demonstrating pathological fatigue.

'Dr O'Reilly? May I ask Mrs Bishop something?'

'Go right ahead.'

'Is it hard to chew?'

'Aye,' she said. 'And I love my vittles, so I do.'

Barry smiled at her. 'This is going to sound a bit daft, Mrs Bishop, but could you raise your arm above your head about thirty times?'

She started to do as she was asked.

Barry watched Mrs Bishop start to sweat, and after twenty repetitions she heaved a deep breath and said, 'I can do no more. My arm's banjaxed.' It hung limply by her side.

Bishop said, 'Didn't I tell you she gets tired?'

'Indeed you did, Bertie,' O'Reilly remarked.

'Dr Laverty,' she said, 'I think I can get my arm up again.' She lifted it.

'That's grand,' he said. 'Thank you.'

Her symptoms and how she tired rapidly but recovered equally rapidly were typical of—he knew, he knew—but damn it, he still couldn't quite remember what the disease was. Barry glanced at O'Reilly, who simply shook his head.

'Mrs Bishop,' Barry said, hating to have to admit defeat, 'I think we've a pretty good idea what ails you.'

'About bloody time,' the councillor grunted. 'What is it then?'

'I'm not exactly sure but—'

The councillor stood. 'A right waste of time this, O'Reilly, so it is.'

'I think,' said O'Reilly, 'Dr Laverty said he wasn't *sure.*'

'Aye. Laverty's a useless bugger.'

Barry ignored Bishop. 'Mrs Bishop, I'm almost certain I know what ails you, but I need to talk to a colleague. Could you come back on Friday?'

He saw her glance at Bishop, who shook his head.

'Or,' said Barry, 'we could send you up to the Royal in Belfast for a second opinion from one of the consultants.'

'Do both,' snapped Bishop.

Barry had to admit that the suggestion made sense. He saw O'Reilly nod in agreement.

'All right,' he said. 'Mrs Bishop, come back on Friday, and in the meantime I'll arrange things at the Royal.'

'Are you done?' Bishop demanded.

'I am, Mr Bishop.'

'Come on then, Flo.' Bishop grabbed his wife's arm and hustled her to the door. 'I've to get things sorted out about the Black Swan.'

'And a very good morning to you too, Councillor,' O'Reilly said to the departing backs. 'Do close the door after you.'

The door swung shut.

'So,' O'Reilly asked Barry, 'what *do* you think's the matter?'

Barry hesitated. 'I never was much of a hand at neurology.'

'Nor me,' said O'Reilly.

Barry suddenly smiled. 'I have it,' he said. 'She's almost certainly got myasthenia gravis.'

O'Reilly whistled. 'I don't believe I've ever seen a case.'

It was all coming back. Barry rattled off what he had remembered. 'A disease afflicting neuromuscular transmission. Characterised by fatigue of striped muscle and rapid recovery after a period of rest.'

'You showed she's got that all right.'

Barry carried on. 'Seldom fatal, but can be debilitating. The symptoms may be associated with thyrotoxicosis and with carcinomatous neuropathy.'

'That's right . . . but I don't think a woman of that size could be riddled with cancer, do you?'

'I doubt it very much. And she has no other symptoms. Carcinomatous neuropathy doesn't usually show up until the cancer is really advanced, usually way past being treatable. Any patient that sick would be skin and bone by now . . .' Barry hesitated. He'd made one mistake with Major Fotheringham by making assumptions that had turned out to be wrong. 'But we should have her thyroid hormone levels measured. Just to be sure about that. And for primary myasthenia there's a simple test we can do right here in the surgery, but I can't remember exactly what it is,' he said. 'I could go up to Belfast and have a word with Professor Faulkner at the Royal—'

'Why not just phone him?'

'Professor Faulkner *never* takes phone calls, at least not from very junior doctors, but I could catch him after he makes his ward rounds tomorrow afternoon.'

'You go right ahead. I'll look after the shop while you're away,' O'Reilly said. He stood and shook Barry's hand. 'If you're right, son, it'll be Laverty ten, Bishop nil, and it'll work wonders for your reputation. I'll see to that.'

'I'd not mind putting one over the dear councillor.' Barry laughed. 'Thanks, Fingal.'

'Huh. Never mind thanks. Nip along . . .'

'I know, and see who's next.' Barry headed for the door, quite happy to do O'Reilly's bidding. As he left, he heard the doctor musing, 'I wonder what Bishop meant about getting things sorted out at the Black Swan?'

BARRY USHERED an elderly woman out through the surgery door. After the Bishops had left, the morning had flown by. O'Reilly had let Barry handle the work. Boys with sniffles, sore muscles; men with arthritis, angina, haemorrhoids, upset stomachs. Mothers with fractious babies, difficulty breastfeeding; children with earaches.

Barry's confidence grew. He just wished that the results of Major Fotheringham's post-mortem would arrive soon.

He opened the waiting-room door. One last patient, a young woman, sat on a bench. He guessed she was in her early twenties, a pretty, red-haired, freckled girl with emerald-green eyes. She wore white cotton gloves, a short white raincoat (the cuffs of a long-sleeved blouse peeping out past the ends of the sleeves) and a tartan, ankle-length skirt.

'Good morning,' he said. 'Will you come with me, please?'

She rose. 'Dr Laverty?'

'That's right.' He let her precede him into the surgery.

'Come on in, Helen Hewitt,' he heard O'Reilly say. 'Would you mind if I asked Dr Laverty to take a look?'

Barry saw her shake her head. 'I'm embarrassed, so I am.'

'I know, Helen,' O'Reilly said, 'but I'd guess what I've been giving you isn't working. Dr Laverty may have some new ideas.'

She half turned, stared at Barry. Then she said quietly, 'I suppose so.' She took off her raincoat and gloves and rolled up one of her long sleeves. She pointed at the crook of her elbow. 'It's that there,' she said.

Barry hunched forward. Her lower arm was, like her face, freckled. There was a rash on the skin there and on the skin of her palm. It was angry red, weeping and scaly.

'It itches something ferocious,' she said.

'And is it the same on the other side, and behind your knees?' Barry asked. She nodded.

That would explain the gloves, the long sleeves and the ankle-length dress.

'You've got eczema,' Barry said. 'How long have you had it?'

'About two months.'

'Have you changed your diet recently?' Eczema could be caused by some foods and cosmetics.

'Not at all.'

'Helen and I have worked our way through her soaps, detergents, lip-sticks and nail varnishes,' O'Reilly added. 'And she doesn't use hair dye.'

'And Dr O'Reilly made me stop wearing stockings . . .' O'Reilly nodded. 'And my bra.' She swallowed, clearly discomfited. 'He said the nickel on the clips on it or on my suspender belt could be the cause.'

Barry hesitated. He'd been taught that some cases of eczema could be stress-related, but to raise the question, to suggest that someone might not be entirely in control, was fraught with risk. Any hint of mental illness was treated as the gravest insult by country folk. He tried to think of a tactful way to broach the subject.

'Has anything changed in your life in the last few months?'

'Aye,' Helen said. 'I got a new job about three months ago.'

'Would you like to tell me about it?' Surely O'Reilly would have found this out or even known about it before she had consulted him.

'I went to work for Miss Moloney. In her dress shop.'

'How do you get along with her?' He saw fires burning in the depths of those green eyes.

'She's a holy terror and she hates the young ones. She's a whey-faced oul' nag-bag . . .' She covered her mouth with her hand.

Barry knew he'd struck the mother lode. He coaxed her gently. 'It's all right, Helen; whatever you say in here stays in here.'

Helen looked at Barry. 'She's driving me daft, so she is.'

'It doesn't sound as if you're very happy there.'

'I'd be happier hanging up by my thumbs. And don't bother saying I should get another job,' she said. 'Dr O'Reilly's already told me he thinks working with the old witch has given me this.' She pointed at the rash.

'So why not just leave?' It seemed simple to Barry.

'I wish I could, but I can't do it.'

'Why not?'

'Wee Mary Dunleavy, Willy Dunleavy's girl.'

Barry frowned. He recognised the name but didn't recall seeing a patient called Willy. Willy? He'd got it. The licensee and barman at the Black Swan.

'What's Mary got to do with it?' he asked.

She sniffed. 'Huh. Mary works part-time there. That Miss Moloney has a tongue on her like a drayman's whip, she has. She never leaves the poor wee girl alone. Sure I couldn't leave wee Mary to face that by herself. She's been looking for something else. She needs the money, but there's not that many part-time jobs here and she can't leave Ballybucklebo. Her dad needs her to help out behind the bar, so he does. He can't afford to take on a full-time barman until he knows what's going to happen with the Duck.'

It was all getting too complicated for Barry. 'Oh.' He looked at O'Reilly, who held out both hands, palms up. 'What have you tried, Dr O'Reilly?'

'Calamine lotion when the rash first blew up, then Lassar's paste, and when it didn't work, medical coal tar.' O'Reilly shook his head. 'By the look of your arm, Helen, the tar's not doing a great deal either.'

That left only the newer hydrocortisone ointment, and that would not get at what Barry was sure was the root cause. He made one more try. 'Are you sure you couldn't find work somewhere else?'

'Not as long as wee Mary's there. And she will be as long as her da needs her.' She frowned. 'Mind you, that might not be for much longer. She's main scared someone's trying to get ahold of the Duck and put her da out of a job. Then she'd have to ask Miss Moloney for a full-time job.'

'Why would she think someone was after the pub, Helen?' O'Reilly asked. Barry heard the seriousness in O'Reilly's voice.

'Bedamned if I know, Doctor.'

'Mmm,' said O'Reilly. 'Never you mind about the old Duck,' he said. 'You try not to let Miss Moloney upset you.'

'Aye, Doctor, but you try to stop the tide coming in.'

'Fair enough.' O'Reilly laughed. 'Now,' he said, 'maybe Dr Laverty here has a notion for a new ointment.'

Barry watched as she stared at him; then to his surprise she said, 'Back there a wee while, Dr Laverty, you was trying to puzzle out how to ask me if I was astray in the head, weren't you?'

'Well, I—'

'And you were right tactful about it, so you were. So write you me the script and I'll give it a wee try.' She waited until Barry filled in a prescription. 'Thanks very much,' she said when he handed her the slip. She rose.

'I can't promise it'll work,' Barry said.

'Sure don't I know that? You're only a doctor . . .'

Any feelings of pride Barry might have had for winning the young woman's confidence were stifled, but at least her expectations were realistic.

'Can you come back and see us in a month?' Barry asked.

'Aye, certainly, Dr Laverty, but I'd better be running along now.' She curled her lip. 'The Wicked Witch of the West'll be having carniptions if I'm not back to give her a hand.'

As Helen left, O'Reilly clapped Barry on the shoulder. 'Come on. Lunch. I'm famished. And we'll see what Kinky has in store for us for home visits this afternoon.'

'HERE YOU ARE NOW, doctors.' Mrs Kinkaid set a tureen on the table. 'I'll be back in a minute with the bread and cheese, so.'

O'Reilly lifted the lid and a rising cloud of steam momentarily blocked Barry's view of a rich red soup, a whorl of white cream and sprinkles of parsley on its surface.

'Gimme your plate,' said O'Reilly. The ladle made a clinking sound against the dish's bottom. 'Here.' He passed it to Barry, who lifted a spoonful to his lips. The flavour of tomatoes was subtly complemented by a hint of ham and celery.

Kinky reappeared and placed a carving board bearing a loaf of wheaten bread, brown and nuggety, and a wedge of crumbly Cheshire cheese beside the tureen. She stood, waiting. 'Well?'

Barry didn't hesitate. 'It's wonderful, Kinky.'

He looked at O'Reilly, who was spooning soup and taking great bites from a slice of bread, butter and cheese, liberally scattering crumbs of Cheshire on the table. Barry expected him to have words of praise for Kinky, but O'Reilly said nothing. He didn't look at all content.

Mrs Kincaid put a hand on her hip. 'It's not your usual big lunch, Dr O'Reilly dear, but moderation in all things is good for a man, and you're getting a belly on you like a poisoned pup.'

O'Reilly sighed and said, 'I suppose you're right, Kinky.'

'I am,' she said. 'Now brush up those cheese crumbs, and don't you get your tie in the soup.'

Barry smiled to himself at how O'Reilly let his housekeeper mother him.

'I've nothing for you for after your lunch,' Mrs Kincaid continued. 'Nobody phoned so you can have the afternoon off. A bit of quiet will do you both a power of good.'

O'Reilly shook his head. 'We promised to call in on Mrs MacVeigh,' he said. 'And it's a grand day for a drive, so when we're done there I think we'll run on down to Bangor and see how Sonny's getting along. We'll be a bit late for supper.'

'Oh?' said Barry.

'I think the pair of us should nip into the Duck on our way home.'

'Why?'

As if Barry didn't know. Fingal Flahertie O'Reilly never needed an excuse to drop in for a quick pint.

'Because Helen said Willy's worried that someone's after his place *and* Bertie Bishop said something about sorting things out about the Black Swan.' O'Reilly picked up his glass and eyed Barry. 'I think "something is rotten in the state of Denmark."'

'Ah,' said Barry, nodding. '*Hamlet.*'

BARRY SAT in the passenger seat. He was disappointed that Myrtle MacVeigh had not seemed to be very far along the road to recovery. Reluctantly, he'd had to agree with O'Reilly when he'd told Myrtle she'd have to be patient and wait for the new antibiotics to take effect.

O'Reilly was driving at less than his usual frenetic pace because even he was cautious enough not to try to overtake the large private coach on the narrow back road to Bangor.

'Bloody American tourists,' he grumbled. 'Coming over here by the coach load to li'l' ol' Ireland to find their roots, taking up half the bloody road and giving the local shopkeepers an excuse to jack up their prices.'

There was some truth to what O'Reilly said. Ever since the fifties, as air travel became more accessible, increasing numbers of Americans had been coming to Ireland. No wonder. Half their eastern seaboard had been populated by the Irish.

Barry stared out of the window at a field of ripening barley where the breeze sent ripples through the golden, bearded grain, making dull patches here and there. A single wood pigeon swooped low over the crop before climbing to land on top of one of the massive elms that grew behind the dry-stone walls flanking the road. The boughs touched the trees opposite, roofing the thoroughfare and filtering light through to the tarmac in dappled golden ponds and silent, dark pools.

The car moved from the wood into full sunshine. Barry wound down his window and inhaled a mixture of the scents of mown hay, fertiliser, and exhaust fumes from the coach ahead.

Fair play to the Americans, he thought, for wanting to see the place where their forebears had come from. He knew he'd never have to undertake such a pilgrimage. Nothing would make him leave Ulster. And yet— what if Patricia won that scholarship?

O'Reilly changed down and screeched past the coach, which had conveniently pulled in to a lay-by.

The fields gave way to where the fringes of the town of Bangor began to encroach on the farmland. Rows of semidetached chalet bungalows stood in ranks where Barry remembered fields. The new estates seemed to have been grafted uncomfortably onto the old Bangor he'd grown up in. But when the car wound its way past the old landmarks, Barry began to feel at home. Bangor Abbey, built on the sixth-century site of St Comgall's

Monastery, sent its narrow spire towards heaven at the corner of Upper Main Street. The dumpy McKee Clock, built of sandstone blocks, still stood at the bottom of High Street, close to the three piers and the Old Customs House, built in 1637.

O'Reilly finally turned into the drive of a large and graceful two-storey building. A sign outside read: BANGOR CONVALESCENT HOME.

Barry followed O'Reilly up a broad flight of steps, through double doors and into a linoleum-floored hall. His nose was assaulted by the smell of boiled cabbage wrestling with the stink of disinfectant.

O'Reilly stood in front of a semicircular desk. Behind it, a bored receptionist filed her nails while indulging in a conversation with a young man in a grubby white uniform. She barely acknowledged his presence.

'Ahem.' O'Reilly leaned over the desk.

The young woman turned her back.

Barry noticed a small bell on top of the counter, the kind with a button on top of a metal half-sphere. O'Reilly's great fist smashed onto the button. He saw the orderly jump. The young woman turned slowly in her chair, looked at O'Reilly and curled her lip. She pointed to a sign on the desktop. 'Can you not read? Visiting hours is over.' She started to turn away.

'I can read the sign, and I can read your badge, Miss . . . Weir.' His nose tip was alabaster.

'Aren't you the clever one?' she said over her shoulder.

'No.' His next words would have been audible on the foredeck of the old *Warspite* if they had been uttered on her bridge. 'But I *am* Dr O'Reilly. I *am* entitled to see *any* of my patients in this miserable apology for a nursing home at *any* hour, day or night. And, I am quite willing to report to the matron what a miserable, impertinent, slatternly, idle apology for a human being you are, Miss Weir.'

'Oh,' she said, standing. 'Who's it you'd like to see, sir?'

'Sonny Houston . . .'

She started to flick through the pages of a ledger.

The young man in a grubby white uniform interrupted. 'He's the old recovering heart failure and pneumonia in Two-C.'

'No,' said O'Reilly, 'he's the grey-haired gentleman with the PhD who lives in Ballybucklebo and is temporarily making use of your premises.' He turned to Barry. 'Come on, Dr Laverty.'

Barry followed O'Reilly up a staircase, along a corridor and through the doorway of room 2C.

Four beds, two to each side, separated by the narrowest of aisles filled the room. Screens surrounded one of the beds, and from behind them came a man's reedy voice repeating over and over: '*Nurse.*' Elderly men occupied two of the other beds, one man wearing a cloth cap, the other flat out, his toothless mouth open wide, snoring loudly.

Barry recognised Sonny in the near bed to the left. O'Reilly had already perched himself on its foot.

'How are you, Sonny?' Barry asked.

Barry saw the old man's face split into a smile. 'Thank you for coming, Dr O'Reilly. I'm very well, thank you.'

'Are you?' said O'Reilly, taking the man's pulse.

Barry was pleased that Sonny's cheeks were no longer the slate-blue colour they had been and the man's breathing was easy, not at all the way it had been two weeks ago when O'Reilly had had him rushed into the Royal.

'And they're treating you well?'

Sonny glanced down. 'I mustn't complain.'

O'Reilly hauled a stethoscope from his jacket pocket and listened to Sonny's chest.

'You're sound as a bell,' O'Reilly said, pulling the stethoscope from his ears. 'But you hate it here, don't you?'

'It could be better. It's noisy at night—'

'And in the daytime,' O'Reilly remarked, wrinkling his nose, 'the place stinks, the grub's rotten, you miss your dogs and you want to go home.'

Barry watched as the old man nodded and his eyes glistened.

'Right,' said O'Reilly, 'we'll see about that.'

'I could go back and live in my car.'

'That's why you got pneumonia in the first place.'

'Perhaps Maggie could take you in,' Barry suggested.

'Oh, no, sir.' Sonny shook his head. 'We're not married yet.'

O'Reilly stroked his chin. 'You can't go back to your house. It's not ready. You're right about not going to Maggie's . . . but I'm buggered if I want you to stay here.' He paced into the narrow aisle. Then turning, he said, 'So, then, I'll have a word with the staff, persuade them to take better care of you . . . Meanwhile I'll think of something.'

'I'd appreciate that, Dr O'Reilly.'

'Now,' said O'Reilly, 'you get a bit of rest. Dr Laverty and I have to get back to Ballybucklebo. We've a bit of planning to do.'

'Out,' said O'Reilly, stopping the Rover in the lane behind his house. 'I'll shove the car in the garage. We'll walk to the Duck.'

When O'Reilly shut the garage doors, Barry could hear joyous barking as Arthur Guinness greeted his lord and master by slamming himself against O'Reilly's back gate.

'Hang on,' said O'Reilly. 'He wants his walk.' He opened the gate only to be ignored by his canine devotee, who rushed at Barry.

'Sit!' yelled Barry, feeling as King Canute must have when he ordered the tide to forget about coming in.

Arthur rose, put both forepaws on Barry's chest and licked his face.

'*Gerroff!*' O'Reilly yelled, yanking on Arthur's collar.

The dog obeyed.

Barry used the back of his hand to brush the mud from the front of his sports jacket.

'Och, sure he's only an affectionate big lump, aren't you, Arthur?'

'*Aarow*,' said Arthur, looking adoringly at O'Reilly.

'You're just full of the joys of spring and missing your exercise.' O'Reilly glanced at his watch. 'Tell you what; we've plenty of time, Barry. You go on down to the Duck and I'll take Arthur for a walk and meet you there later.'

Barry hesitated. 'Why don't I wait for you at the house?'

'Because,' said O'Reilly, 'I don't want to waste time coming back here. I'll be going past the pub on my way home from the shore. I'll be ready for my pint and Arthur'll want his bowl of Smithwicks.'

'*Aaargh*,' Arthur agreed, furiously wagging his tail.

The bloody dog understands English, Barry thought, at least when it comes to beer.

'Come on,' said O'Reilly. 'Heel.' He strode off.

Barry wasn't sure if the last remark was addressed to him or to Arthur, but the dog kept his nose exactly in line with O'Reilly's leg, and Barry trotted at O'Reilly's shoulder.

The traffic light changed and O'Reilly strode across the road. 'Won't be long,' he said, 'but I've got to get this great lummox fit. Duck season starts next month.' Barry remembered O'Reilly saying he and Arthur enjoyed a day's wildfowling as much as Barry enjoyed time on a trout stream. 'You trot on to the Duck.'

Before Barry could answer, O'Reilly had set off at a jog.

Barry walked the short distance to the Black Swan, took a deep breath and pushed his way through the batwing doors.

After the brightness of the day, the dim light in the bar made it difficult for him to see. He could hear the low hum of conversation, and how it faded. As his eyes adjusted he could make out the details of the single room, the black ceiling beams, the tiled floor, the bar with rows of spirits on the shelves behind it. O'Reilly had once told him the building dated back to 1648, when it had been part of a coaching inn.

Two men Barry did not know stood at the bar. In the room itself, all but one of the few tables were empty. It was mid-afternoon and most of the regulars would still be at work. Three other men, all in collarless shirts and moleskin trousers, occupied a table at the back of the room.

The publican, Willy Dunleavy, as ever sporting his floral-patterned waistcoat, stood behind the bar.

Barry moved to the bar. ''Afternoon, Willy.'

'Aye,' said Willy. 'Hot out.'

'Indeed it is,' said Barry, waiting to be asked, 'What'll it be?' Finally he said, 'I'm expecting Dr O'Reilly to join me.'

'Is that a fact?' The usual Ulster barman's response, 'Will you have something while you're waiting,' was not forthcoming.

'Not too busy today, Willy,' Barry said.

'No.'

Trying to drag any conversation out of Willy Dunleavy today was like trying to pull teeth without an anaesthetic. Barry was hot and thirsty.

'I'll have a pint please, Willy.'

The barman started to pour.

Barry put a pound note on the counter. 'Put one in the stable for Dr O'Reilly and . . .'—why not?—'a Smithwicks for Arthur.'

Willy nodded, took the money, made change and gave it to Barry. Not a word was spoken.

Barry carried his pint to a vacant table and hung his jacket over the chair back. He took a pull of the stout.

He considered his situation. His stock was not high in the village since the news had broken of Major Fotheringham's sudden death. Many of O'Reilly's patients had treated Barry with suspicion. Not all of them, but it was too early to know if the antibiotics he'd prescribed for Myrtle MacVeigh would work. They should. There was no reason to suspect little Colin Brown's sutured hand wouldn't heal properly. The jockey Fergus Finnegan's acute conjunctivitis ought to be better by Friday. Julie MacAteer and Helen from the dress shop had seemed to be grateful for his efforts.

On balance, perhaps O'Reilly was right about Barry keeping his head tucked in and simply getting on with his job.

But then there was Patricia. For her sake, he knew he really wanted her to win the scholarship. But for his? He could see clearly that deep in him he wanted Patricia to fail. To stay at Queen's in Belfast. To stay close by him.

He heard the doors creak open and slam shut, heard O'Reilly announcing, 'Afternoon, all.'

Barry was surprised that there was virtually no response.

'It's like a bloody morgue in here,' said O'Reilly.

Willy said quietly, 'Good afternoon, Dr O'Reilly. I've one on the pour for you.'

'Good,' roared O'Reilly. 'My tongue's hanging out.'

Barry was aware of something bashing against his leg. Arthur stood beside the table, trying to beat Barry to death with his tail. 'I've called a Smithwicks for Arthur.'

'I should bloody well hope so, and your glass is empty.'

Barry saw O'Reilly lean across the bar. 'You, Willy Dunleavy, have a face on you like a bulldog that's just licked a nettle. What's up?'

Barry strained to hear, but Willy had lowered his voice and was muttering into O'Reilly's ear. He had no difficulty making out O'Reilly's side.

'Och, Willy, have a titter of wit. He can't do that. He's trying to bamboozle you . . . I don't believe it.' With that, O'Reilly grabbed his pint and Barry's second, headed for the table and called over his shoulder, 'Don't forget Arthur's.' He smacked Barry's glass down. Then he sat in his chair and sank half his pint in one swallow.

Willy appeared with a basin and shoved it under the table. Arthur flopped down and Barry could hear the slurping noises.

'Welcome back.'

'Some bloody welcome. No wonder the place is half empty,' O'Reilly said. He finished his pint. 'One more, Willy.' O'Reilly fished out his briar pipe. 'You remember Helen said Mary was worried someone was trying to take over the pub?'

'Yes.' Barry made a quick deduction. 'Bishop?'

'None other than.'

Willy appeared with O'Reilly's pint. 'We'll pretend it's your birthday, Doctor. On me.' He walked away.

O'Reilly shook his head. 'Willy's worried, and he's a bloody good reason to be.' He lit his pipe. 'The Duck's on a ninety-nine-year lease that started in 1865. It expires next month.'

'Surely Willy can renew it?'

'You'd think so, but would you care to take a stagger at who holds the title to the property?'

'Bishop?'

'None other than himself, and do you know what he wants to do?'

'Take over the pub?' Barry looked round a room that went back more than 300 years.

'That's only half of it. He wants to gut it and redo it with chrome and plastic and piped music.'

The thought saddened Barry.

O'Reilly banged his fist on the table. 'We'll have to stop it or he'll lose all the local trade. The Duck's the heart of Ballybucklebo.'

'So why does he want to do it?'

'Remember the coachload of Yankees we saw? Bishop wants to go after the tourist trade. Can't you just see it? A big neon sign in fake Celtic script outside saying "Mother Macree's Olde Irish Shebeen", and maybe Donal Donnelly outside the front door dressed like a leprechaun.'

The image of Donal, despite Barry's concern, made him laugh.

O'Reilly said, 'Finish up. It's time we were home. As if looking after the sick and suffering wasn't enough, now we've to find a place for Sonny. *And* do something about Bishop and the Duck.' He rose and called, 'Heel, Arthur.'

Having seen Bishop in action, Barry thought perhaps O'Reilly was setting an impossible goal for them. But then, if anybody could bring Councillor Bertie Bishop to heel, it was Dr Fingal Flahertie O'Reilly.

6

B arry stopped Brunhilde, his elderly Volkswagen Beetle, waited for a gap in the heavy traffic and turned left to enter the grounds of the Royal Victoria Hospital.

It had been agreed the day before that Barry would come here to consult Professor Faulkner about Mrs Flo Bishop's suspected myasthenia gravis. Last night after supper, Barry had suggested to O'Reilly that he'd not only see the prof but also take the opportunity to try to meet his old schoolfriend Jack Mills. O'Reilly had a soft spot for Mills because they were both devotees of rugby football.

Barry had phoned Jack and they'd agreed to meet for lunch in the hospital cafeteria. He'd also called Patricia. To his delight, although she had classes until five, she said she would be happy to meet him for a Chinese meal and then be driven back to the Kinnegar.

Barry pulled into a parking spot, got out and started to walk to the back entrance of the Royal, the teaching hospital where he had spent three and a half years as a student and one year as a houseman. He crossed the cloisters beneath the ward units and went in by the basement entrance, past the door to the cafeteria, up a winding flight of stairs and onto the main corridor.

He saw a crowd of blue-uniformed nurses, red-uniformed sisters, white-coated lab techs, checked-uniformed floor cleaners and brown-coated porters going about their business. Housemen and registrars in long white coats and medical students in short white jackets strode purposefully. The precise place of everyone in the hospital caste system was identifiable by their clothes.

Barry stood, getting his bearings, then he started to walk, pausing only to acknowledge greetings from staff members who recognised him. His destination was Ward 22. When he got there, he found the nurses' desk was deserted except for the unit clerk, a brunette whose hair fell to her midback.

She looked up, smiled broadly and said, 'Look what the cat's dragged in. What brings you here, Barry?'

'How are you, Mandy?'

'All the better for seeing yourself,' she said, smiling.

'I need to see the prof.'

She rolled her eyes. 'Do you know about camels and needles?'

Barry laughed. 'It's easier for a camel to go through the eye of a needle—'

'Than for anyone to see the great man.' She gestured along the ward to where Barry could see a group of people clustered round the foot of a bed. All the medical personnel danced attendance on a diminutive man, bald as a billiard ball. The high priest of neurology, Professor Malcolm Faulkner, MD, FRCP, Regius Professor of Neurology at Queen's University, Belfast.

'Don't worry,' Mandy said. 'He's in a good mood this morning. I'll grab him for you before he leaves.'

'Thanks, Mandy. It'll only take a minute or two.' Barry remembered the promise he'd made to Councillor Bishop. 'I don't suppose you could speed up an appointment for one of my patients?'

'I could try. How urgent is it?'

'It's for the woman I want to ask Professor Faulkner about this morning. She may not need to be seen here if I'm right about her and can fix her up back at home. But if I'm wrong . . .'

'Tell you what,' she said. 'See how you get on with your patient. If she doesn't need an appointment, you'll not need to worry. If she does, give me a ring and I'll find her a cancellation. Now, go on into the office. I'll tell the professor you're waiting.'

'Thanks, Mandy. I owe you.'

Eventually, the door opened and Professor Faulkner, accompanied by his senior registrar, Dr Bereen, entered the office.

'Laverty. Mandy says you're a GP somewhere in the bogs and you want a word.' The prof's accents were very upper-class English.

'I'll . . : I'll . . . only take a minute, sir,' Barry stammered.

'It's all you'll get. I've a very important meeting with the dean.'

Rapidly, Barry described Mrs Bishop's symptoms and the physical findings. 'I think she's got myasthenia gravis.'

'And you're sure it's not due to an underlying cancer or thyroid disease?'

'We've excluded cancer pretty well, and we'll be measuring her thyroid hormone levels when she comes back to see us, sir.'

'You seem to have remembered something I taught you.' Professor Faulkner frowned. 'Mmmmm. Could be primary myasthenia, I suppose.'

'When I was a student you taught us about a simple test that would confirm the diagnosis, sir. I'd appreciate it if you'd tell me about it.'

'Tell him, Bereen.'

'You give an intramuscular injection of neostigmine, 2.5 milligrams, along with atropine, 1.0 milligrams, to prevent abdominal colic. The increase in power is quite striking in about twenty to thirty minutes.'

'Thank you, Dr Bereen,' Barry said.

'Will that be all, Laverty?' The prof began to open the door.

'Yes. I can remember the treatment,' he said formally.

'I should hope so.' With that, Professor Faulkner swept out.

Dr Bereen said, relaxing, 'I'd rather work for Adolf Hitler.'

'You have my sympathy,' Barry said. 'My boss isn't a bit like that.' O'Reilly might be unpredictable, given to storms and tempests, but never once had Barry seen him condescend to any living creature, and that included Arthur Guinness and Lady Macbeth. 'I appreciate the help, and I'd appreciate it even more if you'd tell me how to treat myasthenia.'

Bereen laughed. 'I thought you said you knew.'

'I did, but actually I don't.'

Bereen flopped into a chair, pulled out a sheet of paper and began to scribble. He handed the sheet to Barry. 'There you are, mate. Good luck with your patient.'

'Thanks, and good luck to you with the prof.'

'Right,' said Bereen, rising, 'I've to go and do the prof's clinic.'

'I'll walk with you. I'm meeting an old pal for lunch.'

Barry followed Bereen out of the ward, and as they walked along the corridor a thought struck him. If he was successful in treating Mrs Bishop, would O'Reilly be able to use that as a bargaining piece in the coming struggle with Councillor Bishop and his plans to take over the Duck?

THE QUEUE at the cafeteria counter was short. Barry picked up a cheese sandwich and a cup of coffee, then carried his tray to a vacant table. The facility was open twenty-four hours a day and catered to junior staff. Many of the tables were occupied.

Barry chewed slowly, listening to the buzz of conversation and the clink of utensils on crockery. He saw Jack Mills—tall, his broad shoulders stretching the seams of his long white coat—leave the counter and head over. Jack plonked his tray down and sat heavily on the other side of the table.

'Dr Livingstone, I presume?'

'Good to see you too, Jack.' Barry noticed that Jack's normally ruddy, farmer's complexion looked pale, and he had dark circles under his eyes.

Jack shovelled in a forkful of Irish stew. 'How's life abusing you in darkest Ballybucklebo?'

Jack was the one man from whom Barry kept no secrets, hadn't needed to since they'd shared a study as schoolboys at Campbell College and then digs as medical students. 'Could be better,' he said.

Jack yawned. 'Couldn't be any bloody worse than being a surgical registrar. Apparently sleep is only for the upper classes.'

'My heart bleeds. You picked surgery.'

'If there's any truth to this reincarnation business, I'm coming back as a galley slave. Should be easier. Three appendixes last night, and a perforated duodenal ulcer. I don't think the ulcer's going to make it.' Jack did not seem unduly concerned.

'Doesn't that bother you?'

Jack shook his head. 'Nah. We don't let ourselves get too close to the victims. Some of 'em pop their clogs. That's life.'

'One of mine did.'

'Fell off the perch? So?'

'It's different in a village. You get to know the people. And losing my patient hasn't done my reputation a bit of good . . . I may have to leave.'

'And you like it there, don't you?'

'Very much.'

There was a hint of concern. 'So. Tell your uncle Jack what happened.'

Barry briefly went over the major's history. 'And we're still waiting for the post-mortem results.'

'And you're hoping something else helped your victim "shuffle off this mortal coil"?'

'Yes, but it's taking for ever to find out.'

'Help,' said Jack, 'is at hand. 'Scuse me.' He rose.

Barry watched his friend make his way past several tables, stop, say something and then return accompanied by a young man, whose pure white hair made him look older than his years.

'You remember Harry Sloan?' Jack said.

'Hi, Harry,' Barry said. 'How are you?'

'Rightly, so I am.'

'Harry's a budding pathologist, and purely by chance he's in the morgue this week assisting at the PMs.' Jack yawned again. 'Barry wants to know about one of your customers.'

'Who?'

'A Major Fotheringham. He'd had a cerebral aneurysm clipped two weeks ago, then died suddenly on Sunday morning,' Barry said.

Harry frowned. 'Coroner's case?'

'That's right.'

'We did the autopsy yesterday. I remember it . . .'

Barry held his breath.

'Didn't find nothing except for the brain surgery, and it looked good. No signs of any more bleeding.'

Barry felt his hopes rise. But that was only half the answer to his dilemma. He was hanging on to the belief that something for which he could not be held responsible had been the reason for the man's demise. 'And there was nothing else to see?'

'Nah.' Harry shook his head. 'Mind you,' he said, 'it's only the macroscopic findings. We'll have to wait for the histology.'

All the vital organs would be preserved in formalin and representative samples taken to be mounted on glass slides, stained and examined under the microscope.

'How long will that take?'

Harry knitted his brows. Then he said, 'Couple of weeks.'

'Oh,' Barry said. 'Thanks.'

'Barry's worried,' Jack said.

'I don't want to hold out false hopes,' Harry said, 'but once in a blue moon someone has a massive coronary—'

'But,' Barry asked, 'would that not show up with blood clots and damaged heart muscle you could see?'

'Aye, you'd think so, but it's not true. If the victim dies more or less at once, we can't see anything at all.'

'But it would show up on the slides?'

'Oh, aye.' Harry seemed to brighten up. 'As soon as the slides are ready, I'll take a quick look-see myself, and if I think there's anything, I'll get one of the senior blokes to take a shufti. Have you got a phone number?'

'Here.' Barry fished out a small notebook from an inside pocket and scribbled down O'Reilly's number.

'Good to see you again, Laverty.' Harry turned to leave. 'I'll be in touch, but it could be next week.'

'Decent lad,' Jack remarked after Harry had gone. 'He'll see you right.'

'I hope so.'

Jack pushed back his chair. 'You know, Laverty, sometimes you worry too much. If this Ballybucklebo's what you want . . .'

'Professionally it is.'

'O'Reilly'll see you right.'

'I hope so, but there's something else.'

'Not by any chance a certain black-haired damson called Patricia?'

Barry nodded. 'And it's damsel, not damson. That's a plum.'

'I know. Your Patricia's more of a peach. What's got you worried?'

'She's trying to get a scholarship to Cambridge. She'd be in with a bunch of very bright undergraduates there. Mostly men.'

Jack whistled. 'If she's that good at what she does, she's far too bright for the likes of you anyway.'

'Do you think so?' Barry knew he sounded worried.

Jack frowned. 'The truth? She may be. I've only met her once, but she didn't strike me as the kind of lass who'd be happy to sit at home getting the old man's tea.' He frowned. 'What'll you do if she does go to England?'

Barry shrugged.

'If you're that serious about her, why not propose to her?'

'Do you mean it?'

'Why not? If a bird's wearing an engagement ring, it's as good as saying, "Private property. Hands off."'

BARRY PUSHED through the door to the restaurant. The room was decorated with heavy, red-flock wallpaper, Chinese dragons and pagodas embossed on the material. Tasselled paper lanterns hung from the ceiling. He could smell exotic spices coming from the kitchen at the back.

A smiling Chinese hostess approached. She was dressed in a green bro-cade cheongsam. She greeted Barry and ushered him to a table. 'Would you like a menu?'

'Please,' Barry said.

'I'll only be a wee minute, so I will.'

Barry smiled. The woman's features were classically Chinese, her accent pure Sandy Row.

Three other tables were occupied. Five thirty was early for the Belfast dining public. Barry heard the chimes over the door jangle, turned and saw her. She wore black trousers with a maroon sweater. Her hair was done up in a ponytail.

'Hi, Barry.'

'Patricia.' He rose and held her chair. 'Glad you could make it.'

'So,' she said, 'am I.'

Barry took his seat opposite her. 'Busy day?'

'Nonstop. I hate architectural drawing.'

Before he could say something sympathetic, the hostess reappeared. She poured green tea into two porcelain cups. 'Here you are,' she said, handing them menus. 'I'll give you a wee minute to think about what you'd like.'

Patricia opened her menu. 'Good Lord,' she said, 'this thing's about as big as the Domesday Book. How on earth are you meant to pick something?'

Barry watched her flip over the pages as she muttered, 'Wontons? Moo goo gai pan?' She reached across the table and took his hand. 'Barry, I've never been to a Chinese place before. You'll have to help me order.'

'All right.' Barry squeezed her hand, surprised yet pleased that Patricia, normally so self-possessed, would ask for help. 'Jack and I used to come here quite a bit. We'd order two or three dishes and share.'

'Let's do that. What would you suggest?'

'Do you like chicken and pork?'

She nodded.

'Right. Leave it to me,' he said, and he realised how much he enjoyed saying it.

The hostess had come back. 'Would you care to order?'

'Please,' Barry said. 'Deep-fried wontons, chicken fried rice and sweet-and-sour pork.'

The hostess left. Barry picked up his chopsticks and glanced at Patricia. 'Do you know how to use these?'

'No.'

He leaned across and took her hand, admiring her slim fingers. 'Hold them like this.' He positioned the two slim, tapered pieces of wood. 'Then use them like tweezers.'

'Easy for you to say,' she said, but she soon seemed to get the hang of it.

A waiter arrived and set three dishes on the table.

'Those,' said Barry, pointing, 'are wontons. Pick one up with your fingers and dip it in the plum sauce.' He pushed a small bowl to her.

Patricia dunked a wonton in the sauce, popped it into her mouth, chewed, frowned and swallowed. 'That's rather good.'

Barry took her plate and filled it with chicken fried rice and sweet-and-sour pork. 'The fried rice goes better with soy sauce,' he said.

He watched her eat, enjoying her obvious pleasure. Finally she put her chopsticks down and said, 'I'm stuffed. And thank you. It really was delicious. Now,' she said, 'tell me about your day.'

'I went up to the Royal, saw one of the profs. I had lunch with Jack and an old classmate. He's a junior pathologist. He's trying to get me some quick answers about the patient I mentioned the other night.'

'The one who died?'

'Yes.'

Her hand covered his. 'It'll be all right. I'm sure.'

'I hope you're right, but I have to wait for more tests.'

'That makes two of us,' she said.

He knew she was referring to her imminent examinations. Jack had suggested Barry propose, but . . . he couldn't. Not yet.

'Cambridge seems like a very long way away,' he said. He fiddled with his napkin. 'Is going there really so important?'

She pursed her lips. 'Getting yourself re-established in your practice is important to you. Going to Cambridge is very important to me. Do you know they only started giving women the right to be awarded degrees in the Senate House with the men in 1948? That's only sixteen years ago.'

'No. I didn't.'

'There are three women's colleges, but half of the other colleges still won't admit us.' She was warming to her theme, leaning forward over the table. 'Until we get more women into Cambridge, ones who'll do as well as or better than the men, those colleges will never change. We're going to see that they do.'

Barry saw how her eyes flashed. He wished she would seem to feel as passionately about him. '"To strive, to seek, to find, and not to yield",' he said quietly.

'What?'

'Tennyson. *Ulysses*.'

'I don't see what that's got to do with—'

'It's on a cross in Antarctica near Captain Robert Falcon Scott's base camp. He didn't make it back from the South Pole.'

'Barry, we're not talking about polar exploration.'

'No,' he said quietly, 'but we are talking about pioneers.' He stared into her eyes and said as gently as he could, 'I'm being selfish. I don't want you to go. I . . .' He couldn't bring himself to spit out, 'I love you.'

'I understand that,' she said. 'It'll be hard for both of us, but surely you could get over to England for the odd weekend? I'll be coming home for the holidays. It would only be for three years.'

'Would it?'

She stared at the tablecloth. 'I'll not lie to you, Barry. Three years is a long time. Either one of us could meet someone else.'

'I suppose,' he said. He wouldn't. He knew that. The prospect of ending up like O'Reilly, still carrying a torch for one woman after twenty-three years, was daunting. 'I'm not going to persuade you to stay, am I?'

'I'm sorry, Barry.'

The silence hung.

'Right,' he said, beckoning the hostess. 'Time I got you home.'

The hostess presented the bill and took Barry's money. 'Thank you, sir.'

He rose, left a tip, then stood behind Patricia's chair, waiting for her to stand. Then he held open the door for her as they left the restaurant.

'The car's down there,' Barry said, pointing. He slowed his step to match hers.

He opened the passenger door and waited. Instead of getting in she faced him. 'Thank you for a lovely dinner.'

'My pleasure.' But Barry felt it had been more like the Last Supper.

She put her arms round his neck and kissed him, so hard that he had to take one step back. He was breathless when she pulled away. 'Barry, please, *please* try to understand.'

'I am trying,' he said. 'Honestly.'

She kissed him again, and like a child who'd been taken to the circus to comfort it before a trip to the dentist, he let himself savour the moment and dismiss what the future might hold. He held her from him. 'I do understand, Patricia, that anything you've ever really wanted to do, you've done. You're not going to stop now, are you?'

She bowed her head. 'No.'

'All right. Hop in the car and I'll take you home.' He shut the door after her, went round and climbed in. Before he started the engine he turned to her. 'One wee thing.'

'What?'

Her kisses had lifted his spirits. 'This always doing what you set out to do?'

'What about it?'

'Don't ever try to put toothpaste back in the tube.' As he started the engine he heard her chuckle, and felt her punch his arm lightly. 'Right,' he said. 'Next stop the Kinnegar, then on to Ballybucklebo.'

THE GENTLE LIGHT in the upstairs sitting room came from a lazy sun, still visible through the bay windows. It seemed to be taking its own sweet time deciding if it should slip behind the distant Antrim Hills. O'Reilly sat in an armchair, jacket off, tie unknotted. Barry saw he was reading a James Bond novel, *From Russia with Love.*

Lady Macbeth, fast asleep, lay on the hearth-rug curled up with her nose beneath her tail, her white fur bright in a rectangle of sunlight. They made a picture of domestic tranquillity, Barry thought.

''Evening, Fingal.'

'Welcome home.' O'Reilly set his book on the side table. 'Kinky'll be up in a minute with a cup of tea.'

Barry sat in the other big chair. He should tell O'Reilly about the day's events at the Royal. 'I saw Professor Faulkner,' he said.

'A rare treat, no doubt.'

'You know him?'

'Indeed,' said O'Reilly. 'He went to some minor public school, picked up his plummy accent there. He was in my year at Trinity. Worst student in the class. Anyway. Did he give you any helpful hints about Flo Bishop?'

'His senior registrar did.'

O'Reilly laughed. 'Juniors do all the work.'

But not in your practice, Barry thought as he heard the door open. He turned and saw Kinky come in and set the tea tray on the table.

She lifted the lid from a small cake stand. 'I hope you'll enjoy my cherry cake. Now drink up your tea before it gets cold.' She turned to leave.

'I want to hear about what you learned at the Royal,' O'Reilly said, through a mouthful of cherry cake.

Barry fished in his pocket for the note Dr Bereen had scribbled, and gave it to O'Reilly, who read it, brow knitted, then handed it back. 'Interesting,' he said. 'Certainly worth a try.'

'I wonder,' said Barry, 'if we shouldn't ask Mrs Bishop to come in tomorrow? The sooner we have an answer, the better.'

O'Reilly raised one eyebrow. 'Better for whom?'

'Well . . .' Barry understood the question. O'Reilly was wondering if Barry was more interested in being proved right than in helping Flo Bishop. 'The patient,' Barry said firmly.

'Aye,' said O'Reilly. 'I hoped you'd say that.'

'There's something else. It occurred to me that if we do fix Mrs Bishop, the councillor might feel he owed us, well . . . a bit of gratitude.'

'And leave the Duck alone?' O'Reilly finished his tea. 'You could be right,' he said. 'It's worth a try.' He rose. 'Let's mull it over, see Flo on Friday, and see what happens when you fill her full of neostigmine and atropine.'

ON FRIDAY, O'REILLY MADE straight for the surgery and Barry went to call the first of the morning's patients. Today he'd be seeing cases he'd treated earlier in the week, and he was eager to find out how his patients had fared.

He opened the waiting-room door. Barry was surprised not to see Councillor and Mrs Bishop. Had they decided not to come back?

''Morning, Doc.' Fergus Finnegan rose, snatched off his cap and walked to the door. 'Me first,' he said.

Barry turned to follow Fergus. The little man had a spring in his step. 'Grand stuff that golden ointment,' he said, as he turned into the surgery. ''Morning, Dr O'Reilly.'

'Fergus, how are you?'

'Right as rain. Your man here, Dr Laverty, has done me a power of good, so he has.' He smiled.

'Let's have a look.' Barry led Fergus over to the bow window. 'The light's not hurting?'

'Not at all.'

The conjunctiva was clean and shining. The infection had been cleared up by the penicillin.

'Looks like it's done the trick,' he said.

O'Reilly coughed. 'In that case, Fergus, you owe me a quid.'

'Right enough, sir.' Still smiling, Fergus stuck his hand into his trouser pocket and pulled out a note. 'Here y'are.'

Barry had quite forgotten about the bet.

'Thank you, Fergus.' O'Reilly took the pound.

Barry saw the little man wink. 'I've more than that for the pair of you, sirs,' he said. 'Are you for the races the morrow?'

'Indeed,' said O'Reilly. 'Wouldn't miss them.'

'Pop you round to the paddock before the third. I'll give you the nod. I'm riding in that one myself, so I am.'

'I'll see you then,' said O'Reilly. 'Now, off you trot.'

Fergus turned to Barry. 'Thanks a lot, Doc. You done rightly for me, so you did. I'll not forget.'

Barry opened the door. 'My pleasure,' he said, and he meant it.

He heard the front door close as the jockey left. He walked down the hall and came back with Mrs Brown and Colin.

Barry was surprised to find O'Reilly was not in the surgery. He closed the door. 'So, Colin,' he said, 'how's your paw?'

The little lad held out his right hand.

'Is it sore?'

The boy shook his head.

He's scared I'm going to hurt him, Barry thought. He lifted Colin and sat him on the wooden chair. He took the boy's hand in his own. The Elastoplast dressing was grubby, but the palm was cool and not swollen. 'Now,' said Barry, walking over to get the instrument trolley, 'I'm going to see if the stitches can come out.' He poured Savlon into a metal basin. 'Can you stick your hand in there, Colin?'

The child hesitated, glanced at his mother and then slowly put his hand into the solution. He stared at Barry, who had laid out swabs, fine-nosed forceps and a pair of scissors.

'Now,' he said, 'let's get the Elastoplast off.' He lifted Colin's hand and, using the forceps, started to tease the adhesive strip off. It came away cleanly. Colin didn't flinch. The wound edges were clean and healing well. It was time to take out the four black silk sutures. Barry picked up the forceps and Colin pulled his hand away.

'No,' he said. 'Jimmy Hanrahan says it hurts.'

'It's all right. Give me your hand,' said Barry, 'and if it hurts, I'll stop.'

'Promise?'

'Promise. Lay it on the towel there.'

The boy did as he was told. Barry seized the end of one of the sutures with the forceps, lifted it gently so the loop gaped, slipped one blade of the scissors under the loop, snipped and pulled. The stitch slid out.

'That wasn't too bad. Was it?'

'No.' The little boy's eyes were wide.

'Right,' said Barry, 'let's do the rest.' The other three stitches slid out easily. 'All done,' he said. 'You can take him home, Mrs Brown.'

'Thanks very much, Dr Laverty.'

O'Reilly, who had appeared in the doorway, tousled Colin's hair as he left with his mother.

'Sorry I had to nip out, but Kinky needed me to have a word on the phone with Bertie Bishop,' said O'Reilly. 'Seems he and the missus are much too busy to come in this morning and could I not see them after lunch?'

Barry waited. If O'Reilly had agreed, he'd have broken his first law of practice by letting Bishop get the upper hand.

'I told him to be here at one thirty.' O'Reilly slumped into his swivel chair. 'And before you think I'm going soft in my old age, it suits me fine. I'm as curious as you are to see what happens.'

Are you? Barry wondered. Or are you bending your own rules to give me a chance to be right?

'But,' said O'Reilly, 'that's after lunch. Nip along . . .'

Barry came back with a stranger. He was tall and thin, with immaculately brushed silver hair, watery grey eyes, a sharp nose, a clipped silver moustache and a receding chin. He wore an expensive three-piece suit, and a striped tie Barry was pretty sure was that of a Guards regiment.

'O'Weilly?' the man asked. 'I'm Captain O'Bwien-Kelly.' His replacement of the letter 'r' with a 'w' marked him as one of a group of upper-class Englishmen who still affected a pronunciation left over from Regency days.

'Indeed,' said O'Reilly.

'M'yes. Gwenadier Guards ectually, but I didn't come to discuss the awmed fawces. I shall be here for some time. Guest of His Lawdship, the Mawquis. His son, the Honouwable, is a subaltewn with me.'

'Comfy, are you, in the big house?' O'Reilly enquired.

'Living in his gate lodge, ectually. Quite cosy. I may need medical attention duwing my sojourn. His Lawdship assures me you're well qualified.'

'Nothing special,' said O'Reilly. 'Just a country GP. Like my colleague Dr Laverty here.'

'On occasions, beggars can't be choosers.'

'I've heard the rumour,' O'Reilly said, a tiny hint of pallor appearing in his nose tip. 'Now, Captain, I'd appreciate it if you'd start telling me what's bothering you.'

'Me? Fit as a flea. Just wanted to make contact. Just in case. One never knows.'

'No, indeed,' said O'Reilly, rising. 'Will that be all?'

'Indeed. Pleasant to meet you, young man,' he said to Barry.

O'Reilly held the door open and asked, 'Are you by any chance a sporting man?'

'The horses? Yes, indeed. Your Iwish animal Awkle's doing vewy well.'

'Himself? Oh, indeed,' said O'Reilly. 'It occurred to me that as a sporting man you might like to take a run-race down to the local meet here tomorrow.'

'Imagine it could be wather fun . . . for a wustic affair. I'll see if I can pop down. Jolly good. Cheewio.'

'And pip-pip,' said O'Reilly to the departing back. He glanced at his watch. 'The fellah's a waste of space,' he said, 'and of our time.'

Before Barry could comment, O'Reilly said, 'We're running late, and we've still the surgery to finish, lunch, the Bishops, anything Kinky has for us for this afternoon and Myrtle MacVeigh to see.'

'I'll go and get the next one,' Barry said. 'But a quick question. Why were you so polite to Captain O'Brien-Kelly? Inviting him to the races?'

'Ah,' said O'Reilly, 'I'm sure he'll have a lovely day there. And he's just the kind of man who could benefit from meeting one of the local peasantry.'

'You don't mean—'

'Indeed I do. The captain should get along famously with Donal Donnelly. After all, they're both great fans of Arkle.'

7

Fingal O'Reilly looked balefully at the bowl of salad Mrs Kincaid set on the dining-room table. 'Is that it?' he asked.

'It is, so,' she said. 'It's full of vitamins and it's very filling.' Barry could see her eyeing O'Reilly's belly. 'It'll do you a power of good and it'll keep you regular.'

'Mrs Kincaid,' O'Reilly growled. 'I don't think my bowel habits are in your bailiwick.'

Barry saw her purse her lips. But she ignored O'Reilly's remark. Turning to Barry, she said, 'When you're done, Dr Laverty, come out to the kitchen. I've your corduroy trousers mended.'

'Thanks, Kinky.'

She turned to O'Reilly. 'You've to see Myrtle this afternoon.'

'And that's all?' O'Reilly asked.

'No. I was saving half a dozen more as a surprise, so.'

'Come on, Kinky,' O'Reilly said. 'The salad's grand.'

'Huh.' She turned and left.

O'Reilly speared a piece of lettuce. 'Bloody rabbit food,' he grumbled. 'I think, to quote P. G. Wodehouse, Kinky is showing a distinct lack of gruntle today.'

Barry sliced into a hard-boiled egg. 'I don't think she appreciated being told to mind her own business, Fingal. She worries about you, you know. And I think she may be a little cross with me.'

'Why?'

'Something I said on Sunday about going to church.'

'Oops. Kinky's not one of the evangelical types, but she is devout.' O'Reilly shoved another lettuce leaf round his plate. 'Maybe we should make a peace offering?'

'She'll be going to Maggie's wedding?'

'Indeed.'

'I wonder if she'd like a new hat.'

'Now there's a thought.' O'Reilly shoved his hard-boiled egg in whole.

'We could pop in to Miss Moloney's, take a look at her stock . . . and see how Helen's getting on.'

'Good idea. Maybe we could fit that in later.' O'Reilly stared at the sideboard. 'Nothing but bloody oranges,' he said, rising, grabbing one and peeling it. 'I suppose this'll keep me regular too.'

'Well, at least you'll not get scurvy,' Barry said.

'No,' said O'Reilly as the front doorbell jangled. He glanced at his watch. 'That'll be the Bishops.' He strode to the door, held it open and said, 'Your patients. I'll watch.'

'Right.' Barry rose and went into the surgery to find Councillor and Mrs Bishop ensconced on the wooden chairs. ''Afternoon,' he said. 'How are you, Florence?'

'How the hell would she be?' Bishop demanded. 'You've not done nothing for her.'

'Not quite true, Mr Bishop. I have consulted my colleague. He thinks I may be right. Could you stand up, please, Florence?'

She rose heavily.

'Now,' said Barry, 'I'd like you to raise your arm as often as you can. Just like the last time.'

'She's done all that before,' grumbled Bishop.

'She has, Mr Bishop, but I'd like Florence to do it again.'

After a few attempts Mrs Bishop conceded failure.

'That's fine,' Barry said. 'I'm going to give you an injection, but get your breath back first.'

Barry prepared the neostigmine and atropine injections. Then he led Mrs Bishop to the couch and closed the screens.

'If you could just lift your skirt, pull the top of your knickers down and bend over the couch?' He swabbed a piece of white flesh with methylated spirit and gave the two injections. 'Maybe you'd like to rest on the couch?'

'Thank you, Doctor.'

Barry pushed back the screens. 'Now,' he said, 'we have to wait thirty minutes for the medicine to work.'

'*How long?*' Councillor Bishop shot to his feet.

'Half an hour,' said Barry pleasantly, relishing having the upper hand.

'Do make yourselves at home,' said O'Reilly. 'Dr Laverty and I have an urgent case to deal with, but we'll be back in plenty of time.'

Barry frowned. Urgent case? He followed O'Reilly through the door. When it closed, he asked, 'What's urgent, Fingal?'

'I'd forgotten there's a rugby game on the telly tonight. If we walk to Miss Moloney's now, we can come back for the Bishops, scoot out to see Myrtle and be back in time for the game.'

'Fair enough.'

Barry followed O'Reilly through the door onto Main Street, turned left and headed to the centre of the village. The sun struggled to break through clouds that hung low over the lough. Barry noticed the first brown leaves among a stand of elms on the Ballybucklebo Hills. Autumn was coming.

Barry recognised a man in a striped apron coming towards them.

''Afternoon, Doctors,' said Archibald Auchinleck.

'How's the back, Archie?' O'Reilly asked.

'I think it's on the mend. Them pills is great.'

'Good. And the boy?'

The milkman's face split into a great grin. 'I'd a letter yesterday. Rory's getting leave next week, and he'll be coming home.'

'That is good news, Archie,' O'Reilly said.

They walked on until they came to a narrow red-painted door beside a window in which were two mannequins dressed in floral skirts and sweaters. Hats were displayed on glass shelves. A sign above the door read: BALLYBUCKLEBO BOUTIQUE. The bell jingled as O'Reilly opened the door.

A gaunt, middle-aged woman, her pepper-and-salt hair pulled back in a severe bun, rushed out from behind a glass display case. Her thin lips were drawn up into a smile but her hazel eyes were unsmiling.

She clasped her hands. 'Dr O'Reilly. What a great pleasure, and this must be the young Dr Laverty? How can I help you gentlemen today?'

'A hat,' said O'Reilly. 'For Mrs Kincaid.'

'I've just the thing.' She fluttered, turned and screeched in a voice that Barry felt could have opened a tin of sardines: 'Helen . . . bring the blue box.' She turned her forced smile on O'Reilly. 'My assistant's a simple girl. She's in the back.' Then she yelled, '*Helennn.*'

Helen appeared through a bead curtain under an arch at the back of the store. She carried a blue hatbox.

'Not that one, you stupid girl. The navy-blue one.' She tutted. 'So sorry to keep you waiting, Doctor.'

Barry had already noticed that Helen was still wearing a long-sleeved blouse, a long skirt and white cotton gloves. It didn't look as if the hydrocortisone ointment was working. She reappeared with a navy-blue box.

Helen glanced at Barry and set the box on the glass counter.

'Don't just stand there. Open it.'

'Yes, Miss Moloney.' Helen lifted the lid, pulled out handfuls of tissue paper and lifted a hat onto the countertop. Emerald green, it was made of what looked like felt, shaped like a man's trilby with a wide brim, and turned down at the front and up at the back. The hatband was of darker green satin.

'Isn't it lovely?' Miss Moloney cooed.

'A thing of beauty,' O'Reilly agreed, with a perfectly straight face. 'What do you think, Barry?'

'It's not what I think, it's what Kinky will think,' Barry said.

'If you'll forgive me,' Miss Moloney simpered, 'I think Mrs Kincaid will love it. Positively love it.'

'Right,' said O'Reilly. 'We'll take it.'

'Wonderful.' She barely glanced at Helen. 'Get it parcelled up. At once, girl.' She moved behind the counter. 'I'll just make out the bill.'

Barry saw Helen sigh. 'How are you, Helen?'

She shrugged. He was disappointed. The ointment couldn't be having much effect. No wonder if the poor girl had to put up with being treated the way she was. 'I'm sorry.'

'Have you not finished yet?' Miss Moloney glared at Helen.

'Yes, Miss Moloney.'

'Then don't stand around. Get into the back room and get those other hatboxes stacked.'

Helen left, and Miss Moloney smiled again at O'Reilly. 'Here you are, Doctor,' she said, pushing the hatbox to O'Reilly. 'And here's your bill.'

'Give them both to Dr Laverty,' O'Reilly said, and before Barry could protest, O'Reilly fixed him with a stare. 'It was your idea, Laverty.'

The chimes over the door jingled as Barry sighed and pulled out his wallet. He was still worried about Helen. 'Excuse me, Miss Moloney. I wonder if you're not being a bit hard on Helen.'

'I beg your pardon?' It was as if the temperature in the shop had plummeted by a good ten degrees. 'Young man, when I have the impertinence to come into your surgery and tell you how to practise, you may come in here and tell me how to run my business.'

'I . . . that is . . .' He glimpsed Helen peering out from between the beads and had no difficulty understanding what she was mouthing: 'Thanks, Doc.'

'Good afternoon, Dr Laverty,' Miss Moloney said.

As he left he heard Miss Moloney yell, 'Helen, get in here this instant.'

Barry quickened his pace to catch up with O'Reilly.

O'REILLY WAS WAITING in the hall. 'Shove that in the dining room,' he said, nodding at the hatbox. 'We'll give it to Kinky later.'

'We? I paid for it,' Barry said, dumping the box on the nearest chair. 'He who pays the piper—'

'Calls the tune.' O'Reilly opened the surgery door, then remarked, 'Let's see if you've called *this* tune right.' He went in.

Barry followed. He saw Councillor Bishop stumping up and down. 'You said half an hour. It's been thirty-five minutes.'

'Dear me,' said O'Reilly. 'How time flies.' He took his usual chair.

Barry went to the couch. 'Let's get you up,' he said. He helped Florence get off the couch. 'How many times can you work your arm now?' he asked.

'Not again,' Bishop growled.

Barry ignored him and watched as Mrs Bishop raised and lowered her arm, seemingly without any difficulty. 'That's fine. You can stop now.'

'It's a miracle.' She looked at Laverty wide-eyed.

'Your wife, Councillor,' Barry said, 'is suffering from a disease called myasthenia gravis. Severe muscle weakness.'

Bishop frowned.

'Florence, you'll need to take some tablets. One as soon as you get up, and one or two every time you start to feel weak, but I promise you you'll be right as rain in no time.'

'Honest to God?' she asked.

'I promise,' he said, 'and if Dr O'Reilly would let me get at the prescription pad . . .'

'Right.' O'Reilly stood and moved aside.

'I'll write you a script.' Barry sat at the desk and filled in the blank form.

'Thanks, Dr Laverty. It'll be grand to get back on my feet.' As Barry handed her the script he saw the glistening of a tear on her left cheek.

He put a hand on her shoulder. 'My pleasure,' he said. 'Come back and see me next week. I'd like to know how you're getting on.'

'I will.' She smiled weakly. 'Maybe I can get a few pounds off too.'

'It's a couple of stone you need to lose.' Councillor Bishop strode to the door. 'Come on, Flo,' he said. 'We've been here long enough, so we have.'

'Just a minute,' O'Reilly said levelly, glancing at Barry as he spoke. 'I want to ask you about the Black Swan, Councillor.'

Bishop spun round. His eyes narrowed. 'What about it?'

'A little bird told me you're not going to renew Willy Dunleavy's lease.'

'That's none of your business, O'Reilly. Tell your wee bird to go and pluck itself.'

Barry saw two simultaneous colour changes. Bishop's cheeks flushed bright red and the tip of O'Reilly's nose blanched. He was surprised when O'Reilly said calmly, 'Folks in the village would like you to reconsider.'

'They can "like" away to their heart's content. Business is business.'

'I see,' said O'Reilly. He sighed. 'Pity.' It was the first time Barry had ever seen the big man accept defeat.

'Dr O'Reilly,' Mrs Bishop interrupted. 'Bertie doesn't—'

'Houl' your wheest, woman.' Bishop grabbed his wife's hand. The surgery door slammed as they left.

Barry turned to O'Reilly. 'You gave it a shot, Fingal.'

'Aye,' said O'Reilly, 'and missed . . . and, Barry, I'm stuck. Ever since we found out about the Duck, I've been racking my brains about how to get the wee bastard to change his mind.'

'Don't worry, Fingal. I'm sure something will turn up.'

O'Reilly shook his head. 'Sometimes,' he said, 'I think I should stick to the doctoring but . . . this bloody place gets under your skin.'

'I know,' Barry said quietly.

O'Reilly grunted. 'Anyway,' he said, 'I'm proud of you. You *were* right about Flo. She did have me foxed.'

'Thanks, Fingal.'

'The trouble is, I promised you if you were right I'd see to it that it worked wonders for your reputation, but without Flo or Bishop saying something, I can't tell anybody.'

'Patient confidentiality. I know about that,' Barry said. 'It's all right. I've had a couple of successes: the jockey and wee Colin Brown's hand. I think you were right, Fingal, about me just getting on with my job.'

O'Reilly clapped Barry on the shoulder. 'We'll see,' he said. 'And on the credit side, at least Bishop's getting on with *his* job at Sonny's. We should be grateful for small mercies.'

Barry heard the hall telephone ringing, Kinky's voice, and the *ting* as she replaced the receiver. He watched as the surgery door opened.

'Yes, Kinky?' O'Reilly asked.

'It was Myrtle MacVeigh. She says she's up and running around, not to bother calling, and thank Dr Laverty for them nighties-fer-aunties.'

'Thanks, Kinky.' Barry turned to O'Reilly. 'Should we not maybe pop in on Myrtle anyway?'

'I don't think so,' he said. 'If we don't go, we'll have lots of time now before supper . . .' He glanced at Kinky.

'I've crab cakes on the go,' she said, 'and if you like, I'll fry some chips.'

'That,' said O'Reilly, 'would hit the spot.'

'And you'd have plenty of time to see your rugby later, Fingal,' Barry said, quite looking forward to a lazy hour or two.

'And,' said O'Reilly, 'we could visit Maggie. See how the old girl's doing, and ask if she has any notions about where Sonny could go until his house is ready.'

BARRY SHOOK HIS HEAD. Their visit to Maggie MacCorkle's had been mixed. Happily, her headaches were gone, but she had no suggestions for a place for Sonny to live before the wedding.

O'Reilly stopped the Rover in the lane behind his house. Barry climbed out and let himself into the back garden. Immediately he was greeted by Arthur Guinness, who barked joyously, trotted proudly to his kennel and returned with a green Wellington boot. He sat and deposited it at O'Reilly's feet, the picture, Barry thought, of a gun dog making the perfect retrieve.

'Where in the hell did you get this?' said O'Reilly.

'Arf,' said a smiling Arthur, and wagged his tail.

'Idiot,' said O'Reilly. 'Now I'll have to go out after supper and drive around until I find the other one.' He marched to the back door, calling over his shoulder, 'Come on, Barry. I'm famished.'

Mrs Kincaid was on her hands and knees scrubbing the tiled kitchen floor. 'We've had a little accident, so.'

'Not my crab cakes?' O'Reilly asked.

'No. But that cat . . .' She blew out her cheeks. 'She ate a whole half pound of butter, and then she started to make a noise like a cement mixer and sicked the whole lot up over my clean floor, so.' She stood slowly. 'I didn't know whether to comfort her or kill her dead.'

'As long,' said O'Reilly, 'as she didn't steal the crab cakes.'

Kinky shook her head. 'No. They're in the oven. Run along now, and I'll have them and the chips ready in no time.'

O'Reilly turned into the dining room. He picked up the hatbox from where Barry had left it. 'I think,' he said, handing the box to Barry, 'our timing in the peace-offering stakes couldn't be better.'

'I hope so. I much prefer to see Kinky cheerful.'

'Do you, so?' Kinky brought in two plates, each with four crab cakes and a pile of chips. Rather than dig straight in, Barry rose.

''And is there something the matter with your supper?' Mrs Kincaid stood, arms folded.

'No, Kinky.' Barry grabbed the hatbox and gave it to her. 'I—that is, Dr O'Reilly and I—have a wee something for you.'

'Why? It's not my birthday or Christmas.'

'No,' said O'Reilly. 'It's because we love you.'

'Less of your soft soap, Doctor dear.' But Barry could tell by the way she smiled that the gift and O'Reilly's words had pleased her. 'Now, eat up before it gets cold, and I'll run off and have a look in this.'

'I will,' said O'Reilly. The better part of a crab cake vanished.

Barry tucked in. The cakes had a flavour of fresh Dungeness crab, the chips were golden, crisp and firm.

Barry was still eating when O'Reilly set his knife and fork on his empty plate, smiled at Barry and said, 'Just the job to set a fellah up for a lonesome Wellie boot hunt.' O'Reilly rose and headed for the door. 'I'm off to see if I can find the brother to the one Arthur nicked. Keep an eye on the shop, and I'll be back as quick as I can. I still want to see that rugger game.'

'Right.' Barry was pleased to be left in charge.

'Excuse me, Dr Laverty.' Kinky stood in the doorway. 'How do you like the look of that?'

The green felt trilby was set on the centre of her silver hair.

'It suits you, Kinky,' Barry said. 'It really does.'

'It's just what I needed for Maggie's wedding,' she said.

'You'll be the belle of the ball. Kinky, it's by way of saying I'm sorry for that crack on Sunday and Dr O'Reilly's sorry for turning his nose up at your lunches.'

'It's nice of the pair of you to worry about my feelings. Do you mind if I sit down?'

'Please.'

Mrs Kincaid sat on a dining-room chair. 'I have been a bit grumpy lately, but it's nothing to do with you or himself, so don't you fret.' She looked straight into Barry's eyes. 'I told you a bit about myself and Paudeen.'

She'd confided in Barry about how she'd lost her husband, a Cork fisherman, years ago. 'Yes,' he said quietly.

'It was August he was drowned. Sometimes it comes back to me, so.'

'I'm sorry, Kinky.' She still grieved after all these years.

'What's done's done,' she said. 'I just wanted you to understand.'

'Thanks, Kinky.'

'Not at all. It's me to be thanking you for the hat. Imagine Sonny and Maggie. There's a thing.'

Sonny. Barry wondered if Kinky could help. 'Kinky,' he said, 'Sonny's stuck in that home in Bangor, and Dr O'Reilly wants to get him out, but he can't find a place for Sonny to stay. You wouldn't happen to know of anybody with rooms to rent?'

'I did. Brie Lannigan had a room but she let it to Julie MacAteer when the wee lass left employment at the Bishops'. But I'll ask about.'

And Bishop. Kinky might just be able to help there too. 'There's another wee thing. Have you heard about the councillor and the Duck?'

She snorted. 'Who hasn't?'

'He and Mrs Bishop were in here earlier, and Dr O'Reilly asked the councillor to change his mind.'

'Bertie Bishop? Change his mind?'

'I know but it's all to do with the lease, and when Dr O'Reilly broached the subject, Mrs Bishop started to say something—"Bertie doesn't . . ."— but that's as far as she got.'

Mrs Kincaid frowned. 'He doesn't what?'

'I don't know, but could it be possible, just possible, that the councillor's claim to the title isn't sound?'

She laughed. 'Anything's possible in Ballybucklebo, and that councillor's crooked as a corkscrew.'

'It's only a glimmer of an idea, but could you do a bit of sniffing around with Mrs B?'

'I will, so. And now the dishes won't wash themselves.' She rose. 'And if you see that wee cat, tell her she's forgiven.'

Before Barry could reply, O'Reilly came in through the back door.

'Found it,' he said, beaming. 'On the back step of Donal Donnelly's mother's. He lives with her, you know. There was the other boot, all alone, just waiting for its opposite number. Nobody saw me put it back.'

'A good thing too,' said Barry. 'I can just see the headline . . . WELLIE BOOT SNATCHER FOUND: EMINENT PHYSICIAN ON BOOTNAPPING CHARGES.'

'Get away with you, Dr Laverty,' Kinky said, smiling. 'Now go on, the pair of you, and watch your rugby match.'

8

The Rover bounced over a rutted lane to a five-bar gate. Ahead Barry could see cars, estate wagons, Land Rovers and horseboxes parked in ranks on a grassy hillside. A steward in a cloth cap, brown grocer's coat and armband was directing traffic.

'Last row on your left, Dr O'Reilly.' The steward opened the gate.

'Right.' O'Reilly drove slowly up a gentle hill, past six rows of parked vehicles and along the aisle between the sixth and seventh row. He pulled in beside the last car and stopped. 'Here we are,' he said. 'Out.'

Barry stepped onto the springy turf and looked around. A blackthorn hedge surrounded the field. Beyond the hedge the little Ulster fields, most bordered by dry-stone walls, rolled like gentle waves. These hillocks, he knew, were called drumlins, rounded hills left by the last ice age. Someone had once described County Down as looking like a basket of green eggs. Cloud shadows hurried across the fields.

In the distance he could make out the tall, Georgian chimneys and slate roofs of Bucklebo House peeping over small beech woods. It was, he knew, home of the Marquis of Ballybucklebo in whose demesne lay these fields—and the all-important racetrack.

Barry looked over the rows of parked vehicles, each surrounded by its passengers. Men in jodhpurs, cavalry twill trousers, hacking jackets, all wearing camel-hair caps, many with binoculars slung round their necks; women in slacks, tweed skirts, heavy woollen pullovers and blazers, most wearing gay silk headscarves that fluttered in the breeze.

'Three miles and two furlongs,' said O'Reilly. 'That's the start there. They run on the track for half a mile, then out into the country, back round the other side of the track, round a curve, and finish back at the start line.'

At the foot of the hill Barry could see the first hurdle between the hedges.

'The jumps are four and a half feet high, and there's a tributary of the Bucklebo for a water jump.'

O'Reilly opened the Rover's boot. 'Let's see what Kinky's put in for us.' He wrestled a wicker hamper onto the boot's door. 'None of your salad,' he said with a grin as he opened the lid. 'I think the hat worked wonders.'

Barry waited as O'Reilly arranged a cold roast chicken, hard-boiled eggs, whole tomatoes, slices of baked ham, buttered wheaten bread, plates, knives and forks, salt and pepper, and two bottles of Bass ale on a checked tablecloth. 'Dig in.' He handed a bottle to Barry.

Barry helped himself to ham, an egg and a tomato.

There was a crowd milling around a series of raised daises. On each was a desk like something out of a Dickensian counting house. Above, mounted on two stout poles, was a signboard announcing the owner's name in garishly painted colours: 'Honest Sammy Dolan—Best Odds', 'William McCardle and Sons, Turf Accountants'. Blackboards hung from the marquees, with the time of the race in chalk at the top and the horses' names and odds in a column beneath. The bookies were calling the odds. 'Pride of Copelands, two to five on . . .'

'That'll be the favourite,' O'Reilly explained. 'You'd have to put five pounds down to win two.'

'I understand that,' said Barry, sipping his Bass.

O'Reilly wiped his mouth with his napkin. 'Have you had enough?'

Barry nodded.

'Right.' O'Reilly shoved the hamper into the boot. 'Let's take a run-race down to the paddock and see if Fergus Finnegan's about the place.'

Barry followed O'Reilly down the hill, their progress constantly inter-rupted by having to stop and exchange pleasantries with this one and that one. He was pleased to see how many strangers clearly knew who he was and by how they all seemed to treat him with good-humoured civility.

Barry saw a familiar figure approaching. He'd not mistake the carroty hair and buckteeth nor, he smiled, the green rubber boots the man was wearing.

'Donal,' boomed O'Reilly, 'how the hell are you?'

'Seamus and me got the day off from the roof job at Sonny's. It's coming on a treat, by the way. I reckon another two weeks'll see us done. Anyway,' said Donal, 'I'll have to run on. I've a job as bookie's runner for Willie McCardle. I'm making a few more bob for Julie and me.'

'How is she?' Barry enquired.

Donal frowned. 'She'd a wee tummy upset this morning, but she says it's normal. Is it?' He looked at O'Reilly.

'Indeed.'

Barry remembered that he'd had some concerns about Julie's uterus last week, but before he could ask Donal anything O'Reilly was asking, 'Have you found any Englishmen yet, Donal?'

'Not yet, but if I do I'm ready.' Donal winked at O'Reilly.

'Good. Dr Laverty and I may just know the fellah you're looking for. Where can he find you?'

'At Willie's stand.'

'I'll send him along if I see him.'

'Great.'

Donal scurried away.

'And,' O'Reilly rubbed his hands, 'if Fergus sees us right, it is my sincere hope that a certain Honest Sammy Dolan won't remember taking my bet on Donal's dog, Bluebird, last month, but will be well prepared to shell out again later today.'

'You made four hundred pounds on that, Fingal.'

'Money well earned,' said O'Reilly. 'And if you remember, I gave the same tip to His Lordship. He won something too.' O'Reilly turned to walk on, but then stopped. 'And speak of the devil and he's sure to turn up.'

Barry saw two men approaching: Captain O'Brien-Kelly and an older gentleman with a mop of ill-trimmed grey hair sticking out from under a hat. He looked like a gardener, dressed as he was in a darned cardigan, collarless shirt, corduroy trousers and mud-splattered Wellington boots.

''Afternoon, O'Reilly,' the older man said. 'Grand day for the event, isn't it?' Barry heard the gentle inflections of a public-school-educated Ulsterman. There was no aping the accents of the English upper classes. 'I think you've already met my guest, from my son's regiment.' He indicated the captain. 'And you must be Laverty?'

Barry frantically tried to remember the correct form of address for a marquis and settled for 'Yes, sir.'

'And you, Fingal, we'll be beating the outer coverts in a couple of weeks. The pheasants have done very well this year. Would you be able to get free and bring your gun and Arthur Guinness?'

O'Reilly's smile was bright. 'I'd love to.'

'I say, Bertie,' Captain O'Brien-Kelly addressed the marquis. 'Can't we twot on? I'd weally like to put something on that filly in the first.'

Barry saw the marquis frown. Clearly, he disapproved of bad manners, but he said, 'You run along.'

'Captain,' O'Reilly said softly, 'there's a fellah here you should meet, another Arkle fancier. That's him there. Donal Donnelly.' He pointed to Donal at the bookie's stand. 'Tell him I sent you, but you'll have to speak slowly. He's a bit dim.'

'Will do.' The captain hurried off.

'Getting on well with the young man?' O'Reilly asked.

The marquis sighed. 'When Sean asked if I'd let the man come over for a few days, it was very difficult to refuse.' The marquis was too much of a gentleman to criticise his guest, but his evasive answer spoke volumes.

'Your Lordship, I've an odd kind of request,' O'Reilly said.

'Please?'

'Have you met Sonny?'

'The recluse who lives in his car?' The marquis smiled. 'Yes, indeed. Marvellous chess player, and he knows more about early Nabataean civilisation than anyone else I've met. They're the chappies who built Petra. It's been an interest of mine since I was up at Cambridge.'

'That's Sonny,' O'Reilly said. 'He's stuck in a home in Bangor, and I'm looking for temporary accommodation for him.'

The marquis frowned. 'Ordinarily I'd be delighted, but we've a big house party this weekend—folks over for the races. But if any of them go home early, I'll let you know.'

'That's very generous of you, sir.'

'Nonsense,' said the marquis. 'I'd much prefer Sonny's company to . . .' He inclined his head to where Barry could see the captain deep in conversation with a grinning Donal Donnelly.

Barry saw Donal give something to the captain and in exchange accept what appeared to be a number of banknotes. He was so intent on watching the scene unfold he didn't notice the marquis leaving.

'Come on, Barry,' O'Reilly said. 'The one thirty's just about to start.'

O'REILLY SHOULDERED his way through the throng milling round the near side of the start line. Barry followed in his wake.

'Tuck in there,' said O'Reilly, indicating a space beside him at the white painted fence.

Barry leaned on the wooden railing. It was clear that the first 200 yards were fenced; then the fairway ran between chest-high, boundary hedges and led to the first jump.

'That,' said O'Reilly, pointing, 'is the finishing post. If we wait here, we'll be able to see the start *and* the finish.'

A rope stretched between the starting post and a raised platform surrounded by low railings. Barry watched as a figure in a cloth cap and long coat climbed a ladder to the platform.

'Starter,' said O'Reilly. 'Won't be long. Here they come.'

Barry saw a procession of eight horses approaching in single file. Each was led by a groom. The jockeys sat upright in their saddles. Each rider sported a different coloured shirt, his racing silks. Every stable and every owner had their own pattern.

'See that fellah on the big gelding?' O'Reilly indicated a jockey whose shirt was divided into four equal squares, two green, two scarlet. 'Those are the marquis's colours.'

The grooms led their charges to the starting rope, where the animals lined up shoulder to shoulder. The crowd was quiet now, and Barry could hear the jingling of tack, horses snorting, hoofs stamping on the turf.

Barry saw the man on the platform raise a red flag. Every jockey crouched forward, gaze fixed on the track. He heard the jangling of a bell, saw the starter slash his flag down. The rope was dropped and the horses flew forward. The sound of hoofs thundering on the turf was deafening and the earth where Barry stood shook underfoot. Already one had taken the lead.

Barry craned to watch the leader and then the pack hurl themselves at the first hurdle. The leading horse flew over, pursued by several others. Then the sound of hoofs faded as the horses headed out into the countryside.

Barry turned, stared back along the track and waited. In what seemed like no time he began to hear the distant hammering of hoof on grass. Above the perimeter fence he could see the tops of jockeys' and horses' heads pounding rhythmically as they rounded the final turn to gallop to the last fence.

Two animals were neck and neck. Their jockeys crouched, belabouring their mounts with their crops, straining forward in the saddles as if by sheer physical force they could urge their mounts ahead.

From where Barry stood it appeared as if the larger horse had won, and its jockey wore the green and scarlet of the marquis.

'That's a very satisfactory result to the first,' said O'Reilly. 'His Lordship will be pleased. Pity about Whinney Knowes. She refused at the first.'

'Do you know her owner?'

'Not at all,' said O'Reilly, 'but I do know someone who was in a hurry to put a bet on her.'

And Barry remembered Captain O'Brien-Kelly.

'Come on,' said O'Reilly. 'Let's go and find Fergus.'

BARRY FOLLOWED O'Reilly into a meadow. Already the entrants from the first race were returning. As the jockeys dismounted, grooms took off the saddles, curried the horses' flanks, draped them with blankets and led them to waiting horseboxes.

'There's Fergus,' O'Reilly announced, striding across the grass. ''Afternoon, Fergus. How's the eye today?'

'Couldn't be better.' Fergus Finnegan winked at Barry. 'Three of the stable lads want to come in for to see you, so they do.'

Barry was pleased.

'What's the word for the third?' said O'Reilly.

Fergus dropped his voice. 'The favourite's a wee mare, Nancy's Fancy, but I'm riding a ringer. Come 'ere 'til you see him.' He started to walk away, O'Reilly in hot pursuit and Barry bringing up the rear.

A groom stood holding a horse's bridle. Barry stopped dead. It was the biggest horse he'd ever seen.

'This here's Battlecruiser. He's eighteen hands. Show him a fence or a hedge and he's over it like a madman. He's never been out before so nobody's got a notion of his form, and the bookies have him at ten to one.'

O'Reilly chuckled. 'Thanks, Fergus. Now I think it's time for a wee word with Honest Sammy Dolan.'

As they made their way back to the bookies, Barry scanned the names of the other horses. His eyes widened. At five to one was an animal called Patricia's Pleasure. Once in a while, Barry could be superstitious.

Sammy Dolan's voice, already overused from calling the odds, was hoarse. O'Reilly stood in front of him. 'Fifty pounds to win on Battlecruiser.' After the proffered notes were grabbed and stuffed in a satchel, a ticket was issued.

'Good luck, sir. Next,' Dolan said.

O'Reilly stepped aside. 'I'll see you at the start, Barry.'

Barry handed over five pounds and said, 'Patricia's Pleasure to win.'

By the time Barry reached the fence, O'Reilly was already there. The horses running in the third race jostled behind the rope. Barry could see Battlecruiser and Fergus Finnegan. He turned to a man standing beside him. 'Excuse me. Which is Patricia's Pleasure?'

'That one there.' The man pointed to a small roan. The jockey wore silks of vertical green and white stripes.

'Thanks,' Barry said. He heard the bell.

'They're off,' O'Reilly roared. 'Jesus, would you look at Battlecruiser?'

Barry did. The great horse was already two lengths ahead, his jockey moving him over to hug the inside rail. The animal pounded along the course, speeding past the white fence.

Battlecruiser soared effortlessly over the hedge, clearing the top by what Barry reckoned was a good six feet. There was only one difficulty. The minute he left the white railing behind, Battlecruiser spotted the perimeter hedge, accepted the challenge and ran halfway across the ploughed field in the middle of the course, determined, it seemed, to travel all the way to County Antrim.

'Fifty quid down the pipe. It would make the bloody angels weep,' O'Reilly roared, ripping up his betting slip.

Barry felt it wiser not to laugh.

'Right,' said O'Reilly. 'No point staying to the end. Coming?'

Barry shook his head. 'I'd like to see the finish anyway.'

He turned back to the track. The first horse over the final jump was ridden by a jockey wearing vertical green and white stripes. It was leading by a good four lengths, and it kept that lead as it passed the finishing post.

Barry made his way to the bookies and collected thirty pounds. Then he climbed slowly up the hill. He saw O'Reilly, open bottle of Bass clutched in one hand, in conversation with Captain O'Brien-Kelly.

'. . . it's all a bit awkwawd,' the captain was saying. 'I seem to have wather misjudged the fawm on a couple of waces. I was hoping you might be able to help me out.'

'I'd like to,' said O'Reilly smoothly, 'but my horse should be somewhere near the Holywood Arches by now, not in the winner's circle, so at the moment I'm skint.'

'Pity.' The captain's shoulders sagged. 'I'd be all wight if I hadn't spent one hundwed pounds with that chap you wecommended.'

'Mr Donnelly.'

He produced a silver coin. 'Do you know what that is?'

O'Reilly glanced over at Barry, then peered at the coin. 'Begod, you'd swear it was the spit image of Arkle himself.'

'It is, and I was able to get him to sell them to me for a pound apiece. He wanted two pounds, but the man hasn't a clue how to haggle. I took his entiwe stock.'

'No market here,' said O'Reilly, 'but I'm sure you'll clean up with your regiment back in England.'

The captain beamed. 'I will, won't I?' His smile faded. 'Twouble is I could use a bit of the weady. Wight now, in fact.' Barry followed the direction of the man's gaze and saw a heavyset man, shirtsleeves rolled up, leave Honest Sammy's stand and stride purposefully in their direction.

'Weally must be wunning,' the captain said.

When O'Reilly stopped chuckling, he said to Barry, 'So who won?'

Barry hesitated. 'I did, Fingal. At least my horse did.'

'What? Well, I'll be damned.' O'Reilly threw an arm round Barry's shoulders. 'Good for you, Laverty. Here'—he rummaged in the picnic hamper—'have a Bass.'

'Thanks, Fingal. Sorry about your horse.'

'Och,' said O'Reilly. 'I'm still three hundred and fifty pounds ahead, and you know what they say, "Unlucky at the horses . . . lucky in love."'

Barry started to laugh but it struck him that as *he'd* been lucky with the horses, the logical conclusion was not something he wanted to consider.

'Aye,' said O'Reilly, 'there's the rub, isn't it?' He opened a beer. 'Do you feel like running the shop on your own tonight?'

'Well, I—'

'Good, because I don't feel like it. I'd like to take a wander over to the Duck and have another word with Willy Dunleavy.'

'If you think so, Fingal.'

'Good. If you do that, I'll take care of things tomorrow and maybe . . . maybe you could see if that Miss Spence of yours is free.'

9

Brunhilde's near-side tyres scraped against the kerb of the Esplanade as Barry parked opposite Number 9. When he'd phoned Patricia the night before, she'd sounded tired but agreed that a day away from her studies would be a good idea. She said she'd make a picnic, and perhaps today, Sunday, they could take a trip to the country.

He rang the doorbell to Flat 4. His hand slipped unbidden to his crown to smooth the tuft of fair hair he knew would be sticking up.

'Good morning, I . . .' he blurted, but his breath caught in his throat. Patricia stood in the doorway, her hair in a ponytail. A dimple appeared in her left cheek when she smiled at him. She was carrying a picnic basket in one hand.

'Good morning, yourself.' She kissed him lightly.

'Come on.' He took her hand and led her across the street, slowing his stride to accommodate her limp. 'Give me the basket,' he said, walking round to the driver's side and putting the picnic on the back seat. By the time he'd climbed in, she was sitting in the passenger's seat. Patricia Spence wasn't a young woman to wait for any man to hold a door open for her.

'Where are we going, Barry?'

'I thought we'd take a drive down to Strangford.'

'Lovely.' She settled back in her seat. 'I'm going to enjoy the ride. It'll be my last break before the big day.'

'The exam?'

'Tuesday . . . then I'll have to wait for the results.'

Barry thought, You'll not be the only one waiting. He would be hearing soon from Harry Sloan about the histology report. The way things had been going in the last week was helping him feel more at home in the practice. But he still wanted to know what had killed Major Fotheringham. Once the question was answered, he'd have only one more conundrum to sort out: Patricia and what to do if she was successful.

He glanced at her. She was staring out of the window, frowning a little. Patricia wasn't one of those girls who felt it necessary to fill every moment with inane chatter. It was one of the things he liked about her.

He swung the car onto the road that ran through Ballybucklebo, then onto the Six Road Ends. His destination, Gransha Point, lay at the mouth of Strangford Lough. It was a narrow peninsula, stretching for three-quarters of a mile into the shallow waters. It was about half an hour's drive away.

As he concentrated on the road, he became aware of a low musical sound and glanced over. Patricia's lips were moving, and as he strained to hear he recognised the words of 'My Lagan Love', one of the most beautiful of all the Irish love songs. He'd had no idea how rich a voice Patricia had. He felt the hairs on the nape of his neck tingle, and he listened enraptured until the last line: '"And sings in sad, sweet undertone/The song of heart's desire."'

My heart's desire, he thought. 'That was lovely,' he said. 'I didn't know you could sing. With a voice like that you should be on the stage.'

She shook her head and laughed. 'Nonsense. I just sing for the fun of it.'

He saw that the turn to Gransha was coming up ahead, turned right onto it from the Portaferry Road and drove slowly along a rutted lane. He came to a broad, flat expanse of scutch grass in front of a lichen-encrusted, dry-stone wall. He stopped the car close to a stile where a rock step abutted a vertical slab of flat slate.

'Here we are,' he said. 'Hop out.' He climbed out.

'Gosh,' she said, 'it's warm.'

He collected the picnic basket from the back seat, and an old blanket from the boot of the car. 'We'll have to walk from here.'

'Grand.' She took his hand. 'Let's go.'

As he led her to the stile, Barry felt the sun hot on his back. Bees murmured in the gorse flowers and the grass was springy under his feet.

He climbed onto the step, clambered over the slate and hopped onto the grass. He put the basket and blanket on the ground and waited for her to jump down beside him. When she did, he caught her, held her and kissed her. Then he pointed ahead. 'Do you see that collection of tumbled stones about halfway along the Point's shore?'

'Yes.'

'That's where we're going. Come on.'

He guided her along the Point, past brackish pools of peat water the colour of stewed tea.

He jumped when a brace of small ducks exploded from beneath his feet, wings clattering as they strained for altitude.

'Teal,' said Patricia, as a flock rose from the water's edge, wheeled and jinked. Then it turned in unison and flew low over the waves.

'Not far now,' Barry said. The air was redolent of salt, and the scent of its sea tang pleased him.

'Thank you for bringing me here. It's lovely.'

'Glad you like it, madam.' He made a mock bow.

The wind blowing up to Newtownards at the lough's head fluttered the grass, and he watched her ponytail sway to the breeze's caress. Dear God, but she was beautiful.

'How's this?' He led her to the lee of the old sheepcote. 'It's cosy here out of the wind.' He bent and spread the blanket, setting the basket at one edge. She sat, arms clasped round her bent legs, chin resting on her knees.

Barry sat down and put an arm round her shoulders. He felt her snuggle closer and rest her head on his shoulder. 'I'll bring you here any time you like.' If you're still in Ulster, he thought.

'I'd like that, but—'

'No buts,' he said. 'Not today.' He laid his hand on her cheek, feeling its smoothness, turned her face to him and kissed her slowly.

He waited for his breathing to slow. Then he said, 'It's a little too early for lunch. Would you like to walk out to the end of the Point?'

They got to their feet and, hand in hand, they walked to where the strip of land narrowed and slipped into the waters. Barry was so full of her he felt no need to speak.

The wind was warm, the tide high. 'Here we are,' he said, halting at the water's edge. 'Land's end.'

'What a wonderful view.'

'Down there, off in the distance to our left . . .' He gazed across little whitecaps, green waters and low islands to where mountain peaks stood sentinel over the southern part of County Down. He noticed clouds building above the highest, Slieve Donard, and hoped they weren't the harbingers of one of the sudden summer squalls that could sweep the lough.

'Those're the Mountains of Mourne,' she said, and sang, '"But I'd far rather be, where the Mountains of Mourne sweep down to the sea."'

He stared at her, knowing those words were true for him, wishing they were true for her.

'I hear you'll find Cambridgeshire's pretty flat,' he said, and waited to see how she'd respond.

'If I get to go there.' She tossed her head. 'I thought we weren't going to talk about that today. And anyway it is true. I'd far rather be here in Ulster, but even if things do work out for me, the Mournes'll still be here sweeping down to the sea when I come back.'

And so will I, Barry thought. He pulled her to him and kissed her. 'Right,' he said, knowing he had to change the subject. 'Let's go and have a bite of lunch.'

BARRY LOWERED the empty bottle of warm Harp Lager. He put it back in the hamper that earlier had held sandwiches, buttered barmbrack and a couple of apples. 'Feast fit for a king.' He moved across the blanket to sit by her.

'It's been a lovely day,' she said.

'Hasn't it?' He bent, kissed her, and gradually, still kissing her, pushed her backwards until she lay on her side on the blanket. He moved his lips to her neck and felt hands behind his head holding him to her. He slipped one arm behind her, caressing her through the satiny material of her blouse.

Barry knew they were going to make love here on the blanket on the soft grass. 'Patricia, I—'

The lid of the picnic basket slammed shut with a crash. He opened his eyes to see the edges of the blanket flapping as wind battered through the gaps in the stones. The dry dune grasses at the sides of the sheepcote were flattened. Waves pounded the shore.

Barry stood up and glanced at the sky. The clouds had marched across the lough like companies of storm troopers. A single lightning bolt flared across the sky, and seconds later a roll of thunder beat on his ears. He hated thunderstorms.

The rain started, heavy stinging drops, soaking his hair. He felt Patricia get up and stand beside him. He put his arm round her. 'Sit down close to the stones,' he said. 'Try to get a bit of shelter.'

She shook her head and pulled away, then raised both arms above her head and turned her face up to the sky. 'I love storms,' she shouted.

'And I love *you*, Patricia,' Barry shouted, but his words were drowned out by the thunder's crash.

He felt the raindrops, lighter now. The wind was easing. Out over the islands a sunbeam burst through as the storm moved past Gransha Point.

She turned to him, her grin wide, dimple deep. 'Whew,' she said, 'that was wonderful.' She looked at his trousers and started to laugh. 'You're sodden,' she said, 'but it wouldn't be a day out with you if you could keep your trousers dry.'

Barry was forced to agree. Almost every time he'd been with her, some disaster—from Arthur Guinness cocking his leg on him to Barry spilling a pint on himself—had left him with soaked britches. He laughed, but his gaze lingered on the sight of her breasts beneath her wet blouse. He feared the spell had been broken for her.

'We're both soaked,' she said, glancing down at herself. She crossed her arms. 'Would you look at me? I think we should be getting back.'

No. But he swallowed, took a deep breath and said, 'All right.' He began to fold the sodden blanket.

She knelt beside him to help, and she turned and kissed him quickly. 'You are patient,' she said, her voice low and husky. 'Thank you.'

'I love you, Patricia.' He waited.

She looked at him, unsmiling. He closed his eyes. He couldn't bear to watch if she walked away, but instead she hugged him, kissed him, and whispered, 'And I love *you*, Barry Laverty, even though I know I shouldn't.'

AN IRISH COUNTRY VILLAGE | 227

BARRY PARKED BRUNHILDE in the lane. He was relieved to see no sign of Arthur Guinness in the back garden. He opened the gate, crossed the grass and let himself into the house. The smell of roasting duck filled the kitchen and Kinky stood at the sink, peeling potatoes. He crossed the tiled floor, grabbed her and spun her round.

'Put me down, Dr Laverty.' Kinky laughed. 'Put me down this instant.'

'I'm in love, Kinky.'

'Huh,' she said, still grinning. 'For a learned doctor it's taken you a brave while to catch on. Didn't I know that from the first time I saw you and Miss Spence together? I'm glad for the pair of you . . . and for himself.'

'Dr O'Reilly? Why?'

'Sure, sometimes you're as easy to see through as a window. Haven't I known you were thinking of leaving? And I'd not like to see you go, nor would the big fellah. He's no spring chicken any more, and he needs your help . . . and so do the buck eejits who live here, only some of them are too *cadránta* to see it.'

'*Cad* what?'

'Bloody-minded. Never you mind them. You can't please everybody.' She sniffed. 'There's a brave clatter of folks who think you're doing just fine. And if your Miss Spence would make another good reason for you staying, more power to her wheel.'

'Thanks, Kinky.' He was pleased by what she had just said about his being needed, yet somehow unsettled. Since he'd recovered from his initial elation over Patricia saying she loved him, the thought of her going away kept gnawing at him.

'Kinky?'

She was bent over the oven, wreathed in a gust of steam, scooping the melted fat off the duck. 'What?'

He was going to tell her about Patricia, the exam and Cambridge but decided not to. Instead he asked, 'Is Dr O'Reilly in?'

She closed the oven door. 'He is not. His Lordship phoned a while back. Dr O'Reilly went tearing off with a great big grin on his face. He said he was off to Bangor to get Sonny, but don't ask me what it's all about. Well, he'd better hurry back. I'd not want this duck to spoil.'

'I'll be ready on time, Kinky. I'll go and change right now.'

Barry left and ran upstairs. From below he heard the doorbell ring. He hesitated with one leg in his corduroys, and tried to hear what was being said. A man was talking to Kinky.

Barry finished changing his trousers, grabbed the damp pair and hurried back downstairs.

Kinky looked round as he arrived in the hall, where Donal Donnelly stood, cap in hands. 'It's Julie, Doctor.' His words tumbled out. 'Can you come quick? She's bleeding something fierce.'

'I'll get my bag.' Barry shoved his wet trousers at Kinky, ran into the surgery and grabbed his bag. 'Where is she, Donal?'

'At Brie Lannigan's. I'd gone round to have my tea with her, like, and all of a sudden she grabbed her belly and let a howl out of her.' Barry could see tears on Donal's cheeks. 'And then there was this great big red stain on her dress . . . I got her up to bed as quick as I could. Brie's no phone, so I come round here as fast as I could pedal.' Donal grabbed Barry's hand and tugged him to the open door. 'Come on quick, Doctor.'

'Round the back,' Barry yelled to Donal. 'My car's there.'

Barry started the engine, waited for Donal to slam his door and then drove off. 'Which way?'

'Turn left here on Main Street, right at the maypole, along Station Road for about a mile.' Donal hunched in his seat.

Damn it, Barry'd been right to worry when he'd examined Julie last week and thought her uterus didn't feel quite right. Mind you, he told himself, if a miscarriage is going to happen, there's not a thing can be done to stop it.

'I'm scared, so I am, Doctor.' Donal lowered his voice. 'She . . . she couldn't die, could she?'

'Of course not, Donal.' Barry tried to sound confident.

Donal thumped a fist on the dashboard. 'It's all my fault. It's a judgment, so it is.'

'For what?' Barry swerved to avoid a cyclist.

'For putting Julie in the family way before we was married.'

'I'd not worry about that now, Donal.'

'If it wasn't for that, then it was for foxing the English gentleman. I took a hundred pounds off him, so I did, but it was for Julie and the wean.'

Barry said, 'Nobody forced him to buy the half-crowns.'

'Pull in there, Doctor. At that red-brick semi.'

Barry parked, reached for his bag and followed Donal up a path to the right-hand house. Donal had opened the door. Barry followed into a narrow hall and up a flight of stairs. Donal's back disappeared through a doorway.

Julie lay on the bed. She was pale and sweating. A scarlet stain crept across the sheet that covered her lower half. He knew from experience that a little blood went a very long way, but to Julie and Donal it must look as if the bleeding was torrential. He glanced under the bed to see if there were ropes of clots forming from blood that had soaked through the mattress. Good. No clots. She hadn't bled that much—yet.

'Julie,' Barry said, 'can you tell me what happened?' He sat on the bed beside her. 'It's all right.' He took her wrist between his thumb and first two fingers. The skin was clammy, her pulse rapid and very feeble. She was on the edge of going into shock.

'It is now you're here, Doctor.' She forced a weak smile. 'I started getting these wee cramps yesterday. But about an hour ago they got to be fierce, and then I started to bleed down below.'

Barry opened his bag and took out a paper packet of sterile gloves and a green-wrapped pack. He tore open the paper. 'Where's the bathroom?'

'On the left,' Donal said.

Barry left, washed his hands and returned. 'I have to examine you, Julie.' He slipped on the gloves. 'Would you wait outside, Donal?'

Barry could feel the partially open cervix. Julie was aborting, but she had not expelled the tiny foetus and placenta—and until she did, the bleeding would not stop. His patient was going to need a dilatation and curettage and that had to be done in a hospital.

Barry tried to keep his face expressionless. 'I'm sorry, Julie, but you're having a miscarriage. We'll have to get you to the Royal.'

'All right,' she whispered. Then she moaned in pain.

Patients with an incomplete abortion, which was what Julie had, and who were in or close to being in shock, which she was, should not be moved until after they'd had a blood transfusion. To do so could kill the patient. Send for the 'flying squad'—the specially equipped ambulance staffed by professionals who would bring blood and transfuse the patient before transport—had been drummed into him. But sending for the squad would take too much time. Donal had said there was no telephone in the house.

Barry had to do something—and do it at once. He took a deep breath. He went to his bag and found what he needed: morphine to deaden the pain of the uterine contractions and ergometrine to make the uterus contract and to constrict the open blood vessels long enough, he hoped, for him to get Julie to the Royal before she bled again.

He charged two syringes and in quick succession stabbed the needles into her thigh. Within five minutes Julie's breathing had gone from short sharp gasps to a steady rhythm, and the flow of blood had eased to a trickle. 'Come in, Donal.' He heard footsteps.

'Is she dead?'

'No. I gave her morphine. It's knocked her out. I need a hand to get her to my car.'

'Doctor, has she lost—?'

'I'll explain later,' Barry snapped. The practical must take precedence over the emotional. He needed Donal now. 'Get a clean blanket.'

Donal scurried away and returned with a bundle in his arms.

'Right. Help me get it under her.'

With Donal's help, Barry manoeuvred Julie onto the blanket. Together, using the blanket as a makeshift stretcher, they carried her downstairs and into the back seat of the Volkswagen. 'Get in with her and put her head on your lap. I'll be back in a minute.' Barry collected his bag, chucked it in the passenger seat, climbed in the car and started the engine.

HE COULD REMEMBER little about driving to Belfast. He'd stopped the Volkswagen outside the entrance to the Casualty Department, and he'd charged in through the swinging doors. A couple of uniformed ambulance drivers were sitting in the foyer having a smoke and cups of tea.

'Can you give me a hand?'

One of the men looked up. 'We're on our break, so we are.'

Barry pictured O'Reilly at the front desk of the convalescent home in Bangor. He steeled himself and said, 'Listen, you. I'm Dr Laverty. I've a woman outside bleeding to death. Get a bloody stretcher . . . and get it now.'

The men jumped to their feet. 'Sorry, Doctor. Right away.'

Barry waited until the men returned with a wheeled stretcher. 'Out here.' He supervised as they loaded Julie onto the canvas sling and wheeled her straight into the nearest cubicle. He strode through the entry hall to the desk. Behind it, a nursing sister and a doctor were sitting chatting. He recognised the doctor. She'd been in his class.

'Ruth, can you come and see a patient of mine?'

She smiled at him. 'Hello, Barry. Sure. What's up?'

'Incomplete abortion. She's lost a lot of blood. A lot.'

Ruth was on her feet, issuing directions as she headed for the cubicle. 'Right. Sister . . .'

Sister rose. 'Nurse Corrigan, get the intravenous kit . . .' A blue-uniformed nurse hurried down the hall. Sister picked up the telephone. 'I'll send for the blood technician, get the gynae registrar.'

Barry let his shoulders sag. Now that Julie was in good hands he could feel some of the strain slip away. He followed the young doctor and stood watching silently as she rapidly checked Julie's pulse and blood pressure. It seemed like only seconds after Sister appeared pushing a small, wheeled trolley that saline was dripping from an intravenous set into Julie's arm.

'Right,' Ruth said, 'what's the history, Barry?'

He rapidly briefed his colleague.

'Sounds to me as if you're spot on, Barry.' She smiled. 'BP's coming up. The blood'll be cross-matched in no time, we'll get a couple of pints into her, quick D and C, and she'll be fine.'

'Thanks, Ruth.' He bent over Julie and saw her eyes flicker.

'Dr Laverty?'

'It's all right, Julie. You're in the hospital. You're going to be fine.'

'Thanks, Doctor. Is Donal all right?'

'I'm going to see him now, Julie. Tell him what's happening.'

She didn't reply. She'd drifted off to sleep.

Barry spoke to Ruth. 'I'll go and have a word with . . . her husband.' Donal would want to see Julie, but the visiting rules were strict. Immediate family only. 'Then I'll be off home for my supper.'

Ruth smiled. 'You ran her up here in your own car?'

Barry nodded.

'Devotion over and above the call of duty. There are plenty of GPs would have just phoned for the ambulance.'

'Not Dr O'Reilly,' Barry said, without thinking.

'PITY YOU MISSED the duck,' O'Reilly remarked. 'The sherry trifle was good too. I left you some of that.'

Barry looked longingly at the remains of the duck carcass and then at a tureen containing a few dried-up green peas. A Waterford crystal bowl held half a sherry trifle.

'Kinky says you dashed off with Donal.' O'Reilly looked apologetic. 'It would have been a shame for me to wait for you and let dinner get cold.'

Barry shrugged and said, 'Julie aborted. She's in the Royal.' He sat down. 'I had to run her and Donal up there.'

'Good for you. Mind you, it's what I'd expect.'

Barry made a tiny bow with his head.

'That's a shame about Julie,' O'Reilly said. 'But she'll have plenty more.'

'Donal reckons he's being punished for gypping Captain O'Brien-Kelly with the Arkle medallions.'

'Punished? Donal should get a medal of his own.'

Mrs Kincaid came in carrying an empty tray. Barry saw her glance at the remains of the duck.

'I've time to make you an omelette,' she said to him.

'Lovely, Kinky. Thank you.'

'Right.' She loaded the tray with the dirty dishes and left. 'I'll be back in a little minute.'

O'Reilly rose and went to the sideboard to pour himself a whiskey. 'The way Kinky's looking after you, Barry, I think she's adopted you.'

Barry smiled. If anyone in this house had adopted Barry, it was the big man. 'I could do worse,' he said. 'You know my folks are in Australia for a year, and I'm kind of an orphan until they get back?'

'I do.' O'Reilly took a pull of his Irish. 'It's a country I'd not mind seeing myself. I hear there are grand opportunities there for young doctors.'

'There are, so Dad says. There're opportunities in Ulster too.' Barry wished he could reassure O'Reilly that he'd made up his mind to stay.

'I'm glad to hear you say that.'

'Fingal, you just said Donal should get a medal. Why?'

'God,' said O'Reilly, 'moves in a mysterious way . . .' He refilled his glass. 'You know we've not been much use trying to find digs for Sonny until his place is ready or until he and Maggie are wed? It was just a shot in the dark when I asked His Lordship for help. Now I'd *like* to take the credit for what's happened since, but it has nothing to do with me.'

'What *has* happened?'

'You remember when the captain tried to touch me for a loan yesterday?

He'd some financial obligations to Honest Sammy Dolan? Well, it seems that our yeoman of the guard eventually found the marquis, who didn't have more than a few quid on him, so apparently Captain O'Brien Kelly was on the Belfast-to-Liverpool ferry last night.'

Barry laughed.

'The marquis would usually have settled any guest's gambling debts at once. Sorted it out with the offender later. The old boy has a very finely tuned sense of honour.'

'Then why didn't he do it?' Barry asked.

'Oh, he did, but not until after the captain had left. O'Brien-Kelly'll get a bill in the post from His Lordship,' said O'Reilly, 'but as the marquis told me on the phone this afternoon, he couldn't stand the man and was happy to see the back of him. And he would be delighted to let Sonny have the gate lodge. He'll even send down meals from the Big House.'

'Wonderful, Fingal.' Barry added, 'The Lord's not the only one round here to work in a mysterious way. If you hadn't encouraged Donal to go ahead with his crackpot scheme, and if you hadn't taken the trouble to ask the marquis if he could help, Sonny would still be in the home.'

O'Reilly grunted. 'Och, all's well that ends well. Sonny's pleased as Punch, and Maggie's like a cat with ten kittens.'

'Did you drop in to tell her?'

'Not at all. I stopped and took Maggie down with me when I went to collect him. It was worth the price of admission just to eavesdrop on them when I had them in the back of the Rover. Maggie's been planning the wedding. She may call her cat the General but the way she has things organised for next Saturday she could be Montgomery himself. She was worried about where to hold the reception after.'

'You haven't offered your garden again like you did for Seamus Galvin?'

'No. The marquis came down to the gate lodge to see Sonny settled in. When I left to run Maggie home, the pair of them were blethering away about some new Nabataean dig in Jordan, and land titles in Ireland under the Normans. But the important thing is that His Lordship promised they can have the hooley in his grounds.'

'That's great.'

'It's just a pity there won't be two weddings. I don't see Julie MacAteer being well enough to tie the knot with Donal for a week or two yet. I've wondered what a pretty girl like Julie sees in an eejit like Donal, but then there's no accounting for love.'

Barry could see the quizzical way O'Reilly was looking at him. 'You're right, Fingal. There's not. I know that.'

'Aha.' O'Reilly walked round the table and dropped a hand on Barry's shoulder. 'She's a gem that Patricia Spence of yours. I'm delighted.'

'Thanks, Fingal.'

The door opened, and Mrs Kincaid stood there in her coat. 'Now,' she said, setting a plate in front of Barry, 'there's your omelette. I need to run on or I'll be late for the Women's Union meeting at the church.'

O'Reilly asked, 'Will you be seeing Mrs Bishop, Kinky?'

'Aye, so.'

'I believe Dr Laverty asked you to have a word with her?'

Barry had mentioned his idea to Fingal.

'I will, so, and I've not forgotten. I'll see what she knows about Bertie and the lease for the Black Swan.' She turned to leave. 'Oh, and, Dr O'Reilly, somebody's left something for you on the front doorstep. It's a single, solitary Wellington boot.'

'IF THAT BLOODY DOG retrieves one more Wellie, I'll get him a muzzle,' O'Reilly grumbled. 'I was all over hell's high acre last night looking for the other half of the pair. I didn't find it until I was away up in the Ballybucklebo Hills.' He opened the surgery door, then hesitated. 'Tell you what; I'm tired, so I'll go and get the victims this morning. You do the work.'

'Fine.' Barry went into the surgery and sat on the swivel chair.

O'Reilly came in, pursued by Donal Donnelly. O'Reilly hopped up on the couch.

''Morning, Donal,' Barry said.

''Morning, sir.' He cradled his right hand in his left.

'How's Julie?'

'They were great at the Royal after you left, so they were. She had her operation, and she was sitting up with a wee cup of tea in her hand when I went home last night.' He managed a small smile.

'I'm sorry about the baby.'

'Aye, well. The lady doctor there told me you done everything right, sir, and likely the baby wasn't forming properly. Maybe it is for the best.'

'Maybe it is, Donal.'

'In fact, it's not Julie I've come about. I've buggered my finger.' Donal sat and stuck his right hand under Barry's nose. 'I gave it a ferocious wrench lifting a load of slates working at Sonny's.'

Barry could see the right middle finger was bent at the first joint, bruised and swollen. 'Can you move it at all?'

'No, sir.'

Barry took hold of the tip and tried to extend it.

Donal snatched his hand away. 'That hurts.'

'Sorry, Donal.' Barry was sure that the long tendon had been damaged. 'I'll have to splint it.' He went to fetch the instrument trolley.

'I'll get the water,' said O'Reilly.

'How long's it going to take to get better, Doctor?'

'You'll be in the splint for six weeks. It could be quite a while after that before it recovers completely.'

O'Reilly put the bowl of warm water on the trolley top.

'Six weeks?' Donal whistled. 'It's going to hold up getting Sonny's roof done. I'm no use. I can do nothing.'

'Don't you fret about that, Donal,' O'Reilly said. 'Seamus and Maureen and baby Fingal are off to California next week, so it'll get held up anyway. What *we* have to do is get the councillor to hire more men to finish the job.'

Donal sneered. 'Bertie Bishop's too bloody wrapped up making plans to get his hands on the Duck, so he is, to be bothered with a roof job.'

Barry was busy fashioning a tube from the plaster-of-Paris bandage.

'We,' said O'Reilly, 'will see about that, and anyway, Sonny has a place to stay now.'

'Aye. But it's still not going to get the roof done.' Donal's brows knitted together. 'I'll maybe have a word with a few of the lads. I seen an American movie once, and a whole bunch of country folks all got together and they had a fellah's barn up in no time flat.'

'You'd be saving Bishop money,' O'Reilly said.

'Bugger Bertie Bishop. It'd be for Sonny and Maggie.'

Barry slipped the plaster tube over the finger from the tip to the base.

Donal peered at the cast. 'Thing of beauty that, sir.'

'It should do the trick.' Barry felt the cast. 'It's drying nicely. Come in and see me tomorrow. I'll need to make sure the plaster's not too tight.'

'All right, sir.' Donal stood. 'I think I'll take my bike to Sonny's, tell Seamus I'll not be back to work and get him to come to the Duck with me tonight.' He grinned. 'I think Seamus could get most of the boys in the Ballybucklebo Highlanders Pipe Band to chip in for the roofing job.'

'You do that,' said O'Reilly.

'Right, sir, and thanks again, Dr Laverty.' Donal left.

O'Reilly shook his head. 'I'm amazed. Who'd have thought Donal Donnelly would be the soul of Christian charity?'

'Could he really organise a work party, Fingal?'

'I don't doubt it for one minute.' He walked to the door. 'And speaking of work parties . . . do you think we might get on with the morning's business?'

THE TELEPHONE was ringing in the hall, and Barry heard Mrs Kincaid answer. It had been another uneventful surgery. Lunch was over. O'Reilly was muttering under his breath about how if he had to eat one more salad . . .

Mrs Kincaid came in. 'Only one call again today, so. Mrs Finnegan rang, worried that Declan's taken a turn for the worse.'

'The man with Parkinson's disease and the French wife?' Barry asked.

'You remember them?'

'Of course.' Barry felt a tinge of pride in remembering the patient's name and not just the disease.

'That's them,' O'Reilly said. 'Is that her on the phone now?'

'No, she called earlier. It's Mrs Fotheringham, and she insists on speaking to you, Dr O'Reilly.'

'Oh Lord,' O'Reilly said. 'Right. I'll see to it.' He left.

Barry twisted in his chair and wondered what the woman could want. Certainly Dr O'Reilly had gone out when her own doctor wasn't available last Sunday, but Dr Bowman of the Kinnegar should be on duty today. And if Mrs Fotheringham had been sufficiently distraught to leave the practice because Barry had misdiagnosed her husband's cerebral haemorrhage, she'd hardly be wanting anything to do with it now, not since his death.

Minutes later O'Reilly returned. 'Bloody woman,' he said. 'She demands to know what killed her husband. I can't budge her. She's adamant.'

'But the results of the post-mortem aren't in yet.'

'I tried to explain that to her, but she's convinced you were responsible.' O'Reilly laid a hand on Barry's shoulder. 'She says if she doesn't get an answer soon, she'll have to be having a word with her lawyer.'

'What?' Barry heard his voice rise sharply. 'She's going to sue me?'

'She is if we don't get some answers.'

Being sued was every doctor's nightmare. It would utterly shatter the reputation Barry had been trying so hard to rebuild. He looked up into O'Reilly's craggy face.

'I know what you're thinking, son. If it goes to court, it won't matter if they find in your favour. Just being sued puts the mark of Cain on a physician. We'll have to hope to hell the post-mortem finds something.'

Barry's head drooped. He'd not told O'Reilly what Harry Sloan had said to him. He'd meant to when he'd come back from Belfast last Wednesday, but somehow he'd forgotten. 'So far nothing's shown up,' he said.

'What?'

'I had a word with a pathology registrar last week, an old acquaintance. He was at the initial examination and he told me that everything looked pretty normal. He said we'd have to wait for the microscopic examination of the tissues.'

'That could take a couple of weeks.'

'I know, but Harry, my friend, said he'd look at the slides himself. I hope to hear from him either today or tomorrow.'

O'Reilly paced to the far end of the dining room, then back again. 'Right.' He rubbed his hand across his face. 'Here's what we need to do . . .'

Barry waited, wondering what the hell anyone could do.

'You go and see Declan Finnegan. If he's worse, and he probably is, we'll have to get him up to see the neurosurgeons.

'I don't see what that's got to do with Mrs Fotheringham—'

'Listen, will you? If you think it's what he needs, go on up to the Royal, get hold of the head of neurosurgery, Professor Greer, tell him I sent you—we played rugby together—and ask him to see if he can get Declan in soon.'

'All right.'

'While you're doing that, I'll go and see Mrs Fotheringham and pour a bit of oil on her troubled waters, try to persuade her to hold hard before she goes trotting off to a lawyer.'

'Would you?'

'Of course I bloody would,' O'Reilly said. 'One thing I've learned, if a patient's really angry, the longer you keep them waiting the worse they get.

Maybe I can get her to understand there was no more bleeding in the major's head, and so whatever killed him wasn't because you were slow off the mark making that diagnosis.'

'Fingal, I hope you can get her to see reason.'

'I don't know if I can, but I'll try. The best defence is attack. Get some solid facts that prove it wasn't your fault.'

'I could go and see Harry when I'm up at the Royal.'

'Son, you're like Saul on the road to Damascus. You've just seen the light.'

10

Barry hurried along the Royal's main corridor, heading straight for Ward 21, the neurosurgery unit. His first priority was to arrange things for Declan Finnegan. Barry had called at the Finnegan house earlier. It had been apparent that the man's Parkinsonism had deteriorated badly; Declan needed to be seen by a specialist soon.

Barry stopped at the front desk of Ward 21. He didn't know the strikingly handsome, fiftyish, red-uniformed nurse who sat there. 'Good afternoon, Sister,' he said.

Her pepper-and-salt hair peeped out from under her fall, the huge, starched triangular white headpiece worn in the Royal only by those of 'staff nurse' rank or higher.

She smiled at him and he noticed the amber lights in her grey eyes. 'Can I help you?'

'Please. I'm Dr Laverty. I was wondering how I could get hold of Professor Greer. I'd like to talk to him about a patient with Parkinson's disease. Dr O'Reilly sent me.'

'Dr O'Reilly? Fingal Flahertie O'Reilly?'

'Yes. He's my boss.'

'Good God! How is the oul' reprobate?' Her accent was pure Dublin.

'He's fine. You know him?'

'I used to,' she said. 'I knew him when I was a student nurse in Dublin before the war and he was at Trinity College. He wasn't a half bad-looking

lad when him and Professor Greer played rugby together.' There was definitely something wistful in her voice. 'And you want to see the prof?'

'Please.'

She looked at the watch pinned to her apron. 'He'll be in his office dictat-
ing consultation notes.' She rose. 'I'll see if he can give you a few minutes.'

Barry waited until she returned.

'You're in luck. I'll show you the way.' She led him along a short corridor, and then held open the door to a small office.

'Thank you, Sister,' Barry said.

'Come in, Laverty.' Professor Greer rose from in front of a paper-strewn
desk. His coppery eyebrows matched his shock of shaggy red hair. He
offered his hand. His grip was firm but gentle. 'Here,' he pulled a chair
closer to the desk. 'Have a pew.'

'Thank you, sir.'

'What can I do for you, Laverty?'

'Dr O'Reilly wondered if you could help us with a patient?'

The professor laughed. 'Another one? I did a cerebral artery aneurysm
for the pair of you last month.'

'I know,' Barry said. 'He died last Sunday.'

'Did he, by God?' Greer hunched forward and looked into Barry's face.
'Another bleed?' He sounded concerned.

Barry shook his head. 'The early PM results didn't show that. They
haven't shown anything. We're waiting for the histology report.'

'I'm glad it wasn't the surgery.' He sat back in his chair. 'Anyway, it must
be someone else you've come about.'

'We've a man, Declan Finnegan, with very severe Parkinson's. He and
his wife can't cope any more. Dr O'Reilly was wondering if you could see
Finnegan with a view to surgery?'

'How old is he?'

'Sixty-four.'

'No history of encephalitis?'

'Not that I know of, sir.'

'Is he incontinent?'

'I'm afraid so.'

'Probably due to hypertension or atherosclerosis.' The professor consulted a large diary. 'Give me his name and address.' Barry did and Greer

scribbled in his ledger. 'Can you get him up here on Wednesday at six? I'll fit him in as an extra after the clinic. There might be something we can do.'

'That's very kind of you, sir.'

'It goes with the job, but I'm sure being a GP, you know that? Unless Fingal's changed, he'll be working the legs off you.'

Barry had to smile. 'He is.'

The professor leaned forward. 'You're enjoying it?'

'I am, but—'

'But you still get upset when you lose a patient? It's not your fault, lad.'

Barry sighed, looked into the older man's eyes and saw understanding. 'This one might have been. I missed the diagnosis initially. Perhaps if we'd got him here sooner?'

'I doubt it. I remember the case. Small aneurysm. Small bleed. It was easy enough to repair, and the results were very good.'

Barry blurted out, 'His wife's talking about suing me.'

'Bloody lawyers.'

'Dr O'Reilly's gone to see the man's wife. See if he can get her to wait until we know for sure what killed her husband.'

'Good. If anyone can talk her out of going ahead, it's Fingal O'Reilly. And with a bit of luck the histology results'll let you off the hook.'

'I hope so.'

'If they don't, you can call on me as an expert witness.'

'Thank you, sir.'

'Take my advice . . .' The man grinned. 'Hope for the best but be prepared for the worst. And if the worst does come . . .' He walked to one wall and indicated a framed photograph of a group of young men in muddy boots, shorts and green shirts with shamrocks on the right breast pockets. 'Irish side, 1939, at Lansdowne Road in Dublin. We beat Scotland twelve to three. Look.' He pointed.

In the middle of the first rank, two youngsters stood smiling at the camera. One had flaming ginger hair; the other was obviously O'Reilly. Sister had been right. He'd not been a bad-looking lad.

'You'll have the backing of the two best second-row forwards ever to come out of Ireland.' Greer opened the door. 'I'd like to chat longer, but . . .' He nodded to a Dictaphone. 'Bloody paperwork.'

'I understand, and thanks for seeing me, sir.'

'Everything go all right?' Sister asked from behind her desk.

'Fine.'

'Good and . . . Dr Laverty? When you see Fingal Flahertie O'Reilly, tell him Caitlin O'Hallorhan said "hello".'

'I'll do that.' Barry left the ward feeling a bit more cheerful after his chat.

After letting Mandy know he'd not need an appointment for Mrs Bishop now that he had her myasthenia under control, Barry left the neurosciences department and went down the main corridor to the pathology department. He had to find Harry Sloan.

THE DEPARTMENT of pathology was lodged in the Clinical Sciences Building. Barry was struck by how quiet the place was after the bustle of the clinical areas of the hospital. He pushed through the glass doors. On his right the door to an office stood open. Three secretaries sat at three desks.

'Yes?' A small, bespectacled woman looked over her typewriter at him.

'I'm looking for Dr Sloan. I'm Dr Laverty.'

'Harry's down the hall. Third on your left.'

'Thank you.'

He left and walked along the linoleum. Barry knocked and opened the door. Harry Sloan sat on a swivel chair in front of a flat workbench. He lifted his head from the eyepieces of a binocular microscope, rubbed his eyes and said, 'Hiya, Barry. You want that aneurysm's histology results, don't you?' He frowned. 'I'm dead sorry, so I am. I've not had a minute. I did try, but two of the technicians have flu. I don't even know if the aneurysm's slides are made yet.'

Barry tried not to let his disappointment show.

'It's important, isn't it?'

'When I asked you about it last week, it was mostly for my own satisfaction. But I just heard today that if I can't explain why her husband died, the widow's going to sue me.'

'That's desperate. I'll see what I can do.' Harry picked up a telephone, dialled and said to Barry, 'I'll have a wee word with the head tech.'

Barry listened as Harry spoke.

'Hello? Hughey? It's me, Dr Sloan. You remember the coroner's PM? The one who'd had a subarachnoid . . .? Aye . . . Look, I need the cardiac slides as quick as you can get 'em . . . I'll hang on.' He shrugged at Barry.

'Hello. What do you mean they're still not done? I understand. Hughey, I need a wee favour. A mate of mine could have a lawyer breathing down his neck unless I can get some answers for him . . . Right . . . Right . . . I owe you a pint.' Harry hung up and said to Barry, 'He says he'll get on it right away, but it'll take a day or two.'

'Thanks, Harry.' Barry turned to leave. 'I don't want to put you under more pressure but—'

'No bloody buts. I'm glad it's not me facing a lawyer.' He gave a half-smile. 'But then my customers don't have the get-up-and-go to sue anyone any more.' He bent back to his microscope. 'I'll be in touch the minute I have anything. I've still your phone number.'

Barry left. He'd done all O'Reilly had asked him to do at the Royal, but he remembered he was supposed to give Patricia a call to wish her luck for the next day. Call be damned. He'd drop in to see her.

A STEADY DRIZZLE blackened the tarmac of the Esplanade. Barry turned up the collar of his jacket, hurried across to Number 9 and rang the bell.

'Barry?' Patricia came to the door. 'Come in out of that. You're soaking.'

He followed her upstairs and through the doorway of Flat 4. 'Sorry to barge in like this. I just wanted to wish you good luck for tomorrow.' Her small dining table was strewn with open engineering texts.

'Sit down,' she said.

He sat on the sofa. 'Big day tomorrow. Have you got pre-exam wobblies?'

She nodded. 'I thought I could do some last-minute cramming today, but I can't concentrate.'

He patted the sofa. 'Come and sit down.'

She sat beside him and took his hand.

He kissed her gently. 'Do you know what "fey" means?'

She nodded. 'The gift. The second sight.' She looked into his eyes. 'Surely you don't believe in it? You're a scientist.'

'I honestly don't know. But I have the weirdest feeling that you're going to ace the thing.' He had had no such feeling, but it was worth telling her to see the laugh lines deepen at the corners of her eyes.

'I don't know whether to believe you or not.' But she kissed him. 'Thanks for saying it anyway.' She rose. 'Would you like to stay for a while? I was going to make scrambled eggs.'

He'd like nothing better, but he'd not arranged with O'Reilly to be away from the practice for any longer than it would take to run up to the Royal. Barry got to his feet. 'I'd love to, but . . .'

She sighed. 'But duty calls . . . and your patients.' She took his hand and said, her voice low, 'It's one of the things I love about you, Barry Laverty. I think I'd be lucky to be one of your patients.'

Should he tell her he might be facing a lawsuit? No. He wished she could lend him some comfort but this was not the time to burden her with his troubles. 'I love you, Patricia,' he said. He kissed her. 'Now,' he said, 'I'll expect to hear from you tomorrow night.'

'I'll phone.'

'And I want to hear the minute you get the results.'

She pursed her lips. 'I promise.'

'Good.' He headed for the door. 'Are you going home to Newry, or will you still be here on Saturday?'

'I'll be here.'

'Good, because I'd like you to come with me to a wedding. Two lovely old folks.'

'I'd like that.'

'Great.' He opened the door. 'I'll be thinking of you tomorrow.'

THE KITCHEN WAS WARM after the rawness of the day outside. Barry shifted the bag he was carrying and closed the door behind him. The smell of brandy was overpowering. Mrs Kincaid stood at the counter, vigorously stirring the contents of a bowl that she held under one arm. The bowl's contents were grey, glutinous-looking and studded with dark nuggets. He noticed a half-empty bottle of brandy close by.

'You're back, so,' she said.

'I am.' He moved closer and peered into the bowl. 'What's that, Kinky?'

'It's this year's Christmas cake,' she said. 'I like to get it done a few months ahead so it's got time to mature. Here.' She held out the bowl and gave him the wooden spoon. 'Give it a stir for luck.'

Barry plunged the spoon into the mixture, but it was like stirring half-set cement. He handed the bowl back. 'Is Dr O'Reilly in?'

'He is, and he's waiting for you.'

'Right.' He went upstairs to the lounge. He could only hope that O'Reilly had been more successful this afternoon with Mrs Fotheringham than he had been with Harry Sloan. He tucked his bag under one arm and went into the lounge.

O'Reilly stood in front of the fireplace, holding a glass of whiskey. He stared down at Lady Macbeth, who sat on the carpet at his feet. He bent and scratched the cat's head. She rose, arched her back and started to weave back and forth, thrusting her side against the back of O'Reilly's now motionless hand. He grinned up at Barry. 'I call this "going on autostroke".'

Barry could hear the animal purring.

O'Reilly straightened up and waved at the sideboard. 'Help yourself; then come and sit down.' He dumped himself in an armchair.

Barry set his bag on the nearest chair, poured himself a sherry and took the other armchair. 'I saw Harry Sloan. He still hasn't got any results. He's going to try to hurry things up, but it'll still take a day or two. He'll phone.'

O'Reilly looked directly at Barry. 'Will he deliver?'

'I think so.'

'He'd better.' O'Reilly rose. 'I saw the widow this afternoon.'

Barry felt his hand tighten round the stem of his glass.

'I've not seen such naked anger for a very long time.' O'Reilly went to lean against the mantel. 'It's normal, of course. When people lose somebody dear, they want to lash out. I spent an hour with her. I *think* I managed to calm her down a bit, get her to understand why she was so mad at you. But I still couldn't make her understand that suing you won't bring the major back, won't make her feel any better if she wins the case.'

'Could she? Win, I mean.'

O'Reilly shrugged. 'Who can predict what'll happen in a court of law? I did get her to agree that if we can give her a satisfactory explanation, she'll drop it. But she has an appointment with her solicitor next Monday.'

'Monday?' Barry stared up into O'Reilly's face.

O'Reilly nodded. 'I'm pretty sure she'll wait until then, but there'll be no stopping her if we haven't come up with some results by the weekend.' He motioned to Barry's sherry and said, 'Get that into you, son.'

'Thanks, Fingal,' Barry said quietly.

'All right,' O'Reilly said, 'enough despondency. What else did you do?'

Barry finished his sherry and went to refill his glass. 'I saw your friend Professor Greer. He'll see Declan Finnegan on Wednesday.'

'That's Charley. Did you arrange for the ambulance to come for Declan?'

'Not yet, but I will. Your friend talked to me about Major Fotheringham—he did the major's surgery. When I told him what was happening, he said if I needed an expert witness, he'd be happy to testify.'

'With a bit of luck it won't come to that, but if it does it'll be good to have Charley in our corner. He's a bloody tough fighter.'

'He showed me your photograph . . . the Irish rugby team.'

O'Reilly laughed. 'Boxing, rugby . . . it's a bloody miracle I ever qualified from Trinity.'

Barry remembered the look in the eyes of the neurosurgery ward sister when he'd mentioned he worked with a Dr O'Reilly. 'I met someone else from your university days, Fingal.'

'And who would that be?'

'A ward sister. Caitlin O'Hallorhan.'

O'Reilly's glass stopped halfway to his lips. 'Who?'

'Caitlin O'Hallorhan. She said to give you her regards.'

'I'll be damned. Kitty? I haven't seen her for years.' Barry heard a softness in O'Reilly's voice. 'I wonder what she's been up to all these years.'

'Why not give her a call?'

O'Reilly harrumphed and took a great swallow of whiskey. 'Because I'm much too busy,' he growled. 'Never mind the practice, I've still to try to sort out Bertie Bishop and the Duck. We've still to see Mrs Bishop and make sure your treatment's working, and Helen's eczema's not getting any better. We'll be running around for the rest of the week, and the first chance we'll get for a bit of time off is next Saturday for Maggie and Sonny's wedding.'

'Oh.'

'I told you. This isn't a Butlins Holiday Camp.'

'I know. It's just . . . Patricia writes her exams tomorrow. I told her she could phone me if she was worried, but I'd rather go and see her if I can.'

O'Reilly sighed. 'All right. When you need time off, ask.'

'Thanks, Fingal.'

'Just don't ask for too much . . . because after all these years running this shop on my own, I've got used to having you about the place, Dr Laverty.'

Barry heard O'Reilly's words, looked up and saw the affection in the big man's eyes. He felt a tiny inner warmth and knew it wasn't coming from his second glass of sherry.

11

'Come on, Barry. Up.' Someone was shaking his shoulder. O'Reilly threw the attic bedroom curtains open and then stamped out.

Barry climbed out of bed, stumbled along to the bathroom, completed his ablutions and dressed hurriedly.

He trotted down to the dining room.

O'Reilly was already tucking into his breakfast. 'Help yourself.' He waved his fork to a silver chafing dish on the sideboard. 'And get a move on.'

Barry lifted the lid, blinked through the cloud of steam, shoved a brace of kippers on a plate and took his seat.

'Here.' O'Reilly pushed a cup of tea along the table. 'Bad night?'

Barry nodded. Then he accepted the tea and put in some milk.

'I'm not surprised. Being sued hits doctors hellishly hard,' O'Reilly observed, helping himself to a piece of toast. 'All of us went into medicine because we need folks to think well of us. Even me.'

O'Reilly never before had confessed any of his own feelings. 'Have you ever been sued, Fingal?'

'Me?' O'Reilly reached for the marmalade. 'No, I haven't. And I'll be damned if I'll let it happen to you.'

'I don't see how you can prevent it.'

'*I* bloody well do. One . . .' He stabbed at Barry with the toast. 'Your mate may well come up with some answers.'

It was suddenly clear to Barry that when O'Reilly had refused to sign the death certificate for Major Fotheringham, thus forcing the need for a post-mortem, he had somehow foreseen what might happen. O'Reilly had immediately taken precautions to try to protect Barry—and, of course, the reputation of his own practice.

'Two . . .' O'Reilly took a bite out of his toast. 'If I have to, I'll go and see the widow again. Who knows? I sowed the seeds yesterday. Maybe when they've had time to germinate she'll have second thoughts about going to the law.'

'If you believe it would help.' Barry knew he sounded doubtful.

'I'll think on it,' said O'Reilly. He took another mouthful of toast. 'Where was I? . . . Aye, right. And three, I'll be buggered if I'll let you stew over this until we know for certain what's going to happen.'

'It might be easier said than done.'

'There's only one cure, and that's to keep busy working at something you love. I'm going to keep you so damn busy until we hear the histology results that you'll not have time to wonder what day of the week it is.'

'All right,' Barry said. 'I'll go along with that.'

'Good,' said O'Reilly. He polished off the last of his toast and rose.

'Thanks, Fingal.'

O'Reilly said, 'The only thanks I want is for you to get that cup of tea and those kippers into you as quick as you can. In case you've forgotten, it's time to start morning surgery.'

'YOU'RE ON THE HELM this morning.' O'Reilly strode out through the surgery door.

He came back, pursued by Donal Donnelly.

''Morning, Donal. Let's have a look.'

Donal proffered his hand. Barry could see that the finger cast was already grubby, but the exposed fingertip was pink. The cast wasn't too tight. 'Looks grand to me, Donal.' Barry turned to the desk and scribbled on a form. 'The cast'll need to come off in six weeks.' He handed Donal the note. 'There you are. That's a certificate for the unemployment people. I imagine you could use the money now you're not working.'

'Thank you, sir, but I am working.'

'What at?' O'Reilly asked.

'Well, not for any money, sir.' Donal tucked the paper into a pocket. 'Seamus and me've got a bunch of the boys lined up to come round to Sonny's place in the evenings after their work. They want me to be gaffer, so they do. Supervise, like.'

'Good for you, Donal,' Barry said.

'Well, Sonny's a decent oul' codger. And all I have to do is sit on my backside and give orders. I reckon one more week and the place'll be as good as new. You'll not say nothing to Sonny, will you, Doctors? We'd like for it to be a surprise.'

'You've our word on it, Donal,' O'Reilly said.

''Scuse me, sir. There's just one other wee thing.'

'Go ahead.'

'Julie's on the mend. She reckons if you hadn't been so quick off the mark she could've died. And she's heard a wheen of rumours that you don't know your stuff . . .' Donal stuck his cast under Barry's nose. 'Her and me knows better, and she says for me to tell you we're lucky to have the pair of you here, so we are.'

It was quite a speech for Donal. Barry felt warmth in his cheeks. 'Thank you,' he said, 'but it's my pleasure.'

'Right,' said Donal. 'I'll be off.' He made for the door. 'See you Saturday.'

'PHEW,' SAID O'REILLY, when the last patient left what had been a crammed surgery. Barry was pleased that he'd seen the three stable boys Fergus Finnegan had said would be coming in.

O'Reilly stood and stretched. 'Right,' he said, heading for the dining room. 'Food.'

Kinky was waiting. 'You're late for your lunches, Doctors,' she said, setting a plate in front of Barry and moving to give O'Reilly his. 'But it's only a cold quiche lorraine, so it's not spoilt.'

Barry glanced at O'Reilly, who took a small mouthful and broke into a wide grin. 'That's delicious, Kinky.'

'Would it be otherwise?' she asked, smiling.

'You're a marvel, Mrs Kincaid,' Barry added.

'I'm no such thing, so.' But her smile widened. 'Well,' she said, 'maybe at the cooking . . .' Barry was about to agree when she added, 'I've not done so well with Mrs Bishop.'

'Oh?' said O'Reilly in mid-chew.

'I tried to find out about the lease of the Black Swan, but I don't think there's much that she really knows.'

'So we're no further on?' O'Reilly said.

'Well, maybe a bit, but I can't make head nor tail of it. He's told her that he'll get the Duck as long as nobody finds out about the stream, and she's not to mention it to anybody.'

'Stream?' Barry asked. 'What stream?'

Kinky shook her head. 'She didn't know.'

'Nor me,' said O'Reilly, 'but I've a half-notion who might. Do you have the afternoon's list?'

'I do.' Kinky pulled a sheet of paper from her apron pocket.

O'Reilly scanned it rapidly. 'Not too bad,' he said. 'We'll need to nip in and tell Declan Finnegan about his appointment, and I'd like to finish up in the gate lodge.'

'To make sure Sonny's all right?'

'Something like that,' O'Reilly said noncommittally. He added, 'And we need to get back here by teatime. You've to phone your Miss Spence.'

Dear Lord. Today was the day of Patricia's examinations. He'd been so wrapped up in his own woes it had slipped his mind.

BARRY SAT in the passenger's seat as O'Reilly hurled the Rover along the Bangor-to-Belfast road. They had given a relieved Mrs Finnegan the news that her husband, Declan, would be seen by the nerve specialist tomorrow. An ambulance would collect them both and take them into town.

O'Reilly ignored yet another cyclist and slammed the big car round a sharp curve with two wheels on the grass verge.

'Right,' said O'Reilly, slowing down. 'Here we are.' He parked outside the gate lodge of the marquis's estate.

Barry stepped out onto the gravel. The high ornate wrought-iron gates were open, and at the head of a long drive Barry could see the Georgian portico of the Big House. A half-timbered shooting brake was parked outside the lodge. He assumed it would belong to the groundsman.

O'Reilly hammered on the door at the lodge. 'Anybody home?'

The door was opened by the marquis himself. Dark brown eyes smiled from under the iron-grey hair. 'Ah, O'Reilly and young Laverty. You've driven over to see Sonny? Come in.'

Barry followed the two men along a short, parquet-floored hall, through an open doorway into a small, tidy sitting room.

Sonny, dressed in a woollen cardigan over a white shirt and neatly creased black trousers, was sitting on an armchair but rose to greet O'Reilly. A brass-topped table stood in front of the chair. The chessboard on the table bore the irregularly placed chessmen of a game in progress.

'Dr O'Reilly,' Sonny said. 'What a pleasant surprise.'

'Sit you down, Sonny.' O'Reilly took Sonny's pulse.

Barry could see that Sonny's eyes were bright and he had no difficulty breathing, although there was a hint of grey above his cheekbones. Even before he'd been taken seriously ill, the man had suffered from a minor degree of chronic heart failure but O'Reilly had it well controlled.

'Your ticker's going away like a well-tuned steam engine, Sonny,' O'Reilly said. 'Do you still have the heart pills we gave you?'

'Yes, Doctor.'

'Keep on taking them. You've a big day coming on Saturday.' He turned to the marquis. 'Will you be arranging for Sonny to get to the church, sir?'

The marquis smiled. 'I'm the best man. I'll run him there in the Rolls.'

Sonny coughed. 'Could I ask you for a favour, Dr O'Reilly? Maggie's too shy to ask you herself.'

'Fire away.'

'Her da's dead and she wants everything done properly. She wanted me to ask you . . . would you walk her up the aisle and give her away?'

'Me?' O'Reilly's grin was vast. 'I'd be delighted.' He glanced sideways at Barry, who heard the wicked edge to his senior colleague's voice when he asked, 'Would she like Dr Laverty here to be her pageboy?'

Sonny and the marquis joined O'Reilly's laughter.

'I think,' said the marquis, 'all this talk of weddings calls for a glass of sherry.' He moved to the sideboard. 'Please be seated, gentlemen.'

'I don't suppose you'd have a drop of John Jameson's, Your Lordship?' O'Reilly asked, moving the table and the chess set aside and lowering himself onto a small sofa.

'Naturally, Fingal, and is it all right for Sonny to have something?'

'Indeed,' said O'Reilly, accepting his glass but refusing the marquis's offer of water. Barry sat beside O'Reilly and took his sherry.

The marquis remained standing. 'To the happy couple.' He raised his drink.

'That's a grand drop,' said O'Reilly, swallowing half the whiskey in the glass. 'Better than the stuff Willy pours at the Duck.'

The marquis said, 'The Duck? I've been hearing rumours about the Black Swan. Something about a takeover bid by that man Bishop.'

O'Reilly nodded. 'The lease runs out soon, and Bertie Bishop is the landlord. He's refusing to renew and wants to turn the old Duck into a tourist trap. Rip out the old stuff and stick in chrome and plastic.'

'Good Lord. That's horrible. Can't we stop him?'

'I've tried,' O'Reilly said, 'but he'll not listen to reason. He owns the property the Duck's built on.'

Barry heard Sonny clear his throat. 'Excuse me, Your Lordship. You remember, sir, we were discussing Norman land titles in Ireland?'

'I do indeed.'

Sonny nodded. 'If I recall correctly, you told me that when John de Courcy conquered Ulster for Henry the Second, your ancestor was granted all the rights to the townland of Ballybucklebo.'

'True. But we've had to sell off a great deal. That's how the land the Duck was built on was lost ninety-nine years ago.' He frowned. 'Somehow Bishop's been able to buy the title from the descendants of the original purchasers. He can do whatever he likes when it comes to renewing or not renewing Willy Dunleavy's lease.'

O'Reilly fiddled with one of the chess pieces. 'Mrs Kincaid says Mrs Bishop told her that Bertie's keeping mum about something to do with a stream.'

'Is he, by Jove?' The marquis began to smile. 'A stream?'

Sonny stood, almost spilling his sherry. 'I'll bet your family didn't sell the salmon rights, sir.'

'Indeed not. That would have been unthinkable.'

'And I know,' said Sonny, 'that a small branch of the Bucklebo River had to be roofed over in a culvert because it flowed, indeed still flows, under the crossroads and . . .'

'Under the Duck? Hah.' O'Reilly sank the rest of his whiskey in one swallow. 'And the fish still use it to come inland and spawn?'

'Oh, yes,' said Sonny.

'I'm sorry,' Barry said, 'but I don't understand.'

'It means, Dr Laverty,' the marquis said levelly, 'that when my forebears sold the property—the property Bishop now owns—the deed would carry a codicil that no structural alterations could be made to any buildings there if they might interfere with the salmon run. At least not without our family's permission.'

'So Councillor Bishop can't go ahead with his plans for the Duck unless you allow him to, Your Lordship?'

'I'm sure gutting the place would qualify as structural alterations. But I suppose he could get his lawyer to challenge me on that point.'

'Would you fight him, Your Lordship?' O'Reilly asked.

'Of course I'd *like* to, but the legal costs would be enormous.'

O'Reilly glanced back at the marquis. 'But legally, *legally*, you could threaten to stop him? And Bishop's astute enough to work out for himself how much it would cost him to fight. He'd be crippled financially.'

'You're right. All I need to do is *threaten* to go to court.' The marquis's grin was almost as broad as O'Reilly's. 'Here,' he said, stretching out his hand, 'your glass is empty. Let me refill it.'

O'Reilly shook his head. 'No, thank you, sir. Dr Laverty and I have to drop in at the Duck on our way home . . . have a word with Willy. And I'd not be surprised if he'll want us to have a wee half-un to help him celebrate.'

THE DUCK'S BATWING DOORS creaked shut behind Barry. There was none of the usual hum of conversation. He saw two figures standing at the bar: Archie Auchinleck and a tall, suntanned young man in a khaki uniform. Barry guessed the soldier was Archie's son.

''Evening, Doctors,' Willy said. 'What'll it . . .?'

'Whiskey,' O'Reilly called. 'And, Barry?'

'Sherry, please.'

Barry went to the nearest table and waited as O'Reilly strode to the bar. ''Evening, Archie. 'Evening, Rory. Home on leave? Nice to see you.'

'I got home last night. It's great to be back, Doc,' Rory said. He smiled and lifted his straight pint glass of Guinness. 'You can't get a drop like this in Cyprus.'

O'Reilly said to Archie, 'Willy, give young Rory and his da a pint on me.'

'Thanks a lot, Dr O'Reilly,' Archie said.

O'Reilly ignored the thanks. 'How's the back, Archie?'

Barry saw the milkman's face split into a great smile. 'Right as rain. Them pills was cracker, so they were.'

'Good,' said O'Reilly, with a glance at Barry. 'And I'm sure it doesn't hurt to have your young fellah home for a while either.'

He's at it again, Barry thought. The man's never really off duty.

A glass of whiskey and a schooner of sherry were set on the bar. O'Reilly paid and took his change. 'Business still slack, Willy?'

'It picked up a wee bit in the last day or so,' Willy said, 'and come nine o'clock the place'll be bustin'. The Rooftop Rangers Regiment'll be in.'

'Who?'

Willy smiled. 'That's what I call all the lads from the Highlanders who go straight to Sonny's after work. Donal Donnelly has them hard at it, and not just the bandsmen. Just about every able-bodied man in the village wanted to help when the word got out. Donal says it's the village's wedding present to Sonny and Maggie, and he wants for it to be a surprise.'

'Good for them,' said O'Reilly, picking up his glass.

'Aye,' said Willy, 'and do you know something else, sir?'

Willy lowered his voice, and although Barry strained he couldn't make out what was being said.

'Bloody marvellous!' O'Reilly roared. He downed his whiskey and put the empty glass on the table. 'Willy. There's a hole in this glass. It's empty.'

'Sorry, Doc. Will I . . .?'

'Of course you will; then bring it to the table and you come over and sit with us. Dr Laverty and I have something to tell you.'

He ambled over to the table and gave Barry his sherry. 'Here. Get that into you.' O'Reilly hauled out a chair and sat.

'Cheers.' Barry sipped.

O'Reilly hunched forward. 'You'll never believe what Willy just told me. Not only are the lads doing their damnedest to finish the repairs at Sonny's by Saturday night, but Sonny's got no furniture . . .'

'A man who lived in his car hardly would have, would he?'

'Not so much as a footstool. So Seamus and Maureen Galvin have a table and a clatter of cutlery they're not taking to America. Mr Coffin, the undertaker, has half a dozen chairs. This one has sheets, that one has a bed, the other one has pots and pans. The plan is to have Sonny's place ready to live in by the time the wedding's over.'

'That's fantastic.'

'Aye,' said O'Reilly. 'Everyone knows that the pair of them *could* squeeze into Maggie's cottage at a pinch, but it's too small for two people, five dogs and Maggie's cat. When Sonny proposed to Maggie years ago, they planned to move into his place, and they would have but for the row with Bertie Bishop about the roof.'

'And the roof's getting fixed now.'

'It's more than that,' O'Reilly said seriously. 'The whole place's boiling about Bishop's takeover plans for the Duck, and they know he wasn't overexerting himself to get the roof job done. I think it's the village's way of telling Bertie Bishop that they don't need him and—'

'Sorry to interrupt, sirs.' Willy handed O'Reilly a full glass. 'You said I was to join you?'

'Sit down, Willy.' O'Reilly pulled his legs out of the way.

'It's a drop of port, sir,' Willy said, nodding at his own glass. '*Slàinte.*'

'*Slàinte mHath.*' O'Reilly sipped, then said, 'Willy, that's Black Bush . . .'

Barry knew it was the best whiskey produced by the Bushmills distillery in County Antrim.

'I'm finishing up my stock,' Willy said. 'I have to be out of here when the lease is up.'

'Do you now?' said O'Reilly. 'That's what Dr Laverty and I wanted to talk to you about, Willy.'

Willy sat rigidly. 'Have you got Bishop to change his mind?'

'No,' said O'Reilly, 'not yet. But . . .'

O'Reilly explained the details of the stream under the pub, and most importantly, that His Lordship would make damn sure the Duck wasn't mucked about with by Bertie Bishop.

'I don't know what to say.' Willy's eyes were wide.

'Ah,' said O'Reilly, 'that's exactly what I want you to do. Say nothing to *anybody.*'

Willy nodded.

'You see,' O'Reilly continued, 'if you don't mind, I think I should be the bearer of the glad tidings to the worthy councillor, and I don't want him to get a whisper of what's in store.'

'I'll houl' my tongue, Doctor, but there is one wee thing.'

'What?'

'Can I tell my Mary? You see, Mary's having a godawful time with that Miss Moloney over at the dress shop. If I can be sure . . . You are absolutely certain, sir, that we'll be able to stay on? I can give her a full-time job and she can get away to hell out of that place.'

'Willy, nothing's *sure* in this life except death and taxes, but the marquis says he'll fight Bishop to the extent of his resources.'

True, Barry thought, but those resources weren't limitless. O'Reilly was gambling on Bishop's being frightened off. But what if he wasn't?

O'Reilly glanced at Barry. 'Willy, you go ahead and tell Mary.'

Willy stood, sank his glass of port in one swallow and said, 'Get those into you, Doctors. There's more coming.' He headed for the bar.

'We shouldn't really be doing this, Fingal,' Barry said. It wasn't having another drink he was thinking about.

'I,' said O'Reilly, who by his scowl had followed Barry's line of reasoning perfectly, 'could not disagree with your diagnosis more, Dr Laverty. We bloody well should. And we're going to drink to it and to the good ship Ballybucklebo and all who sail in her. She's a grand wee place.' He finished his drink. 'I for one wouldn't want to be anywhere else on God's green earth.'

Barry hesitated. Then he said, very seriously, 'You know, Fingal, I could drink to that myself.'

'Right,' said O'Reilly, 'but it will be the last one. Kinky'll read us the riot act if we're late. And you,' he said to Barry, 'have to phone your Patricia.'

IN THE KITCHEN, Kinky stood wiping flour from a pastry board. O'Reilly was nowhere to be seen.

Barry sniffed. 'What's that you're cooking, Kinky?'

She smiled. ''Tis a beef stew with suet dumplings.'

'Lovely,' Barry said. Then he asked, 'Kinky, have there been any phone calls for me?'

'Not the one.'

It was six fifteen now so he could forget about hearing from Harry Sloan.

'Were you expecting to hear from somebody?' Kinky looked him straight in the eye. 'You will hear,' she said quietly, 'and you'll hear exactly what you want to hear. I don't know what that is, but it'll not be for a day or two yet.'

'How do you know, Kinky?'

She smiled. 'I can't tell you that. I just do. Now, I've work to do so trot along and get ready for your supper like a good lad.'

Barry wondered as he climbed the stairs what the blazes Kinky had meant. That Major Fotheringham's post-mortem had turned up the needle in the haystack? That his future was assured in Ballybucklebo?

He washed his hands and headed downstairs into the hall.

O'Reilly was talking on the telephone.

'. . . Right. I'll pick you up at ten thirty on Saturday. Bye.' He replaced the receiver with a loud *ting*, smiled broadly, turned and saw Barry. 'None of your business,' he said.

Barry held up both hands. 'I wasn't going to ask.'

'Good,' said O'Reilly. He nodded at the receiver. 'Your turn.'

'Thanks, Fingal.' Barry lifted the receiver, dialled and waited. 'Hello. Patricia?'

'Barry?'

He thought she sounded tired. 'How did it go?'

She sighed. 'It was awful. I told you that I hate architectural drawing. Two of the six questions involved drawing up plans. I can't have won the scholarship.'

He thought she sounded close to tears. 'Patricia, listen. I'm an expert in sitting exams. I'll bet you're going through exactly what I did, and what all my friends did. If we hadn't learned much about the subject, we were always sure we'd passed. We were too ignorant to know how much we *didn't* know. Those were the exams some of us failed. Once in a while some of us really did have a firm grip on the subject.' He had to smile. In his own case and in Jack Mills's, that hadn't been too often. 'Immediately after those tests we were convinced we'd failed because we were acutely aware that no matter how much we knew, there was always a hell of a lot more we should have known. But that didn't mean we hadn't done well.'

'Honestly?'

'Of course. I'll bet you're doing the same thing. I'll bet you've aced it.'

He heard her sigh. 'I'm not so sure.'

'Cheer up. Even if you're right'—he glanced around to be sure he couldn't be overheard—'I'll still love you . . . darling.'

'I know and . . . I love you, Barry. I'd like to see you soon, but I can't. Dad and Mum think I should be home in Newry now to wait for the results.'

Damnation, he thought. But he said, 'It's maybe not such a bad thing to head home.' He'd not mind being able to have a few words with his folks about his own troubles, but they were in Australia.

'I knew you'd understand. Dad's picking me up here at seven, but I'll be back on Saturday morning. If I get any results before that, I'll phone you.'

'I'm as anxious to hear as you.' Even, he thought, if my reasons are a bit different from yours. 'Try not to worry too much, and I'll see you on Saturday. I'll pick you up at one. The wedding's at two.'

12

Wednesday morning had flown by. Barry had had no time to dwell on anything else.

'Any calls for this afternoon, Kinky?' O'Reilly asked, when Mrs Kincaid came into the dining room.

'Two,' she said, 'but neither's urgent.' She handed the list to O'Reilly and set a willow-pattern tureen on the table.

'Just soup again?' O'Reilly was pouting.

'With all the dumplings you put inside you at dinner last night, you need something lighter for your lunch,' she said. 'But there's buttered barmbrack for after. I've to run along and toast it.' She hesitated in the dining-room doorway. 'Maybe the raisins in the brack'll sweeten you up, Doctor dear.'

'I suppose so.' O'Reilly sighed and passed his plate. 'What's Kinky given us this time?'

Barry lifted the tureen's lid and inhaled a mixture of the scents of garlic, cloves, onion and rich meat. 'Smells like mock turtle to me.' He returned the full plate to O'Reilly, then helped himself.

'Huh.' O'Reilly sniffed, filled his spoon and shoved it in his mouth. 'It is,' he said, smiling. 'And it's bloody good.'

Someone rang the front doorbell and Barry heard Kinky open the door. He thought he could hear Bertie Bishop's voice. O'Reilly had arranged for the Bishops to be seen at one o'clock.

Kinky came in with a plate of barmbrack and a pot of tea. 'Now don't take too long over your tea. I've just let Bertie and Flo Bishop into the surgery. He's as irritable as a dog with fleas.'

O'Reilly grinned at Kinky. 'Dr Laverty and I have a surprise for him.'

'Aye, so?' She cocked her head to one side.

'Yes,' said O'Reilly, 'and we've you to thank for it. It was you who found out from Flo about the stream that runs under the Duck.'

'A stream under the Duck? Now there's a thing.'

'Yes. And that stream, small as it is, is going to be Bertie Bishop's down-fall. He'll not be able to do anything with the Duck.'

You *hope* it's going to be his downfall, Barry thought.

'If you say so, Dr O'Reilly. Just don't let him know who told me. He's a vindictive little bashtoon, and I'd not want him to go after Flo.'

'Don't worry about that, Kinky,' O'Reilly said. 'Flo and her secret are safe with us.' He grinned at Barry. 'But Bertie Bishop isn't, is he?'

'I hope not, Fingal.'

O'Reilly rose and headed for the surgery. 'Come on, Dr Laverty,' he called. 'It's a terrible shame to keep the Bishops waiting. They're both your cases.'

Barry rose, eager to see how Mrs Bishop was doing but uncertain about how he should handle the councillor. This was O'Reilly's scheme.

The councillor and Mrs Bishop were seated on the wooden chairs. Bertie Bishop was dressed in his black suit, holding his bowler hat by the brim. Mrs Bishop wore a simple blue dress and a little hat with a half-veil. Barry thought she looked brighter, less lethargic. The councillor half turned when Barry said, 'Good afternoon.'

'About time, Laverty,' the councillor grumbled.

'And a very good afternoon to you too, Bertie,' O'Reilly said pleasantly, entering the room. He hoisted himself on the examining couch.

Barry took the swivel chair. 'Hello, Mrs Bishop. How are you today?'

'Dr Laverty.' She positively beamed at him. 'It's a miracle, so it is. I've been taking them wee pills, and I'm running round like a bee on a hot brick, and I've all my energy back.'

'Too much, if you ask me,' the councillor said.

'And I can do all my housework, and I'm not one wee bit tired, and I've my appetite back, but I haven't put on an ounce, and . . .'

'See what I mean? I can't get a word in edgewise,' the councillor said.

Barry glanced at O'Reilly and immediately had to look away. It would *not* be appropriate for Barry to laugh. 'I'm very glad to hear you're feeling better,' he said. 'Now, Flo, you remember the last time you were in I asked you to lift and lower your arm?'

'Like this?' Her arm went up and down effortlessly.

'That's excellent, Flo,' Barry said. 'You're on the mend. I'm very pleased.'

'Not near as pleased as I am, Dr Laverty.' She turned to her husband. 'You said these two doctors were a couple of quacks, and that there was nothing wrong with me, and I was just idle, and—'

'Yes, dear,' the councillor said. He raised his eyes to the heavens, then looked at Barry. 'Could you maybe cut the dose down a bit, Doctor?'

'I'm sorry,' Barry said, 'but I don't think so.'

'I don't want you to,' Flo said, 'and I want to ask you, Doctor, if you've any other pills? I'd like to lose a bit of weight. Cissie Sloan says when she was all slowed down and you give her tablets that fixed her thyroid, she lost weight, and—'

'Hold on, Flo,' Barry interrupted. He was beginning to feel a tad of sympathy for the councillor. 'I can't discuss another patient with you.' Last month Barry had diagnosed Cissie's hypothyroidism. 'The pills I gave her won't do for you unless there's something wrong with your thyroid gland.'

'Oh.' Mrs Bishop looked crestfallen.

'Perhaps,' Barry said, 'we should get it checked just in case.' He'd forgotten to order the test last week. 'I'll write the forms. They'll do the blood tests down in Bangor.'

'Great. Bertie, you can run me down this afternoon and I could do a bit of shopping.'

'I can do no such thing,' Councillor Bishop snapped. 'I've to see Willy Dunleavy at two and get the Duck wrapped up.'

If Barry was going to bluff Bertie Bishop, this would have to be handled with as much confidence as he could muster. 'That would be the matter of the lease, Mr Bishop?'

'It's none of your bloody business, Laverty, but, yes, it is.'

'When you were in here last, Dr O'Reilly said a little bird had told him you were going to chuck Willy Dunleavy out, and you told us the little bird could go and pluck itself.'

'I did and I meant it, so I did.'

Barry took a deep breath. 'Mr Bishop, Dr O'Reilly and I have been having a word with a much bigger bird. Much bigger.' Barry fixed Bishop with a glare. 'The Marquis of Ballybucklebo owns the salmon rights to the stream that runs under the Black Swan.'

Bishop's eyes widened. His face turned puce.

'Who the hell told you about the stream?'

Barry clenched his fists. They'd promised Kinky they would protect her. 'It came out in a conversation when His Lordship and Sonny were discussing Norman land titles. Sonny knew all about the stream.' He was bending the truth again, but it was in a very good cause. 'His Lordship told us you can do nothing to the Duck without his permission.'

'We'll see about that, so we will. I'm going to lose a fortune if I can't go ahead. I'll take him to court.' Bishop stood.

The man's response was exactly as O'Reilly had predicted. If Barry was going to checkmate him, he'd have to force Bishop to believe that a lawsuit wasn't going to work.

'The marquis is quite prepared for you.'

'Prepared? I know for a fact all his money's tied up in running the estate.'

'Councillor, His Lordship said he would fight you to the limit of his resources.'

Bishop's brow wrinkled. 'Did he say that?'

Barry nodded.

'You're not having me on? The limit?'

'Mr Bishop,' Barry said. 'I'm a doctor. What would I have to gain by lying to you?' This victory, the Duck, Willy's and Mary's futures, and the preservation of O'Reilly's reputation, that's what. Barry held his breath.

The rotund little man scowled at Barry. 'I'd go bust.'

Barry exhaled. He'd won and the feeling was grand.

'It's all that ould goat Sonny's fault. I should never have let you two talk me into fixing his bloody roof.'

'Actually,' Barry said, 'you're not. Since last night Donal has had a work crew from the village hard at it . . .'

'And,' O'Reilly added, 'apart from the materials it's not costing you a penny, Bertie. You're getting the labour for free now.'

'Free? Nobody does nothing for free. What are they after?'

'The whole village,' said Barry, 'would like you to leave the Duck as it is.'

'I don't have much choice about that then, do I?'

'No,' said O'Reilly, 'you don't, but you could turn it to your advantage.'

Bishop's eyes narrowed. 'My advantage?'

'Well,' said O'Reilly, 'your stock went up when you agreed to fix Sonny's roof. Nobody need know about the deeds. Just tell the village you've changed your mind. It's your duty as a councillor. You and Flo'll be at the wedding, won't you? It would be a grand time to make the announcement.'

'I suppose.'

'You could say something else too, Bertie.' Mrs Bishop turned to Barry. 'I'm sorry, Dr Laverty, but some folks round here have been saying you don't know your job. But I think you done a miracle for me.'

'Hardly a miracle,' he said.

'Well, *I* think it was, and didn't you tell me you couldn't discuss Cissie Sloan?' The words rattled out. 'So you can't go round blowing your own trumpet about fixing me up, can you?'

'No, I can't.'

'But *you* could, Bertie. It wouldn't hurt to say a word or two about Dr Laverty and me, and . . .'

'All right, Flo.' The councillor sighed. 'I'll say the words on Saturday, but you doctors won't say nothing about the deeds?'

'Not a word,' said O'Reilly.

'In that case,' said Bishop, 'come on, Flo. I'll take you to Bangor.'

The couple left.

O'Reilly slipped down from the couch. 'Well done, Barry.'

Barry inclined his head. 'Thank you for rowing into the discussion, Fingal.'

'I hardly needed to. It's just like when I was boxing. Nothing beats the old one-two punch.'

Barry grinned. 'You fixed the councillor again, Fingal.'

'No. *You* fixed him, Barry. I just gave the last nail in his coffin lid a wee tap. We're a good team, but we should say no more about this. We can let Bertie's moment of glory come as a surprise to the locals.'

'Fair enough.'

O'Reilly grinned. 'And once he's made the public announcement . . .'

'He'll not be able to retract.'

13

'It'll be easier when the kiddies go back to school next month,' O'Reilly remarked. Thursday morning's surgery had seemed to Barry like a paediatric outpatients' clinic. Summer colds, hay fever, one case of severe sunburn and one little boy with a marble stuck in his left nostril.

O'Reilly had let Barry do the consulting, barely offering a word or a nod of encouragement, never questioning Barry's judgment. Just as well he made me work, Barry thought, while O'Reilly went to fetch the next patient. His prescription for keeping me too busy to dwell on unpleasant matters is working—up to a point.

O'Reilly held the surgery door open. 'Go on in, Helen,' he said. 'I'll be back in a minute.' He closed the door.

'Hello, Helen. Have a seat.' Barry noticed she wasn't wearing gloves or a long-sleeved blouse. 'How are you this morning?'

'Better,' she said, 'much better.' She held out her arms. 'See?'

The angry, red, scaly rashes had faded. 'How about behind your knees?'

Helen stood, turned and hitched up her skirt.

The skin behind her knees was no better. 'That's not so good.'

She dropped her skirt. 'It's not as bad as it was, and it'll really start to improve by tonight.'

'Why this evening, Helen?'

'I'll be handing in my cards after work today.'

Barry heard the door open, looked up and saw O'Reilly enter.

'You'll be giving your notice, Helen?' Barry turned his attention back to the patient.

'Now that wee Mary's going to be all right, so she is.'

Barry glanced at O'Reilly, who stood in the background.

'Mary's da's able to find more work for her,' Helen said. 'Don't ask me how, with that man Bishop going to take over the Duck.'

'He's a sound man, Willy Dunleavy,' O'Reilly said, with a wink to Barry.

'Anyhow,' Helen said, 'Mary'll be all done tonight. She's only part-time so she can go any time. I'll be gone then too.'

Barry took one of her hands, and inspected the healing rash. 'It really does look as if the eczema's clearing up. To be honest, I don't know if it's the treatment or the fact you'll be leaving Miss Moloney's that's doing the trick, but I think you should keep on using the ointment for a while longer.'

'I'll do that, Dr Laverty. I just thought I'd pop in today to let you know I was getting better. I'll maybe see you both on Saturday?'

'You will that,' O'Reilly said.

Barry closed the surgery door. 'Who's next?'

'Helen was the last. But I've a bit of news for you. I went out a minute ago to make a call. I had a wee word with Charley Greer. He saw Declan last night. He's sorry he didn't phone us then, but there was a car crash and he was in the operating theatre half the night. Anyway, he was waiting until he had the results of some tests before he phoned.'

'What did he say?'

'Charley reckons Declan's a good candidate for surgery. He says the X-rays of the arteries show only a tad of atherosclerosis. He can't cure that, but at least he's pretty sure he can give the old boy a bit of relief from his Parkinson's symptoms.'

'I'm glad to hear that. His wife will be pleased.'

'She's not the only one. I've known Declan and Mélanie since I came here. They're a lovely couple. It's been miserable watching the poor old fellah go downhill.' O'Reilly tapped his pipe mouthpiece against his lower teeth and said, almost to himself, 'I wonder should I have sent him up to see Charley sooner?'

Barry wasn't sure what to say. He knew he was young and inexperienced, was bound to have doubts, but he had never suspected that O'Reilly was troubled by those kinds of questions.

'It's always a bugger,' O'Reilly said quietly, 'trying to decide when to hold back and when to act. Declan and Mélanie won't have that many years left together. Maybe if I'd sent Declan for surgery sooner, the years would have been better.' He shoved his briar back into his mouth. 'I did ask Charley and he didn't think he would have done anything back then. It's a pretty narrow margin between improvement and making things worse. He isn't too keen to operate unless the symptoms are seriously advanced.'

'And they are now. Declan's tremors are much more pronounced.'

O'Reilly stared out through the surgery window. 'That's what makes Charley Greer such a fine surgeon. He doesn't just know how to operate . . . he knows *when* to operate and that's important.' He turned and headed for the door. 'Charley's not sure what day he'll do it, but he's agreed to keep Declan in. Mélanie needs the rest.' O'Reilly opened the door. 'We'll go round and let her know, then deal with whatever's on Kinky's list.'

'OUR AMERICAN COUSINS,' said O'Reilly, 'have an expression, TGIF. Thank God it's Friday.' He stood at the sideboard, pouring predinner drinks. 'I, for one, agree.'

Barry stared through the windows of the upstairs sitting room, barely listening. It was all very well for O'Reilly to be talking about celebrating the end of another routine working week. There was still no word from Harry Sloan, and Mrs Fotheringham's deadline of Sunday evening was rapidly approaching.

'Sherry?' said O'Reilly, reaching for the decanter.

Barry shook his head. 'No, thanks. I'll have an Irish.'

'Good man,' said O'Reilly, pouring. He handed Barry the glass, then lowered himself into the other armchair. 'All right, Barry. You've had a face on you all afternoon. Cheer up.'

'I'm sorry.'

'You've done well in trying not letting this business get the better of you and carrying on with your work. It's a lesson all doctors have to learn. You have to keep your own troubles to yourself because, trite as it may sound, the customers come first.' There was brightness in his deep eyes when he said, 'And, son, for a young man, you've all the makings of a good doctor . . . Experience is a wonderful thing. It lets you recognise the same mistake when you make it again . . . and again, until one day you stop making that bloomer.'

O'Reilly's words made Barry smile.

'That's better,' O'Reilly said. 'I thought you were going to tell me your mind was on other things.'

'Well . . .' There was no point dissembling. He looked O'Reilly in the eye. 'I was hoping Harry would have been in touch by now.'

O'Reilly nodded. 'Any point you trying to get hold of him?'

Barry shook his head. 'He'll have gone home and I don't have his number. I don't even know where he lives.'

'Pity,' said O'Reilly. 'I said that if I thought it necessary I'd go and see Mrs Fotheringham again. I haven't.'

'Do you think it would help?'

'Honestly, Barry? I don't know.'

'Then why bother?'

'Because you don't give up a fight in the middle of the tenth round.' He looked enquiringly at Barry. 'But she's promised me she'll drop the suit if we have evidence it wasn't your fault.'

'But we don't have the evidence.'

'Not yet,' O'Reilly said. 'What do you think? Should I go and see her?'

Barry wasn't sure how to answer. 'It won't be easy.'

'For who? Me? For Mrs Fotheringham?'

Barry shook his head. 'No. For me.'

'You?' O'Reilly frowned. 'Why you?'

'If anyone has to talk to her, it's me. It's my responsibility.'

O'Reilly clapped Barry on the shoulder. 'I knew you'd say that. I'm proud of you, Barry. And you'll not be going alone. If we haven't heard by Saturday, we'll drop in on her on Sunday.'

'Thanks, Fingal. I appreciate . . .'

Barry heard Kinky's voice, and then her footsteps coming upstairs. She stuck her head round the door. 'Dr Laverty. There's a call for you, so. It's your Miss Spence. She sounded all excited.'

Barry took the stairs two at a time and grabbed the receiver. 'Hello. Patricia? Where are you?'

'In my flat.' She did sound excited.

'But I thought you weren't coming up to the Kinnegar until tomorrow.' He heard her laugh. 'You've won, haven't you?'

'Yes. I have. You were right. Isn't it wonderful?'

'Amazing.' He swallowed. 'Well done. Congratulations.'

'Can you come over? I wanted to see you so much I got Dad to run me up tonight.'

Barry hesitated. 'I don't know. I'll ask O'Reilly. Hang on.' He set the receiver on the hall table and turned to the stairs, but heard O'Reilly bellow from the landing.

'Well? Has she won? Kinky said she was excited.'

'Yes. She has. She's back and she's in her flat.'

'Bloody marvellous.' O'Reilly held his hands clasped above his head like a prize fighter who had scored a KO. 'Well, don't just stand there. Go and see her and give her a big hug from me.'

THE VOLKSWAGEN'S WIPERS struggled back and forth, trying and failing to clear the windscreen of drizzle. Barry hunched forward and concentrated on where he was going, along the winding road to the Kinnegar.

It was difficult to see ahead, and not only through the streaked windscreen. He knew he loved her. You were meant to rejoice when someone you loved won a victory, and he did—for the success itself—but the thought of Patricia's going away tore at him. Jack had urged him to propose, mark her as his property, but he couldn't. Was it because he was scared of the idea of marriage, because he thought he was too young at twenty-four? Or was it because one of the things he loved about her was her spirit, which, like a wild pony, should be tamed only when the animal was ready? Damned if he knew.

But the fact was she'd won the scholarship and she'd be going to Cambridge. The question was, did she love him enough to save herself for him? Time, he supposed, would tell, but he already knew how much he hated uncertainty and waiting for answers to questions over which he had no control. And time, in this case, was going to be three long years. It would seem like for ever. He decided not to dwell tonight on the implications of her win, but to celebrate with her.

When he parked in the Esplanade and stepped out of Brunhilde, the steady drizzle made Barry shiver. He huddled into his jacket and hurried down the road to Number 9, where he rang the bell to Flat 4, and waited. Almost immediately, he heard the sound of running footsteps.

'Barry! Barry!' Patricia flung open the front door and threw her arms around him. He grabbed her and kissed her hard, before drawing back.

'I'm delighted, darling. Congratulations.'

Patricia laughed excitedly, then took him by the hand and led him into the flat, where a bottle of Chianti and two glasses sat on the table in the living room.

Patricia picked up the corkscrew and began to open the wine. 'You don't mind that I'll have to go away?' she asked shyly.

Of course he minded, but this was not the time for selfishness. 'I told you, I'm delighted and very, very proud of you.'

She smiled and twisted the corkscrew home, and then pulled the cork. 'I love you, Barry.'

'I know, and I love you.' He kissed her cheek. Then, not wanting her to dwell on their forthcoming separation, he said, 'Come on, I want to hear all the details.' He took the bottle and corkscrew from her and set them on the coffee table.

'I got the letter in the afternoon post,' she said. 'It had a Cambridge postmark and a Cambridge crest on the envelope.' She smiled. 'I had to ask Mum to help me. My hands were shaking so much I couldn't open it.'

'I'll bet they shook more when your mum told you the results.'

She nodded. 'I couldn't believe it. I had to read it for myself.' He heard awe in her voice. 'I've done it, Barry. I've actually done it.'

'It's wonderful.' Barry picked up the bottle and poured two glasses of wine. 'I'm so proud of you. Here'—he handed her a glass—'come and sit down.' He waited for her to join him on the sofa, then raised his glass. 'To your success.' Together they drank.

Patricia lowered her glass. 'And I'd promised to tell you as soon as I heard. I'm sorry I blurted it out over the phone, but I couldn't keep it to myself. Then telling you on the phone wasn't good enough.' She hugged him and kissed him so hard he almost spilt his wine. 'I had to see you. Dad understood. He ran me up . . .'

'I'm very glad of that,' he said, seeing the joy in her eyes, loving their brightness.

'I still can't believe it. The award covers all my fees, books, equipment, and board and lodge for three years. I'll be living at Girton. That's one of the all-women colleges . . .'

He let her prattle on, understanding her excitement.

'I'll have to pay, or at least Dad and Mum'll have to pay my travel expenses.'

'I suppose that means you'll only come home for the long holidays?'

'That's right. I'll be off to England in the first week of September, but I will be home for Christmas . . . and Easter, and I'll have two months off in the summer . . . if I'm not doing some kind of practical course.' She took another drink. 'Isn't it wonderful, darling?'

The 'darling', spoken with such naturalness, should have warmed him, but he felt a chill, already imagining her whispering it to some intense, long-haired undergraduate, or, worse, to some junior don.

He tilted his head back and stared into her eyes. 'It *is* wonderful,' he said, 'and I love you.'

She took his hand and said quietly, 'Thank you.'

'For what? For loving you? That's easy.'

'Yes, but for more. I know you think we'll drift apart . . .'

Barry lowered his gaze.

'But we won't. How could I not love, and go on loving, a man who's been dreading my winning, but who has not said a word about it and has celebrated with me? You have a gift, Barry Laverty. It's no wonder O'Reilly thinks you're one of the finest young doctors that he's met in years.'

'O'Reilly said that?' O'Reilly said *that*?

'He did. When I was chatting to him a couple of weeks ago at the big party in his garden. He said your gift is to be able to feel what other people are feeling. And it's more than that. You act on those feelings, just as you did when you learned I'd won the scholarship. You put yourself second.'

'If it's true about feeling things and O'Reilly said it, then all I can say is, "It takes one to know one." I swear Fingal's telepathic.'

'And you admire him for it, don't you?'

He nodded.

She picked up her wine and sipped. 'If you can read minds like O'Reilly, what am I thinking now?' She smiled and cocked one eyebrow at him.

'Right now? I haven't the foggiest notion.'

'Huh,' she said, 'some mind-reader.' Suddenly her arms were round his neck and she was pulling him to her, kissing him. She took his hand and held it to her left breast, and he felt the pressure of her hand and the warmth beneath it.

He cupped her breast, feeling his whole body tingle; he screwed his eyes tightly shut and then felt the loss of her as she gently stood up, still holding his hand.

'Bring your wine,' she said, and he opened his eyes and looked up at her smile. 'If you *had* known what I was thinking, you'd have beaten me along to the bedroom. It's the first door on the left.'

14

'I know it's only ten thirty, but it's such a lovely day.' Barry followed Patricia through the front door of Number 9 and into her flat. He closed the door behind him, took Patricia in his arms and kissed her, wanting her even more than he'd wanted her so few hours ago.

She pulled back and said slightly breathlessly, 'I don't mind that you're early, but look at me, I'm a mess. I'm just out of the bath.'

'You're beautiful,' he said, even though her hair was damp and she wore no make-up. She was in an old dressing gown and pink, fluffy slippers.

'And you're nuts if you think that right now.' She shook her head. 'There's coffee in the pot,' she said, moving away from him. 'Would you like a cup?'

'Please.'

She poured his coffee and put in some milk. She knew how he liked it. It was as if they were a long-married couple, comfortable in their morning ordinariness. She handed him a cup.

He took it, set it on the table and held her to him. 'Last night was wonderful. Thank you.'

She kissed him, then smiled into his eyes. 'Mmm.'

He strangled the urge to untie the gown's belt. God, he wanted her, but now was not the time. He moved back, sat on the sofa and gulped a mouthful of coffee.

'You wait here and I'll go and get ready.'

'Fine.'

She went along to the bathroom and closed the door. He heard the humming of a hair dryer.

He stood up, then walked to the window to gaze past the tiny front garden where the rough, salt-burnt grass straggled in brown tufts. He looked across the narrow road and the sea wall to where a fleet of racing yachts tacked close-hauled to the upwind mark, their white sails taut, straining against the wind. It seemed to be a very long time since he'd had a chance to race, and he'd loved his sailing.

He heard the bathroom door open and close, turned and glimpsed Patricia slipping across to her bedroom.

'I'll not be much longer,' came from the bedroom.

'Take your time,' he called. He was happy to wait and went to sit on the sofa again. 'I came early because O'Reilly's gone off to pick up someone in Belfast, and Kinky's holding the fort until the service. I reckon everyone's too busy getting ready to see Sonny and Maggie get hitched to be bothered to get sick.'

'It's going to be quite the do, isn't it?'

'The whole village is buzzing.'

She came back into the room. 'How do I look?'

He eyed her up and down over her patent pumps, knee-length tartan kilt, bottle-green blouse and almond-shaped eyes. 'Stunning,' he said.

'Thank you, kind sir.' She dropped a little curtsy.

'Look,' he said, 'we've time before the ceremony. I thought we'd go to Sonny's house. Donal Donnelly—he's one of our patients—and a bunch of the boys have been fixing it up. It's to be the village's surprise wedding present to the happy couple, and I'd like to see how they've finished the job.'

'I'd really like to see the place,' she said. 'Hang on. I'll get my handbag.'

BARRY PARKED close to Sonny's gate.

'What on earth is that?' Patricia asked, pointing to Donal Donnelly's bike of many colours propped against the gatepost.

'Donal must be here,' Barry said. 'That's his machine. Let's go and inspect the great project.'

He barely recognised Sonny's house. The scaffolding had vanished. The new slate roof glowed darkly in sunlight that brightened the green-painted front door and window sashes. He was pleased to see window boxes on the lower sills. Maggie would like that.

When he pushed the gate open, the hinges no longer creaked.

The lawn had been newly cut, and the air smelt of grass clippings. He could hear a combine harvester working in the distance and the lowing of a cow. Two birds, black-caped and white-flanked, with long, broad tails, swooped overhead, their cries harsh giggles.

'Magpies,' Patricia said. 'Two of them. That's lucky.'

'Dr Laverty, sir.' Donal Donnelly stood in the open doorway, his shock of ginger hair untidy, his buckteeth white in the middle of his grin.

''Morning, Donal. Donal, this is Miss Spence,' Barry said. 'Patricia. Donal Donnelly.'

'Pleased to meet you, Miss,' Donal said. 'If you'll excuse me, I'll be running along. I've to get into my uniform. Me and the rest of the Highlanders are going to be a guard of honour after the wedding, so we are.'

'Would it be all right if Miss Spence and I had a look around inside?'

'Aye, certainly. Help yourself.' Donal trotted off.

Barry led Patricia into the hall. There was a smell of fresh paint. The walls were cream. A rug covered the floorboards. The door to his left stood ajar. 'What's in here?' He pushed the door open.

'The dining room,' Patricia said.

Sun's rays coming through the front windows made dust motes twinkle between a cut-glass chandelier and a pine table surrounded by four wooden, hard-backed chairs. Two places were set on a checked tablecloth. A vase of freshly cut flowers sat flanked by two brass candlesticks in the middle of the table. A hand-drawn card read: *Welcome home, Maggie and Sonny. Your dinner's in the fridge.*

Patricia stood wide-eyed. 'It's lovely. Your friends must have worked like Trojans. It's as if the fairy godmother from *Cinderella* had waved her wand.'

'Somehow,' he said, 'I've a bit of difficulty casting Donal as the fairy godmother, but you're right. And I'll bet—'

He recognised a deep voice that came booming into the room. 'Helloo. Anyone home?'

What on earth was Fingal doing here? Probably, Barry thought, just as curious as I am to see the place. 'Just us, Fingal.'

O'Reilly stood in the doorway, dressed ready for the wedding.

''Morning, Fingal,' Barry said. 'You've met Patricia Spence.'

O'Reilly nodded in her direction. 'And what the hell are you doing here, Laverty?' He didn't seem pleased.

'Just having a look around.'

O'Reilly turned and said, 'It's all right. It's just young Laverty. Come on in, Kitty.'

Caitlin O'Hallorhan walked through the doorway.

Barry's mouth opened. So *that* was who O'Reilly had been talking to on the phone the other evening. Well, well.

'Sister,' Barry said with a small bow, 'nice to see you again. This is Patricia Spence. Patricia, Sister O'Hallorhan.'

As the two women were exchanging the to-be-expected noises, Barry had a good look at the ward sister, who'd known O'Reilly when he'd been a student. The first time Barry had met her, he'd thought her a handsome woman. But out of uniform she was striking. Her hair, now freed from the confines of her starched uniform headdress, was shining silver. Her well-tailored maroon suit complemented her figure. In the sunshine, the amber flecks in her grey eyes seemed golden, and the laugh lines in the corners of her eyes deepened as she smiled and said to Barry, 'I see you're a man of your word, Dr Laverty.'

'I'm sorry?'

'You did give Fingal here my regards.'

O'Reilly's collar must be too tight, Barry thought, watching him tug at it. 'Well,' he said, 'old *friends* from student days should keep in touch.'

'Och, indeed, Fingal,' she said, with a wicked grin, 'to be sure. What's twenty-five years to old friends?'

O'Reilly made a harrumphing noise.

'We've only just got here and as far as we can tell, Donal and his merry men have done a superb job,' Barry said.

O'Reilly asked, 'Is this all you've seen?'

'So far,' Barry said.

O'Reilly said to Patricia, 'You show Kitty the rest.' He grabbed Kitty O'Hallorhan's hand. 'You go with Miss Spence, please. I need to have a word with my young colleague.'

O'Reilly had said 'please'? Barry waited for the women to leave, and said, 'Yes, Fingal?'

But O'Reilly was staring at Kitty O'Hallorhan's retreating back, saying quietly, 'I haven't seen that girl for years and she hasn't changed one scrap.'

Barry coughed. 'You said you wanted a word, Fingal?'

'Yes. I'm glad I ran into you. I need a hand. I should've asked you earlier, but it slipped my mind. Someone has to drive Kitty to the reception.'

Did it slip your mind, Fingal? Barry wondered. Or did you not want to tell me who you were bringing?

'You see, Sonny's still pining for his dogs. They're at Maggie's. I want to nip over and bring them to His Lordship's . . .'

'And you want me to bring Kitty?'

O'Reilly nodded. 'Aye, and I'd like you to pick up Arthur Guinness too.'

'I can do that.'

'Good lad.' O'Reilly clapped Barry on the shoulder. 'I knew I could count on you.'

Kitty and Patricia came in. Both were smiling broadly.

'It's wonderful,' said Patricia. 'The kitchen's all set up. Two of the bedrooms are unfurnished, but the third has a huge brass bed, chintz curtains and a view down over the fields to the lough in the distance. Sonny and Maggie're going to get a great start.'

'Good,' said O'Reilly, avoiding looking at Kitty. 'It's bloody well time the pair of them got together.' He fixed Barry with a glare. 'I'm sure, Barry, you and Miss Spence would like to have a bit of time on your own . . .'

And even if we didn't, we're going to get it, Barry thought.

'I'm going to take Kitty to the Old Inn in Crawfordsburn for lunch. We'll see you in the church.' He held the door open and waited for Kitty to precede him through the door.

Barry watched O'Reilly hold the car door open and saw Kitty climb in. Then he distinctly heard her saying, 'Now you will drive carefully, won't you, Fingal? You know you nearly hit a cyclist on the way down here.'

15

Sonny and Maggie were now man and wife 'til death did them part. Sonny kissed the bride; the minister gave the benediction.

Barry let Kitty and Patricia precede him as they left their front pew to head for the porch. Much of the rest of the congregation had already vanished. They would be hurrying to the reception at the marquis's estate.

Barry was blinded by the sunlight and deafened by the roaring of the great Highland bagpipes. Two columns of Highlanders, distended bags under their arms, drones on their shoulders, flanked the pavement. Donal Donnelly held a silver-headed mace aloft, clearly not discomfited by the cast on his finger. He was revelling in the exalted position of drum major.

Barry beckoned to the two women. It was useless trying to make himself heard over the racket. He headed for the back lane where Brunhilde was parked. Behind Number 1 the sounds of the pipes were muted, but in the garden Arthur Guinness sat, head thrown back, yodelling horribly out of tune with the band.

'I'm sorry,' Barry said to Kitty, 'but I'm afraid one of you is going to have to share the back seat with the Hound of the Baskervilles.'

'I'll do it,' Patricia said. Barry held the seat forward and helped her to climb in. Arthur Guinness climbed in beside her.

Barry flipped the seat upright. 'You're next, Sister O'Hallorhan.'

'It's Kitty,' she told him, getting in.

He ran round the car and got in. 'Next stop, the reception.'

Well-wishers stood cheering on both sides of Main Street. Up ahead Barry saw a small jaunting car. Maggie, Sonny and the marquis, as best man, were perched on its benches. A becapped Fergus Finnegan sat in the driver's seat, urging a small donkey to plod along. A sign on the back of the vehicle said: JUST MARRIED.

The gates of the estate were wide open, and Barry drove slowly along the gravelled drive. He found a place to park, got out and went round to open the passenger door. As soon as Patricia climbed out of the back seat, Arthur followed and galloped off.

He took Patricia's hand and nodded to Kitty. 'Come on. It's not going to be easy finding Fingal in this mob.'

Half of the lawn was occupied by a head table that ran at right angles to several other long tables. The rest of the lawn was packed with a milling scrum—the entire village must have arrived.

Barry could smell meat cooking. He craned over the throng until he could see that a curl of smoke wafting past the Georgian façade of the Big House was coming from a whole pig being roasted on a spit. Kinky was keeping a watchful eye on the proceedings. He could make out the bright green of her new hat. He waved at her, but she mustn't have seen him. Oh, well, he'd catch up with her soon enough to ask if Harry had called.

Barry had been so busy trying to attract Kinky's attention that he bumped into Helen Hewitt. She was wearing a short-sleeved blouse and a very short skirt.

Barry had to put his ear close to her mouth to hear over the din.

'I hear that ould targe Miss Moloney's not too happy,' she said, with a wicked grin. 'Serves her right. She's a personality like a bagful of hammers, so she has.' He saw the fire in her green eyes. 'Anyhow, I'll not be staying long. I've got a job in a Belfast linen mill, and I start on Monday.'

'I'll be sorry to see you go.'

'Aye. Well, it's for the best, and . . .' She beckoned and Barry bent lower. 'My rash is nearly all gone, so it is, since I quit that shop.'

He nodded and mouthed, 'Good.'

'I hope to God I never need a doctor again, but if I do, I'll be coming back here to see yourself, so I will. I'm right glad you come to work here with the ould fellah. He works himself far too hard.' She squeezed his arm. 'Now, run away on with your lady friend. She's lovely, so she is.'

Helen left as Patricia drew level. 'And who was that?' There was just a tiny edge in her voice.

'One of my patients.' The truth was, a country GP in a place like Ballybucklebo was never off duty—and it wasn't such a bad thing.

'Oh,' she said, 'that's all right then.'

Was she becoming possessive? If she was, Barry didn't mind one bit.

He saw Patricia point, and he followed as she and Kitty headed to where O'Reilly was parked at the head table. As the women arrived, O'Reilly pulled out a chair for Kitty.

'Come and sit down, Barry,' O'Reilly roared. He held a large glass of whiskey in one hand. 'The bride and groom should be here in a few minutes, so if anyone wants a drink before the formalities start, it's speak now or for ever hold your peace.'

'Glass of white wine for Patricia,' Barry said, seeing her nod of approval. 'And . . .' He almost ordered a sherry, but changed his mind. 'A small Bushmills, please.'

O'Reilly held up one thumb. 'Come on, Barry. I'll need a hand.'

Barry shrugged at Patricia. 'I'll be back in a minute.'

'Lord,' said O'Reilly, 'she's not going to run away. And, Patricia?'

'Yes, Fingal?'

'Keep that seat on the corner for Kinky. I see her heading this way.'

Barry had to run to keep up with O'Reilly, who went straight to the head of the queue, raising not a single protest from those waiting.

Barry moved to O'Reilly's side, took a tray of full glasses and headed back to the table.

Kinky was seated there, beaming as she adjusted her new hat.

Barry handed out the drinks, then took his seat beside Patricia. He raised his glass to her. 'To the new scholarship winner.'

She smiled, but said quietly, 'No, Barry, just "to us".'

He felt her take his hand under the table.

'Excuse me, Dr Laverty,' Kinky said. 'Himself is blethering away to that nice Dublin lady, but when you've a wee minute will you tell him what a great success my new hat is?'

'Of course, Kinky.'

'And there's one more wee thing I've to tell you. That friend of yours, Dr Mills, phoned from the hospital just before I left for the church . . . And he said for to tell you . . .'

But Barry couldn't hear. The air was rent by the music of the pipes, the battering of the drums and the howling of Arthur Guinness, who had crept under the table at O'Reilly's feet.

Donal Donnelly led the procession. Behind him came the Highlanders, kilts swinging, bags inflated, cheeks red and bulging. Two tenor drummers whirled their woolly-headed drumsticks. Side drummers played paradiddles and rolls. Behind them came the donkey, pulling the little cart where the marquis perched. Sonny seemed bewildered by all the fuss, but Maggie, in her white wedding dress, had a smile from ear to ear.

Behind ran the children, skipping over the grass. One little boy—Barry thought he recognised Colin Brown—was happily turning cartwheels. Sonny's five dogs appeared from wherever O'Reilly had left them and ran jumping and barking beside the car.

Barry wanted to talk to Kinky, but until the pandemonium died down, he was going to have to wait.

Boom-boom. Boom-boom. The big drummer gave the double beat to signal the end of the tune. The wailing of the pipes died, and for the first time in that noisy gathering silence fell.

The marquis, every inch a peer of the realm in his morning coat, dismounted and stood to hand Maggie down from the car. Barry smiled when he noticed that her now thrown-back veil was held in place by a demure circlet of artificial lilies of the valley, but in the circle, front and centre, was a wilted orange nasturtium. The day Maggie MacCorkle *doesn't* have a dead flower in her hatband, he thought, will be the day the sun fails to rise.

The marquis led Maggie and Sonny to the head table. The moment he took his place and the bridal party was settled, cheering filled the air.

Barry tried to attract Kinky's attention, but she was deep in conversation with the woman sitting opposite her.

O'Reilly was on his feet, pounding a fork on the side of an empty glass. 'I want your attention,' he roared. 'I've been asked to compere this afternoon's festivities to celebrate the wedding of two of Ballybucklebo's finest residents.'

'Hear, hear!' someone yelled, as applause started.

O'Reilly battered the glass. 'We'll start with grace, then we'll eat. There's a buffet set up beside the bar. Head table first, then each table in turn, starting with the one on my right. Is that clear? Once you've all been fed and watered, there'll be a bit of speechifying. So I'll ask you all to rise and bow your heads while the reverend says the words.'

Barry stood with everyone else and waited until grace was finished, then immediately leaned over the table. 'Kinky? Kinky?'

'What?'

'What did Dr Mills say?'

'He said, Dr Laverty, for to tell you your friend Harry's had the flu. He was very sorry, so—'

'Sorry?' Did that mean Harry hadn't found anything?

'He'd been up all night and he'd slept late, but he was on his way to see Harry and he'd come straight on down here after. Is that all right, sir?'

Barry sighed. 'Fine,' he said. 'Thanks for telling me.'

'Dr Laverty? I told you you'd hear what you want to, so just you bide and be patient.'

He stared at her. 'I'll try to,' he said.

'Good, so,' she said. 'Now run along and get Miss Spence a bite to eat.'

BARRY PUSHED his plate away and said to Patricia, 'Would you like to meet the happy couple?'

'I'd love to.'

She rose and together they moved along the top table.

'Excuse me,' Barry said. 'Maggie, Sonny, may I present Miss Patricia Spence?'

Sonny stood and bowed. 'Charmed, Miss Spence.'

'So *you're* the one I've been hearing about,' Maggie said, head cocked to one side. 'You're even prettier than I heard tell. You've been the talk of the village, you know.'

Barry had never seen Patricia discomfited before. She blushed as she stuttered, 'Th . . . thank you, Maggie.'

'I think, Dr Laverty, this young lady's too good for you.'

'I'm sure you're right, Maggie,' Barry said.

O'Reilly was on his feet, ringling-dingling his fork on a glass. 'Pay attention. I know some of you are still eating, but it's time to get things moving along.'

Barry led Patricia back.

O'Reilly said, 'It's time to get on with the proceedings, but before we do,

I want to say on behalf of everyone here a huge thankyou to the Marquis of Ballybucklebo for allowing us to use his grounds.'

The roar from the crowd was deafening.

'I agree,' said O'Reilly, 'but now with no further ado I call on His Lordship to propose the toast to the happy couple.'

O'Reilly sat and the marquis rose. 'Ladies and gentlemen, we have all known Maggie MacCorkle and our friend Sonny for many years. Sonny: chess player, expert on Middle Eastern pottery and'—he looked straight at Bertie Bishop—'Norman land titles.'

Barry looked over and saw the councillor scowl.

'Maggie: cat fancier; window-box gardener *extraordinaire*; and—some of you may not know this—winner of the silver medal in the All-Ireland springboard diving championship in 1922.'

Barry certainly hadn't.

'And here she is, once again taking the plunge, but this time—' he inclined his head towards Sonny—'I think she's won the gold.'

No one laughed. Instead the sound of hands clapping in sincere agreement was loud.

'Congratulations to you, Sonny, and every happiness to you, Maggie.' He raised his glass. 'I'll ask you all to charge your glasses and rise with me and drink a toast. Long may they be happy together and the sun shine every day on their marriage. To the bride and groom.'

'To the bride and groom,' roared the chorus.

O'Reilly called, 'Sonny will now reply on behalf of the happy couple.'

Sonny rose. 'My lord, ladies and gentlemen. I've very little to say on behalf of . . . my wife and I . . .' He smiled down at Maggie. 'But there are a number of people I should like to thank. First, I want to thank His Lordship for his generosity to me in so very many ways.'

There was polite applause.

'Next I want to thank Councillor Bishop . . .'

Barry heard a communal in-drawing of breath. Everyone present knew of the long-running feud between the two men.

'I trust that from now on he and I can let bygones be bygones.' He looked straight across to Bertie Bishop. 'Finally,' Sonny said, 'I want to thank Maggie for waiting for me for all these years and consenting to be my wife.'

The cheers were deafening as Sonny sat.

Before O'Reilly could speak, Maggie had risen. In Ulster the bride was meant to sit demurely by her new husband's side and say nothing. 'I know, I know, I'm meant to keep my trap shut, but His Lordship proposed a toast to both of us, and I want my turn to thank His Lordship and Councillor Bishop. If he hadn't fixed Sonny's roof, I'd still be alone with my cat.' She grinned. 'I've advice for some of you.' She let her gaze fall on Barry and then turned to O'Reilly and Kitty. 'Sonny and me are a pair of stubborn old goats who once fell out over a stupid roof and wasted a few years when we could have been together. Don't you young folks be as daft as us.'

Barry glanced at Patricia, who was looking, with one eyebrow raised, at Maggie. He saw O'Reilly frown and stare at the back of Kitty's head.

Maggie bent and planted a wet kiss on Sonny's forehead. Then she sat down to a round of applause.

Barry was aware of someone standing behind him. Turning, he saw Donal Donnelly. Julie MacAteer, looking pale but happy, stood by his side.

Barry rose. 'How are you, Julie?'

She smiled at him. 'Well on the mend, Doctor. I just wanted to say thanks.'

'No need.'

'And cheerio for a wee while. I'm going down to Rasharkin for a couple of weeks to see my folks.' She looked at Donal. 'And when I get back him and me have to make our plans.'

'Good for you.'

'We'd best be running along, Doctor,' Donal said.

O'Reilly roared, 'Next on the agenda, I'll ask Councillor Bishop to come up here.'

The councillor stumped to the head table. A voice called, 'What about the Duck then?'

The councillor stood with his legs braced apart. 'My lord, ladies and gentlemen,' he intoned. 'Unaccustomed as I am to public speaking . . .' He paused as if waiting for laughter, but it failed to materialise. 'One of you asked a very important question—'

'Aye. What about the Duck?'

'I have,' said Bishop, stealing a glance at O'Reilly, 'been giving this matter serious consideration. I have listened to your concerns and I'm going to take the sound advice of Drs O'Reilly and Laverty, so I am.'

'To run away off and chase yourself?'

'No,' Bishop said, smiling. 'I'm a bit on the heavy side for running.'

That did provoke a few chuckles.

'So I've made up my mind, and I've told Willy Dunleavy he and his family can have the lease for another ninety-nine years.'

The cheering almost drowned out Bishop's next words.

'And if Sonny's ready to bury the hatchet, then so am I.'

Bishop bent down and he and Sonny shook hands.

'And don't none of you forget it when the local elections come round. That's all I have to say.'

The cheering increased.

'Bertie.' Barry turned to see Flo Bishop waving at her husband. 'Bertie, it is not all you've to say. You promised.'

'Right. Right, Flo. I did near forget. I'm sorry.' He pointed at Barry. 'My Flo's been awful sick, and it's a very rare thing she's got. But our Dr Laverty here, he sussed it out in no time flat, and he's her fixed up right as rain, so he has. Flo and me's very grateful, Doctor.'

A hush had descended.

'My toast was going to be to friendship, and of course to Sonny and Maggie,' Bishop said, 'but I'll ask you all to rise . . . and drink to our two doctors as well.'

'Well done, Bertie,' O'Reilly said, as Bishop went back to his place to the sound of cheering. 'And,' said O'Reilly, 'that leaves one last speaker before we can get down to the serious business of the day. Will you welcome, please, Donal Donnelly?'

Donal came forward. 'First of all, me and Julie want to thank Dr Laverty too. You all know what he done for her . . .'

There was a muted round of applause.

'But most important, me and the Highlanders, and a brave clatter of the other lads, have a wee present for Sonny and Maggie.'

Sonny gave Maggie a puzzled look.

'On behalf of the village of Ballybucklebo, it gives me great pleasure to give you the key to your new and fully furnished house that we managed to get finished this morning.' He handed a huge artificial key, crafted from cardboard and covered with silver aluminium foil, to Sonny.

Barry saw the look of sheer amazement on Sonny's face, and tears ran freely down his cheeks. Barry felt a lump rising in his own throat. How could any young doctor in his right mind think of leaving Ballybucklebo? He directed his attention to what Donal was saying.

'Here you are, Maggie.' Donal gave her a real set of keys. 'I'm giving these to you because as any of the married men here'll tell you . . . they may be the legal heads of the household, but they all know who really wears the trousers, so they do.'

The wave of laughter started low, and grew and grew as a tidal wave gathers strength as it nears the shore.

A hand on Barry's shoulder made him turn to find himself staring up into the open, country face of Jack Mills. 'Sorry I'm late, mate, but better late than never.'

'Jack.' Barry stood up as he stared at Jack's face for any hint of what the news might be. 'Have you seen Harry?'

'Och, aye. You'd have to feel sorry for the poor bugger. He looks like the wreck of the *Hesperus*. That flu's a nasty one.'

'I'm sorry about that. Did he have the report?'

'Aye.' Jack's face was expressionless. He fished an envelope from the inside pocket of his jacket and handed it to Barry. 'Have a gander at that while I find myself a drink.'

Barry grabbed the envelope. He knew how Patricia had felt when her examination results arrived. He ripped the flap open, fished out a form, unfolded its two pages and began to read.

Major Fotheringham's name and identifying information headed the pages. Next came the histological report. Barry flipped over to the second page to the section headed SUMMARY.

There is striking evidence of atherosclerotic occlusion of three of the four major coronary arteries . . .

He dropped his gaze to the final section, CONCLUSIONS.

Cause of death: massive coronary occlusion of sufficient magnitude to result in sudden death prior to the formation of obvious macroscopic pathological changes.

Major Fotheringham had died of a coronary, a condition that had nothing whatsoever to do with his earlier cerebral haemorrhage. Barry exhaled.

'You all right, Barry?' Patricia stood by his side.

'Fine. Yes, thanks. I'm fine.'

'Good, because you went white as a sheet.'

'I . . . I've been waiting for this report.' He grabbed her and hugged her. 'I'll tell you what it's all about later.'

'So that's two of us with things to celebrate, isn't it?'

'Damn right it is.' He kissed her. 'Now,' he said, 'I have to go and tell O'Reilly. He's been waiting too.'

'Go ahead. He's over there with Kitty, but come back and tell me soon. I'm dying to hear.'

'I'll be back.' Barry started to walk to where O'Reilly stood deep in conversation with Kitty O'Hallorhan.

He heard Jack call, 'Good news? Harry told me what it said.'

'It's exactly what I wanted to hear. Why the hell didn't you tell me at once if you knew?'

'And spoil the surprise? Don't be daft, and it was worth it just to see that idiotic grin on your face.'

Barry shook his head, laughed and made a beeline for O'Reilly. Sonny's five dogs were clustered around O'Reilly and Kitty. There was no sign of Arthur Guinness. Nor of Sonny and Maggie. They must be getting changed into their going-away clothes.

O'Reilly and Kitty O'Hallorhan stood close together, O'Reilly's arm round Kitty's waist. Barry waited for them to finish speaking.

Kitty chuckled. 'And then you put me out of the fifth-floor window of the students' residence in the sling of that fire-escape device . . . and it only reached to the second floor.'

'At least the warden didn't catch you.' O'Reilly took his arm from Kitty's waist. 'Just . . . h-hem . . . talking about old times,' he said. 'What can we do for you, Barry?'

'Fingal, Jack Mills brought me the post-mortem report.'

O'Reilly's shoulders stiffened. 'And?'

'Massive silent coronary.'

'Bloody marvellous. Wonderful. Tough on the major, but that's life.' He grabbed Barry's hand. 'We'll see the widow tomorrow. She'll keep her promise now we have the facts. No lawsuit. I'm delighted for you, son.'

'I'm sure you'll explain all this in a minute, Fingal,' Kitty said.

'I will, but first this calls for a jar. Whiskey, Barry?'

'Just a small one, but later. I've left Patricia on her own, and I promised I'd explain to her what this is all about.'

'Right.' O'Reilly took command. 'You wait here, Kitty. I'll get the drinks. Barry, you bring Patricia over here. She'll want another wine.' He charged off, singing to himself a lyric Barry recognised came from *The Mikado*. 'The threatened cloud has passed away . . .'

'You've known him for years, Kitty. Was he always like this?'

'Worse,' she said. 'He's mellowing with age.'

She really had the most delightful smile.

'I'd better go and see Patricia,' Barry said. 'And thanks.'

'What for?'

'You know.' Barry hesitated. He meant for being with Fingal.

'Get on with you,' Kitty said, clearly having understood his meaning. 'We're just old friends.'

Patricia was waiting. 'Sorry about that,' he said. 'It's a long story, but that report I just got has saved my bacon. I was threatened with a lawsuit and it looked as if my partnership with O'Reilly might fall through.'

'Good God. You never said anything about it.' She frowned.

He shook his head. 'No. You'd enough on your plate.'

'The exam?' Her cheeks reddened.

Barry held up both hands. 'There was nothing you could do. I had to wait for the results of a post-mortem.'

'And you just got the results a few minutes ago?'

'That's right.'

'And it wasn't your fault.' She kissed him. 'Wonderful. So you'll stay?'

Should he tell her he'd been thinking of looking for a post in Cambridge to be near her? No.

'Yes,' he said. 'I can stay.' He looked into her eyes. 'But what about us?'

'Us?' She didn't answer at once. 'I love you, Barry. I really do.'

'And I love you. But three years is a hell of a long time.'

She took his hand. 'We both have our careers to think of. We're both of us far too young to get married, if that's what you have in mind.'

'I know all that,' he said, 'but—'

'There aren't any buts, Barry. Listen. If you love me as much as you say you do, you'll wait. Some people do, you know.'

'Sonny and Maggie?'

She nodded. 'I'll come back to you. Never worry about that.' She came closer, flung her arms round her neck. 'Don't you *ever* doubt it.'

He laughed, kissed her and said loudly, 'I believe you, Patricia. I love you and I don't give a hoot who knows.'

He was going to say more but was interrupted by cheers and the clattering of tin cans on gravel. The marquis's Rolls-Royce, strings of cans tied to its rear bumper, had drawn up to the portico of the big house.

'Come on,' he said. 'We have to go and see the happy couple off.'

They crossed the lawn and arrived just in time to see the marquis walking down the front steps with Sonny, now dressed in a neat, double-breasted grey suit, and Maggie in a heather-mix twin set, smart pleated wool skirt and straw hat with a single rose in the hatband. She carried her bouquet.

Well-wishers lined the steps.

Maggie threw her bouquet at the crowd. Barry wished Patricia had been the one to catch it, but the roar of approval from the crowd, and the look of bewilderment on O'Reilly's face when it flew straight to Kitty O'Hallorhan, made up for his disappointment.

Sonny helped Maggie into the back of the Roller, and the marquis, as befitted his position of best man, drove them away, accompanied by the clattering of cans and the music of a single piper.

'Tell me again, how long did you tell me Maggie had waited for Sonny?' Patricia asked.

'More than fifteen years,' Barry said without thinking.

'Now there's a thing,' she said, cocking her head slightly to the side, one eyebrow raised and a smile on her lips.

And Barry heard the unspoken promise and slipped an arm round her shoulders. 'Indeed it is,' he said.

He heard O'Reilly call, 'Barry, get over here this instant.'

O'Reilly was sitting with Kitty and Mrs Kincaid. Barry had forgotten that there were drinks waiting for Patricia and him. Taking her hand, he walked to the table. He noticed that Arthur Guinness lay underneath it, slurping from his stainless-steel bowl.

'Here you are.' O'Reilly handed the white wine to Patricia and the whiskey to Barry. 'Slàinte.'

'Slàinte mHath,' Barry replied.

'Right then,' said O'Reilly. 'The jollifications here are really going to get going now, but I've a half-notion you youngsters might like to slip away?'

Barry glanced at Patricia, who smiled up at him.

'Good,' said O'Reilly. 'In that case, I'll take call tonight.'

'Thanks, Fingal.' Barry set his glass on the table, but he was halted when O'Reilly bellowed, 'Not yet, you goat. You've not finished your drink. And before you gallop off, I've a job for you.'

Barry shrugged and picked up his whiskey.

'Now,' said O'Reilly, 'if I'm going to take call, I'll need to be near the phone.' He looked at Kinky. 'Do you think, Mrs Kincaid, you could put together a bite of supper for Sister O'Hallorhan and me?' He turned to Kitty. 'You might like to see how an old country GP lives?'

'That would be lovely.' She nodded her agreement.

'Supper is it?' Kinky asked, staring at O'Reilly's straining waistcoat buttons. 'I've all the makings of a wonderful salad, so.'

Barry had to smother a laugh.

O'Reilly grunted and bent down to reach under the table. Still bending, he fixed Barry with a stare. 'Dr Laverty,' he said slowly. 'I've not asked you about your plans for the future, but I'm going to take a chance now. In view of your recent news, will you be accepting my offer?'

'I will, Dr O'Reilly, and thank you.'

'Grand, so. Grand.' Kinky's chins wobbled as she laughed.

'And,' O'Reilly continued, 'I assume you'd like to work unsupervised?'

'Well, I . . .' It certainly was what he'd been dreaming of two weeks ago. 'Yes, Fingal. You would be right.'

'Good. Because I've your first independent case for you, Dr Laverty.'

Barry felt a pride in O'Reilly's obvious confidence. He'd rather be taking Patricia somewhere at once, but if there was a patient to be seen . . . He was relieved to see her nodding at him. 'Who is it, Fingal?'

'Not who . . . what.' O'Reilly guffawed as he straightened up. He pulled a single Wellington boot from under the table and thrust it at Barry. 'You find a home for that bloody thing, Dr Laverty . . . and you'll not have me breathing down your neck while you do.'

PATRICK TAYLOR

Born: August 23, 1941
Home: County Roscommon, Eire
Medical field: obstetrics and gynaecology

RD: Do you have a favourite bar in Ireland?
PT: There are four within walking distance of home. The grub's best at Donnellan's but it and The Water Splash are only open four days a week. Henry's and Clancys open seven days. I'm not going to pick a winner. It's a small community. And they do all keep their Guinness in good order.

RD: What three food items would you request, as treats, if you were stranded on a desert island?
PT: Melton Mowbray pie, scampi (that's Dublin Bay prawns), and roast, wild mallard duck.

RD: What sort of music drives you mad?
PT: Piped music, anywhere, that I have not asked for but am forced to listen to.

RD: And what's the worst book you've ever read?
PT: One called *A Peck of Salt,* which ran to 800 pages and detailed medical under-graduate life. It is still in a dusty box somewhere in my study.

RD: What was the happiest day of your life?
PT: I don't know. I have been so amazingly lucky, in so many ways, I hesitate to pick one. And, who knows, perhaps it is yet to happen?

RD: And what is guaranteed to bring peace to your heart?
PT: The love of a good woman, fifteen knots on the beam on a sunny day, the voice of Luciano Pavarotti, the constellations on a cloudless night, the poetry of William Butler Yeats—and healthy royalty cheques.

RD: Do you have a favourite spot in Ireland?
PT: Strangford Lough in County Down. I used to go there wildfowling with my father when I was a boy, and latterly by myself when I was a student and young doctor.

RD: Can you pick three famous people you'd like to meet?
PT: Ernest Shackleton and Oscar Wilde who were Irish, and Charles Dickens who was not—but should have been.

RD: Can you name a book you've never forgotten?
PT: I can name quite a few, but one? If only for its masterly storytelling and the way

in which it captures a time and place now long gone, *Shogun* by James Clavell.

RD: Money you should never have spent?

PT: When I was forty, on a sports car—I'll not mention the make—when I couldn't afford it and it was a bucket of bolts anyway.

RD: And a person you'd secretly like to be . . .

PT: Mark Twain. I'd kill to be able to tell stories like that man.

RD: The most inspiring words you've ever heard?

PT: Spoken by the Dean of the Faculty of Medicine at Queen's University, Belfast, when I was a student there in 1961. He said: 'And I don't care how hard you want to study, how much you want to be physicians, you will not be whole human beings if you don't read at least two non-medical books every week. I myself have a great attachment to Winnie the Pooh . . . although I do prefer it in Latin as *Winnie Ille Pu*.'

RD: And the best thing about the Irish, as a race?

PT: The craic, lively conversation, and a deep sense of their own history.

RD: If you won £1 million, what would you spend it on?

PT: A house each, here in Ireland, for my two grown-up children.

RD: And what legacy would you most like to leave to the world . . .

PT: I'm not really important enough to leave anything as grand as a legacy, either in the medical or literary fields. If my tombstone reads: *He did his best, he made us laugh, he wasn't a bad oul' hand, and he had a heart of corn*, I'll rest content.

MRS KINCAID'S SODA FARLS

INGREDIENTS :
1lb (450g) plain flour
1 tsp salt
1tsp baking soda, heaped
10–15fl oz (300 to 450ml) of buttermilk
Preheat oven to 425°F/220°C/Gas mark 7.

METHOD:
Sieve the dry ingredients into a bowl. Make a well in the centre and gradually add enough buttermilk to give a soft, but not sticky, dough. Turn onto a well-floured board and shape into a round cake 1.5ins (4cm) thick. Transfer to a floured baking sheet and mark into 4 to 6 wedges (farls). Bake for 30 to 35 minutes. For a crunchy crust, put on a rack to cool. For a softer crust, wrap cake in a clean dishcloth. The farls can be separated once the soda bread has cooled. Delicious served warm, sliced or split, with butter and homemade jam.

All the
Colours
of Darkness

PETER ROBINSON

When DCI Banks is called back from
an idyllic weekend away with his
girlfriend to lead a double murder
investigation, his reaction is one
of annoyance. Especially since the
motives for the deaths seem to be
straightforward: a crime of passion
followed by a guilt-ridden suicide.
But once Banks learns that one of
the victims was a former secret
service agent, his curiosity is
aroused and he can't resist
digging deeper for answers . . .

Chapter One

Detective Inspector Annie Cabbot thought it was a great shame that she had to spend one of the most beautiful days of the year so far at a crime scene, especially a hanging. She hated hangings. And on a Friday afternoon, too.

Annie had been dispatched, along with Detective Sergeant Winsome Jackman, to Hindswell Woods, just south of Eastvale Castle, where some schoolboys spending the last day of their half-term holiday splashing in the River Swain had phoned to say they had seen a body.

The river ran swift, broad and shallow here, the colour of freshly pumped beer, frothing around the mossy stones. The scent of wild garlic filled the air, clusters of midges hovered over the water, and on the other side the meadows were full of buttercups, pignut and cranesbill.

Four schoolboys, all aged about ten or eleven, sat hunched on the boulders by the water, draped in towels, strips of pale skin, white as tripe, exposed here and there. They'd told the police that one of them had chased another off the path into the woods above the river, and they had stumbled upon a body hanging from an oak tree. One of them dialled 999 on his mobile, and they waited by the riverside. When the police officers and the ambulance crew arrived and took a look at the body, they agreed there was nothing they could do, so they radioed for the heavy brigade. Now it was Annie's job to assess the situation and decide on what action should be taken.

Annie left Winsome to take statements from the kids and followed the patrol officer up the slope into the woods. Before long, just over the rise, she caught a glimpse of a figure hanging from a length of yellow clothes line on a low bough ahead of her, its feet about eighteen inches off the ground. It made a striking contrast to the light green of the woods because it—Annie couldn't tell yet whether the shape was a man or a woman—was dressed in an orange shirt and black trousers. The tree was a gnarled old oak that stood alone in a small copse. The area around it had been taped off.

'You checked for any signs of life, I assume?' Annie asked the young constable who was making his way through the undergrowth beside her.

'The paramedic did, ma'am,' he answered. 'But you don't have to get that close to see that he's dead.'

A man, then. Annie ducked under the police tape and inched forward. As she stopped about ten feet away, she could see for herself that he was a man. His head was closely shaved, and what hair remained had been dyed blond. She guessed his age at somewhere between forty and forty-five. He wasn't twisting at the end of the rope, the way corpses do in movies, but hanging heavy and silent as a rock from the taut yellow clothes line. He seemed to have a lot of blood on him for a hanging victim.

Most hangings were suicides, Annie knew, not murders, for the obvious reason that it was very difficult to hang a man while he was still alive. If it was a suicide, why, Annie wondered, had the victim chosen this particular place to end his life? This tree? Did it have strong personal associations for him, or had it simply been convenient?

Annie knew that she needed the scenes-of-crime officers here as soon as possible. She took out her mobile and rang Stefan Nowak, the crime scene manager, who told her to wait and said he would organise his team. Next, she left a message for Detective Superintendent Catherine Gervaise, who was in a meeting at County HQ in Northallerton, to let her know what was happening.

Then there was Banks—Detective Chief Inspector Alan Banks, her immediate boss. Should she call him? He had taken off early for the weekend, driving down to London that morning to stay with his girlfriend. Annie couldn't complain. Banks had plenty of time off due to him, and she herself had recently got back from a two-week stay with her father in St Ives.

She decided that Banks could wait. It was time to get back to the river and see what Winsome had found out from the kids. Poor buggers, Annie thought as she tottered back down the slope. On the other hand, kids were resilient, and when they got back to school on Monday morning, they'd have one hell of a story to tell their mates.

AFTER THE SCHOOLCHILDREN had been sent home to their parents, Annie leaned against a tree in companionable silence with Winsome and watched the SOCOs work the scene in their disposable white oversuits.

The kids hadn't known much. About the only piece of interesting information Winsome had gleaned from them was that when they had first approached the shallows along the riverside path from Eastvale at about one o'clock, just after lunch, and run up the slope, there had been no sign of the hanging man. It was 3.17 p.m. when the 999 call had been logged, which gave a window of just over two hours.

DI Stefan Nowak slipped off his face mask and goggles, ducked under the tape and ambled towards Annie and Winsome. 'You're in luck,' he said.

'Suicide?'

'The post-mortem should verify our findings, but from what Dr Burns and I saw, the only wounds on his throat were those caused by the rope, and it was in exactly the place you'd expect it to be. Of course, there's no saying he wasn't poisoned first, and we'll certainly ask for a full toxicology report, but there are no visible signs of serious physical trauma to the body other than those that can be related to the hanging.'

'What about all the blood, if that's what it was?' asked Annie.

'It was. We've taken samples, of course. The only thing is . . .' Nowak frowned. 'Well, it *could* have come from the superficial scratches he got when he climbed the tree, but there's rather a lot more blood than I would have expected from a few scratches. We can get typing done pretty quickly, but as you know, DNA and tox screens take quite a bit longer.'

'Soon as you can,' Annie said. 'The rope?'

'Cheap nylon washing line, the kind you can buy almost anywhere.'

'And the knot?'

'Perfectly consistent with the kind of knot a potential suicide might tie. It was on the left side, by the way, which indicates a left-handed person, and given that he was wearing his wristwatch on his right hand . . . I'd say all the indications we have here point to a suicide by hanging.'

'Any idea who he was? Did he have a wallet with him? Keys?'

'No. It's my guess that he drove out here and left them in his car, maybe in his jacket. He wouldn't have had any further use for them, would he?'

'I suppose not,' said Annie. 'We'll have to find out who his next of kin is. Any signs of a suicide note?'

'Not on or near him, no. Again, it's possible he left something in the car.'

'We'll check when we find it. I'd also like to know what his movements were this afternoon. As far as we know, he killed himself sometime between one and three. Most of all, we need to know who he was.'

'That's easy,' said one of the SOCOs, a civilian soil expert by the name of Tim Mallory. Annie hadn't noticed him come up behind them.

'It is?' she asked.

'Sure. I don't know his second name, but everyone called him Mark. He worked at the Eastvale Theatre. You know, the one on Market Street.'

'I know where you mean,' said Annie. The town council had recently restored an old Georgian theatre that had fallen into disrepair. For the past year and a half, it had been the centre for all thespian endeavours in town, along with the occasional concert. 'What did he do there?' she asked.

'Something to do with props and scenery. My wife's a member of the amateur operatic society,' Mallory added. 'That's how I know.'

'Know anything else about him?'

'Nah, not really,' Mallory said. 'Except that he's gay. It's pretty common knowledge around the place.'

'Know where he lived?'

'No, but one of the theatre crowd would.'

'I don't suppose you know what kind of car he drives, do you?'

'Sorry.'

'OK. Thanks.' What Mallory and Nowak had told her should certainly make her job a lot easier. She nudged Winsome. 'Come on, let's get over to the theatre,' she said. 'There's nothing more we can do here.'

Just then a young PC came trotting up the path, out of breath. 'Excuse me, ma'am, but we think we've found the car. Want to see it now?'

THE CAR WAS a dark green Toyota, an even earlier model than Annie's old purple Astra, and it had definitely seen better days. It stood in the parking area between the river and the main Swainsdale road. They couldn't be certain it belonged to the victim yet, but the key left in the ignition had drawn the attention of the uniformed officers. Maps, petrol receipts, sweet wrappers and CD cases littered the passenger seat, and in the back, along with what looked like some theatrical props, was a black zip-up windcheater.

Annie found the victim's wallet in a side pocket of the windcheater, along with a set of keys. He had forty-five pounds in notes, credit and debit cards in the name of Mark G. Hardcastle, a couple of business cards, a driving licence complete with photograph and an address not far from the centre of town, along with a date of birth that put his age at forty-six. There was no suicide note. Annie went through the pile of stuff on the passenger seat and on the floor, under the seats. Nothing. Next she checked the boot and found a cardboard box full of old newspapers for recycling, and some antifreeze.

Annie took a deep breath of fresh air. 'Do you think he just happened to be carrying a length of clothes line with him?'

'Unlikely,' Winsome answered. 'But it could have been a theatrical prop.'

'True. But if he was planning to hang himself, and he *didn't* have any rope conveniently stashed in his car, he'd have had to buy some, wouldn't he? We'll get Harry Potter to check the local shops. It shouldn't be too difficult to trace.' Annie showed Winsome a handful of receipts from Hardcastle's wallet. 'Three of these are from London—Waterstone's, HMV and a Zizzi's restaurant. All dated this past Wednesday. There's also a petrol receipt from an M1 service station at Watford Gap dated Thursday morning.'

'Any signs of a mobile phone?' Winsome asked.

'None.' Annie glanced back at the car. 'I think we'd better make a few enquiries around the theatre,' she said. 'But first we should call at his home. God forbid there's someone there waiting for him.'

BRANWELL COURT branches off Market Street just a hundred yards or so south of the square. The houses, among the oldest in Eastvale, are all weathered limestone with flagstone roofs, cheek by jowl but varying greatly in width and height. Many have been divided into flats.

Number 26 had a purple door with the name MARK G. HARDCASTLE engraved in a brass plate beside the doorbell to the upper floor. Annie rang the bell. Nobody came down the stairs. She tried the keys she had taken from the pocket of Hardcastle's windcheater. The third one fitted, and led them into a whitewashed hall. A few letters lay scattered on the floor. Annie picked them up to examine later, and they climbed the narrow staircase.

The upstairs flat was tiny. There was hardly space in the living room for the television set and sofa, and the dining area was a narrow passage with a table and four chairs, between the living room and the small kitchen. A ladder led up from the dining area to the converted loft. Annie climbed up.

There was barely room for the double bed, bedside table and a chest of drawers. Very quaint, Annie thought, but almost uninhabitable.

'Strange place to live, isn't it?' said Winsome, catching up with her in the attic and standing with her head bowed, not in reverence, but because she was over six feet tall and there was no way she could stand upright.

'Definitely bijou.'

The bed had been slept in, its flower-patterned duvet askew, but it was impossible to tell whether one or two people had lain there. Winsome checked the dresser drawers and found only socks, underwear and a few T-shirts.

Downstairs again, they checked the kitchen cabinets, which held pots and pans, and some tins of mushroom soup, salmon and tuna. The fridge was home to several wilting lettuce leaves, an almost empty tub of Flora, some wafer-sliced ham with a sell-by date of May 21, and a carton of milk.

In the living room, there were no family photographs on the mantelpiece, and there certainly wasn't a convenient suicide note propped up against the brass clock. In the bookcase next to the television were a few popular paperbacks, several historical books on costumes, a cheap complete works of Shakespeare, and a few DVDs and CDs. Hanging over the fireplace was an old poster for a Stoke-on-Trent repertory production of *Look Back in Anger* with Mark Hardcastle's name listed in the stage credits.

Annie scanned the letters she had picked up earlier. The oldest was postmarked the previous week, and they were either utility bills or special offers.

'What do you think?' Winsome asked.

'There's nothing really *personal* here, have you noticed?' Annie said. 'It's as if he only lived here part-time, or he only lived part of his life here.'

'Maybe he did,' Winsome offered.

'Then let's see if we can find out where he lived the rest of it,' said Annie. 'Fancy going to the theatre?'

THE EASTVALE THEATRE was a masterpiece of restoration, Annie thought, and it managed to pack a great deal into two storeys hardly more than forty feet wide. A wine bar and café had been added to the side of the original building in the same stone and design. Only the large, long plate-glass windows on the addition bowed in the direction of a more modern style. Beside the entrance were posters for the major production now running, the Eastvale Amateur Dramatic Society's version of *Othello*.

Annie and Winsome went into the foyer, and showed their warrant cards to an overly made-up woman in the box office.

'Excuse me,' Annie said. 'Is the manager here?'

The woman smiled. 'Do you mean the stage manager, dearie?'

'I mean the person in charge,' said Annie.

'There isn't one, really. I mean, there's the stage manager, but he's not—'

'How about someone who works with the props, sets?'

'Ah, that'll be Vernon Ross. He's in charge of all the technical stuff.' The woman squinted at Annie. 'What's this about?'

'Please?' said Annie. 'We're in a hurry.'

The woman frowned and nodded towards the theatre entrance. 'If you walk through those doors down the aisle to the stage, you should find him there. They'll be getting ready for tonight.'

'OK. Thanks,' said Annie.

They headed through the double doors. The house lights were on, and several people in jeans and T-shirts were shifting pieces of furniture and backdrops. A young woman glanced up. 'Sorry, we're closed,' she said.

'I know,' Annie said. 'I'd like to talk to Vernon Ross. Is he here?'

A man came down from the stage and walked towards her. Older than the rest, he had curly grey hair and was wearing khaki overalls and a checked work shirt. 'I'm Vernon Ross,' he said. 'How can I help you?'

Annie shook Ross's extended hand. 'DI Annie Cabbot and DS Winsome Jackman, Western Area Major Crimes.'

Ross frowned. 'Well, that's quite a mouthful,' he said. 'But, as far as I'm aware, we haven't had any major crimes around here.'

'No,' said Annie with a smile. 'At least we hope not.'

'What's it about, then?'

'Were you a friend of Mark Hardcastle's?'

'*Was* I? We all are. Yes. Why?' His forehead creased into a frown. 'What is it? Has something happened to Mark? Has there been an accident?'

Annie became aware that work had ceased on and around the stage. 'Do you happen to know if he has any next of kin?' she asked.

'My God,' said Ross, 'so this is serious?'

'Sir?'

'No, no,' said Ross. 'His parents are dead. He did once mention an aunt in Australia, but I don't think they were at all close. Why? What—?'

Annie turned to face everyone. 'I'm sorry to be the bearer of bad tidings,' she said, 'but it seems that Mark Hardcastle has been found dead in Hindswell Woods.'

As Annie had expected, a deep hush followed her announcement. Vernon Ross turned pale. 'Mark? But how? *Why?*'

'We don't have the answers yet,' said Annie. 'That's partly why I'm here. Did any of you see Mr Hardcastle today?'

'No. He didn't come in,' said Ross. 'I . . . I'm sorry, but I can't quite manage to take this in right now.'

'That's understandable, sir,' Annie said. 'Would you like to sit down?'

'No, no. I'll be all right.' He rubbed the backs of his hands across his eyes. 'Please, carry on with your questions. Let's get this over with.'

'Very well. Was Mr Hardcastle expected in today?'

'Well, he said he was going to try and come by. He'd been down to London for a couple of days with Derek Wyman, the am dram director.'

'Is Mr Wyman here today?'

'No. He's still in London. He's due back tomorrow.'

'You don't need him for tonight's performance?'

'No.' He gestured to his co-workers. 'Mark and us are the only ones actually employed by the theatre—along with the box-office staff, of course. The amateur dramatic society has its own director and cast. And everything's in place for tonight. We can manage without Derek for a couple of nights.'

'So Mr Wyman isn't employed by the theatre, but Mr Hardcastle was?'

'That's right. Derek teaches drama at Eastvale Comprehensive. Amateur dramatics is only his hobby, as it is for the actors. Mark trained professionally in theatrical costume and set design.'

'I'll need to talk to Mr Wyman when he gets back.'

'Of course. Sally in the box office will give you his address.'

'When did Mark Hardcastle go to London?'

'Wednesday. He was supposed to be driving back up yesterday afternoon.'

'Weren't you concerned when he didn't show up for work today?'

'Not really. As I said, Mark's our set and costume designer. His job is mostly done by opening night. He creates the vision of the production, the blueprint of how it should appear. Along with the director, of course.'

'In this case Derek Wyman?'

'Yes. For some reason, they settled on German Expressionist sets for

Othello. That's why they went to London, actually. There's a celebration of German Expressionist cinema at the National Film Theatre.'

'Do you know if Mark Hardcastle had a mobile phone?'

'No. He hated them. Used to go spare every time one went off during a performance. What's happened to Mark? You say he's been found dead. Has there been an accident? Did someone kill him?'

The others all sat on the edge of the stage listening closely.

'What makes you think that?' Winsome asked.

Ross looked at her. 'Well, *you're* here, aren't you? Major Crimes.'

'We don't know what we're dealing with yet, Mr Ross,' Winsome said. 'In all cases of suspicious death there are certain protocols to follow.'

'So he didn't just drop dead of a heart attack, then?'

'No, he didn't. Did he have a bad heart? Was he ill?'

'It was just a figure of speech. His health was fine,' said Ross. 'As far as we knew. I mean, he was always full of energy. He loved life.'

'Did he take drugs?' Annie asked.

'Not that I was aware of.'

'Anyone?' Annie glanced around the room. They all shook their heads. 'Can any of you tell me anything about Mr Hardcastle's recent state of mind?'

'Did he commit suicide?' asked one young woman. She had a pleasant, heart-shaped face, and her light brown hair was tied back in a ponytail.

'And you are . . . ?' Annie asked.

'Maria. Maria Wolsey.'

'Well, suicide is a possibility. Was he depressed or upset about anything?'

'He'd been a bit edgy lately,' Maria said. 'That's all.'

'Edgy? In what way? Why?'

'I don't know. Just . . . like there was something worrying him.'

'I understand that Mr Hardcastle was gay,' Annie said.

'Mark was quite open about his sexuality,' said Vernon Ross.

'This trip to London with Mr Wyman,' Annie went on. 'Anything in it?'

'Good Lord, no,' Ross said. 'Derek's a happily married man. With children. Has been for years. They're just colleagues with shared interests, that's all.'

'Did Mark Hardcastle have a partner?'

'I think so,' said Ross, clearly a bit embarrassed by the whole idea.

'Maria?'

'Yes, he did. Laurence. I don't know his surname.'

'Was this relationship recent?'

'Six months or so, I think,' said Maria. 'He was very happy.'

'What was he like before?'

Maria paused, then said, 'I wouldn't say he was unhappy, but he was definitely more restless and superficial. He lived for his work.'

'Did you ever meet Laurence?'

'A few times, when he came to the theatre.'

'Could you describe him?'

'About six foot, handsome, a bit sort of upper class. Dark hair with a touch of grey at the temples. Slender, athletic. Very charming, but rather remote. Maybe a bit of a snob. You know, a sort of public-school type.'

'Do you know what Laurence does? What his job is?'

'Mark never mentioned anything. I think he might be retired.'

'How old?'

'Early fifties, I'd say.'

'Do you know where he lives? We really need to find him.'

'Sorry,' said Maria. 'I don't know. I think he's fairly well off, though—at least his mother is, so he's probably got a posh house. Mark was spending more and more time with him. They were practically living together.'

Annie saw Winsome make a note of that. 'This change you noticed in Mr Hardcastle lately,' she went on, 'can you tell me more about it?'

'He'd just been a bit moody this past couple of weeks, that's all,' Maria said. 'About a week ago he shouted at me for putting a table in the wrong place on the stage. He never usually does that.'

Ross glared at Maria. 'Just a lover's tiff, I should imagine,' he said.

'Lasting two weeks?' Annie said.

'It didn't appear serious at the time,' Ross said. 'Mark was just in a bad mood. It happens to all of us. There was nothing that would drive him to *suicide*, for crying out loud.'

'If he did commit suicide,' said Annie, 'do any of you know if Mr Hardcastle had someone he might have talked to, shared his problems with? Other than Derek Wyman.'

No one said anything.

'Anyone know where he was from?'

'Barnsley,' said Maria. 'He was always making jokes about it, said he had to support the local football team when he was growing up or people would think he was a poof. His dad worked down the pit. I got the impression it was a tough place to grow up gay.'

'I should imagine so,' said Annie. 'Is there anyone else here who was close to Mark Hardcastle?'

One of the other girls spoke up. 'We all felt close to Mark. He made you feel special. You could talk to him about anything.'

'Did he talk to you about his problems?'

'No,' the girl said. 'But he'd listen to yours and give you advice if you wanted it. He was so wise. I just can't believe it. I can't believe any of this.' She started crying and took out a handkerchief.

Annie glanced at Winsome to let her know they were done. Then she took some cards from her briefcase and handed them out.

'If any of you think of anything, please don't hesitate to call,' she said. Then she looked at Vernon Ross again and said, 'Mr Ross, can I ask if you would mind coming to the mortuary with us now, to identify the body?'

Chapter Two

'Got it!' said Annie, punching the air in victory. It was half past eight on Saturday morning, and she and Winsome were in the Western Area HQ squad room with DC Doug Wilson. They had called it a day at seven o'clock the previous evening, after Vernon Ross had identified Mark Hardcastle's body. After a quick drink they had each gone their separate ways home.

Wilson had canvassed the local shops and discovered that Mark Hardcastle had bought the yellow clothes line from a hardware shop owned by a Mr Oliver Grainger at about a quarter to one on Friday afternoon. He had blood on his hands and face, and Grainger had thought he might have cut himself doing some carpentry. He had also smelt strongly of whisky, though he hadn't acted drunk. According to Grainger, he had appeared oddly calm and subdued.

Now, while sorting through the SOCO reports on her desk, Annie discovered that a thorough search of Mark Hardcastle's car had produced a letter mixed in among the newspapers and magazines in the boot. The letter was nothing in itself, just an old special wine offer from John Lewis, but it was addressed to a Laurence Silbert at 15 Castleview Heights.

'Got what?' asked Winsome.

'I think I've found the lover. He's called Laurence Silbert. He lives in the Heights.' Annie got up and grabbed her jacket. 'Could you hold the fort?'

'Of course,' said Winsome.

Annie turned to Doug Wilson, whose youthful looks, along with the glasses, had earned him the nickname 'Harry Potter' around the station. With his hesitant manner and tendency to stutter when under stress, Doug Wilson wasn't ready to conduct interviews, but all he needed, Annie reckoned, was a bit more self-confidence, and only on-the-job experience would give him that.

'Want to come along, Doug?' she asked.

'Yes, guv,' he said. 'Absolutely.'

'Don't tread on any toes up there,' said Winsome. 'And you'll ring me and let me know what happens?'

Annie smiled. 'Yes, Mother,' she said as she turned to leave.

DC Wilson put on his glasses, and dashed out of the door behind her.

CASTLEVIEW HEIGHTS had the reputation of being an exclusive club for Eastvale's wealthy and privileged. You wouldn't get much change from a million quid for a house up on the Heights, Annie thought, as DC Wilson parked outside number 15. That is, if the tenants' association and neighbourhood watch committee approved of your credentials. Laurence Silbert must have had both money and status.

Getting out of the car, Annie could see why the locals did their best to protect their habitat from the hoi polloi. The view was magnificent. To the south stood the ruined castle on its hill, and below that the River Swain tripped over a series of little waterfalls. Directly across the water stood the Green, with its Georgian semis and mighty old trees. On the left riverbank, beyond the castle, Annie could also see the beginnings of Hindswell Woods, where Mark Hardcastle's body had been discovered.

Annie breathed in the air. It was another beautiful day, fragrant and mild. DC Wilson stood waiting for instructions, hands in his pockets, and Annie turned to the house. It was an impressive sight: a walled garden with a black wrought-iron gate surrounded the gabled mansion, built of local limestone, with large mullioned windows and ivy and clematis climbing up the walls. A short gravel drive led from the gates to the front door. Just to the right was a garage, converted from an old coach house. The double doors were open, and inside was an extremely sleek and expensive silver Jaguar.

So Mark Hardcastle hadn't only got lucky in love; he'd found himself a rich boyfriend into the bargain. Annie wondered how much that had mattered to him. It was a long journey for the son of a Barnsley coal miner.

Annie banged the brass lion's-head knocker on the front door. The sound echoed through the quiet neighbourhood. From inside there was nothing.

'Shall we try round the back, guv?' asked Wilson.

Annie peered in through the front windows but could see only dim, empty rooms. 'Might as well,' she said.

The path led between the coach house and the main building into a spacious back garden complete with hedges, well-kept lawn and flowerbeds. On their way, Annie put her hand on the Jaguar's bonnet. Cool.

'Seems like this Silbert bloke's away, doesn't it?' said Wilson.

'But his car's in the garage,' Annie reminded him.

'Maybe he's got more than one. Bloke this rich . . . Range Rover or something? Visiting his country estates?'

Wilson had imagination; Annie had to grant him that. There was a conservatory at the back of the house. She tried the door and found that it was open. A small pile of newspapers lay on the table, dated last Sunday.

The door that led through to the main house was locked, however, so she knocked and called out Silbert's name. Her attempts were met with an eerie silence. Something was wrong; she knew it. Could she justify breaking in without a warrant? She thought so. A man had been found dead, and a letter in his possession clearly linked him to this address.

Annie wrapped her hand in one of the newspapers and punched out the pane of glass directly above the area of the lock. She was in luck. Inside was a large key that opened the dead bolt when she turned it. They were in.

She found herself in a cheerfully decorated living room, with vibrant, modern paintings on the walls. The only furniture was a three-piece suite, a black grand piano and a series of bookcases built into the walls. They walked through to the spotless kitchen, all gleaming white tiles, brushed-steel surfaces and every utensil a master chef would ever need.

A broad, carpeted staircase led from the hallway upstairs. As they walked up, every once in a while Annie called out Silbert's name but she was met with that same chill silence. Their feet made no noise on the thick patterned carpet on the landing as they padded around, checking the rooms.

It was behind the third door that they found Laurence Silbert.

Fortunately, they didn't have to do anything more than stand at the threshold to see the body that lay on the sheepskin rug in front of the hearth. Silbert—or at least Annie assumed it was Silbert—lay on his back, arms spread out, making the shape of a cross. His head had been beaten to a pulp, and a dark halo of blood soaked into the sheepskin around it. He was wearing tan chinos and a shirt that had once been white but was now mostly dark red. The area between his legs was also bloody.

Annie became vaguely aware of Wilson's grunt and the sound of him being sick on the landing before he managed to get to the bathroom.

Pale and trembling, she shut the door and reached for her mobile. First she rang Detective Superintendent Gervaise. Something big like this, you let the boss know immediately. Gervaise said she would call in the SOCOs, photographer, police surgeon. Then she said, 'And DI Cabbot?'

'Yes?'

'I think it's time we called DCI Banks back. I know he's on holiday, but things could get very messy up here, and this *is* the Heights. We need to be seen to have a senior officer in charge. No criticism implied.'

'None taken, ma'am,' said Annie. 'As you wish.'

As she watched an ashen Wilson sitting on the stairs with his head in his hands, she picked Banks's mobile number from her BlackBerry's address book and pressed the call button.

ALAN BANKS STRETCHED and almost purred as he reached for the lukewarm cup of tea on the bedside table. The sun was shining, the glorious morning warmth rolling in through the slightly open window, the net curtains fluttering. Tinariwen were singing 'Cler Achel' on the alarm clock's iPod dock and all was well with the world.

Sophia had had to go to work, unfortunately, but just for the morning. That evening, they were hosting a dinner party, and they would spend the afternoon shopping for ingredients at one of her favourite farmers' markets, probably Notting Hill. He loved to watch her choosing strangely shaped and oddly coloured fruits or vegetables, an expression of pure childlike wonder on her face as she felt their firmness and the texture of their skin.

In the evening, he would offer to help make dinner, but he knew that Sophia would only shoo him out of the way. At best he might be allowed to chop a few vegetables, or prepare the salad. The special alchemy of cooking was reserved for Sophia alone, and he had to admit that she did it with flair.

Banks put his cup down and lay back. He could smell the pillow where Sophia had lain beside him, her hair like the memory of apples he had picked in the orchard with his father one glorious autumn afternoon of his childhood. His fingers remembered the touch of her skin, and that brought back the one little wrinkle on the mantle of his happiness.

Last night, making love, he had told her that she had beautiful skin, and she had laughed and replied, 'So I've been told.' It wasn't the little vanity that bothered him but the thought of the other men who had been close enough to tell her that before him. That way madness lies, he told himself, or at least misery. No matter how many lovers she had had, whatever he and she did together, they did for the first time. That was the only way to think of it. John and Yoko had it right: *Two Virgins*.

Enough lounging around and slipping into dark thoughts, Banks told himself. It was nine o'clock, time to get up. After he had showered and dressed, he made his way downstairs. Sophia's terrace house was in a narrow street off the King's Road. Its pastel blue façade reminded Banks a little of the blue of Santorini—perhaps deliberate, as Sophia was half Greek. Though it looked narrow from the outside, the plot was deep and the space opened up when you went inside: living room to the right, stairs to the left, dining room and kitchen at the end of the hall, and a little garden at the back. On the second level were the two bedrooms, one with an en-suite shower and toilet, and Sophia used the converted attic as her home office.

The house was full of *things*. Spindly legged tables inlaid with ivory or mother-of-pearl held artfully arranged displays of fossils, amphorae, stone jars, Victorian shell boxes, crystals, agates, seashells and smooth pebbles that Sophia had collected from all over the world. She collected masks, too: dark wooden ones from Africa, coloured bead ones from South America, painted ceramic masks from the Far East. They hung between the bold abstract paintings that covered the walls. There were also peacock feathers, dried ferns and flowers, a chunk of the Berlin Wall, tiny animal skulls from the Nevada desert and worry beads from Istanbul. Sophia said she loved all these things and felt responsible for them; she was merely taking care of them temporarily, and they would continue long after she was gone.

Quite a responsibility, Banks had said, which was why Sophia had installed a top-of-the-line security system. He set the security code before he left the house. Sophia would never forgive him if he forgot and someone broke in. Insurance was no good. None of the stuff was valuable, but to her everything was priceless. It was also just the sort of stuff on which a burglar, finding nothing he could fence, might take out his frustrations.

Banks stopped at the newsagent's and bought the *Guardian*, then headed to the local Italian café for an espresso and a chocolate croissant. No sooner had he sat down to read the film reviews when his mobile buzzed.

He put the phone to his ear. 'Banks.'

'Alan. Sorry to bother you on your weekend off,' said Annie, 'but we've got a bit of a crisis brewing up here. The super says we could use your help.'

'Why? What is it?'

He listened as Annie told him what she knew.

'It sounds like a murder-suicide to me,' said Banks. 'For Christ's sake, Annie, can't you handle it? Sophia's organising a dinner party tonight.'

He could hear Annie's intake of breath. 'The last thing I'd want to do is spoil Sophia's dinner party by stealing you away,' she said. 'But it's orders from above. Besides, it could turn into something big and nasty. There's money involved—Castleview Heights—and the gay community. Yes, I agree, it *looks* like a murder-suicide so far, but we haven't got the forensics back yet and we don't know a great deal about the victims, either.'

'You won't get forensics until the middle of next week. Maybe you should have waited until then before calling me.'

'Bollocks, Alan,' said Annie. 'I'm only the messenger. Just get up here and do your job. And if you've got a problem with that, talk to the super.'

And she left Banks listening to the silence, chocolate croissant halfway to his mouth.

ANNIE STOOD BEHIND the crime-scene tape that zigzagged across the door of the drawing room and watched Dr Burns, the forensic medical examiner, go to work for the second time in two days. Annie was still inwardly fuming at Banks, but on the outside she was all business. She had been shaken by what she had seen and had overreacted, simple as that. Even so, who the hell did Banks think he was, telling her what to do and what not to do?

Stefan Nowak was running the show for the moment. He stood beside Annie with a clipboard in his hand, his SOCO team kitted up and ready to go. Everyone, even Annie and Wilson, was wearing full protective clothing. As soon as Dr Burns had finished his external examination, Nowak sent in the trace experts to take blood, hair and any other samples they could find.

Annie went in with them. She needed a closer look at the body. She didn't blame Wilson for being sick. She had seen quite a few crime scenes in her time, but this one had shaken her, too: the sheer frenzied violence of it, the blood and brains splattered everywhere, the sense of pointless overkill. The place was a shambles; antique tables had been knocked over, vases smashed, mirrors and crystal ware shattered. Amidst it all, Annie could make out a framed photograph on the floor, its glass spider-webbed with cracks, showing Mark Hardcastle with his arm round the shoulder of the dead man. Both were smiling into the camera.

She ducked under the tape and went back out to join Dr Burns on the landing. He was busy making notes in a black book.

'Jesus Christ,' Burns whispered, putting the notebook away and looking at her. 'I've rarely seen such a vicious attack.'

'Anything you can tell me?' Annie asked.

'According to body temperature and the progress of rigor,' Burns said, 'I'd estimate that he's been dead about twenty to twenty-four hours.'

Annie made a quick calculation. 'So between nine a.m. and one p.m. yesterday. Cause of death?'

Dr Burns glanced back to the body. 'You can see that for yourself. Blows to the head with a blunt object. I can't say yet which blow actually killed him. Dr Glendenning should be able to tell you more at the post-mortem. There are defensive wounds on the backs of his hands, as if he held them over his face to protect himself.'

'Is the arrangement of the body natural?' she asked.

'You're thinking of the cross shape, did someone arrange it that way?'

'Yes.'

'I doubt it. I think when he gave up the ghost he just let his arms fall naturally the way they did. A posed body would appear more symmetrical. See how crooked the right arm is? It's broken, by the way.'

'Weapon?'

Burns jerked his head back towards the room. 'The SOCOs have it. A cricket bat.' He gave a harsh laugh. 'One signed by the entire England team that won back the Ashes in 2005. Read what you will into that.'

Annie didn't want to read anything into it. Not yet. 'What about the other wounds?' she asked. 'You know . . . between his legs?'

'On a cursory examination, I'd say they were also done with the cricket bat, and the blood you see there was transferred from the head wounds.'

'So that happened *after* he was dead?'

'Well, he may have still been clinging on to some vestiges of life, but it was done *after* the head wounds, I'd say, yes.'

'Sex crime?'

'That's for you to decide. I'd certainly say that the evidence points that way. Otherwise why attack the genitals after the head?'

'A hate crime, perhaps? Anti-gay?'

'It's possible,' said Burns. 'Or it could simply be a jealous lover. The element of overkill points in that direction. Whatever it is, you're certainly dealing with some high-octane emotions here.'

You can say that again, Annie thought. 'Any sexual interference?'

'As far as I can tell, no, but I'd suggest you wait for the full SOCO report and Dr Glendenning's post-mortem before forming any conclusions.'

'Thank you, Doctor,' said Annie. 'I will.'

And with that, Dr Burns marched off down the stairs. Annie was just about to follow him when Stefan Nowak came over, a small leather-bound book in his gloved hand.

'Thought you might find this useful,' he said. 'It was on the desk.'

Annie took the book from him and looked inside. It was an address book. There weren't many entries, but two in particular interested her: Mark Hardcastle on Branwell Court, and one written simply as 'Mother', with a phone number and address in Longborough, Gloucestershire.

'Thanks, Stefan,' said Annie. 'I'll inform the locals and make sure someone goes out there to break the news.'

Annie bagged the book and then went downstairs. She needed some fresh air. In the back garden, she found Doug Wilson talking to Detective Superintendent Gervaise, who had just arrived. To Annie's surprise, Chief Constable Reginald Murray was also there.

'Ma'am, sir,' said Annie.

'DI Cabbot,' said Gervaise. 'The chief constable is here because he was a friend of the victim's.'

'I wouldn't exactly say friend,' said Murray, fingering his collar. 'But I knew Laurence from the golf club. A murder on the Heights. This is a terrible business, DI Cabbot. The quicker we get to the bottom of it, the better.' He glanced at Gervaise. 'I assume DCI Banks has been informed?'

'He's on his way, sir.'

Murray nodded and wandered off.

Gervaise turned to Annie. 'How goes it so far? Any thoughts?'

Annie handed Doug Wilson the address book and asked him to go back to the station and get in touch with the Gloucestershire police. He seemed relieved to be leaving the Heights. Then Annie turned to Gervaise, 'Not much yet, ma'am.' She summarised what Dr Burns had told her. 'The timing certainly fits a murder-suicide theory,' she added.

'You think Mark Hardcastle did this?'

'Possibly, yes,' said Annie. 'As far as we know, he drove back to Eastvale from London on Thursday. He could have gone back to his flat in Branwell Court and come up here Friday morning, or come straight here and stopped over Thursday night. All we know is that Silbert was killed between nine a.m. and one p.m. on Friday, and Hardcastle hanged himself between one and three p.m. the same day. Also, the amount of blood on Hardcastle's body was inconsistent with the few scratches he might have got climbing the tree to hang himself. The man who sold him the rope said he had blood on him when he called in at the shop, and that he was subdued and smelt of whisky.'

'So it may be cut and dried, after all,' said Gervaise, almost to herself. 'Well, let's hope we didn't drag DCI Banks back for nothing.'

'Yes, ma'am,' said Annie, through gritted teeth. 'Let's hope not.'

GETTING OUT OF LONDON was bad enough, but the M1 was an even worse nightmare. There were roadworks near Newport Pagnell, where the motorway was reduced to one lane for two miles. The Porsche ticked along nicely, and Banks was glad he'd decided to keep it. It was shabby enough now for him to feel comfortable in it. The sound system was great, too.

Banks was still annoyed at Detective Superintendent Gervaise for giving the order to call him back. He knew it wasn't Annie's fault, no matter how much she seemed to have relished the task. This was the first time he had been called away on urgent business since he and Sophia had been together, he realised. It was something that had happened with monotonous regularity throughout his career and marriage, and something that his ex-wife, Sandra, had complained of more than once, until she decided to leave him.

But things had been quiet recently. Until now. It *would* be this weekend.

He had been making excellent time for a while, and just past the Sheffield cooling towers his mobile buzzed. It was Sophia.

'What is it?' she asked. 'What's wrong? I just came out of the studio and got a message from Tana to call you. Where are you?'

'Just north of Sheffield,' said Banks.

'What?'

'Nothing's wrong. I'm fine. I've just been called in to work, that's all.'

'That's all! But I don't understand. It's your weekend off, isn't it?'

'They're not sacrosanct, unfortunately. Not in this job.'

'But the dinner party?'

'I know. And I'm sorry. I promise I'll make—'

'Oh, this is too much. It's too late to cancel at this point. And Gunther and Carla are only over from Milan for the weekend.'

'Why should you cancel? Go ahead. Enjoy yourselves. I'm sure I'll get another chance to meet them. Offer my apologies.'

'A fat lot of good they'll do. Oh, shit, Alan. I was looking forward to it.'

'Me too,' said Banks. 'I'm sorry.'

There was a short pause, then Sophia's voice came back on again. 'What is it, anyway? What's so important?'

'Nobody's sure yet,' said Banks, 'but there are two people dead.'

'Damn and blast your job! Couldn't you have said no?'

'I tried.'

'Not very hard, obviously. How long will you be gone?'

'No idea. You can still come up next weekend as planned, though, right?'

'And risk spending it by myself? I don't know about that.'

'You know plenty of people up here. And aren't we supposed to be having Sunday lunch with your parents?'

'A weekend with my parents isn't quite what I had in mind.'

'I'm sure I'll be around. Sophia, this isn't my fault. Do you think I wouldn't rather be with you right now than on my way to work?'

She paused again, then replied rather sulkily, 'I suppose so. But I'll miss you. The dinner won't be the same without you.'

'I'll miss you, too. Call me later?'

'If I've got time. I'd better get moving. I've got a lot to do now.'

'Soph—' But she had already ended the call. Banks cursed. He knew he had warned Sophia that things like this might happen, but how seriously do people take warnings like that when everything is going blissfully well? Perhaps it was for the best that Sophia had found out about the demands of his job sooner rather than later.

He turned up the volume on his stereo. Bowie was singing 'Where Have All the Good Times Gone?' Banks hoped it wasn't prophetic.

Chapter Three

Tea and custard creams were served in the boardroom of Western Area Headquarters just after five o'clock that Saturday afternoon. Four of them sat around the end of the long oval table: Banks, Annie, Stefan Nowak and Superintendent Gervaise.

'It seems to me,' said Banks, when the others had brought him up to speed, 'that the first thing we need to do is get the forensic results on the blood.'

'What would that prove?' asked Annie.

'If the blood on Mark Hardcastle's body is Silbert's, and no one else's, then it would go a long way towards proving the murder-suicide theory.'

'A long way, but not the whole way,' Annie argued. 'If Hardcastle found Silbert dead, his natural instinct would be to touch him, hold him, try to revive him, something like that. Maybe that's how he got Silbert's blood on him. But someone else could still have killed Silbert first. Then we'd have a murder *and* a suicide, but we'd also have a murderer still loose.'

'A good point, DI Cabbot,' said Gervaise. 'DCI Banks?'

'I still think forensics should be able to tell us a great deal more about what happened. What about fingerprints, Stefan?'

'The only fingerprints Vic Manson's lifted from the cricket bat so far are Mark Hardcastle's. The bat belonged in the room, by the way. There was a special stand for it by the sideboard, brass plaque and all. We have unidentified prints from the sitting room and other parts of the house, of course, but they could take for ever to eliminate. We'll be running them all through NAFIS.' Nowak paused. 'I hesitate to express an unsupported opinion here, but this crime scene doesn't look like a murder committed by an interrupted burglar. The attack on that body was emotional and deeply personal.'

'Any signs of forced entry?' Banks asked Annie.

'No,' she said. 'Only by us. I had to break a window in a door to get in.'

'What about the neighbours? Anybody see or hear anything?'

'Uniform branch has talked to most of the people on the Heights this afternoon, and so far nobody admits to seeing or hearing anything,' Annie said. 'But that's hardly surprising. The houses are detached, and the people are insular, cautious. The one bright spot is that some of the houses have surveillance cameras, so if we can get hold of the tapes . . . Anyway, one or two reporters were sniffing around this afternoon, too, so word is spreading. We've told them we can't release the victim's name until next of kin has been informed, but they'll be able to work out whose house it is easily enough. We've left a couple of PCs guarding the gate.'

'Good,' said Gervaise. 'I'll handle the press. Do we know anything about the mother?'

'Not yet,' said Annie. 'We're following up on that now.'

'Have we found anyone who actually *knew* Silbert and Hardcastle yet?'

'We're still working on that, too,' Annie said, a trace of irritation in her voice. 'Certainly no one we've talked to so far admits to having them over for drinks or dinner on a regular basis. Judging by the kitchen at Castleview Heights, Silbert probably did a fair bit of entertaining. He was sophisticated, obviously well educated and probably quite wealthy. On the other hand, Mark Hardcastle was the son of a Barnsley coal miner and he wasn't, as far as we can gather, at all coy about his sexuality.' Annie glanced at Gervaise. 'Did Chief Constable Murray have anything to add about Laurence Silbert?' she asked. 'Idle chatter at the nineteenth hole or something?'

Gervaise pursed her cupid's-bow lips. 'Not much. They weren't close; they simply made up a foursome from time to time. But the CC has other friends on the Heights, so he'll be watching over our shoulders. What do you think of all this, DCI Banks? You're the closest we've got to fresh eyes.'

Banks tapped the end of his yellow pencil on the desk. 'I think we just keep on asking questions while we're waiting on forensics,' he said. 'Try to build up a picture of Hardcastle and Silbert's life, of everything they did during the last two or three days.'

'One of Silbert's neighbours says she's noticed that a green Toyota has become something of a fixture at Silbert's house lately,' Annie added, 'which seems to confirm the living-together bit. I saw a lot of Hardcastle's personal stuff when I had a quick look around Silbert's house,' she went on. 'He used one of the upstairs rooms as a sort of office.'

'Why hang on to the flat, then?' Banks asked. 'Hardcastle can't have been making that much money at the theatre. Why waste it on the flat?'

'Any number of reasons,' said Annie. 'Insecurity. A bolt hole. A little private space when he needed it.'

'You and DCI Banks can have a good poke around the house tomorrow,' Gervaise said. 'With DI Nowak's permission, of course.'

'All right with me,' Nowak said. 'I'll probably still have a couple of men working there, but if you don't get in each other's way . . .'

'See what you can dig up,' Gervaise went on. 'Personal papers, bank books, stuff like that. What about Hardcastle? Did he have any family?'

'A distant aunt in Australia,' Annie said.

'Phone records?'

'We're working on it. Hardcastle didn't have a mobile, hated them apparently, but we found one in Silbert's jacket pocket, along with his wallet. Nothing out of the ordinary on it so far. In fact, nothing much at all.'

'No call log, address book or stored text messages?' Banks asked.

'None.'

'That's a bit odd in itself, isn't it?' said Gervaise. 'I understand you talked to the cleaning lady?'

'Yes,' said Annie. 'Mrs Blackwell. She wasn't much help. Said Mr Hardcastle was around more often than not these days, when Mr Silbert was at home, at least. Apparently he travelled a lot. They were a nice couple, always paid her on time, blah, blah, blah. If she knew any deep, dark secrets, she wasn't telling. We can talk to her again if we need to.'

'What brought the two of them together? I wonder,' Banks asked. 'What on earth did they have in common? Was it the theatre, or was it simply the money? How rich was Silbert exactly?'

'We haven't had time to examine Silbert's bank accounts yet,' said Annie.

'But, like I said, he must have had a bob or two to live where he did. The car's no old jalopy, either. Which reminds me.' Annie took a slip of paper sheathed in a plastic folder from her file. 'We found this in the glove box of the Jag. It's a parking receipt from Durham Tees Valley Airport timed nine twenty-five a.m. Friday. The car had been parked there for three days, and from the restaurant receipts in his wallet it looks as if he was in Amsterdam.'

'Interesting,' said Banks. 'Durham Tees Valley. That would fix his arrival at Castleview Heights around . . . quarter past to half past ten.'

'And by one o'clock he was dead,' added Superintendent Gervaise.

They all sat in silence for a moment to let that sink in, then Banks said, 'And Hardcastle was definitely in London on Wednesday and Thursday?'

'Yes,' said Annie. 'He was there with Derek Wyman, the director of *Othello*, the current production. Hardcastle had a restaurant receipt in his wallet from Wednesday evening, and one for petrol dated Thursday afternoon, two twenty-six p.m. Northbound services, Watford Gap.'

'On his way home, then,' said Banks. 'If he was at Watford Gap at two twenty-six, he'd be here by about half past five. What's the restaurant?'

'One of the Zizzi's chain, on Charlotte Street. Pizza trentino and a glass of Montepulciano d'Abruzzo. A large one, going by the price.'

'Hmm,' said Banks. 'So Hardcastle probably ate alone. Or he and Wyman went Dutch. Any idea where he stayed on Wednesday night?'

'No,' said Annie. 'We're hoping Derek Wyman might be able to tell us. He's not back yet. I was planning to interview him first thing tomorrow.'

'Any idea what Hardcastle did on Thursday evening after he got back to Eastvale?' Banks asked.

'Who knows?' Annie said. 'He was probably at Castleview. The downstairs neighbour at Branwell Court hasn't seen him since last week. He wasn't at the theatre. All we know is that the next day, around lunchtime, he went into Grainger's shop, bought a length of clothes line and went and hanged himself in Hindswell Woods. So between late Thursday afternoon and Friday morning, he'd had a few drinks and possibly killed Laurence Silbert.'

'Anything else of interest in Silbert's wallet?' Banks asked.

'Credit cards, a little cash, a business card, sales receipts, driving licence. He was born in 1946, by the way, which makes him sixty-two. Nothing yet to give a hint of his profession or sources of income.'

'Business card? Whose? His own?'

'No.' Annie slid the plastic folder over to him.

'"Julian Fenner, Import-Export",' Banks read. 'That covers a multitude of sins. It's a London phone number. No address. Mind if I hang on to it?'

'OK by me,' said Annie. 'Maybe it's another lover?'

'More speculation,' said Gervaise. 'What we need is solid information. Is there much else on in Major Crimes at the moment?'

'Not much,' said Annie. 'Couple of gang-related incidents on the East Side Estate, a spate of shoplifting in the Swainsdale Centre. And the traffic cones, of course. They're still disappearing. CID's dealing with it.'

'Good,' said Gervaise. 'Any idea when Dr Glendenning might get around to the post-mortems?'

'I've spoken to him,' said Annie. 'He's been in his office catching up on paperwork. He's keen to get started whenever he gets the go-ahead.'

'Wonderful,' said Gervaise. 'He's got his wish.'

'Just one point,' said Banks. 'Might it make sense if Dr Glendenning autopsies Silbert first? I mean, everyone's pretty sure that Hardcastle hanged himself. There's no evidence that anyone else was with him, is there, Stefan?'

'None,' said Nowak. 'And everything about that scene is consistent with suicide by hanging. Textbook case.'

'So are we working on the assumption that if Hardcastle *didn't* kill Silbert himself, then someone else did?' asked Banks. 'And that Hardcastle found the body and hanged himself from grief?'

'Makes sense,' said Gervaise. '*If* he didn't do it himself. Any objections?' No one had any.

'In the meantime, then,' Gervaise went on, 'as DCI Banks suggested, we try to plot out their movements, the hours leading up to their deaths. We dig into their backgrounds, family history, friends, enemies, ambitions, work, finances, previous relationships, travels, the lot. OK?'

They all nodded. Superintendent Gervaise gathered her papers and stood up. 'I'll try to keep the media at bay for as long as I can. Remember, this is the Heights. Tread carefully. Keep me informed at every stage.'

AFTER THE MEETING, Banks sat in his office and studied his copies of the materials gathered from Silbert's wallet and Hardcastle's car. It didn't add up to a hell of a lot. He glanced at his watch. Just after 6.15. He wanted to talk to Sophia, see if she had forgiven him, but now would be the worst possible time. She would be right in the midst of her dinner preparations.

Idly, he dialled the number of Julian Fenner, Import-Export, the card found in Laurence Silbert's wallet. After only a few rings and several distant clicks and echoes, an automated voice came on the line tell him that the number was no longer in service. He tried again, in case he had misdialled. Same result. After a few attempts to find a matching address through reverse directories, he gave up. It appeared that the number did not exist. He made a note to put technical support on to it.

The internal phone rang. It was Annie. 'PC Wythers called in from Castleview Heights. Apparently a woman has just turned up there claiming to be Laurence Silbert's mother. Want to come along?'

'Of course,' he said, picking up his car keys. 'I'll follow you in my car.'

LAURENCE SILBERT'S MOTHER was sitting in the driver's seat of a racing-green MG sports car outside number 15 Castleview Heights smoking a cigarette and chatting with PC Wythers when Banks and Annie arrived. There were still plenty of media people around the area, but Banks and Annie ignored the call for comments and turned towards the MG.

The woman who got out had once been at least as tall as Banks, but age had given her a slight stoop. Even so, she was a commanding presence, and the grey hair drawn back tightly from her forehead, her high cheekbones and twinkling blue-grey eyes spoke of a beauty not long faded. In fact, she was still beautiful, and there was something vaguely familiar about her.

'Good evening,' she said, offering her hand to both of them in turn. 'I'm Edwina Silbert, Laurence's mother.'

Banks stepped back. '*The* Edwina Silbert?'

'Well, I suppose I did attract a certain amount of notoriety at one time,' she said, dropping her cigarette on the ground and stepping on it. She was wearing black high heels, Banks noticed. 'But that was a long time ago.'

Annie looked puzzled.

'Mrs Silbert started the Viva boutique chain in the sixties,' Banks explained. 'And it went on to become enormously successful.'

'Still is,' said Annie. 'I shop there myself sometimes. Pleased to meet you.'

'I'm very sorry for your loss,' Banks said.

Edwina Silbert inclined her head. 'Poor Laurence. I've been thinking about him all the way up here. It's still very difficult to take in. Can I see him?'

'I'm afraid not,' said Banks.

'That bad?'

Banks said nothing.

'I'm not squeamish, you know. I saw many things during the war that would turn your stomach. I was a Queen Alexandra nurse.'

'Mrs Silbert—'

'Edwina. Please.'

'Edwina. I'll be frank with you. I think seeing him the way he is now would cause you far too much pain. Best to remember him as he was. We think we have enough to go on to make a positive identification for the time being.'

She was silent for a moment or two. 'Very well,' she said finally. 'But there is something that might help. Laurence has a distinctive birthmark on his left arm, just above his elbow. It's dark red and shaped like a teardrop.'

'Thank you,' said Banks. 'We'd also like to take a DNA swab. Later, when you're feeling up to it.'

'You're more than welcome to take your sample whenever you wish. Look, I don't know about your rules and regulations, but I've come a long way and I could do with a drink. There's a delightful little pub close by.'

THE BLACK SWAN, with its horse-brasses, framed Stubbs prints and polished brass rails, was not one of the pubs that attracted the rowdies on a Saturday night. In fact, it attracted hardly anyone except people from the immediate neighbourhood.

'Shall we sit outside?' Edwina suggested. 'I could do with a cigarette.'

They found an empty bench and table on the patio that offered a magnificent view over the town and the distant hills, dark green as the evening light weakened. Banks went back inside to pick up some drinks. Edwina wanted a gin and tonic and Annie a Diet Coke. Banks studied the pumps and chose a pint of Timothy Taylor's Landlord. He carried the drinks on a tray back to the table, where Edwina Silbert was already smoking. She accepted the gin and tonic eagerly.

'You shouldn't have come all this way,' Banks said. 'We were going to drive down and see you soon, anyway.'

'Don't be silly,' she said. 'I'm perfectly capable of driving a few miles. What else was I supposed to do? Sit at home and twiddle my thumbs?'

If Silbert was sixty-two, Banks thought, then Edwina was probably in her eighties, and Longborough was 200 miles away. She looked much younger, but then so had her son, by all accounts.

'Where are you staying?' he asked.

She seemed surprised at the question. 'At Laurence's house, of course.'

'I'm afraid that's not possible,' said Banks. 'It's a crime scene.'

Edwina Silbert gave her head a slight shake. Banks could see tears glistening in her eyes. 'Forgive me,' she said. 'I'm not used to this. What's that nice hotel in town? I stayed there when the house was being decorated.'

'The Burgundy?'

'That's the one. Do you think I'll be able to get a room?'

'I'll check for you,' said Annie, taking out her mobile. She walked over to the edge of the patio to make the call.

'Were you and Laurence close?' Banks asked.

'I'd say so,' Edwina answered. 'I mean, I would like to think we were friends as well as mother and son. His father died when he was only nine, you see, killed in a car crash, and Laurence is an only child. I never remarried. Of course, when he left university he travelled a lot and there were lengthy periods when I didn't see him at all.'

'How long had you known Laurence was gay?'

'Ever since he was a boy, really. All the signs were there. Of course, he was always most discreet. Apart from the odd peccadillo at public school or Cambridge, I very much doubt that he was sexually active until his twenties, and by then it was perfectly legal.'

'It didn't bother you?'

She gave Banks a curious look. 'What an odd thing to say.'

'Some parents get upset by it.'

'Perhaps,' said Edwina. 'But it always seemed to me that there's no point in trying to change a person's nature. A leopard's spots and all that. No. It was what he was. His cross to bear and his path to love. I hope he found it.'

'If it means anything, I think he did. I think he was very happy these past few months.'

'With Mark, yes. I like to think so, too. Poor Mark. He'll be devastated.'

'You knew Mark?'

'*Knew?* Oh my God, is there something you haven't told me?'

'I'm sorry,' said Banks. 'I thought you would have heard. Please forgive me.' Why he had assumed that the Gloucestershire police would have told her about Mark Hardcastle, he didn't know. 'I'm afraid Mark's dead, too. It seems he committed suicide.'

Edwina seemed to shrink in her chair as if she had taken a body blow. 'But why?' she said. 'Because of what happened to Laurence?'

'We think there's a connection, yes,' said Banks.

Annie came back and gave Banks a nod. 'We've got a nice room for you at the Burgundy, Mrs Silbert,' she said.

'Thank you, dear,' said Edwina, reaching for a handkerchief in her handbag. She dabbed her eyes. 'Excuse me, this is really very silly of me. It's just rather a lot to take in all at once. Mark, too?'

'I'm sorry,' Banks said. 'You liked him?'

She put her handkerchief away, took a sip of gin and tonic. 'Very much,' she said. 'And he was good for Laurence. I know their backgrounds were very different, but they had so much in common.'

'Was Laurence interested in the theatre?'

'Very much so. That's where they met. He and Mark. Didn't you know?'

'I know very little,' said Banks. 'Please tell me.'

'I visited Laurence just before Christmas, and he took me to the panto here. *Cinderella*, I believe. During the intermission we got talking to Mark in the bar, as you do, and I could see that he and Laurence hit it off immediately. I made my excuses and disappeared to powder my nose, or some such thing, you know, just to give them a little time to exchange telephone numbers or whatever they wanted to do, and that, as they say, was that.'

'How would you characterise their relationship?' Banks asked.

'I'd say they were in love and they wanted to make a go of it, but they moved cautiously. They'd both been through painful relationships and split-ups before. Strong as their feelings were for one another, they weren't going to jump into something without thinking.'

'Mark hung on to his flat,' Banks said, 'yet it seemed they were practically living together at Castleview. Is that the kind of thing you mean?'

'Exactly. I imagine he would eventually have given it up and moved in with Laurence completely, but they were progressing slowly. Besides, Laurence has a pied-à-terre in Bloomsbury, too.'

'Would you give me the address?'

Edwina gave him an address near Russell Square. 'It really is very tiny,' she said. 'I couldn't imagine the two of them staying there together.'

'But would Mark have stayed there alone when he was in London?'

'I can't see why not.'

'Did you ever sense tension between them? Did they argue? Fight?'

'No more than any other couple. Actually, they laughed a lot.' She paused. 'Why? You're not . . .? Surely you can't . . .?'

'We're not suggesting anything, Mrs Silbert,' Annie said quickly. 'We don't know what happened. That's what we're trying to find out.'

'But that you can even believe there's a possibility of Mark's . . . of Mark's doing something like that.'

'I'm afraid it *is* a possibility,' said Banks. 'But that's all it is at the moment. As Annie said, we don't know what happened. All we know is that your son was killed in his home, and that shortly afterwards Mark Hardcastle committed suicide in Hindswell Woods.'

'Hindswell? Oh my God, no. Oh, Mark. That was their favourite spot. They took me to see the bluebells there once, back in April. Grief, Mr Banks. That would be why he killed himself. Grief.'

'That occurred to us, too,' said Banks. 'And your son?'

Edwina hesitated and Banks sensed that something had crossed her mind, something she didn't want to share yet. 'A burglar, perhaps?' she said.

'We're working on it. What we need, though, is a lot more background on your son and Mark. We know so little about them, their life together.'

'I'll tell you what I can,' said Edwina. 'But can it wait until tomorrow? Please? I'm feeling suddenly very tired.'

'I don't suppose there's any hurry,' said Banks, disappointed but trying not to show it. She was an old woman, after all.

Edwina got up to leave and Annie stood. 'Can I drive you?'

'It's all right, dear,' Edwina said, touching Annie's shoulder. 'I think I've got just about enough energy left.' And she walked away.

'Should she be driving?' Annie asked.

'Probably not,' said Banks. 'But I wouldn't recommend you try to stop her. Sit down. Finish your Coke.'

'I suppose you're right,' said Annie. 'She'll be OK.'

Annie shivered, and Banks offered her his jacket to put over her T-shirt. Her tousled chestnut hair hung over her shoulders, and her complexion was smooth and free of all but the lightest make-up.

'So what do you think about that pied-à-terre?' Banks asked.

'I don't know,' she said. 'I suppose it was worth hanging on to if he could afford it, and if he used it often enough.'

'We should check the place out. If Hardcastle stayed there on Thursday night, he might have left some sort of clue behind as to his state of mind.'

'I suppose we should,' Annie said. 'And we'll have to ask Edwina about her son's finances tomorrow. She's certainly an interesting woman, isn't she?'

'She was quite beautiful in her day. I remember seeing pictures of her in the papers. She was right in the thick of things, party-going with all the big names, being seen at all the right clubs. I didn't even know that she had a son. She obviously kept him well out of the limelight.'

Annie yawned.

'I'm boring you.'

'Long day.'

Banks finished off his beer. 'Then let's call it a night.'

'Good idea,' Annie agreed, handing Banks back his jacket.

They walked to their cars, still parked outside Laurence Silbert's house, where a few die-hard reporters lingered. They said good night, and Banks watched Annie drive away in her old Astra before starting the Porsche and heading for Gratly. Cameras flashed in his rearview mirror.

IT FELT LIKE WEEKS since Banks had been home, but it had only been a couple of days. One night away, he realised. Only one night with Sophia. Even so, his isolated cottage greeted him with a silence that felt even more profound and oppressive than usual.

He turned on the lamps in the living room. There was one message on the answering machine: his son Brian saying that he was back in London for a couple of weeks, if Banks happened to be down there and fancied dropping by the flat in Tufnell Park.

A dark turquoise afterglow shot with orange and gold remained in the sky over Gratly Beck. Banks gazed at it for a few moments, drinking in the beauty, then closed the curtains and went through to the kitchen. He realised he was hungry, hadn't eaten since breakfast, unless he counted that custard cream at the meeting. He made himself a toasted cheese sandwich, which he carried into the entertainment room, along with a glass of wine.

Banks lounged back in the armchair and put his feet up, his mind on the case. He found himself wondering what Laurence Silbert had been doing in

Amsterdam. Perhaps Edwina would be able to help tomorrow. Her sadness over the loss of both Laurence and Mark seemed genuine to Banks, as did her absolute shock at the idea that Mark could have had anything to do with her son's murder. Banks also wondered if Mark's trip to London with Derek Wyman had played a part in the events that followed, however innocent it might have been. Was it so innocent? Had Laurence Silbert found out, and flown into a jealous rage? Was that what had led to both their deaths? Banks and Annie would talk to Wyman in the morning. It was Sunday, but there would be no time off for Banks. A DCI didn't get paid overtime, so the best he could hope for was a little time in lieu, then maybe he and Sophia could manage a long weekend in Rome or Lisbon. That might just make up for missing the dinner party.

It was half past eleven when the phone rang. It was Sophia, and she sounded a little tipsy.

'How did it go?' Banks asked.

'Great,' she said. 'I did Thai and everyone seemed to like it. They just left. I thought I'd leave the dishes. I'm tired.'

'I'm sorry I'm not there to help you,' said Banks.

'Me too. Just sorry you're not here, I mean.'

'I had a drink with Edwina Silbert this evening.'

'Edwina Silbert! From Viva? What's she like?'

'Interesting. She's definitely got charisma. And she's still very beautiful.'

'Should I be jealous?'

'She's eighty if she's a day.'

'And you prefer younger women. I know. How did you get to meet her?'

'She's the mother of one of the victims. Laurence Silbert.'

'Oh dear,' said Sophia. 'The poor woman. She must be devastated.'

'She managed to put on a brave face, but yes, I think she was.'

'How's the case going?'

'Slow, but we're making some progress,' said Banks. 'Chances are it might lead in the direction of London before too long.'

'When? I've got a really busy week coming up.'

'I'm not sure. It's only a possibility at the moment. More important, what about next weekend? Are you still coming?'

'Of course I am. But *do* promise me you'll be around.'

'I'll be around. Don't forget, I've got tickets for *Othello* next Saturday night. The Eastvale Amateur Dramatic Society.' He didn't want to tell her that the case was connected to the theatre; he had got the tickets well before he had ever heard of Mark Hardcastle.

'An amateur production of *Othello*,' said Sophia with mock enthusiasm. 'I can hardly wait. You sure know how to treat a girl well.'

Banks laughed. 'Drinks and dinner before at one of Eastvale's finest establishments, of course.'

'Of course. The fish and chip shop or the pizza place?'

'Your choice.'

'And after . . .?'

'Hmm. Remains to be seen.'

'I'm sure we'll think of something.'

Banks laughed. 'I'm glad you called.'

'Me too,' Sophia said. 'I wish you'd been here, that's all. Anyway I'm going to hang up now. I'm really tired. Miss you. Good night.'

'Good night,' said Banks. He put down the phone and drained the last of his wine. A wave of tiredness rolled over him. He felt more alone and further away for having just talked to Sophia than he had before her call, but it was always like that. He hadn't told her he missed her, too, and he wished he had. Too late now, he thought, putting the glass down and heading for bed.

Chapter Four

Derek Wyman's household at half past ten on Sunday morning reminded Banks of his own before Sandra and the kids had left. In the spacious living and dining area, pop music was blasting out from a radio or stereo, a teenage boy lay on his stomach on the carpet in front of the television playing games that involved killing futuristic armour-clad soldiers, while his shy, skinny sister chatted away on her mobile. The smell of bacon lingered in the air as Mrs Wyman cleared away the breakfast table. Outside, the wind lashed sheets of rain across the street.

Derek Wyman had clearly been sitting in his favourite armchair reading the *Sunday Times* Culture section. How he could concentrate with all the noise going on, Banks had no idea. The front section of the newspaper lay on the chair arm, open to the news of the apparent murder-suicide in Eastvale. It wasn't much of a story. Laurence Silbert hadn't been named, Banks knew, because his body hadn't been identified officially, although the birthmark Edwina had told them about confirmed Silbert's identity in Banks's mind.

'So much for the fine weather,' said Wyman, after Banks and Annie had showed him their warrant cards. He nodded towards the paper. 'I suppose this is about Mark?'

'Yes,' said Banks.

'Quite a shock to come home to, I must say. Dreadful business. Please, sit down.' Wyman cleared away some magazines and offered them the sofa. 'Dean, Charlie,' he said, 'why don't you go up to your rooms and play. We need to talk. And turn that damn music off.'

With slow, drawn-out movements, both kids gave their father a long-suffering look and went upstairs, Dean switching off the radio on his way.

'Teenagers,' Wyman said, rubbing his head. 'Who'd have 'em? I spend most of my days with them at school, and then I come home and have to deal with two of my own. Must be a masochist. Or mad.'

Wyman seemed to Banks like a man with the energy and patience necessary to deal with teenagers on a daily basis. Tall, thin, wiry even, with a closely cropped scalp and an elongated bony face with deep-set, watchful eyes, he taught games as well as drama.

A few framed photographs graced the mantelpiece, mostly Wyman and his wife and kids, but Banks noticed one in which a slightly younger Wyman stood next to an older man in army uniform outside a train station, the man's arm draped over his shoulders. 'Who's that?' he asked.

Wyman saw where he was looking. 'Me and my brother, Rick,' he said.

'Where is he now? Is he still in the army?'

'He's dead,' said Wyman. 'Killed in a helicopter accident in 2002.'

'Where did it happen?'

'Afghanistan. On manoeuvres.'

'Were you very close?'

Wyman glanced at Banks. 'He was my big brother. What do you think?'

'I'm sorry,' Banks said.

'Well,' said Wyman, 'that's what you sign up for when you join the bloody army, isn't it?'

Mrs Wyman finished clearing the dishes away and sat at the table. She was an attractive brunette in her late thirties, a little careworn, but she obviously worked at keeping her figure and preserving her smooth complexion. 'You don't mind me being here, do you?' she asked.

'Not at all,' said Banks. 'Did you know Mark Hardcastle?'

'I met him a few times,' she said, 'but I wouldn't say I *knew* him. Still, it's terrible, what's happened.'

'Yes,' Banks agreed, turning back to her husband. 'I understand you were in London with Mark just last week?'

'Yes,' said Wyman. 'I go there whenever I can get away. Theatre and film are my passions, so London's the place to soak it all up.'

'Were many of these London trips made with Mark Hardcastle?'

'Good Lord, no! This was the first. And I wasn't really *with* him. I took the twelve-thirty train from York on Wednesday. Mark drove down by himself.'

'Why was that? I mean, why didn't you travel together?'

'We were leaving at different times. Besides, I rather enjoy travelling by train. I can get some reading done, or just watch the world go by.'

'And the purpose of the trip was?'

'The German Expressionist retrospective at the National Film Theatre.'

'For both of you?'

'Well, we were both interested in it, certainly, but we didn't spend that much time together.'

'Can you tell me what you actually *did* do together?'

'Yes, of course. We met for a bite to eat at Zizzi's on Charlotte Street that first evening, about six o'clock, before the showing. It was a pleasant evening, and we managed to get a table on the pavement out front.'

'What did you have to eat?'

If Wyman was puzzled by the question, he didn't show it. 'Pizza.'

'Who paid?'

'We went Dutch.'

'Do you still have your receipt?'

Wyman frowned. 'It might be in my wallet. I can check, if you like.'

'Later will do,' said Banks. 'And after dinner?'

'We went to see the films. *The Cabinet of Dr Caligari* and a rare showing of Dmitri Buchowetzki's *Othello*. It's very interesting, but not among the best. You see, I'm directing—'

'Yes, we know about that,' said Banks. 'What about afterwards?'

Wyman looked a little sulky at being denied his directorial bragging rights. 'We had a quick drink in the bar, then we went our separate ways.'

'You weren't staying in the same hotel?'

'No. Mark's partner owns a small flat in Bloomsbury. He stayed there.'

'What about you?'

'I stayed at my usual bed and breakfast near Victoria Station. Cheap and cheerful. A small room, but it does all right for me.'

'Do you have the address?' Banks asked.

Wyman seemed puzzled, but gave Banks an address on Warwick Street.

'You mentioned Mark's partner,' Annie said. 'Did you know Laurence Silbert well?'

'Not well. We met a couple of times. They came to dinner once. They reciprocated and we went to their house.'

'When was this?' Annie asked.

'A couple of months ago.'

'Did Mr Hardcastle appear to be living there at the time?' Banks asked.

'More or less,' said Wyman. 'He practically moved in the day they met. Well, wouldn't you? Bloody big house on the hill.'

'You think it was the grandeur that attracted him?' Banks said.

'No, I was just being facetious. But Mark certainly appreciated the finer things in life. He was one of those working lads who've gone up in the world. You know, more your Château Margaux and raw-milk Camembert than your pint of bitter and a packet of cheese and onion crisps. They were well matched, despite their difference in background.'

Mrs Wyman came back in with the tea at this point, and they all helped themselves from the tray. Banks thanked her and resumed the questioning.

'What about the next day, Thursday? Did you see Mark then?'

'No. He said he had to go home. I was staying until Saturday, as you know. I wanted to fit in a few exhibitions, too, while I was down there. And some book shopping. I can give you the details if you like.'

'Ticket stubs?'

'Yes, probably.' Wyman frowned. 'Look, you're questioning me as if I'm a suspect or something. I thought—'

'We just want to get the details clear,' said Banks. 'As yet there aren't any suspects. So,' he continued, 'you stayed in London until when?'

Wyman paused. 'Yesterday. I checked out of my B & B about lunchtime, had a pub lunch, did a bit of book shopping and went to the National Gallery. Then I caught the five o'clock train back to York last night. Got home about . . .' He glanced towards his wife.

'I picked him up at the station around quarter past seven,' she said.

Banks turned back to Wyman. 'And you're sure you didn't see Mark Hardcastle after he left the bar on Wednesday evening?'

'That's right.'

'Was he driving?'

'No. We took the tube to Waterloo after dinner.'

'And going back?'

'I walked back to Victoria along the embankment. I assume Mark caught the tube to Goodge Street. He could easily walk to Bloomsbury from there.'

'What time was this?'

'About half ten, quarter to eleven.'

'Where had he left his car?'

'No idea. Outside the flat, I suppose, or in the garage, if he had one.'

'What did you talk about over your drinks?'

'The films we saw, ideas for sets and costumes.'

'What kind of state of mind would you say he was in?'

'He was fine,' said Wyman. 'That's why I can't understand—'

'Not depressed at all?' Annie asked. 'Edgy?'

'No.'

Banks picked up the questioning again. 'Only we've been given to understand that he'd been a bit moody and irritable over the past couple of weeks or so. Did you notice any signs of that?'

'No, sorry.' Wyman shook his head. 'If he was depressed, he hid it well.'

'Did you sense that he and Laurence might have had a falling-out?'

'He didn't talk much about Laurence. He was always secretive about his private life. Not about the fact that he was gay or anything—he was very up-front about that. Just about who he was sharing his life with.'

'I don't mean to be indiscreet here,' said Banks, 'but did Mark ever make a pass at you or show any undue interest in you?'

'Good Lord, no! Mark was a colleague and a friend. He knew I was married, heterosexual. He always respected that.'

'Was he a jealous person?'

'Well, I got the impression once or twice that he felt a bit insecure.'

'In what way?'

'I think he had a jealous nature—this is just an impression, mind you—and I reckon he sometimes felt that Laurence was a bit out of his class, kept thinking the bubble would burst. I mean, a Barnsley miner's son and a wealthy sophisticate like Laurence Silbert. Go figure, as the Yanks say.'

'Was Mark jealous about anyone in particular?'

'No, he didn't mention any names. He just got anxious if Laurence was away or something. Which happened quite often.'

'I gather that Mr Silbert was in Amsterdam while you were in London?'

'Yes. Mark did mention that.'

'Did he say why?'

'No. Business, I assumed.'

'What was his business?'

'Retired civil servant. He'd worked for the foreign office, travelled all over the place. I think Mark was worried about the nightlife in Amsterdam, you know, the Red Light district. It does have a bit of a reputation.'

'Indeed,' said Banks. 'So Mark *was* anxious?'

'I didn't mean it like that. It was just part of his nature to worry. He even joked about it. I told him he could always go to Soho or Hampstead Heath if he wanted a bit of fun himself.'

'How did he react to that?' Annie asked.

'He just smiled and said those days were over.'

'So nothing out of the ordinary happened on this trip you and Mark Hardcastle made to London?' Banks said.

'No. Everything happened exactly as I said it did. All we did was share a meal and go to the pictures.'

'And absolutely nothing occurred that night that could have set in motion the events of the next three days?' Banks asked.

'Not that I know of. Who knows what he got up to after he left me?'

'Got up to?' said Banks.

'It's just a figure of speech. Bloomsbury isn't far from Soho, is it? And there are plenty of gay clubs there, if you like that sort of thing.'

'I thought you said he told you those days were behind him?' Annie said. 'Was Mark in the habit of being unfaithful to Laurence Silbert?'

'I've no idea. Like I said, he didn't confide in me about his love life. But if you want my honest opinion, no, I don't think Mark was the type for a bit of hanky-panky in the back room of a Soho club. That's why I could joke about it. But what do I know? It's not a world I belong to.'

'Is there anything else you can tell us?' Banks asked.

'Not that I can think of,' said Wyman.

His wife shook her head. Banks had been watching Carol Wyman's face from time to time throughout the interview, checking for signs of concern, or belief that her husband might be lying when the matter of Hardcastle and Wyman being away together came up, but she had shown nothing but polite interest and vague amusement. She obviously had no fears on that score.

There was nothing more to be learned from Derek Wyman right now, Banks thought, so he thanked him and gave Annie the sign to leave.

BANKS AND ANNIE managed to grab an early lunch at the Queen's Arms, already busy with earnest people in waterproof walking gear that warm, wet Sunday in June. The sun was breaking through gaps in the cloud.

Banks snagged a table for two in a corner, while Annie went to the bar and ordered roast lamb and Yorkshire pudding for Banks and veggie pasta for herself. Conversations buzzed around them. Banks eyed his grapefruit juice with disdain and raised his glass to clink with Annie's Diet Coke.

'Here's to working Sundays.'

'It has been a while, hasn't it?'

'I think we've got a pretty good head start, at any rate,' Banks said. 'What did you think of Derek Wyman?'

'A bit of a trainspotter, really, isn't he? An anorak.'

'You always say that about someone with a passion. There's nothing anoraky about the theatre. And it's a bit more cerebral than trainspotting.'

'Oh, I don't know,' said Annie. 'Don't you think there's something rather romantic about standing there in the wind and rain at the end of the platform, writing down the numbers of the diesels that zoom by?'

Banks studied her expression. 'You're winding me up again.'

Annie smiled. 'Maybe just a little bit.'

'Very funny. Now what about Wyman? Was he telling the truth?'

'He had no real reason to lie to us, did he? And he knows we can check his alibi. He got all those receipts for us before we left, as well.'

'Yes,' said Banks. 'They turned out to be very handy indeed.'

'So what is it?'

'Nothing,' said Banks. 'Just my bloody scar's itching, that's all.'

'How *did* you get that scar?'

Banks ignored her. 'Do you think there was something going on between them? Wyman and Hardcastle?'

'No, I think he was telling the truth about that. And his wife didn't react. If she had her suspicions, I think she'd have found it hard to hide them.'

'What about Derek Wyman and Laurence Silbert?'

'I doubt it,' said Annie, as the waitress arrived with their food. 'It doesn't sound as if Silbert was much of a mixer.'

'Then what, for crying out loud, are we missing?'

'I don't think we're missing anything,' said Annie. 'Like I said, he's a bit of an anorak, that's all. He can probably name every gaffer and best boy on every film he's seen, but I doubt that makes him a killer.'

'I didn't say he was,' Banks argued after a bite of lamb. 'Just that there's something niggling me about this murder-suicide business, that's all.'

'But that's just what it is: a murder-suicide. You're annoyed because you got dragged away from your romantic weekend, and you can't find a good mystery to make it worthwhile.'

Banks shot her a glance. 'Wouldn't *you* be?'

'I suppose I would.'

'It's all so inconclusive,' said Banks. 'I mean, was Hardcastle upset or wasn't he? Maria Wolsey said he was. Wyman said he wasn't, but that he was generally insecure and jealous about Silbert's travelling. There are just too many questions.' Banks put his knife and fork down and started to count them off on his fingers as he spoke. 'Why did Silbert travel so much if he'd retired, and what was he doing in Amsterdam? Had Hardcastle and Silbert had a fight or hadn't they? Did either or both of them play away or not? Who's Julian Fenner, and why doesn't his phone number connect? People don't just beat their lovers to death then hang themselves for no reason.'

'But the reason could be insignificant,' Annie argued. 'You know as well as I do that the most inconsequential of things can spark off the worst violence in people. Maybe Hardcastle had had too much to drink, and Silbert chastised him for it. Something as simple as that. People don't like being told they've had too much to drink. Maybe Hardcastle was a little pissed, already aggressive, and before he knew it Silbert was dead.'

'What about the damage inflicted on Silbert's genital area?' asked Banks. 'Doesn't that suggest to you a sexual motive?'

'Perhaps.' Annie pushed her plate aside. 'It's nothing we haven't seen before, though, is it? If there's sexual jealousy involved, the killer will go to the area that symbolises it. Maybe they argued about Hardcastle going to London with Wyman, or about Silbert going to Amsterdam. Whatever the motive—jealousy, infidelity, criticism of drinking habits—the result's the same: an argument turned violent and one man was left dead. The survivor couldn't bear what he'd done, so he committed suicide. There's nothing sinister about that at all. Sad to say, it's very commonplace.'

Banks sighed. 'Maybe I am just trying to justify losing my weekend,' he said. 'Or maybe *you* want to get this sorted quickly so we can concentrate on something important, like all those traffic cones that have gone missing.'

Annie laughed. 'Well, at least you're thinking along the right lines.'

'Come on,' Banks said. 'Let's go have a shufty around Silbert's house. Then we'll have another word with Edwina. I get the impression that she's got something else on her mind, too.'

'Sounds like a plan to me,' said Annie.

A COUPLE OF SOCOS were collecting the remaining trace evidence in Silbert's upstairs drawing room when Banks and Annie arrived.

'We've had a good look around,' Ted Ferguson, one of the SOCOs, told them, 'and there are no hidden safes or compartments anywhere in the house. The only rooms with any personal stuff and papers in them are this one and the study down the hall.' He handed them some latex gloves. 'We've got a few more things to do downstairs, but we're done up here for now. We'll leave you to it. Wear these.'

'Thanks, Ted,' said Banks, opening the seal and slipping on the gloves.

The SOCOs went downstairs, and Banks and Annie stood on the threshold and took stock.

Even though the body and the sheepskin rug it had lain on were gone, the blood spatter left on the walls and the traces of fingerprint powder on every surface now marked it as a crime scene. The photo in the shattered frame still lay on the floor. It showed Mark Hardcastle smiling, standing next to Silbert. Banks picked it up carefully and studied Silbert's face. Handsome, certainly, cultured, slender and fit, he had a cleft chin, a high forehead and clear blue eyes. He wore a light blue cashmere jumper and navy chinos.

Annie pointed at a framed blown-up photograph on the wall. 'That's Hindswell Woods,' she said. 'On the left is the tree Mark Hardcastle hanged himself from. It's very distinctive.'

They gazed at the picture for a few moments. Then they started to search.

Silbert's computer showed nothing out of the ordinary on a cursory examination, but it would have to be checked by technical support if the evidence pointed towards a killer other than Mark Hardcastle. The desk drawers held only stationery and a few files full of bills and business receipts.

A set of keys in the middle drawer unlocked an antique wooden cabinet beside the desk. Inside, Banks and Annie found the deeds to the house, bank statements and all the other papers they needed to discover that Silbert had been in the millionaire-plus bracket. His civil-service pension certainly didn't account for it, but investment income and regular cheques from Viva did. There were also a few large transfers from foreign bank accounts, Swiss mostly, the nature of which remained unclear. There was no will, so unless Silbert had left one with his solicitor, his fortune would go to his mother.

On the bottom shelf of the cabinet, Banks found a bundle of personal letters held together by a rubber band. The first was dated September 7, 1997, and was from someone called Leo Westwood at an address in Swiss Cottage. Banks read through it quickly, Annie looking over his shoulder. It was written in a neat, sloping hand, and most of the contents dealt with the death of the Princess of Wales. There were also references to an afternoon's antique hunting and a delicious meal at a Michelin-starred restaurant in the West End, where one of Tony Blair's Cabinet ministers was spotted dining with an out-of-favour colleague. The letter, like the rest, had been sent to Silbert, as diplomatic post, at the British Embassy in Berlin. Banks wondered if it had been read by censors. Gossipy as it was, there was nothing seditious in it, nothing likely to bring the wrath of HMG down on Westwood or Silbert. When Annie had finished reading it, Banks put the letter back in its envelope and returned it to the pile.

'Do you think these could have caused a row?' Annie asked.

'It's possible,' Banks said. 'But why now? I mean, they've probably been lying around since the late nineties.'

'Maybe Hardcastle did a bit of prying on Thursday evening while Silbert was still away, and jealousy got the better of him.'

'Hmm,' said Banks. 'Let's go have a look down the hall.'

The room was clearly Hardcastle's study, and it was much less tidy than Silbert's. Most of what they found was related to Hardcastle's work at the theatre—notes, sketches, books and working scripts. On his laptop was a computer program for generating various screenplay formats, and it appeared that Hardcastle himself was writing a movie script.

In the top drawer of the desk, on the latest copy of *Sight & Sound*, lay a memory stick of the type most commonly used in a digital camera.

'That's odd,' Annie said, when Banks pointed it out to her.

'Why?'

'Hardcastle has a digital camera. It's over here on the bottom bookshelf.' She picked up the small silver object and carried it over to Banks.

'So?' he said.

Annie sighed. 'Can't you see? This is a Canon camera,' she said, as if explaining to a five-year-old. 'It takes a compact flash card.'

'And this thing here isn't a compact flash card,' said Banks.

'Bingo. It's a memory stick. It's for Sony digital cameras. So where did it come from? Silbert didn't have a Sony, either. He's just got an old Olympic. I saw it in his study.'

'Interesting,' said Banks eyeing the small, wafer-thin stick. 'Let's check it for fingerprints.' He went to the landing and called one of the SOCOs.

The officer came up and dusted the stick. He peered at it and shook his head. 'Too blurred,' he said, then went back downstairs.

'Let's have a look at it, then,' Banks said to Annie.

She sat down at the laptop and slipped the stick into a slot in its side. A series of dialogue boxes flashed across the screen. Within seconds, Banks was looking at a photograph of Laurence Silbert sitting on a park bench with another man. In the background was a magnificent two-domed building. Banks thought they were in Regent's Park, but he couldn't be certain. Next, the two men were pictured from behind walking down a narrow street past a row of garages on the right. Above the garages were gabled houses, or apartments, with white stucco fronts. The final shot showed them entering through a door between two of the garages, the unknown man in profile, his hand resting lightly on Silbert's shoulder. It could have been a simple gesture of courtesy, the man ushering Silbert into the house first. To a jealous lover, though, it could conceivably have appeared as a sign of affection.

Whoever the man was, he certainly wasn't Mark Hardcastle. Maybe he was Leo Westwood, Banks thought. He looked about the same age as Silbert and about the same height. The photos were dated a week ago last Wednesday.

'OK,' said Banks. 'Can we get these printed up back at the station?'

'No problem,' said Annie. 'I can do it myself.'

'Let's call back there first, then. I've got a pal in technical support who might just be able to enhance the image enough to identify the street name that's on the sign on the wall in the background. There's obviously a damn good reason that memory stick was there.'

Banks pocketed the letters while Annie took the memory stick out of the slot and turned off the laptop. They were just about to head back to the station when Annie's mobile rang. Banks glanced round the room as she dealt with the call but saw nothing he thought of any significance.

'That was Maria Wolsey, from the theatre,' Annie said, putting her phone away. 'She wants to talk to me, so I said I'd drop by her flat.'

'OK,' said Banks. 'Why don't we go and get the photos printed first, then you can talk to her while I have another chat with Edwina Silbert?'

THE MORNING'S RAIN was long gone by the time Banks arrived at the Burgundy Hotel. Edwina Silbert was taking a gin and tonic and a cigarette in the small, quiet courtyard at the back of the building, one of the Sunday style supplements open before her, her gaze fixed on the distant hills.

Banks pulled up a chair and sat opposite. 'Comfortable night?' he asked.

'As well as could be expected,' she said.

Banks ordered a lemon tea from the hovering white-coated waiter. Edwina was looking her age this morning, he thought. Or closer to it. She was wearing a black woollen shawl over her shoulders, and her grey-white hair and pale, dry skin stood out in stark contrast.

'Where's that pretty girlfriend of yours today?' she asked.

'DI Cabbot isn't my girlfriend.'

'Then she's a damn fool. If I were twenty years younger . . .'

Banks laughed.

'What? You don't believe me?' Her expression turned serious. 'Anything new to report?' she asked.

'Not much, I'm afraid,' said Banks. 'I just called in at the station and discovered that your son's blood type is A positive, like about thirty-five per cent of the population. The only blood types we found on Mark's person were A positive and B positive, which is much rarer, and happens to be his own.'

'So you're saying it looks more and more as if Mark killed Laurence?'

'We've a long way to go to be certain of that yet,' said Banks, 'but blood typing certainly supports the theory.'

Edwina sat in silence. Banks felt that she might be debating with herself whether to tell him something, but the moment seemed to pass.

Banks slipped the photos that Annie had printed out of their envelope. 'Any idea who the other man is?' he asked.

Edwina studied the photos. 'No,' she said. 'Never see him before.'

'It's not Leo Westwood?'

'Leo? Good Lord, no. Leo's far more handsome than the man in this photograph, and not quite so tall. How do you know about Leo?'

'We found some letters from him to Laurence. When were they together?'

'About ten years ago. Late nineties until the early two thousands.'

'Do you know what happened?'

She stared at the distant patterns of dry-stone walls. 'Whatever usually happens to split people apart. Boredom? Someone new? Laurence didn't tell me. He was broken-hearted for a while, then he got on with his life.'

'Do you know where Leo is now?'

'I'm afraid not. We lost touch after he and Laurence split up. He might still be living in the same place, I suppose. He owned a flat in Swiss Cottage. I had dinner with them there on several occasions.'

'Were there any other serious relationships?' Banks asked.

'I'd say Leo was the only one until Mark came along. He was the only one I knew about, at any rate. There were casual lovers, of course.'

'Did you ever hear Laurence mention a man called Julian Fenner?'

Edwina frowned. 'Fenner? No, I can't say I have.'

Banks's lemon tea arrived. He thanked the waiter and took a sip. Refreshing. Edwina took the opportunity to order another gin and tonic.

'We've also been thinking,' Banks went on, 'that Mark may have found out that Laurence was having an affair.'

'I wasn't privy to all Laurence's comings and goings, but I would very much doubt it,' said Edwina. 'While Laurence could be as promiscuous as the next man when his feelings weren't engaged in a relationship, well . . . when he was in love, it was a different matter.'

'What about the man in the photo?' Banks said. 'They're touching.'

'I shouldn't think that means anything, would you?' Edwina said. 'It's just a natural gesture when you usher someone through a door before you.'

'But a jealous person might not see it that way.'

'True, but I wouldn't have said Mark was jealous. Just a little insecure.'

'What about Laurence's business interests?' Banks asked. 'I gather he was a retired civil servant?'

Edwina paused. 'Yes,' she said.

'But he also helped you with Viva, didn't he?'

She almost spilt her gin. 'Where on earth did you get *that* idea?'

'I thought it might explain his frequent trips to London, if he worked for you as a business consultant. And he received regular cheques from Viva.'

'I gave Laurence a share in the business, but he played no part in the running of the company. If he had, we'd have been bankrupt by now. Besides, our head office is in Swindon. Office space in London is far too expensive.'

'There were also a number of transfers from Swiss bank accounts we've been unable to account for. Would they have anything to do with Viva?'

'I very much doubt it,' Edwina mumbled, lighting another cigarette 'Though I imagine that someone in the employ of the foreign service for that many years would have squirrelled a certain amount away.'

'Expenses?'

She looked away, up at the hills again. 'Expenses. Contingency fund. Mad money. Escape hatch. Call it what you will.'

Banks's head was beginning to swim. Edwina seemed to have wrapped herself in a cloud of verbal smoke, as well as the real stuff. He felt as if the interview was slipping away from him, and he didn't know why. 'Do *you* know why he went down to London so often, then?'

'I'm afraid not.'

'Or why he went to Amsterdam last week?'

'I have no idea. Old friends, perhaps? Contacts. He had them all over the world. They were his life's blood.'

'What do you mean? I don't understand you.'

When she gazed at him, he sensed a guarded look in her eyes. 'It's perfectly clear,' she said. 'Laurence had no business affairs. Whatever he did down in London after he retired, it wasn't business.'

'Could it have had anything to do with his former job?'

'Oh, I should imagine so. One never really retires fully from that sort of thing, does one, especially in times like these?'

'What do you mean? What was it exactly that he did?'

Edwina sipped her gin and tonic and remained silent.

'Edwina,' Banks said in exasperation, 'you're keeping something from me, I can tell. What on earth is it? What are you holding back?'

Edwina paused and sighed. 'Oh, very well. I suppose you'd find out sooner or later.' She stubbed out her cigarette and looked him in the eye. 'He was a spy, Mr Banks. My son, Laurence. He was a spook.'

MARIA WOLSEY'S FLAT reminded Annie of where she had lived when she was a student. She glimpsed an unmade mattress on the floor in the bedroom, and the bookcases in the living room were made of planks separated by bricks. Posters of the Arctic Monkeys and the Killers vied for space with playbills for the RSC and the Eastvale Theatre on the walls. Eastvale, it turned out, was Maria's first job after leaving university, and her interest was in theatre history, costume design and set production.

'You could say Mark was a sort of mentor to me,' she said, cradling her mug. She wore a loose off-the-shoulder top, and she sat in an old armchair with her legs crossed, feet bare below the frayed hems of her jeans.

'Did the two of you spend much time together?' Annie asked.

'Quite a bit, yes. We'd often go for a drink or a bite to eat after work.'

'So you were close? Is that why you rang me?'

Maria's brow furrowed. 'I didn't want to talk in front of everyone. And Vernon acts like he's the boss, you know. He's always putting me down. I think he feels threatened by a competent woman.'

'What about a competent gay man? How did he like working for Mark?'

'Vernon's like a lot of men. He thinks he's OK with it, but really he's a homophobe. The whole idea of it terrifies him, threatens his manhood. But basically he and Mark got along all right.'

'What about Derek Wyman?' Annie asked. 'He and Mark went to London together last week. Had they done anything like that before?'

'No. To be honest, it came as quite a surprise to me. I mean, I know they met socially occasionally, but it wasn't as if they were the best of friends.'

'You mean they didn't get along?'

'No, I'm not saying that. I think Mark just got frustrated with Derek sometimes, because he kept trying to do Mark's job, telling him how the production should look and all that. I mean, Derek *is* the director, but Mark's a professional. He's done courses and everything.'

'I thought they were agreed on the German Expressionist set?'

'Well, they were. But it was Derek's idea, and he wasn't always receptive when Mark brought fresh perspectives to it. Mark was very creative, and he saw a production as more of a collaboration. Between all of us, really. He was always asking our opinions on things. The actors, too. But Derek just gave orders.'

'You said Mark had been a bit strange the past couple of weeks. Do you have any idea why?'

'No. We didn't really have chance to get together for a chat or anything during that period, what with one thing and another.'

'Did he ever tell you if something was bothering him?'

'There were a couple of occasions when he let his guard down.' She stifled a giggle. 'Usually when we'd had a bit too much to drink.'

'And what did he talk about on these occasions?'

'Oh, you know. Life. His feelings. His ambitions.'

'Can you tell me more?'

'Well, you know about his background, don't you? He was an only child, and he didn't turn out to be exactly the sort of son his father wanted. His father was a miner, very macho apparently, played rugby and all that. Mark wasn't very good at sports. Worse, he wasn't even interested.'

'What about his mother?'

'Oh, Mark *adored* her. But she broke his heart.'

'How?'

'She was so beautiful and so artistic, so sensitive and tender. She acted with the am drams, took him with her to concerts. But his father used to mock everything they liked to do. It sounds as if he was a drunken brute. In the end, she couldn't take it any more, so she left them. Mark was only ten. He was devastated. I don't think he ever got over it.'

Annie could hardly believe it. 'She left him with a brutal, drunken father?'

'I know. It sounds terrible. But there was another man in her life, apparently, and he didn't want any children hanging around. They ran off to London. It tore Mark apart.'

'Go on,' said Annie. 'What happened after his mother left?'

'Well, Mark was left with his father, who just sank even deeper into the booze and became more and more vicious. Mark lasted till he was sixteen. Then he hit him with an ashtray and ran away from home.'

'He hit his father with an ashtray?'

'It was in self-defence. His father beat him regularly, usually with a thick leather belt, Mark said. The kids at school used to bully him, too, spat on him and called him a sissy. His life was hell. That one time, he told me, it just all came surging up in him and he lashed out.'

'What happened to his father?'

'Mark didn't hang around to find out. He never went back.'

Annie could see why Maria had not wanted to talk about this in front of the others. If Mark Hardcastle had shown an inclination towards violence, poor anger control, then it certainly supported the theory that he had killed Laurence Silbert in a jealous rage and was then overcome with remorse.

'He did very well for himself, then,' Annie said. 'But it sounds as if he had a lot of inner demons to overcome.'

'And prejudice. Don't forget that. We might think we're living in an enlightened society, but as often as not you'll find it's only skin-deep.'

'I know what you're saying,' said Annie. 'Hypocrisy's everywhere. But it doesn't sound as if Mark suffered a great deal from anti-gay prejudice here, at the Eastvale Theatre. I mean, Vernon may have been uncomfortable, but he didn't actively harass Mark, did he?'

'Oh, no. I didn't mean to imply that. It was a great place for him to work. And he had such great ideas. He was going to make so many changes.'

'What do you mean?'

'The theatre. Mark had a vision of starting the Eastvale Players. A professional company made up of some of the best local actors along with jobbing actors. The idea was that Eastvale would be their home base, but they'd tour and we'd have reciprocal visits from other groups of players. Mark would be the artistic director and he said he'd put a good word in for me with the board, so I could have the job he's got now. Had.'

'And Vernon?'

'He'd do the same as he's doing now.'

'But wouldn't he be upset if you became his boss?'

'I don't see why. Vernon's not ambitious. He'd still be paid, wouldn't he?'

Annie thought that Maria was being deliberately obtuse, given her earlier comment that Vernon seemed to have problems working *with* a competent woman, let alone *for* one. 'What about the amateur groups?' she asked.

'They'd do what they were doing before the theatre was restored, I suppose: putting on their plays in the community centre and church halls.'

'And Derek Wyman?'

'He'd still be their director.'

'I know, but it'd be a bit of a step-down for him, wouldn't it?'

'But it's not as if it's his life, is it? Or even his real job. He's a schoolteacher. The theatre's just a hobby for him.'

Try and tell that to Derek Wyman, Annie thought, remembering her talk with him that morning. 'And who was going to finance this little venture?'

'Laurence Silbert, Mark's partner, was going to help us get started. Then the idea was that it would mostly pay for itself, maybe with a little help from the Arts Council lottery money. Laurence was on the board, and he thought he could convince them.'

'Interesting,' Annie said. 'Just how far had all this got?'

'Oh, it was still only in the planning stages,' Maria said. 'That's another reason this is all so tragic. Now nothing will change. I don't even think I have the heart to stay here without Mark being around.'

'You're young,' said Annie. 'I'm sure you'll do fine. Is there anything else you can tell me?'

'Not really,' said Maria. 'That was about all I had to say.'

Annie stood up. 'Thanks for your help, Maria.'

'Think nothing of it,' the young girl said, seeing her to the door. 'Just don't tell Vernon what I said about him being homophobic and all that. I'm sure he thinks he's the very model of tolerance.'

'Don't worry,' said Annie. 'I won't.'

EDWINA'S STATEMENT hung in the silence ready to burst like a piece of overripe fruit on a tree. Banks had had his suspicions that Silbert was up to *something* clandestine, but not this. Not espionage. He knew that it changed the whole focus of the case, but it was too early to say exactly how.

'I shouldn't have told you,' Edwina said. 'It'll only muddy the waters.'

'On the contrary,' said Banks. 'You should have told me the first time we talked to you. It could be important. How long had this been going on?'

'Oh, all his life. Well, ever since he graduated from university.' Edwina sighed and lit another cigarette. 'His father, Cedric, worked for military intelligence during the war. I don't think he was very good at it, but at least he survived. After the war he got involved in a number of ill-advised business ventures, one after the other. I'm afraid my late husband wasn't much good at anything, Mr Banks. His main interests were fast cars and faster women. We stayed together for appearances' sake, but God knows how long it would have lasted if it hadn't been for his accident. He died in October 1956, right at the height of the Suez Crisis. I think he was involved in the oil business then. The only bright spot in my life at that time was Laurence.'

Banks noticed the tears in her eyes. 'The spying,' he said gently. 'How did that come about?'

'Oh, yes, that. Would you believe it, Dicky Hawkins—an old war colleague of Cedric's—actually *asked me* for permission to recruit Laurence? This was in his last year at Cambridge, 1964. He'd shown a remarkable facility for modern languages—German and Russian in particular—and a keen grasp of contemporary politics. He was good at sports, too. Not for Laurence the Beatles, marijuana and revolution. He was about as dyed-in-the-wool blue as you could get.'

'So you told this Dicky Hawkins that it was all right to recruit him?'

'The question was a mere courtesy. I can't say I was happy about the idea, but I told him he was welcome to give it a try, that I wasn't Laurence's keeper and wouldn't stand in his way. The next thing I knew Laurence was off on training courses for a couple of years and I didn't see much of him.'

'Do you know which branch of the intelligence services he worked for?'

'MI6. His facility for languages sealed it. I remember his first real assignment was in Prague in 1968. I assume he had to mingle with the students and help make things difficult for the Russians, or report on developments. After that . . . who knows?'

'Where was Laurence living during this period?'

'Oh, it varied. We're talking about quite a long time, you know. Forty years: 1964 to 2004. He had a beautiful house in Kensington. He lived there for over twenty years, when he was in the country.'

'What happened to it?'

'He sold it when the market was good. That was what enabled him to buy the large house in Yorkshire and the little pied-à-terre in Bloomsbury.'

'Did Mark know about his past?'

'I would imagine so. They would have had to have him vetted.'

'Why didn't you tell me about Laurence before?'

Edwina looked away. 'I don't know. It didn't seem relevant.'

'You know that's not true. You know a hell of a lot more than you're saying. Why didn't you tell me, Edwina?'

She lowered her head and whispered, 'Why are you asking me this when you know what the answer is already?'

'Because I want to hear it from you.'

Edwina paused for a moment, then leaned forward and grasped the edge of the table with talon-like hands. Her voice was dry and sibilant. 'Because I'm not convinced that Laurence had completely retired, nor do I trust the people he was working for. There, how's that for you?'

'Thank you,' said Banks, standing up to leave.

'There's something else,' Edwina said, relaxing back in the chair. 'If you're going to proceed with this business, then I'd advise you to be very careful. These men don't play by your rules. Believe me. I know.'

'I'm sure you do,' said Banks. 'And I'll remember that.' He shook her limp hand and left her to stare out at the hills, lost in memories.

Chapter Five

Built in the sixties, the East Side Estate had been steadily declining ever since. Certain areas were a wasteland of burnt-out cars and abandoned supermarket trolleys, dogs running rife and a population suspicious of all strangers, especially the police. A row of uniformed officers held back the curious crowds at about half past ten on Wednesday evening. Ambulance lights spun blue in the humid night air near the mouth of what the locals called 'glue-sniffers' ginnel'. A fifteen-year-old boy called Donny Moore lay bleeding on a stretcher from stab wounds as the paramedics hovered over him. Annie Cabbot and Winsome had been called to the estate to assess the situation for Major Crimes.

'What's the damage?' Annie asked one of the paramedics, as they manoeuvred the stretcher into the back of the ambulance.

'Hard to tell at this point,' he said. 'Three stab wounds. Chest, shoulder and abdomen.' He lowered his voice. 'Don't quote me, but I think he'll live.'

'Thanks,' said Annie. 'When will we be able to talk to him?'

'Not until tomorrow at the earliest.' He climbed in the back of the ambulance and shut the doors, and they sped away.

The man who had reported the incident, Benjamin Paxton, paced beside his modest grey Honda, clearly anxious to get away. His wife was still sitting in the car with the doors locked, staring straight ahead. Annie asked Paxton to tell her what had happened, while Winsome took notes.

'I did my duty as a citizen,' said Paxton, eyeing the crowd anxiously. 'I reported the incident and waited here till the police arrived, as I was asked to do. Isn't that enough? Can't we just go home?'

'Where's home?'

'We live in South Shields, but we're renting a cottage near Lyndgarth. This is supposed to be a walking holiday.'

Annie glanced around at the dilapidated terrace houses. 'What brought you down here, then?' she asked.

'We got lost, that's all. We had dinner at a pub in Kilnwick we read about in the guidebook and took the wrong road on the way back.'

'Can you tell me exactly what happened, sir?' Annie asked.

'We were driving down the street and Olivia thought she saw something moving on the waste ground at the end of that passage under the railway lines there. I . . . well, I wasn't going to stop, quite frankly, because I didn't like the look of the place, but it was unmistakable. A person on the ground there, rolling, you know, as if he was in pain.'

'So you stopped to help?'

'Yes. I got out and . . . well, as soon as I saw the blood I got straight back in the car and phoned the ambulance and police on my mobile.'

'Did you see anyone else around?'

Paxton paused. 'I'm not really sure. I mean, it was dark, even then. But I thought I saw a hooded figure running up that passage.'

'Could you give a description?'

'I'm afraid not. It was too dark to make anything out clearly.'

'I understand,' said Annie. 'Did you see anyone else?'

'I got the most fleeting impression . . . I don't know, just before we saw the figure on the ground, that there was a group of people sort of scattering.'

'Could you describe any of them?'

'No. They were all either in the shadows or wearing hoodies.'

There were two gangs operating on the East Side Estate, Annie had learned, and though ASBOs abounded on both sides, they had never caused any serious problems outside the odd scrap, graffiti and shoplifting. But the mood had been changing lately; knives had arrived, and there were rumours of heavier drugs coming in from Manchester.

'Did you see anything or anyone else?' she asked.

'No,' said Paxton. 'I went back to the car and waited.'

'OK,' said Annie. 'You can go home now. Leave an address with DS Jackman here and we'll be in touch about a formal statement.'

As she walked away, she heard Paxton ask Winsome, 'Er . . . do you think you could possibly tell me the way to Lyndgarth?'

ON WEDNESDAY EVENING, Banks was in the kitchen in his jeans and an old T-shirt putting together an Ikea storage unit for his collection of CDs and DVDs. Stanford's *Symphony No. 2* was playing in the background, and the agitated movement he was listening to at the moment echoed his frustration with Ikea. He had got the top the wrong way round and wasn't sure he could get the back off to fix it without ruining the whole thing. When he heard the knock at the door and got up off his knees to go and answer it, he realised that he hadn't heard a car. That was odd. His cottage was at the end of a long driveway and nobody walked there except the postman.

Banks answered the door and found a man of around sixty standing there, with thinning grey hair and a neat grey moustache. Though it was a warm evening, the man was wearing a light camel overcoat on top of his suit.

'Mr Banks?' he said. 'Detective Chief Inspector Banks?'

'Yes.'

'I'm sorry to bother you at home. My name is Browne, with an "e". Er . . . may I come in?'

'I don't mean to be rude,' said Banks, 'but I'm busy. What's it about?'

'Laurence Silbert.'

Banks paused for a moment, then stood aside and gestured for Mr Browne to enter. He did so, and followed Banks through to the kitchen.

The storage unit lay on the floor, the untreated wood that formed its top plain to see. 'You've got the top the wrong way round,' said Browne.

'I know,' Banks grunted.

Browne grimaced. 'Quite a job to put it right. I know. I've done it myself.'

'Look, I appreciate your advice, but I do know the problem I'm facing. Please, sit down.' Banks gestured to a bench. 'Would you like a drink?'

'Thank you,' said Browne, wedging himself into the breakfast nook. He hadn't taken off his overcoat. 'A small whisky and soda wouldn't go amiss.'

Banks found a bottle of Bell's and added a touch of soda. He poured himself a small Macallan eighteen-year-old with the merest threat of water.

Browne raised his glass as Banks sat opposite him. '*Slàinte.*'

'Slainte,' Banks said. 'You told me you came about Laurence Silbert. Whose interests do you represent?'

Browne played with his glass, swirling the amber fluid. 'I suppose you could say that I represent Her Majesty's government,' he said finally.

'You're one of Laurence Silbert's old bosses?'

'Please, Mr Banks. Surely even you must know that MI6 doesn't operate on British soil. Haven't you seen *Spooks*?'

'MI5, then,' Banks said. 'I stand corrected. I suppose seeing some identification is out of the question?'

'Not at all, dear chap.' Browne took a laminated card out of his wallet. It identified him as Claude F. Browne, Home Office Security. The photo could have been of anyone of Browne's general age and appearance.

Banks handed it back. 'So what is it you want to tell me?' he asked.

'Tell you?' Browne sipped some more whisky and frowned. 'I don't believe I mentioned wanting to tell you anything.'

'So why are you here? If you don't have anything to say relevant to the case under investigation, you're wasting my time.'

'Don't be so hasty, Mr Banks. There's no need to jump to conclusions. I was simply wondering what point your investigation has reached.'

'I can't tell you that,' said Banks. 'It's not our policy to discuss active investigations with members of the public.'

'Oh, come on. I'm hardly a member of the public. We're on the same side.'

'Are we?'

'You know we are. All I'm interested in is whether we're likely to encounter any potentially embarrassing situations, any unpleasantness.'

'And how would you define that?'

'Anything that might embarrass the government.'

'What did Silbert do? Put Strontium 90 in someone's tea?'

'Very funny. I'm afraid I can't tell you what he did,' said Browne. 'You know I can't. That information is protected by the Official Secrets Act.'

Banks sipped some Macallan. 'Then we're at a bit of an impasse, aren't we? You can't tell me anything and I can't tell you anything.'

'Oh dear,' said Browne. 'I was hoping it wouldn't be like this. We *are* on the same side, you know. Our methods may differ but our ends are the same.'

'The difference is,' said Banks, 'your organisation believes the ends justify the means. The police try to operate independently of that, of what governments need to get done on the quiet so they can stay in power.'

'That's a very cynical assessment, if I might say so,' said Browne. 'And I'm more than willing to bet that you've taken a short cut or two in your time to make sure someone you *knew* to be guilty got convicted. But that's by the by. Like you, we're mere civil servants. We sometimes have to do things that go counter to what one would deem right.'

'Why? That's what I said about the ends and the means, isn't it? Is that what Silbert did? Was he a government assassin? Did he betray people?'

Browne finished his drink and edged out of his corner to stand by the kitchen door. 'You're letting your imagination run away with you. I simply came here seeking some sort of reassurance that, for the good of the country, your investigation into the death of Laurence Silbert wasn't likely to cause any . . . any further ripples that might embarrass the government. That it could be swiftly and neatly concluded, and you could head off back to Chelsea to see your lovely young girlfriend.'

At the mention of Sophia, Banks felt a chill crawl up his spine. 'Are you telling me that you think there's something about Silbert's murder that could stir things up internationally?' he said. 'Is there a terrorist connection? A Russian Mafia connection? Was he a double agent? Is that where the Swiss bank accounts come in?'

Browne stared at Banks, his eyes hard and cold. 'If you can't give me the assurances I seek, I'll have to seek elsewhere.' He turned to leave.

Banks followed him through the living room to the front door. 'As far as I know,' he said, 'it looks like a simple murder-suicide. Silbert's lover killed your man, then he killed himself out of grief.'

Browne turned. 'Then there's no need for a messy investigation, is there, no chance of anything uncomfortable slipping into public view at a trial?'

'Well, there probably wasn't,' said Banks. 'Not until you turned up, that is. I only said that's what it *looks* like.'

'Good night, Mr Banks, and grow up,' said Browne. He shut the door firmly behind him. Banks didn't hear a car engine start until a few minutes later, far away, at the end of the lane.

ON THURSDAY MORNING, Detective Superintendent Gervaise called a meeting in the boardroom, at which Banks, Winsome, Annie and Stefan Nowak were in attendance. After tea and coffee had been sorted, everyone turned to Nowak for his forensic summary.

'I just got the DNA results this morning,' he said, 'and on the evidence of the DNA comparison with the mother, we can state that the identity of the deceased found at Castleview Heights is definitely Laurence Silbert. According to the post-mortems, Hardcastle died of ligature strangulation— the clothes line he hanged himself with—and Silbert was killed by a series blows to the head from a hard, flat object—which we've matched to the cricket bat found at the scene. The first blow was to the back of the head, the left side, so he was moving away from his killer at the time.'

'Does that fit with the idea of a lover's tiff?' Gervaise asked.

'I don't see why not,' said Banks. 'People turn away from one another in rows sometimes. Silbert must have misjudged the depth of Hardcastle's rage. But it could also fit other possible scenarios.'

'We'll leave those for the moment,' said Gervaise. 'Go on, Stefan.'

'We think Mr Silbert turned as he fell to his knees, and his assailant hit him on the right temple and in the throat, breaking the hyoid bone, crushing the larynx and knocking him backwards into the position we found him. One or more of those blows killed him. There was then a series of blows, post-mortem.'

'And Mark Hardcastle was left-handed,' said Annie.

'Yes,' said Nowak. 'Given that the only fingerprints we found on the bat belonged to him, I'd hazard a guess that he's your man. DNA analysis confirms that the only blood at the Silbert crime scene belonged to Silbert himself. And the blood we found on Hardcastle was mainly Silbert's, with a small amount of Hardcastle's own, caused by scratches as he climbed the tree.'

'What about toxicology?' asked Gervaise.

'Nothing but alcohol in Hardcastle's blood,' said Nowak. 'Neither Hardcastle nor Silbert was drugged.'

'Was there evidence of anyone else at the scene?' Banks asked Nowak.

'Not at the scene specifically, no. Just the usual traces. You know as well I do that there's always trace evidence of whoever's been in the room—friends, cleaners, relatives, what have you—all over the place.'

'I think it's time you put your curiosity to bed,' said Gervaise to Banks. 'I'd say we've got our answer. You can't argue with DNA.'

'Begging your pardon, ma'am,' Annie said, 'but it doesn't prove anything, does it? I mean, the fact that we haven't found Hardcastle's blood at the scene simply means that he didn't shed any there. And if *he* didn't shed any—'

'—then another killer might not have shed any. Yes, I can see where you're going with this, DI Cabbot,' said Gervaise. 'But we have a lot of evidence to suggest that Hardcastle killed Silbert and then hanged himself, and none whatsoever to suggest that someone else did it. No one was seen entering or leaving the house, and no other suspects have suggested themselves. I'm sorry, but it sounds very much like case closed to me.'

'But someone from the theatre might have had a motive,' Annie said. 'Maria Wolsey reckons—'

'Yes, we know all about that,' said Gervaise. 'Vernon Ross or Derek Wyman might have had a motive if Hardcastle and Silbert got their new players' group together. I read your report.'

'And?' said Annie.

'I just don't believe that either Ross or Wyman would have had the ability to kill Silbert and make it look as if Hardcastle had done it.'

'Why not?' Annie protested. 'They're both theatrical types. They're used to manufacturing illusions.'

'Very clever, but I'm sorry, I don't believe it. Surely someone would have seen them coming or going. What about the CCTV cameras?' Gervaise looked towards Nowak.

'We've checked all the footage and there's nothing out of the ordinary,' he said. 'Number fifteen wasn't covered directly.'

'It's a very insular neighbourhood,' said Banks. 'Maybe the locals would notice a tramp, or some kid in a hoodie, but not someone who blended in with the neighbourhood. I agree with DI Cabbot. Hardcastle could have gone out, and while he was gone, someone else—Ross, Wyman, some spook—could have entered and killed Silbert. When Hardcastle returned and found the body, he became distraught and committed suicide. He could have picked up the cricket bat then, after the murder, after the real killer had wiped it clean. Given that we have a photograph of Laurence Silbert in London with an unknown man, that Silbert was known to be an MI6 agent and that they're pretty good in the dirty-tricks department—'

'That's neither here nor there,' snapped Gervaise. 'I don't suppose you've identified this mystery man in the photograph, have you?'

Banks glanced at Annie.

'We've shown it around to a few people,' she said, 'but nobody admits to recognising the unknown man.'

Gervaise turned to Banks. 'Have you learned anything yet about the location in the photographs?'

'No, ma'am,' said Banks. 'I'm pretty certain the first two were taken in Regent's Park, but I haven't heard back from technical support on the others. Or on Julian Fenner's dodgy phone number, either.'

'It seems as if you're getting nowhere fast, doesn't it?' Gervaise said.

'Look,' said Banks, 'I don't think it's irrelevant that Silbert was a spook or that Mr Browne, if that's his real name, came to see me last night and basically told me to lay off. You know as well as I do that we've run into a brick wall every time we've tried to find out anything about Silbert this week. The local police said they'd handle the Bloomsbury pied-à-terre business, and the next day they phoned us back, said they'd checked it out, and that there was nothing out of the ordinary. What does that mean, for crying out loud? And can we trust them? Perhaps if there was something out of the ordinary they made it disappear? How do we know that the police who checked out Silbert's flat weren't Special Branch?'

'Now you're being paranoid,' said Gervaise. 'Why can't you just accept that it's over?'

'Because I'd like some answers.'

Nowak cleared his throat. 'There is one more thing,' he said.

'Yes?' said Gervaise.

Nowak avoided Banks's gaze. 'Well, perhaps we should have done this earlier, but . . . things being the way they were . . . Anyway, we ran Hardcastle's and Silbert's fingerprints through NAFIS and we got a result.'

'Go on,' said Gervaise.

'Well, ma'am, Hardcastle's got form. Eight years ago.'

'For what?'

'Domestic assault. Apparently Hardcastle flew into a jealous rage and beat up the man he was living with.'

'Serious?'

'Not as bad as it could have been. He stopped before he did too much damage. Still put the bloke in hospital for a couple of days. And got himself a six-month suspended sentence.'

Gervaise said nothing for a few moments. Then she slammed her Silbert-Hardcastle folder shut and said, 'That's it, then. I'll be talking to the coroner. Case closed. DCI Banks, could you stay behind a moment, please?'

When the others had left, Gervaise sat down again and smoothed her skirt. 'I'm very sorry we dragged you back from your holiday,' she told Banks. 'We can't always tell when something's going to be a waste of time, can we?'

'It would make our lives easier if we could,' said Banks. 'But with all due respect, ma'am, I—'

Gervaise put her finger to her lips. 'No,' she said. 'This isn't a continuation of the meeting. As I said, case closed.' She laced her fingers together on the table. 'What plans do you have for the next week or so?'

'Nothing in particular,' Banks said, surprised at the question. 'Sophia's coming up tomorrow. We're going to see *Othello* on Saturday.'

'Only I was feeling guilty,' Gervaise went on. 'About dragging you back up here for nothing on the evening of your big dinner party.'

Christ, Banks thought. She wasn't going to invite them to *dinner*, was she? 'It wasn't for nothing,' he said. 'But that's all right. Water under the bridge.'

'Only I know how much trouble this job can cause a couple sometimes, and it must be really hard when you're just starting out.'

'Yes, ma'am.' Just where on earth was she going with this?

'So, er . . . Alan . . . I'd like to make it up to you for calling you back. I'd like you to pick up your holidays where you left off. As of this weekend. A week, shall we say?'

'Next week off? But—'

Gervaise held up her hand. 'But me no buts. Please. I insist. No reason you shouldn't enjoy the rest of your leave. Now bugger off and enjoy yourself. That's an order.'

And with that she walked out of the boardroom and left Banks sitting alone at the long polished table wondering just what the hell was going on.

Chapter Six

'So what do you think?'

It was hot and crowded in the theatre bar at intermission. Banks felt the sweat prickle on his scalp as they stood by the plate-glass window, looking out at the evening light on the shops across Market Street. He glanced at Sophia. She was wearing her hair loose tonight, and its lustre framed her oval face, the olive skin and dark eyes showing her Greek heritage. Not for the first time, he felt like a very lucky man.

'Well,' said Sophia, taking a sip of red wine, 'it's hardly Olivier, is it?'

'What did you expect?'

'The lighting's good, all that chiaroscuro and whatnot, but I'm not convinced about the whole German Expressionist idea.'

'Me neither,' said Banks. 'I keep expecting Nosferatu to jump out from behind one of those big curved screens and flash his fingernails.'

Sophia laughed. 'Seriously, though, I *am* enjoying it. It's a long time since I've seen *Othello*. Come to think of it, it's a long time since I've seen *any* Shakespeare play on stage. It takes me back to my student days.'

'You studied Shakespeare?'

'Long and hard.'

'We did *Othello* for O-level English.'

'Pretty tough when you're only sixteen. It's a very grown-up play.'

'Oh, I don't know. I understood jealousy even then.' Banks thought of the other night, down in Chelsea: Sophia saying, *So I've been told.*

'But that's not what it's really—Oops, damn!'

Someone had accidentally jogged Sophia's arm and she had spilt a little red wine on her roll-neck top. Luckily, it was a dark colour.

'Sorry,' the man said, turning to her and smiling. 'There *is* a bit of a crush in here, isn't there?'

'Good evening, Mr Wyman,' said Banks. 'Haven't seen you for a while.'

Derek Wyman turned, and Banks detected a cautious expression come into the drama teacher's eyes.

'It's all right,' Sophia was saying.

'No, let me get some soda,' Wyman said. 'I insist.'

'Really, it's all right. It was only a drop. And you can't even see it now.'

Banks wasn't sure that he appreciated the way Wyman was staring at Sophia's chest. 'I'm surprised you've got time to mingle with the punters,' he said. 'I'd have thought you'd be backstage giving the cast a pep talk.'

Wyman laughed. 'It's not like a football match, you know. I don't go into the dressing room and yell at them at half time.' He held his hand out to Sophia. 'I'm Derek Wyman, by the way, director of this modest little effort. I don't believe we've met.'

Sophia took his hand. 'Sophia Morton,' she said. 'We were just talking about how much we're enjoying the play.'

'Thank you,' Wyman said.

'While you're here,' Banks said, pulling out the photograph that had become a fixture in his pockets. 'We weren't able to track you down during the week. Do you recognise the man with Laurence Silbert?'

Wyman studied the photograph and frowned. 'No idea,' he said. 'I wouldn't know why you'd expect that I should.' He seemed anxious to get away.

'Just that you were in London with Mark Hardcastle, that's all.'

'I've already explained all about that. Look, I—'

'Do you own a digital camera?'

'Yes.'

'What make?'

'It's a Fuji. Why?'

'Did you have any idea that Laurence Silbert had worked for MI6?'

'Good Lord, no. I really must go. They'll be starting again in a minute.'

'Certainly,' said Banks, edging back to let Wyman by.

'That wasn't very nice of you,' said Sophia, when Wyman was out of earshot. 'You didn't have to interrogate the poor man in the theatre bar.'

'You call that interrogation? You should see me when I really get going.'

'You know what I mean. You don't think he's guilty of murder, do you?'

'I doubt it. But I wouldn't be surprised if he was mixed up in it somehow.'

'Mixed up in what? I thought there was no case. You said they'd dragged you back from London for nothing.'

'That's what *they* say,' said Banks. 'Only I'm not so sure.'

The bell started ringing to announce that the performance was due to recommence. Banks and Sophia headed for the theatre entrance.

'THERE'S SOMETHING funny about that new bookcase you've got your CDs in,' said Sophia, from the sofa of Banks's entertainment room.

Banks was flipping through his CD collection, trying to find something suitable for the late hour and the post-*Othello* mood. He decided that Mazzy Starr would do nicely.

'The bookcase, yes,' he said. 'I messed it up. It's the top. It's the wrong way round. I can't get the damn flimsy back off without ruining it, so I thought I might stain the top. I just haven't got around to it yet.'

Sophia put her hand to her mouth to stifle her laughter.

'What?' Banks said.

'Just the thought of you on your knees with an Allen key in your hand cursing to high heaven.'

'Yes, well, enough of that. Did you enjoy this evening?'

'It's not over yet, is it?'

'Certainly not.' Banks bent over and kissed her. A taste of things to come.

Sophia out held her glass. 'I'll have one more glass of that spectacular Amarone before you sit down,' she said. 'Then I think it'll be bedtime.'

Banks poured the wine and passed her the glass, then filled his own.

'I've been thinking about the play,' Sophia said, turning to face him as he sat down beside her. 'What do you think it's about?'

'*Othello*? Oh, jealousy, betrayal, envy, ambition, greed, lust, revenge. The usual stuff of Shakespearean tragedies. All the colours of darkness.'

Sophia shook her head. 'No. I mean, well, yes, it *is* about all those themes, but there's something else, a subtext, if you like, another level.'

'Too deep for me.'

Sophia slapped his knee. 'No, it's not. Listen. Remember when Iago and Rodrigo wake up Desdemona's father and tell him what's going on?'

'Yes,' said Banks.

'Well, the language Iago uses is very powerful, very visual. It plants images in the hearer's imagination. Remember, he talks about Desdemona being *covered* by a Barbary horse. That's the language of the stud farm. Just imagine what sort of images it must have put into her father's mind, how unbearable it must have been to think of, to *see*, his daughter that way.'

'That's how Iago works,' said Banks. 'He plants ideas, pictures, lets them grow, bides his time.' Banks thought of Sophia saying, *So I've been told*, and the images it created in *his* mind.

'Exactly. That's what I'm getting at. *Othello* is a play about the power of language, about the power of words and images to make people *see*, and what they see can drive them insane. Iago uses exactly the same technique on Othello later. He presents him with unbearable images of Desdemona's sexual activities with another man. Not just the idea of it, but *images* of it, too. I mean, what real evidence does Othello have of his wife's unfaithfulness?'

'There's the handkerchief,' said Banks. 'But that was planted. Then Iago tells him that Cassio had a dream about Desdemona, said things in his sleep. Did things.'

'Yes, and that while he was having this dream Cassio tried to kiss Iago, and get his leg over, thought he *was* Desdemona. Othello's already half crazed with jealousy by then, and bit by bit Iago feeds him even more unbearable images until he's over the edge. And he kills her.'

'Of course,' Banks said, 'you could argue that Othello did the same thing with Desdemona, too. He even admits to winning her over by telling her stories of battles and exotic places and creatures. Putting pictures in her mind. Cannibals. The Anthropophagi. Men with their heads below their shoulders. Real life and soul of the party.'

Sophia laughed. 'It worked, though, didn't it? As chat-up lines go it can't have been such a bad one. Language can impress *and* it can inflame the passions. It works both ways.'

Banks sipped the last of his rich, silky Amarone. 'And in the end,' he said, almost to himself, 'Iago succeeds in talking Othello into murdering Desdemona and killing himself.'

'Yes. What is it, Alan?'

'What?' Banks put his glass down. 'Just a glimmer of an idea, that's all.' He reached out for her. 'But then a better one came along. How would you like to hear a story about a particularly grisly murder I solved once?'

'Well, you certainly know how to get a girl in the mood, don't you?' Sophia said, and moved into his arms.

SUNDAY MORNING dawned clear and sunny, the sky as blue as the grass was green, a perfect late-spring day. After breakfast, Banks and Sophia drove to Reeth, parked on the village green, then headed past the old school and turned up Skelgate. At the top, they went through the gate onto open moorland and walked high along the daleside below Calver Hill. Curlews soared above the moors, making their curious piping calls. Banks and Sophia walked hand in hand back down to the river, which they crossed by a small swing bridge and continued on to the old Corpse Way into Grinton.

Sophia's parents were already waiting in the pub when they got there. They had taken a table by the window, settling themselves on the comfortable padded bench. Banks and Sophia sat in the cushioned chairs opposite them, and they could see St Andrew's, the beautiful twelfth-century Norman church across the road, through the low bay window.

'We haven't ordered yet,' said Victor Morton, Sophia's father. 'Just got here ourselves. Thought we'd wait for you.' He was a fit, slim man in his early seventies, not an ounce of fat on him.

'Let me order,' said Banks. 'Everyone know what they want?'

The choices were fairly predictable for a Sunday pub lunch—roast beef and Yorkshire pudding for Banks and Victor, roast lamb for Sophia and pork for her mother, Helena. It was easy to see where Sophia got her looks, Banks thought, glancing at Helena as he went to the bar to order. She must have been quite a beauty in her day, and Victor was no doubt a dashing, handsome young diplomatic attaché. Banks got along well with Helena, but he sensed Victor's disapproval of him. He wasn't sure if it was the age difference, his job, his background, or the fact that he was divorced, but he felt it.

Sophia helped him carry the drinks back. Beer for Victor and himself, wine for the women. Banks sat back and enjoyed his drink through the small talk. Somehow, nothing tasted quite as good as a pint of well-kept ale after a long walk.

When the food came, they all ate in silence for a few moments, then Victor looked up at Banks and said, 'Nasty business, that Hindswell Woods and Castleview Heights. You involved?'

'I was,' said Banks, with a sideways glance at Sophia.

'Funny chap, Laurence Silbert.'

Banks paused, glass halfway to his mouth. 'You *knew* him?'

'Well, sort of. Years ago. Bonn. Back in the old days, before the Wall came down.' He nodded towards Sophia. 'She was still at school,' he said, then turned back to Banks as if his words were some sort of challenge.

Banks said nothing.

Sophia looked at her mother, who said something in Greek. The two of them started chatting quietly.

Between mouthfuls of food, Victor went on. He lowered his voice and leaned forward as he spoke. 'Anyway, I say I knew him, but it was more by reputation than anything. It was the eighties, '86 or '87. The embassy was in Bonn then, of course, not Berlin. Interesting times.'

Victor needn't have worried about people overhearing, Banks thought; the pub was noisy with chatter, laughter and the shrieks of children. There was a man at the bar, Banks had noticed, who kept glancing over, but he wouldn't be able to hear their conversation.

'Were you involved in intelligence work?' Banks asked.

'No, not at all. We weren't all spies, you know. Some of us were genuine diplomats, not like the Russians. Spies to a man, that lot.'

'Why do you remember Laurence Silbert in particular?' he asked.

'His reputation, I suppose. We used to call him 007 around the office, just between ourselves. A little joke. Bit of a James Bond. Not the girls, of course, he was never interested in that direction, but he had the good looks, the coldness, ruthlessness, and he was tough as nails.'

'He killed people?'

'Oh, I'm sure he did. Not that I ever had any evidence, mind you. Just rumour. But he worked on the other side a lot, so he's bound to have faced danger and . . . well . . . I'm sure you can imagine what it was like.'

'Yes,' said Banks.

Sophia kept glancing sideways at Banks, and he could tell from her expression that she was half annoyed that he was talking shop with her father, but also pleased that they were getting along. He turned and smiled at her while Victor was cutting off another lump of Yorkshire pudding.

Sophia smiled back. 'Shall I get more drinks?' she asked.

'I'll have one, please,' Banks said. 'Victor?'

Victor picked up his empty glass. 'Please, dear.'

He watched her go to the bar, then turned his watery grey eyes back on Banks. He seemed on the verge of saying something about the relationship.

'How long were you in contact with Silbert?' Banks asked quickly.

'Oh, it wasn't real contact,' Victor said. 'As I told you, I had nothing to do with that sort of thing. Then the Wall came down and things changed. We moved to Berlin, for a start, in '91. Of course, that wasn't quite the real end of things, as some people think, more the symbolic one, which was the face presented to the world.'

'But did you know anything about what Silbert did, what operations he was involved in?'

'No, nothing like that. As I said, I only knew him by reputation, really.'

Sophia came back with the drinks. They had all finished their meals by now, and Sophia's mother was studying the dessert list.

'Helena, dear,' said Victor, 'would you be so kind as to pass me the pudding menu? I fancy something hot and sticky with lashings of custard.'

Banks could read an 'end of discussion' signal as well as the next man, and he turned to Sophia, asking her if she was going to have a dessert. Then Helena joined in, and the conversation moved on to her and Victor's travel plans for the winter, which included a three-month visit to Australia. Soon it was well into the afternoon and the lunchtime crowd was thinning out. Time to go. Sophia had to drive back to London that evening.

Victor said he would drop them off at their car in Reeth village green. As they picked up their bags, Banks couldn't get Victor's story out of his mind. It was a bygone age, or so it seemed to him, the world he knew about only from reading Le Carré and Deighton. But Laurence Silbert had lived it. He wished Victor had known more details. Could Silbert's, and by extension Mark Hardcastle's, death be in any way connected with that clandestine world? And if so, how on earth could Banks find out about it?

Before they left, Banks glanced at the man at the bar, who was reading a *Mail on Sunday* and sipping a half-pint of ale. The man looked up as they passed and gave them a vague smile. Something about him seemed out of place. He wasn't dressed for walking, and he wasn't one of the locals. Banks put it out of his mind as Victor drove them the half-mile or so to Reeth, back to the car, and he and Sophia said goodbye to her parents.

'Well,' said Sophia, as she settled into the Porsche, 'even a simple family lunch becomes quite an adventure with you.'

Banks shrugged. 'Anything to stop him getting on to my job prospects.'

ANNIE CABBOT wondered what Banks wanted with her as she slipped out of the squad room at four o'clock on Monday afternoon and headed for the Horse and Hounds, which had become the secret getaway for anyone who wanted to enjoy a contemplative pint during the day.

Most of her working time had been taken up with the East Side Estate stabbing. She had spoken briefly with Donny Moore at the hospital on

Friday. His injuries weren't life-threatening, but he claimed to remember nothing of what happened the night he was stabbed, except that he was just innocently walking along the street when a big bloke in a hoodie came at him. Winsome and Doug Wilson had tracked down most of the gang members they suspected had been present and, as expected, discovered nothing. None of them was particularly large, being just kids, but Winsome had nonetheless noted that one or two of them merited a follow-up visit, and Annie intended to be in on that over the week.

Annie had also gone for a radical haircut on Saturday, swapping her tumbling mass of auburn waves for a short, layered style. She wasn't sure whether she liked it yet, worried that it perhaps made her appear older, but she also thought it made her seem more professional, which couldn't be a bad thing for a detective inspector.

Banks was waiting for her, a copy of *The Independent* spread on the table in front of him and a pint of Black Sheep bitter in his hand.

He folded up the newspaper when he saw her. 'Are you alone?' he asked, glancing towards the doorway behind her.

'Of course I am,' she said. 'Why? Who else are you expecting?'

'You weren't followed?'

'Don't be silly.'

'Drink?' Banks asked.

Annie sat down. 'Britvic orange, please.'

Banks went to the bar. She got the feeling that he was checking out who was in there. He came back with her drink and settled down opposite her.

'So why all the cloak-and-dagger stuff?' Annie asked.

'Well, Laurence Silbert worked for MI6, so it makes sense, doesn't it?'

'Alan, I hate to tell you this, but it's over. Superintendent Gervaise said so the other day. You're on leave, remember? Whatever Silbert did for a living, it had nothing to do with his death. Mark Hardcastle killed him and then hanged himself. End of story.'

'I don't think it's as simple as that.'

Annie could hear the drone of voices from the bar. The barmaid laughed at one of her customer's jokes. 'All right,' she said. 'What *do* you think?'

Banks sat back in his chair. 'Have you ever read *Othello*?'

'Years ago. At school. Why?'

'Well, Sophia and I went to see it at the Eastvale Theatre on Saturday night. The one Derek Wyman directed and Mark Hardcastle did the sets for.'

'How was it?'

'The German Expressionist sets were a real distraction, but the acting was pretty decent. But that's not the point. The thing is, Sophia and I were talking later and she pointed out that the play was more about the power of words and images than about jealousy and ambition, and I think she's right.'

'That's what an English lit. degree will do for you. I can't say we ever got much further than ambition and jealousy at my school.'

'If you think about it . . . well, it really makes sense.'

'How? What?'

Briefly, Banks tried to explain what Sophia had said about the use of language to create unbearable images in the mind.

'Alan, this is all very stimulating and everything, but I've got ironing to do at home and I still don't see what this has to do with us.'

'It got me to thinking about the case,' Banks went on. 'About Hardcastle and Silbert. Everyone's pretty much decided how it happened, even though you pointed out that the absence of anyone's blood other than Silbert's didn't really prove anything.'

'Right,' Annie agreed.

Banks leaned back. 'In actual fact, I think it happened exactly as Superintendent Gervaise and Stefan say it did. Mark Hardcastle beat Silbert to death with a cricket bat, then went out and hanged himself out of grief.'

'So you agree with the official version?'

'Yes. But I also don't think that's the point.'

'What is, then?'

'Listen.' Banks leaned forward, and Annie saw that gleam in his blue eyes that she always associated with his fanciful theories, though she had to admit that sometimes they were right. 'Hardcastle and Silbert hadn't been together all that long. Six months. By all accounts, they were very much an item, practically living together, but the relationship was probably still a little fragile, vulnerable. We know Hardcastle was a bit insecure, and he may have had a short fuse. What if someone worked on him?'

'Worked on him? On Hardcastle?'

'Yes,' said Banks. 'The way Iago worked on Othello. Plagued him with unbearable images of Silbert's infidelity.'

'So you're saying that someone goaded him into this?'

'I'm saying it's a possibility. But it would be bloody difficult to prove. It's a hands-off murder. Murder from a distance, murder by proxy.'

'I very much doubt that you could call it murder, even if it did happen that way,' said Annie. 'But why do it?'

'To get rid of Silbert.'

'Any idea who would want to do that?'

Banks sipped his beer. 'Well,' he said, 'I suppose anyone who was close to one or both of them could have done it, really. Vernon Ross or Derek Wyman, for example. Or Carol, Wyman's wife. There's no shortage of possibilities.' Banks paused. 'On the other hand, it could have been someone acting for one of the secret intelligence services. It's just the sort of labyrinthine plot they would come up with.'

'Oh, come off it, Alan! That's a bit far-fetched, even for you.'

'Not necessarily.'

'But hold on a minute,' Annie argued. 'Who could have known that Silbert was seeing someone else, if he was?'

'It doesn't matter. If information like that hadn't somehow fallen into the killer's lap, he could have made it up. After all, that's what Iago did.'

'OK, but how could the killer be certain of the result?'

Banks scratched his temple. 'You have a point there,' he said. 'I've been grappling with that one. But I'll bet you MI6 knew about Hardcastle's previous form for violence against a partner. Push someone far enough and their reactions can be pretty predictable. People resort to patterns they've followed in the past.'

'I know,' said Annie, 'but as a method of murder, it sucks. It's not reliable.'

'I can see it's a flawed hypothesis. But I still think it has possibilities.'

'OK, then,' said Annie. 'Let's assume for a moment that you're right. Then we come to the matter of motive. Why?'

Banks sat back on the bench and sipped some beer before he spoke. 'Well, that one's easy enough,' he said. 'It goes right along with who.'

'I know what you're going to say, but they just don't—'

'Hear me out, Annie. This Mr Browne with an "e" comes to see me and basically tells me to lay off, that any publicity around the Silbert murder would be courting disaster. What sort of disaster? I ask myself. Now, we know Silbert was an MI6 agent, and Lord knows what sort of things he got up to in his heyday. What if the government wanted rid of him for some reason? Say he knew too much? Something embarrassing? Maybe he was involved in something that shows MI6 and the government, or a friendly foreign government, in a bad light, and with an election coming up . . .'

'They'd stop at nothing?'

'Something like that. If they felt threatened.'

'I still don't swallow it, Alan. OK, so the victim was a spook. When these people want rid of one another, don't they just stab them with poisoned umbrellas or slip them a dose of radioactive isotopes or something? They'd hardly be likely to go for such an unreliable method as trying to make Silbert's partner jealous and just hope he does their job for them when they could just . . . well, push him under a bus. No, I'm sorry, but it won't wash.'

Banks seemed deflated. 'Has someone got to you?' he asked.

Annie's jaw dropped. 'I resent that. Don't we play devil's advocate as a matter of course? How could you even *think* something like that?'

'I'm sorry,' said Banks. 'Maybe I am getting paranoid. But look what happened. The day after Mr Browne's visit, Madame Gervaise says the case is closed, keeps me back after school and tells me to take some leave. Are you saying she hasn't been got at? And I thought someone was watching me in the pub yesterday. Things are just . . . confusing.'

'Well, *I* haven't been got at. I'm just trying to take a rational perspective on some of the half-baked ideas you're coming up with.'

'Can't you accept that it *might* have happened the way I just outlined?'

'I don't know that I can, Alan.' She said nothing for a moment. 'So what are you going to do?' she asked eventually.

'I still need a couple more pieces of information,' he said. 'Then I think I'll head down to London, check out the pied-à-terre for myself, dig around, see what I can find. I've still got a few days' holiday left.'

'I don't know,' said Annie. 'It could be dangerous. I mean, if you're right and they *are* capable of knocking off one of their own, they'd hardly think twice about killing a troublesome copper, would they?'

'Thank you,' said Banks. 'I was trying not to think of that. Anyway, what else can I do? Madame Gervaise has closed the case.'

'I think you should be very careful.'

'I will be.'

'I suppose you'll be staying with Sophia?'

'I suppose so. Why?'

'It's just that . . . Well, should you be involving her in all this?'

'I'm not involving her. Besides, they already know about her. Browne mentioned something about my lovely young girlfriend in Chelsea. But don't worry, I'll be careful. For me and for Sophia.'

'So what is it you want from me?'

'I'd like you to be my eyes and ears up here while I'm away. Keep a lookout for anything out of the ordinary. And if I need any information, some record tracked down, another chat with Wyman and the theatre people, I'd like to think you might help.'

'Might as well be hanged for a sheep as a lamb,' said Annie.

'I'll be buying a new mobile as soon as I get down there. Pay-as-you-go, throwaway. I don't want my calls traced, or any troublesome records kept. I'll ring you and let you know the number.'

Annie frowned at him. 'Just like a criminal. You're serious about all this cloak-and-dagger stuff, aren't you?'

'You didn't meet Mr Browne. And there is one more thing before we go.'

'What's that?'

'What did you do with your hair? It looks great.'

THOUGH BANKS didn't expect any further visits from the likes of Mr Browne, he nonetheless kept his alarm system on and his ears open at home that evening. After a Marks and Spencer's beef Wellington washed down with a 1998 Shiraz, he settled down to an evening's reading in the entertainment room. Banks spent most of his time in this room these days. It had been added to the cottage, along with an extra bedroom and a conservatory, as part of the rebuilding work carried out after the fire, over three years ago.

The phone rang shortly after half past nine. It was Sophia.

'Have a good journey home?' Banks asked.

'Fine. Just boring, that's all. I think I'll take the train next time. At least then I can get some work done, read a book.'

He thought he could hear her stifle a yawn. 'Tired?'

'Long day.'

'How's your week shaping up?'

'Lots of interviews. A fifteen-minute special on that new James Bond book by Sebastian Faulks, including a few comments from Daniel Craig.'

'Don't tell me he's coming to the studio.'

'Don't be an idiot. But a girl can always dream.'

'Hmph. Right. Well, I hope to be down your way in a day or so. Could you maybe give Daniel Craig a rain check and find a bit of room in your busy schedule to fit me in? I can easily get a hotel, if . . .'

'Of course I can, you idiot. You've got a key. Just come over. Is it business or pure holiday?'

'A bit of both, really.'

'That case you were quizzing Dad about, with all the spooks?'

'One of the victims was an MI6 agent, that's all.'

'How exciting. With you around, who needs Daniel Craig? Bye.'

Always, at the end of their telephone conversations, Banks was tempted to say, 'I love you,' but he never did. The 'L' word hadn't been mentioned yet, and Banks got the feeling that it would only cause complications at this point. Best go on as they were and see where it led.

After he'd hung up, Banks had a sudden urge to go outside to sit on the wall beside Gratly Beck. This was one of his favourite spots, especially when the weather was warm. Before he could open the door, though, the phone rang again. Thinking it might be Sophia phoning back, Banks hurried to pick it up.

'DCI Banks?'

'Yes?'

'It's Ravi here. Ravi Kapesh. Technical support.'

'Oh, Ravi. It's a bit late for you to be working, isn't it?'

'Par for the course these days if you want to get ahead,' said Ravi, resignedly. 'Anyway, I think I might have something for you.'

Banks felt a tremor of excitement. 'You do? Great. Look, I know this might sound a bit weird, but can you call me back on my mobile?'

'Sure. When?'

'Right now. I'm hanging up.' Banks didn't know if his mobile was any more likely to be secure than his land line, but he thought it might be.

'OK, let's have it,' he said, when the mobile rang.

'I managed to enhance the street sign on the photo enough to get a name,' said Ravi. 'It's a little street called Charles Lane, off the High Street in St John's Wood. Ring any bells?'

'None,' said Banks, 'but I can't say I expected it to. Thanks a lot, Ravi. What about the phone number? Fenner.'

'Drew a blank. According to all my efforts, it's a number that has never actually been assigned in the UK. Maybe it's for somewhere overseas?'

'Maybe,' said Banks, 'but I doubt it. Just one more favour.'

'Yes?'

'Keep it under your hat, OK?'

'OK,' said Ravi. 'My lips are sealed.'

'Bye.' Banks hung up.

St John's Wood. Well, that was a posh enough area, he thought. What was it all about? A fancy man? Sharing government secrets with the other side? Whatever it was, Banks felt sure it had contributed to Silbert's death.

Perhaps Annie was right in that the Iago method couldn't absolutely guarantee results, but if it did work, it would be the perfect murder. A murder that wasn't even murder.

Banks picked up his wine and stepped outside. It was after sunset, but there was still a glow deep in the cloudless western sky, dark orange and indigo. The stone he sat on was still warm. The smell of grass and manure mingled with something sweet, perhaps a flower that opened only at night.

Banks thought he heard a sound from the woods, and he had the odd sensation that he was being watched. It was probably some nocturnal animal, he told himself. After all, he heard them often enough. He mustn't allow his nerves to get the better of him. He sipped some more wine, and listened to the beck flowing down the terraced falls, the wind in the trees, a sheep baaing on a distant daleside. Like the streets, the woods were full of shadows and whispers. After a while, even those sounds ended and he was left in a silence so profound that all he could hear was his own heart beating.

Chapter Seven

The fine weather had brought out the crowds by Wednesday lunch time, and as Banks walked along Tottenham Court Road, he realised there was no way he would spot someone following him. He put his hand in his pocket and touched the spare key to Laurence Silbert's Bloomsbury flat. He knew it was the right one because it had been marked with a neat label when he found it in Silbert's study drawer that morning. The rules called for Banks to get in touch with the local police, ask permission to visit the house, but he hadn't done so. No sense inviting trouble, he thought.

He turned up at Montague Place between the British Museum and the university and found the street he wanted off Marchmont Street. Banks had driven down that morning by an indirect route and had parked the Porsche, legally, outside Sophia's house. He had left his grip in the house, then took the tube to Tottenham Court Road, where he had bought a cheap pay-as-you-go mobile in one of the electronics shops.

The house he wanted was divided into flats, and the names under the brass number plates still listed an L. Silbert in flat 3A. It was a well-appointed building, with dark, thick-pile carpets, flocked wallpaper and a hovering scent of lavender air-freshener.

The door opened into a tiny vestibule, hardly bigger than a hall cupboard. There were three doors leading off, and a quick check told him that the one on the left led to a small bedroom, just big enough for a double bed, wardrobe and chest of drawers, the one on the right to a shower room, and the door straight ahead to the living room with a tiny kitchenette.

Banks started in the bedroom. The blue and white duvet was ruffled and the pillows creased. On impulse, Banks pulled the duvet back. The linen sheets were clean but wrinkled, as if someone had slept on them. More than likely, Mark Hardcastle *had* spent his night in London here.

There were a few clothes in the wardrobe and the chest of drawers, but Banks found nothing hidden on the top or at the back of the wardrobe, or among the socks and underwear. The middle drawer of the chest held an assortment of old theatre-ticket stubs and programmes, restaurant and taxi receipts, a few cheap ball-point pens. The room had a Spartan feel about it, as if it were somewhere merely functional, a place to sleep.

The shower room held no surprises, and the living room was every bit as neat and clean as the bedroom. In the kitchenette Banks found an empty Bell's whisky bottle and an unwashed glass.

There was nothing here for him, he decided. Either Silbert had been very careful or someone had already removed anything of interest.

Just before Banks left, he picked up the phone and pressed redial. Nothing happened. Either it wasn't working properly or it had been erased—most likely, he thought, the latter.

ANNIE TOOK WINSOME with her when she went to talk to a fifteen-year-old boy called Nicky Haskell after school. She felt more than one pair of eyes following them as she drove along the winding main street of East Side Estate. The Haskells lived in Metcalfe House, which had one of the worst reputations of any area on the estate.

It was soon clear that they needn't have waited for the end of the school day to make their visit.

'Got a cold, haven't I?' Nicky said, turning his back after letting them in.

'I don't know,' said Annie, walking into the living room behind him. 'Do you? You sound fine to me.'

Nicky sank back onto the battered sofa he had probably been lying on all day, if the empty crisp packets, overflowing ashtray and can of lager were any indication. He drank from the can, then reached for his cigarettes.

'I'd prefer it if you didn't drink or smoke in our presence,' Annie said. 'You're underage.'

Haskell smirked and put the cigarettes down next to the lager. 'I can wait till you're gone,' he said.

Annie sat on a wooden chair because she didn't like the look of the stains on the armchairs, and Winsome did the same.

'Where are your parents?' Annie asked.

'Mum's at work; Dad's at the pub.'

Technically, as he was only fifteen, they weren't supposed to talk to him unless his parents were present. But as he wasn't a suspect—Donny was one of his crew, after all—and most likely he wasn't going to say anything useful, Annie wasn't inclined to worry much about that.

'We've been over all this before,' said Haskell before she even started. 'It's time to move on.'

'Someone stabbed Donny,' Annie reminded him, 'and we're not moving on until we find out who it was.'

'Well, it wasn't me. Donny's me mate. He's all right, isn't he?'

'He'll be fine. And we know he's your mate. That's why we thought you might be able to help us. You were there.'

'Says who?'

'Nicky, we know there was a scuffle down by glue-sniffers' ginnel. We know you and your mates hang out there every night, and we know you wouldn't take kindly to Jackie Binns's crew muscling in, but we know they did. So why don't you make it easy for us and just tell us what happened?'

Haskell said nothing. He may have thought he was looking tough and defiant, Annie thought, but she could see a slight trembling in his lower lip.

'What are you scared of, Nicky?' she said.

'Nothing. I ain't scared of nothing. I don't know why you bother coming here, anyway,' Haskell went on, a sneer on his face. 'Didn't you ought to be spending your time taking care of those rich folk up on Castleview Heights? They're the ones doing all the murder and shit these days.'

'What do you know about Castleview Heights?' Annie asked.

'You'd be surprised,' Haskell said, tapping his nose and grinning.

'If you know something, you should tell me.'

'You were asking me about Donny Moore and that ratshit Jackie Binns. Not about them two shirt-lifters on the Heights. What you got for me?'

'What if I were to ask you about Laurence Silbert and Mark Hardcastle?' Annie went on. 'What would you be able to tell me about them?'

'That Mark Hardcastle, he the one from the theatre?'

'That's right,' Annie said.

'I been there. School trip, few months ago.' Nicky eyed them defiantly, as if to say that he *did* go to school sometimes. 'Some Shakespeare shit, man. *Macbeth*. Dudes offing each other all over the stage. That man, that Hardcastle, he answered some questions after the play, him and Mr Wyman. That's why I knew him when I saw him the next time.'

'Where did you see him the next time?' Annie asked.

'Like I say, what you got for me?'

Annie felt like saying that she had a clip round the ear for him, but instead, she reached for her purse and pulled out a five-pound note.

Nicky laughed. 'You must be joking. That don't buy shit these days.'

Annie put the five back and pulled out a ten.

'Now we talking the same language,' said Nicky, and reached for it.

Annie held it away from him, so that he would have to get up from the sofa to grab it. As she expected, he didn't. 'Before I give you this, you're going to tell me where you saw Mark Hardcastle the second time.'

Haskell nodded, and grinned. 'Was in a pub, wasn't it? The Red Rooster.'

'The Red Rooster? Down in Medburn? When was this?' Annie asked.

'Dunno. Two or three weeks before he offed himself.'

'What was he doing when you saw him?'

'That's why I noticed him, man. I was just there having a quiet drink, you know, chillin' with my friends, and then I see my teacher and I have to get out real fast, or he'll bring all kinda shit down on me.'

Annie frowned. 'Your teacher?'

'Yeah. Mr Wyman.'

'Let me get this straight,' Annie said. 'You saw Derek Wyman in the Red Rooster with Mark Hardcastle a short time before Hardcastle died?'

'You got it.' He glanced at Winsome. 'Hey, give the lady a prize.'

'What were they doing there?' Annie went on. 'Were they looking at anything? Photographs or anything?'

'You mean, like *porn*? Pictures of men—'

'Nicky!'

'No, they didn't look at nothing.'

'Was anyone else with them? Or did anyone join them?'

'Nope. Can I have my money?'

Annie gave him the ten-pound note. She wanted to ask if there was anything intimate about the meeting, any closeness, but somehow she didn't think Nicky would be attuned to such subtleties. She asked anyway.

'Don't know nothing about all that stuff, man,' Nicky said, 'but that Hardcastle, he sure seemed angry. Mr Wyman had to cool him down.'

'Did they appear to be arguing?'

'Arguing? No. Like they were friends.'

'What happened next?'

'I got out of there, man. Before he saw me.'

'Is there anything else you can tell me?'

'No. Like I told you, Mr Wyman say something and got Hardcastle all upset, then he chill him right down again.'

'Mr Wyman upset Hardcastle in the first place?'

'The way it look. They was in the other bar, so I figure they couldn't see me, but I wasn't taking no chances. Why'd I want to hang around a pub where my teacher's drinking, man?'

'Nicky, the amount of time you spend in school, he probably wouldn't even recognise you,' Annie said.

'Ain't no need to be sarcastic. I do OK.'

Annie couldn't help but laugh, and Winsome laughed with her. They got up to leave.

'Back to Jackie Binns and Donny Moore for a minute,' Annie said at the door. 'Are you certain you can't tell us anything more about what happened? Did you see Jackie Binns with a knife?'

'Jackie didn't have no knife, man. You got that all wrong. Jackie didn't do nothing. I didn't see nothing.' He turned away, picked up the remote control and turned up the volume on the television set.

When they got to the car, Annie said, 'How about a drink?'

'Anything to get the taste of this place out of my mouth.'

'How about the Red Rooster?' Annie suggested.

AS IT WAS SUCH a beautiful evening, Banks decided to follow Silbert's route and walk through Regent's Park to St John's Wood. He found Charles Lane easily enough. It was a secluded mews, and from the High Street it looked as if it ended at a brick house with a narrow white façade, but that was just a little dogleg, and beyond it he came to the garages in the photograph. He realised this must have been the corner where the photograph was taken from. The door he wanted was between the sixth and seventh garages along.

Before anyone could find his loitering suspicious, he strolled down the street, crossed to the house in question and rang the bell.

After about thirty seconds, a woman opened the door on its chain and peered at him. He reached for his warrant card. She made him hold it close to the narrow strip that was all the chain allowed and spent so long studying it that he thought she wasn't going to let him in. Eventually the door closed, and when it opened again, it opened all the way, revealing a neatly dressed, grey-haired woman in her sixties.

'You're a long way from home, young man,' she said to Banks. 'You'd better come in and explain yourself over a cup of tea.'

She led him upstairs into a small, cluttered living room above the garage, where a man of about her age sat in an armchair reading the newspaper. He was wearing a suit, complete with white shirt and tie.

'It's a policeman,' the woman said to him. 'A detective.'

'I'm sorry to intrude like this,' Banks said, feeling awkward.

'No matter,' said the woman. 'I'm Mrs Townsend, by the way. You can call me Edith. And this is my husband, Lester.'

Lester Townsend looked over his newspaper and grunted a quick hello.

'Pleased to meet you,' said Banks.

'Sit yourself down,' Edith said. 'I'll just go and put the kettle on. Lester, put your newspaper away. It's rude to sit and read when we have guests.'

Edith left the room and Townsend put his newspaper down, staring suspiciously at Banks before reaching for a pipe on the table beside him, stuffing it with shag and lighting it. 'What is it we can do for you?' he asked.

Banks sat down. 'Can we wait until your wife comes back with the tea?' he said. 'I'd like to talk to both of you.'

Townsend grunted round his pipe. Smoking contemplatively, he stared at a spot high on the wall until his wife returned with the tea tray.

'It's not often we get visitors,' she said. 'Is it, darling?'

'Hardly ever,' her husband said, glaring at Banks.

'I really am sorry for interrupting your evening,' Banks said, balancing the teacup and saucer on his lap, 'but this address has come up in connection with a case I'm working on back up in North Yorkshire.' It wasn't entirely true, but they weren't to know that the investigation had been closed.

'How exciting,' said Edith. 'In what way?'

'How long have you lived here?' Banks asked.

'Ever since we were married,' her husband answered. 'Since 1963.'

'Do you ever rent out the house, or any part of it?'

'What a strange question,' Edith said. 'No, we don't. This is our home.'

'Have you been on holiday recently?'

'We took a Caribbean cruise last winter.'

'Have you been away even for a few days over the past month or so?'

'No,' Edith said. 'Lester still works in the City. He should have retired by now, but they say they still need him.'

'What do you do, Mr Townsend?' Banks asked.

'Insurance.'

Banks put his cup and saucer down and took out the photographs. He passed them first to Edith. 'Do you recognise either of these men?' he asked.

Edith examined the photo closely, then passed it to her husband. 'No,' she said. 'Should I?'

'You, sir?' Banks asked Townsend.

'Never seen either of them in my life,' he answered.

'You do agree it's this house, don't you?' Banks asked.

Edith took the photograph again. 'Well, it certainly *looks* like it,' she said, passing it back to her husband. 'But it can't be, can it?'

'What on earth is all this about?' asked Townsend. 'What's going on? You come barging in here upsetting my wife and showing pictures of . . . of I don't know what, asking damn fool questions.'

'I'm sorry, sir,' Banks said. 'I didn't mean to upset anyone. One of our technical-support officers was able to enhance the photograph I just showed you and read the street name. This street name.'

'Couldn't he have made a mistake?' Townsend said, handing the photo back. 'After all, it's a bit blurred.'

'Mistakes *are* made,' said Banks. 'But not this time. I don't think so.'

Townsend stuck out his chin. 'Then what's your explanation? Eh?'

Banks pocketed the photograph and stood up to leave. 'I don't know, sir,' he said. 'But one way or another I'll get to the bottom of it.'

'I'm sorry we couldn't help,' said Edith as she led him to the door.

'Have you ever heard of a man called Julian Fenner?' Banks asked.

'No.'

'Laurence Silbert? Mark Hardcastle?'

'No, neither of those names is familiar to me. Now, I'm afraid you'll have to leave. We can't tell you anything more.'

And Banks found himself standing on the doorstep scratching his head.

MEDBURN WASN'T much more than a postwar council estate with a pub, a post office and a garage clustered round the green, where bored kids lounged on the benches and scared off old folks. The Red Rooster wasn't too busy around five thirty on a Wednesday afternoon, and Annie and Winsome had no trouble getting a couple of drinks and putting in an order for food.

'What's all this about, then?' Winsome asked when they sat down. 'I thought the Hardcastle business was over and done with.'

'It is. At least officially.' Deciding that she could trust Winsome not to tell anyone, Annie put her in the picture.

'So DCI Banks is in London following this up instead of on leave?' Winsome said, when Annie had finished.

'Yes. Well, he's officially on leave, but . . . he's not convinced.'

'And he wants you to help at this end?'

'Yes.'

'And that's why we're sitting in this lame pub, waiting for some naff food.' Annie smiled. 'That's just about it, Winsome. Want in?'

Winsome muttered something under her breath, then said, 'It looks like I'm stuck here, doesn't it? You've got the car keys.'

'There's always the bus.'

Winsome held her palm up. 'OK, all right, I'm in. Unless you start crossing any serious boundaries.'

'What's a serious boundary?'

'One you know when you're crossing it.'

Annie paused for a moment as their food arrived, a beefburger and chips for Winsome and a mini pizza margherita for her.

'What did you think of Nicky Haskell this time?' Annie asked as she picked up a slice of pizza. 'It's the third time we've talked to him and his story hasn't changed. The mention of Hardcastle was the only thing that was new, and he'd obviously seen something about that on TV.'

'Dunno,' said Winsome around a mouthful of burger. 'It was on the news the night before last. Silbert and Hardcastle.' She dabbed her lips with the serviette. 'Did he seem more scared this time to you?'

'He did,' Annie said. 'And he's a tough enough nut himself that I really don't think he'd be scared of Jackie Binns or his mates.'

'So what is it?' Winsome asked.

'Could be there's someone else involved he really is scared of.'

'Now *that* would be an interesting development.'

They ate their meals in silence for a while. Then Winsome asked, 'Does DCI Banks really think the Secret Intelligence Service goaded Hardcastle into bumping off Silbert for some sort of twisted government reason?'

Annie nodded. 'Thing is, what Nicky Haskell just told us changes things.'

'It does? Derek Wyman?'

'Well, yes. If it was Wyman did the Iago bit, it might have had nothing to do with Silbert's MI6 career. Wyman probably didn't even know about that. But he did stand to lose his position at the theatre if Hardcastle got his new group of players going, and Hardcastle needed Silbert's backing for that.'

'So why did this Browne bloke pay DCI Banks a visit, then?'

'A fishing expedition? To see which way the wind was blowing? They're bound to be interested if it was one of their blokes who copped it, aren't they? Silbert probably knew all kinds of secrets, did all sorts of nefarious deeds that could bring down the government, or at least bring about a clean sweep of the intelligence services, if they became public.'

'But you're saying that may not be the case?'

'I don't know,' Annie said, pushing her plate aside. 'But if Wyman was the one who stirred up the hornet's nest, the motivation might be a whole other thing, mightn't it? Professional jealousy. Revenge.'

'Maybe Wyman and Hardcastle were having an affair. They were in London together, and Nicky Haskell said he saw them having a tête-à-tête.'

'He said he thought he saw Wyman say something to upset Hardcastle, then calm him down. It certainly fits,' Annie said.

'They could have met on some other occasion, later, and Wyman could have given him the memory stick.'

'But when and how did Wyman get the photos?'

'I don't know,' said Winsome. 'Maybe he followed Silbert to London on one of his trips and got lucky. Maybe he just wanted to turn Hardcastle against Silbert so he could have him for himself.'

'And it backfired,' Annie said. 'Hardcastle overreacted. Finished?'

Winsome drained her glass. 'Uh-huh.'

'Let's have a word with the barman on the way out. He's not too busy.'

The barman's name tag identified him as Liam, and he immediately assumed a serious air when Annie showed him her warrant card. At the same time, he could hardly stop looking at Winsome. He was a gawky lad with slightly bulging eyes, rubbery lips and a gentle face, so easily flustered and so easy to read he wouldn't have made a good poker player.

'How long have you been working here?' Annie asked.

'Six months. Give or take.'

Annie fanned out photographs of Hardcastle and Silbert on the bar. 'Recognise either of these men?'

Liam pointed to the photograph of Mark Hardcastle. 'He's the bloke who hanged himself in Hindswell Woods. Nasty business.'

'Have you ever seen him in here?' Annie asked.

'He's been here once or twice, yes.'

'Recently?'

'Past month or so.'

'Alone or with someone else?'

'With another bloke.' Liam gave a quick description that resembled Derek Wyman. 'They had a drink or two, and mostly they just talked.'

'Ever see them arguing?'

'No. But the bloke that hanged himself, Hardcastle, got a bit agitated once or twice and the other bloke had to calm him down.'

It was exactly as Nicky Haskell had described. 'Did they ever come with anyone else, or did anyone else join them?' Annie asked.

'Not when I was on duty.'

'Did you ever see anything change hands?'

Liam drew himself up to his full height behind the bar, which was still a few inches less than Winsome's. 'Never. That's something we don't countenance in this establishment. Drugs.' He spat out the word.

'I'm impressed,' said Winsome, and Liam blushed.

'Ever see them looking at photos?' Annie asked.

'No,' Liam said. 'But they were usually here when we were pretty busy. I mean, it's not as if I was keeping an eye on them or anything.' He looked at Winsome again. 'But if you want me to, I can keep my eyes and ears open. You know, if they come in again. I mean, I know Hardcastle can't, like, he's dead, right, but the other one, whoever he is, and I'll certainly—'

'It's all right, Liam,' Annie said, though he seemed to have forgotten her presence. 'We doubt very much he'll be back. Thanks a lot for your help.'

They were laughing as they went outside. '"Countenance in this establishment," for crying out loud,' said Winsome. 'Where'd he get that from?'

'You got him all flustered, Winsome,' Annie said. 'You know, I think he fancies you. You might be in with a chance there.'

Winsome nudged her in the ribs. 'Get away with you.'

BANKS MET SOPHIA in their local wine bar on the King's Road just after eight o'clock that evening. It was always crowded by then, but they managed to get a couple of stools at the bar.

'He was *terrible*,' Sophia was saying, finishing a story about a radio interview she had produced that afternoon. 'I mean, most crime writers are nice enough, but this bloke came on like he was Tolstoy, and complained about not being nominated for the Man Booker. If you even hinted that he wrote crime novels, he'd practically go apoplectic. And he swore all the bloody time!' She knocked back a healthy draught of Rioja and patted her chest. Her face was a little flushed. 'So tell me about your day, Mr Superspy.'

Banks put his finger to his lips. 'Ssshhh,' he said, glancing towards the bartender. ' "Keep mum, she's not so dumb." '

'You think the Rioja's bugged?' Sophia whispered.

'Could be. After today, I wouldn't be surprised.'

'What happened today?'

'Nothing really. I went to this house in St John's Wood. We had evidence that Laurence Silbert and an unknown man entered it together about a week before Silbert died . . .' And Banks told her about Edith and Lester Townsend.

'How very *North by Northwest*,' said Sophia when he had finished. 'Are you sure your technical-support people didn't make a mistake?'

'I'm sure. You can see it's the same place as soon as you stand outside.'

'They must be lying, then,' said Sophia. 'Perhaps they run a gay brothel?'

'Or maybe they're simply a part of it all,' Banks said.

'A part of what?'

'The plot. The conspiracy. Whatever's going on.' He tossed back the rest of his drink. 'Come on, let's go for that meal and talk about something else. I'm sick of bloody spooks already. It's doing my head in. And I'm starving.'

Sophia laughed and reached down for her handbag. 'Talking about doing your head in,' she said, 'if we hurry, Wilco are playing at the Brixton Academy tonight, and I can get us in.'

'Well, then,' said Banks, standing and holding out his hand for her. 'What are we waiting for? Have we got time for a burger on the way?'

Chapter Eight

Sophia left for work early on Thursday morning while Banks was still in the shower. The Wilco concert had been great, and they'd had a drink afterwards with some of Sophia's friends, which had made for a late night. At least Banks had remembered to charge his new mobile, and he planned on phoning Annie later to let her know his number.

Banks dried himself, got dressed and went down to the kitchen, blessing Sophia for leaving some coffee in the pot. He poured himself a cup, toasted a slice of wholemeal bread, then spread it with butter and grapefruit marmalade and sat on a stool at the island.

He had to work out his day. What he needed was information about

Laurence Silbert, and it wasn't going to be easy to get. There was, however, one place he could start.

He washed his breakfast dishes and made sure he had everything he needed in his briefcase. At the front door, he paused and set the alarm system. Then he headed up to the King's Road towards Sloane Square tube station. It wouldn't take long to get to Swiss Cottage. His first task would be to find out if Laurence Silbert's old lover Leo Westwood still lived there.

BANKS FOUND a Starbucks on Finchley Road and phoned Annie. She was on her way to meet Winsome at Wyman's comprehensive.

'Storm clouds gathering,' said Annie. 'You're definitely persona non grata around these parts.' She sounded a bit breathless, as if she'd had a shock.

'What's wrong?' Banks asked.

'It's Gervaise. She knows where you were yesterday, who you talked to.'

'The Townsends?'

'Yes.'

That surprised Banks. He hadn't expected them to call the police. When he thought about it, though, it made sense. Another way of getting him put back in his cage before he did any damage. 'What's the bottom line?' he asked.

'What do you think? She called me in and told me in no uncertain terms that, if I value my career, I'll stay out of it and let her know if you get in touch. Then I'm supposed to let you hang out to dry. Why don't you just take Sophia to Devon or Cornwall for a few days, Alan, make everyone's life a bit easier, including your own?'

'*Et tu*, Annie?'

'Oh, sod off, you idiot. I didn't say I was going to do what she asked, did I? Look, I'm almost at the school and I've got something to tell you before I have second thoughts. It might change things.'

Banks's ears pricked up. 'What?'

'Nicky Haskell mentioned seeing Mark Hardcastle drinking with Derek Wyman in the Red Rooster a couple of weeks ago.'

'The Red Rooster? That's a kids' pub, isn't it? Why would they go there?'

'I have no idea. But there's more.' Banks listened as Annie went on to tell him about Wyman calming Hardcastle down.

'But nothing changed hands?' Banks said. 'No pictures, no memory stick or anything?'

'Not that Nicky Haskell saw. Or Liam, the bartender.'

'Maybe you could find someone else who was there. If Gervaise is watching, you'll just appear to be following up on the East Side Estate stabbing.'

'I *am* following up on the stabbing. Look, I'm at the school driveway now. I have to go.'

'You'll ask around?'

'I'll ask around.'

THE ADDRESS on the letter they'd found in Laurence Silbert's house from Leo Westwood was for a flat in Adamson Road, near Swiss Cottage tube station. The building was one of a row of imposing three-storey houses with white stucco façades, complete with porticos and columns. The list of tenants showed that Leo Westwood still lived there, on the third floor. Banks pressed the bell beside the name and waited. After a few seconds, a voice crackled over the intercom. Banks identified himself and the reason for his visit and found himself buzzed up.

Leo Westwood stood at the door of his flat. He was a short, pudgy man with silky grey hair and a smooth, ruddy complexion, somewhere in his early sixties, wearing a black polo-neck jumper and jeans. Banks had expected an antique-laden apartment, but the living area was ultra-modern, all polished hardwood floors, chrome and glass.

Westwood bade Banks sit on a comfortable black leather armchair and offered coffee. Banks accepted. When Westwood went into the kitchen, Banks looked around. There was only one painting on the wall, an abstract of geometric shapes. On a small case beside the sound system was a mixture of books, mostly architecture and interior design, some DVDs of classics by Truffaut, Antonioni and Bergman, and numerous opera boxed sets.

'I like to keep the space relatively uncluttered,' Westwood said from behind him, putting a silver tray bearing a caffetière and two white cups down on the glass coffee table before them. He then sat at a right angle to Banks. 'I was sorry to hear about Laurence,' he said, with a slight lisp, 'but you must realise it was a long time ago. Ten years.'

'You were close then, though?'

'Oh, yes. Very. Three years. It might not sound like long, but . . .'

'If you don't mind my asking, why did you part?'

Westwood passed him a cup of coffee. 'I suppose it was his work, really.

I mean, he was always heading off somewhere and he couldn't tell me where. Even when he got back I'd no idea where he'd been. I knew that sometimes his missions involved danger, so I would lie awake and worry, but I rarely got a phone call. In the end . . .'

'So you knew what he did?'

'To a degree. I mean, I knew he worked for MI6. Beyond that, though . . .'

'Was he unfaithful?'

'I don't think so,' Westwood said. 'He could have been, of course. He was away often enough. But I think I would have known. I do believe that Laurence truly loved me, at least as well as he could love anyone.'

'What do you mean by that?'

'There was a large part of his life that he kept secret from me. Oh, I understand it was his job, national security and all that, but nevertheless it still meant that I only got a small part of him. The rest was shades of darkness, shadows, smoke and mirrors. You couldn't pin him down.'

'When did you last see him?'

'Years ago, when we split up. He went off on one of his trips and I never saw him again.'

'Did you meet any of his colleagues?'

'No. They didn't exactly have office parties. I tell a lie, though. I was vetted, of course, and interviewed. They came here once. Two of them. They asked me about my job, what sort of people I worked for, how I felt about my country, about democracy, communism, that kind of thing. They treated me with the utmost respect and politeness, but there was an edge, you know. There was a veiled threat. "We'll be watching you, mate. Any funny business and we'll have the electrodes on your balls before you can say shaken not stirred."' He laughed. 'Well, something like that.'

Hardcastle had probably got the same treatment, Banks imagined. 'Have you heard of someone called Fenner?' he asked. 'Julian Fenner.'

'No, I can't say I have.'

'What about a couple called Townsend?'

'No, again the name doesn't ring a bell.'

Banks showed Westwood the photograph of Silbert with the man in Regent's Park, but he said it didn't mean anything to him.

'How did you find out about me?' Westwood asked.

'We found some old letters from you in Mr Silbert's safe.'

'Ah, I see . . . Do you think, perhaps, when this is all over . . .?'

'I'll see what I can do,' said Banks. He noticed a tear glisten in Westwood's right eye. He didn't think there was anything more to be gained from talking to him. He finished his coffee, thanked Westwood and stood up to go. It seemed that every time he thought he was taking a step closer to Laurence Silbert he was actually moving further away from him. It was like trying to grasp a handful of smoke.

'THEY'RE WAITING for us in the staff room,' Winsome said, when Annie arrived at the front entrance of Eastvale Comprehensive. Some of the pupils paused and gawked at them, Winsome in particular, and more than a few giggles and wolf whistles echoed in the high corridors.

They found the staff room close to the administration offices. Three teachers, a woman and two men, one of them Derek Wyman, sat on battered sofas and armchairs around a low table littered with the day's newspapers.

'So you've found our secret lair,' said Wyman, standing up.

'I phoned. The school secretary told me where you were,' said Winsome.

'I can see you're not a detective for nothing,' said the other man.

Winsome and Annie exchanged glances.

Wyman obviously noticed their reaction. 'I apologise for my colleague,' he said. 'He spent all morning with year ten and he hasn't recovered yet.'

'That's all right,' said Annie, positioning herself so she could see them all and take control of the interview. Winsome sat next to her with her notebook.

'This shouldn't take long,' Annie went on. 'You're here because you all teach at least two of the pupils we think might be involved in the stabbing of Donny Moore. We're still trying to form a picture of exactly what happened that night, and you might be able to help us. Can you start by telling us who you are and what you teach?'

'Well, you know who I am,' said Wyman. 'I teach drama and games.'

The man who had made the bad joke said, 'I'm Barry Chaplin and I teach science and PE, for my sins.'

'I'm Jill Dresler,' the woman said, 'and I teach maths. No sports.'

'And you all know Nicky Haskell and Jackie Binns?' Annie asked.

They nodded, and Jill Dresler added, 'When they can be bothered to come to class.'

'And what can you tell me about Donny Moore?' Annie asked.

'Donny wasn't a bad student,' said Dresler. 'He was more of a follower than an instigator. Not a scrapper.'

'Not at all,' agreed Chaplin. 'Not like Haskell.'

'So Nicky Haskell likes to fight?' Annie pressed.

'Well,' said Chaplin, 'I wouldn't say he picks fights, as such. I mean, he's not a bully. But people sometimes pick on him because he's a bit shorter than the rest, and they usually get a hell of a surprise.'

'He's good at games, too,' Wyman added. 'Strong, fast, quick-witted.'

'We believe Haskell might be a witness, but he's not talking.'

'That figures,' said Chaplin. 'I mean, he wouldn't, would he? He'd lose face. These kids don't rat out each other, even their worst enemies.'

'It's just that he seems scared.'

'Of Jackie Binns?' said Chaplin. 'I don't believe it. I've seen them tangle on the football field and Haskell has never shown any fear of him.'

'So you don't think he'd lie out of fear of what Binns might do to him?'

'Absolutely not,' said Chaplin. 'Binns isn't that tough. He's all bluster.'

'Is there anything else you can tell us?' Annie asked.

'I don't think so,' said Jill Dresler. 'I know what you probably think, but they're not bad kids, really. Not all of them. I mean, OK so they do break the law and sell drugs, but they're not big-time dealers, and you don't have to shoot anyone to belong to their gangs or that sort of thing.'

'I suppose we ought to be thankful for small mercies,' Annie said, getting to her feet. 'And I appreciate your defence of your kids. But somebody's lying, and until we find out the truth, we can't get to the bottom of this. Things are getting a bit tense on the estate, as I'm sure you can imagine.' She reached in her bag. 'So if you do think of anything that might help us, here's my card. Don't hesitate to phone. Mr Wyman, a word, please.'

'Of course. I'll walk to the door with you,' said Wyman.

Once they were out in the noisy corridor, Annie let Winsome get a few feet ahead, then turned to Wyman. 'Can you tell me what you were doing in the Red Rooster with Mark Hardcastle a couple of weeks ago?'

Wyman seemed surprised, but he answered quickly. 'Having a drink. I told you we got together for a drink every now and then.'

'Yes,' said Annie. 'But the Red Rooster is a kids' pub, and it's hardly just round the corner.'

'Well, the food's OK, and the beer's not bad.'

'Look, Mr Wyman,' said Annie. 'It's out of the way—at least two miles from Eastvale; the beer might be passable, but the food's crap. Anyone would think you went there because you didn't want to be seen.'

'Well, to be quite honest,' said Wyman, 'knowing the way tongues start wagging, and given Mark's . . . er . . . sexual inclinations . . . I will admit that somewhere a little out of the way seemed more suitable.'

'Come off it, Derek. Your pupils drink there. You expect me to believe—?'

'Now, look here.' Wyman stopped in his tracks and turned to face her. 'I don't have to explain to you why I drink where I do. Or who with.'

'What was Mark Hardcastle upset about?'

Wyman carried on walking. 'I don't know what you're talking about.'

'Something you said upset him. Then you calmed him down. What was it?'

'That's rubbish. I don't remember anything remotely like that happening.'

'Don't you?' said Annie. She was at the door, and Wyman stopped again. 'Funny, that,' she went on. 'Other people remember it very well.' She pushed the door and walked out towards Winsome, who was waiting on the steps. 'Bye, Mr Wyman,' she said over her shoulder. 'I'm sure we'll talk again.'

AFTER A QUICK BURGER and chips and a pint of Sam Smith's at Ye Olde Swiss Cottage, a rambling pub that looked rather like a large ski chalet stuck in the cleft of busy traffic between Avenue Road and Finchley Road, Banks made his way to the tube station and negotiated his route to Victoria.

He found Wyman's bed and breakfast hotel easily enough, about five minutes' walk from the underground. A sign in the window offered vacancies from thirty-five pounds per night, which sounded remarkably cheap to Banks. Surprisingly, the place turned out to be quite charming. The entrance was clean and the decor fresh. The man who answered Banks's ring was a rotund Pakistani with a moustache and a shiny head. He introduced himself as Mohammed and asked with a smile how he could help.

Banks took out his warrant card and Mohammed scrutinised it.

'No trouble, I hope?' he said, a worried expression corrugating his brow.

'Not for you,' Banks said. 'It's just information I'm after, really.' He described Wyman, and told him the dates he said he'd last stayed there.

'Ah, yes, Mr Wyman,' Mohammed said. 'He's one of my regulars. Very fine gentleman. Please, let me check for you.' He went behind the reception desk and thumbed through a large book. 'Yes, here it is. He arrived on

Wednesday afternoon the week before last, and he left on the Saturday.'

'Was he any different than on previous visits?'

'In what way?'

'I'm not sure,' said Banks. 'Excited, depressed, on edge, anxious?'

'No, not that I noticed. He seemed quite . . . quite happy.'

'What time did he leave?'

'Checkout time is eleven o'clock.'

That squared with what Wyman had told them. He said he had gone for a pub lunch, then done some book shopping and visited the National Gallery before catching the five o'clock train back to York.

'Do you have any idea where he went while he was here?'

Mohammed frowned. 'I don't spy on my guests, Mr Banks,' he said.

'I understand,' said Banks. 'But you must have noticed him coming in or going out at certain times. Did he sleep here every night?'

'As far as I know. His bed was always slept in.'

'I don't suppose you know what times he came and went?'

'No. He usually went out after breakfast, and he might call back at some point for an hour or so in the middle of the afternoon, perhaps to rest, and then he would go out again at tea time, like any other tourist.'

'Did he have any visitors?'

'We don't encourage visitors in the rooms. I suppose he *could* have sneaked someone in the room if he'd wanted, but I don't think he did. In fact, he's a model guest. He never makes any noise. He is always polite.'

'Good,' said Banks. 'This might sound like an odd request, but can I have a look at the room he stayed in the last time he was here?'

Mohammed stroked his moustache. 'As it happens, you're in luck. That room is empty now. Though what you hope to find there I have no idea. Other guests have stayed since Mr Wyman, and everything has been cleaned and washed. I can vouch for that. I take care of the cleaning myself.'

'Did you find anything odd or interesting when you cleaned the room after Mr Wyman left last time?'

'No. I . . . Wait a minute,' said Mohammed. 'It had slipped down the back of the radiator. It's always difficult to clean behind there.'

'What was it?' Banks asked.

'Just a business card. It got stuck on the end of the vacuum cleaner. I remember thinking it must have fallen out of the top pocket of his shirt when he took it off to go to bed. Mr Wyman was usually a most tidy guest.'

'Do you still have it?'

'No. I put it in with the rest of the rubbish.'

'I don't suppose you can remember what the card said, can you?'

'Oh, yes,' said Mohammed. 'It was the name, you see. "Tom Savage". Wouldn't you remember that?'

'I suppose I probably would,' said Banks.

'And,' Mohammed went on, beaming, 'you would certainly remember it if it said "Tom Savage Detective Investigations". Like Magnum P.I. or Sam Spade. I'm a fan of the American detectives, you see.'

'Could it have been dropped there before Mr Wyman came to stay?'

'No, I'm most thorough. I clean every nook and cranny between guests.'

'I don't suppose you remember an address or telephone number?'

'I'm sorry.'

'That's OK,' said Banks. 'It should be easy enough to find out.'

'Do you still want to look at the room?'

'Yes, please.'

'Very well. Follow me.'

Mohammed took a key from a hook on the wall, led Banks up three flights of carpeted stairs and opened a door off the landing. The room was small, but clean and cheerful. Banks spotted the radiator. A wooden chair stood right next to it, a natural place to lay out one's clothes for the morning. Easy for a card to slip out of a pocket and flutter behind the radiator.

There was no television set and only a single bed, but the room was snug and comfortable and at that price Banks would probably stay there himself.

'It's charming,' he said to Mohammed. 'I can see why he liked it. Mind if I have a look around?'

'Please. There's nothing here.'

Banks could see what he meant. A quick glance under the bed revealed nothing, not even the dust balls one might usually expect to find there, and the wardrobe, too, was bare.

'I'm sorry to have troubled you,' Banks said. 'Thanks a lot for answering my questions and for letting me see the room.'

Mohammed led him down the stairs. 'I do hope Mr Wyman isn't in any trouble,' he said as they shook hands.

'So do I,' said Banks, taking Mohammed's card. 'So do I.'

Chapter Nine

The detective agency looked like a one-man operation housed in a nondescript sixties office tower on Great Marlborough Street, between Regent Street and Soho. Banks had got the address easily from the Yellow Pages. He took the jerky lift up to the fifth floor and found the door marked TOM SAVAGE DETECTIVE INVESTIGATIONS.

When he walked into the room, he was almost expecting a rumpled, hung-over, smart-mouthed tough with a bottle of Scotch in his filing cabinet, though none of the private investigators he'd met had ever matched that particular stereotype. Savage had a receptionist, but she wasn't sitting behind her desk polishing her nails; she was actually stuffing papers in folders in a filing cabinet. She had to bend over to do it, too, and her low-slung, tight jeans didn't leave much to the imagination.

On hearing Banks arrive, she stood up, smoothed her jeans and blushed. She knew exactly what he'd been looking at. 'Can I help you?' she said.

'Mr Savage in?'

'Do you have an appointment?'

'I'm afraid not.'

'Then I'm sorry—'

Banks pulled out his warrant card and showed it to her.

She gave him a sharp glance and said, 'Why didn't you say?'

'I just did,' said Banks. 'Does it make any difference?'

She read the card again. 'Are you . . .? Alan Banks . . . You're not . . .? Are you Brian Banks's father?'

'Yes. Why?'

'Oh my God!' She put her hands to her cheeks. Banks thought she was going to jump up and down. 'You are. You're Brian Banks's father!'

'I'm sorry,' said Banks. 'I don't . . .'

'I just *love* the Blue Lamps. I can't believe it. I only saw them a couple of weeks ago. Your Brian was terrific. I play a bit of guitar myself and write my own songs. Just an amateur, like, but . . . When did he start playing? How often did he practise?'

'In his mid-teens, and way too often, when he should have been doing other things,' said Banks. 'Like homework.'

She managed a quick smile. It lit up her face, which was very pretty, a pale oval with good cheekbones, clear, direct emerald eyes and a smattering of freckles framed by shoulder-length blonde hair. 'I'm so sorry,' she said. 'What must you think of me, acting like a silly schoolgirl?' She stuck out her hand. 'Tom Savage. Pleased to meet you. Actually it's Tomasina, but I don't think that would go down very well in this business, do you?'

Banks tried not to show his surprise. 'How did you know who I was?'

'I read an article about the band, an interview, and your son mentioned that his father was a detective chief inspector in North Yorkshire. There can't be that many called Banks. I'm sorry. I didn't mean to gush.'

'That's OK,' said Banks. 'I'm very proud of him.'

'Let's go through to the main office. It's more comfortable in there.' She gestured around the reception area. 'It's a one-woman show at the moment, I'm afraid. I don't have any client appointments today, hence the casual wear. It's office clean-up day.'

Banks followed her into the office and sat down opposite her.

'So.' Tomasina rested her palms on her desk. 'What can I help you with?'

'Maybe nothing. I found your card in a hotel room that may have been used by a murder suspect.' Banks was embellishing the truth, but he thought it might be the best way of getting her to talk.

'And what?' She pointed at her chest and blinked. 'You think I . . . I mean, you think he hired *me* to kill someone?'

'No doubt he picked you on the basis of your name in the telephone directory. It sounds tough. But I'm not accusing you of murder.'

'Well, thank the Lord for that.'

'I just want to know if you accepted an assignment from a man called Derek Wyman, and if you did, what exactly it consisted of.'

She picked up a pencil and started doodling. 'You know, there are issues of confidentiality involved here. I can't tell you who my clients are or what they want me to do. None of it's illegal. I can assure you of that.'

'I'm sure it's not.' Banks paused. 'Look, you can really help me here. I'm going out on a limb on this, but if I am right . . .'

'It could lead to a court case in which you'd expect me to testify.'

'It won't come to that.'

'Yeah, and you'll still respect me in the morning.'

'You're very cynical for one so young.'

'I'm only trying to protect my interests.' She gave him a direct look. 'As you can see, the place isn't exactly crawling with clients. Truth be told, I'm hard pushed to make ends meet. Now you expect me to throw away my reputation because of some limb you're out on?'

'Why not try another career? A more lucrative one?'

'Because I like what I do. And I'm good at it. I started out with a big agency, and I did my ABI training and got my advanced diploma. I've got degrees in law and criminology, and I've had five years on-the-job experience. Why should I search for another career?'

'Because you don't have any clients and you can barely pay the rent?'

She glanced away, her cheeks flushed. 'They'll come.'

'I'm sorry,' said Banks. 'I'm not trying to browbeat you or anything. To be honest, I'm rather in the same boat as you on this one.'

'You mean this isn't an official investigation?'

'Not exactly.'

'Oh, that's priceless.' She dropped her pencil. 'Not only do you come in here pushing me to give you confidential information, but it's not even part of a sanctioned investigation. Why don't you stop wasting my time?'

'You've got plenty to waste. Or would you rather get back to your filing?'

'Why?' she said. 'So you can have a good ogle at my arse again? Don't think I didn't notice.'

'It's a very nice arse.'

She glared at him, then leaned back in her chair, linked her hands behind her head and started to laugh. 'You're a prize specimen, you are,' she said.

'Does that mean you'll help me?'

'I know the rules,' she said. 'I know I'm supposed to cooperate with the police if the situation merits it. Tell me about this situation.'

'Have you read anything about the two deaths in Eastvale recently?'

'The two gay guys? Sure. Murder-suicide, wasn't it?'

'So it would appear.'

'But you don't believe it?'

'Oh, I believe that Mark Hardcastle beat Laurence Silbert to death with a cricket bat, then hanged himself. I just don't believe he did it without help.'

'I'm listening.'

Banks tried to explain his *Othello* theory, aware of how absurd it sounded every time he did so. Tomasina sat with her brow furrowed and her fingers steepled on the desk for a full minute or so after he'd finished.

'What evidence do you have for your theory?' she asked eventually.

'None.' Banks wasn't going to bring the Secret Intelligence Service into his discussion with her. He had already decided on that.

'Motive?'

'None that I'm aware of right now, other than professional jealousy.'

'So the only thing even approaching evidence you have is that this Wyman character was directing *Othello*, that he met up with Hardcastle in London the day before the killing, that they had some professional differences and that they were seen drinking together in an out-of-town pub?'

'And there's the memory stick with pictures of Silbert with another man. Neither Hardcastle nor Silbert had a camera that took such a card.'

'What about Wyman?'

'He didn't have one, either. His is a Fuji.'

'And that's all you've got?'

'Yes, but when you add it all up together it's damn suspicious. Why go two miles to a grotty pub when there are plenty of good pubs in Eastvale? And how did Wyman get Hardcastle upset and then calm him down? Why?'

'There's no way anyone could have known what effect playing Iago would have on two people.'

'That's what Annie said. DI Cabbot. She and I were working together on the case until we were told to drop it. Orders from above.'

'She's right, though.'

'I know that. Maybe it went wrong.'

'Then it wasn't murder. Some sort of malicious trick backfiring. At the most, you'd be able to charge him with incitement; that's if you can prove that he incited anyone to a criminal act.'

'It doesn't matter,' Banks said. 'The result's the same. Two men are dead.'

Tomasina studied him for what felt like a long time. Then she said, 'I took those photos. The ones on the memory stick.'

Banks's jaw must have dropped. 'Just like that!'

'Well, it wasn't quite that easy. I had to stay out of sight.'

'No, I mean you're admitting it just like that. I appreciate your help, really I do.'

Tomasina shrugged. 'When a cute man—and the father of my rock hero, no less—says nice things about my arse, I can't hold out on him, can I?'

'I'm sorry about that. It just sort of slipped out.'

She laughed again. 'It's all right. I'm only teasing. But you'd better be careful. Some women might not appreciate it as much as I do.'

'I know. You're one in a million, Tomasina.' In fact, just about every woman he knew would have given him hell for a comment like that. What had he been thinking of? 'Will you tell me about it?' he asked.

'There's not much to tell, really. Derek Wyman wanted me to do a simple surveillance job.'

'Do you remember when he first came to you?'

'I could find out. Hang on.' Tomasina got up and walked back out to her filing cabinets. In a moment she was back, consulting a buff folder. 'It was the beginning of May.'

'That long ago,' Banks mused. 'What did he ask for?'

'He gave me an address in Bloomsbury. On certain occasions—he would phone me first—I was instructed to watch it, follow the man who left, find out where he went and take photos of him with anyone he met.'

'Did he tell you why he wanted you to do this?'

'No.'

'And you just assumed it was all above board?'

'He seemed all right. I thought maybe he was gay and he thought his lover was having an affair. It wasn't as if he was asking me to hurt anyone.'

Images of Silbert and Hardcastle in the mortuary flashed through Banks's mind. 'There's more than one way of hurting someone.'

Tomasina flushed. 'You can't blame me for what happened.'

'I'm not blaming you. But in the wrong hands, photos can be as deadly as a gun. Maybe they were intended for blackmail? Didn't you think of that?'

'To be honest, I didn't. Like I said, he seemed nice enough.'

'You're right,' said Banks. 'You were simply doing your job.'

She was studying his face, he felt, looking for signs that he was telling the truth and not winding her up. In the end, she reached her decision and relaxed visibly. 'It was easy enough,' she said. 'In the early evening, seven o'clock, the man in question would walk to the Boating Lake in Regent's Park. Always he would sit on a bench and another man would join him.'

'How many times did you follow him?'

'Three.'

'He met the same man every time?'

'Yes. They didn't talk, but they'd get up and walk together to St John's Wood. You know, the High Street where the cemetery is.'

'I know it,' said Banks. 'And from there they would walk to Charles Lane and enter a house together.'

'Yes. You know all about it?'

'We identified the house from one of your photos. How long did they stay?'

'Almost two hours every time. When they came out, they parted ways. My man usually walked to the tube on Finchley Road. But once he walked all the way back to Bloomsbury.'

'And the other man?'

'I never followed him. But he headed north. Towards Hampstead.'

'When they got to the house on Charles Lane, who had the key?'

'Nobody,' said Tomasina. 'They knocked on the door and someone let them in. She was always in the shadows and didn't show on the photos.'

'She?'

'Oh, yes, it was definitely a woman. Grey-haired, maybe in her sixties. I could see that much. I just couldn't describe her features. But she was quite small, smartly dressed.'

'Edith Townsend,' said Banks.

So the Townsends *had* been lying to him, he thought, which meant they were something to do with Mr Browne and the spooks. Or the other side. What had Silbert been up to? It wasn't an affair, Banks was almost certain of that, but were the photos enough to convince Hardcastle that it was? With the added Iago-style innuendoes and rhetoric, perhaps they were.

'Do you know her?' asked Tomasina.

'In a way. When did you give your client the memory stick?'

'Wednesday afternoon. The end of May. Two weeks ago.'

'Did you give him prints, too?'

'Yes. Do *you* know what it's all about?'

'Not really,' Banks said. 'I have a few vague ideas, but that's all they are.'

'Will you tell me, or is this a one-way street?'

Banks smiled at her. 'It's a one-way street for the moment, a cul-de-sac, too, as far as I can see.'

'Is this it, then? You walk out of here and I never see you again?'

'This is it.' Banks stood up. 'But if you need to get in touch, you can call this number.' He scribbled down his new mobile number on the back of his card, handed it to her and walked over to the door.

'Wait,' she called out. 'Will you do just one teeny little thing for me?'

Banks paused at the door. 'It depends on what it is.'

'The Blue Lamps. Can you get me a ticket for their next show?'

Banks looked back at her. 'I'll see what I can do,' he said.

IT WAS A FINE EVENING, and the little park in the centre of Soho Square was filling up. Banks decided to call Annie, to bring her up to speed. He sat on the grass, found her number and pressed the call button.

'So what were Silbert and his pal up to?' Annie asked, when he'd finished telling her about Tomasina and the photographs.

'My guess is that they were working on something together. Some intelligence service project. I've been to that house and the old couple who own it are definitely dodgy; they lied to me through their teeth.'

'So he was still spying? He hadn't retired?'

'Something like that. Or he was working for the other side, whoever that is. But imagine what it would seem like to Hardcastle, Annie, especially with the help of Wyman's sly innuendoes and graphic images.'

'But if Wyman poisoned Hardcastle against Silbert,' Annie went on, 'there's no reason to believe that Silbert was the intended victim. Wyman hardly knew him. He *did* know Hardcastle quite well, though.'

'So you're saying Mark Hardcastle was the victim?' Banks said.

'I'm saying he could have been. And you still have to consider the fact that Wyman could not have been certain of the effects of his actions.'

'I agree he couldn't have known that Hardcastle would kill Silbert, then himself. But he did know he was stirring up a volatile situation, and that someone might get hurt.'

'True. Even if only emotionally, even if his only intention was to split them up.'

'Is that what you're suggesting?'

'It makes sense, doesn't it? Isn't it what you'd expect if you convinced someone his partner was being unfaithful, rather than bloody murder and suicide? And Wyman had plenty of reason to be upset with Hardcastle over developments at the theatre. Though not enough to kill him, obviously.'

'Perhaps,' said Banks.

'In which case, all this spooks business is beside the point.'

'What about Mr Browne?'

'You pissed in his swimming pool, Alan. For God's sake, we'd be swarming around quickly enough if it was one of our blokes died that way.'

'Julian Fenner and the mysterious phone number that doesn't ring?'

'Tradecraft? Part of what Silbert was up to in London? I don't know.'

'And us being warned off?'

'They don't want publicity. It does so happen that Silbert was a member of MI6, and he'd probably been involved in a fair bit of dirty business over the years. They don't want to take the slightest chance that any of that might come out. It was all neatly wrapped up. Murder-suicide. Sad but simple. No need for further messy investigations. Until you come along crying foul.'

'I'm still not convinced.'

'But you admit that it could have been all about Hardcastle, not Silbert?'

'It could have been. Why don't you nose around into Wyman's and Hardcastle's backgrounds a bit more deeply, see if you can come up with anything? Who knows? Maybe you'll find the missing link.'

CHARLOTTE STREET was packed with people: smokers crowding the pavements outside pubs, tourists searching for somewhere to eat. Not quite sure what he was going to do, Banks made a quick dash when he saw someone leaving one of the outside tables at Zizzi's, getting there before a couple of Americans, who had also had their eye on it. The woman glared at him, but her husband tugged her sleeve and they walked away.

Banks hadn't made any arrangements for dinner with Sophia, wasn't even sure what time she'd be home, so as he was hungry, he decided he might as well order a pizza and a glass of wine. The wine soon arrived, a nice large glass, and Banks settled back to sip and watch the pageant.

This was pretty much what Derek Wyman and Mark Hardcastle must have seen when they sat out here about two weeks ago, Banks thought. What had they talked about? By then, Banks guessed, Derek Wyman would have picked up the memory stick and prints of the digital photographs it contained from Tom Savage. Had he given them to Hardcastle here? And what had Hardcastle's reaction been? Had they gone to the cinema as planned, or was that another lie?

When the waitress reappeared with his pizza diavola, Banks asked her if she had a spare moment. She was clearly busy, but the sight of his warrant card, discreetly shown, drew a curt nod, and she leaned closer.

'Were you working here on Wednesday night, two weeks ago?'

'Yes. I work every day same shift.'

'Did you notice two men sitting at an outside table about six o'clock?'

'There were many people,' she said. 'Very busy. Long time ago.' Her accent was Eastern European, Banks thought. She glanced over her shoulder, apparently worried that her boss was watching her.

Banks hurried on. 'Two men together. One gave something to the other. There might have been an argument or a fuss of some sort.'

She put her hand to her mouth. 'The man who tear the photographs?'

'What?' Banks said.

'I am delivering order to table over there, and this man—I think he dye his hair blond—he look at photographs, then he get angry and tear them up.'

'Did you see the other man give him the photos?'

'No. Very busy. I just notice he tear them.'

'Did they leave then?' he asked.

'They pay me. Separate bills. Very strange. Then he leave, the one who tear the photographs.'

'And the other?'

'He gather up the pieces and stay longer. I must go.'

'Thank you,' Banks said. 'Thank you very much.'

The waitress scurried away and Banks sipped some more wine and began to eat his pizza. So Wyman *had* given Hardcastle the photos at the restaurant, and he had reacted by tearing them up. Which was why they hadn't been found at Castleview Heights.

Banks realised that Annie could very well be right about Hardcastle, not Silbert, being the intended victim, which left the whole espionage business on the sideline. But that shady and much misunderstood world existed, all right, and Banks had apparently become fixed on its radar. He needed to find out why. The problem was that while they could always find you when they wanted to, you could never find them.

There was one person he could talk to, though. Detective Superintendent Richard 'Dirty Dick' Burgess had been working with some elite antiterrorism liaison squad for a while now. Even their acronym was so secret that if you heard it you had to die, he had joked. Burgess and Banks went back a long time, and there was a chance he might know some of the people involved.

As he finished his wine, Banks was convinced that the young couple who had just passed by again on the opposite side of the street had not had to walk up and down Charlotte Street six times in the past hour, as they had done, simply to find an outside table at a restaurant. Who was it who said that paranoia simply means being in possession of all the facts? Banks gestured to the waitress and reached for his wallet.

BY THURSDAY EVENING, Annie had had enough of Eastvale Comprehensive and the East Side Estate's problems. She didn't want a drink, but she did want a bit of peace and quiet, so she bought a Britvic orange and hid herself away in the back room of the Horse and Hounds. As usual, there was no one else around. It was dim and cool, the perfect place to collect her thoughts.

'Ah, DI Cabbot. So this is your little hideaway. Mind if I join you?'

Annie looked up to see Detective Superintendent Gervaise standing in the doorway. 'No problem, ma'am,' she said.

'Drink?' Gervaise asked as she plonked her pint down on the table.

Annie glanced at her watch. Just after six.

'You're officially off duty, aren't you? Besides, a senior officer is asking you to have a drink with her.'

'OK. Thank you, ma'am. I'll have a pint of Black Sheep, please.'

'Good choice. And there's no need to call me ma'am. We're just a couple of colleagues having a drink after work.'

Somehow, that sounded more ominous to Annie than Gervaise had probably intended. Though she wasn't sure about that. She still hadn't quite got a grasp on the superintendent yet. Gervaise was tricky. You had to be careful. One minute she could come on like your best friend, and the next she was all business again, the boss. Annie decided it was best to remain as passive as possible and let Gervaise lead the way.

Gervaise came back with the beer and sat opposite Annie. She looked around the small room, its dark, varnished panelling glowing in the soft light, and said, 'Nice here, isn't it? I always think the Queen's Arms is just a little too noisy at times, don't you? I can't say I blame you for coming here instead.'

'Yes, m—Yes,' said Annie, just remembering herself in time. So the game was up. Gervaise knew about the Horse and Hounds. Pity.

'You're a good copper, Annie, I like you,' Gervaise began. 'You appear to have your head screwed on the right way, and at a guess I'd say you're fairly ambitious, am I right?'

'I like to do a good job and be recognised for it,' said Annie.

'Exactly. You acquitted yourself well in that business you were involved in on detachment to Eastern Area. You kept your head and your wits about you.'

Annie didn't feel that she had kept her head at all, but you didn't throw such praise back in the face of the person who gave it to you. Especially Superintendent Gervaise. 'Thank you,' she said. 'It was a difficult time.'

'I can well imagine. Anyway, that's behind us now. As is the Hardcastle and Silbert business. In fact, the chief constable himself has taken a personal interest in that whole business, and he thinks it's in the best interests of all concerned—his very words—that we toss the file in the solved cabinet—he really thinks we have such a thing, you know—and put it out of our minds, deal with the situation on the East Side Estate before it escalates. This *is* tourist season, you know.'

'And let's not forget the traffic cones,' said Annie.

Gervaise gave her a disappointed look. 'Yes, well. My point is that if you were doing your job, if you were following instructions—'

'I *am* working on the Donny Moore stabbing.'

'I know you're working on it, Annie, but I'm not convinced you're giving it your full attention.'

They both drank more beer in silence.

'Let me tell you a story,' Gervaise said. 'A few years ago, I was working on the Met, and we sometimes had to work with Special Branch and MI5. I know they can be arrogant and devious bastards, but we're all fighting a common battle, a united front against the forces of evil. Well, one of the lads on our team, let's call him Aziz, was a Muslim. His family came from Saudi Arabia, and he'd grown up here, spoke like an Eastender, but they still went to the local mosque, said their prayers, the whole thing. This was all in the wake of the July bombings in London and the unfortunate shooting of that Brazilian on the tube. Tempers were a little frazzled all round, as you can imagine. Anyway, Aziz made some criticism of the way our local Special Branch–MI5 liaison officer handled a situation at a mosque, said something to indicate that he thought we were all being a bit heavy-handed about it all, and the next thing you know he's got a file as thick as your wrist. They'd fitted him up with a legend—a complete alternative life history. It was all in there, the training camps in Pakistan, the meetings with terrorist-cell leaders, all documented, photographs, the lot. And every word, every image of it, was a lie. Aziz had never left England in his life. But there it was, in glorious technicolour, the life of a terrorist. We all knew it was crap. Even MI5 knew it was crap. But they had a point to make and they made it.'

Gervaise paused to drink some beer. 'Of course, they searched his flat, interrogated him, pestered his friends and colleagues. This was something that could happen to any one of us who stepped out of line, they were saying. Aziz just happened to be dark-skinned, happened to be a Muslim, but we weren't immune just because we were white police officers.'

'What happened to Aziz?'

'His career was over. They took back all the files about training camps and stuff, of course—that was all for effect—but they'd made their point as to what they *could* do. A week later Aziz jumped off an overpass on the M1. I mean, I don't suppose it's fair to blame MI5 for that. They couldn't have predicted how deeply unstable he was. Or could they?'

'What are you saying?'

Gervaise sipped more beer. 'I'm just telling you a story, Annie, that's all.'

'You're warning me off.'

'Warning you off what? You're reading too much into what I'm saying. If I'm doing anything at all, Annie, I'm telling you to be very careful, and you can pass that on to DCI Banks the next time you talk to him.'

'There's something else,' Annie said. 'I don't know what it is, but there's something else. Don't you think there's something odd about the Hardcastle-Dilbert business, something that doesn't quite fit? You do, don't you?'

'There are always things that don't quite add up. But whatever baroque theories you and DCI Banks might have dreamed up, scientific evidence, proved beyond all reasonable doubt that Mark Hardcastle killed Laurence Silbert and then hanged himself. You're not arguing with the facts, are you?'

'No. I'm—'

'Then there is no case to pursue.' Gervaise looked at Annie. 'Let's say, just for the sake of argument, talking of baroque theories, that DCI Banks had some outlandish idea about someone putting Hardcastle up to it, making innuendoes, getting him all riled up, that sort of thing. I went to see *Othello* the other night, and I understand DCI Banks took his girlfriend last weekend. Maybe he got it from there. It's really quite a powerful story. Of course, Iago turned a man against his wife, but there's no reason that shouldn't translate into homosexual terms, is there, especially given the element of overkill we sometimes find in gay killings?'

'What?' said Annie. She knew she was on dangerous ground now. She hadn't wanted to reveal the *Othello* theory to Gervaise for fear she of being mocked, but now the woman was quoting it to her.

Gervaise gave her a sideways glance and smiled. 'Oh, don't be so disingenuous, Annie. I'm not so green as I'm cabbage-looking, as I believe they say around these parts. Can you think of any other reason why you, or DCI Banks, would think it a case worth pursuing other than that you thought someone put Hardcastle up to it? I'm sure the two of you know as well as I do that our security services have any number of psychological tricks up their sleeves. As for DCI Banks, well, you probably know as well as I do that if you tell him to do something, he does the opposite. I just hope he realises what happens to spies who go on missions behind enemy lines. What's wrong, Annie? Lost your voice?'

THE TUBE WAS HOT and crowded again, and Banks was relieved to get off at Sloane Square. He walked down King's Road in the evening light, instinctively slowing down to look in a shop window and check for anyone who might be following him, then turned into Sophia's street.

If Sophia was home, perhaps they would have a glass of wine and then go to the cinema or a concert. Even spending the evening at home together would be perfect as far as Banks was concerned. When he got to the steps, he noticed that the living-room light was on, which meant she was in.

He put his key in the lock and was surprised when the door opened at his touch. It hadn't been locked. That wasn't like Sophia. He checked the handle and lock for any signs of forced entry and found none. Calling her name, Banks turned right from the hall into the living room and stopped dead on the threshold. She was sitting on the floor leaning back against the sofa, her head hanging on her chest, her long legs stretched out into the heap of broken things piled at the centre of the carpet. *Her* things. When he called her name again, she lifted up a tear-stained face to him.

Banks couldn't tell exactly what was there: a slashed landscape painting that had hung on the wall above the stereo; an antique table on which she had displayed various objects, its spindly legs splintered, mother-of-pearl inlay smashed; a broken Eskimo soapstone sculpture; a shattered ceramic mask; dried ferns and flowers tossed willy-nilly over the whole mess like a parody of a funeral.

Sophia sat clutching a piece of exquisite gold-rimmed pottery in her hand. 'This belonged to my mother. Her grandmother gave it to her. God knows how long she'd had it.' Suddenly she flung the shard of pottery at Banks. It hit the doorjamb. 'You bastard!' she screamed. 'How could you?'

Banks made to move over to her but she held up her hands. 'Don't come near me,' she said. 'Don't come near me or I don't know what I'll do.'

'Sophia, what is it?' he asked. 'What happened?'

'You know damn well what happened. Can't you see? You forgot to set the alarm and'—she gestured around the room—'*this* happened.'

Banks crouched across the heap from her. His knees cracked. 'I didn't forget to set the alarm,' he said. 'I've never forgotten to set it.'

'You must have. The alarm never went off. I came home as usual. The door hadn't been broken open or anything. And this was what I found. How else could it have happened? You forgot to set the alarm.'

Banks walked down the passage to where the back door opened off the kitchen. Nothing. No sign of forced entry, no sign of any kind of entry.

He went back to the living room. Sophia hadn't moved. 'Have you called the police?' he asked.

'I don't want the bloody police. What can the bloody police do? It's the *police* that caused this in the first place.' She gave him a look as full of loathing as any he had ever received, and it cut him to the heart.

'Even so,' he said. 'They might be able—'

'Oh, just go away. Why don't you just go away?'

'Sophia, this isn't my fault. I set the alarm as usual this morning.'

'So how do you explain all this?'

'Was anything taken?'

'How should I know?'

'It could be important. You should make a list for the police.'

'I told you I don't want the police here. What can they do?'

'Well, the insurance company—'

'Bugger the sodding insurance company! They can't replace any of this.'

Banks stared at the heap of broken treasures and knew she was right.

Everything here was personal, none of it worth a great deal of money. He also knew that there was only one explanation for all this, and in a way it *did* make him guilty. There was no point calling the police. The people who had done this were shadows, will-o'-the-wisps, to whom fancy alarm systems were child's play. Mr Browne had known where Sophia lived, all right. Banks knelt down beside the wreckage. Sophia wouldn't meet his gaze.

'Come on,' he said, sighing, 'I'll help you clean up.'

BANKS WAS IN A QUANDARY when he left Sophia's. He sat in the Porsche, his heart still pounding, wondering what to do. Sophia had insisted that he go, but he hadn't wanted to leave her alone. In the end, he had persuaded her to phone her best friend, Amy, and spend the night at her place. Reluctantly, Sophia had agreed, and Amy had driven over to pick her up. Banks was glad of that. Amy was sensible and strong, and Banks felt he need have no worries about Sophia tonight. His dilemma was whether or not he should stay in London to be around for her tomorrow, in case she had changed her mind about him.

Then he remembered the woman across the street, who was a bit of a nosy parker, always at her window. He got out of the car and went to knock on her door. If she was up to form, she would have seen him coming.

The door opened shortly after his knock. 'Yes?' he said.

She was younger than he had imagined from the vague figure he had seen from a distance, and there was an air of loneliness about her.

'I'm sorry to bother you,' Banks said, 'but it's just that we were expecting someone to come and service the computer across the street. I wonder . . .'

'The man and the woman?'

'Yes,' said Banks.

'They've already been.'

'What time, do you remember?'

'Just after four o'clock.'

'Did they knock?'

'Yes. Then one of them took out a key and they just walked in. It did appear odd, but they didn't act suspiciously at all.'

'That's all right,' Banks lied. 'We did leave a key with their company in case we were both out. They just didn't leave an invoice. Can you describe the couple for me? I'd like to put in a good word for them.'

'Just a man and a woman,' she said. 'Nicely dressed. Late thirties.'

At least it wasn't Mr Browne, thought Banks. But then, he wouldn't do something like this himself; he would send operatives.

'I'm sorry, but my dinner's in the oven.' She started to close the door.

Banks muttered good night and went back to his car.

Just as he had sat down, his new mobile rang. It was Annie.

'Alan?'

'Yes. What's happened?'

'Don't ask me how, but Gervaise found me in the Horse and Hounds.'

'What did she say?'

'I don't really know. She told me a story about a young Muslim police officer drummed out of the force after pissing off the spooks. She told me the chief constable in particular wanted an end to the Hardcastle–Silbert business. She told me there was no case to be investigated.'

'All to be expected,' said Banks. 'Anything else?'

'Plenty. She said she'd been to see *Othello* and thought you might have based some theory of events on it.'

'She *what*?'

'My reaction exactly.'

'Did you tell her about Tom Savage? The photos? The Red Rooster?'

'Of course not. But she's no fool, Alan. It's only a matter of time.'

'Damn. I didn't think it would all turn to shit so soon.'

'What do you mean?'

'Nothing. It doesn't matter. Just be careful, Annie.'

'That's what she said, too. She told me to pass on the warning to you.'

'She didn't tell you to lay off, then?'

'Well, she told me the *chief constable* had said to lay off. I think she was just telling us not to expect any mercy if we get caught.'

'Annie, you can get out of this right now,' said Banks. 'Just back off and be seen to throw all your energies into the East Side Estate business.'

'You must be joking.'

'I've never been more serious. Why don't you call Winsome, stay at her place tonight?'

'I might do just that,' said Annie. 'I've certainly had too much to drink to drive home, and it would be nice to have the company, if she'll have me.'

'I'm sure she will,' said Banks. 'Give her a ring.'

'OK, boss.'

'I'm serious. Remember, be careful. Good night.'

Annie started to say something, but Banks pressed the end-call button. He thought about turning off the phone altogether, then he realised it probably didn't matter, when it came down to it. If they wanted to find him, they would find him. Or anyone else he came into contact with.

Banks sat with his hands on the wheel. He didn't think he had ever felt so alone in his life. He was beyond even music. He started the car and drove. He had no idea where he was going, only that he had to move on. Bad things happened when you stood still for too long in this game.

Chapter Ten

B anks didn't feel any better at nine o'clock on Friday morning. After driving around for an hour or so the previous evening, keeping a close eye on his rearview mirror for any telltale signs that he was being followed, he had checked into the first decent hotel he had seen.

He had thought of going to Mohammed's bed and breakfast, but he wanted a room with a shower and a bit of space, somewhere safe to park his car, a decent television set and a well-stocked mini-bar. He had got all of this at a little over £150 in a place off Great Portland Street. At least he hadn't got completely pissed and ended up with a hangover. Physically, he felt OK after a long shower and a pot of room-service coffee.

Over a latte and a cranberry muffin at a nearby Caffè Nero, Banks decided to head up back to Eastvale. Surely even Superintendent Gervaise would agree, after hearing Tom Savage's story, that they had enough to bring him in for questioning. If Banks could convince her that the business was nothing to do with Silbert and the spooks, then maybe she would see the point in trying to find out exactly what had happened.

Banks was about to try Sophia on the pay-as-you-go mobile when it rang.

'Mr Banks? It's Tom. Tom Savage.'

'Tomasina. What is it?'

'Some people were here. They were waiting when I got in this morning. They've taken stuff. I . . . I'm scared, Mr Banks.'

Banks gripped the phone tightly. 'You're still at the office?'

'Yes.'

'Stay right there. I'll be over in about ten minutes. Don't move.'

'Thank you. I'm not usually so . . . a baby . . . I just don't . . .'

'It's OK, Tomasina. Hang on. I'll be there.'

Banks turned off the phone and hurried out, cursing as he went.

'I'M SORRY to disturb you at work,' said Annie, 'but do you think you could spare me a few moments?'

Carol Wyman turned to the young girl beside her behind the medical-centre reception desk. 'Can you cover for me, Sue? I'm just off for a coffee.'

Sue seemed a little surprised, but she smiled and said OK.

Carol grabbed her handbag and ducked under the flap. 'There's a nice coffee shop just over the road,' she said. 'If that's all right.'

'Perfect,' said Annie. It was nine o'clock on Friday morning, and she was ready for her second cup of the day.

'What's it about, by the way?' asked Carol as they crossed the street.

'Just a few routine questions,' said Annie.

The coffee shop was fairly quiet, and they found a small table by the window. A young waitress scribbled their orders after apologising that the espresso machine wasn't working. Annie settled for café American and Carol went for a cup of herbal tea. Both also ordered toasted tea cakes.

'You've changed your hair since you were over at the house,' Carol said, smiling. 'It looks nice. Have you ever thought of going blonde?'

'I don't know if I could handle more fun,' said Annie, as their drinks arrived. 'Still, it's a thought.' She blew on her coffee. 'Actually, it's your husband I wanted to talk to you about. We need to know a little more about his relationship with Mark Hardcastle and Laurence Silbert.'

'I thought that was all over. Your superintendent said so on the news.'

'Just tidying up a few loose ends,' said Annie, smiling. 'Sometimes the job's nothing but paperwork.'

'I know what you mean,' said Carol. 'Mine's just the same.'

'How long has your husband been directing plays for the theatre?'

'Ages now,' said Carol. 'I mean, not so much for the theatre, but the amateur dramatic society. They used to put on performances at the community centre, even the church hall sometimes.'

'He seems very passionate about his work.'

'Oh, he is,' Carol said. 'Sometimes I think he's more passionate about his work than he is about me. No, that's not fair. He's a good husband. And a good father. It's just that the teaching wears him down and—'

'I thought he liked it.'

'Well, he does. I mean, it gives you a chance to make a difference, doesn't it? To inspire future generations.' She glanced around the room and leaned forward, lowering her voice. 'But a lot of them just don't care. Don't even bother turning up for school. It's hard when you really care about something, to be constantly surrounded by people who mock it.'

'Why doesn't Derek consider another line of work?'

'You try that at forty-two, when you've been a teacher for more than twenty years. If he didn't have his theatre, I don't know what he'd do. It makes him feel just that bit more important. And he loves working in a real theatre rather than a village hall.'

'I know what you mean. He must feel like a real professional.'

'Yes. And he works so hard. Anyway, what is it you want to know?'

'Has your husband ever mentioned going to the Red Rooster pub?'

'The Red Rooster? In Medburn? But that's a chain pub. Derek is strictly a real-ale man. He wouldn't be seen dead in a place like that. Why?'

'It doesn't matter,' said Annie, even more curious now. 'As I said, I'm just tidying up loose ends. You get swamped with information in a case like this, and you have to sort out the wheat from the chaff.'

'I suppose so,' said Carol slowly.

Annie could see that she was starting to lose her. Any more questions that implied Carol's husband was up to something and that would be the end of their pleasant little chat. 'It must have been terrible for Derek when his brother died,' Annie said, making an abrupt turn, remembering the photograph in the Wymans' living room.

'Oh God, yes,' said Carol. 'Derek simply *adored* Rick. Hero-worshipped him. He was just devastated, gutted. We all were.'

'When exactly did it happen?'

'October the 15th, 2002. I won't forget that date in a hurry.'

'I'll bet you won't. Did you know him well?'

'Rick? Of course. He was a lovely fella. You know, you think these SAS chaps are all macho like someone out of an Andy McNab book, and a lot of them probably are, but Rick was as gentle and considerate as could be.'

'Your husband's brother was in the SAS?'

'Yes. I thought he said.'

'No.' Even Annie knew that the SAS carried out covert operations, and if Laurence Silbert had worked for MI6, he would probably have had some contact with them. They were back in Banks territory again.

'Was Rick married?' she asked.

'No. Rick told me that he just couldn't do it, get married, given his job, like, the risks, and the kind of world he operated in.'

'So Rick was away a lot, was he?'

'I wouldn't say a lot. He had a lovely house in the country. Ross-on-Wye. He did a lot of training, but he did go on missions, yes. That was what did for him, of course.'

'What?' said Annie. 'I thought it was a helicopter accident.'

Carol lowered her voice again. 'Well, that's what they *have* to say, isn't it? The official line. They don't want people to know what it's *really* like out there, what's *really* going on, do they?'

'What happened?' asked Annie.

'I don't know the full story.'

Annie could feel Carol pulling away again, but she didn't want to let go of this line of questioning. Not just yet. 'We never do, do we?' she said. 'Even in my job, the bosses hold their cards close to their chests. Half the time we don't know why we're following the lines of enquiry we're told to.'

'Well, in this case I really *don't* know. All I do know is that it was a secret mission, not an accident. Something went wrong.'

'How do you know that?'

'Derek told me. He'd talked to a couple of Rick's mates after the funeral, when they'd all had a few. They didn't give much away, either, but Derek said he got the impression that Rick's mates wanted him to know that his brother hadn't died in some stupid accident, but that he'd died in action, a hero.'

Annie didn't know if this had any relevance at all, but it was something that Derek Wyman had skirted when they first talked to him.

'I realise this is a bit of a cheeky question,' Annie said, 'and please don't take it the wrong way, but didn't it ever worry you, your husband being close to a gay man?'

'Why should it?'

'Well, some people . . . you know . . .'

'Perhaps if I didn't feel *secure* with Derek, it might have done,' she admitted. 'But let's just say I have no worries on *that* score,' she said, reddening.

'I'm sorry for asking,' said Annie. 'How is Derek doing now?'

'Oh, he's all right. I mean, he's still a bit upset about Mark, a bit quiet and moody. Well, it's not every day a good friend goes and hangs himself like that. I mean, someone you've had over to dinner and all.'

'How did they go? The dinners? What did you talk about? What did Mark and Laurence talk about?'

'Oh, you know, after a couple of bottles of wine, the conversation starts to flow. And Laurence told all sorts of stories. He'd been everywhere. Chile. Russia. Iran. Iraq. Australia. South Africa. It must have been so exciting.'

'Yes,' said Annie. 'I heard he was a well-travelled man. Did he mention Afghanistan at all?'

'As a matter of fact, he did. It came up when we were talking about Rick.'

'Of course. What did he say about it?'

'I got the impression that he didn't like it very much.'

'Dangerous place, I suppose,' said Annie. 'Is everything else OK with your husband?'

'Yes, of course. Except this gang business is getting him down.'

'It must be,' said Annie. 'I talked to him yesterday about a couple of his lads involved in that East Side Estate stabbing.'

'Did you? He didn't say.'

Well, he wouldn't, thought Annie. 'It wasn't important.'

'Anyway, like I said, you do it because you think you can make a difference, but . . .' Carol glanced at her watch. 'Ooh, is that the time? I must be getting back or Sue will be going ballistic.'

'I'll walk with you,' said Annie.

TOMASINA WAS SITTING behind her desk when Banks arrived. She had clearly been crying, but she had stopped now. A box of tissues lay on the desk by her hand next to a large mug of tea. On a cursory glance, the office looked the same as it had on his last visit. Either Tomasina had already done a good job of tidying up or her visitors had been very neat.

'I'm sorry for being such a blubberer on the phone,' she said.

'That's all right,' said Banks. He sat opposite her.

'No, it isn't. But you wouldn't understand.'

'Why don't you tell me what happened?' Banks said.

She drank some tea, holding the mug with both hands. Her hands were shaking. 'They came just after I got here, about nine. Two of them searched through everything, while the other two . . . well, they called it an interview.'

'Did they say who they were?'

'They just said they were from the government.'

'Did they show any identification?'

'I didn't get a good look. It was all too fast. But one was called Carson or Carstairs, maybe. And the woman was Harmon or Harlan. I'm sorry. I should have been paying closer attention, but they took me by surprise.'

'Don't blame yourself. They're well trained in that sort of thing. One of them was a woman?'

'Yes, one of the interrogators.'

'What were they like, the two who questioned you?'

'Oh, very proper. Nicely dressed. Trendy. He was wearing a dark silk suit and a fifty-quid haircut. Handsome in a Hugh Grantish sort of way. She wasn't exactly dressed by Primark, either. Blonde. Early thirties.'

'What did they want to know?'

'Why you came to see me yesterday.'

'What did you tell them?'

She blushed. 'Well, I said you were my boyfriend's father, and you were in town on business so you just dropped by to say hello. It was the best I could do on the spur of the moment.'

'What did they say to that?'

'They didn't believe me, so they asked all their questions again. I stuck to my story, and so blondie started threatening me with prosecution. When I asked what for, she said it didn't matter and they could shut down my business as easy as swatting a fly. Is that true, by the way?'

'Yes. They can do anything they want. But they won't. They've no reason to, and those things usually cause more trouble than they're worth.'

'Who are they?'

'Well, there's a question. These people are ruthless and powerful, make no mistake about it, but they won't harm you. You're no threat to them. They just want to know what you were up to, why I visited you.'

'How did they know?'

'They must have followed me. That's my fault. I'm sorry. I've been trying to be careful, but it's a crowded city. What were the other two doing while the man and woman were interviewing you?'

'Searching everything. They took some of my files. And my laptop. They said everything would be returned when they'd finished with it.'

'The Derek Wyman file?'

'Yes.'

'Were the photos in it?'

'Yes. I made copies. And my report.'

'Shit. Then it won't take them long to work out why I was here. I'm really sorry to bring all this down on you, Tomasina.'

'Forget it. It's all part of a day's work. But what will they do when they work out the truth?'

Banks thought for a moment. 'They'll probably put a tail on Derek Wyman now. Do a thorough background check, that sort of thing.'

'And me?'

'You were just a professional doing a job. They understand that.'

'But why are they doing all this?' Tomasina asked.

'I don't really know,' said Banks. 'But it's to do with the man in the photo. He was one of theirs. First they wanted to hush up what had happened, intimidate everyone involved into dropping the investigation. Now they're interested, though. And that's all I can tell you.'

'I see. At least I think I do.' She frowned. 'But let me get it straight. Mr Wyman hired me to take photos of a spy who met another spy in Regent's Park and went to a house in St John's Wood. Is Mr Wyman a spy, too?'

'No,' said Banks. 'At least, I don't think so.'

Neither spoke for a few moments; then Tomasina's stomach rumbled. 'I'm hungry,' she said. 'I think you owe me at least lunch for this.'

'Burger and chips?'

She squinted at him. 'Oh, I think you can do better than that. Bentley's isn't far, and it's early enough to get a table in the bar.'

BANKS'S WALLET was about £130 lighter when he walked out of Bentley's with his two companions later that Friday afternoon. But he had eaten the best fish and chips he had ever tasted, and it was worth every penny to see the smile on Tomasina's face when his son Brian had joined them for lunch.

Not only had he been available at a moment's notice—his girlfriend Emilia being away in Scotland filming—but he was also more than willing to share his father's company with a stranger in need. Or so Banks had put it when he called him from Tomasina's office. Tomasina had been tongue-tied at first, of course, but Brian's natural charm had worked its magic and they were soon all chatting away like old mates.

Now they stood outside the restaurant on Swallow Street between Regent Street and Piccadilly ready to go their own ways. If they were being watched, it was from a distance. The street was so short and narrow that Banks would have immediately spotted any suspicious activity.

'Sorry,' said Brian to Tomasina, 'but I must dash. It's been a pleasure to meet you.' He reached into his inside pocket. 'We're playing the Shepherd's Bush Empire next week, so here's a couple of comps and a backstage pass. Come and see us after the gig.'

Tomasina took the tickets. 'Thanks,' she said. 'That's great. I'll be there.'

'Look forward to it,' said Brian. 'Got to go now. See you later, Tom. See you, Dad.' He disappeared in the direction of Piccadilly Circus.

'Thank you so much,' said Tomasina to Banks. 'That was really nice.'

'Feeling better?'

'A lot. But I've had enough of the office for today. I'm going home.'

'Where's home?'

'Clapham. I'll get the tube from Piccadilly. Thank you again.'

Then she gave Banks a quick peck on the cheek and dashed off along Swallow Street, a spring in her step. How resilient are the young, Banks thought, as he walked up Regent Street towards Oxford Circus. Around Great Marlborough Street, the crowds of tourists got too thick, so he turned right to avoid Oxford Circus altogether. He wanted to call at Borders and HMV, anyway, before driving back up north. He was somewhere between Liberty and the Palladium when he heard an almighty explosion, and the pavement shook beneath him as if there had been an earthquake. High windows shattered, and glass and plaster fell into the street.

For a moment, the world seemed to stop, freeze frame. Then Banks became aware of people screaming and running past him, confused and terrified expressions on their faces. To his left, up the narrow side street, he could see a pall of black smoke mixed with dark orange flames. Alarms sounded everywhere. Without thinking, he ran up Argyll Street, against the panicking crowds, to Oxford Street. There he found himself in a scene of carnage that might have come straight out of the Blitz.

There were fires all over the place. The dark, thick smoke stung his eyes. It smelt of burnt plastic and rubber. Plaster dust filled the air. Broken glass crunched underfoot. At first, everything happened in slow motion. Banks was aware of sirens in the distance, but where he was, in the smoke, felt like a sort of island separated from the rest of the city. It was as if he had arrived at the still centre of darkness, the eye of the storm.

Wreckage lay everywhere: bits of cars; twisted bicycles; gaudy souvenirs and cheap luggage strewn over the road; a man lying halfway through his windscreen, still and bleeding. Then, out of it all, a figure stumbled towards Banks, an elderly Asian woman in a bright-coloured sari. Her nose was gone and blood streamed from her eyes.

'Help me!' she cried. 'Help me! I can't see! I'm blind!'

Banks took her arm and tried to murmur words of comfort as she gripped onto him for dear life. Everywhere people were staggering about in the haze, their arms flailing like zombies in a horror film. Some were shouting, some screaming, and some were just lying, moaning in pain. He stumbled on and tripped over a leg. It wasn't attached to a body. After he had got the Asian woman out of the smoke and sat her down on the pavement to wait until help came, he picked his way back through the wreckage. He found a disorientated boy of about ten or eleven and half dragged him away to where he had left the Asian woman. Then he went back and guided the next person he saw out of the carnage.

He didn't know how long he went on doing this, taking people by the arm and leading them to the edge of Oxford Circus, where the air was still full of the stink of burning plastic but was at least breathable.

A burning taxi lay on its side and a pretty young blonde in a bloodstained yellow sundress was trying to climb out of the window. Banks went to help her. She held a Selfridges bag, which was almost too big to get through the window. She got out, but she wouldn't let go of the bag handle. Banks feared the taxi might explode at any moment. In the end, she pulled the bag free and tottered back into Banks's arms on her high heels. It took him only a quick glance to see that the driver was dead. The woman clung to Banks as they edged their way towards the cleaner air. He left her sitting by the roadside crying, and went back.

The next thing he knew the area was full of dark shapes in protective gear, wearing breathing equipment with oxygen tanks strapped to their backs, some of them carrying submachine guns. Someone was calling over a loudspeaker for everyone to evacuate the area. Banks carried on searching for survivors until a hand rested on his shoulder and pulled him away.

'Best get out of here, mate, and leave it to us,' said the voice, muffled by breathing apparatus. 'One of the cars might go up any moment.'

The strong, steady hand guided him gently but firmly round the corner to Regent Street. 'Are you all right?' the man asked him.

'I'm OK,' said Banks. 'I'm a policeman. I can help.' He reached for his warrant card, and the man had a good look at it.

'There's nothing you can do without the right equipment. It's too dangerous,' the man said, guiding him away. 'Did you see what happened?'

'No,' said Banks. 'I was in Great Marlborough Street. I heard the explosion and came up to see if I could help.'

'Leave it to the pros now, mate.'

Down Regent Street, Banks could see the massed fire engines, police cars, ambulances and armed response vehicles, and the street swarmed with uniforms. The area was cordoned off as far as Conduit Street.

Banks walked on through the crowds, back the way he had come he couldn't say how long ago. The emergency rescue worker had been right; there was nothing more he could do. He would only get in the way.

He didn't know where he was going now, or care, only that he was moving away from the carnage and chaos. His breathing had almost returned to normal, but his eyes still stung. People gawped at him as he passed, everyone aware now that something serious had happened nearby, even if they hadn't seen it themselves.

When Banks got past Piccadilly Circus, he knew what he wanted. A bloody drink. Or two. He made his way up Shaftesbury Avenue, turned into Soho and tottered into an old pub on Dean Street.

'Jesus Christ,' the barman said. 'What happened to you, mate? You look like you've just . . . Oh, bloody hell. You have, haven't you?'

Other people looked away from the TV screen, which showed images of the carnage around Oxford Circus, and glanced at Banks. He nodded.

'Whatever you want, mate, it's on the house,' said the barman.

Banks wanted two things. He wanted a pint to slake his thirst and a double brandy to steady his nerves. He said he'd pay for one of them but the barman wouldn't have any of it.

'If I was you, mate,' the barman said, 'I'd pay a quick visit to the Gents first. It's just behind you. You'll feel better if you clean yourself up a bit.'

Banks took a quick gulp of beer, then pushed open the wooden door of the Gents. One look in the mirror was enough. His face was smudged black with smoke; his eyes were two staring holes in the darkness. The front of his white shirt was burnt and smeared with blood and God knows what else. Luckily his navy windcheater wasn't too bad. He gave his face and hands a good wash and tried to cover up his shirt by zipping up his jacket.

'That's better, mate,' the barman said when he returned.

Banks thanked him and drained his pint. When he put his glass down, he started working, more slowly, on the brandy.

'Suicide car bomber, they think,' the barman said. 'Bastards.'

'How many injured?' Banks asked.

'They don't know for sure yet. Twenty-four dead and about the same seriously injured is the latest count. You *were* there, weren't you?'

'I was.'

'What was it like?'

Banks took a sip of brandy.

'Sorry. I should know better than to ask,' said the barman. 'I've seen my share. Ex-para. Northern Ireland. For my sins.' He stuck out his hand. 'Joe Geldard's the name, by the way.'

Banks shook hands. 'Good to meet you, Joe Geldard,' he said. 'Alan Banks. And thank you for everything.'

'It's nothing, mate. How you feeling?'

Banks drank some more brandy. He noticed that his hand was still shaking. His left hand was slightly burnt, he saw, but he couldn't feel any pain yet. 'Much better for this,' he said, hoisting his glass. 'I'll be all right.'

Joe Geldard moved to the end of the bar to keep an eye on the TV with the rest. Banks was left alone. He thought about Brian and Tomasina. They would be fine. Both were taking the underground from Piccadilly Circus. It entered his head that they might be worried about him, too.

And Sophia? Christ, she often worked at Western House, up Great Portland Street, unless she was at another studio or out somewhere producing live interviews. She might have wandered down to Oxford Street to go shopping on her lunch break. She never did, though, Banks remembered. Said she hated it, with all the tourists. He'd phone her, though, not least because he wanted a chance to put things right between them.

A wave of nausea came over him and he took a gulp of brandy. It made him cough, but it helped. When he glanced in the mirror behind the range of spirits and wine bottles, he hardly recognised the face that stared back at him. It was time to make a move.

His car was parked at the hotel, but he didn't want to drive back to Eastvale, he realised. He would buy new clothes, then take a train home and come back for the car when he felt better.

Then he realised that all the underground and mainline stations would probably be closed for a while, so he wouldn't be going anywhere yet. The alcohol was slowly calming him down and blotting out some of the horrors of the last hour, so he called out for another pint and told Joe Geldard to have one on him.

Chapter Eleven

Annie wondered why Banks wanted her to drive out to his Gratly cottage early on Saturday morning. She had assumed that he would be staying in London with Sophia, at least for the weekend, but obviously not.

All her attempts to phone him the previous evening had been frustrated, as he had been unable or unwilling to answer either mobile. After work, she had simply gone home and watched in horror the events unfold on television after the Oxford Circus bombing. Anti-terrorist units were already on the move in Dewsbury, Birmingham and Leicester; three people had been arrested and one London mosque raided. Al-Qaeda had already claimed responsibility.

Still, it was a lovely morning for a drive into the dale, she thought, putting the news images aside. The Leas lay spread out to her right, flat wetlands around the River Swain, which meandered slowly through the meadows of buttercups, cranesbill and clover. She had her window rolled down and a Steely Dan greatest-hits CD playing on the stereo. Banks probably wouldn't approve, but she didn't give a damn.

Winsome had caught a break on the East Side Estate business when one of the local thugs had let slip that there was a new player on the block, 'an Albanian or Turk or something', just up from London, and all the kids who had previously had free rein in what petty dealing of drugs went on were now expected to work for him, or . . . perhaps get stabbed. There were also rumours that the newcomer, who went by the name of 'the Bull', had connections and was planning on importing heroin into Eastvale in a big way. Catching the Bull would definitely be a feather in their caps.

Annie drove along Helmthorpe High Street, past the church, and turned left up the hill to Gratly. She had never ceased to marvel at what an isolated and beautiful place Banks had chosen to live in after his marriage broke up. The renovations he had made after the fire had given him a lot more space, but it had all been tastefully carried out in the same local limestone, and the place probably didn't look much different from how it had when it was built—in 1768, according to the gritstone door head.

Banks answered her knock and took her through the living room into the kitchen. 'Coffee?' he asked.

'Please.' He knew how she liked his, Annie noted. Black and strong. He liked the same.

'Let's go out to the conservatory,' Banks said.

Annie followed him through the kitchen door. Honeyed sunlight poured in through the glass, and there was a breeze through the open windows. The view up the daleside to the limestone scar at the top, like a skeleton's grin, was stunning, and sheep were dotted all over the hillside. She sat on one of the deep wicker armchairs and set her coffee down on the low glass table beside the morning papers, which hadn't been touched yet. That wasn't like Banks. He wasn't so much of a news hound, but he liked to read the music and film reviews and grapple with the crosswords. Perhaps he had slept in.

'What time did you get back last night?' she asked.

'Late.'

He seemed more gaunt than usual, his bright blue eyes less full of sparkle. He also had a bandage on his left hand.

'What did you do to yourself?' she asked.

He lifted his hand. 'Oh, this? Burnt it on the frying pan. The doc always told me my diet would kill me. It's nothing. I was going to come back in to the station this morning, but I've changed my mind. That's why I asked you to come out here instead.'

'Because you hurt yourself?'

'What? No. I told you, this is nothing. It's something else.'

'What?'

'I'll tell you later.'

'OK,' Annie said lightly. '*Be* mysterious. See if I care. We've got a lead on the East Side Estate stabbing.' She told him about the Bull, but when she sensed his attention drifting, she said, 'What is it, Alan? Why am I here?'

'I thought we should talk about Wyman,' Banks said. 'We should consider bringing him in. Things are getting out of hand.'

Annie listened as Banks told her about Hardcastle tearing up the photos, and what had happened at Sophia's house on Thursday evening, and in Tomasina's office yesterday. When he'd finished, all she could say was, 'You were down in London yesterday, weren't you? You can't have been far from Oxford Street when it happened.'

'Just down Regent Street,' he said. 'They closed all the stations for about four hours. That's why I was so late back.'

'Why didn't you stay with Sophia?' she asked.

'She's with a friend.' Banks stared at Annie, and she thought for a moment that he was going to tell her to mind her own business. Then he said, 'As a matter of fact, she didn't want me around. She sort of blamed me for what happened, for not setting the alarm. I did, but she wouldn't believe me.'

'So did you tell Sophia the truth, who you think it was?'

'No. What's the point in frightening her? Besides, they won't hurt her. Or Tomasina. They could have done that any time, if they'd wanted to. Me, too. No, they've delivered their message and that's all they wanted to do. For now. They're just trying to scare us off. That's why it's time to bring Wyman in.'

'But they *haven't* scared you off. Me neither, for that matter.'

Banks managed the beginnings of a smile. 'What did you find out?'

'A couple of interesting things.' Annie told him about her talk with Carol Wyman.

When she had finished, Banks said, 'This business with Rick Wyman is interesting. SAS, indeed. You know where they get their orders from, don't you? MI6, I'll bet. This could be the link between Wyman and Silbert's world. What if Wyman thinks Silbert was responsible for his brother's death? What if he was? What if it's something MI6 want to cover up?'

'They'll do everything in their power to prevent you from uncovering it.' Annie reached for her coffee. 'Besides, just how do you plan on finding out?'

'Before you arrived,' Banks said, 'I got a return phone call from a Detective Superintendent Burgess. Dirty Dick Burgess.'

'I remember him,' said Annie. 'He's a sexist, racist, homophobic pig who thinks he's God's gift.'

'That's the one,' Banks admitted. 'I'd been trying to reach him for a couple of days, leaving cryptic messages. I thought I hadn't heard back from him because I'm *persona non grata* with his bosses. As it happens, I am, and he knows it, but that wasn't the reason. He's not in London at the moment; he's in Dewsbury.'

'Dewsbury,' Annie echoed. 'But isn't that where . . .?'

'One of the bombers, or planners, lived. Yes, I know. And that's probably why he's there. The point is, he's agreed to meet me.'

'Where? When?'

'This morning, up at Hallam Tarn. It might be our only chance of finding a link between Wyman and Silbert. 'I know you still think Hardcastle was the intended victim and professional jealousy was the motive, and you could be right. But bear with me a while longer.' Banks reached for a pen and notepad from the bookcase beside him. 'Have you got any more details about Rick Wyman?'

Annie told him all she knew, which wasn't much.

'Should be able to track him down from that,' Banks said. 'You're sure about the date of the incident? October the 15th, 2002?'

'That's what Carol Wyman told me. But what's next? If they're on to Wyman, as you say they must be now after ransacking this Tom Savage's files, isn't he in danger?'

'It depends how much of a threat he is to them. But yes, I agree, we need to act fairly quickly, bring him in and get to the bottom of it.'

'We need to talk to the super first.'

'Can you do that?' Banks asked.

'Me? Jesus Christ, Alan!'

'Please?' Banks glanced at his watch. 'I have to meet Burgess soon, and I don't think we should waste any more time.'

'But . . . I . . .'

'Come on, Annie. She knows you've been on the case, doesn't she? Just present her with the evidence. Stress the theatre business and play down the intelligence-service angle. That's the only thing that really worries her. She'll go for it otherwise.'

'All right, all right,' Annie said, standing up to leave. 'I'll have a go.'

'I'll be in later. I'll phone for a driver when I'm ready. Bring Wyman in after you've talked to Gervaise and let him stew for a while.'

'On what charge?'

'You don't have to charge him; just ask him to come along voluntarily.'

'What if he won't?'

'Then bloody arrest him.'

'For what?'

'Try for being a lying bastard, for a start.'

'If only . . .'

'Just bring him in, Annie. It might get us a few answers.'

WHEN HE WAS ALONE again, Banks poured himself the last cup of coffee. It was almost time to go out now and, tired as he was, this was an appointment he didn't want to miss. Wondering why he bothered with security, he locked up the cottage and struck out up Tetchley Fell to Hallam Tarn.

He hadn't slept a wink the previous night; his mind had been full of the scenes he'd witnessed at Oxford Circus, and he could still smell burning flesh and plastic. Certain images, he knew, would be lodged in his mind for ever.

After he had left Joe Geldard's pub, he had bought new clothes in a Marks & Spencer's and made his way on foot through the Bloomsbury backstreets to King's Cross Station. It was after five o'clock when he got to the station, and service was still suspended. Crowds of people milled around the announcement boards, ready for the dash when their gate was announced.

While he waited, Banks phoned Brian and Tomasina, who were both fine, though shaken at having been so close to disaster. He also phoned Sophia at home and got no answer, as expected. He left a message asking her to pick up his car from the hotel and said he hoped she was all right. He wasn't going to tell anyone about his afternoon—not now, probably never.

As luck would have it, the first train to the north left the station at 6.35, and Banks was on it. He stared out of the window for the whole journey, without a book or even his iPod to take his mind off the memories. He wouldn't have been able to concentrate on words or music anyway.

He had taken a taxi home from Darlington, which had cost a fortune. All in all, it had been an expensive day, what with the hotel bill, lunch, new clothes and train ticket. Thank God everyone took plastic, he thought.

When he got home, Banks had poured himself a generous glass of red wine and sat down in front of an old Marx Brothers movie to distract himself. He realised that he didn't feel sad or angry or depressed. Perhaps that would come later. What had happened that day had taken him to a new place inside himself, a place he didn't know. His world had changed, its axis shifted. It was the difference between knowing these things happened, watching them happen to other people on television, and being there, in the thick of it, seeing the suffering and knowing there's very little that you can do.

Yet for all the fear and sorrow, he also felt a deep calm, a sense of inevitability and of letting go that surprised him. It was like the walk he was on now. There was something simple and soothing about putting one foot in front of the other and making slow progress up Tetchley Fell. The sun shone in a bright blue sky, but a light breeze to take the edge off the heat. Even so, Banks was panting and sweating when he reached the top of the hill. Now he only had to totter down the other side of a steep bank to get to Hallam Tarn. It was nothing much, just a hollowed-out bowl of water about a hundred yards wide and two hundred long, with a path around the tarn offering a scenic walk. Five or six cars were parked in the space at the far end where the road up from Helmthorpe came to a full stop at the water's edge.

As Banks reached the car park, he saw the familiar figure of Detective Superintendent Dirty Dick Burgess standing at the water's edge.

When he caught sight of Banks, Burgess clapped his hands and rubbed them together. 'Banksy,' he said. 'Who's been a naughty boy, then?'

IT WAS TYPICAL that Banks would give her the job of talking to Gervaise, Annie thought, as she pulled up outside the superintendent's house later that morning. Gervaise had been a tad tetchy on the phone—her husband had taken the children to the cricket, and it was her gardening day, she said—but had agreed to give Annie five minutes of her time.

When Annie knocked on the door, she heard a voice call, 'I'm round the back. Just come down the side.'

A narrow path ran down the side of the house to the back garden, where the superintendent stood in a broad-brimmed hat, baggy man's shirt, white shorts and sandals, with a pair of secateurs in her hand. There were four chairs and a round table on the lawn.

'Sit down, DI Cabbot,' said Gervaise. 'Barley water?'

'Thank you.' Annie accepted the glass, sat down and took a sip.

'Have you thought about blonde highlights?' Gervaise asked.

'No, ma'am.'

'Maybe you should. They'd look good in the sunlight.'

What was all this? Annie wondered. First Carol Wyman had suggested she go blonde, now Gervaise was talking about highlights.

Gervaise sat down. 'So what have you come to see me about, DI Cabbot?'

Annie shifted in her chair. 'Well, ma'am, you know we were talking, the other day, about Derek Wyman?'

'You mean Banks's Iago theory?'

'Yes. Well, what if there's something in it? I mean, *really* something in it.'

'Like what?' asked Gervaise.

'Well, I was talking to Mr Wyman's wife, Carol, and she—'

'I thought I told you to leave them alone. It's over.'

Annie took a deep breath and blurted out, 'I'd like to bring Derek Wyman in for questioning.'

Gervaise's silence was unnerving. A wasp droned near her barley water. Finally, the superintendent said, 'You? Or DCI Banks?'

'Both of us.' Now that Annie had said it, she was gathering courage fast. 'I know you've been warned to lay off,' she went on, 'but there's evidence now. And it has nothing to do with the intelligence services.'

'Oh, really?'

'Yes. DCI Banks found the private investigator who took the photos of Silbert with the other man.'

'A *private investigator*?'

'Yes. He also talked to a waitress in Zizzi's who remembered seeing a man we assume to be Hardcastle tearing up some photos.'

'Assume?'

'Well, Wyman did tell us he'd had dinner at Zizzi's with Hardcastle before going to the National Film Theatre. And he commissioned the photos.'

'But why?'

'To stir up Hardcastle.'

'Or so you assume?'

'Why else would he go to all that expense? He wasn't a rich man.'

'Why would he want to do it in the first place? He didn't even know Silbert very well, did he?'

'Not well. No. They'd met once or twice, had dinner, but no, he didn't really know Silbert. The target was Hardcastle, I think, but when you set things like that in motion, you can't always predict their outcome.'

'I'll say. Do go on.'

'I gather from talking to Carol Wyman that her husband's sick of his teaching job and he's got a passion for theatre. If Hardcastle and Silbert had succeeded in setting up their acting company, there'd have been no room for Wyman. Hardcastle himself wanted to direct. Wyman would have been back at square one. That kind of humiliation can really hurt a man's pride.'

'And you're saying that's Wyman's motive for killing two men?'

'I don't think he intended to kill anyone. It was just a nasty prank that went wrong. What he really wanted was to split up Hardcastle and Silbert so that Hardcastle would leave Eastvale and abandon the theatre.'

'It still sounds a bit far-fetched,' said Gervaise. 'And correct me if I'm wrong, but I don't see what crime has been committed.'

'Even if he hadn't anticipated the outcome, Wyman may have incited Hardcastle to do what he did, harassing him with images and innuendoes the way Iago harassed Othello.'

'I suppose there's a certain low-level plausibility to it all,' Gervaise admitted. 'But even so, we'd never prove it in a million years.'

'Unless Wyman confessed.'

'Why would he do that?'

'Guilt. If he didn't mean to really hurt anyone, what happened must be a burden for him. I'll bet it's weighing on his mind.'

'All right, DI Cabbot,' said Gervaise. 'Let's accept that Wyman did cook up some scheme to get at Hardcastle, and that it backfired. Can you guarantee that this was nothing at all to do with the intelligence services?'

Banks was right, Annie thought. With the intelligence services out of the picture, Gervaise was more willing to go along with the idea. 'Yes,' she said.

Gervaise sighed, took off her hat and used it as a fan for a moment. 'Hmph. Do you know how much pressure I've had from above to drop this?

The chief constable is adamant. I don't want this on my plate. Bring in Wyman, by all means. Have a chat with him. And if he admits anything that supports your theories, send the file to the CPS and see if they can come up with a criminal offence to charge him with. Just make damn sure that there's no room here for things to go pear-shaped.'

'Yes, ma'am,' said Annie, draining her glass and standing up before Gervaise changed her mind. 'I'll do that.'

'Where *is* DCI Banks, by the way?'

'He's finishing his holiday at home,' said Annie.

'Things not work out in London?'

'I suppose not.'

'Well, let's hope they improve. The last thing I want is a lovesick DCI moping about the station. Go on, then. Get to it. I've got to get back to my herbaceous border before Keith and the kids get back wanting their dinner.'

'THIS IS A BLOODY godforsaken hole you've chosen for a meeting place,' said Burgess as they walked around the scenic footpath.

'It's supposed to be a spot of great natural beauty,' said Banks.

'You know me. I'm a city boy at heart. I have to tell you, though, Banksy, Dewsbury is a boil on the arse of the universe. You know, two of the young lads involved in planning yesterday's bombing live there. Twenty-two years old, the kid who actually did it. Bright lad, by all accounts. Islamic studies degree from Keele. And he drives two hundred miles wearing an explosive suit wired to a bootful of explosives, knowing he's going to die at the end of it. The score's forty virgins for him, forty-six dead, fifty-eight injured, and seventy-three orphans for London.' Burgess paused. 'I counted. Do you know, when they raided one of the flats, they found plans for similar attacks on Piccadilly Circus, Trafalgar Square and the front of Buck House?'

Banks said nothing.

'Hang on a minute, you were in London yesterday, weren't you?'

'Yes,' Banks said.

'Were you anywhere near? You were, weren't you?'

'I was there,' Banks said. He hadn't planned on telling anyone, but Burgess always had an uncanny knack of knowing these things anyway.

Burgess stopped and stared out over the water. Its surface was ruffled by the light breeze. 'Bugger me,' he said. 'I won't ask you . . .'

'No,' said Banks. 'Don't. Thanks. I don't really want to talk about it.' He could feel a lump in his throat and tears prickling in his eyes, but the sensations passed. They continued walking.

'Anyway,' Burgess went on, 'what is it you want to see me about?'

Banks told him what he knew about Wyman, Hardcastle and Silbert, along with what had happened at Sophia's house and Tomasina's office.

Burgess listened as they walked, and when Banks had finished he said, 'No wonder you're red-flagged.'

'It's not just me,' Banks said. 'If it were only me, I could deal with it. They go after your loved ones as well.'

'Well, the terrorists don't discriminate either. These are interesting times, Banks. Bad things happen. There's a darkness out there. You should know.'

'Yes, and the struggle is to *keep* it out there.'

'That's too metaphysical for me. I just catch the bad guys.'

'So you're defending their actions? I mean MI5. What they did in Sophia's house, Tomasina's office?'

'What makes you think it was MI5? Silbert worked for MI6. The two don't exactly work hand in glove, you know. Half the time they're not even talking to each other.'

'So you think MI6 are more likely to be involved in this than MI5?'

'I'm only saying that it's possible. I'm on a wholly different detachment. I don't know those people.'

'But I thought MI6's brief was working *outside* the country?'

'It is. Usually. But I'd imagine they'd want to investigate the murder of one of their own. Can we stop for a minute?' Burgess sat down on a bench. Banks joined him. 'But why didn't they come directly after me?'

'Well, they did, didn't they? This Mr Browne you told me about.'

'He came once, got pissed off when I wouldn't cooperate, and left.'

Burgess started to laugh. 'Oh, Banksy, you're priceless, you are. Did you expect more? Another polite visit, perhaps? "Please, Mr Banks, do cease and desist." They don't mess around, these buggers—5 or 6. This is the new breed. They're a lot nastier than the old boys and they've got a lot of new toys. They can erase your past and rewrite your life in the blink of an eye. I tell you in all seriousness, Banksy, do not piss them off.'

'A bit late for that, isn't it?'

'Then back off. They'll lose interest in time.' He paused. 'I did talk to someone in the know after I got your message, to see if I could find out what was going on. He was very cagey, but he told me a couple of things. For a start, they're not sure about Wyman, and they don't like to be not sure.'

'Why haven't they questioned him?'

'Surely you can work that out for yourself? First of all, they tried to warn you off. They wanted you to shut down the investigation. But when they get the photos from the private detective woman they start wondering about Wyman. What he might have been up to. Who he might have been working for. What he might know. And more important still, what he might *tell*. Now they're letting you do their job for them, watching you from a distance. You could still just let it drop and walk away. Nothing will happen to you or your girlfriend. There's nothing to be gained by antagonising them any further.'

'But there are still a few things I need to know.'

Burgess sighed. 'It's like talking to a brick wall, isn't it?' he said.

'Wyman had a brother called Rick,' Banks went on. 'SAS. He was killed in Afghanistan on October the 15th, 2002. According to the press it was a helicopter crash on manoeuvres, but according to other sources, Rick Wyman was killed on active duty, on a secret mission.'

'So what? It's standard procedure to downplay your casualties in a war.'

'What concerns me,' said Banks, 'is that Silbert might have had something to do with the intelligence behind the mission. Maybe Wyman *blames* Silbert. I need to know when Silbert was in Afghanistan and why.'

'Even if Silbert was responsible for Rick Wyman's death, how on earth could Derek Wyman know about it if it was a secret mission?'

'I don't know. Pillow talk? Silbert lets something slip to Hardcastle in bed after one of those dinners, and Hardcastle passes it on.'

'Crap. Silbert and his kind are better trained than that. What you're asking could possibly bring a whole lot of grief on the intelligence services, including me, who really don't need that right now, thank you very much.'

'Look, Derek Wyman set in motion a chain of events that ended in the violent deaths of two men. I want to know why he did it.'

'Why does it matter? Why don't you just beat a confession out of him and leave it at that?'

'Because I want to know what it takes to drive a man to a cold-blooded act like that. Can't you understand that?'

'Well, seeing as you put it like that, Banksy, how can I refuse?'

'You'll do it?'

'I was joking. Look, it's easy enough to find out about Silbert's background, in general terms, but it might be harder to find any connection with a specific mission. I think the best I can do for you is find out if Silbert was working in an area and in a capacity that made it at all likely he could have a connection with SAS missions in Afghanistan in 2002. That shouldn't be too highly classified. Will that do you?'

'It'll have to, won't it?'

'Is your phone safe?'

'It's a pay-as-you-go.'

'How long have you had it?'

'Week or so.'

'Get rid of it as soon as you hear from me. I mean it.' Then, muttering, 'I must be a bloody lunatic,' under his breath, he got up and walked back to his car, leaving Banks to sit alone on the bench in the sun.

Chapter Twelve

'What's this all about?' Derek Wyman asked Banks after Annie had picked him up and kept him waiting in the interview room for an hour. 'I have to be at the theatre. I've got a play to direct.'

'They'll manage without you,' said Banks. 'They did before, when you were in London. And we'll try not to keep you too long.'

'Are you charging me? Do I need a solicitor or anything?'

'You're not under arrest. You're not being charged with anything. You can leave at any time. You're here simply to answer a few questions. I should also tell you that you do not have to say anything, but it might harm your defence if you do not mention, when questioned, something you later rely on in court. Anything you do say may be given in evidence.'

'My *defence*? In *court*?'

'It's a formal caution, Mr Wyman. Standard procedure. To protect all of us. As for the solicitor, that's up to you. Do you think you need one? You're certainly entitled, if you think it would help, in which case you can either drag your own solicitor off the golf course, if you have one, or one will be provided for you.'

'But I haven't done anything.'

'Nobody's saying you have.'

Wyman chewed on his bottom lip for a few moments, then he said, 'OK. I'll answer your questions. I've got nothing to hide.'

'Good,' said Banks. 'Shall we start now?'

Wyman folded his arms. 'All right.' He looked stiff, tense.

Banks gave Annie the signal to begin the questioning. 'How would you characterise your relationship with Mark Hardcastle?' she asked.

'I don't know, really. I didn't have one. Not in the way you mean.'

'Oh? What way do I mean?'

'Don't think I'm not aware of the subtle insinuation behind what you say. I direct plays. I know all about subtle insinuations.'

'I'm sure you do,' Annie said, 'but actually I wasn't insinuating anything. I was being quite straightforward. You say you didn't really have a relationship, but you were friends, weren't you?'

'Colleagues, really, more than friends.'

'But you went for a social drink every now and then, didn't you? And you had Mark Hardcastle and his partner, Laurence Silbert, over for dinner with your family. You also went with your wife, Carol, to their house in Castleview Heights once. Isn't that correct?'

'Yes. You know it is. I'm not prejudiced about people being gay.'

'So why do you constantly play the whole relationship down? Is there something you're not telling us?'

'Not. Everything is just as I said it was.'

'But it *was* more than just a working relationship, wasn't it?' Annie went on. 'Not only did you go to London with Mark Hardcastle, you went drinking with him on several occasions in the Red Rooster. We just want to know why you didn't tell us about that earlier, when we first questioned you.'

'I didn't think it was important where we went for a drink, that's all.'

'And perhaps you didn't want to get involved?' Annie suggested. 'I mean, people often want to distance themselves from a murder investigation. It does get rather dirty and that dirt can sometimes rub off.'

'Murder? Who said anything about murder?' Wyman seemed flustered.

'Laurence Silbert was certainly murdered,' said Annie, 'and we do believe that someone engineered the argument between him and Hardcastle. Perhaps they only expected a falling-out, but even that's nasty, isn't it?'

'Maybe. But I don't know anything about it.'

'Remember, Mr Wyman. If you don't tell us something now that you later rely on, it could go badly for you. This is your chance for a clean slate.'

'I've told you all I know.'

'What were those drinks in the Red Rooster all about? It's hardly a place for sophisticated men of the world like you and Mark Hardcastle to hang out. Why there? Was it the karaoke? Fancy yourself as the new Robbie Williams?'

'There was no karaoke when we were there. And they do a decent pint.'

'The beer's rubbish,' said Banks. 'Don't expect us to believe that's why you went there.'

Wyman looked imploringly at Annie, as if she were his lifeline.

'What happened there, Derek?' she asked gently. 'Go on, you can tell us. We heard that Mark was upset by something you said and you were calming him down. What was it all about?'

Wyman folded his arms again. 'Nothing. I don't remember.'

'This isn't working,' said Banks. 'I think we'd better move on to a more official legal footing.'

'What do you mean?' Wyman asked, glancing from one to the other.

'DCI Banks is impatient, that's all,' Annie said. 'We just hoped this informal chat would resolve our problems. We don't want to move on to matters of detention, home searches or anything like that yet.'

'You can't intimidate me,' Wyman said. 'I know my rights.'

'Was it about work?' Annie asked. 'Your discussion in the Red Rooster.'

'It might have been. That's what we usually talked about.'

'I understand that you were a bit upset about Mark wanting to direct plays himself and to start up a professional acting troupe at Eastvale Theatre,' Annie said. 'That you thought it would threaten your position as director.'

'Mark Hardcastle couldn't direct his way out of a paper bag.'

'But he was the up-and-coming star,' Banks said. 'He had big ideas. As artistic director he would have put the Eastvale Theatre on the map. You're just a schoolteacher moonlighting as a director. No contest.'

Wyman squirmed in his chair. 'I don't know where this is leading, but—'

'Then let me show you,' said Banks. 'DI Cabbot might want to go gently with you, but I've had enough pissing about.' He took some photographs from an envelope in front of him and slipped them across the table.

'What are these?' Wyman asked, glancing down at them.

'Surely you recognise Laurence Silbert?'

'It could be him. It's not a very good photo.'

'Bollocks, Derek. It's a perfectly good photo. Who took it?'

'How should I know?'

Banks leaned forward and rested his arms on the table. 'I'll tell you how you should know,' he said. 'These photos were taken by a young private detective called Tomasina Savage. On your instructions.'

'That's privileged! That was a private . . . It . . . You can't . . .'

'Privileged? You've been watching too many American cop shows,' Banks said. 'Why did you employ Savage to follow Laurence Silbert and take those photographs? We know you gave them to Mark at Zizzi's and he tore them up as soon as he saw them, but he kept the memory stick. Did he really go to the cinema with you after that? Or was that a lie?'

'May I have some water?'

Annie poured him a glass from the pitcher on the table.

'Why did you pay Savage to take those photographs?' Banks repeated.

Wyman sipped his water. For a moment he said nothing, seemed to be coming to a decision. Then he said, 'Because Mark asked me to. That's why. But as God is my witness, it was not my intention that anyone should die.'

WINSOME WAS GETTING sick and tired of traipsing around the East Side Estate with Harry Potter by six o'clock on Saturday evening. But at least they were getting close to finding the Bull.

So far, they had discovered that one of Jackie Binns's recent recruits, Andy Pash, a fifteen-year-old wannabe trying to ingratiate himself with the rest of the gang, had told the Bull that Donny Moore had called him a big ugly Arab bastard and said he was going to get what was coming to him. Apparently, Moore had said nothing of the kind—he was neither stupid nor suicidal—but the Bull believed that he had and had gone after him. Nobody had actually witnessed the stabbing—or so everyone said—but they all knew who did it, and someone had eventually let the name slip.

Pash lived with his mother and two sisters on one of the nicer streets on the estate. The woman who answered the door, a bleached blonde wearing a micro skirt and too much make-up, turned out to be his mother, Kath. If she was surprised to find a six-foot-plus black woman and a detective constable who resembled Harry Potter at her door at just after six on a Saturday evening asking to talk to her son, she didn't show it.

'He's up in his room,' she said. 'Can't you hear the bloody racket? And I'm off out.'

'You should be present while we question him,' Winsome said.

'Why? He's a big boy. Help yourselves. And close the door behind you.'

She brushed past them. Winsome and Doug Wilson exchanged glances.

'Did she just give us permission?' Wilson asked.

'I think so,' said Winsome, stepping inside.

In the living room, a young girl of about thirteen lounged on the sofa, watching *The Simpsons*. She had just lit a cigarette.

'Hey, you're too young to be smoking,' said Winsome.

The girl jumped. The television was so loud that she hadn't even noticed them enter. 'Who the fuck are you?' she said. 'I'll call the cops.'

'No need, love, we're already here.' Winsome showed her warrant card. 'And mind your language,' she said. 'Now put that cigarette out.'

The girl glared at her, but dropped her cigarette into a half-empty mug on the coffee table, where it sizzled and went out.

It was a small victory, Winsome knew, and as soon as they were out of the way the child would light up again, but of such small victories the war is sometimes won. 'We're off up to see your brother,' she said.

'Lucky you,' said the young smoker, turning back to the TV.

Winsome and Wilson climbed the stairs. The noise was coming from the second door on the right, but before they could knock, the door across the landing opened and another girl peered out at them. She was younger than her sister, perhaps about nine or ten. She was holding a book in her hand.

'Who are you?' she asked, looking at them with curiosity.

Winsome squatted so she was at eye level with her. 'My name's Winsome Jackman. I'm a policewoman. And this is Doug. What's your name?'

'Winsome's a nice name. I've never heard it before. I'm Scarlett.'

'We've come to see your brother.'

'Oh,' said Scarlett, as if it were an everyday occurrence.

'What are you reading?' Winsome asked.

The girl clutched the book to her chest as if she feared someone was going to steal it from her. '*Wuthering Heights*.'

'I read that at school,' said Winsome. 'It's good, isn't it?'

'It's *wonderful*! I've read *Jane Eyre*, too!' said Scarlett proudly. 'But sometimes it's just so noisy it's hard to follow the words. I wish Andy didn't play his music so loud.'

'We'll see what we can do,' Winsome said. 'See you later, Scarlett.'

'Bye-bye.' Scarlett shut her bedroom door.

After a swift tap, Winsome opened Andy Pash's door and walked in.

'Hey,' said Pash, getting up from his unmade bed. 'What's all this? Who the fuck do you think you are?'

'Police,' said Winsome, flashing her card. 'Your mother let us in. Said we could ask you a few questions. Do you want to turn that music off?'

Glumly, Andy Pash turned off the music. The first thing Winsome noticed, glancing around, were the bookcases against one wall—or, more specifically, the rows of traffic cones that stood on them, painted different colours.

'Quite the artist, I see, Andy,' said Winsome.

'Oh, that . . . yeah, well . . .'

'I suppose you know what you've done is theft?'

'They're just traffic cones, for fuck's sake. It was just a lark.'

'Glad you can see the funny side of it. And don't swear when I'm around.'

Pash peered at Wilson. 'Anyone ever tell you that you look like—?'

'Shut up,' said Wilson, pointing a finger at him. 'Just shut right up.'

Pash held his hands up. 'All right. OK. It's cool, man. Whatever.'

'Andy,' said Winsome, 'have you ever heard of a bloke in the neighbourhood called the Bull?'

'The Bull? Yeah. He's a cool dude.'

American television had a lot to answer for, Winsome thought. 'Know what his real name is?' she asked.

'No. I think it might be Torgi or Tory or something like that, some sort of Arab or Turkish name. But everyone calls him the Bull. He's a big guy.'

'Andy, did you tell the Bull that Donny Moore, Nicky Haskell's right-hand man, had called him an ugly Arab bastard?'

'Donny Moore is mental. He deserved everything he got.'

'He deserved to get stabbed, did he?'

'Dunno.'

'Do you know who did that to him, Andy?'

'No idea. Not one of us.'

'What did you have to do to become a member of Jackie's crew?'

'Whaddya mean?'

'You know what I mean, Andy. Usually you have to perform some sort of task, prove your courage, before you can be accepted into a gang. What did Jackie Binns ask you to do to become a member of his gang?'

'He didn't ask me nothing.'

'You're lying, Andy.'

Pash turned away and stared sulkily at the wall. For all his surface bravado, Winsome thought, he was just a confused and scared kid.

'OK,' Pash said. 'OK. Nicky and Jackie, they never got along, right? Then along comes the Bull, and he's, like, bigger than both of them. Jackie thought maybe it would be a good idea to set them against each other, so, yeah, he said I should tell the Bull that Donny had badmouthed him. But I never saw anything. I don't know who stabbed Donny.'

'Does the Bull carry a knife?'

'The Bull got a blade, yeah.'

'What's his address, Andy? Where does the Bull live?'

'I don't know no address. But he lives in the flats. Hague House. Second floor. It's got a green door, the only one there with a green door. Side facing the castle. But don't tell him I sent you.'

'Don't worry. I wouldn't think of it. But first, I'd like you to come down to the station so we can get down what you've told us all nice and legal.'

'Do I have to?'

'Well, let me put it this way,' said Winsome. 'Right now, I'm inclined to be lenient about the traffic cones, but if you start giving us any trouble, I'll arrest you for being in possession of stolen property. Is that clear enough?'

Pash didn't say anything. He just grabbed his jacket from the floor and followed Wilson downstairs.

'Think of it like this,' Winsome said. 'It'll give your little sister a bit of peace and quiet to read *Wuthering Heights*.'

'NOW LET ME GET THIS STRAIGHT,' Banks said to Derek Wyman in the hot and stuffy interview room. 'You're telling us now that Mark Hardcastle asked you to spy on his lover, Laurence Silbert, because he suspected that Silbert was cheating on him, right?'

'That's right,' said Wyman.

'Why not do it himself?'

'He didn't want to be seen.'

'Why did you hire Tomasina Savage?'

'Because I simply couldn't get down to London on every occasion Laurence went there. And he knew me, too. There was always a chance he might spot me. I just looked in the Yellow Pages and liked the name.'

'And those conversations with Mark in the Red Rooster?'

'It was somewhere out of the way, that's all. I didn't know the kids from school had started to drink there. Mark was telling me all about his suspicions. No wonder he seemed upset. He was. He loved Laurence.'

'So you just helped Mark in this out of the goodness of your heart?'

'Well, yes.'

'Without any idea of what the repercussions might be?'

'Obviously not. Like I said, I never intended for anyone to get hurt.'

'It's not so obvious to me, Derek,' said Banks. 'At the very least, you knew what you were doing might cause Laurence Silbert great pain. It clearly caused Mark pain.'

'Well, Laurence deserved it, didn't he, if he was cheating on Mark? And I was only doing what Mark asked. A favour. As a friend. I didn't . . . I mean, what happened is awful. I would never have . . .'

'And you're certain there was nothing else in it for you, that you had no other reason to want any harm to come to Laurence Silbert?'

'No. Why should there be?'

This was sticky ground. Superintendent Gervaise had insisted that they should not refer to Silbert's occupation, but Banks thought there was no harm in taking a little digression. 'When you saw the pictures and heard Tomasina's report, what did it bring to your mind?' he asked.

'That Mark was right. Laurence *was* meeting another man.'

'But they sat together on a park bench and walked to a house in St John's Wood, where an elderly woman opened the door to them. Are you telling me that this looked to you like a man meeting his lover?'

'I don't know. Maybe the bloke was taking him to meet his mother?'

'Do you know what made Mark think that Silbert was being unfaithful in the first place?'

'He didn't say. Just little things, I suppose.'

Banks knew he probably shouldn't be asking his next question, but he just couldn't help himself. 'Did Mark give you any reason to believe that Silbert had anything to do with your brother's death?'

Wyman's jaw dropped. 'What?'

'Derek, I know that your brother, Rick, died on a secret mission in Afghanistan, not in a helicopter accident. I'm just wondering if there was something extra in this for you, an element of revenge, shall we say?'

'No, of course not. That's ridiculous. I didn't even know that Laurence had worked for MI6 before you told me in the theatre bar, so how could I connect him with Rick's death? This is way out of line. I told you, I only did it because Mark asked me to. I haven't committed any crime.' He checked his watch. 'I'd like to go to work now. You said I could leave whenever I wanted.'

Banks glanced at Annie again. They both knew that Wyman was right. Even if he'd been responsible for the deaths of two men, there was nothing they could do about it, nothing they could charge him with. With a deep sigh, Banks brought the interview to a close and told Wyman he could go.

GLAD TO BE AWAY from the station and home for the evening, Banks slipped in the Sarabeth Tucek CD he'd got to like so much over the past few months, poured himself a drink and went out to the conservatory to enjoy the evening light on the slopes of Tetchley Fell.

Even though the Hardcastle case was really over, there were still a few loose ends he wanted to tie up, just for his own peace of mind. He picked up the phone and dialled Edwina Silbert's number.

After about six rings she answered. 'Hello?'

'Edwina? It's Alan Banks here.'

'Ah,' she said, 'my dashing young copper.'

Banks could hear her breathe out smoke. 'I don't know so much about that,' he said. 'How are you?'

'Coping. You know they released the body? The funeral's next week. If you had anything to do with it, thank you.'

'I can't claim any credit,' said Banks, 'but I'm glad.'

'Is this a social call?'

'I wanted to let you know that it's officially over.'

'I thought it was officially over last week?'

'Not for me it wasn't.' Banks explained what Wyman had done, and why.

'That's absurd,' said Edwina. 'Laurence wasn't being unfaithful.'

'But Mark thought he was.'

'I don't believe it. Mark knew perfectly well that Laurence was still involved with the service. He knew the trips to London and Amsterdam were work-related. Your Mr Wyman must be lying. I think he did it off his own bat, out of pure vindictiveness.'

'You could be right,' Banks said, 'but unfortunately, it doesn't matter now. I can't prove it, and even if I could, he hasn't committed any crime.'

'What a world,' said Edwina, with another sigh of smoke. 'Two dear people dead and no crime committed. Was that why you rang?'

'Partly, yes.'

'There's something else?'

'Yes. Remember when you first told me that Laurence worked for MI6? It crossed your mind then, didn't it, that they might have somehow been responsible for his death?'

'At first, I suppose, yes,' Edwina said. 'They are a devious crowd.'

'Was that because of Cedric?'

'What?'

'When you spoke about your husband, you told me he had worked for military intelligence during the war, and that he still had connections. He died in a car crash at the height of the Suez Crisis, when he was involved in some oil deal. Didn't that set off any alarm bells?'

'I suppose it did,' said Edwina. 'Cedric was a good driver, and there was no investigation. But that's the problem with these people, Mr Banks. You just never know, do you? And now I really must go. I'm tired. Good night.' She hung up.

When Banks put the phone down, he could hear Sarabeth Tucek singing 'Stillborn', one of his favourites. So the Hardcastle–Silbert case, such as it was, was over. Two men were dead, Wyman was responsible for their deaths, whether intentionally or not, and he had walked away a free man.

Nearly an hour passed, and Banks had just switched Sarabeth for Cat Power's slow, unbearably sad version of '(I Can't Get No) Satisfaction' when his phone rang. He didn't immediately recognise the voice.

'Alan? This is Victor, Victor Morton. Sophia's father. How are you?'

'I'm fine,' said Banks. 'What can I do for you?'

'You can tell me what's going on, for a start.'

'What do you mean?' Banks asked.

'I had a very interesting conversation with an old colleague yesterday,' Victor went on. 'We met just by chance, in the street, if you can believe that, and he suggested we have a drink together.'

'Who was it?'

'His name doesn't matter. It was someone I knew from Bonn, someone I never liked, someone I always suspected of being a bit . . . well, rather like the fellow we were talking about the other day.'

'Silbert? A spy?'

'Do you have to spell everything out for whoever's listening?'

'It doesn't matter,' said Banks. 'The case is closed. Hardcastle suspected Silbert was having an affair and hired someone to get the evidence. It was just jealousy, after all, and it went terribly wrong. It's over.'

'Well, perhaps someone should tell my colleague that.'

'What do you mean?'

'It started off as a pleasant enough conversation, old times, retirement and the like, then he started to ask about you, what I thought about you as a detective, how I felt about your relationship with my daughter.'

'And?'

'I don't like being grilled, Alan. I told him nothing. Then he moved on, in a roundabout sort of way, started asking if I knew anything about a man called Derek Wyman. I said no. Do you know this person?'

'He was the one who Hardcastle asked to get the evidence. But as I said, it was all to do with jealousy, not government secrets.'

'Well, he harped on about this Wyman for a while, then he asked after my "lovely" daughter Sophia, how she was doing. I told him fine as far as I knew, and got my things together to leave. I'd had enough by then. Just as I was about to go, he grabbed my sleeve and told me to be careful. That's all. No overt threat. Just "Be careful, Victor." Now what was that all about?'

'Melodrama,' said Banks, nonetheless feeling his flesh crawl as he tried to shrug it off. 'They love melodrama.'

'Well, I hope so, Alan. I sincerely hope so. Because if anything happens to my daughter, I'll—'

'If anything happens to your daughter, you'll have to get in line, and I'll be the first in the queue.'

'Just as long as we understand one another.'

'We do,' said Banks. 'Goodbye, Victor.'

THE SHADOWS were lengthening when Winsome and Doug Wilson, along with two of the uniformed officers they had drafted in, approached Hague House. If the Bull was armed, then he might be dangerous. One of the officers was carrying a miniature battering-ram, affectionately known as a 'big red door key', which they would use to break the door down if they got no answer. More uniforms were stationed at the bottom of the stairwells. Andy Pash had reluctantly given an official statement, which gave them sufficient cause to bring the Bull in as a serious suspect in the Donny Moore stabbing. They had also managed to dig up the Bull's real name, which was Toros Kemal, and his criminal record, which was lengthy.

The lifts were out of order, as usual, so they had to climb the stairs to the second floor. One or two lurkers in the shadows scarpered when they saw the uniforms. Winsome found the green door easily enough.

'Step back a bit, ma'am,' said one of the uniformed officers. 'We'll take care of this part.'

'Be our guest,' said Winsome. She and Doug Wilson stepped back towards the stairwell, about twenty feet away.

The officer rapped on the door. 'Toros Kemal. Open up. Police.'

Nothing happened. He knocked again. People started to appear at the doors of neighbouring flats, and a small crowd gathered on the stairwell.

Finally the green door opened and a tall man stood framed in the doorway, stripped to the waist, wearing only a pair of track-suit bottoms and trainers. He rubbed his head as if he had just woken up. 'Yeah, what is it?'

'Mr Kemal,' said the officer. 'We'd like you to accompany us to the station for questioning in the matter of the stabbing of Donny Moore.'

'Moore. Don't know him,' said Kemal. 'Just let me get my shirt.'

'I'll accompany you, sir,' one of the officers said. They went inside.

The other officer lowered his battering-ram, clearly disappointed. Winsome stood by the stairwell, Wilson behind her, when Kemal came out with the uniformed officer. He was wearing a red T-shirt.

'I've gotta tie my laces, man,' he said in the doorway, and knelt. The officers stepped back, behind him. In less than a second, he had a knife in his hand, pulled from a sheath strapped to his lower leg. The officers took out their extendable batons, but they were too slow. The Bull wasn't hanging around. Winsome and Wilson were the only ones blocking his way to the stairs, and Winsome was standing in front. The Bull came charging straight for her as if he'd just come into the ring, letting out an almighty yell and with his arm stretched out, pointing the blade directly at her as he ran.

Winsome felt a chill run through her, then her self-defence training took over, pure instinct. She stood her ground, readied herself, let him come to her. She grabbed his outstretched knife arm with both hands, let herself fall on her back, and using the impetus he'd built up, she wedged her feet in his solar plexus and pushed with all her might.

Kemal was travelling fast enough that it all happened as one seamless, choreographed movement. There was a gasp from the crowd as he flipped heels over head in the air, then his back bounced against the flimsy balcony, and he disappeared over the edge with a scream.

Winsome lay on her back on the concrete, gasping for breath. In seconds, Doug Wilson and the two uniformed officers were standing over her, muttering apologies and praise. She waved them aside and stood up. The crowd round the stairwell was silent, awe-struck. Winsome just felt lucky. One minor misjudgment and she would have had a knife through her chest. They should have handcuffed and searched Kemal before bringing him out. Well, it would all go down in the reports, and bollockings would be freely handed out. For the moment, Winsome was just happy to be alive. She turned and looked over the balcony, down at the courtyard. The Bull was lying on his back in a twisted way, a darkening stain spreading slowly around his head.

Chapter Thirteen

The rain started to come down hard on Sunday morning, and it was still pouring on Monday, when Banks took the newspapers and his second cup of coffee into the conservatory. The weather suited Banks's mood well enough. The music, too. Underneath the noise the rain made on the glass roof, Billie Holiday was singing 'When Your Lover Has Gone'.

He had slept hardly at all the past three nights. The images seared in his mind's eye wouldn't go away. As a policeman, he had seen death before in all its gruesome forms, but what had happened on Friday was different. Someone had done it deliberately to inflict as much as pain and suffering as possible on innocent people. He had met criminals who had done that before, too, of course, but not on this scale, in this *random* way.

The music had finished and he needed more coffee, so he went to the kitchen and refilled his mug. Just as he had settled down to the crossword, his telephone rang. It was Sophia.

'Alan, I moved your car. You're lucky the police didn't impound it. Things are still crazy around there. Anyway, it's just down the street. Do you know you left your iPod in there, too?'

'Yes,' said Banks. 'How are you?'

'I'm fine.'

'I'd like to come and see you. I've still got some free time and things have quietened down up here.'

'I'm glad to hear that, but I don't know. I'm really busy this week.'

'We've always worked around that before.'

'I know, but . . . it's just . . . well, I think I need some time, that's all.'

'Time away from me?'

She paused, then said, 'Yes.'

'Sophia, I *did* remember to set that alarm.'

'Then how did someone just manage to walk into my house and break my things without alerting the police?'

'The people who did it are very adept. They can get in anywhere.'

'I don't know what's worse,' Sophia said. 'You not setting the alarm or these paranoid delusions you've got about the secret service. Is it some kind of elaborate excuse you've come up with? Because if it is—'

'It isn't an excuse. It's true. I told you about them before. Laurence Silbert was a retired MI6 agent. Semi-retired.'

There was a pause, then Sophia said, 'Anyway, it's not even that.'

'What is it, then?'

'I don't know. It's all been too fast. I just need some time. If you care at all about me, you'll give me some time.'

'Fine,' he said, exhausted. 'Take your time. Take all the time you want.'

'I'M SORRY for disturbing you, honest I am,' said Carol Wyman, opening the door to Annie, 'but I'm really beside myself.'

She looked it, too, Annie thought. Hair unkempt, no make-up, dark circles under her eyes. 'It's all right,' Annie said. 'What's the problem?'

'Come in,' Carol said, 'and I'll tell you.'

The living room was untidy, but Annie managed to find a place to sit on the sofa while Carol made some tea. Annie had stopped off at the Wymans' on her way to Western Area Headquarters, where Superintendent Gervaise wanted the whole team assembled at twelve o'clock for a meeting. As she waited, Annie glanced around the room and noticed that the photograph of Derek Wyman with his brother was missing, as were several others.

'What is it?' Annie asked, when Carol brought the tea and sat next to her.

'It's Derek,' she said. 'I don't know where he is. He's disappeared.'

She started crying, and Annie put an arm round her shoulder and passed her a tissue from the box on the coffee table. 'When was this?' she asked.

'He didn't come home last night, after the evening performance. I haven't seen him since he went out for the matinée at two o'clock. He usually comes home between performances, but yesterday he didn't.'

'Did he phone or anything?' Annie asked.

'No, nothing. That's just not like him.'

'Did you phone the police station?'

'Yes, this morning. But they wouldn't do anything. They said he was a grown man and he had only been missing for one night. I told them about Saturday, when he was there talking to you, and that he'd been upset ever since, but they didn't even know he'd been at the station. So I phoned you.'

'It's all right,' Annie said. The Monday-morning desk officer wouldn't have known that Wyman had been in the station on Saturday; he hadn't been arrested or charged, so his name wouldn't appear on the records. 'You did the right thing. Have you any idea where he might go? Any friends or anything?'

'No. I've already phoned all his colleagues at school and from the theatre. They said he didn't show up for last night's performance.'

'But he was there for the matinée?'

'Yes. It ended about half past four. Maria said he left the theatre, and she just assumed he was coming home for tea. But he never turned up here.'

'Is his car gone?'

'As far as I know. It's not parked on our street, at any rate.'

'You'd better give me some details.' Annie noted down what Wyman had been wearing, along with the make, colour and number plate of his car.

'Something must have happened to him,' Carol went on. 'I think it was something to do with those people who came.'

'What people?' Annie asked.

'Late yesterday afternoon, while Derek was at the theatre. A man and a woman. They were something to do with the government. Anyway, they were a bit abrupt. Pushy. Wanted to know all sorts of things, personal things. Wouldn't tell me why. They went through the house from top to bottom. Took some stuff with them. Papers, photographs, Derek's computer.'

'They took those family photographs, too, from the sideboard?'

'Yes. They do work for the government don't they? I haven't been stupid, have I? I haven't been burgled? I don't know what's going on any more.'

'No,' said Annie. 'They are who they say they are.' Not that that helps at all, she thought. 'Did Derek know about this visit?'

'He can't have done. He was at the matinée.'

Unless he'd been on his way home and seen them from the end of the street, Annie thought. That might have caused him to do a runner.

'His mobile wasn't working,' Carol went on. 'Maybe it was the battery. He's always letting it run down. Oh, what can have happened to him?'

'I'm going to the station to report him missing and see about initiating a search,' said Annie. 'In the meantime, if there's anything else you can think of, don't hesitate to phone me again.' Annie stood up. 'There's probably a simple explanation. Let me get working on it.'

'Oh, I do hope he's all right. *Please* find him for me.'

'Don't worry,' said Annie. 'We'll find him.'

THERE WAS MORE than a little tension in the boardroom, Banks sensed, as the Major Crimes squad congregated round the impressive oval table.

'Right,' said Gervaise, standing and leaning forward, her palms on the table. 'I notice that DI Cabbot hasn't seen fit to join us yet, but let's get down to business. It's wrap-up time. We'll start with you, DS Jackman.'

Winsome almost jumped. 'Yes, ma'am.'

'That was a very stupid thing you did on Saturday evening, wasn't it? You should have taken more back-up and you should have stayed out of the way until the suspect had been subdued and handcuffed.'

'But, ma'am, we had no reason to think he'd go crazy like that.'

'Where drugs are involved, DS Jackman, it's folly to try to predict what someone will or will not do. Toros Kemal was high as a kite on metham-phetamine, and you should have been ready for that. There are no excuses.'

'No, ma'am.' Winsome looked down, her lower lip trembling.

Gervaise let a little time pass, then she turned to Winsome again and said, 'I hear your fancy footwork was quite a sight to behold. Well done.'

Winsome smiled. 'Thank you, ma'am.'

'But don't even think of trying a trick like that again. We don't want to lose you. How is our wild man?'

'Well,' said Winsome, 'I did call by the hospital yesterday, and he's out of danger. He's got a broken collarbone, broken arm, broken leg and a minor skull fracture, along with untold cuts and bruises.'

'Not least to his ego,' said Annie.

Gervaise turned to Banks. 'Now, DCI Banks, make my day and tell me I have no reason to fear any more fallout from this Hardcastle–Silbert business you've been probing against my orders.'

'It's over,' said Banks. 'Derek Wyman admitted to hiring a private investigator to take photographs of Laurence Silbert with whoever he met. When we questioned him yesterday, he told us that Hardcastle asked him to do it. He'd become suspicious of Silbert's frequent trips to London, thought he'd found a lover. It was jealousy, pure and simple. Wyman didn't tell us earlier because he felt guilty about it all, and he didn't want to get involved.'

'I see,' said Gervaise. 'And do you believe him?'

'Not entirely,' said Banks. 'Edwina Silbert assured me that Mark Hardcastle knew her son was still working on the occasions he visited London and Amsterdam, so why ask Wyman to follow him? But it doesn't matter what we believe. There's nothing to charge him with.'

'And the involvement of the intelligence services was purely tangential?'

'Well, you can never be entirely certain with these people,' Banks said, echoing Edwina. 'But yes, ma'am, we're pretty sure that Silbert's intelligence work had no relevance to the murder-suicide.'

'So I can tell the chief constable, and whoever's been on *his* back, that it's all over?'

'Yes,' said Banks. 'Though I would imagine the chief constable is well aware of that already.'

Gervaise looked at him suspiciously, but didn't follow up on the remark because, at that moment, Annie Cabbot rushed in and sat down.

'Ah, DI Cabbot,' Gervaise said. 'Good of you to join us.'

'Sorry, ma'am,' said Annie. 'I was out on a missing-person call.' She glanced towards Banks and said, 'Derek Wyman's disappeared.'

'When did this happen?' Banks asked.

'Yesterday afternoon. He left the theatre after the matinée and didn't turn up for the evening performance. And there's another thing.'

'Yes?' said Gervaise.

'Two people went over to Wyman's house yesterday afternoon. A man and a woman. They scared the sh—the living daylights out of his wife, took photographs and papers away. Said they were from the government.'

'*Shit!*' said Gervaise. 'This was yesterday?'

'Could he have got back from the matinée in time to see these people enter his house?' Banks asked Annie. 'Do you think they picked him up?'

'It's possible,' Annie said. 'The timing's close enough.'

'But DCI Banks just assured me that this mess was over and done with,' said Gervaise.

'Well, it was,' said Annie. 'It might still be. I mean, maybe he's just . . . I don't know . . . another woman? Or he's done a runner. These things happen. Just because he's missing it doesn't have to mean that MI6 carted him off to one of their secret interrogation camps.'

'There are no such places,' said Gervaise.

'Very well, then. One of their secret *nonexistent* interrogation camps.'

'Very clever. Don't let your imagination run away with you, DI Cabbot,' snarled Gervaise.

'Have these government people had access to any of our case files?' Banks asked Gervaise.

'Not through me,' she answered. 'Or through anybody else in this office.'

'Has the chief constable been around much lately?'

Gervaise paused. 'A bit more often than he usually is. What are you trying to suggest, DCI Banks?'

'I think you know, ma'am. You might not like to admit it, but you know. They took an interest in this as soon as they realised I wasn't going to stop investigating. They've been following me around. Annie, too, perhaps. They probably know what we know. Given that we didn't tell them, I'm wondering how they found out. It's my bet they went straight to the top. The chief constable's ambitious, and he has political aspirations.'

'Do you know what you're saying?' said Gervaise. 'And why on earth would they be interested in a schoolteacher cum amateur theatre director?'

'Because he hired a private detective to take photographs of Silbert meeting a man in Regent's Park,' Banks said. 'And then there's the brother.'

'Brother?'

'Wyman's brother, Rick. He was SAS. He was killed on a secret mission in Afghanistan in 2002. The press covered it up. Called it an accident during manoeuvres. Silbert has visited Afghanistan. There's a chance that he might have been involved on the intelligence side, and Wyman might have found out about it through Hardcastle, blamed him for Rick's death.'

'Oh, this just gets better and better.' Gervaise glared at Banks. 'We'd better discuss this later, in my office, when we've got a bit more information.'

'Yes, ma'am.'

Gervaise got to her feet. 'I suppose we ought to count our blessings as well as lick our wounds,' she said. 'At least we've got Donny Moore's assailant and maybe done a little bit towards keeping more heroin and methamphetamines off the East Side Estate.'

Doug Wilson spoke up. 'And don't forget, ma'am. We've got the traffic cones back, too.'

Gervaise gave him a withering glance.

BANKS HAD DUG OUT his old portable CD player, in the absence of his iPod, and he listened to Laura Marling's *Alas, I Cannot Swim* on the train down to London that Monday evening. He needed his car back, and despite what had been said on the phone, he thought that if he could just see Sophia for a few minutes, he could convince her to stay with him. He didn't want to let her go. Annie was heading the search for Derek Wyman, running through the list of friends and relatives. So far nobody had seen any trace of him.

Banks's pay-as-you-go vibrated discreetly in his pocket. He took his earphones out and answered it.

'Banksy?'

'Ah, Mr Burgess.'

'Right. I'll keep this brief. Are you listening?'

'I'm listening.'

'Laurence Silbert operated strictly in Cold War territory, primarily Berlin, Prague and Moscow. His only visit to Afghanistan was in 1985, when the Russians were there. It was a joint operation with the CIA, probably to do with supplying backing to the anti-Russian Taliban forces. This particular bit of knowledge isn't classified, by the way, but keep it under your hat.'

'Of course.'

'Basically, he was a Cold War warrior. He never had anything to do with the situation in the Middle East.'

'What about after his retirement?'

'I'd have thought it was pretty obvious. We all know the old KGB and Stasi agents have turned up in one form of organised crime or another, or have become "businessmen", as they like to call themselves. They're operating openly in the West now. Silbert was part of that world for a long time. He knew all the players, their strengths, weaknesses, trade routes, the lot.'

'So they're using his old knowledge?'

'Yes. I'd say so. Just a guess, mind you.'

Banks kept his voice low. 'Why all the secrecy? The Regent's Park meetings. The house. Fenner's phone number. The Townsends. Why didn't he just go and have a chat at Thames House when they wanted to pick his brains?'

Banks heard Burgess chuckle down the line. 'That's not the way they do things, Banksy. When he was ready for a meeting, Silbert would ring a phone number they gave him, an untraceable number, and all he'd get would be a line-disconnected message, but they'd know he was ready. They'd also know if anyone else phoned the number, too, which I assume is what tipped them off to your meddlesome presence in the first place.'

'Maybe,' said Banks. 'Julian Fenner, Import-Export, I suppose.'

'Anyway,' Burgess went on, 'they clearly didn't want the other side to know that they were using Silbert because they would change any plans or routines or personnel accordingly.'

'Is that all?'

'I can't think of anything else. Don't forget what I said: dump the phone. You owe me, Banksy. I must get back to bugging Muslim MPs now.'

The phone went dead. Banks switched it off and put it in his pocket. He'd dispose of it later, in the Thames perhaps, with all the other secrets that had been dumped there over the years.

IT WAS A MUGGY EVENING on the London streets. The rain that had been falling steadily since Sunday morning had stopped by the time Banks was walking down King's Road at about half past eight, but a warm, heavy mist hung in the air, muffling the sounds of the street.

Banks had sensed an odd mood in the city as he made his way on the tube and by foot. London was still in shock from Friday's bombing, but at the same time people were determined to get on with life as usual, to show that they weren't going to be intimidated. Banks felt a part of that, too. But most of all he wanted to find Sophia.

He felt his chest tighten as he rang her doorbell. No answer.

She was probably working. Often her job demanded that she attend evening events—readings, openings, premieres—so he decided to pass the time in their local wine bar, just round the corner. As usual, it was crowded and nobody paid him any attention, including the bar staff.

Then, through the crowd, Banks saw a profile he recognised at one of the tables. *Sophia.* She was unmistakable, her smooth cheek, the graceful curve of her neck, her dark hair tied up and held in place by that familiar tortoise-shell comb. She was in half-profile and would only be able to see him if she turned round. But she wasn't going to do that.

Opposite her sat a young man with lank, longish fair hair and the kind of scruffy beard you get after not shaving for four or five days. Banks hadn't seen him before, but he knew that Sophia had many friends in the arts he hadn't met. He was just about to walk over when he noticed Sophia leaning in towards the man, the way women do when they're interested. Banks froze. Anxious not to be seen, he edged towards the exit. The next moment he was out in the street, heart pounding, not sure what to do.

There was a pub just down King's Road called Chelsea Potter, and in a daze Banks wandered inside and bought a pint. There were no seats left but there was a shelf running below the front windows where he could rest his drink. From there he could see the end of Sophia's street. He decided that if she went home alone he would approach her, but if she went with the man from the wine bar he would head back to Eastvale. Someone had left an *Evening Standard* behind, and he started reading an article on the aftermath of the bombing, keeping one eye on the street.

Banks had been in the pub perhaps an hour and a half, had finished reading the paper and was into the dregs of his second pint, when he saw Sophia and her friend turn into the street. He left his drink and went outside. From the corner he could see them approach Sophia's front door. They stood for a moment, chatting, then she put her key in the lock and opened the door. The man put his hand on the small of her back and followed her inside.

ANNIE CURSED THE RAIN as she walked round the parked car. The way the wind blew slantwise rendered her umbrella close to useless, and in the end it was easier just to close it and get wet.

She was looking at Derek Wyman's 2003 Renault, which was parked in a lay-by across from the Woodcutter's Arms, a couple of miles outside the village of Kinsbeck, about twenty miles southwest of Eastvale.

A local patrol car had discovered it about an hour ago and called it in. Now Annie and Winsome were on the scene, shooing away the sheep. The patrol officers, a couple of surly buggers by the name of Drury and Hackett, were leaning against their car, smoking, clearly eager to get on their way.

The Renault was locked, and glancing through the window, Annie could see that the keys were gone, and there was nothing out of the ordinary in the interior. No blood. No signs of a struggle. Nothing. She turned to PC Drury. 'It's an unusual place to leave a car, isn't it?' she said. 'Any ideas?'

'Maybe he ran out of petrol,' said Drury. 'Want me to check?'

'Good idea,' said Annie, happy to let the man do what was clearly man's work and dig out a dipstick to measure the level of fuel.

'Nary a drop left,' he said when he'd finished.

'Do you think he may have walked to the garage to get petrol?'

'Possible,' said Drury. 'The garage is three or four miles down the road that way.' Then he checked his watch. 'Though I doubt it'll be open now.'

It was after eight o'clock. 'Would you go down there and check for us?' Annie said. She gestured over to the pub. 'We'll be in there.'

Drury glared at her, but he had a word with his partner and they got in their patrol car and drove off down the road.

Winsome and Annie walked into the welcome shelter of the lounge bar, which was deserted apart from an old man by the fireplace, and two farm labourers enjoying their pints at the bar. Everyone looked round.

'Evening all,' said Annie, smiling as she walked up to the bar. 'Two Cokes, please,' she said to the barman. 'Nasty night out there.'

'Seen worse,' the barman muttered.

'My colleague and I are from Major Crimes, Eastvale,' Annie said, flashing her warrant card. 'We're here about that car parked over the road.'

'Been there since yesterday, it has,' said the barman, handing her the drinks.

So Derek Wyman clearly hadn't just gone down the road for petrol. Or if he had, something had stopped him from coming back.

'Yesterday, you say?' she said. 'Any idea what time?'

'Well,' said the barman, 'at a guess, it'd probably be about the time the bloke who was driving it came in.'

The farm labourers snickered. Ah, thought Annie, a true Yorkshire wit.

'Did he look anything like this?' she asked, taking Wyman's photograph from her briefcase.

The bartender scrutinised it. 'Aye,' he said finally. 'That's him.'

'What time was he here?'

'About seven o'clock Sunday evening.'

Annie remembered that Carol had told her the matinée finished at half past four. It certainly didn't take two and a half hours to get from Eastvale to here, so he must have been somewhere else first, maybe just driving around aimlessly, unless the MI6 pair had been chasing him.

'How long did he stay?' she asked.

'Two drinks.'

'How long's that?'

'Depends on how long a man takes to drink them.'

Winsome leaned over the bar. 'Would you prefer to come to Eastvale to answer these questions, because that can be arranged, you know?'

That shocked him. The farm labourers laughed, and the barman blushed. 'Hour and a half, maybe.'

'What state of mind was he in?' Annie asked.

'How would I know?'

'Try to remember. Was he upset, jolly, aggressive? Flustered? What?'

'Just kept himself to himself, like. Sat in the corner and drank quietly.'

'What else was he doing? Did he have a book? A newspaper? A mobile?'

'Nowt. He just sat there. Like he was thinking or something.'

'Did he talk to you or anyone else at all?' Annie asked.

'No.'

'Did anyone come in and talk to him?'

'No.'

'What about after he'd gone? Did anyone come looking for him then?'

'Only thee.'

'Did you see where he went when he left?'

'How could I? You can't see the road from the bar.'

'OK,' said Annie. 'Any idea where he might have gone?'

'How would I know?'

'Is there anywhere near here a traveller might spend the night?'

'Well, there's a youth hostel up the lane. And there's Brierley Farm. It's a bed and breakfast. It's half a mile back towards Kinsbeck. You can't miss it.'

At that moment the door opened and the two patrol officers entered.

'Any luck?' Annie asked.

'No. He wasn't there. They were closed, anyway.'

'Right,' said Annie, finishing her Coke. 'Let's make a start by doing a house-to-house of the area—the youth hostel and Brierley Farm being first on our list. All right, lads?'

'But we've got our patrol route to cover,' one of the officers protested.

'Want me to clear it with your superior?' Annie asked.

'No,' the officer mumbled. 'Don't bother. Come on, Ken,' he said to his partner. 'Let's start with Brierley.'

IF TRUTH BE TOLD, Banks probably hadn't been fit to drive, he thought as he pulled up outside his Gratly cottage at some ungodly hour in the morning. But all he knew was that he couldn't stay in London. After he had tossed his pay-as-you-go mobile into the Thames, he felt that he had to get away.

The drive home hadn't gone too badly. He had wanted loud, raucous sixties rock and roll, not mournful torch ballads, so he set his Led Zeppelin collection on random. The first track that came on was 'Dazed and Confused', which just about said it all. He didn't really remember the M1 at all now, just the rain, the loud music and a swirling haze of red brake lights ahead and the glaring headlights coming towards him on the other side.

As he drove, he told himself that he should have gone over to Sophia and her friend in the wine bar, that it was all innocent, just a drink with an old friend. But there had been something about the body language, the ease between them, that he just didn't believe it, and he couldn't shake the images of Sophia in bed with the young man, the bed where *they* slept.

When he finally shut the door behind him, he felt exhausted, wrung out. The last time he had felt like this was when Sandra had left him.

He poured himself a large glass of wine and went to sit in the conservatory. He hadn't eaten since lunch time, and his stomach growled, but he couldn't be bothered to go and see if there was anything in the fridge. It didn't matter. If he drank enough wine, he would find sleep. Or oblivion.

Chapter Fourteen

'So just what the bloody hell is going on?' Superintendent Gervaise asked Banks in her office on Tuesday morning at an 'informal' meeting over coffee. The rain was still pouring down, Derek Wyman was still missing, and Banks's head was pounding. Oblivion had come to him in the week hours of the morning, but not before he had downed enough red wine to give him a headache even extra-strength paracetamol couldn't touch.

'We think Wyman might have made it to a town,' said Banks. 'Harrogate, Ripon. York, even. Maybe hitched a lift or caught a bus. Annie and Winsome are checking the bus and train stations. We've also got his picture in the paper and it's coming up on the local TV news this evening. His credit and debit cards are covered, too. If he uses them, we'll know where.'

'It's the best we can do, I suppose,' said Gervaise.

Banks poured himself a second coffee. 'Something obviously put the wind up him,' he said. 'Maybe Mr Browne got the thumbscrews out.'

'There's no call for flippancy. It was expressly to avoid something like this happening that I told you to lay off over a week ago.'

'With all due respect, ma'am,' said Banks, 'that wasn't the reason. You told me to lay off because MI6 told the chief constable, and he passed the message on to you. Your hands were tied. But I'd hazard a guess that you knew damn well that the best way to get me asking questions on my own time was to tell me to lay off. You let me do the dirty work for you while keeping me at arm's length. Only you didn't expect Wyman to do a runner.'

Gervaise said nothing for a moment, then she allowed a brief smile to flicker across her features. 'Think you're clever, don't you?' she said.

'Well, isn't it true?'

'It doesn't matter now. The point is what are we going to do?'

'We're going to find Derek Wyman first,' said Banks, 'and then we'll work on calming everyone down. I think we should just sit down and thrash it out with MI6. It doesn't matter whether Wyman upset the applecart because of his brother or because he was angry with Hardcastle. He hasn't broken any laws and it's about time everyone knew that.'

'You think it's that easy?'

'I don't know why it shouldn't be. Get the chief constable to invite his pals to the table. He's in with them, isn't he?'

Gervaise ignored his barb. 'I don't think they're concerned right now about why Wyman stirred up Hardcastle and Silbert,' she said, 'but what and how much he knows about matters of a top-secret nature.'

'I don't think he knows anything,' said Banks.

'You've changed your tune,' said Gervaise.

'Not particularly. I've had a chance to think it through. I've got a contact who does know about these things, and he told me that Silbert had nothing to do with Afghanistan except for some joint mission with the CIA in 1985, and that his recent work involved the activities of the Russian Mafia.'

'You believe him?'

'About as much as I believe anyone in this business. Maybe Silbert *was* a double agent and that's why they wanted rid of him. We'll probably never know. But there's no evidence they killed him and there never will be. I'm sick of the whole damn business. The point now is to stop all this before it gets worse. If Wyman hasn't found shelter, food and water, do you realise that the poor bastard could die of exposure out there? And for what? Because a couple of jumped-up Boy Scouts in suits have ransacked his home and scared the shit out of him the way they did with Tomasina Savage?'

'But what if Wyman's working for the other side?' Gervaise asked.

'The Russian Mafia? Oh, come off it,' said Banks. 'What use would a puny schoolteacher like Derek Wyman be to a bunch of neckless ex-KGB agents? And why would he hire a private detective if he was in with them? They'd have their own surveillance people. It's just common sense. And I think we all left a little bit of our common sense at home on this one, including me.'

'Perhaps,' said Gervaise. She glanced at her watch. 'I've got a meeting with the chief constable in half an hour. I'll put your idea to him. I doubt that he'll go for it, but I'll try.'

'Thank you,' said Banks. He topped up his coffee and carried his cup back to his own office, where he stood by the window and watched the rain slanting across the market square below. Banks thought of Wyman, alone and frightened out there somewhere, hoped he was dry and sheltered in some cosy bed and breakfast, despite all the trouble he had caused. This business had started with a suicide; he hoped it wouldn't end with one.

DARKNESS CAME EARLY that night, and by ten o'clock it was pitch-black outside Banks's cottage, and still raining. There had been no progress in the search for Wyman that day. If they didn't find him soon, it would be time to concentrate on the moors again, maybe drag Hallam Tarn.

Several times over the course of the evening, Banks had been on the verge of ringing Sophia, but every time he had backed off. She had wanted time, she said, and she also seemed to have another relationship she wanted to pursue. Often the two went together. But had he misinterpreted the situation last night? Had it actually been perfectly innocent? How would he ever know if he didn't ask her?

He tidied away the remains of his takeaway vindaloo and took a generous glass of red wine through to the conservatory. He was just about to go ahead and ring her when he thought he heard a noise out in the back garden. He held his breath. There it was again. Something, or someone, out there in the bushes. He was about to pick up a kitchen knife and go outside to see what was happening when he heard a light tapping at the conservatory door. Banks walked over and put his hand on the handle.

'Who is it?' he asked. 'Who's there?'

'It's me,' a familiar voice whispered back. 'Derek Wyman.'

Banks opened the door and Wyman stumbled in, soaked to the skin.

'Bloody hell,' said Banks, switching on the table lamp. 'Look at the state of you. I'll find you a towel and some dry clothing. Drink?'

'A whisky wouldn't go amiss,' Wyman said through chattering teeth.

They went through to the kitchen, where Banks poured him a healthy shot of Bell's, then they went upstairs and Wyman dried himself off in the bathroom while Banks dug out some old jeans and a work shirt. Finally, they went back downstairs and into the conservatory.

'Where've you been hiding?' Banks asked, when they were sitting down.

'Moors,' said Wyman. 'I used to do a lot of walking and caving around here. I know all the spots.'

'Have you eaten anything?'

Wyman shook his head.

'I've got some leftover vindaloo,' Banks said. 'At least it's fresh.'

'Thanks.'

Banks went into the kitchen, warmed up the vindaloo and half a naan in the microwave and put it on a plate for Wyman. He ate fast, much faster than anyone should eat vindaloo, but it didn't seem to have any adverse effects.

'Would you like to tell me why you ran?' Banks asked. 'The full story.'

'I saw them at my house,' Wyman said. 'The spooks. I was on my way back for tea after the Sunday matinée. They were carrying stuff out. The computer. Papers. Boxes. They don't do that for nothing.'

'How did you know who they were? It might have been us.'

'No. They'd already talked to me once. Warned me what to expect.'

'When?'

'The day before, Saturday, just after I left the police station after talking to you. They were waiting in the square in a car. Put me in the back seat between them. Man and a woman. They wanted to know why you were talking to me, what connection I had to Laurence Silbert's murder. They think I'm hooked up with the Russian Mafia, for God's sake. When I saw them at the house, I just panicked.'

'They must have got to Tomasina's file on you,' Banks said. 'They raided her office on Friday.'

'How did they find her?'

'Through me, I'm afraid. You dropped her card down the back of the radiator at Mohammed's, and he found it.'

'You went to Mohammed's? You didn't tell me this before.'

'There's a lot I didn't tell you. You didn't need to know.'

'And now?'

'It might help you to understand what's going on and why.'

Wyman paused to digest this. 'They knew I'd been to Russia,' he said.

'That wouldn't be hard to find out. When were you in Russia?'

'Four years ago. Moscow and St Petersburg. I was a bloody tourist, for crying out loud. I saved up for years for that trip. They wanted a list of people I'd met and talked to while I was there.'

'What did you tell them?'

'The truth. That I didn't meet anyone. Well, I did, but no one . . . you know . . . I went to museums, galleries, the Bolshoi, the Kremlin . . .'

'And?'

'They didn't believe me. They said they'd be back. Warned me about some of the things they could do to me if they thought I was lying. Lose me my job. Turn my family against me. It was awful. When I saw them at the house on Sunday, I just panicked and took off. But I ran out of petrol. I had a drink or two and tried to think what to do. I realised they'd be searching for my car, so I set out on foot. I've been living rough, up on the moors, ever since. Then I thought of you. I thought if anyone could sort this mess out, you could. I haven't done anything, Mr Banks. I'm innocent.'

'I'd hardly call you innocent. How did you know where I live?'

'The fire a while back. It was in the local paper. And I remembered the place from my walks, when the old lady lived here.'

'So what do you think I can do for you?'

'Get it sorted. Tell them the truth, with a solicitor present, in the police station. I don't trust them. I don't want to be alone with them again.'

Nor did Banks. And he had told Gervaise that he wanted to set up a meeting with them. Perhaps it would be best to take Wyman in. It might give MI6 an extra reason to turn up at the table.

'Why don't you tell me how it really happened first?' Banks said. 'All that about Hardcastle asking you to spy on Silbert, it was crap, wasn't it?'

Wyman hung his head. 'Yes. Mark never suspected Laurence might be seeing someone else. It was me who suggested that. It was all me.'

Banks poured Wyman another tumbler of whisky and himself some more wine. The rain continued to slither down the windows of the conservatory.

'Why did you do it, then, if it wasn't Hardcastle's idea?'

'Does it matter?'

'It does to me, especially if it was nothing to do with the Russian Mafia, or your brother's death, either.'

'Rick? I told you before, I didn't even know what Laurence did for a living. And how could it have been anything to do with Rick?'

'Never mind,' said Banks. 'Carry on.'

'I wasn't interested in Laurence Silbert. He was just a means to an end. Mark loved him. That was who I wanted to hurt, the smug bastard. Mark.'

'Are you telling me this was all about the bloody theatre, after all? Your directing career?'

'You don't understand. With a professional acting troupe there, he was going to end up artistic director of the whole bloody show, and I was going to be stuck teaching the likes of Nicky Haskell and his mates for the rest of my bloody days. And he delighted in letting me know. He used to *tease* me about it. Those plays were my *life*. Do you think I was just going to stand around and have it all taken away from me by some johnny-come-lately?'

'I don't believe this,' said Banks. 'For *that* you destroyed two lives?'

Wyman drank some whisky. 'I never intended that. I just wanted to cause a rift, so maybe Hardcastle would bugger off and leave us all alone. It started as a bit of a lark, really, thinking about *Othello*. Then I wondered if you really could do that, you know, drive someone round the bend through innuendo and images. Mark *was* a bit jealous about Laurence's trips to London, whether they were business or not. I thought I could use that. One time when I was in London at the same time as Laurence I went and watched the flat in Bloomsbury. When I saw Laurence come out, I followed him, I don't know why. I saw him meet a man on a park bench and go to a house in St John's Wood. I didn't have my camera with me. You know the rest.'

'And you hired Tom Savage because you couldn't get down there as often as Laurence Silbert did?'

'That's right. I gave her the address and asked her to follow him and take photographs. She did a terrific job. Mark went spare when I showed him them at Zizzi's. Of course, the photos weren't enough in themselves; I had to embellish a bit on the sort of things I thought they were going to do to one another when they got upstairs. But the hand on the back was a lovely touch. If it hadn't have been for that, it might have looked innocent.'

A harmless gesture. Again Banks wondered about Sophia. Was that all her friend's gesture had been last night? Was he doing his own embellishment? He put her out of his mind. That was for later.

'I never expected what happened next,' Wyman said. 'You have to believe me. I've been a wreck ever since. Ask Carol. Poor Carol. Is she all right?'

'You should ring her,' Banks said. 'She's worried sick about you.'

'I can't face that just now,' said Wyman. 'I need to get myself together.'

Banks finished his wine. 'Look,' he said, 'as far as I can tell, technically you haven't committed any crime. The CPS will make the final decision on that, of course, but I honestly can't see what the charge would be.'

'You've got to take me in,' said Wyman. 'We've got to get it sorted before I can go home. I don't want them coming to my house again. Carol. The kids. I'm willing to accept whatever punishment you think I should have, but I want you to help me get them off my back. Will you do that?'

Banks thought for a moment. 'If I can,' he said.

Wyman put his tumbler down and got to his feet. 'Now?'

'We'll ring your wife from the station,' Banks said.

As THEY WALKED OUT to the car, Banks thought he had probably had too much to drink to be driving—a can of beer with dinner and then a couple of glasses of wine. But it *was* almost midnight, and he didn't feel at all impaired. He knew he wasn't destined for sleep tonight, anyway, so he might as well take the silly bugger to the station, put him in a cell for a night, then arrange for a solicitor to attend in the morning to thrash it all out.

There were no streetlights on the road to Eastvale, and only Banks's headlights cut through the darkness and the steady curtain of rain ahead.

Then he noticed the distorted glare of headlights in his rearview mirror, too close and too bright for comfort. They started flashing.

'Shit,' said Banks. He realised that they must have been watching his place, hoping either that he would lead them to Wyman or Wyman would fetch up there looking for help after they'd put the wind up him. *Parasites*.

'What is it?' Wyman asked.

'I think it's them,' Banks said. 'I think they were staking out my house.'

'What are you going to do?'

'It seems as if they want us to stop.' Banks readied himself to pull over at the next lay-by, which was a good half-mile ahead. He was still driving quite fast, but the car behind was gaining.

'Don't stop,' Wyman said. 'Not till we get to town. I don't trust them. I want a solicitor present when I talk to them.'

Banks felt anxious himself. He remembered the callous brutality these people had shown at Sophia's, and how they had frightened Tomasina. It was still possible that they could have been responsible for Silbert's murder.

Call me paranoid, Banks thought, but I don't want a confrontation with MI6 out here in the middle of nowhere, with no witnesses. If they wanted to have it out, they could bloody well follow him to Eastvale and have a nice cosy chat in the police station, just the way he and Wyman wanted it.

But they had other ideas. As soon as Banks overshot the lay-by and put his foot down, they did the same, and this time they started to overtake him. The Porsche was powerful enough, but their BMW wasn't lacking in power either. There was a corner coming up, but they obviously didn't know about that when they started to edge to the left, about half a car length ahead. No doubt they intended to bring Banks to a smooth halt, but either because of the rain or not knowing the bends in the road, or both, they misjudged terribly and Banks had to turn the wheel sharply to avoid a collision. He knew this part of the road well, so he braced himself as the Porsche broke through a section of dry-stone wall and flew over the steep edge.

Banks was strapped in the driver's seat, and he felt the jolt of the seat belt as it absorbed the impact. Wyman, in his distracted state, had forgotten to fasten his belt, and he shot forward through the windscreen, so he lay half on the bonnet, his lower half still in the car. For some reason, the air bags hadn't released. Banks unbuckled his seat belt and staggered out to see what had happened.

Wyman's neck was twisted at an awkward angle, and blood pumped all over the bonnet from where a large sliver of glass had embedded itself in his throat. Banks left it there and tried to hold the wound closed around it, but he was too late. Wyman shuddered a couple of times and gave up the ghost. Banks could feel him die right there in front of him, feel the life go out of him, his hand resting on the dead man's neck.

Banks fell back against the car's warm bonnet, slick with blood, looked up to the heavens and let the rain fall on his face.

Two people were walking towards him, a young man and a young woman carrying torches, the slanting rain caught in their beams of light.

'Bit of a mess, isn't it?' the young man said when they got to the Porsche. 'Nice car, too. We only wanted to talk to him again. Find out why he put a tail on one of our men. You should have stopped when we flashed you.'

'He couldn't tell you anything,' said Banks. 'He was just a bloody schoolteacher.'

The man shone his torch on the bonnet of the Porsche. 'Dead, is he? We'll never know what he was up to now, will we?'

Banks could think of nothing to say to that. He just shook his head. He felt dizzy and weak at the knees.

'You all right?' the young woman asked.

'I'm fine,' said Banks.

'We'll take it from here,' she went on. 'We'll get this cleared up and have your car back outside your cottage again by tomorrow morning, as good as new.' She paused and looked at the Porsche. 'Make that the day after tomorrow,' she said. 'It can sometimes be hard to get replacement parts for foreign cars. We'll make sure they fix the air bags, too.'

Banks gestured towards Wyman. 'What about him?'

'Best let us take care of it. He was distraught over what he'd done. He went walkabout and either he jumped or he fell off a cliff. We don't want any fuss, do we? I'd just go home if I were you. Walk away.'

Banks stared at her. She was pretty in a slightly hard-faced sort of way, but her eyes didn't flinch; there was no milk of human kindness in them. 'But he didn't do anything,' said Banks. 'And you killed him.'

'Now, wait a minute,' said the young man, squaring up to Banks. 'You were driving way too fast. You've obviously been drinking. And he wasn't wearing a seat belt. Your air bags malfunctioned, too.'

'And you wouldn't know anything about that, would you?'

'Don't be ridiculous. If we wanted you both dead, you'd be dead in easier circumstances to clean up than this. It was an accident. Besides, don't forget he was responsible for the death of one of our best men, and if you'd had your way, he simply would have walked away. Hardcastle didn't ask him to put a tail on Silbert. The whole thing was his own twisted, crazy plan.'

'How do you know?'

'What?'

'I can understand you probably got the transcripts of the interview. The chief constable would have given you those. But how did you know that was all a lie, that Wyman . . .?' Banks paused as the truth dawned on him. 'You bugged my cottage, didn't you? You bastards.'

The man shrugged. 'You're away a lot. Access isn't a problem.'

Banks looked back at Wyman's body. 'Is *this* your idea of justice?'

'It's justice of a kind,' the man said. 'Look, Silbert helped us bring down some pretty big players—sex traffickers, drugs dealers, killers for hire. He even helped put some terrorists behind bars. And this piece of scum you're defending basically killed him.'

'I'm not convinced about that,' Banks said. 'Oh, Wyman stirred Hardcastle up all right, but you lot could still have killed Silbert. Wyman just makes a good scapegoat because he's so full of guilt.'

'Why would we do that? I told you, Silbert was one of our best men.'

'Maybe he was a double agent. What about those Swiss bank accounts? People led me to believe that agents feather their nests when they're in the field, but who knows? Maybe he was playing for both sides.'

'Then maybe the other side killed him. Whatever happened, you'll never know, will you? Anyway, this is getting us nowhere. Look, the best thing you can do is—'

But he never got to end the sentence. Banks felt the urge begin in his solar plexus, and the next thing he knew his fist was connecting with the man's jaw. It happened so quickly the man never had a chance, no matter what fancy martial arts he had been trained in. Banks heard a satisfying crunch. He could also sense that he'd probably broken a knuckle, maybe two, but the pain was worth it to vent some of his anger—anger about Wyman, about Sophia, the bombing, Hardcastle, Silbert, the Secret Intelligence Service. The man crumpled and fell like a sandbag to the earth.

'Carson,' the woman said, bending over him. 'Carson? Are you all right?'

Carson groaned and rolled over. Banks kicked him hard in the ribs. The man groaned again and spat out a tooth. Banks was just about to kick him in the stomach when he realised that the woman was pointing a gun at him.

'Stop it,' she said. 'I don't want to use this, but I will if I have to.'

Banks glared at her, then took a few deep breaths. He looked at Carson again and felt no desire to inflict any more pain. He leaned back on the car and caught his breath, cradling his right hand in his left.

'The truth is that none of this happened,' the woman said. 'We weren't even here. You'll get your car back as good as new. His body will be found at the bottom of a cliff, and nothing changes. You can tell all the stories you want, but I guarantee you that nobody will believe a word you say. If necessary, we'll give you a legend that will land you in jail for the rest of your days. When we've finished with you, even your family and your closest friends will never want to talk to you again. Do I make myself clear?'

Banks said nothing. What was there to say? Any insults and threats of retribution he might want to make would just be empty bluster in the face of the power these people had. He knew he'd had all the satisfaction he was going to get from the punch he'd landed.

The woman held her gun in one hand and her mobile in the other. Both hands were perfectly steady. 'Walk away,' she said. 'Do it. Now.'

Banks's legs were still a bit wobbly, but they worked. He didn't say anything, just made his way up the slope to the road. The night was a dark, wet cloak around him. There was only one place he wanted to be now, only one place left for him to go. A little unsteady at first, but gaining strength and momentum as he went, Banks started the long walk home. He wasn't sure whether the wetness he felt on his face was rain, blood or tears.

PETER ROBINSON

Born: March 17, 1950
Homes: Toronto and the Yorkshire Dales
Former profession: lecturer

RD: You said once that you are more interested in character than plot. Does that mean that you didn't know the ending of *All the Colours of Darkness* when you started to write it?

PR: No idea! I know a lot of people find this hard to believe, especially of a crime writer, but it's true. All I have when I begin are a lot of loose ends that I want to tie up.

RD: What was it that triggered the idea for this story?

PR: *Othello*, really, and the image of a man in brightly coloured clothing hanging from a tree in the woods. From such simple beginnings are complicated plots born.

RD: And did it develop in surprising ways?

PR: In many, as always. Characters came and went, minor characters became major, and the motivation changed, as did the entire background of one of the victims. But this isn't unusual for me. I find I get far better ideas when I'm actually sitting down and writing than I do when I'm trying to plan something out in advance. Of course, that means a lot of revision.

RD: You came from a working-class home—your father was a factory worker and your mother a charwoman—did that mean little access to books at home? Where do you think your passion for storytelling came from?

PR: Working-class culture shouldn't necessarily be equated with a deprived or a philistine background. There was a wealth of learning in our street, and a lot of keen readers, just none of the middle-class trappings of formal education. There were also a lot of stories. We didn't have a television until I was about twelve, by which time I had developed a lifelong reading habit and a love of radio serials and comedy. Though the family wasn't bookish—I was the first to go to grammar school and university—my father was, and still is, a keen reader of crime fiction.

RD: Can you remember favourite books from childhood?

PR: My mother used to read to me in bed when I was little. I wouldn't go to sleep without a story. The first one I remember is *Black Beauty*. I learned to read quite young and raced through Enid Blyton, the William and Jennings books, Billy Bunter, *Kidnapped*, *Treasure Island* and a lot of science fiction before the television came, but even that didn't stop me from reading; it simply gave me new ways of enjoying stories and perhaps of escaping the everyday.

RD: Has living in Canada coloured your writing in any way?

PR: It must have done. Canada has developed a very strong literary tradition (one thinks of Margaret Atwood, Alice Munro and Alistair MacLeod) but no one has yet fully explored why so many of us, when we get to Canada, suddenly feel the urge to write about where we came from. Writing in Canada gave me a more objective and slightly nostalgia-tinged view of Northern England. Now that I live in Richmond, Yorkshire, part of the time, I can feel that changing.

RD: And what do you miss about Yorkshire?

PR: Not so much any more, because I'm here a lot, but I remember missing the sense of humour, the depth of tradition and layers of history, the countryside, the beer and the fish and chips.

RD: Banks has a passion for alternative music at the moment, and lots of interesting artists are mentioned. Are you into this too?

PR: I'm into all kinds of music and it's becoming impossible to mention everything. Sometimes artists even send me CDs. It's a fun sideline for me to pick out what Banks might be listening to at any given time, and I know a lot of readers enjoy it too.

RD: Who is your latest musical discovery?

PR: The Fleet Foxes.

RD: What top three tips would you/do you give to would-be writers?

PR: Bum on seat, fingers on keyboard, and don't give up.

RD: And what aspect of being a writer do you most dislike?

PR: Copy-editing and proof-reading. It makes me feel like a stupid schoolboy getting back an essay all marked in red. I see nothing but my errors.

RD: Is there a crime story that you've never forgotten and would like to have written?

PR: I probably have written it! I just hope nobody realises. After all, how many motives and methods are there?

RD: Finally, if you ruled the world for a day, what would you change?

PR: There's so much to do that it's hard to know where to start. But just like a Miss Universe contestant, I think that eliminating poverty and war would perhaps make a good beginning. As the songwriter said: 'What's so funny 'bout peace, love and understanding?'

How Starbucks Saved My Life

Michael Gates Gill

Picture this:

rich kid from top-notch family goes to a fine university, walks into a great job, lives the high life . . . then, in his fifties, loses the lot. One day, sitting alone with a coffee in Starbucks, he is mistaken for a job applicant. Soon, he's a barista, learning how to clean floors and make lattes.

Nightmare or dream?

For Michael Gates Gill, starting from scratch was 'physically rejuvenating and redemptive' and a profound lesson in life. This is his inspirational story.

1
From Drinking Lattes to Serving Them Up

This is the true, surprising story of an old white man who was kicked out of the top of the American Establishment, by chance met a young African-American woman from a completely different background, and came to learn what is important in life. He was born into privilege on the affluent Upper East Side of Manhattan, she into poverty in the projects in Brooklyn. He once had a high-powered advertising job and now had nothing; she came from the streets and now had succeeded—so much so that she was able to offer a stranger a chance to save himself.

This is *my* story and, like all surprising stories, it starts with an accident.

March

I should not have been anywhere near the location of that transforming experience. But on that particular rainy day in March, I could not resist the urge to go back in time.

Have you ever wanted—when life is too hard to bear—to return to the comfort of your childhood home? I had been the only son of adoring if often absent parents, and now I wanted to recapture some sense of the favoured place I had once occupied in the universe. I found myself back on East 78th Street, staring across at the four-storey brownstone where I had grown up.

I had a sudden image of a crane hoisting a Steinway grand piano into the first-floor living room. My mother had decided I should learn to play the piano, and my father had thrown himself into the project. Nothing was too good for his only son, and he had bought the biggest, most expensive model. The problem became how to get this magnificent instrument into our home, a 100-year-old house with narrow, steep stairs.

My father hired a crane and then had the men raise it up to the first floor, where, by opening the French windows and turning the piano on its side, they could just get it inside. My father had been terribly proud of his accomplishment and my mother delighted. Of course, I had been secretly happy to be the reason for all this unusual activity.

Today, as I gazed at the stately building that had once been my home, I thought of how much all that extravagant effort must have cost. How far I had fallen from those happy times. I had come a long way from my childhood, when money was never mentioned. I was now nearly broke.

Turning away from the comforts of the past, I looked for some comfort in a latte. One of my last remaining treats. A Starbucks store occupied the corner of Lexington and 78th. In my depressed daze, I did not notice the sign in front reading HIRING OPEN HOUSE—not that it was the kind of sign I would have noticed anyway. Later, I was to learn that Starbucks has hiring events at different stores every week or so in New York. Managers from the area come in to interview prospective employees. Looking back now, I realise that the good fortune which had left my life returned the moment I stepped into the store at the corner of 78th Street.

Still in my own cocoon of self-pity and nostalgia about lost fortune and family, I ordered my latte and made my way over to a table. I sat down and did not look at anyone nearby. Staring into my interior space, I tried to make sense of a life that seemed to have completely escaped me.

'Would you like a job?'

I was startled out of my reverie. The speaker sat at the table next to mine, shuffling some papers with professional efficiency. She was an attractive young African-American woman in a Starbucks uniform. She was wearing a silver bracelet and a fancy watch and seemed secure and confident.

I was struck dumb. I wasn't used to interacting with *anyone* in Starbucks. For the last few months, I had been frequenting many Starbucks stores around the city, not as places to relax or chat but as 'offices' where I could call prospective clients—although none were now answering my calls. My little consulting company was rapidly going downhill. Marketing and advertising is a young man's business and, at sixty-three, I was starting to find that my efforts were met with a deafening silence.

'A job,' the woman repeated. 'Would you like one?'

Was I that transparent? Despite my Brooks Brothers suit and expensive leather briefcase, could she see that I was really one of life's losers? Did I, a former creative director at J. Walter Thompson Company, the largest advertising agency in the world, want a job at *Starbucks*?

For one of the few times in my life, I could not think of a polite lie. 'Yes,' I said, 'I *would* like a job.'

I'd never had to seek a job before. After starting at Yale in 1963, I'd had a call from James Henry Brewster, IV, a friend of mine in Skull & Bones (the Yale University secret society).

'Gates,' he said assertively, 'I'm setting you up at J. Walter Thompson.'

Jim was working for Pan American, the largest airline in the world at the time and a major client of J. Walter Thompson, the advertising firm known as JWT in the business. The two of us had a good time together at college— wouldn't it be a gas to work together now!

Jim set up the interview. And when I went to meet the people at JWT, my connection with him proved invaluable. Advertising was regarded as a glamorous profession. Lots of people wanted to get into a business in which you could make plenty of money but also have a creative edge. JWT's training programme was regarded as the best in the business, and it hired only one or two copywriters a year.

I was one of those hires.

It had been love at first sight. All I had to do was talk and write—skills that came naturally to me. I was good at my job and the clients appreciated my creative ideas.

I also found that I enjoyed making presentations, and doing them in original ways to bring some life and laughter into what could be boring meetings. For example, because we had created the line 'The Marines are looking for a few good men', we were asked to pitch for the Department of Defense's multimillion-dollar recruiting account. The presentation was held in a war room at the Pentagon. As I walked in, I saw a row of bemedalled men sitting behind a table looking like stone statues, clearly unhappy that they had been dragged into such a frivolous marketing meeting.

I marched up to the front of the room carrying my portfolio case. I reached inside and pulled out a bow and arrow. Someone else from my team walked to the opposite end of the room with a target I had drawn with

Magic Marker on a piece of Styrofoam. I wanted to dramatise the fact that we believed in targeted advertising. I also wanted to make sure that, since we were the first of thirteen agencies these men would be seeing, they would remember us.

I pulled back the arrow and let it go. By the grace of God, it hit the bull's-eye. For a minute there was dead silence in the room. Then the military leaders broke into applause. We won the account.

In addition to liking the work, I worked extremely hard. I received promotions early and often, moving from copywriter to creative director and executive vice-president on a host of major accounts, including Ford, Burger King and IBM.

I was willing to go anywhere to help our clients. I had no hesitation in uprooting my growing family—somehow between ads I had found time to marry and have four children—and moving to offices in Toronto, Washington, DC, and Los Angeles.

Yet, with terrible irony, I flew many hundreds of thousands of miles to spend time with clients, and hardly saw my children. My clients became my children, and my children grew up without me. Was that really my pudgy baby, Annie, now a beautiful young woman graduating from high school? I realised with a pained clarity that I had missed so many precious moments with her, and with all my children.

And yet I convinced myself—even then—that the sacrifice was worth it, because JWT supported me. My salary was high and my benefits were excellent, so now that the kids were moving on to college and the bills were about to become even more insane, I didn't need to be terribly concerned. In the back of my mind, I even congratulated myself: this is why you were smart to dedicate yourself to one company—the stability and the pay.

Loyal to a fault, I was always ready to adjust my personal schedule for my clients' needs. I remember getting a phone call from a client one Christmas Day when my kids were little. I had just been getting ready to spend a rare day at home, having a chance to play with Elizabeth, Annie, Laura and Charles and enjoy a few moments of being a real family. The client wanted to do a New Year's sale event and could I shoot some commercials?

'Sure,' I answered. 'When?'

'Now,' he said.

I heard those emphatic words and knew I had to go, leaving my children in tears, their presents just unwrapped. But I was a loyal JWT man, and so I got a taxi to the airport and flew to Detroit.

I was full of pride that I had never refused any effort JWT ever asked of me. It was a true shock, then, when twenty-five years into my career, I received a call from young Linda White, a senior JWT executive.

'Let's have breakfast tomorrow,' came her directive.

I liked Linda. A few years earlier, I had convinced the old-boy network that we needed an intelligent young woman. Linda had done well, and I had helped to get her on the board of directors. The only woman on the board. In fact, Linda was now president, having passed me in the corporate hierarchy.

She was a favourite of the new owner of JWT, a Brit in his early forties named Martin Sorrell whose bookkeeper background made him particularly attentive to the bottom line. I had once been in a meeting when Martin said bluntly, 'I like young people around me.' I really should have listened to him and seen what was coming.

On the morning of our breakfast, Linda showed up late. A bad sign. She had red eyes. It looked like she had been crying. Yet another bad sign. I knew that Linda liked me, and I knew that she felt some gratitude towards me for helping her career, but I also knew that in modern corporate life there was no room for sentimentality. The facts that I was still good at my job, and was honest, and had spent my whole adult life helping JWT to become successful were irrelevant.

I had met Linda at a party. She had just graduated with an MBA from Harvard and held an undergraduate degree in art history. As I told her, it was a winning combination in advertising—she would be strong in creative ideas, while making sure the whole process made a profit. I had helped Linda focus on the hard substance of the business—money and an unforgiving attitude toward cutting 'overhead', which, in advertising, was always people. Now the overhead was *me*.

I smiled at her over the table. Yet my heart hurt. I felt really sad. And angry with myself. Why hadn't I seen the signs? Linda went forward and upward in her career at JWT. I stayed in place. Martin liked Linda. In a polite, British way, it was clear Martin could not stand being in the same room with me. With my sparse white hair, I was an embarrassment to the kind of hard-charging, young company he wanted to run.

'Michael,' Linda said, 'I have some bad news.'

I fiddled with my muffin, willing myself to meet her eye.

The waiter came up to me to see if we needed anything else. Waiters still think that the old guys have the money and run the show. I shook my head and he backed off.

'Let me have it,' I said stoically. I wasn't going to beg for mercy. I knew it would not do any good.

'We have to let you go, Michael.' She pronounced the words robotically. To her credit, she had a hard time getting them out, especially that phoney corporate 'we'.

'It's not my decision,' she hastened to add, and a tear started down her cheek. I don't think she was acting. I think she was genuinely unhappy that I had been fired and that she had been chosen to do the dirty deed. From the bottom-line point of view, it was, as they said, a 'no-brainer'. Plenty of young people could write and speak as well as me—for a quarter of the cost. If Linda had refused to fire me, then she could not be part of the management mafia.

Linda told me that I would get paid a week's salary for every year I had spent at JWT, adding that she was sure I had saved something during all the good years.

Fat chance! I said to myself. I have a house full of kids to educate!

'OK,' Linda said, rising. 'It's not necessary for you to go back to the office to pack up. We'll handle that.'

The 'we' again. Linda was ready for prime time.

The thought passed through my mind of suing JWT, or writing nasty letters to clients. But Martin and Linda had already thought of that. 'You will probably want to become a consultant of some kind,' Linda continued, 'and Martin and I would, of course, give you fabulous recommendations.'

Being fired is not the best way to start a consulting company. Yet I knew I needed the goodwill of JWT in order to have a chance of getting any business from my old clients, or anyone else.

The pesky waiter came up again and I waved him off.

Then Linda turned and strode out of the restaurant.

The waiter returned, one last time, and presented me with the bill.

Outside, the sun was shining. I suddenly, desperately, realised I had nowhere to go. For the first time in twenty-five years, I had no clients waiting for me. At fifty-three, I had just been given a professional death notice.

I knew in my heart it was going to be a bad time to be old and on the street.

And so it turned out.

'Yes, I'd like a job.' I hadn't said those words for thirty-five years. It had been thirty-five years since I had taken my entry-level job at JWT. And it had been ten years since I'd been fired. I had set up my own consulting company, and I got a few good jobs right away from my old clients. Then, slowly, fewer and fewer of my calls were returned. It had been months since my last project. Even a latte was becoming a luxury I could no longer afford.

Now, looking across my latte at this confident, smiling Starbucks employee, I felt sorry for myself. She seemed carefree to me, so young, so full of options. Later, I would learn that she had seen more hardship in her life than I could imagine. Her mother, who died when she was just twelve, was a dope addict. She had never known a father. When her mother overdosed, she had been sent to live with an aunt, who already had several of her own fatherless children. She would later tell me of the horrifying time when she had fallen down the cement stairs of the project in Brooklyn where she lived. Her hip was broken, but her harried aunt just screamed at her for being clumsy and refused to send her to a hospital. The bone set, but in a way that guaranteed constant pain. Despite the confidence that she projected to me that day, she was even then in pain.

But at that moment I was still at the centre of my own universe, and my own problems were all-consuming.

To me, this young woman had great power—the power to employ me. *Yes, I would like a job.* As soon as the words had come out of my mouth, I was horrified. What was I doing? Yet, at the same time, I knew I wanted a job. I *needed* a job. And, I presumed, I would easily get a job at this Starbucks store . . . or would I?

The Starbucks employee arranged the papers in front of her, her smile disappeared, and she gave me a hard look. 'So, you really want a job?' she said incredulously.

It suddenly struck me: her invitation to a job had been a kind of joke. But to her surprise, I had taken her up on her invitation.

She eyed me sceptically. 'Would you be willing to work for me?'

I could not miss the challenge in her question: Would I, an old white man, be willing to work for a young black woman?

She later confided to me that her angry and bitter aunt had told her repeatedly as she was growing up: 'White folks are the *enemy*.' From her point of view, she was taking a risk in even offering me a job. She was not willing to go further until she was sure I would not give her any trouble.

I, too, was ambivalent. The whole situation seemed backward to me. In the world I came from, I should have been the one offering her a job, not the one supplicating for the position. My world had turned upside down.

New York City, 1945. My parents always seemed to be going out to parties. I was a lonely little boy. As usual, they were not home when I returned on the bus from Buckley School, but there was Nana, as always, waiting for me with arms outstretched and a big smile on her face. This old woman, who lived with us in our imposing brownstone on East 78th Street, was the love of my young life. She was my family's cook and my closest companion. I spent all of my time with her in the warm and delicious-smelling basement kitchen. I had buckteeth and big ears, but Nana said, 'You are a handsome boy.' She told me I was going to be a real heartbreaker.

One day, I overheard my parents talking in the library. Their voices were low. I crept up to the door to hear them better.

'Nana is getting too old to climb the stairs,' Mother said.

'Yes, it is becoming too much for her,' Father agreed.

Weeks later, when I came back from school one afternoon, Nana wasn't waiting for my bus. She was gone. Mother had hired a refugee from Latvia to be our cook. She was nineteen, and Mother told me she was doing a good deed in hiring her. The Latvian worked hard, but she barely spoke any English and didn't talk to me. I wished that Nana would come back.

Less than a hundred yards from the brownstone I had lived in from the ages of one to five, as I applied for a job at Starbucks, I was suddenly feeling the hole in my heart for a woman I hadn't seen for almost sixty years. Nana had been much older than the Starbucks employee facing me today. Nana was loving and large and soft. This young woman was professional, small, with a great figure and a perfect smile. Nana was like a mother to me. This woman would be my boss.

There was really nothing these two women had in common—except they were both African-Americans. Like so many white people I knew, I appreciated the idea of integration, and yet it seemed that in my social circle, white people stuck with white people, black people with black people. For me to relate to an African-American woman on a personal, honest level opened memories of the only truly close relationship I had ever had with an African-American woman.

This young Starbucks employee did not realise that, because of Nana, I was emotionally more than willing to work for her—I could not help but trust her. 'Would you be willing to work for me?' she had asked.

'I would *love* to work for you.'

'Good. We need people. That's why we're having an open house today, and I'm here to interview people for jobs as baristas. It's just a starting position, but there are great opportunities. I never even finished high school and now I'm running a major business. Every manager gets to run their own store and hire the people they want.'

She handed me a paper.

'Here is the application form. Now we will start a formal interview.' She reached out her hand. 'My name is Crystal.'

I was still sitting with my latte and papers at my corner table. My briefcase on the table fell to the floor as I rose awkwardly partway out of my seat, shook her hand, and said, 'My name is Mike.'

I had called my business Michael Gates Gill & Friends because I was in love with the sonorous sounds of my full name. But here I felt that 'Mike' was the only way to go.

'Mike,' Crystal said, shuffling her papers. 'All Partners at Starbucks go by their first names, and all get excellent benefits.'

She handed me a large brochure.

'Look through this and you will see the health benefits.'

I grabbed the brochure. The position offered health insurance. Rates had got too high for me to afford my health insurance and I had let it go, a mistake that I had recently found out might have serious repercussions. Any remaining ambivalence I had about the job went out of the window.

A week before, I had had my annual check-up with my doctor. Usually, he gave me a clean bill of health. But this time, Dr Cohen shook his head slightly and said, 'It is probably nothing, but I want you to have an MRI.'

'Why?'

'I just want to make sure. You said you had a buzzing in your ear?'

'A *slight* buzzing,' I hastily replied.

'Get an MRI,' he said, 'and then go see Dr Lalwani.'

I had the MRI. Dr Cohen told me that it would only take a 'few minutes'.

I lay there for at least half an hour. And I also did not like the fact that I heard other doctors come in and out of the room.

'What's going on?'

'Nothing,' the young orderly told me. 'We will send the MRI up to Dr Lalwani. He wants to see you.'

I was angry. Angry with Dr Cohen for insisting on this stupid MRI. I had been healthy all my life. And I was not about to stop now. I could not afford any ill health.

Dr Lalwani kept me waiting for most of the afternoon. I saw people go in and out of his office. Finally he appeared, smiling from ear to ear. Was that a hopeful sign? Lalwani gestured me into his office. It was small and cramped and piled with papers.

'Mr Gill,' he said. 'I have some bad news for you . . . but then you knew something must be wrong, am I correct?'

I knew something must be wrong? Was he crazy? I thought everything was all right.

'What are you saying?' I could barely contain my anxiety.

'You have a rare condition. Fortunately, it is in an area that is a specialty of mine. You have an acoustic neuroma. It is a small tumour on the base of your brain that affects your hearing.'

For a second, I could not see or hear anything. It was as though I had been given a blow to my head.

Dr Lalwani, sensing my distress, hurried on. 'This condition is not fatal. I can operate. But I must tell you the operation is very serious.'

I recovered sight and sound just in time to hear those ominous words. 'Serious' coming from a surgeon was not something I wanted to hear.

'What do you mean?'

'We bore into the skull and it is an operation on the brain. Literally, this is brain surgery.'

He was so confident. I hated him for wanting to operate.

'Your hearing may not be restored. The tumour is causing the buzzing. It will be one or two weeks before you can leave the hospital,' he said.

'Before I can leave the hospital?' I repeated numbly.

'And several months before you will be fully recovered. But the rate of recovery is high. Fatalities are very rare. Only a few actually die.'

A few . . . die? Was he mad?

'When do I have to have the operation?' I stammered out.

'I would do it right away . . . but you might wish to wait several months, come back, have another MRI, see if the tumour has grown. You might have a very slow-growing tumour.'

Finally, a ray of hope. Like everyone, I hated the idea of hospitals. Friends had died in hospitals. Not to mention I was broke. Any postponement was a gift from God.

I got up quickly, shook Dr Lalwani's hand, left his office, and immediately called Dr Cohen.

He was not reassuring. 'Sounds like you should have the operation,' he told me.

'Yes,' I said, 'but I will wait for another MRI.'

I was buying time.

Giving up health insurance for myself was bad enough, but not to be able to afford it for my children was much worse. I wondered if the tumour was in some karmic way a punishment for my behaviour.

Now, sitting across from Crystal, I read the Starbucks brochure about the insurance benefits. They seemed extensive. I looked up at Crystal, hopeful, 'Does this cover children?'

'How many kids do you have?'

'Five,' I said, thinking about how I was used to saying 'four'.

Crystal smiled almost kindly. 'You've been busy.'

'Yes.'

I did not want to say any more; it was way too complicated to explain in a job interview.

'Well,' she went on, 'your five kids can *all* be covered for just one small added deduction.'

What a relief. My youngest child, Jonathan, was the main reason I was so eager for work. It wasn't his fault. It was all my fault.

I had met Susan, Jonathan's mother, at the gym, where I had started to go shortly after I was fired. One morning, I had been lying down on a mat, resting. I was in an empty room occasionally used for yoga classes. Susan had come in. It was clear she had not noticed me. She was crying.

'Are you OK?' I asked.

She was startled, but did not stop crying.

'My brother is dying of cancer . . . just days to live . . .'

'That's tough,' I said, sitting up on my blue mat, getting ready to leave.

'And last year I lost my father to lung cancer.'

'Tough,' I repeated, standing up. I should have continued out of the door, but I did not feel I could just leave her with her sorrow.

'Don't worry,' I said, not knowing where these words came from. 'You will soon be happier than you ever have been before.'

She looked up. Susan was small, barely more than five foot, with lots of dark hair and brown eyes. I am over six foot, with little hair and blue eyes. We were a study in contrasts.

Susan rubbed her tears away. 'What?' she said.

I could not believe what I had said. But I repeated the words. 'You will be happier than ever.'

She nodded, as though understanding at some level.

I turned to go.

'I like a man who does yoga,' she said. 'It shows flexibility.'

Susan and I started our relationship on totally false assumptions. She had taken me for someone interested in yoga. I had no interest in yoga. I did not like to stretch: it made me feel even more *inflexible*. I was rigid about many things. Physically. Mentally. Emotionally. I liked old songs, old ways. Until now, my past had worked well for me. Susan had no idea about what I was really like. Meeting me in the yoga room, she thought I was a flexible, perceptive person who could understand the more positive profundities of life.

It is funny, sometimes, how wrong people can be.

Susan was wrong about me, and I was wrong about Susan. I took her for a sad waif, a person who needed comfort and protection. Yet I learned later that she was an established psychiatrist with a large group of patients.

I thought she needed me.

She thought I could help her.

We were both so wrong.

Yet there was an immediate attraction between us.

Since I had been fired, I had found it impossible to make love to my wife, not that we tried that often. Like many married couples, we made love only occasionally. Still, it had scared me when I had tried to perform last time and failed. That physical failure compounded my recent professional failure—one more sign of my seemingly irreversible decline.

Until I met Susan.

'Would you like to have a cup of coffee?' Susan asked.

I found myself saying, 'Sure, let's have a cup of coffee.'

What could be the harm? We could get a latte at Starbucks and I could cheer her up.

But instead of Starbucks, she suggested her apartment. I went with her and I was hooked. After that, I saw Susan two or three mornings a week.

Susan was not that young. In her mid-forties. She told me that her gynae-cologist had told her she could not have babies. So she said she saw no point in getting married.

'Marriage is for having kids,' she said. 'Not to mention you already *are* married,' she reminded me, glancing at my ring to confirm the fact.

I acknowledged her point with a significant amount of guilt. I loved how Susan made me feel, but I loved my wife and wanted my four kids to live in a stable family environment.

Then one morning, Susan called me at home—something she had never done before. 'I have to see you.'

'When?' It was 7.30 a.m.

'Now.'

She was standing in her apartment, the curtains open to the East River. 'Michael,' she whispered, 'I'm pregnant. And God has told me I should have this baby.'

I had kept my relationship with Susan secret, but when Jonathan was born, I told my wife. She could not stand it.

'An affair is one thing,' she said. 'A child is another.'

Betsy is very clear-headed.

'I just can't do it,' she told me. 'I'm not made for this kind of thing.'

So we got an 'amicable' divorce, although she was rightly furious with me for being so stupid.

'I thought we would spend the rest of our lives together,' she said. I felt terrible.

My kids, now practically grown-ups, were understanding in a grown-up way, but hurt and angry, too. I had given Betsy our big house, and she had family money, but I knew it wasn't just about money. I had ruined her life.

And ruined my own life as well.

I took a small apartment in a New York City suburb. Desperately wanting to do the right thing after doing all the wrong things, I resolved to try to be there for Susan and my new child, Jonathan. I would go round at 4 or 5 a.m. and play with Jonathan so Susan could have a little sleep.

One day, when I was putting him back in his crib, Jonathan smiled at me. He opened his mouth and out came the beautiful sounds: 'Da da'. Two simple, heartbreaking syllables. Thinking back to how I had missed such magical moments with my other children caused a physical pain in my chest. And for what? For a company that rewarded my loyalty with a pink slip.

I spent less and less time chasing new clients, and more and more time with Jonathan. He loved me, and he needed me. I was somebody wonderful in his eyes.

Jonathan seemed to be the only one who felt that way these days. Susan had gradually lost interest in me. In a peculiar way, the more available I became to her—after divorcing my wife, and having fewer clients and work to do—the less appealing I was to her.

Jonathan was my last fan and my best pal. But now he had started school, so I was left with more time on my hands, fewer excuses for not finding work, and a greater need for a job.

How had I managed to be so incompetent in all of my relationships? I tried to clear my mind of all my negative thoughts and focus on Crystal and this surprising interview. She had given me a chance—maybe my last chance—to stop my downward spiral. I did not want to blow it.

I looked up at Crystal and tried to give her a confident smile.

She wasn't buying it. Convince her, I told myself. Convince her that this is a match made in heaven. I willed myself to be positive.

'Now I want to ask you some questions about your work experience,' Crystal said in a cool, professional tone.

I was suddenly worried. After finding out about the health benefits, I really wanted this Starbucks job.

'Have you ever worked in retail?'

Her question startled me. I tried desperately to think.

'Like a Wal-Mart?' she said, trying to help. I sensed, for the first time, that Crystal might have decided to be on my side. Yet I could not even grab the saving rope she had tossed me in this job interview. I had never even been inside a Wal-Mart.

Crystal made a little mark on her paper and moved on. I felt very nervous. This was not going well.

'Have you ever dealt with customers in tough situations?' Crystal read the question from the form and then looked up at me. But her eyes were softer; now she seemed to be willing me to answer this question correctly.

I remembered I had done advertising for Burger King and worked at a store one morning to get a feeling for the business. 'I worked at Burger King,' I said.

Crystal gave me a big smile. 'Good,' she said. 'And how did you handle a customer when things went bad?'

'I listened carefully to what the customer was saying, then tried to correct what was wrong and asked if I could do anything more.' I spouted gibberish from some forgotten brochure I had written on how to handle bad situations.

Crystal smiled again and made a mark on the paper.

'Have you worked with lots of people under tough time pressures?' she asked.

'Yes,' I said, keeping it vague. Working late on an advertising campaign was different from serving lattes to hundreds of people on their way to work.

Crystal ticked down the list. 'What do you know about Starbucks? Have you visited our stores?'

I was off and running. I had been in many Starbucks around New York, and I leapt at the opportunity to show my knowledge. 'The Starbucks stores in Grand Central are always busy, and *none* have seats, so I can never sit down, but the store on Fifth Avenue at Forty-fifth Street is really comfortable, and—'

'OK, Mike,' she said, cutting me off. 'I get it.' She smiled. 'And what is your favourite drink?'

Once again, I was enthusiastic. I love coffee and Starbucks was my favourite place to get it.

'What's the difference between a latte and a cappuccino?' Crystal asked.

Here she had me. I liked both drinks, but did not know the difference. 'I don't know. The cappuccino has less milk or something?'

'You'll learn,' she said, marking my form again, but I thought that response was positive, a confidence-builder. I had almost given up on the thought that I could do anything new, or that anyone would invest time in helping me learn a new job.

Crystal stood up. The interview was clearly over.

I stood up as well. We shook hands. 'Thanks, Crystal,' I said.

She laughed. She was obviously now getting a kick out of the whole situation. And me. Maybe I had shown her that the 'enemy' was someone she could easily handle. Maybe she had discovered that I was not just an old white man, but also a real person whom she could help.

But then she got serious. 'The job is not easy, Mike.'

'I know. But I will work hard for you.'

She smiled, and maybe there was a little bit of pride in her smile. Later, I would learn the reason. Eight years earlier, when she had been on the street, she could never have conceived that in the future, she would have a Waspy guy all dressed up in a suit begging her for a job.

'I will call you in a few days, Mike,' she said, 'and let you know.'

2
Reality Shock

April

Several agonising weeks went by, and I heard nothing from Crystal. Every moment I was consciously or unconsciously waiting for her to call. I continued going to the Starbucks store at 78th and Lexington, hoping to catch sight of her, but she was never there.

I also kept calling potential clients for my marketing business, but my voicemail remained empty. More than ever I needed a job, any job. I realised that Starbucks offered me a way—perhaps the only way—to handle the costs of my upcoming brain-tumour operation and to support my young son and my other children. To support myself. I was facing the reality, in my old age, of literally not being able to support myself. I had left my former wife with our large house, was down to the last of my savings, and was facing the possibility that I might not be able to meet next month's rent. I was even more desperate than I had been just a couple of weeks ago. Whenever my phone rang, I found myself almost praying it was Crystal.

Had I done something wrong during the interview? I wondered. Or was I just the wrong gender, race or age?

I thought back to when I did the hiring. I chose people who were like me, with backgrounds like mine. Now, as the days went by and Crystal still did not call, I had a sinking feeling that maybe Crystal operated in the same way: do the easy thing, stay clear of anybody different.

Then, one morning when I was in Grand Central Terminal, my cellphone rang.

'Mike?'

'Yes?' I answered with some suspicion. The person on the other end didn't sound like anyone I would know.

'It's Crystal.'

My guarded attitude changed instantly. 'Oh, hi!' I said enthusiastically. 'So good to hear from you!'

'Do you still want a job'—she paused, and then continued coolly—'working for me?' It was as though she were eager to hear a negative response and get on with her day.

'Yes, I do want to work with you,' I almost yelled into my cellphone. 'I am looking forward to working with you and your great team.'

Calm down, I told myself. Don't be overenthusiastic. And why had I said 'team'? Crystal had talked about 'partners'. I knew that every company had a vernacular that it was important to reflect if you wanted to be treated well.

'OK,' she said. 'Show up at my store at Ninety-third and Broadway at three thirty p.m. tomorrow.'

'Ninety-third and Broadway?' I echoed, surprised by the address.

'Yes.' She sounded like she was instructing a three-year-old. 'Ninety-third . . . and . . . Broadway. Don't be late.'

I was confused. 'But we met at Seventy-eighth and Lex.'

'I met you there 'cause we had a hiring open house going on. That's the way we do things at Starbucks.'

Crystal had taken on a tone I knew well. I had used this corporate by-the-book attitude when dismissing people I did not want to deal with.

'At Starbucks,' she continued, 'we pick a store, have an open house, and the managers who need people interview. But that doesn't mean that's the store you will work in. I'm the manager of the store at Ninety-third and Broadway.' She paused, and added, 'Do you have a problem with that?'

'No problem,' I hastened to assure her. I could sense she was not enjoying this job offer. 'I'll be there tomorrow, and on time.'

I sounded—even to myself—like an old guy speaking like a new kid at school. How embarrassing!

'If you want to work, wear black trousers, black shoes and a white shirt. OK?'

'OK,' I answered.

She hung up. She did not even say goodbye.

The call made me feel really depressed. Through those days of waiting for Crystal to call, the prospect of working at Starbucks was humiliating, but I told myself at least I'd be working in a nice neighbourhood. A location that would help me in my transition from a member of the ruling class to a member of the serving class. In the midst of my obvious, impossible-to-deny fall from financial and social heights, 78th Street was a comforting place to be.

Now I was going to be working at 93rd Street and Broadway in what I envisioned could be a dangerous neighbourhood. It was certainly far from the Upper East Side, where I felt at home.

And I also didn't like Crystal's attitude toward me. She acted as though I were some dummy. Then I remembered with remorse that I had treated a young African-American woman who had once worked for me at JWT with exactly the same kind of dismissive attitude. Jennifer Walsh was part of a push we made in the 1970s to hire minorities.

I was supposed to be her mentor. Yet now I realised with a sinking heart how casually prejudiced against anyone different I had been in my reactions at JWT. At the agency, we thought we were the elite of the advertising business. Hiring anyone who hadn't gone to the crème de la crème of universities we saw as lowering the status of our club—and that included many taken on in the minority-hiring initiative.

Jennifer was nice, but she had graduated from some junior college with a two-year degree, and I never took her career at JWT seriously. I had told her to read ads, then I gave her a newspaper ad to write for Ford. Her very first ad.

Jennifer came into my office. It was clear that she was scared, even petrified, as she approached my big desk. Which made me feel that she was wrong for JWT; we had to project self-confidence to our clients. When I read her draft of an ad, I noticed that she had copied a paragraph from some other Ford ad I had given her to read. This was a form of plagiarism that we really hated at JWT. Perhaps because we were called copywriters, we could not stand anyone who copied someone else's work. Jennifer had just committed an unpardonable corporate sin. At least as far as I saw it.

Thinking back, I realise that she might not have known this was against policy, and I certainly didn't point it out to her. I went to management and told them that Jennifer might make a great secretary someday, but she did not 'have what it takes' to master the higher art of advertising. I had no time for her, or the idea of diversity.

I realised with a kind of horror now, recovering from Crystal's casual handling of a job opportunity that meant so much to me, how casually cruel I had been in 'helping' Jennifer. I had derailed her attempt to penetrate my little world just because she was an African-American without the education or experience that mattered to me.

Jennifer had been moved into some clerical job in personnel and had gone from my mind until this very moment. Now I felt terrible. I imagined Crystal thought I was some dumb old white guy whom she had mistakenly offered a job. I wouldn't fit into her world or be a good match for her needs—just as I had felt about a young black woman several decades ago.

I also kicked myself for not listening to my daughter Laura over many years. Laura had a beautiful halo of brown hair that echoed the sparkle of her hazel eyes, and I had a picture of her now shaking her head in angry frustration as I refused to 'get it'. Laura had a dynamic, positive energy; she laughed easily, but she also had a feeling for how unfair life could be. I had dismissed Laura's feelings and ideas of how to help others less fortunate as 'hopelessly naive'. I had been secure in my bubble of self-congratulation—convinced that my job and my affluence were my just reward for being a great, talented guy. Laura and I had a running argument when she was growing up. It seemed like from the time she was about ten years old, she took my whole affluent lifestyle as an affront when so many people had so much less.

Now I realised with a painful awareness how wrong I had been to try to stifle Laura's view of the 'real world' as unfair to those not born in the right class with the right skin colour. Finally, I was 'getting it' as I faced a new reality of what the world could be like.

But was my hard-won knowledge too late to change my fate?

Maybe there *was* bad karma, I thought to myself. I certainly deserved it. But I was not about to turn down Crystal's offer—whatever her attitude. I woke early the next day and realised with a shock that I was just weeks away from my sixty-fourth birthday. As I struggled into my black trousers for my Starbucks job, I shook my head in disbelief that I was probably going to celebrate my birthday by working as a lowly coffee server.

I didn't know whether to laugh or cry at my feeling of trepidation as I hurried from my inexpensive apartment in suburbia and leapt on a train to Grand Central. Then I ran as fast as I could with the mass of people for the subway shuttle over to Times Square, where I transferred to a crowded train heading up to 96th Street. Squeezing in just as the door was closing, I found myself pressed against people, forced into a kind of primal physical proximity. All faces were unfriendly. How did I get to this place in my life?

Soon the doors opened and I was forced out onto the dirty platform. I climbed the steep stairs with a pumping heart, beginning to sweat, although it was a cold day at the beginning of April.

Emerging from the subway, I struggled against the wind as I approached the Starbucks store at the corner of Broadway and 93rd Street. Icy rain made the pavement slippery. I paused. Now that I was there, I was in no hurry to open that door.

As I stared at the Starbucks sign, the reality of my situation hit me with a sickening impact. Yes, I was going to join a big international company, but in reality as nothing better than a waiter with a fancy name. I would have the very public embarrassment of being Michael Gates Gill, dressed as a waiter, serving drinks to people who could have been my friends or clients. It was like the old days when the Pilgrim Fathers put sinners in the stocks in the public square as a visible example to others to watch their ways.

The Puritan minister Jonathan Edwards had said: 'We all hang by a thread from the hand of an angry God.' Maybe there was an angry Puritan God who had decided to punish me for all my sins. During every minute of the past few years, I had felt the heavy weight of guilt for hurting so many I loved. My former wife, my children, and even those few friends I still had.

Yet I had to admit that my reality was more mundane and sad. I could not pretend that I was living out some kind of mythical biblical journey. I was not a modern Job; I was looking for a job. And I had to face the fact that I was here because of my own financial mismanagement and my sexual needs that had led me to stray. I was not some special person singled out for justice by God. I was, and this really pained me to admit, not even that *unique*. It was hard for me to give up my sense of my special place in the universe.

Now I was forced to see a new reality. What I was experiencing, as a guy too old to find work, was a reality for millions of ageing Americans today who could not support themselves and were no longer wanted by the major corporations. In this state of anxiety, ambivalence and forced humility, I opened the door to the Starbucks store.

Inside, all was heat, noise, and a kind of barely organised chaos. There was a line of customers almost reaching the door. Mothers with babies. Businesspeople checking cellphones. Schoolkids lugging backpacks. College kids carrying computers. All impatient to be served their lattes.

As I looked behind the bar at the servers, one of my worries was confirmed: virtually all the Partners were African-American. For the first time in my life, I would be a visible member of a real minority. I would be working with people of a totally different background, education, age and race.

And it was also clear from what was going on in the store that I would be working hard. Three Starbucks Partners punched at the cash registers taking money and calling out drink orders to other people at the espresso bar. The people at the bar called back the drink names while quickly, expertly, making the drinks, juggling jugs of hot milk while pulling shots of espresso. In rapid-fire order, they then served them up to the customers with an emphatic 'Enjoy!'

This coffee business clearly was not a casual one. There was a frantic pace and much focused noise. This store had that athletic atmosphere of people operating with peak adrenaline.

Suddenly I was very worried. Not just about race or class or age. Now I had an even more basic concern. I had originally thought that a job at Starbucks might be below my abilities. But now I realised it might be *beyond* them. This job could be a real challenge for me—mentally, emotionally and physically.

I had never been good at handling money—it was a major reason I needed a job so badly now. Math was a subject I had never mastered at school. All that money changing hands so rapidly at the Starbucks registers terrified me.

I had lost hearing in one ear due to my brain tumour. Hearing the complicated drink orders could be a problem for me. Yet it was clear I was expected to master the exotic language of 'Starbucks Speak'.

In that first instant, I realised with humiliation that my new job might be a test I could easily fail. I had worn the black trousers with a white shirt, no tie. I was feeling lonely and afraid. Then Crystal appeared in a swirl of positive energy.

'Let's share a cup of coffee,' she said, guiding me over to a table. 'Sit here, I will bring you a sample.'

Crystal seemed much friendlier than she had on the phone. Perhaps, I thought, she had come to terms with hiring me and did not hate herself or me for taking this chance. Soon I was sitting with Crystal, sipping a delicious cup of Sumatra. 'This coffee has an "earthy" taste . . . but I call it "dirty".' Crystal laughed. Today, she had her hair up under a Starbucks cap, making her look sophisticated, even glamorous. Two diamond earrings caught the light.

Maybe it was the coffee, more likely it was Crystal's ability to put me at my ease, but I was feeling a lot better.

Still, I was a long way from being *comfortable.* Out of nowhere, I had a sudden image of myself in a long past life, basking in the comfort of family and friends on a dock at a lake in Connecticut.

I remembered as a young boy throwing apples at the poet Ezra Pound. Pound's publisher owned the camp next door and had brought the poet down to the lake for the day. Pound sat like a kind of statue at the end of the dock. At one point, he rolled up his suit trousers and dangled his white legs into the water, still not speaking. His legs looked like the white underbelly of a frog. There was something about his proud strangeness that got to my young cousins and me. We picked up some apples and started throwing them at him, missing him but sending up water to splash against his dark, foreign clothes.

Ezra Pound did not move or speak. My father laughed and kind of encouraged us in our behaviour. He had written a best-selling book, *Here at The New Yorker*, about his years at the magazine. In the opening, he had stated his philosophy: 'The first rule of life is to have a good time. There is no second rule.' Having a good time for my father meant upsetting apple carts. He had no love for Pound's politics and enjoyed the scene.

My father had won his place on this lake by marrying into my mother's family, who had vacationed there for a hundred years. He had brought new money, earned by his Irish immigrant father, into her *Mayflower* ancestry. At the lake, there was a powerful combustion of gentle Wasp politeness meeting up with my father's purposefully provocative Celtic rebel style.

My father loved to speak; he loved to write; and he loved, above all, to be the centre of attention at parties. 'Everything happens at parties,' he would say. So there was a continuous party on our dock at this exclusive, rustic lake.

My father was a spendthrift with his time as with all his many talents. He gave himself away to so many that there was never enough time at home for *me*. When I was grown and I had moved away from home, he invited me to his parties, and that is the only way we saw each other. When he died, my need to go to parties died as well.

Now I found myself sipping coffee with Crystal—worlds away from the parties during those summers on that exclusive lake—yet as I laughed with her, I could actually feel my spirits rise a bit. Maybe it was the caffeine, but I felt at ease in this totally new scene, having coffee in a crowded, upbeat bar as a way of beginning a new job. It was all so bizarre. I was stepping out from my old status quo and, as a result, I felt better than I had in months.

Crystal's voice broke through my daydream. 'Mike, it is important you learn the differences between these coffees.' I no longer had the luxury of philosophical self-concern. The bell had rung. It was time to get involved. Keeping up with customers' orders was my new job. I had to give up spending so much time thinking about the past and what I had lost. It was going to be a challenge just to keep up with the present. I was about to discover that at Starbucks it was not about me—it was about *serving others*.

Crystal had a serious look on her face and launched into a lecture as though I were some eager student of coffee lore: 'Sumatra coffee is from Indonesia; the Dutch took it there hundreds of years ago and it's part of a whole category of coffees we call "bold".' Crystal leaned forward as though to confide a great personal secret. 'This is the way we welcome all new Partners. Coffee is our business. So we welcome all new Partners with coffee-sampling and coffee stories.'

Crystal sat back with a smile, and I smiled back at her. And I felt that maybe—just maybe—Crystal really was going to give me a chance to prove myself. As I sampled the rich Sumatra brew, I was beginning to feel that I could handle this part of the Starbucks business. I loved coffee. I loved learning about the history of things. I glanced over at the Partners behind the counter, all working hard yet seeming to have a great time.

The store door swung open. In stepped a scowling African-American guy, well over six foot tall, with bulging muscles under a black T-shirt. He had a moustache and was wearing a do-rag scarf wrapped round his head and fastened at the nape of his neck. He was the kind of person that in the past I had crossed the street to avoid.

Crystal called to him: 'Hey, Kester, come over and meet Mike.'

Kester walked slowly over to our table. I noticed a bruise on his forehead. He reached out a big hand.

'Hi, Mike,' he said in a low baritone. Then he smiled. His smile transformed his whole face. Immediately, I felt welcomed.

'Kester, where did you get that?' Crystal said, pointing at his forehead.

'Soccer.'

'Soccer?'

'Yeah, some friends got me into a game. It turns out they think I'm pretty good.' Kester laughed.

Crystal got back to the business at hand. Her face took on what I was coming to know as her hard, professional look. I got a sense that Crystal always liked to be in control. 'Mike is a new Partner,' she explained to Kester, 'and I was wondering if you could do me a favour. Would you be willing to be his training coach?'

I was to learn that nobody at Starbucks ever *ordered* anyone to do anything. It was always: 'Would you do me a favour?' or something similar.

'Sure,' Kester replied, 'I'll change and be right back.'

When Kester returned, dressed in a green apron and black Starbucks cap, he still looked pretty intimidating . . . until he smiled. Crystal got up and gave him her seat.

'I'll bring you two some more coffee.'

She returned with a cup of Verona for each of us and some espresso brownies. I was surprised by the enthusiastic way she served us. I had never served anything to any subordinate in all my years in corporate life. But Crystal seemed to be genuinely enjoying the experience. She launched into a detailed description of Verona, telling us it was perfect with chocolate. 'But, then,' Crystal explained, 'all coffees go well with chocolate; they're kissing cousins.'

She left us to enjoy our coffee and brownies. The Verona coffee with the espresso brownies was a delicious combination—Crystal was right.

Then Crystal brought us a Colombian coffee with a slice of pound cake.

'This is in the "mild" category,' she said. 'Can you taste the difference?'

'It sure seems lighter than Sumatra,' I said.

'Right, "lighter" is a good word, Mike,' she said as though she were a teacher congratulating an apt pupil. 'Don't worry, you'll learn all about lots of different coffees here. By the way, you are going to be paid for the time you have been sitting here drinking coffee and having cake with Kester. Not bad for your first day on the job!'

Crystal left me with Kester. Though she had seemed so relaxed, I realised it might be just part of her management style. She was probably just putting a 'new Partner'—me—at ease.

'Here's how it works,' Kester said matter-of-factly. 'We call it training by sharing. It just means that we do things together. I learn from you by helping *you* learn.' He picked up my cup in his and stood up. 'OK, now that you've had your coffee, I'll show you how to make it.'

I followed him behind the bar.

Later, I came to know that Kester was the best 'closer' at Starbucks. Closing the store late at night is a big challenge because you're responsible for totalling up all the registers and making sure everything is perfectly stocked for the next day. Kester always made sure he got everything done on time and done right.

I didn't know any of this on my first day on the job. I also did not know that one late night, months later, Kester would save my life.

3

One Word That Changed My Life

May

I stood at the Bronxville station waiting for the 7.22 train to New York. I was not due to start my shift until 10.30 that morning—but I wanted to give myself more than enough time. The train from Bronxville to Grand Central took thirty minutes. The shuttle from Grand Central was another ten to twenty minutes to Times Square. From there I would jump on an express up to the West 96th station. I could then walk the block or so to my store. I was anxious. I had not mastered the commuting routine and did not want to be late. I did not think I could afford any mistakes at my new job.

Waiting on the platform on that May morning, I looked around Bronxville. The little suburban village had changed in the last few days as the spring colours arrived. There were masses of bright red and white tulips. The forsythia was a burst of yellow. Trees had that first green tint that was like a soft mist against the blue morning sky.

I sighed and then, out of nowhere, began to cry softly. The tears silently ran down my cheeks as I tried to suppress them. I did not want to draw attention to myself in that mass of energetic commuters. The men and women all seemed confident about their lives. I hated them for the ease with which they faced their commute.

I knew I was relatively invisible to them. In my black trousers, shirt and Starbucks hat, I looked like what I was—a working guy heading for a service job. I tried to brush the tears away, but they would not stop.

There was something so incongruous and sad about my standing on that platform, waiting for a train in my uniform, so many decades after I had first arrived in this exclusive town. My father had decided, after my mother had several more children, that we had to leave the city.

My father chose a huge Victorian mansion in Bronxville because it was close to the city and had a good public school. But Bronxville was not a happy place for me. When I got to school, I was in for daily humiliation. Try as I might, I could not learn to read. I really tried. All my classmates learned. It was terrible to be sitting there in the midst of my classmates and not see what they could see. The words in the books seemed to be created in some secret code that I could not break. The sentences jumped before my eyes. I tried to will myself to break the code, but could only guess what those black lines meant.

How horrible it felt to me to be singled out for this public demonstration of my own stupidity. My failure was impossible to ignore.

Miss Markham was the principal in the elementary school. She was a terrifying figure, marching down the halls issuing commands in a deep voice. I was brought to her attention. She called my parents to come in and speak to her.

My mother was embarrassed; my father was clearly angry. I had ruined his day.

'Why couldn't she see us at some other time?' my father asked my mother. 'It's right in the middle of my morning!'

For some reason Miss Markham took my side. She had decided, despite all signs to the contrary, that I would turn out all right. Right in front of me, she told my parents, 'Michael will read when *he* wants to. Stop badgering him.'

Her apparently irrational faith was eventually justified, although reading came to me, not through any act of concentration, but gently, easily, one summer in the country when I was ten.

Every summer, we would leave Bronxville for a small country town in the mountains of Connecticut. Mother was happier there. She had gone to Norfolk for summers when she was young, and there were still many friends from her youth who summered there. Her best friend from childhood had a house a few fields away, and her son became my best friend. We would ride our bikes down the old dirt roads and go for swims in the lake.

Mother would get me out of bed in the morning to see the dew sparkling in the sun. 'Elves' jewels,' she would say, hugging me with delight. 'Is there anything more beautiful in the world than a summer morning in Norfolk?'

But my happiest memory was sitting with Mother on a rug while she read to me. Across the field I could see a group of birch trees, their leaves fluttering green and silver in the soft breeze.

We lived in a little bungalow built by her father in the midst of a huge field and backed by an endless forest. That secluded woodland was a refuge for me. I would wander with a bow and arrow, telling myself I might shoot something (although I never did), and the silence of the old trees would comfort me.

I also liked the country because I could spend some time with my father. In Bronxville he had enthusiastically renovated a thirty-five-room mansion, bragging, 'This is the biggest house anyone in the family has ever owned.'

He took the profits from selling our brownstone on 78th Street in Manhattan and poured it all into this huge house. There was an acre of tiled roof to repair. He built a two-storey library. I overheard him telling his friends, 'I always wanted to have a private library with a ladder like this,' demonstrating the ladder that could move along the bookcases to reach the highest volumes.

He had volumes of old *New Yorker* magazines there. I would climb up the ladder and take them down. It was as though I were communing with my father, although he was almost never home. Despite his apparent pride in the house, he seemed always eager to get away, back to his city life. I never saw him come into the library and actually read a book. Once we moved to Bronxville, he spent less and less time with his family. He would leave early in the morning and come home after I had gone to sleep.

But I liked looking through the old *New Yorkers*—the cartoons, and even the way the print marched across the page. Although I could not understand what it said, I caught a glimpse of something my father was proud to be part of.

One afternoon in the country, I came into the bungalow from wandering in the woods. Mother was having a nap, and my sisters were visiting friends. I was by myself in the old living room. I pulled out an ancient book. Since this was a summer cottage, most of the books had been bought many decades ago and been left to grow musty and damp on the shelves.

I took down a book that was very thick but which had photographs. I opened a page at a photograph.

'General Grant,' I read. I could actually *read* his name. I could read! First a few words and then more and more. Suddenly, the black print made sense in my brain. I did not say anything to anybody, but by the time we returned to Bronxville that fall, I had learned to read many words. I was even confident enough to read aloud at school.

Despite the fact that I was by now in the sixth grade and was only now achieving what my classmates had accomplished years ago, Miss Markham was terribly pleased. I had justified her crazy faith in me. One afternoon, she asked me to come to her home and she served me tea. Then she took out a note and showed it to me. 'Read it,' she instructed in her bold voice.

'Michael Gates Gill is destined to be great,' I read.

I looked up. Was this a test? 'Is there any more?' I asked.

'No more to read,' Miss Markham said, reaching forward and holding my hands in hers.

I noticed she had big eyebrows and bright brown eyes. 'You, Michael,' she said, as though making a formal public statement, 'are destined for *greatness*. I don't care what you do, or what you don't do. I don't care if you go to some prestigious college, or don't go. I just know: you *are* great.'

She sat back, dropping my hands, smiling. 'Maybe you won't know what this note means now,' she said, intuiting my mystification, 'but keep it in a drawer somewhere. Take it out once a year and read it. Now that you can read!'

She laughed, and then became serious again. 'You didn't think you could ever learn to read, did you?' she asked me.

'No,' I said.

'But I knew,' she said. 'And I know that you are great. Just remember I told you so.'

She rose and walked me to the door, once again the Miss Markham of energetic forward motion and dynamic action.

We shook hands almost formally. I left, and for some reason stopped at the corner and looked back.

She was watching me. She waved.

I waved back.

I kept Miss Markham's words for several years, but lost them when I went away to college and Mother threw out a lot of my old stuff. But I remembered that afternoon vividly, and still do.

Miss Markham might well have expected what happened. After I learned to read, I developed a passion for books. Starting when I was ten, I read for hours every day. I loved to escape into that world of words and books.

For life was still very lonely for me. My father would visit for weekends during the summer, but during the winter he was too busy to do things with me. I had a few friends, but to me there was something horrible about this elite suburban town. In New York City, even when Nana left and I felt alone, I could still look out of the window of our home at a wide range of people passing on the sidewalk outside. Old people. Kids. Policemen walking. Teenagers running down our block. In Bronxville, in our huge house, there was no one even walking by.

I fared better in the country. In Norfolk, there would be weekends when my father would let me caddy for him when he played golf. And he came to the lake with the family, and I could spend a whole day in his company.

Sometimes he would sing songs: 'The Minstrel Boy'. 'Danny Boy'. Old Irish tunes. At other times, during family meals, he would recite poetry to us; sad poetry. '"Nothing to look backward to with pride",' he would intone from Robert Frost's 'The Death of the Hired Man'. 'Isn't that a sad summation of a life?' he would ask.

As a young boy, I had no idea what he was talking about.

Even later, at Yale, when I met Robert Frost, I failed to understand the sadness beneath his poetry. Of course, Robert Frost presented himself as a kind of jolly country gentleman. I remember running from a late class to a sherry party in honour of this famous poet. I did not have to change my clothes. I was, like all undergraduates in those days, wearing a jacket and tie. My professors addressed me as 'Mr Gill' and my English professor had invited me to 'have a glass of sherry with Robert Frost'.

Professor Waite greeted me at the door and ushered me in. There were already half a dozen other undergraduates gathered round a large man standing in the centre of the room. Frost wore a thick tweed jacket and had a shock of white hair that seemed windblown despite the fact we were inside an overheated faculty lounge.

He greeted me with a strong grip and laughing eyes.

None of us asked him any questions about his 'work'. It would not have been polite in that social context, like asking a doctor to do a diagnosis at a cocktail party.

In fact, I don't remember discussing poetry and writing itself with *any* poet I met at Yale. Having a drink with W. H. Auden, we wound up discussing the proper way to make a particular drink. When I was invited to meet T. S. Eliot, who had come to New Haven to give a lecture one evening, I was specifically told by my professor, 'Don't ask him any questions. Rumour has it that he is dying of cancer and is on a lecture tour to try to raise money for his wife.'

Part of the social obligation at Yale, as it had been in my home life, was not to ask too many direct questions.

So as a young boy growing up, I would never have thought to ask my father what he meant when he quoted Frost, or any other poet. I was a receptive audience but was not encouraged to be more than that.

Almost every day, my father would say, '"Stay with me beauty for the fire is dying."'

I asked him once what that meant.

'It's a line from a poem,' was all he would say.

It was clear that my father did not feel comfortable talking with me or even just being with me. I overheard him telling Mother once, 'I can't wait until Michael Gates grows up and I can have a decent conversation with him.'

My father was more a part of the family during weekends in the country than he ever was in Bronxville. And when he was away from us 'working hard in the city' during the summer weekdays, I could swim and walk in the woods, and smell the pines and taste the amazing, fresh Norfolk air.

But Bronxville had no such charms for me.

How had I ended up here, standing at the Bronxville station, living in a tiny apartment, without family or friends? I brushed more tears away.

Once I got the job at Starbucks, I tried to find an apartment near my store in New York City and discovered there was no way I could afford one. I started to look outside Manhattan, out to the Bronx, or up to Mount Vernon. There didn't seem to be anything I could afford.

One day, during my apartment search, I stopped in Bronxville to have a hamburger at a restaurant owned by an old high-school friend. Phil told me he had kept his parents' house and had a small attic apartment on the third floor. 'The house is right by the railroad tracks,' Phil told me, 'but it's convenient, and I'll give it to you at a good price.'

I jumped at the chance. The little apartment suited me. I liked climbing the old stairs and living in the attic of an old house.

The train arrived.

I got on, shuffling behind the herd of eager-beaver commuters. I knew that being morose was no way to start the day, and so I tried to recall *happy* memories about Bronxville.

My father would have great parties at our Bronxville home. He would make a point of introducing me to someone I might enjoy. When I was young, he had me meet E. B. White because I had so loved *Stuart Little*. E. B. White was diminutive, kind and curious. Just like Stuart Little.

Then, when I was older, he invited Brendan Behan, the wild Irish playwright, to the house so I could meet him. I loved Behan for his crazy song that the bells of hell might go 'ting-a-ling-a-ling for you but not for me'.

I told myself now that I had had happy times in Bronxville. But I had to admit that those big parties, and these literary celebrities, really meant very little to me. I would have preferred more time alone with my father.

I'm sixty-four, I reminded myself, I would be dead soon . . . not just singing Behan's song. Did I want to spend the rest of my life mourning my past? It was time for a more positive approach to the few years I had left.

For some reason I thought at that moment, trying to squeeze anonymously into my seat on the way to my new Starbucks job, of F. Scott

Fitzgerald's comment, 'There are no second acts in American lives.'

Was I on some hopeless quest to start a new life? I took a deep breath, straightened up in my seat and tried to think it through.

I really liked working with Crystal. It was hard to admit, but in many ways I enjoyed working at Starbucks more than I had at my high-status job at J. Walter Thompson.

Be honest, Mike, I thought, calling myself by my new Starbucks name. You feel good about what you are doing. Just because you are wearing a green apron rather than a Brooks Brothers suit doesn't mean you can't enjoy it!

By the time we got to Grand Central, I felt good. I rushed off the train, trying to get ahead of the upwardly mobile Bronxville strivers. Few, maybe none, would be heading with me to Times Square and the Upper West Side.

As I stepped into the shuttle, I stood taller. There is nothing wrong with working at Starbucks, I told myself, and a lot right. I would be able to afford my little apartment. It wasn't the huge mansion or the beautiful New England farmhouse I had lived in with my former wife and kids, but it was now home to me. A room of my own.

The express train took me up to 96th Street.

I climbed up the subway stairs into . . . sunlight. It was a beautiful spring day in New York. I saw the green Starbucks sign on the corner of 93rd and headed towards it with growing optimism.

Another Fitzgerald quote came into my mind. Something he had written to his daughter after his wife had died in a mental hospital after years of decline. Zelda had never fulfilled her early promise and Fitzgerald wrote: 'She realised too late that work was dignity.'

Work is dignity, I repeated to myself. That could be my mantra.

Why had it taken me so long to realise this essential truth? Fitzgerald had written his daughter this key perception, yet I had fought my daughter Elizabeth, nicknamed 'Bis', when she had wanted to go to work. When she was just twelve years old, she had been offered a summer job helping a tennis pro with scheduling and teaching, and I had turned down the job offer—without even talking to Bis about it.

'How could you do that, Daddy?' Bis had cried.

'But I want you to just enjoy yourself this summer.'

'But I *like* to work!' Bis had replied angrily.

For me, work was something one had to do, not what one chose to do. I thought I was doing Bis a favour by protecting her from having to work. How wrong I had been.

Bis had always loved to work and be active in the world outside our home. When she was young, she had loved to go to school, and even before her first day of school, Bis had taught herself to read.

Bis was also fortunate in that she was beautiful. A friend put her in a movie because he said she was a 'showstopper', with her halo of blonde hair and large blue-green eyes. But it was her brains and her love of working hard that were really remarkable. After college she went to NYU Film School and then got a job as a gopher for Martin Scorsese . . . not an easy boss. She went on to work for Harvey and Bob Weinstein—an even bigger challenge. Even while working for Scorsese and Miramax, she had found time to make several short films. Then she got a chance to direct a full-length feature. The movie, *Gold in the Streets*, was shot in New York and Ireland. Bis discovered that Ireland was a more open market for female film directors, and she moved there to continue her work.

Working hard had always come naturally to Bis. Why hadn't I profited by her example? Her attitude should have taught me about the dignity of work.

The thoughts of Bis comforted me as I opened the door to Starbucks, looking forward to work. I was hoping Crystal would be there and would give me something to do that did not involve the dreaded cash register. As anxious as I was to prove myself as a new Partner, I hesitated at going out front to deal with customers. I had yet to handle a cash register and the thought terrified me. So I usually just stood there in the neutral zone of Crystal's 'office'. It was a little space with a desk, a chair and a computer. For the last few weeks, Crystal had usually turned to me after I had hung around for a while and asked, 'How do you feel about cleaning today?'

I always responded, 'I would like nothing better!'

Cleaning, I thought, would keep me from those terrifying registers.

'This is grout,' Crystal said on my first cleaning duty day. 'It takes a lot of work to get it out. We have tiles, and we have a grout problem. Or maybe I should say that we have a grout *opportunity*.'

Crystal gave me a special grout brush. Then she showed me how to fill up the mop bucket with hot water and a cleaning solution. I would sweep, then I would mop, then clean the grout with the brush, then mop again.

Once Crystal came by and laughed at me. 'Mike, I have never seen anyone clean with such enthusiasm.'

'I love it,' I said. I could see I was making a difference. Even the other Partners quietly gave me some respect.

Kester came by once and said with his engaging smile, 'Watch out for the bathroom.'

Sure enough, that very day Crystal said, 'Mike, I am going to show you how to really clean a bathroom. You know how sometimes a car wash will say they are "detailing" your car? We are going to "detail" a bathroom.'

Crystal made me put on gloves and gave me super-powerful detergent, and I found myself down under the toilet bowl. I was surprised how little revulsion I felt for a job I would have previously thought too humiliating to even contemplate. But since Crystal seemed to be so positive about it, her respect for the challenge of cleaning a bathroom made me feel differently. It was a worthy effort to her, and who was I to argue with Crystal? I also felt that if I could succeed in doing something for Crystal, I could keep my job—whatever difficulties I might encounter with the other challenges of this fast-moving retail environment. So I was more than happy to do a great job of cleaning a bathroom.

Soon the toilet was sparkling.

Crystal smiled. 'Mike, I've never seen anyone clean like you.'

She did not know I was betting my whole future at Starbucks on getting good at some job nobody else wanted. That way, I figured she couldn't fire me. That was how scared I was that I would lose this job. I didn't want to fail at what I now thought might be my last chance. The average age of the Partners was about twenty. And I knew I wasn't getting any younger.

Yet I found my own advanced age did not make me any more merciful to the old or needy. Understanding, and adapting my behaviour to the Starbucks experience was not easy.

One afternoon, I had just finished "detailing" the bathroom, and it was sparkling. I saw an old African-American man who was clearly a homeless person heading for it. I intercepted him and explained that it was closed for cleaning—a lie I made up because I was afraid of the mess he might make.

Crystal overheard me and gestured for me to follow her back to her office—never a good sign. I had learned that she never criticised anybody in front of the customers, or even other Partners. She would take you aside

—one-to-one—in her office. 'Mike, never refuse the bathroom to anyone,' she said in a low, angry voice.

'But that guy wasn't a customer, he couldn't afford—'

'He might not be a customer, but everyone who walks in that door is a *Guest*. That's what makes Starbucks different.'

For some reason, perhaps because I had just worked so hard to clean up such filth, I argued with her. 'But it's not Starbucks' job to provide toilets for the homeless.'

Crystal did not say anything for about thirty seconds. I could see she was furious.

I shut up. Somehow, I had tripped over a land mine of emotion.

'Look.' I could tell she was fighting not to yell at me. 'In my store, in *our* store, we are . . . *welcoming*. Don't refuse that toilet to anyone, especially someone who really needs a welcome and not another person putting them down.'

She had not said 'not another white person' putting them down, but I read into it that way. I understood that I had made a big mistake. Crystal, and Starbucks, didn't treat people like that.

I went back out front to try to find the guy, but he had gone. My rejection probably meant nothing to him—New York is an unfriendly city to someone trying to use a restroom. But I learned a valuable lesson that day. My old arrogance had come back as soon as I thought I had done a great job. How sad!

The next day, Crystal didn't even mention the incident. I was to learn that she didn't harbour grudges. She let you know when she didn't like something you did, the moment you did it. And she never brought it up again.

'Now we move outside,' she instructed. She had me wash down the sidewalk and all the windows and window ledges.

A week later, she pulled me aside. 'I've decided to make you cleaning supervisor,' she declared. 'Sometimes other Partners will help you, and you can supervise.'

I was elated. Promoted! I had been programmed at J. Walter Thompson to be excited by promotions. Moving from copywriter to creative director and then to vice-president and finally executive vice-president had been a series of great occasions. There was always a raise, a celebratory dinner at a fancy restaurant. But then I realised with a powerful jolt that I was no longer in that world where such things meant something. This isn't some corporate hierarchy where it matters what title you have. You're *cleaning bathrooms*, I thought, laughing at myself . . . something I'd never learned to do before.

Now, standing awkwardly in Crystal's tiny office space, I hoped to do more cleaning today. One more day away from those cash registers.

'Hey, Mike,' Kester said, brushing by, 'how are you doing?'

'Good,' I said. 'I hope to do some more cleaning today.'

'No shit,' Kester said, then we both broke into laughter at his unintentional reference to toilets.

Crystal, in her chair in front of the computer, swivelled to face us. 'No street talk in here,' she said, clearly not amused. Kester gave me a wink and continued on out front.

'He was just joking,' I said, stupidly. Why hadn't I just shut up?

'Mike, let me explain something to you,' Crystal said, pushing her chair back. She pointed to the wall behind me. 'That's a paper with our uncompromising principles on it. . . . Read me the first one.'

Crystal sounded like an angry teacher. I read out the first 'uncompromising principle': 'To create a great work environment and treat each other with respect and dignity.'

Crystal stood up. 'Respect,' she said, reaching past my face to point at that word. 'I don't think it's respectful to use street talk in here.' Her hand dropped. Her voice lowered. 'Mike, I don't mean to go off on you like this. It's just that, before I came here, I wasn't treated with respect by anybody. My mother was a dope addict. She died when I was twelve. I was handed off to an aunt who already had two kids of her own. My aunt hated me. She also hated white people.'

Crystal looked at me as though to say, *Now do you get it?*

'She called white people "the enemy".'

I was shocked. I was silent. It was if Crystal was trying to shock me with her revelations of how disrespectful some people could be.

'My aunt made me feel like some unwelcome stranger in her house. Since I have been here at Starbucks, I have been . . . welcomed.' Crystal turned and sat back down.

'I'm sorry,' I said.

'Don't be sorry, Mike. This respect thing might be new to you, too.' She laughed. 'You don't learn it overnight. I just wanted to explain why it's such a big thing with me.'

'Yeah, I notice people at Starbucks seem polite.'

I had noticed that, even from the first day I stepped through the door at Starbucks, I had been treated with respect. I also realised that I had gained some self-respect by handling the cleaning and some of the tougher parts of the job. But Crystal didn't feel I had quite got the respect idea yet.

'The Partners are a lot more than *polite*,' she said. She was obviously disappointed with my response. In Crystal's eyes I still didn't quite get it. Politeness wasn't the same thing as respect.

'You'll get it,' Crystal said, as though reading my thoughts. 'It takes a while. Hey, I've got a great cleaning project for you today . . . if you would like to? Cleaning up this office space.'

She gestured around her at all the stuff covering every surface.

'I'd love to!' I blurted out. Another day of cleaning—far from registers.

Crystal smiled at my enthusiasm.

'Cool,' she said. 'I've just got to run out front for a few minutes, then I'll be back and we can get this space really clean.'

She stood up, her fancy black shoes catching my eye, then she hurried towards the front of the store. Crystal always did everything with such positive energy.

I could use some of that forward motion, I thought.

I had a sudden memory of my friend Gordon Fairburn, who had been so full of forward motion during his far-too-brief life. I pictured the last time I had visited Gordon, and the leave-taking. I was in the driveway of his home, heading towards my car. He was upstairs in his bed, surrounded by his wife and children, dying of prostate cancer. The window of his first-floor bedroom was open to the spring day. I heard his high, beautiful voice singing out an old song to me: 'Happy trails to you . . . till we meet again!'

I sang the last verse with him. We sang that last song together. Then I got in my car, flung my hand out of the window in a waving salute, and drove away. We had sung many songs since he was at Buckley with me, where he was my only friend. We had also been in the same class at Yale. Many nights in New Haven had ended with Gordon at the piano and me and other friends leaning against it, singing old songs. Even after college, we used to get together just to laugh and sing. Gordon was my oldest friend. That spring day, several years ago, he was dying. Now he was dead.

Why was I suddenly thinking of him after Crystal's talk to me?

I had missed him so this last year when my life was falling apart. Gordon always had a sense of humour, even about the toughest times. He had a good perspective on things. I had gone into advertising, and Gordon had gone on to Yale Divinity School and then became a successful therapist, a job he had loved.

Gordon was physically fragile. Yet he always loved to sing and loved life. How he would have loved still to be alive, I thought. He would have loved to help me with my problems. He would have loved even to have had the chance to *have* my problems.

Maybe it was about time I respected this extra time I had been given. I could still sing and laugh. Maybe, I thought, I had better spend more time singing and laughing, and less time crying about the past.

I had lost a lot. But I was still in the midst of life at this Starbucks store, where I had learned that there was a lot of dignity in the hardest kind of work. I should sing and laugh more. Out of respect for Gordon and his amazing, uplifting life. Out of respect for Crystal and what she was teaching me. Out of respect for myself and my new life.

4

On the Front Lines—Ready or Not

June

During the next weeks, rushing through Grand Central Terminal, I would sometimes be reminded of my previous life when I had helped in a small way to preserve this space. Twenty-five years ago, I had stood in Grand Central with Jackie Kennedy and my father as we talked of plans to save the station from destruction. I had been asked to join them because they wanted me to get the publicity resources of J. Walter Thompson behind this effort—at no cost.

As my father had grown older, he had become more and more passionate about preserving the city he loved, and he always claimed that architecture and buildings were his first love. That day, he stood poised on the steps overlooking the grand concourse, his arms flung wide in a loving embrace of everything he saw.

'We cannot let this great public space be desecrated by the greedy, opportunistic developers,' my father intoned in his melodic baritone. 'It deserves to *live* as a kind of beautiful, open oasis in this crowded, cacophonous city . . . a rare gift of welcoming space for countless *future* generations of New Yorkers.'

Jackie stood at his side, gazing at him with adoring eyes. My father was a successful writer, he was funny and he was a social asset, all qualities that she could admire. Having checked with the powers that be at JWT, I was happy to pledge the company's pro bono support to this effort. Jackie's name was magic to everyone.

I helped to organise a train journey, with Jackie and the media, down to Washington, where the Supreme Court was due to rule on a historic landmarks preservation law. The event was to be followed by an elegant party to which I had invited many notables. Nobody refused my invitation. Vice-President Mondale and his wife, Joan, greeted Jackie as she stepped off the train. We had a reception for her in a small, beautiful room at Washington's Union Station—filled with senators, media and, most importantly, a few wives of the justices on the Supreme Court.

(When I met Justice Potter Stewart at a Skull & Bones event a few months later and thanked him for his positive ruling on the landmarks issue, he said, 'Don't thank me—it was my wife. She told me I could not vote against Jackie!')

Jackie worked the whole room with an amazing talent for connecting with and elevating everyone she spoke to. She even found time for a few words with me at the end of the event.

'Michael, you have been so helpful.'

I leaned forward to hear her and was enveloped in the cocoon of her attention. 'Thank you,' I said, tongue-tied, just as many professional politicians were in her powerful presence. I felt uplifted by those few moments with her and have never forgotten them.

But I remembered now, glancing at the big, newly sparkling clock above the information booth and the gleaming, restored space she had achieved in Grand Central, that I could be late for work. I rushed for the shuttle.

I hurried to my store at 93rd and Broadway and made my way inside, nodding a quick smile at my new Partners. I clocked in and noticed that I had come within minutes of being late. I shuddered at the thought. Why had I wasted precious time in Grand Central contemplating the past?

Less past, more future! I kept telling myself, a kind of mantra I wanted to believe.

I saw Crystal look up from her computer and I realised I must have spoken out loud to myself. I was going nuts! Fortunately, she quickly turned back to her computer screen.

Anxious to prove myself, I still hesitated about going out front with the other Partners. Over two months, and I had yet to handle a cash register. The thought still horrified me. So I just stood there in Crystal's tiny office space, hoping to be assigned more cleaning today. Yet Crystal seemed barely to notice me. She was involved with her computer.

Ever-glamorous, her lustrous hair fell to her shoulders perfectly, and she wore expensive gold jewellery on each hand. I stood behind her, hoping to catch her attention. Over her shoulder, I could see that she was preparing some kind of presentation.

I could not resist trying to help.

'In my previous life, I prepared a lot of presentations,' I told her. 'Maybe I can help.'

She turned to me with an annoyed expression. I realised that—for her—I was an unwanted interruption today. 'Mike, isn't it about time you got out front and onto a register?'

My mouth dropped open.

'You've done the computer simulation, right?' Crystal continued. I had done the training on the computer, but I was sure it was nothing like the actual experience of handling hundreds of dollars while calling drinks and trying to make eye contact with Guests.

'Yes . . .' I reluctantly responded. 'But, Crystal, honest, maybe I could help with your presentation?' I was almost begging to do something I knew how to do, rather than be sent to do something I felt I was certain to fail at.

'How? This is a presentation about the store and a review of the Partners and sales of pastries, and coffee and beans . . . not something you know a lot about.'

She turned back to the screen, trying to dismiss me.

At this point, I wasn't going to let myself be dismissed. I would do anything to not have to go out to register duty. 'Have you heard of KISS?'

'No.' She continued to focus on the computer. 'What does that have to do with what I'm trying to do?'

'KISS is a statement based on research about presentations.'

She turned to me. The word 'research' had always got the attention of clients, and now it worked with Crystal. Any opinion was much more interesting if you preceded it with the idea that there was some scientific study behind it. 'It's not a big deal,' I said. 'KISS just stands for "Keep It Simple, Stupid". Studies show that the best presentations are simple and short. Have you ever wished a presentation were *longer*, or more *complicated*?'

Crystal laughed.

Phew. I had also found in my previous life in advertising that if you could get clients to laugh, they usually bought your ideas. So I was glad that Crystal laughed now.

'So how do I do KISS?' she said, always quick to recognise an opportunity that might help her.

'You could try the three P's.'

She gave me a look as much to say: *Get on with it!*

'People. Product. Profits. You could talk about the new people you've hired; under product could be the pastries and bean sales; and profits is the bottom line.'

'Plus *Place*,' Crystal said, reaching up to slap my hand with a high five. I slapped back, hard and clumsy in my enthusiasm. We did not high-five at JWT.

She turned to her screen.

'Place?' I asked.

'The store. We've done some cleaning here, Mike, as you well know . . . I want to highlight that as well.'

I was thankful and decided to shut up. After *one* more suggestion. 'The best presentations start with some surprising visual or prop, something that they will never forget.'

I was thinking of a presentation I had done about a name change on an airline. No one in the Allegheny Airlines management wanted to change the name. But I hated the name Allegheny. And so did most customers. They called it Agony Airlines. When I had met the chairman, who was a fragile man in his seventies, his first question was, 'What do you think of the name of my airline?'

'If it was neutral you could stay with it, but it's not good to be a joke.'

He didn't buy it at first. Then we did research that showed people would wait thirty minutes to take USAir, an as yet nonexistent airline, rather than Allegheny.

One morning I was asked to present the name-change idea to the chairman and 500 sales reps from across the country. We were in a huge, draughty room, part of an aircraft hangar. Not a great place to make a pitch.

I started with the research. Dead silence. I could sense the room wasn't buying it.

But I had brought props. A baseball bat and a baseball.

I took up the bat and said, 'This name change is going to let us knock the competition out of the park.'

I threw the ball up and tried to hit a long, high-fly ball. Instead, in my nervousness, I hit a powerful straight shot, almost grazing the head of the chairman. He threw himself to the floor. The ball raced to the back of the room and gave off a great *whack* when it hit the metal wall.

There was dead silence, then the whole sales team rose and roared with a deafening cheer. Maybe they were tired of losing to the competition year after year and I had sparked some bloodlust. But whatever the reason, that ball slamming into the far wall had given us a room full of new emotion.

We sold the new name. But we couldn't have done it without the bat and the ball.

'Before you get to your PowerPoint four P's presentation,' I said to Crystal, 'isn't there some prop you could hold up . . . just so they get a sense of who you are? Something to make it memorable. Remember, your audience will be seeing lots of presentations about lots of stores.'

She looked at me. Then I saw her beautiful eyes sparkle with an idea. 'How about this: I still have the first pound of coffee I ever ground, from seven years ago. I keep it in my apartment.'

'Why?' I asked.

'I don't know. Maybe because it was part of joining Starbucks and turning my life around. I kept it. That pound of ground Verona coffee means a lot to me.'

'Perfect. Just start your presentation by holding up the pound of coffee.

Wait till everyone is quiet. Then say how it turned your life around.'

'Cool,' Crystal said, turning back to her computer. 'Now get out to the registers, Mike. Joann is out there. She is patient. Let her help you get going.'

Damn! After all my effort to avoid the register by helping Crystal with her presentation, something I was good at, I was still going to be forced to do the money part of the business, at which I knew I would fail. Dragging my feet, I made my way to the front of the store. Fortunately, it was the quiet part of the afternoon, just after lunch and before the schoolkids piled in.

There were three registers behind the counter. Bianca was on the one closest to the pastry case, there was an empty one in the middle, and Joann was on the register by the bar. I walked by Bianca to the middle register.

'Joann,' I said, 'Crystal told me you'd help me get a register.'

'Sure, Mike.'

Joann was a large, comforting woman and older than most Partners. 'Just punch in your numbers on the screen,' she said, 'then take the register drawer to the back. There's a machine that will weigh the cash—should be one hundred fifty dollars in your drawer. Then come on back.'

A machine that will weigh and count the cash! My heart leapt with joy. Counting out pennies and dollars would have taken me hours, and I would have got the sum wrong. I always did.

I grabbed the drawer and headed towards the back. Crystal was still involved in her presentation, but she looked up with a smile. 'There's the weighing machine,' she said, pointing to a small desktop instrument. 'Just put your coins and paper on that, and make sure it comes out to exactly one hundred and fifty. You'll be responsible for any over or under. By the way, you are not allowed to be, at the end of the shift, more than five dollars over or under.'

'Sounds good,' I said, not realising that when you process $1,000, you can easily be several dollars short or long.

The weighing machine, which was about the size of a large hardcover book, had a metal pocket on top, in which you put your notes. Your coins were already in little pockets in your register, and you just lifted them out and the magic machine weighed them up exactly as well. For example, if you put a bunch of dollar bills on, a little window would read underneath: '$85'. Or if you put a pocket of pennies on from your register, the machine would read: '$0.50'. The machine kept a running count, shown on a little screen beneath the pocket. I was not required to add or subtract anything!

To me, the weighing machine was a miracle. I turned to head back towards the register, a little more confident.

'Hey, Mike,' Crystal called after me.

I stopped and turned my head.

'The presentation looks good. What do I do for an ending?'

I felt pleased she was asking me for advice. That was a first for Crystal and me. I walked back, still holding the drawer of the register.

'The best ending is a summary of what you've said.'

'The four P's?'

'OK.' I smiled inside. She had got it. 'So put up a slide of the four P's, and then an equal sign, then the words "Starbucks Success".'

'That sounds too cold,' Crystal said.

'So what do all those things equal?' I asked.

Crystal thought for a moment and then suggested, 'How about we put up the four P's, and then the equal sign, and then the words "Great Experience for Our Guests".'

'OK,' I said. 'But to me the unique thing about Starbucks is what a great experience it is for the *Partners*. Every Fortune 500 company says they put the customer first. Starbucks puts the Partners first.'

Crystal looked at me. 'OK, how about this: the equal sign leads to "Great Experience for Partners and Guests".'

'Good,' I said, heading out to the registers. Then I stopped. 'How about,' I couldn't resist saying: '"The Best Experience for Partners and Guests"? "Best" is a word that kind of rhymes with "Guest" . . . makes the summation sound more memorable.'

'OK,' she said. '"The Best Experience for Partners and Guests".'

'And when you use the word "the" in front of something like that, it implies a pre-emptive benefit.'

Crystal wasn't listening any more—thank goodness.

'Get out to the registers, Mike,' she encouraged. 'Be sure to make eye contact and connect with conversation.'

I had heard those words on the training video, but I was more concerned with just handling the cash.

Unfortunately, now the kids from school had arrived.

Joann came over and helped me put my drawer in. 'The computer will show you the correct change. You'll do fine, Mike.'

'But I'm terrible with money.'

'So were my first two husbands. Just let the register do the work.'

I smiled. A good mantra.

A kid stepped up to my register to order. 'I want a Tall Mocha.'

I called down to Tawana, an attractive but combative barista on the espresso bar: 'Tall Mocha.'

'Tall Mocha,' Tawana called back to me, confirming she had got the order right.

I looked at the register. On the screen I read the words 'Tall' and 'Mocha', just like on the computer-training module. I jabbed at them with my finger. Sure enough, it worked, and the price came up on my screen.

The boy handed me five dollars.

The screen displayed the option '$5.00' in a box.

I punched at the box.

The register opened, and the screen displayed the exact change I should hand him: '$2.73'. I dug out the change. The kid looked at it, stuck it in his pocket and made his way to the espresso bar to pick up his drink.

My screen read: 'Close your drawer.'

I closed my drawer.

Hey, I said to myself, you can do this!

Then the next Guest stepped up; a young lady who was clearly pregnant. 'A Decaf Tall Coffee,' she said.

I punched in 'Tall', took her money, gave her the change, closed the drawer and turned to get a cup of coffee for her. Fresh coffee was right behind me, with the cups. I gave one to her.

She gave me a big smile, as though I were already a friend. 'My name's Rachel. I have another child on the way. I have to stick to Decaf for a while. Can't wait to get back on the hard stuff.'

I had a sudden realisation that people might treat me the way they were said to treat bartenders. They wanted to engage with someone serving them the good stuff.

The afternoon went surprisingly well, despite the constant stream of Guests. As evening fell, it got even busier, but Joann came over a couple of times to help me out. The line moved smoothly, with people ordering a Single Pump Mocha or a Tall Latte. I was supposed to call out the *size* first, then the name of the drink, and any 'customising'. Often I would get the order wrong, and Tawana would correct me at the top of her lungs, putting the order in the right way. It was humiliating for me, but I learned fast.

Also, it was a gift to me that Tawana had such a large, commanding voice. With my brain tumour affecting my hearing, I had been worried about getting the orders straight. I never missed Tawana's powerful calls. And I found that by leaning over the register, closer to the Guests, I could also hear them clearly.

That night, around 7 p.m., I was surprised to see the store grow really busy. A businessman entered the store and joined the growing line. When I had been on the other side of the bar, I had worked so hard just to get a prospective client like this well-dressed man to return a call. Now my customers were literally waiting in line for my services, I thought to myself. How funny.

The businessman stepped up in line and told me, 'Double Macchiato.'

Starbucks language. I had a hard time figuring out what to punch on the cash-register screen.

'You are new here, right?' the man asked. I looked at him. Was he going to complain and get me fired on my first day at the register?

But he smiled at my look of panic.

'Don't worry, you'll get it.'

He actually took the time to encourage me. Wow. I looked back at the screen with renewed clarity of mind. Double Macchiato. Hit 'Tall' then 'Macchiato'. Simple.

Around eight o'clock, it started to get even busier. I had not realised that people had made Starbucks a part of their nightlife. Crowds of young people were piling in to share time with one another over their lattes.

Focus, I reminded myself. Punch the right button, call out the order, make the right change, smile. A beautiful young blonde woman came up to my register.

'A Tall Skim Latte,' she said.

I intently punched in 'Tall', then 'Latte' on my register, called out the drink to Tawana in the right order, took the young woman's five-dollar bill, and started to hand her back change. When I looked up to smile, I realised it was my daughter, Annie! I had been concentrating so hard on not making a mistake I had not even realised who I was serving.

'Hi, Dad,' she said, smiling. She obviously thought it was funny that I had not recognised her. Maybe she also thought it was funny to see me in a green apron and wearing a black cap—and in a situation where I was so clearly in over my head.

'Annie!' I said. 'Good to see you!'

I felt the blood going to my face. Here I was, in a blue-collar job, serving my daughter. But I remembered what Crystal had said about respect, and tried to stand tall and respect myself, and show respect for my daughter. Annie must have realised I was struggling and confidently took charge of the situation. 'I'll wait. What time are you off?'

'Nine . . . I'll be off at nine.'

'See you then,' she said, heading off to pick up her drink at the bar.

'Double Tall Skim No Whip Mocha,' the next young lady said. I laboriously hit the different keys on the screen and called the drink out to Tawana. She called it back exactly the same way and I was relieved.

You know how it is when you are involved in some sport or physical activity when you can't stop and you can't think about anything else? I remembered when I had played football in high school. Just as now, I really didn't know what I was doing, but the effort carried me along. Probably I was performing the same way now. The rest of the night passed in a blur.

As the night wound down, Joann went home to her child. Crystal appeared. 'It's time, Mike,' she called. 'Pull your till.'

Crystal showed me how to weigh my money out.

'Your "drop" should be the total weighed out, minus one hundred and fifty. Don't worry, the machine will tell you the amount.'

And the machine did. It also said that I was $4.50 short.

'Not too bad for your first time,' Crystal said. 'As I said, you are allowed to be five dollars over or under . . . but most Partners come within a few cents. You'll get it.'

Was she out of her mind? She had no idea of the financial idiot she was talking to. But I was grateful I had just got through the experience, and I was surprised what a high I had got from interacting with the Guests who were so eager to buy from me.

'You did OK, Mike,' Crystal said in review as she oversaw my weighing out. 'But try to call out the drinks correctly. And if you get the time, try to say a few words to the Guests. A lot of people come to Starbucks to feel better. It's part of our job to help them.'

'Sure,' I said, just grateful not to have been hundreds of dollars short.

Crystal looked at her wrist. 'I gotta go,' she said, pulling on a leather coat. 'Punch out, Mike,' she called back to me as she headed to the front. I watched as she stopped on the way out the door to talk with several Guests.

I punched out on the time clock on her computer . . . 9:05. I had put in seven hours. My feet ached and my head was still spinning.

Then I remembered: Annie! She was waiting for me. I pulled off my apron quickly and made my way out front; I found her sitting at a small table, reading a book. 'Hi, Annie.'

'Daddy!' She leapt up from the table and gave me a big hug. 'Let's go. It's late for you.'

Annie knew that I usually liked to get to bed early. I am more of a lark than an owl. When she was growing up, Annie and I would share the early hours together. We would walk down to the lake in Connecticut in the summer mornings. I would splash with her in the shallows, and then we'd walk home and share some cereal before the rest of the family woke up.

We headed towards the door of my store and Annie took my arm. That made me feel better. 'We'll take the subway to Times Square,' Annie said, taking charge, 'the shuttle over to Grand Central, and I can get a subway back to Brooklyn from there. You can get a train to Bronxville.'

Annie had it all figured out. As we rode the rocking subway downtown, we talked over the jangling noise.

'I wanted to see if you were *really* working at Starbucks,' Annie explained. I had told her mother and left a message for Annie that I was working at the Broadway store but telling her to wait for a while before stopping by, until I was better at my job.

But Annie was born without a willing-to-wait gene in her body. So I was not surprised that she had shown up to see me despite my plea.

'I just wanted to see if it was really true,' Annie laughed.

'Well,' I said defensively, 'it's a job.'

'No, don't get me wrong,' Annie said. 'I like it. You look good in that black cap.'

She was teasing a little bit, but she wasn't kidding. Maybe she liked the idea that I was willing to work hard. And it must have been clear to her that I was struggling, which she obviously didn't mind.

'I still don't know what I'm doing,' I said.

'I know!' She laughed. I laughed. I was filled with love for this wonderful person, and with regret.

'Annie,' I said with deep sincerity, 'I am so sorry that I've messed up my life so, and *your* life.'

It was as if I had reminded her of a fact she had forgotten and, suddenly, the goodwill seemed to dissipate. She said angrily, 'I'll never listen to your stupid advice again.'

The subway pulled into Times Square and, as we exited, Annie pointed us towards the shuttle, to which we were transferring.

As we sat in the shuttle, waiting for it to take us to Grand Central, I broke the silence. 'I'm sorry,' I said again.

'Sorry doesn't cut it,' Annie said. She had always had a sharp tongue.

The shuttle filled up with people and then started to move. I let an old lady with five shopping bags take my seat. Annie also stood up. We were squeezed together with hundreds of others.

Annie was wearing an elegantly styled coat, her posture was straight despite the crush of people and the swaying car, and she seemed so bright and beautiful—even under the harsh fluorescent lights. She was so put together. I looked down at my shoes, hating the idea that I had lost the respect of my intelligent daughter by my stupid, selfish acts.

We got out in Grand Central. I remembered Crystal's emphasis on dignity and respect and realised that I had not treated Annie or any one of my children with the respect and dignity that they deserved. I had been a pompous fool, broadcasting advice while my own life was falling apart. I looked into Annie's clear blue eyes and said, 'I am sorry for being such a pompous fool.'

She reached out and gave me a hug. 'You *have* been stupid, but I like your working at Starbucks.'

I felt a great sense of relief. Annie had a quick temper, but an equally fast ability to forgive and move on. I had once told her, 'You are like a summer thunderstorm.'

'What do you mean?' Annie had asked.

'Your temper is so strong and quick.'

'But it's great after that kind of summer storm . . . a fresh new feeling to everything!' Annie had replied, winning the dialogue as usual.

Now she looked up at the big schedule board listing all the trains. 'I am going down this corridor to catch a subway to Brooklyn,' she said. 'Your next train for Bronxville leaves in four minutes. Don't miss it.'

Then she gave me a strong hug and a kiss, and I ran for my train with a lighter heart.

5

Open Wide and Smile—You're on Broadway

July—August

I awoke, sweating. I had no air conditioning and my little attic apartment was sweltering in the summer heat. It was only 3 a.m. I had an hour or so before I had to get up and leave for New York, but I was too hot, and anxious about helping Crystal open the store for the first time, to go back to sleep. The idea of opening was really getting to me. I told myself to calm down, but some conversations I had overheard made me worry. Partners had said, 'Opening is a bitch,' and that made me feel that it might be more than I could handle.

I tried to remind myself that in my previous life I loved challenges. I loved going after new business or meeting a 'tough' client. But opening a store was a physical challenge. I had never been confident physically.

Suddenly, I had a bad memory come into my head of a physical challenge I should have avoided. But the stupid test came at a time when I was still an adolescent and had too much to prove.

Sweating in the summer heat, I remembered a scary time in Spain, in 1959, when I was just nineteen and had taken the summer to go to Europe by myself. I could even now almost feel the hard-packed earth of the campsite on the outskirts of Pamplona, baking in the unforgiving sun. Like many young men of the time, I had gone to Spain seeking Papa, and I found him. That summer Ernest Hemingway sat in the sunny square in Pamplona, surrounded by an adoring circle of fans. He had a handsome face and broad shoulders, with white hair carefully combed over a scar I should never have mentioned.

I stepped up. 'Michael Gill,' I said, shaking his hand. His grip was strong. His eyes were measuring me. He did not ask me to sit down and join the group.

'Janet Flanner sends her regards,' I said to him. Janet Flanner was a colleague of my father's on the *New Yorker*; she was the Paris correspondent, and an old drinking friend of Hemingway's. I had met her a few weeks before. When she found out I was a Hemingway fan, she told me to use her name. She also mentioned that I should ask Hemingway about a scar on his head. Rumour had it he had been hit by a piece of shrapnel in the war, or had been gored by a charging rhino in Africa. All Janet Flanner had told me was, 'There's a good story behind that scar—*if* Ernest will tell it.'

At the mention of Janet, Ernest Hemingway looked at me with new interest. 'She is a friend of my father's,' I explained. 'Brendan Gill.'

'Yes, I know him,' Hemingway said. 'And Janet is an old friend of mine. One of the great reporters of her generation.'

Under his formal courtesy was a hint of aggression.

'Miguel is the son of another friend of mine,' Hemingway announced to the larger group, deciding quickly on his nickname for me. 'Brendan Gill, a colleague of Janet Flanner's on the *New Yorker* magazine.'

A few heads nodded in appreciation.

Looking back now, forty-five years later, as I tossed and turned in my hot bed before my morning Starbucks shift, it occurred to me that I had gone to Hemingway for validation. And at that moment in Pamplona, I had to prove myself.

I looked Hemingway in the eye, remembering Janet Flanner's comment. 'How did you get that scar?' I asked, sensing that this question would annoy him.

Hemingway's eyes went dead—for just a second. Then, ignoring my question, he asked simply, 'Have you run before the bulls?'

'No,' I said, and then stupidly added, 'not yet.' I had not thought a moment before that I would risk my life in such a stupid spectacle.

'Well,' Hemingway said slowly, calculating his verbal punch, 'you run in front of the bulls, Miguel, then come back and we can talk.'

He had treated me like a boy, not yet a man.

I stayed up drinking that night, held aloft by the manic festival atmosphere. By morning, I had decided I *had* to run before the bulls. The bull corral was opened at seven each morning, and those foolish enough to do it raced up a mile of cobbled streets to the arena, bulls in hot pursuit all the way. I dreaded the whole thing.

It was growing light when I got to the corral. I could hear the bulls moving around, occasionally banging against the boards that contained them. I climbed up the side of the corral to look at them. They looked big and dark and mean.

Soon a crowd gathered, mostly young men getting ready for the run.

An old man stood at my side. I nodded to him. He knew I was a stranger here. Although I had very little Spanish, and he had no English, I gradually understood that he was urging me to wait for the bulls further up the street.

I looked up the hill.

The street was a narrow one, lined with large wooden barricades. I decided to take his advice. I walked several hundred yards up the hill and leaned against a barricade to rest for a moment. Then I sat down. I suddenly realised how tired I was. I had not slept well in days. The early sun was just hitting me. I dozed off.

A commotion behind my barricade woke me. The crowd was gathering there, waiting for the imminent release of the bulls. I had an urge to leap over the barricade to safety. Hemingway would never know. I resented him now, for forcing me to risk my life in such a stupid adventure.

Then there was a shout and everyone began to run. I tried to stay up with the leaders, but gradually dropped towards the middle.

As I came round one corner, I stumbled on the cobblestones and slammed into a barricade. Some hands helped me up. My back felt like it was broken, and my hands were scraped as I tried to right myself.

Hands patted my back and pushed me back into the pack. I found myself running for my life. Somehow I had found a second wind, full of pure, unadulterated fear.

I feared I was going to die on that narrow street, surrounded by people I did not know. All in the name of Papa.

I fought my way to the front, lifting my legs high, passing beyond the pain until I was just going on adrenaline. I found myself within two or three men of the very front of the pack. Up ahead I could see the bullfight arena, which seemed to give me extra energy. I gave a final burst of speed and headed in just as the gates opened.

A whole cluster of bulls now charged into the arena. A man fell before them; some bulls stepped over him, and some stepped on him. Another brave fellow had a cape and was trying to make some passes. The crowd roared approval.

After the last of the bulls had entered, I snuck over to the side of a barricade and went out through the same opening the bulls had just come in. I could hear screams but also cheers behind me. I was covered in sweat, still shaking from fear. I found a small alley that was still dark, unlit by the early morning sun, and lay down and slept.

The sun, creeping down the wall, woke me. I went back up to the main square. Hemingway was not at the café at this early hour, so I sat near his big, circular table and ordered a beer. And another.

Soon after one o'clock, Hemingway emerged from the hotel. His swarm of pilot fish followed him, as always in Pamplona. He sat down, raised his big hand to order, and then he caught sight of me. 'Miguel?'

I rose and made myself walk over to his table. (I ached in every joint.) 'I ran in front of the bulls,' I said.

'Good,' Papa said, nodding his head. 'Good.'

He indicated the chair next to him, which had not yet been filled. A great honour. I took it eagerly, almost collapsing into it. Hemingway signalled the waiter to bring me a drink. Then he clinked my glass, toasting me.

He leaned forward and said in a low voice, 'Now I will tell you about that scar.'

Hemingway scraped his chair round and faced me so no one else at the table could hear. 'Some people will tell you I got that scar fighting in the war, or in Africa.'

Papa spoke deliberately, yet as serious as his manner was, his eyes still held a combative sparkle. 'Many people make up many stories about Papa,' Hemingway said with a slight smile, 'but few know the truth. Here is the truth of the scar, Miguel:

'It was in Paris. A group of us had been drinking all day. Later, we ended up back in someone's place. I went to the bathroom, and reached up to pull the chain to flush the old-fashioned toilet. I reached too far, and pulled too hard. I grabbed the lever to a skylight and pulled the whole damn thing down on my head. The glass smashed. There was a lot of blood. Someone panicked and insisted I go to a hospital. A French hospital in the middle of the night. They sewed me up and did a terrible job of it. So I got this scar.

'I never told people of that story, so they made up their own. Like the war. Like an African safari and a lion ripping at my head. But you have heard the true story, Miguel. Now let's have some drinks with our friends.'

He turned back to the larger crowd, signalling with his beefy forearm for another round.

Now, in my little attic room, thinking of Hemingway's story of the toilet and the scar, I got out of bed and hobbled on my sore feet to the bathroom and took a shower. I once ran fast from the bulls, but now I could hardly handle a job serving coffee, I thought to myself grimly.

My feet hurt all the time since I had joined Starbucks. At first I had fancy black brogues. Then I got a pair of black trainers. But my feet still hurt. One of my Partners, a big man named Anthony, told me I'd be better off with paratrooper boots.

'They use 'em to jump out of planes and land on the ground.'

I spent a lot of my hard-earned money on the combat boots, but my feet hurt even more. My sister Holly, who was the closest in age to me, just two years younger, called to ask, 'How's the job?'

'Great, but my feet hurt. I'm on my feet all day.'

'You're just getting old,' she replied frankly. 'The pads on the bottom of your feet get thinner as you age, and your feet hurt more.'

I hung up, feeling even worse. So I went back to my trainers.

I had a sudden memory of my son Charles leaping off the roof of the camp on the lake in the country last summer. He was just seventeen at the time. Yet Charles was already several inches taller than me. He was also a better athlete. Charles had leapt with an easy confidence out into the summer air.

I smiled at the memory of his graceful leap as I staggered with hurting feet out of the bathroom. I got dressed in a white shirt and black trousers, pulled on my black trainers and headed into the city.

Later, coming out of the subway, I saw a neon sign across the way saying it was already ninety degrees. In the summer, the city never slept. As I waited for Crystal on the sidewalk of 93rd and Broadway, a couple of drunks were wandering around, but I kept my head down and hid in the doorway of the store.

Again, I was struck by the incongruity of my life—ten years earlier, as a busy executive, at five in the morning I might have been riding the red-eye back from a trip to LA. Most summer mornings since being fired, I would have been sleeping peacefully in our big old New England farmhouse, dreaming of a day of swimming and golf. Now I was standing in the dark of sweaty New York City, waiting for my twenty-eight-year-old boss and feeling scared that I might not be able to do a good enough job of opening a Starbucks store. My former arrogant self would have been appalled.

When Crystal came up from the subway I was relieved to see her, but she had no time for niceties. Brushing past me, she put her key in the door and told me to 'lock it behind you'.

I realised that every second would count. We had to open at 6 a.m.—just an hour to go.

'Give me a hand,' Crystal said, and I helped her move the crates of pastries to the back. The pastries were delivered fresh each day to every Starbucks store.

'Here are the clean plates. Put the pastries on them. There's a schematic on the pastry case, telling you what goes where. I've got to get the coffee going.'

As I moved to open the first pastry packages Crystal suddenly yelled, 'Stop!' and I jumped.

'Put on some of these plastic gloves,' she said, handing me some. 'Never touch the pastries with your bare hands. OK, get going.'

I put on my green apron, taking a quick look at the schedule that was always posted on the bulletin board. Joann would be in at nine. Joann never came in too early, or stayed too late. She had a child to take care of, and since she was such a dedicated and competent worker, Crystal always gave her the times she needed on the schedule.

Soon the store was filled with the aroma of the delicious coffee that Crystal was brewing. She called to me as she did her different opening steps, helping me learn as she went through the process:

'I brew up today's coffee—Verona,' she called, 'then I brew up a batch of mild coffee: today it's Colombia. Finally I brew some Decaf . . . right now it's Decaf Sumatra.'

I nodded my head as she called these specifics out to me. How did she think I had time to learn? I was doing the pastries as quickly as possible before the store opened.

I ripped open the plastic packages containing the scones. There were four different kinds of scones. There were five different varieties of muffins and three different donuts. Then there were chocolate and oatmeal cookies, marshmallow crispy squares, espresso brownies, and a variety of other items that had to be unwrapped and set up.

I looked at the visual display posted on the case that showed where each pastry should go. This was not like handling a register and trying to make change. I was confident, and after a quick glance, the schematic was clear in my mind. At Yale, I had built up a good visual memory as a history of art major who had to spend many a late night memorising pictures. I smiled to think that my college education was being put to use—forty years later.

Until I hit the bagel packages. The bagels were tricky to get out. The packages were designed to keep the bagels as fresh as possible, but they made it very hard to release them from the plastic coverings. It occurred to me that American civilisation might be remembered for creating the most difficult-to-open plastic packages in the history of the world—all to keep things nice and antiseptic. But Crystal came to my rescue with a scissors. Perhaps I wasn't the only one who had a problem with the bagel bags.

As I cut them open, Crystal called instructions out to me: 'Now I'm making the iced tea. Passion, Black Iced Tea, Green Tea.' I glanced at her to let her know I had registered her lesson.

But there was more to do, and the clock was ticking.

'I'm going to get the espresso bar open,' Crystal said, 'and you do the sandwiches.'

The sandwiches went in the front of the pastry case. I put the egg salad, the tuna and the turkey in the spots that were already marked in the case. While math was something I had never mastered, filling the cases according to a detailed visual was something I could do, and do easily.

I stood when I finished, observing the fully stocked case like it was indeed a work of art.

Crystal smiled at me. 'Good job, Mike,' she said. 'Now assign yourself a register.' I got a drawer from the middle register, weighed it out on the magical counting machine to $150, and put it back in my register just as I saw the first Guest waiting at the door.

'Open the door, Mike,' Crystal called, busy getting the espresso bar ready and pulling a first 'test' espresso drink to make sure everything was working right.

I went over and unlocked the door. We were open for business.

The first Guest ordered a Tall Skim Cappuccino and a plain bagel with jelly.

I remembered Crystal telling me to make eye contact and conversation. I was less worried about screwing up on the cash register by now, so I decided to focus on what I knew I could do. After all, during my twenty-five years at J. Walter Thompson I had been paid extremely well to talk—making conversation was not a problem for me.

'A Red Sox fan?' I asked the Guest, who was wearing a Sox cap.

'Actually, no,' he laughed. I noticed he had white hair and an easy smile. 'My roommate at Harvard Medical School was a rabid Red Sox fan. Over the last decades, I have rooted for the Yanks and he for the Red Sox. And the Yanks have won—every year. But since it's my sixtieth birthday this year and he gave me this Red Sox hat, I promised him I would half root for the Sox.'

'Half root?' I said, and he laughed.

'I wear the hat he gave me. That's as much as he gets.'

He made his way over to a small table in the corner.

The next Guest in line was a young guy with a child that could not have been more than two years old, in a stroller.

I greeted him. 'Good morning.'

'I'll have a Venti Latte, and a plain bagel for Ella.'

'Ella?'

'My daughter, named after Ella Fitzgerald.'

'Venti Latte,' I called down the bar.

'Venti Latte,' Crystal called back to me.

'You're a good father,' I told him as I handed him his change, and he pushed the stroller over to a table. I liked the idea that our Starbucks store was a place he would find comfortable when spending time with his little daughter so early in the morning.

I looked up to see a young mother with a child in her arms. She brightly ordered, 'A Two Pump Grande Decaf Skim No Whip Mocha;' I repeated the drink down to Crystal. 'A Two Pump Grande Decaf Skim No Whip Mocha.'

Crystal called it back to me in a different order. 'Decaf Grande Skim Two Pump No Whip Mocha.' I knew you were supposed to call out the ingredients as they were listed on the cup, in order of importance.

Obviously, decaf was more important than the number of shots of mocha.

The young woman noticed Crystal's correction and was grateful. 'I have to have decaf for now,' she explained. 'I'm pregnant . . . again.'

I was impressed. 'Well, it's great you got up so early, and got her dressed and—'

'My child is a boy. . . . His name is Max. My name is Rachel.'

Suddenly, I remembered that Rachel had introduced herself to me before and had explained about her need for decaf. How stupid I was. I used to pride myself on my recall of names, but at the register, under stress, I was losing it.

'It's great you got Max dressed and out so early . . .' I stumbled out the response.

Rachel smiled at me. 'This is *not* voluntary,' she said. 'I have to have my Mocha in the morning or I am not a good mother or good for anything!' She laughed and moved away, juggling her child and her hot mocha.

Not voluntary, I thought to myself. *What* a great *business*. Starbucks was not something people decided for or against in a casual way. It was obviously a key part of their lives, an important destination for them every single day. Maybe several times a day!

My mood had lifted so much since starting this job. And it occurred to me why: my old job involved sitting as a customer in Starbucks unable to find customers of my own. What a relief it was to me to have customers eager to greet me, rather than my calling for clients and no one wanting to take my calls. I loved greeting these early morning Guests, and serving them.

'Hey, Mike,' Crystal called over to me from the espresso bar. 'You are a natural. You are doing a great job at connecting this morning.'

'Connecting?'

'With the Guests. A lot of Partners just make change, you make *conversation*. And you're funny. You are a funny guy!'

I thought she meant this as a compliment. I felt the pride of a schoolkid whose teacher has praised him.

Crystal laughed as she turned back to her espresso machine.

What was so funny? Was funny good? The Guests and I did seem to be having some laughs as we talked. I was certainly having an enjoyable time, and they seemed to be as well.

When there was a break in the almost constant stream of Guests, Crystal called over and casually but pointedly asked, 'Who was that young girl I saw you with the other night?'

'My daughter.'

Crystal gave me a surprised look and a smile. 'Good for you,' she said. It seemed to me there was a new kindness in her voice I hadn't heard before.

I had no more time to think about it.

'Iced Venti Americano, light on the ice,' the next man told me; he was dressed for business in a pinstriped suit.

I realised there was a real mix of professions here on the Upper West Side. I liked that. Not only did Starbucks have diversity in Partners, they also had diversity in Guests.

I looked up to see a line out the door. The more Guests in line, the less conversation I could have. Nonetheless, it seemed that a sea of positive energy was coming my way.

In my haste to serve the next customer, I gave six dollars instead of sixteen dollars back to a professional-looking young woman carrying a computer in a case over her shoulder.

'I'm so sorry,' I said, correcting my mistake. 'I know you need to get to work.'

'Don't worry,' she took the time to tell me before hurrying off. 'You'll do great.'

Crystal had talked to me about respect, but now I felt it not only from the Partners but also from the Guests.

How different this was from my job in the macho competitive world of J. Walter Thompson! The clients there would sometimes get positive pleasure when things went wrong. I recalled a tense moment after presenting over 200 new layouts of possible car ads to Lee Iacocca—each layout representing many hours of effort—and he simply said, 'Nothing here bites my ass.' The room had erupted in laughter. Everyone lived in fear and loved to see someone else get publicly humiliated.

My first boss at JWT had told me: 'Fear is a great motivator.'

Here at Starbucks both Partners and Guests seemed to agree that everyone should be treated with respect. I had never seen any work environment like it.

By the time Joann arrived at nine, the store was full to overflowing.

Crystal continued to make the espresso drinks at the bar. She never seemed to get flustered, despite the unending line.

'Take a ten,' Crystal called to me at one point. After every couple of hours on the shift, you were allowed to take a break. I was grateful to get out of the front lines for a while, and started towards the back room.

'Hey, Mike,' Joann called. 'Any broken pastries today?'

'I don't know,' I answered. I had been so busy setting them out, I hadn't bothered to check for any damage.

'Go help him check the form,' Crystal told her.

Joann and I went to the back.

'When you put out the pastries, you have to check for any damaged stuff. Then we can call corporate and get credit for 'em.'

Joann spoke in a soft, soothing voice. I loved the way she instructed me.

She pulled out a pair of glasses and put them on.

'New glasses?' I said.

'Yeah, now I can see!' She laughed. 'Starbucks paid for my eye test *and* my glasses.'

'Great,' I said.

'You know Yvette?' Joann asked. Yvette was a new hire. She was going to school on the side. I had not yet had a chance to work a shift with her. She was a tall African-American lady who always seemed in a big hurry.

'Yvette's not here today,' Joann said. 'Got to get her wisdom teeth out. That girl had never been to the dentist before.'

I was dumbfounded. Never been to a dentist, and yet already going to college. I had a realisation that Starbucks was giving people not only unique health benefits, but also encouragement to make sure they took care of themselves.

'Now,' Joann continued, 'did you see any checklist with those pastries you unpacked?'

'I didn't notice anything.'

'You were probably hurrying too much,' Joann said, looking around. Then she came up with a typed list of pastries on a long sheet of paper. 'Let's check this,' she said, taking out a pen. We went through the pastries, making sure they were all right. There was one damaged raspberry scone.

'Mike, would you mind coming back out?' I heard Crystal call from the front. I rushed to help at the registers.

Around ten, Kester came in to relieve Crystal. He gave me a big smile and really handled the bar in an equally magical way. Like Crystal, he seemed to have no problem making the different combinations of drinks. He still stayed relaxed as he called out all the different lattes, cappuccinos, doppios and macchiatos. Then, as the morning wore on and younger Guests appeared, there were calls for caramel, coffee, mocha and all the other different varieties of iced frappuccinos that were a big favourite in the summer.

I took my half-hour meal break and then I was back on my feet working until my shift was done early that afternoon. I pulled off my apron and made my way down to the basement to drop it in the laundry. I had survived my first opening. It made the running of the bulls seem like a piece of cake.

As I went down the stairs, I noticed that Crystal was over in the corner, talking on her cellphone. I didn't want to disturb her, but I had to walk past her to throw my apron in the laundry bag.

She closed her cellphone, shook her head and passed her hand through her black hair. I couldn't help but notice she was crying.

I didn't want to intrude, but I also couldn't just be silent in the face of her distress. 'What's the matter?'

Crystal sighed. 'It's Winston. My cousin. He's had to go to the emergency room. They think it might be his heart.'

'That's bad,' I said stupidly. My comment made Crystal look even more distressed. I wanted to help. I had an idea. 'Why don't I call my doctor? He really knows his stuff. Maybe he can help your cousin.'

'Winston is overweight. He has high blood pressure. Don't bother, there's plenty of doctors at the hospital.'

'But this guy is good at cutting through the nonsense some hospitals talk. He'll find out what's really wrong.'

'OK,' Crystal said reluctantly.

I dialled Dr Cohen's office number and found out that he was at home on vacation in his Park Avenue apartment. I tried that number.

Dr Cohen answered on the first ring.

'Hello.'

'Hello. Doctor, I'm sorry to bother you—'

'Who is this?'

'Michael Gill . . .'

'How's the exercise going? Are you doing the stretching exercises I gave you every morning? Did you break something?'

'No. I'm calling for a friend. A cousin of hers just got taken to an emergency room, and it would be really helpful if you could just give them a call and find out what is happening to him.'

'August is the worst time to go to an emergency room in New York City. What's his name?'

'Winston?' I looked over at Crystal.

'Winston Grove,' she said. 'He's at Mount Sinai.'

I repeated the name and the hospital to Dr Cohen.

'That can be a real zoo,' Dr Cohen said. 'OK, give me the number of your friend.'

I gave him Crystal's cell number. The manager of each Starbucks store always gives her cell number to all the Partners, in case of emergency.

'Do your exercises,' Dr Cohen told me, and then hung up.

(Later, I learned that Dr Cohen had helped sort things out. Winston did have high blood pressure and some slight heart palpitations, but Dr Cohen told Crystal if he went on a diet and got some exercise he would be OK.)

'Thanks, Mike,' Crystal said. 'See you later. I want to go see Winston for myself.' She headed up the basement stairs, then stuck her head back down. 'You did good on the opening,' she said, and then she was gone.

6

The Million-Dollar Punch

September—October

More than a month passed, and I began to get more confident. Handling the opening of the store with Crystal had been a big breakthrough, and I was getting used to calling out drinks and making conversation at the same time. Then one day, when she was making up the schedule, Crystal told me: 'It's time you closed, Mike.'

She could see by my expression that I was worried. I had still not lost the habit of fearing any new challenge.

'Don't worry,' Crystal continued. 'You'll be closing with Kester. He's the best in the business.'

Fall seemed to have come earlier than ever this year, the days growing shorter. I shivered a little as I waited for my train. Partly from the cold, but also from the fact I was going for a check-up on my tumour. I was not due into work until 8.30 that evening. It had been more than six months since I had seen Dr Lalwani and heard the shocking news that there was a 'small growth' at the base of my brain.

I had told my children about the tumour—emphasising that it was not terminal and nothing had to be done right away. I had *not* told Crystal or my other Partners about it. I didn't want them to pity me. My growing confidence and enjoyment in working with them was based in part on the fact that my Partners gave me no quarter and did not make any special allowances for me—despite the fact that I was so much older. I had, I realised now, been deferred to all my adult life.

My Partners didn't care about my background or my age or my education. During a shift at Starbucks, there was such pressure that it was a kind of immediate democracy—no time for anything but equality of responsibility to get the job done, done right, and done quickly. You had to grab that Tall Coffee With Room with speed and cooperate with your Partners, or the whole experience wouldn't work for everyone. I loved that feeling of being part of a well-functioning team—no special treatment for me.

I also didn't tell my Partners about my tumour because I didn't want to think about it myself. Sometimes at night, before I got to sleep, I would hear buzzing in my left ear. I hated the fact that somehow I had, out of all the millions of people, been given this rare affliction. Yet I was also grateful that it was not worse: I could be dead, or dying. My daughter Bis had given me a Bose radio, and I played classical music, which helped to blot out the buzz so I could sleep.

Now I hoped I could postpone the dreaded operation once again.

Dr Lalwani's assistant had set up an MRI and a meeting with the doctor afterwards. The MRI was painless, but afterwards I waited in a kind of suspended agony outside Dr Lalwani's office. He came out and told me, 'Go down the hall and get an ear exam.'

Dutifully, I went down the hall.

I tried every way to fool the person giving me the ear exam, yelling out a firm 'yes!' when I couldn't hear a thing, but she ended up saying that my hearing was just 20 per cent in my left ear.

'But my right ear is perfect!' I said, to put a positive spin on it.

'Not perfect,' the young woman had replied, unfazed by my attempt at optimism, 'but normal for your age.'

'Normal for my age.' I hated those words. Starbucks had given me an increasing confidence that I could almost keep up with people a generation or two younger, and here she was bringing me back to the dreaded fact that I was three score and four years old.

I shuffled down the corridor, carrying my ear-test results back to Dr Lalwani. He ushered me into his office. 'Good news,' he said, slapping the MRI up on his light machine. 'The tumour has hardly grown at all.'

'What does that mean?'

'A smaller tumour makes things easier.'

'But you still have to cut into my head?'

'Yes.'

'And you said it was serious.'

'Any brain operation is serious.'

'But if it'—I couldn't say tumour—'hasn't grown a lot, maybe I don't need the operation right now.'

Dr Lalwani looked at my MRI again. 'Correct,' he said. 'We could continue with another few months of watchful waiting.'

I had heard the term 'watchful waiting' before. It had sounded like bad news. Now I grabbed at the tired phrase like a drowning person reaches for *any* support.

'Sounds good,' I said. I wanted to say, Sounds great! but didn't want to appear too enthusiastic. I didn't want Dr Lalwani to realise that I would do almost anything to avoid going under his knife.

'And your hearing has not degenerated significantly,' he said, more to himself than me, looking at my audio tests.

'No, no,' I leapt in. 'Not degenerated at all. I am able to keep up with all the complicated orders at Starbucks.'

'Starbucks?'

I had forgotten I had not mentioned my job to him.

'What do you do there?' he said, beginning to gather up my MRI and get ready for the next patient. 'Manage a store?'

'No, I just work there.'

He looked at me. The idea didn't make sense to him, but he didn't have time to figure it out. 'OK,' he said, again focusing on me as a patient, not a Starbucks Partner, 'we'll set up another MRI in a few months.'

I got up quickly and shook his hand.

Isn't it amazing in life how one minute you are devastated by some news, but then, a few seconds later, your desperate need to survive at any price kicks in and you can find some way to turn it round in your head? I had heard that I wasn't going to have a major operation for at least a little while, and I was relieved.

I left his office in a hurry, not wanting him to change his mind. I knew that if I had to leave my job at Starbucks at this point, it would be hard on me, and hard on the Partners as well. I was just beginning to understand how to help.

I hadn't even had a chance to close yet!

It was already dark when I got to the store, past eight o'clock. My shift was to be from 8.30 until half past midnight.

Kester was there and greeted me with a big smile. Crystal was in the back, but on her way out she pulled me aside. 'Sometimes there's trouble with Guests during closing,' she said in her professional, no-nonsense voice. 'Whatever you do, don't touch a Guest.'

'Touch a Guest?' I was surprised. What did she mean?

'I'm talking about getting someone to leave, even taking their arm. A Partner here hit a Guest once who wouldn't leave . . . We got sued for a million dollars and I had to fire him. No million-dollar punches.'

I almost laughed. She was talking to a congenital coward. I just said, 'I promise. No punches.'

I thought with a smile back to the one and only fight experience of my life.

'What's so funny?' Crystal asked, seeing me smile.

'Nothing,' I said. 'I was just remembering seeing Muhammad Ali.'

'You saw Ali?' Kester came over.

'Yeah, I saw his first professional fight in New York, against Doug Jones.'

'Cool,' Kester said.

'Doug Jones was his first fight after winning a gold at the Olympics. He fought at Madison Square Garden.'

'Listen,' Crystal interrupted, clearly not interested in hearing my fight talk with Kester, 'just be careful, Mike. OK?'

I looked at her. 'Got it,' I said.

'See ya.' She headed out of the door.

Kester called, 'Hey, Charlie, come on over. Mike's got a story about Muhammad Ali.'

Charlie, one of the Partners, pulled off his earphones and joined us. Fortunately, there were no Guests waiting to be served.

'Ali's first professional fight,' I said, 'just blocks from here, down at the old Madison Square Garden. He won in ten rounds.'

I could see by the expectant looks on their faces they wanted more. They had probably not even been born when Ali was fighting.

'Ali said that he could "float like a butterfly, sting like a bee".'

'Cool,' Charlie said. 'That almost sounds like rap.' Charlie was into music, and everything to him probably sounded like a possible rap song.

'Sort of,' I said. 'Ali was definitely a poet.'

'How so?' Charlie said.

'He'd make up poems about his fights. He made up one for me. I was working for a magazine and I asked for a poem, and Ali just made one up in the locker room.'

I did not tell them that I had talked my way into Ali's locker room by saying I was 'press'. I had asked him for a poem in my position as editor of the *Yale Literary Magazine*.

'"Old Doug Jones was fat as a hen . . ." Ali said.'

Kester and Charlie started to laugh.

'"But he fooled me, he lasted ten."'

'That's pretty good,' Charlie said. 'Not bad for right off the top,' and he gestured toward his head.

'He was the fastest, smartest boxer ever,' I said.

They liked hearing about Ali, but time on any Starbucks shift is very limited—there is always work to do.

Charlie put his earphones back in, listening to his own CD while he started to clean up the espresso bar, and Kester said, 'Mike, would you like to do the front of the store?'

'Sure,' I said.

'Here, let me get you started. It all starts with a mop.'

We went to the back room. Kester gave me a mop and special soap. 'First you sweep,' he said, pausing once we were in front of the counter. 'Keep sweeping all night, so there's not that much to do in the last hour. Also, your job will be to make sure the condiment bar has all the napkins, sugar and everything. And the bean wall. People will buy pounds of different coffees tonight. You replace them.'

'We can't make the coffee for the morning,' Kester continued, gesturing towards the espresso bar and the urns, 'but we can make sure all the coffee beans are fully stocked. Right now you can take out the garbage. Just get it from the basement and put it outside by the kerb. They'll pick it up later.'

Kester gave me a hit on the back, encouraging me. He never seemed to doubt that I could do what he asked me to. It meant something to me that he seemed to treat me almost as though I were just another guy his age.

But the garbage was a physical challenge for me. The garbage bags were heavy. And I had to climb a steep iron stairway. I could feel my heart pounding as I lifted them up the almost vertical incline, and I started to sweat. I was struggling with the load and about halfway up the stairs when I almost ran into Charlie on his way down. He had his earphones on and was rocking to music, but he saw me in time and quickly backed up the stairs with a casual athletic grace that I envied.

He took his earphones off as I passed him at the top, which I took as a mark of courtesy. 'Can I grab those?' he asked.

'Got it,' I said defensively. I was terrified I would be perceived as too old. If closing the store meant carrying a bunch of heavy garbage bags up steep stairs, I wanted to prove I needed no help.

Charlie seemed not to notice. 'Hey, Mike, you closing tonight?'

'Yeah.'

'Cool,' Charlie said.

Charlie was always full of such upbeat energy. I had worked with him several times already. He would come in early and have a 'red eye', a drink with one shot of espresso in regular coffee. He seemed to literally bounce through his shift, as though powered with extra caffeine.

Charlie had told me several weeks before that he was putting together a 'music company'. Almost every time I saw him he showed me a new CD he had made. The last one had featured a big picture of him on the cover. In the photo he had his shirt open and a big gold cross on his chest.

'From my grandma,' Charlie said. 'Always wear it when I do my stuff.'

He laughed, but I knew he was serious.

Beneath his cheerful jive, Charlie was a serious man. With big dreams. Now he put the earphones back in and ran down the stairs. Ran! I kept moving forward, realising how in many ways in this job I was really out of my league.

I hurried from the back of the store out to the kerb with the heavy garbage bags, trying to make up the time I'd lost. As I got to the door, it was opened for me by a Guest. I had noticed that many of our Guests treated Partners with extra courtesy. I had Guests stop me when I was cleaning off a table to ask, 'How are they treating you?'

'Great,' I replied truthfully. 'Great people, great coffee . . . great benefits.'

The Guests always smiled when they heard this. Perhaps they wanted the whole Starbucks experience to be as positive for the people who were serving them as it was for them. I wasn't entirely sure.

Whatever the reason, I was grateful to whoever was opening the door for me now as I was stumbling along with three heavy bags of trash.

'Thanks,' I said, glancing at his face.

He also looked at me.

'Michael Gates?'

He knew my first name and my middle name. My old friends often called me Michael or Gates or, sometimes, Michael Gates Gill. People at Starbucks called me Mike. So this was someone from my previous life.

'Benjamin?' I said.

'It is you!' he exclaimed with pleasure. It was Benjamin Zucker, a friend I hadn't really seen since Yale. We had first met and bonded when sharing a boring geology class during freshman year. The class was agony for me. But Benjamin took this deadly geology class with a light heart. He seemed to approach Yale with a relaxed spirit, while I was weighed down by the generations of my family who had preceded me. I could not afford to fail. Benjamin didn't even seem to consider that possibility. He was the first of his family to go to Yale, or any school in America. For him it was all a great adventure.

Now I found myself, forty-two years later, meeting him again.

'I can't believe you are here,' Benjamin started, and then he surprised me by finishing, 'this is my neighbourhood Starbucks!'

I had fully expected him to say that he could not believe I was working at Starbucks, carrying garbage. Instead, he was apparently delighted I was working so close to his home.

'I live just blocks away,' Benjamin continued.

'Great,' I said. 'Just a minute.'

I completed my task of taking the garbage bags out to the street.

Out of the corner of my eye, I saw Kester watching me, and decided I had better introduce my friend: 'Kester, this is Benjamin, an old friend.'

Kester looked surprised. It occurred to me that it might be hard for him to imagine that this guy, a well-dressed Guest from the neighbourhood, was a friend of mine. To Kester, I expected, I was just an old guy down on my luck. Benjamin seemed so prosperous and positive—someone who didn't belong in my world. He also looked ten years younger than I did.

'Cool,' was all Kester said.

'I'm working right now,' I said to Benjamin, getting ready to head back to the basement.

'OK, so we'll meet some other time. I come in here a lot. Here's my number.' Benjamin handed me a business card. 'Call me. We'll have a latte.'

I turned to go.

'This is so great,' Benjamin said as I turned to head back downstairs. 'I just live two minutes from here.'

I appreciated the easy way Benjamin had taken to the idea of my working at Starbucks and the positive way he greeted the discovery. The other former friends I had told about my job at Starbucks had reacted in two ways: a kind of shocked silence, the way you might greet a person who told you he had cancer; or, even more painful to me, a kind of condescending encouragement— 'Sounds good. I hear Starbucks is a great company. Are you managing a store, or in marketing?'

'No, I just work as a barista, at the register, cleaning—'

'Sounds great,' they would hasten to say, not wanting to hear the painful details. Working at a low level at Starbucks was a sign I had fallen through the net that was supposed to support the white, upper-middle class. It was as though my disease of poverty were contagious. Most of my friends couldn't wait to get off the phone.

I headed to the basement, leaving Benjamin talking with Kester. As I made my way down the iron stairs, I realised I had spent most of my life trying not to fail; trying to meet my parents' high expectations; terrified of letting my family down. It had all been, I felt now, a terrible burden. And so stupid of me!

I picked up a few more garbage bags and headed back up the stairs. I was relieved to see that Benjamin was gone. I was no longer embarrassed about having my job. Yet I worried that I had not become *good enough* at my job to be seen by people I knew. I wasn't confident enough to invite even my kids to see me work.

When my trash duty was done, I stood back proudly and looked at the great pile of garbage bags I had built on the corner of 93rd and Broadway. I was surprised by the peculiar sense of satisfaction I felt.

Over the sound system, Otis Redding was singing, 'Try a little tenderness.' I promised myself I would try a little tenderness. Starting with myself. I would not be so hard on myself. What was the big deal? I was working, and working hard, and learning a job . . . like most of the rest of the world.

I swept the floor, once, twice, three times. As it neared midnight, Kester came up to me. 'Could you do me a favour, Mike?'

I was reminded again how much I liked that Starbucks style—not ordering someone around, but asking in a courteous way. When I was a big boss at J. Walter Thompson, I would come round late on a Friday and order people: 'You have to work this weekend.'

I never asked them or implied they were doing me a favour by working so hard. It was part of the macho code that you never explained, you just demanded immediate obedience.

Starbucks was so different.

'Sure,' I said to Kester, eager to be of help.

As I was sweeping during the night, the Otis Redding song was played and replayed on the Starbucks sound system. It was true to the spirit of the place. Starbucks seemed to have created a culture that tried to guide Partners with a kind of tenderness. Even Kester had acquired this gentle approach, now asking me to 'do a favour' rather than giving me a direct order.

'Charlie and I will handle the registers and the espresso bar during the closing,' Kester continued. 'Could you clean the bathroom? Crystal says you are the best cleaner ever!'

He gave me his big smile.

I laughed. 'Can do!' I said with pleasure.

I, Michael Gates Gill, was a good toilet cleaner. I couldn't yet make espresso drinks, I struggled carrying heavy garbage, and I still didn't feel good at the register, but I had confidence that I could make the bathroom sparkling clean.

I gathered the mop and bucket, my broom and cleaners and, fully armed for the task, I approached the bathroom door. The little gizmo in the lock read: OCCUPIED.

I was annoyed. It was 11.30 already. I needed to get in. I heard the clock ticking. If I could do the bathroom now, it was one less thing I would have to worry about in the last minutes before closing. I was exhausted after being on my feet since early that morning.

I waited. Ten minutes went by. I restocked the bean wall and the condiment bar, and swept once again. I checked my watch and then the door, but the OCCUPIED sign remained. Finally, I banged on the door.

'Take it easy!' yelled a male voice from inside. Whatever he was doing, I was certain it wasn't going to be making the bathroom any easier for me to clean.

Twenty minutes later, the door finally opened. A kid came out carrying a computer and lugging a huge backpack. What was he doing in there?

On closer look, he wasn't a kid; he was just dressed like a kid. Unshaven, with long blond hair, he looked like a hippie, but his face was full of lines and his bright blue eyes shone with anger. He smelt of cigarette smoke. I suspected he had been using drugs while in the bathroom. He looked at me like I was some kind of bug.

'Go for it,' he said with a sarcastic smile, pushing past me and making his way over to a table in the corner.

At this point, few Guests remained in the store.

I rushed into the bathroom. It was a mess. Toilet paper everywhere. I cleaned with a focused passion, washing the mirror and sanitising the sink and toilet. I emptied the garbage and cleaned the door and replaced the toilet paper. It took me more than twenty minutes and I knew I was already short of time. I still had to check the condiment bar one last time and restock the fresh coffee packages on the wall, and I still needed to clean the windows, the door and the glass of the pastry case. After finishing the bathroom, I asked Kester for the keys.

'What's up? We don't close for another half hour.'

'I thought I'd shut the bathroom now. I just cleaned it.'

'Can't shut it until the store shuts. Mike, you are getting into this cleaning, but don't go over the top! You'll do fine.'

Kester had sensed my impatience and, like a good coach, was trying to calm me down. 'Stay cool. Once the last Guest leaves, you can go for it.'

My watch seemed to move so slowly as we got to the official closing time of 12.30. Finally the dials aligned. I swept for the last time. All the Guests had gone but one.

My nemesis.

I walked up to his table. The guy who had made fun of me and my eagerness to clean the bathroom. He was deep into his computer.

'We're closing,' I told him.

He continued typing on his laptop.

'Sir,' I said, struggling against every natural inclination to yell at him, 'it's past twelve thirty. We've got to close.' I even added a half-felt 'Sorry.'

He looked up. 'Stop bothering me. I'm in the middle of something.'

I stared at him. 'I'm sorry, sir, but you have to leave,' I said. Though I was scared, his dismissive attitude had made my blood boil.

'F— you,' he said, turning back to his computer screen.

I moved closer to him, remembering not to touch. But my move, as timid as it was, aroused something in him. He slammed his computer case. In one fluid motion, he rose and pulled something out of his back pocket. It was a knife, which he flicked open with practised ease. I saw the glitter of the metal and stood transfixed.

I couldn't think. I was frozen. I gripped my mop, maybe with an unconscious desire to protect myself from him.

'One more step,' he said, his voice squeaking with rage, 'and you are one dead old man.'

That really got to me. I hated anyone calling me old. Especially in this job. I took another step towards him and raised the handle of the mop. What was I going to do? Mop him to death?

Kester appeared from nowhere. 'Hey, Mike,' he said, addressing me, 'Charlie needs some help.'

Kester didn't even look at the knife or the man holding it, but I could see the crazy guy look at him. Kester's size and strength were obvious. And the tone in Kester's deep voice was tough. I turned to go, happy to have an out. My heart was racing.

Before I had taken more than a few steps, I saw the man was putting his knife away and picking up his stuff.

Kester watched him silently.

I went to get Charlie, who was cleaning the espresso bar, dancing to some music he was creating in his head. By the time I got to tell Charlie about it, it was all over.

The guy was moving to the door, then he walked out, and Kester, right behind him like a big shadow, locked the door.

Neither Kester nor the guy had exchanged a single word.

I was shaken. I asked Kester how he had known that I had needed help at that moment.

'I always got a feeling for when things go bad,' Kester said. 'OK, get mopping. Time to make your move, Mike.' Kester's voice was now relaxed again and he gave me a smile of encouragement.

I went back and got my mop and bucket and worked hard to get everything as clean as possible. The effort was a great relief to me because I didn't have time to think about what had happened.

'OK, Mike, let's go,' Kester called. 'There's a subway I got to catch.'

I pulled off my apron and made my way downstairs.

Kester and Charlie were changing into their street clothes: do-rags, big caps, baggy pants and boots. When I went back upstairs, I was accompanied by two guys who I would have at one point typed as hip-hop artists or gangsters—probably both. But now I knew that when I saw guys like these, they might be something else, too. They had lives and loves that were as full or fuller than mine. Charlie always seemed to have a lot of girlfriends coming around to see him when he was working, and even many of the female Guests seemed to glow with a special brightness in Charlie's presence.

I had seen Charlie several times locked in serious conversations with Kester before or after he started his shift, and I got the feeling that Kester was trying to talk some sense into him. Kester was just twenty-three, Charlie nineteen, but somehow Kester seemed a lot more mature. Many of the younger Partners seemed to turn to Kester as a father figure or a responsible uncle they had never had.

I don't mean that Kester was all business. I had met his girlfriend, a beautiful, quiet girl. Kester could laugh, and I knew that he played soccer, touch football and other sports with his friends in Central Park at the weekends. Once, he had come in limping and Crystal had said, 'You hurt yourself?'

'No,' Kester had openly lied.

'You've got to stop playing so hard,' she said.

Kester laughed. 'Yes, Mama.'

Crystal had the grace to laugh with him. She was like a tough-love mother to Kester, to all of us.

'Clock out,' Kester told me, bringing me back to the present.

He and Charlie were moving fast. Kester made a quick tour of the store, including the bathroom, to make sure everything was in order.

He locked the door. Then we all turned and ran down to the subway. 'The express leaves in five minutes. If I miss it, I have to wait another half hour,' Kester said.

We stood together on the platform. I was breathing hard. 'Hey, Mike,' Kester said, 'you did a great job on the close.'

I felt a swell of pride.

The uptown subway roared into the station. Kester and Charlie got in. My downtown train took another ten minutes to arrive.

In that time, I went over in my mind all that had happened. I could have got into real trouble, I realised. I promised myself I wouldn't let my anxiety to do a good job interfere with my judgment next time. I had made two mistakes. One was thinking I could confront anyone. Just because I worked with Kester and Charlie did not mean I was 'street smart' or could protect myself in the real world of New York. But my bigger mistake was reverting to my old habit of wanting to be in control, to get people to do things I needed them to do. The backpack guy had threatened my sense that I was in control, and my ability to do a great job.

Give it up, I told myself. You are only cleaning a Starbucks store, not making the world safe for democracy or curing cancer. Then I smiled.

Some of my old friends and family might have thought I *had* contracted cancer by falling so far from the protected and privileged life they led, but the unexpected meeting with Benjamin that day had reminded me that I had also fallen, like Alice through a rabbit hole, into a great world I could never have imagined . . . where people could be nicer, and the work environment better, than I had ever believed possible.

I was tired and sleepy, and thought of my little attic apartment with real longing as I made my way to Grand Central. I caught the last train out to Bronxville and realised I liked my small apartment better than I had ever liked being in the thirty-five-room mansion where I had grown up.

Maybe I was climbing Jacob's ladder, I thought, as I walked up my steep stairs at the end of this long night.

Back off, I told myself. You are not on some high-flying spiritual journey. You are a guy who made a series of stupid mistakes and blew an easy existence. You didn't get religion . . . you got broke.

I admitted at that moment that I would never have found this new world I really loved unless I had had to. I had been caught in a struggle for survival. Which was common for most people in this world, but uncommon for the spoilt prince I had been. Crystal had noticed me, the way you might see someone having trouble swimming, and had given me a hand.

What was that famous poem about swimming by Stevie Smith when she says she was not waving but drowning?

My thoughts ran on as I lay in bed.

The scary knife scene was definitely my fault, I decided.

You've got to stop taking yourself so seriously, I told myself.

Who, really, was crazier? A sixty-four-year-old man who couldn't give up a sense of power even when it came to cleaning bathrooms, or an angry guy who would be happy to have a confrontation with any old fart who tried to act like an authority figure?

Crystal and the Partners at Starbucks, like Kester and Charlie, had given me a chance to work and live and see things a new way. The least I could do was to help them by not reverting to my old, prideful, control-freak self. Yes, I had to admit, I had been a control freak. I had been a real bad boss. It was time to be a real good Partner.

I promised myself that I would not get so pumped up with ambition or crazy self-righteous pride in anything I did that I lost my perspective again. I wasn't some know-it-all authority, a pompous lifeguard ordering people around on a beach. I was just another swimmer, now riding a wave I'd never known existed. Starbucks was giving me an incredible ride on a rising tide.

My thoughts tumbled over themselves as I closed my eyes. 'Try a little tenderness,' Otis had sung.

I had a picture of myself swimming to a sunny shore. And then I slept.

7

Turning Losers into Winners

November—December

'Old age is not for sissies,' Brooke Astor had famously said.

Years ago, in my previous life, full of social events, I had met the glamorous philanthropist at many parties. Once, I could not stop myself from saying how great she looked for her age. 'Growing older requires a better and better sense of humour,' she told me. I remembered her words and smiled as I made my way on a cold, grey afternoon into the welcoming warmth of my Starbucks store. Compared to Brooke, I'm still a kid with a lot of life ahead of me! I told myself. Yet it was absurd to compare my age with the legendary longevity of that society beauty. Mike Gill, working stiff—stiff in almost every muscle after every shift—was no Brooke Astor!

Crystal greeted me as soon as I stepped inside the store.

'Mike, I've got a new idea for you.'

I nodded. The last several months, I had been getting more confident in cleaning, opening and closing the store. But I greeted Crystal's new idea for what I could do with a little trepidation.

In my previous life, when I was younger and was confident of earning a good living, I had loved new challenges.

A boss of mine once said, 'You're going to London to present the idea one-on-one with the client. And don't come back unless you sell our campaign to Marks and Spencer.' My heart had leapt at that kind of challenge. With the arrogance of youth, I didn't think I could fail. Now, with the insecurity of advancing age and many personal and professional failures behind me, I hesitated before *any* new challenges.

Crystal saw the concern in my face. 'Don't worry, Mike,' she said. 'This is right for you. Don't you like coffee?'

'I love coffee.'

'This is your chance to share your love with others. Remember how I gave you a sample of coffee and pastries on your first day?'

'I'll never forget it.' I smiled happily at the memory. 'It really got me excited about working here with you.'

'I know. But believe it or not, Mike, many Partners don't like coffee that much.'

I looked around at the Partners. I knew what Crystal said was true. At the beginning of each shift, every Partner was allowed free libations. The other Partners were all young, and most of them liked frappuccinos and sweet drinks. They rarely ordered real coffee straight, not even lattes and cappuccinos. In contrast to the other Partners, I was always making myself a coffee. Coffee was a real treat for me.

Crystal was right. Maybe there was a way to share my love of coffee with others. But how?

As though reading my mind, Crystal said, 'At Starbucks we have Coffee Masters.'

The very word 'master' set off a memory of when my father had introduced me to Frank Lloyd Wright and had told me that people who worked with the great architect called him 'the Master'. I had felt back then the respect my father had for that title. Now I was to become a 'Master'—a '*Coffee* Master'.The thought made me smile.

But Crystal didn't smile back. 'It's not easy to become a Coffee Master. You have to master knowledge of a lot of coffees, then sample them with Partners and Guests—'

'I would love that,' I interrupted her.

'Exactly!' She laughed. 'Mike, you are funny. That's why I thought of you for this role. See all these beans?'

Crystal gestured at the packages of coffee behind us. She was dressed in a white silk shirt that gleamed against her green apron. Her hair was pulled back, highlighting her high cheekbones.

'There's no point in having all those beans on display unless people know about the coffee.'

It was suddenly clear to me: Starbucks was about coffee, and the more that people could understand and appreciate the coffee, the better off we would all be.

'You get a black apron,' Crystal said, 'and I can just see you on the floor, greeting the Guests, inviting them to sample the coffee while you tell them all about it.'

'Feels good to me,' I said.

'"Feels good" is the right response,' Crystal said, pointing to my heart. 'Follow your heart. And your heart is clearly in the coffee.'

It did feel good. I felt this was something I could do—and enjoy doing.

'Plus,' Crystal added, 'you're great with our Guests.'

Under Crystal's guidance I took a series of computer courses. It was almost like going to coffee college. There were different subject areas: the history, geography, growing conditions and every aspect of great coffee-making. I found out where coffee was first discovered, how it was grown, and harvested, and dried or washed, shipped and then roasted. The roasting, it turned out, was as important as the selection and the growing in determining the final taste.

I also filled out my 'Coffee Passport', a small book with room for taste reactions to many varieties, putting the labels in as I sampled each coffee, giving an opinion as to the flavour, body, acidity and all aspects of aroma and 'mouth feel' of the various blends.

After a couple of weeks of hard study, Crystal told me: 'The holidays are coming up. Why don't you plan some coffee seminars and samplings for our Partners and Guests?'

For my first seminar I chose Yukon because it was a coffee with a great story. I picked a date, an evening in early December. With Crystal's help I put up a sign, inviting people to sample coffee, along with free oatmeal raisin cookies and chocolate chunk cookies.

As I worked nervously to set up for the upcoming Coffee Tasting, for some reason a memory of a blunder at a tea with the Queen of England came into my mind. It was a semiformal event in a tent during a polo match many years ago. I had inadvertently knocked Queen Elizabeth's arm when I reached for a cucumber sandwich on a table beside her. The Queen gave me a bit of a frown, but her husband, the Duke of Edinburgh, just a step behind, dressed for polo, was clearly displeased and physically brushed me back as though I were some kind of intruding barbarian.

Why had that awkward, embarrassing moment come into my mind now? Because I was working so hard to make sure everyone enjoyed the coffee and pastries I would serve, and hoped nothing would go wrong? I told myself the coffee and cookies would be a hit and reminded myself to be confident. How upset could people be after being served cookies and coffee? On the night, I ground up some fresh Yukon and served it in little sample cups, along with the cookies. There were a dozen Guests who came to hear about the coffee and get the free treats.

Rachel's husband, Justin, was there. He often accompanied his wife and child to Starbucks, but they were not with him tonight.

'Where are Rachel and Max?'

'Home. Rachel is still staying on decaf. This is an hour out for me!' He laughed.

Dr Paul had come, without his Red Sox hat.

'Where's the hat?'

'The Sox don't need me any more. Now I'm guilty for having given them the World Series. You can't win!'

There was also a young couple, clearly in love, holding hands. I thought at first they were there by accident, so I asked, 'Do you want to be part of this coffee tasting?'

'That's why we came,' the young man said. 'We met each other here over coffee.'

'And we like coffee,' she said, and they laughed as though she had made a wonderful joke.

I liked their laughter. I remembered Crystal had told me that Starbucks was based on an Italian café. I imagined there would be a lot of laughter in that kind of place.

I had a little silver tray from which each guest picked up a small cup and a cookie.

'We are sampling Yukon coffee this evening,' I announced to the audience. 'First, smell,' I said. 'Then slurp, *then* speak.'

They laughed again—the young couple and the whole little group. I was happy standing there leading this seminar in a subject I had grown to love. 'While you enjoy,' I said, 'here's a little history. There is no coffee grown in the Yukon . . . so why the name?'

Crystal and Kester approached and I served them coffee and pastries. Kester gave me a wink and a big smile.

'The reason it's called Yukon,' I continued, 'is that a fishing boat captain in Seattle, who made trips to the Yukon, came in and said he needed a stronger brew than the popular house blend. So they blended in some bolder Indonesian coffee along with the Latin American beans.'

'It's good,' Dr Paul said.

'Delicious,' Rachel's husband said.

Several other Guests also murmured their appreciation. I noticed that Crystal and Kester had drifted away, back to their Starbucks duties. I took that as a vote of confidence.

'Who discovered coffee?' I turned to greet the question asked by a man I called the Professor. He taught a course at Columbia. He had a white beard and sparkling green eyes. He always had 'a Solo Espresso for here' as he said, and read a book while he sipped his coffee.

'Good question, Professor,' I said. 'Coffee originated in Ethiopia. There is a wonderful story about the beginning of coffee, although it might be a bit metaphorical . . . more of an allegory.'

'I like mystic myths,' the Professor said with a smile.

'One day,' I began, 'hundreds of years ago, a goat herder followed his goats up the hills of Ethiopia. He was a young boy, and the goats led him farther and farther up the slopes. The goats moved so fast that at one point they left the boy behind. He was a poet, and had a flute, and he probably paused to play a song. When he caught up with the goats, they were chewing berries and dancing on their hind legs. The boy was entranced and started chewing the berries, and soon he was dancing, too.' I continued, 'When he came home, dancing and singing, his family also wanted to know what was going on; so they went up the hill to get some of these magic berries. Over the course of centuries, the Ethiopians learned to roast the beans, and other people took the coffee plants from Ethiopia. A Frenchman brought a plant to Latin America in the eighteenth century, and the Dutch brought some to Indonesia even earlier.'

'I love that story,' said the Professor. 'I can't wait to have some Ethiopian coffee.'

'How about we do a sampling next week?' I hadn't checked with Crystal, but why not?

'Great,' Dr Paul said.

'It's a date,' the young couple said, and laughed again.

Gradually the group broke up. Several of the Guests bought pound bags of Yukon to take home.

As I cleaned up, I heard Frank Sinatra on the Starbucks speakers.

'That's life,' Frank sang. I remembered meeting him one night in Toots

Shor's bar in New York. The bar was a favourite for some of us who had just left college and started to work in the big city. Frank had come in when I was drinking with some friends. When you have seen someone's face so often on TV or in the movies, you feel you know them, and as he entered the bar, I instinctively called out as if to a friend, 'Hi, Frank!'

When I realised that he wasn't a friend but *Frank Sinatra* himself, I was embarrassed, but he was kind to us and paused to say hello.

I loved to hear him sing. Now, as I started to sing along, I saw Anthony looking over at me. Anthony was just nineteen, but seemed much older. He always had a kind, confident smile on his face—even when facing a long line; he never lost his classy cool.

'Frank Sinatra's a great singer,' I told him, still full of upbeat energy from the coffee seminar and the music.

Anthony gave me a quizzical look. He had clearly never heard of the man who had been such an icon. I suddenly realised that Frank had died before Anthony was born.

'He's ancient history to you,' I said.

'*You* are a history lesson,' Anthony said.

He could see the stricken look on my face. I hated to be reminded that I was decades older than the other Partners.

'But I *like* history,' Anthony said, eager to make me feel better.

'Me, too,' I said, hoping to make something positive out of this. 'I studied history at school.'

'I plan to go to college and take some history,' Anthony said. 'Starbucks pays for courses,' he told me, as though confiding some special secret, 'and I plan to take all I can.'

Anthony was kind to me, and I was grateful for his courteous style. And I was sure he was the kind of disciplined guy who would graduate. I wasn't so sure about Yvette. She would show up with books, but she was always complaining about not having enough time to study. My heart went out to her. I could imagine what it was like to try to go to college and work the shifts at Starbucks. Starbucks helping out with education was great, but it still took a Partner with a lot of discipline to make use of the opportunity. Anthony didn't seem to be struggling to balance work and college. I was sure he was going to use Starbucks to help him achieve his goals.

I was smiling, thinking about Anthony and his classy style and positive ambition, as I made my way behind the bar. Crystal was still in her little office space. She looked up.

'One happy guy,' she said, noticing my upbeat mood. 'Mike, you *are* funny.'

'What do you mean?' I was still a little defensive about—and confused by—her way of describing me.

'I don't know,' she said, moving around to face me. 'Like you had that whole group laughing at the coffee seminar.'

'It is a pretty funny story about the goat herder.'

'It's not just the story. Guests like it that you're happy here.'

'Yeah,' I said. I moved past her to go downstairs, where I took off my apron and threw it in the laundry pile. I didn't want to think about how happy I was. I was almost superstitious about it. I wasn't used to feeling like this. Back upstairs, I clocked out and headed for the door.

'Great job,' Crystal called after me. 'We'll do a lot more of these. The holidays will be good for us!'

The next sampling I scheduled was a comparison between Sulawesi and Sumatra. Sumatra had a definitive 'earthy' taste, while Sulawesi had a more elegant, complicated set of flavours.

Growing in confidence with the Starbucks experience, I asked Annie to come on the night of the tasting. I was happy to see her in the crowd, and afterwards she came up to me.

'A new star on Broadway,' she said, giving me a big hug and kiss. Annie herself loved the theatre and performing. I saw what she meant. Starbucks was a kind of theatre. A unique place people could come that wasn't work and wasn't home. They could relax and get away from all the details that filled their minds.

Partners *were* kind of performing, greeting people with an upbeat mood that lifted their lives.

I mentioned to Charlie one night that my daughter Bis was making a film in Ireland with 50 Cent. I had never heard of him, but Bis told me: 'Your Partners will know who he is.'

Charlie sure did. '50 Cent!' he yelled. 'Hey, Kester, Mike knows 50 Cent!'

Kester came over. Even though there was a line of Guests waiting to be served, they couldn't resist hearing more about 50 Cent.

'He's supposed to be a nice guy, my daughter says.'

'Let's get back to the line,' Kester said, reminding us all to focus on serving the Guests. Later, at the end of my shift, Charlie came up to me.

'So tell me about 50 Cent.'

'My daughter knows him,' I said. 'I never met him. It's just that my daughter is making a film with him.'

I caught the excitement any connection to such a popular entertainer had for my Partners. I think Charlie, and maybe, in their heart of hearts, all of them, could in some way see themselves making that move from Starbucks Partner to famous entertainer.

I could catch their enthusiasm for the entertainment world. So being on Broadway 'performing' by creating a great experience for our Guests was not far from the natural inclination and ambition of the Partners. In that sense, Starbucks was also very much in the entertainment age, with drinks and music and a warm welcome by Partners who threw themselves into their roles.

I felt better and better about my role in the store: serving coffee I loved to people I really enjoyed talking with.

I went back to clean up.

Crystal was going over some business reports. 'Mike, take a look at this.' She pointed to her computer screen. 'Our bean sales are way up.'

'Good,' I said, staring dumbly at the screen, not really understanding all the numbers I was seeing.

Crystal turned to look at me. 'You're helping the store, Mike.' She paused. 'You're helping me.'

I was so grateful to Crystal for saving me from my downward spiral, and to be able to help her in some small way gave me a great feeling.

'There's an open forum—a chance for the Partners in this region to get together, next week. Kester's coming, Yvette and Anthony. All the Partners in our store and in this region are invited. I'd like you to come with us,' she said.

So the next week I went to the forum, held in the bottom of an old cathedral on the Lower East Side. Hundreds of Partners were there. As I entered the room, I saw that there were tables filled with such popular drinks as pumpkin spice latte and peppermint mocha—all, of course, free for us.

I was stopped as I entered by a man who said his name was Tom from Personnel. He asked me how things were going, and if he could do anything more for me. I told him things were great and asked him if I could do anything more for Starbucks. 'Just find more people with a positive attitude like yours,' he told me. That made me feel good.

I looked around for Crystal and saw her talking with Kester up at the front of the room. Someone grabbed my arm. It was Yvette. Yvette was almost as tall as me. She was wearing a very non-Starbucks type of gold tank top and a small red skirt. I also noticed she had a tattoo of a heart on her arm. I had never seen that before because it was a dress code rule at Starbucks that you had to cover any tattoos when you were on the floor serving Guests.

'Let's go sample some drinks.' We walked over to a table.

'Would you like an Egg Nog Latte?' a young lady asked.

'Sure,' we said.

'Look at that!' Yvette said, pointing across the room. She had seen a booth with a bunch of cute Christmas teddy bears. Starbucks created little bears for every season, popular with Partners and Guests.

Crystal came over and picked up a bear. 'These are beautifully made,' she said. 'I've got a whole collection back at my apartment.'

'You can win a bear,' a young man told us from behind the counter, 'if you answer some questions about Starbucks.'

'Let's win,' Crystal said, typically confident.

'Who is going to play?' the young man asked.

'We will all play . . . a Partner team from Broadway!' replied Crystal

'Good,' the man said. 'This is a kind of Starbucks trivia game. What was the original colour of the Starbucks logo?'

'Brown,' Crystal answered in a heartbeat.

'Where does the name Starbucks come from?'

There was an uneasy silence. Crystal didn't know this answer. Fortunately, as soon as I had joined Starbucks, I had started to read all about it. I loved history, and Starbucks had an unusual one.

'Starbuck was the first mate on a ship,' I said.

'A ship?' the man said. He was not going to let us win a bear so easily.

'Captain Ahab's boat . . . searching for Moby Dick. Starbuck liked coffee, or something like that.'

'Anything else about the name?' the young man asked.

'The name is great,' I said, feeling good now that I had answered his question correctly. 'Starbucks is a name that is *unique*, easy to *pronounce*, and implies key *benefits*.' These were proven rules for names I had written down when I was a creative director for my clients who were interested in inventing new names.

The young man in the booth was staring at me. *Where did this crazy guy come from?* he probably wondered.

Crystal was smiling; she knew me by now and how I could go off into advertising-speak when given half a chance.

'I just meant,' I said quickly, 'everyone wants to be a *star*, and everyone wants to make *bucks*. So Star . . . bucks is a perfect name.'

The man behind the counter laughed.

'You win a bear,' he said, handing over a little bear dressed up as Santa Claus.

I handed the bear to Crystal.

'Look at this,' she said. 'Velvet. Hand-stitched. This is going home!'

Yvette headed off to another part of the room, while Crystal and I walked up and took some seats near the front. She carefully put the bear into her commodious leather bag.

'You really are a funny guy, Mike,' Crystal said. 'Knowing all that stuff.'

'About the name?' I asked.

'I don't mean just funny, in the sense of funny. Although you do make me laugh.' Crystal smiled. 'I just mean the way you enjoy the Guests, and talking with the Partners. You seemed so cold and serious when I first met you. You have really lightened up. I guess that's what I mean by funny. Now you really enjoy Starbucks. I can tell.'

She gave me a kind look.

'I think we are alike that way. You get it, Mike. But it's just kind of weird.' She laughed. 'I just never expected . . . you know, we'd have some laughs. And I never thought you'd get me a *bear*!'

Kester sat down next to me and Anthony also joined us.

'Mike won me a bear,' Crystal said, gesturing towards her bag.

'Cool,' Kester said, giving me a gentle punch on my shoulder. I felt I was in sync with my Partners.

Soon a woman took the stage. She was in her late thirties. She stood tall and straight and was clearly confident about speaking before such a large audience. 'Hi,' she said, 'I'm Kathy. I hope you are all having a good time today.' There was a small cheer from the audience. 'They call me a regional director, but really I'm just a person you can go to when you want some answers. So let's get going! We are here to answer any Partners' questions.'

'How do I get a music CD I made sold in the stores?' a Partner asked. There were other questions along those lines.

'Great question,' Kathy would say and then mention the name of a person the questioner should call. Often that person was there. There were people who represented the music department, and the pastries, and cleaning the stores—all the different aspects of our lives.

After the questions, Kathy and a bunch of people came out dressed as rock stars and danced to a new CD Starbucks was then selling. After the 'show' Kathy announced, 'Now we have a few awards. Let's start with the top award: Best Manager of the Year . . . Moses Thornton!'

A big cheer went up as a young African-American man made his way to the stage.

'Our next award,' Kathy said, 'goes to someone who has done a great job for many years . . . and it is my pleasure to present the Manager of the Quarter Award to Crystal Thompson.'

Crystal gave a little gasp and leapt up. The whole room seemed to come to its feet. She was clearly a popular choice. As she made her way to the stage, everyone started clapping.

Crystal waved to me and Kester, and to all her other friends in the crowd.

The forum was just another example to me of what a wonderful group I was now part of. I was thrilled for Crystal—she was the *true* star on Broadway.

As we moved into the holiday season, I found that doing successful Coffee Tastings and the increased activity of my store were a help to me in my lonely state. In my previous life, when I was still living with my wife and children in Connecticut, my holiday world would have been filled with the comings and goings of family and friends. My New England farmhouse would have been full of the sounds and sights and smells of Christmas.

Living alone in my small apartment by the train tracks in the suburbs was very different. The loudest sound in my apartment was the abrupt honk of the trains as they drove through the station. So I was grateful to leave the confinement of my empty apartment and join in the animated spirit of the holidays at my Starbucks store. Behind the register, and out in front doing my coffee tastings and pastry samplings, I was part of a convivial group, and the constant pain and guilt I felt deep in my heart at all the hurt I had caused—more intense during these 'family holidays'—was subdued or, from time to time, forgotten. The store was crowded, there was more work to do, and I had now learned how to do it better and got some pride in helping my Partners—rather than always being the one who needed help.

I would try to see my son Jonathan once or twice a week. I had bought him some little wooden trains and we would play with these. It was a relief to be with him. He had no painful questions for me and a talent for finding positive wonder in each moment. I could share Jonathan's uninhibited enjoyment and leave my sense of loss and my fear of the future far behind.

My daughter Bis was in Ireland working on her movie, but my other children were home for the holidays—in Connecticut, where I was no longer welcome. I called them, and we talked, but it was often awkward and painful despite our efforts to keep things positive. The one part of my present life they seemed to respect was that they knew I was struggling to make it in a job that was not easy for me and did not reflect my former need for status.

And my job had become much more than simply 'a job' during the holiday season, as Crystal and my Partners filled up the void in my life with a kind of cheerful, purposeful energy. I was not invited to holiday parties in the houses of my previous friends, and I would not have felt comfortable about going if I had been.

My Starbucks store became a refuge for me, a little island of warm welcome in the larger island of Manhattan. In a very real sense it had become my new home for the holidays. I realised now how much affection I felt for Crystal and my Partners. And I felt real admiration for the great job they were doing, and helping *me* to do.

Going out of the door of my store after another successful coffee tasting, I was met with a gust of cold December air. The weather had changed dramatically in the last few days. I pulled down my woollen hat and put on my woollen gloves.

As I walked towards the subway, the lights seemed brighter in the city. They seemed to twinkle magically in the air.

I started walking, then literally stopped with a shock of revelation: 'I am happier than I have ever been,' I said out loud. I put my hand on my heart. I could feel a kind of gentle, inner happiness I had never felt before.

What was going on?

I was almost scared. Afraid to admit to myself how happy I was now . . . with a job as a barista at Starbucks. This was not the high-status job or affluent life my parents, my family and my friends had expected of me. Did this mean that my whole former life had been a joke?

No. I shook my head. I had loved many things. I *still* loved my children. But I had to admit that I felt great relief in the different life I had now, even my little apartment. I felt proud of being able to live and support myself. Still, it did not make sense. I had achieved at the age of sixty-four what most people accomplish by twenty-four. Why was I so happy?

Maybe the mistakes I'd made had helped me to break out of my comfortable cocoon—to get out into a world so much more full of life and light. I didn't know. But I knew what I felt in my heart.

Crystal had said, 'Follow your heart.'

My heart was full of a happiness I had never known before.

8

Fired—Almost

January

As I entered into the warmth of the store one cold January morning, Tawana greeted me with a baleful stare that cancelled the goodwill I was feeling.

'Crystal wants to see you,' Tawana told me with a look of cold satisfaction that stopped my heart.

Those were not good words, especially from Tawana. While other Partners always made an effort, no matter how busy they were, to greet me with a smile and a verbal welcome, Tawana was frosty. Working with adversaries made a good job unpleasant. I couldn't help but remember another scene from my past, sitting in the grand Algonquin Hotel on 44th Street with my father when I was sixteen.

'I despise that man,' my father said, gesturing toward a large, elderly man sitting in a chair across the room. My father reached for the peanuts in the bowl in the centre of the table. He threw a fistful into his mouth. 'That is James Thurber,' he said. 'I hate him, and I think the feeling is mutual.'

James Thurber was regularly published in the *New Yorker.* I had actually studied one of his humorous short stories at school.

'Recently, I told others at the office about a scandalous, funny story Truman Capote had told me about Thurber,' my father continued, 'and aroused Thurber's undying ire. Thurber doesn't have a sense of humour about himself.'

I was familiar with Truman Capote, although I had not yet read any book by him.

'Truman was the most beautiful creature any of us had ever seen when he first appeared at the magazine.' My father smiled, lighting up his face and the mood as he launched into his storytelling manner. His eyes sparkled. My father was at his best when telling a story.

'Thurber treated Truman like an office boy, asking him to do the most degrading things. Thurber is virtually blind. He would have assignations with women in the afternoon, right here in this hotel, and then call Truman over to help him get dressed. One day, Truman, in dressing him, turned his socks inside out so that Thurber's wife would know that he had been undressed during the day.'

I smiled. It sounded funny, and I could picture the discomfiture of the old man when his wife, undressing him that night, had discovered his adultery. I could also understand how my father would think that the story was relatively harmless to pass on. My father loved gossip, especially about famous people, and told such stories with fervour. But I was also surprised that Thurber or anyone at his beloved magazine could hate my father. He seemed so eager every morning to leave the house for his office and he came home so late, I imagined his *New Yorker* colleagues as having one long, happy time, almost a continuous party atmosphere. So Thurber's negative emotion was a new idea for me.

I thought of Thurber and my father's ill will as I walked back to Crystal's little office. While my relationship with Tawana was worlds apart from that of my father and Thurber, I realised that negativity anywhere, from anyone, could drag you down. I was afraid Tawana was trying to sabotage the one good thing to happen to me in a long time.

I told myself to calm down. I was doing the best I could, that would have to be enough. I remembered the times I had given that advice to my kids when they were under pressure: when Bis was having trouble with a teacher at high school, when my son Charles was involved in a lacrosse tournament, I had assured them that all would be well if they just focused on doing the best they could. Now I realised that giving such common sense advice was easy, but taking it was hard.

As I entered the office Crystal looked up, but did not smile. 'Sit down, Mike,' she said. 'Tawana has brought something to my attention.' Crystal paused. 'She has pointed out that you have been more than ten dollars over and, once, more than ten dollars short at different times during the last month.'

Crystal was referring to the cash-register count we did at the end of every shift. I knew you were supposed to be within five dollars over or under—at the most.

I hastened to interrupt. 'I'm sorry.'

'Sorry is good,' Crystal said, 'but you can be written up for this, especially for any financial situation. Enough write-ups can get you fired.'

I suddenly felt pure panic. Not fired! Not again. And especially not from the one place I felt safe and secure.

I had a vision of myself tossed out onto the bleak, grey January street of this cold city. I realised again how far I had come from my former external status supports of a big home, a big job, fancy suits, which I had sought to give me comfort and which had failed me so miserably when things went wrong. Now I had found with Starbucks a better *reality*, not based on status symbols but on a real feeling of confidence and support and admiration for and from the Partners and the Guests. And Crystal. Crystal and Starbucks had saved me. Saved me from my pursuit of empty symbols, but also from my anxiety about a fear-filled superficial life that hadn't been, in the end, helpful or even enjoyable for me.

Unlike Tawana or Crystal, since birth I had been placed on an upward escalator reserved for those few affluent, properly educated, well-spoken and well-dressed peers who would never stop ascending. I had not voluntarily stepped off that easy escalator. I had been pushed and then stumbled further down, and no one seemed to have been able to help me or even notice my great distress.

Of course, that was my fault. When I lost my footing, I could not bring myself to tell family or even my closest friends how unhappy I really was. Or that I was broke. Such a shattering reality was never welcome in my world. I had not been brought up to speak such terrible truths. My mother lived in the full bloom of New England optimistic denial. For her, everything was always for the best in the best of all possible worlds.

She couldn't even bear to tell me that my father had died.

I had received the call early in the morning just days after Christmas seven years earlier: 'We had the most wonderful Christmas,' she began, her voice as usual full of a musical vitality. 'Your father helped Emma put all her toys together.' (Emma was my parents' youngest grandchild.) 'It could not have been a more wonderful Christmas, and your father was such . . .' Her voice paused.

'How is he?' I asked in a routine way.

'He's sick.'

'What's the matter?'

'He died.' My heart dropped from my chest. 'But it could not have been a better Christmas!' She ended on an upbeat, uplifting note.

My mother embraced the Episcopal prayer 'for the means of grace and the hope of glory'. But she did more than hope. She greeted every moment with a conviction that it was glorious.

'O, glorioso!' was her exclamation to any information I might convey.

I could say, 'Gordon is coming for dinner.'

'O, glorioso!' she would respond.

Or, 'I will be going over to the camp for a swim.'

'O, glorioso!' she would reply. Mother lived her life with a kind of passionate desire to view each moment as an incredible gift. She also was careful to keep all bad news buried.

After her phone call reluctantly revealing my father's sudden death, I jumped in the car and drove over to be with her. But she didn't want to talk about what had happened.

I learned later—from others—that my father had felt a back pain and had uncharacteristically gone to a hospital to be checked out. While he was being examined, I think he realised something was terribly wrong and willed himself to die. Another man might have fought for more time, even as a semi-invalid. But my father had watched his mother die an agonising, slow death from cancer when he was just a seven-year-old child. One of his lifelong principles was not to inflict that kind of lengthy suffering on anyone.

'Shoot me if I get like that,' my father would often say, usually in an embarrassingly loud voice, pointing to a doddering relative at a party.

My mother and father were alike in the way they died. My mother also chose a sudden death. She had gone to a doctor and been told that she had an aneurysm. 'What does this mean?' my mother asked.

'You have a choice,' her doctor said. 'You could have an operation, which could be lengthy and difficult. It would take months to recover. On the other hand, if you don't have the operation you could go at any time.'

'Perfect!' my mother had exclaimed with her usual positive force.

She died at Christmastime less than two years after my father. Mother was dressed up, getting ready to go to a concert at church. She looked so beautiful. I wish I could have held her before she died.

I was sad not to have had a chance to tell both my mother and my father how much I loved them before they left me so hurriedly. I hope they knew I had done the best I could to make them happy while they lived.

Yet for all my love for my mother and father, and for all their love for me, I knew that, had they lived, they would probably have been unhappy and uncomfortable with my present job and my current life.

Now that I was living alone, my parents would probably be angry at that idea and accuse me of being selfish. Whenever I had been unwilling to help them at a family party or other occasion, I had been 'selfish'. They had needed me to be a happy performer in the happy play they had created, and nothing I ever did had been quite enough for them.

They would also be puzzled and upset that I was *happy* to work serving coffee and finding pleasure and friendship with people they would hardly notice. They would be surprised that Crystal and her Partners had become such good friends for me.

My mother and father would be very uncomfortable with what to them would have been a shocking truth: I was satisfied with my service job and my simple life. I could not live to make my parents happy any more.

I could not deny the feeling of a growing happiness. I also felt a kind of warmth in my heart in the nurturing silences and lack of any real social life. No more fancy parties. I knew my parents would have wanted me to continue to join in with their view of a wonderful life in a perfect world lived at the highest reaches of the arts and society. I no longer had the energy or the will for it.

Thanks to Crystal and Starbucks, I no longer needed it.

Taking a deep breath and reminding myself how wise she had proved to be in the time I had known her, I told myself that Crystal wouldn't throw me out just because Tawana was trying to get me fired. And I was right.

For then Crystal smiled. 'Mike, I *could* write you up for this, but I don't want to ruin your excellent record.'

Thank you, Crystal, I said silently to myself.

'You have done such a great job with meeting and greeting, and those coffee tastings'—her voice dropped off—'but you do have to be better at managing your register.'

Just then Tawana appeared.

'Hi, Tawana,' Crystal said. 'I've spoken to Mike about the register.'

'He should be written up,' Tawana said. 'Partners can be fired for stuff like this.'

Crystal paused. She was a strong woman. When other Partners had made mistakes, I had watched her being firm but also fair.

'I know my job, Tawana,' Crystal said simply.

Crystal's tone conveyed a feeling of finality. She was not the type to be pushed where she didn't want to go.

Tawana gave Crystal a look of rage and resentment that she had often directed at me.

'Mike is going to do better. I'm sure he can,' Crystal told her, giving me an endorsement I really appreciated.

'You don't have to go to *college* to do the *register*,' Tawana said, and stormed away.

I knew just where that comment had come from. I knew that Tawana had graduated from college and could not believe she had to do such menial jobs as punching a cash register or pulling drinks at the espresso bar.

'OK, Mike.' Crystal turned to me, giving me a serious look. 'Concentrate. I know you can do it.'

I headed back out front, disturbed by how angry Tawana was. Yet I could understand why she felt that way. Just a week ago I had been reminded of the social and cultural divide that still separated me from the lives of most of my Partners. I had come in for a mid-morning shift. When I went down the stairs, I saw Kester talking with Charlie. I thought he was helping him sort out his complicated love life. But it was much more serious than that. It turned out that Charlie was sharing with Kester a scene he had witnessed on the way to work that morning. A younger sister of one of his girlfriends had got into an argument with another sixteen-year-old girl.

'They were yelling at each other and Julie took out a knife, just to threaten her. But the other girl kept yelling and Julie took a stab at her, and the knife went right to her heart. It was an accident. But the other girl is *dead*. Two seconds and Julie's life is over. I mean her life is *over*.'

Charlie's face was white, his voice was shaking.

Kester put his arm around him—a rare gesture.

I had a sudden revelation of how far my world was from theirs. My streets in Bronxville were safe. I had never seen anyone stab anyone. Yet this was a grim reality most of my Partners lived with every day. No wonder Tawana was upset with me. From her point of view, I lived in a protected bubble of privilege. Wasn't it about time I got what was coming to me?

More remarkable was Crystal's attitude. Crystal had grown up in the same tough world, but had somehow found it in her heart to see me as a person—rather than a symbol of a repressive society.

I couldn't help but conclude that part of Tawana's rage at me was because I was an old white guy—part of the group that she felt had oppressed her. I thought how unfair Tawana was being. The rest of the Partners seemed to have accepted me—despite our different backgrounds. They considered me their Partner. Why couldn't Tawana do the same?

Kester stopped me before I reached the front of the store. He put a hand on my shoulder. 'Mike, Tawana's like that with everyone.' He gave me his big smile. 'Don't take it personally.'

That afternoon, I observed her and realised he was right. Tawana dissed all the Partners and even some of the Guests. By the end of the day I could understand that she wasn't attacking me, she was attacking everyone. And I felt genuine sympathy for her. How would I have felt if, after going to college, I couldn't get the job I had imagined for myself? I had been given a big job right out of college without lifting a finger. In that way I was a proper focus for her rage.

But from that moment, with Kester's advice ringing in my ears, I didn't take her rage personally and I knew in my heart that I would do what I could to help Tawana, or any other Partner, to be as successful as they could be.

Not long after, I remembered how at J. Walter Thompson they had told me not to send 'praise memos' because such positive missives could make them vulnerable to a lawsuit if we had to fire the person. In fact, we once had a special meeting when the head of personnel told us: 'You will have to fire many people, so don't commit to them in print.'

Now at Starbucks I could freely express how happy I was, and how much I appreciated my Partners. I started writing notes to other Partners for being so kind and helpful to me. I wrote to Kester, thanking him for his advice and leadership, and calling him a 'great coach'. I wrote to Joann telling her how her quiet, patient competence had helped me make it through the experience of doing everything for the first time.

I wrote to Crystal, saying how much I appreciated not only her giving me a chance, but also her making sure I then succeeded in the new world I had joined. 'You are a true star in Starbucks,' I wrote to her.

I wrote to Charlie the Music Man saying how much I appreciated his upbeat energy. 'There was many a night, Charlie, when your positive attitude was as great an uplift as a great cup of coffee.'

It was such a relief to me to truly express my positive emotions towards my Partners.

I didn't stop with the Partners. Now I set my sights on the Guests to whom I was also grateful. For Guests, when it was their birthday, I would write them a little personal poem. For Dr Paul, I would thank him for all the work he was doing to help little kids with arthritis. For baby Ella, I would say her early chirpings were as good as any songs by her namesake Ella Fitzgerald. For Rachel, I complimented her on Max: 'the Maximum Baby'.

I could be sincere at Starbucks because I was finally in a work environment that valued those precious moments of truly human interaction. From the moment when I admitted I was happy, it had seemed so simple and easy.

From that day when Tawana had tried to get me fired, I did concentrate on the register. I made conversation a little less. Since I saw the world in pictures and words, rather than numbers, I developed a trick to keep my mind focused. I'd call out the face on every note I was given. I would call out 'Abraham Lincoln' if I was given a five-dollar bill, or 'Alexander Hamilton' for a ten. By calling them out, I was forced to concentrate on the money. In addition, when I handed back the change, I would call the amount out loudly to the Guest: 'Four dollars and sixty-five cents.'

I must have sounded like a carnival barker. But, gradually, I became more confident and started to instinctively focus on the money, allowing me to continue with those conversational interactions I'd enjoyed so much before.

About two weeks after Crystal had talked to me, I added up my register in her office. She was on the phone; I was on the weighing machine. This was always a moment of reckoning for me. I punched a button on the computer. *Voilà*: the screen showed that I had taken in over $840, and I was just three cents over. Just three cents! That would be an excellent effort for anyone, even Tawana.

I couldn't resist bringing my great achievement to Crystal's attention. When she got off the phone, I proudly exclaimed, 'Look, I'm only three cents over!'

She glanced over. 'I knew you could do it, Mike.'

To her, it seemed it was no big deal. Then I realised with surprise that it hadn't been that big a deal for her because, unlike me, she had never been worried about me or my ability. Crystal had more confidence in me than I had in myself.

One day, as I was cleaning up the condiment bar after doing one of my coffee tastings, I heard Crystal call to me.

'Mike,' she said, 'have you got a minute?'

I turned. She was with a man who was smiling.

'This is Abe. I have told him how great you are.'

How great I was, I thought; nice words to hear.

'You're due for a ten-minute break,' Crystal continued.

'Yes,' I said, checking the napkins and the sugar. I had found at Starbucks that you worked while you talked. There was always something more to do.

'During your break, Mike, I'd like you to sit down with Abe. He's our new district manager, and he wants to meet our Partners.'

'Sure,' I said. A few minutes later, I joined Abe and Crystal at a table in the back of the store. Crystal got up.

'I'll leave you two alone,' she said. 'I've got work to do.'

I looked at Abe properly for the first time. He seemed to be in his late thirties. 'Mike,' he said with a warm smile, 'Crystal says you are one of the best at delivering legendary service.' Legendary service was Starbucks

HOW STARBUCKS SAVED MY LIFE | 557

shorthand for making positive connections with the Guests through conversation and extra efforts to serve them.

'I enjoy talking with the Guests,' I responded.

'That's great. This is definitely a people business.'

'And I love the coffee,' I said spontaneously.

'I love coffee, too,' he said. 'I grew up on a coffee farm in Costa Rica. My family grows coffee.'

'How did you get to Starbucks?' I asked.

'I worked for Pepsi, then had my own business. A wine business. But I'm happy to have discovered Starbucks.'

Discovered Starbucks, I thought. What a great way of describing it.

'Then you can really appreciate how unique Starbucks is,' I said.

Abe laughed. 'Absolutely. This is the best place I've been.'

'Me, too!' I said.

Abe smiled. 'How did you get here?'

'A random act of kindness,' I said. 'Crystal offered me a job.'

Abe laughed again. It was like we were old friends sharing a wonderful story. 'Where do you live?' he asked, then said, 'Crystal says you are really dedicated, giving us *total availability*, and yet you have a long commute.'

'Total availability' was Starbucks talk for being willing to go to work at any hour of the day or night. I had signed up for 'total availability' when I first met Crystal and she had helped me fill out my job application. I felt that Starbucks was more valuable to me than I was to Starbucks. So I gave my life completely and promised that I would be available whenever they needed me.

My other priority, aside from Starbucks, was my children. I tried to see Jonathan as often as time allowed, which usually meant once or twice a week. My daughter Annie was living in Brooklyn, so she came by the store and I could see her more easily. Once, she starred in an off-Broadway show just a few blocks away from the store, and I was able to go and see her on opening night.

My oldest daughter, Elizabeth, had called herself Bis because when she was small she couldn't pronounce her full name. In a sense, she had given herself her name, which was appropriate. Bis was always a creative force, writing and doing original artwork when she was young, writing and directing films as she got older.

Bis had stopped in once, but she and I stayed in touch primarily through email. She had always been very loving and supportive of what I was trying to do. Now that I was on my own, struggling to start a new life, she was right there with me. I told her in an email that I felt bad I had not been a better father, and she wrote back: 'I have always felt loved, and you have been a great dad.' That made me feel good.

My daughter Laura was away at college most of the year. She had come to the city a couple of times to visit friends and see me, although she told me she was sad that 'I don't see much of you any more.' That made me feel guilty. I felt bad that I couldn't see more of my kids.

My son Charles was also away at school, but I had made a point of going to see him sometimes when he played soccer or lacrosse, and of spending his birthday with him and taking him to a Red Sox game.

Aside from Starbucks and my kids, I hardly did anything. I would go back to my little apartment and make a simple meal of a bowl of cereal or open a can of tuna fish. During my half-hour 'meal break' when I was working in the city, I would run across the street to a twenty-four-hour diner. There I would treat myself to scrambled eggs and bacon or a turkey sandwich. I didn't have much time to savour any food.

Yet my total availability to Starbucks was a kind of gift for me. The challenging work, the daily struggle to get things right, filled my life with so much activity that I was hardly ever lonely. I approached the job at Starbucks as a matter of survival, and I was totally engaged. The 'total availability' I had given to Starbucks had helped to save me from myself.

Abe was looking at me, and I realised I had not answered his question. 'I live out in Bronxville,' I finally said. 'It takes me an hour to make it here.' It was really an hour and a half, but I didn't want to make a big deal of it.

'Bronxville?' Abe said. 'We have a store in Bronxville.'

There was silence. I knew about the Bronxville store. I could see it from the train when I travelled into the city. And I had actually gone in for a latte from time to time.

'You know,' Abe said, 'Starbucks believes in Partners working close to their communities. That's one of our uncompromising principles. Community involvement.'

'Good idea,' I said without thinking.

'Have you ever thought of working in Bronxville?'

'But I love my Broadway store,' I said.

'Yes.' Abe smiled. 'And it's clear that Crystal and the other Partners love you. It's up to you,' Abe said, 'but you might want to think about working in a store closer to your home at some point.'

'I *do* know Bronxville,' I said. 'I went to school there.'

'Exactly,' Abe said. 'Just think about it, Mike. Whatever makes the most sense for you, I'll support *your* decision,' he said seriously. 'At Starbucks we like to help our Partners lead the life they want. Whatever decision you make, Mike, I will make sure it happens.'

I really appreciated Abe's backing. Of course, Crystal had set it up, but I appreciated Abe's confidence that I would make the right decision.

I remembered how at J. Walter Thompson they would call me in and say: 'You're going to work in LA.' Or: 'You're going to work on Ford.'

It was never a question of what was best for *me*. I couldn't remember them asking my opinion or giving me any time to consider options.

Crystal came back to the table. 'You two getting along?'

Abe laughed. 'Great,' he said.

'Now I'd like you to meet Joann, Abe. She has been with us for more than three years . . . one of the most experienced Partners.'

I got up and Joann sat down.

It would be several weeks before Abe's words would return to me and change my life at Starbucks.

9

Crystal Takes Me to the Bar

February

Over a series of weeks, Kester had been preparing me to move to 'the bar', meaning I would make the drinks themselves. The bar was the next step up in the Starbucks hierarchy. It was like going from waiter to head chef. At the bar, you were responsible for delivering Starbucks drinks exactly right—with the correct temperature and weight of espresso and steamed milk.

Kester had shown me how to make sure a thermometer was always in the mug in which you steamed the milk.

'It should be between one hundred sixty and one hundred eighty,' he said. He had also instructed me in how to clean out the mugs, to keep the milk fresh. Then he gave me different tests when we had a few moments without Guests. 'Make me a Grande Upside Down Caramel Macchiato,' he would call out. When I had made the drink, he would take its temperature and weigh it to make sure it had the right proportion of milk and espresso. Once he called out, 'Venti Soy Extra Dry Cappuccino.'

I hurried to get a mug of soy milk ready. I had learned that you should always have the milk ready before you drop in the shot of espresso. Espresso has a short life of great taste, so it should be as fresh as possible when served to a Guest.

I tried to steam the soy milk into a foamy mixture. A cappuccino was basically frothy milk, on top of shots of espresso, yet with the soy milk it was hard to get the proper 'head'. It didn't seem to want to froth up. And then, suddenly, the soy milk almost erupted out of the mug, spilling all over the bar. I had steamed it too hot trying to get it to foam up.

I could hear Kester laughing. 'It's hard to steam soy up for a cappuccino,' he said, hitting me on the back.

'Shall I try again?' I asked, smiling but worried.

'Forget it, Mike,' Kester said. 'Almost no Guests order that, and I'll help you if they do. Now just make a regular Tall Cappuccino.'

I steamed up some frothy whole milk for a Tall Cappuccino, dropped in a shot of espresso, and gave it to Kester to take its temperature and weigh it.

'Perfect, Mike,' he said with a big smile.

Now, as I struggled into my green apron, Crystal asked me: 'Mike, could you jump on the bar today?'

I wasn't sure I was up to the challenge, but at least it was a chance to leave the dreaded cash register. Crystal smiled as she saw my hesitation and moved down to the espresso bar to help me fill the orders.

When Kester had shown me how all the machines worked, it had been during slow times. Now we were in the midst of an afternoon rush, with Crystal, whom I desperately wanted to please. With her watching, any confidence I had quickly left me. Today the espresso bar seemed like a gleaming silver monster belching powerful steam, capable of going crazy with spluttering rage at the tentative touch of an inexperienced hand.

After heating my third jug of steamed milk, I turned too fast, hit it against the side of the espresso machine, and poured milk onto the floor.

Crystal ran and got a mop. She was laughing.

'It happens to everyone,' she said.

Despite her encouragement, I was embarrassed.

It took me many more weeks just to *begin* to get it right. Sometimes I would forget to make the coffee decaf for a particular Guest, and I would have to start the drink all over again. Once or twice, concentrating on the milk and syrup, I forgot to drop in the espresso, and the Guests returned to the bar wondering why there was no coffee in their drinks.

I was finally getting into the flow of making drinks—into a kind of focused concentration where all that mattered was making them right at the right time. I was in the zone. As the drinks were called, I executed with intensity and perfection. I had put two Tall Skim Lattes and one grande caramel macchiato up on the bar. When I looked up to make sure they were taken by the right customers, to my shock I saw Charles, Laura and Bis staring back at me. I did a double take, and then they all laughed.

'I didn't recognise you for a moment,' I said. 'I've got a break in five minutes.'

'Great.'

They took their drinks and headed over to a table.

When I joined them, they were laughing together. I was pleased they seemed to get along so well, especially now, when they were all so grown up. And especially since I had inflicted such pain on them. It was a rationalisation to help ease my guilt, but I told myself at that moment: at least they have one another.

My kids were in the city to see the opening of Bis's new film, *Goldfish Memory*. And now Bis led the way in approving of my new job.

'I love this,' she said, glancing around. 'This is perfect for you.' Bis was in her thirties and the eldest of my kids. She was happy in the life she had created for herself, making movies in Ireland, and I felt she was the most open to this new version of mine.

At that point, Crystal came over. She had grown so close to me in recent months that she was no longer shy about enquiring what was going on in my private life.

I stood up and introduced Crystal.

'She runs this whole place. She is my boss.'

My daughter Laura, with whom I had had many fights about affirmative action, seemed especially tickled to see I was working for Crystal. 'Don't let him get away with anything,' Laura told Crystal.

Laura didn't need to worry! Crystal shot back with a smile, 'I *don't* let him get away with anything.'

And they both cracked up into laughter—at my expense.

Then Crystal made a point of shaking hands with all my kids. 'Mike's doing good,' she said. 'And your father is *funny*. We all like working with him.'

I'm sure my kids had thought of me as a pompous ass on many occasions. It was probably a surprise for them to hear that I was accepted.

Then Kester swung by the table. 'You got a call,' he told Crystal. I introduced the kids again and Kester gave them all a big smile.

'Good meeting you,' Crystal said to my children, and left with Kester to take her phone call. I was happy Crystal was so relaxed with my children, just as she had become with me.

When Crystal left, I turned to my eighteen-year-old son, Charles, who was still at high school. I was worried that of all my kids Charles would have the hardest time with my being a barista at Starbucks. It was not the kind of job you could boast about to your adolescent friends. My father had given me a car when I'd got my driver's licence. That was the kind of thing teenage guys could admire. I could not do anything like that for Charles.

Yet he had assured me, in a quiet way, over the last months when I had talked to him, that he was fine. He had always had a kind of cheerful acceptance of life that was foreign to me.

'What do *you* think, Charles?' I asked him.

'Can you get me a Starbucks card?' he asked. Bis and Laura laughed, and I joined in.

'Yes,' I said, smiling.

'Cool,' he said. I could imagine Charles being happy to offer his friends some free drinks. Maybe, because Starbucks had become so popular among high-school kids, my working there was not a social disaster for him. It was entirely likely that I was projecting my previous anxiety about losing my social standing onto my son—and to him, maybe, it was a non-issue.

I *was* proud of my job, I reminded myself, and the good job I was doing. Charles could see that I was working hard. Maybe that was enough.

I looked at my watch. I didn't want to be late getting back to work, so I made plans to meet again with my children later that night. I stood up. All my kids stood with me, then put their arms round me and gave me a great circle hug.

I felt better as I headed back toward the espresso bar. As it had been with my daughter Annie when she first visited me, none of them seemed embarrassed. What a great relief. Maybe they were putting up a brave front for my sake, but I sensed that they were sincerely happy that I was working hard at making my life better.

I hurried back to the bar, but Crystal gestured for me to follow her. 'Your kids are great, Mike.' She laughed as we headed into her little office. 'You really are Mr Lucky.'

'True,' I said, realising that she was right. It wasn't what *I* had done, or what *I* had failed to do. They were simply good kids. Luck had played a huge role. My kids were all unexpected and undeserved gifts to me.

Despite everything I had stupidly done, and left undone, somehow my children were decent and seemed willing to forgive me. I felt deeply grateful to my children's understanding hearts.

Crystal sat down in the office and gestured to the chair next to her. I noticed she had her hair tied back, and the Starbucks hat on her head almost looked like a fashion statement. Somehow, Crystal gave everything she wore a feeling of glamour.

'I've been thinking about what Abe said.'

Abe? For a minute I could not remember who he was. Then I placed him—the new district manager who had said he would help me in any way he could.

'About the move to Bronxville,' Crystal said.

'I told him I loved *your* Broadway store,' I said.

'I know. That's what Abe said. But I've been thinking about it. What is your commute?'

'About an hour and a half,' I confessed.

'That's long, Mike. Anthony has the second longest. Almost an hour. But I live twenty minutes away, and you know Kester is up at 125th Street.'

'Yes,' was all I could say.

'The commute has got to cost you . . . what . . . over a hundred bucks a month?'

'More,' I said, being honest. Why lie? Crystal would know. In some ways, she knew me better than I knew myself. Another reason I didn't want to leave her.

'So the Bronxville move would make *time* sense and *money* sense for you. Plus, Starbucks has a principle of community involvement. You do a great job here, Mike, and you can stay. But in Bronxville you could help the store and be more a part of the community where you live.'

Crystal did things by the book. I knew that Starbucks principles such as community involvement meant a lot to her. Hadn't she taught me and showed me how the principles of dignity, respect and diversity worked? These weren't casual words to her, but a guide to daily behaviour.

'Hey.' She saw the sadness in my face. 'You don't *have* to go. But moving is the Starbucks way. There are always new opportunities for all of us. Kester will probably move on and up. I might go someplace some day. I was in another store before; I might move any time.'

My heart fell. I had counted on Crystal being here for ever. Still, I could see she was right.

'Starbucks is always on the move.' Crystal smiled.

I had to smile with her. It was true. People were always coming and going. This was a booming business, with new stores opening every day. How could I expect Crystal to stay in one place?

What she said also made sense financially. I was barely able to support myself, living from week to week to pay for rent and food. And it would be much less stress to walk to work rather than ride the train and shuttle and subway. There was many a night, climbing those steep subway stairs on the way back to Bronxville, that I had staggered a bit from physical exhaustion and the pain in my aching feet. At sixty-four I knew I should take it easy on myself if I could. Already I had a brain tumour, and aches and pains I didn't even want to admit to myself, that I had acquired as I got older.

I definitely could do a better job of reaching out to the community in the village where I had gone to high school. So I could do a better job, not only for myself but also for Starbucks in Bronxville.

'Mike, don't worry,' Crystal said, sensing my sadness. 'I'll back you on anything you want to do. It's *your* choice. I'd hate to lose you. The Guests would miss you. The Partners would as well. You're fun to work with.' She paused. '*I'd* miss you too,' she said, smiling.

I appreciated those last words. Crystal had given me a lot of praise in recent days, but the face-to-face statement that she would miss me meant the most.

I felt sad and scared at the idea of leaving the safety of what had become a life raft for me, but what Crystal said now made sense. And Crystal was clearly glad of the opportunity to help me once again.

10

Exit Broadway

March

My last shift did not start until 1 p.m. It was already noon at my little train station in suburbia, yet I knew I could make it to my store in New York City in plenty of time. I leapt onto the express train to Grand Central, ran to the shuttle to Times Square and jumped onto the subway up to 96th Street. I was now able to take all these frantic actions with hardly a thought, yet each forward motion this afternoon reminded me that this was my last day.

We had joked that our Starbucks store was the best show on Broadway. Now I would be moving *off* Broadway to a store right next to my apartment in Bronxville. I would return, sometimes, to say hello to my Partners at 93rd and Broadway, but I would never be working with them again.

While walking up the steep subway stairs towards the cloudy March light, I saw ahead, almost level with my eyes, the curious sight of a pair of Lobb shoes, the most expensive men's shoes in the world. Lobb shoes are easy to spot. They give off a kind of inner light; the leather seems to shine like burnished gold. To get a pair, you have to travel to London and have Lobb take a mould of your feet. The shoes are then made to fit your unique measurements. Each pair costs several thousand dollars.

My eyes travelled from the shoes up to the torso, bound tightly in a double-breasted blue suit with bold stripes that spoke of being handmade by a London tailor. Who would spend so many thousands on his personal appearance and yet ride the subway?

As this overdressed man emerged with me into the dark gloom of the afternoon, I realised there was something about his awkward gait that I recognised. He moved with the same pugnacious arrogance as a classmate of mine at Buckley and Yale who was known to be incredibly rich and incredibly mean: Everett Larkin Fallowes was one who would spend thousands on himself while travelling on the subway to save a few bucks.

A year ago, I might have sought his company eagerly. Everett was a person who exemplified the highest status in my formerly secure past. Before my job at Starbucks, I would have reached out to him in my insecurity as a needed reminder of my old life. Yet today I no longer needed to visit the supposedly secure world I had left.

I passed Everett to get inside my store. I had found that several former acquaintances did not recognise me if they happened to come into my West Side store, which was rare. With my black cap and green apron, I was virtually invisible to them. I had my Starbucks hat on now and Everett Larkin Fallowes did not give me a second glance. As I brushed past him, I had the sensation that I was not just moving round him, but beyond him, as I had already moved beyond other remnants of my past.

I went to the small office area. This space held memories now. I thought back to the day Crystal was worried about giving her presentation. I remembered what a moment of transition it had been for me—and for Crystal. I recalled not just her sceptical look when I had told her about KISS and the three P's, but her look of real joy when she heard from the company president about her job well done. From that moment on, I was someone in Crystal's eyes. It was in this office that Crystal had talked to me about my move to Bronxville. When she had hugged me in excitement, I had hugged her back, tears springing to my eyes.

'You don't have to go, Mike,' Crystal had said, reading my mind, 'but this is better for you.'

'Yeah, I know . . . but I'll miss you.'

'Me, too,' Crystal said, but at twenty-eight years old, departures are not sad. The future beckons and always looks brighter.

I would miss Crystal immensely; her advice, her kindness, her referring to me as 'a funny guy'. I looked at the daily schedule posted on the wall.

Crystal wasn't due to come in. I was disappointed; I had wanted to say a proper goodbye. I also noticed that Kester, my first coach and mentor, wasn't due in until tomorrow. Even Charlie the Music Man was going to miss my shift. I had grown so close to these Partners, and part of me ached that they hadn't worked their schedules to be there with me on my final day.

I went down to the basement to put on my green apron, then made my way upstairs for my last shift with a heavy heart. As I went by the bulletin board on the way into the bar, I noticed that a new 'customer snapshot' had been posted. Crystal had written across the top: *Congratulations, Mike.*

That was me!

A secret 'customer' came in every few weeks to judge our performance and report back to the management of Starbucks. This 'customer snapshot', taken when I had been working behind the bar, was based on key criteria such as: Do you greet the Guest? Do you thank the Guest? Do you initiate conversation?

I had hit all the criteria, and the store had got five stars for 'legendary service'. Five stars were the highest. Our Broadway store had never won more than four before.

I was going out on a high note.

I moved to the front counter. Oops. Tawana was on the espresso bar. The one person I did not want to see today.

'Mike,' she said in her loud, bossy voice, 'take the middle register.'

I punched in at the register and took the drawer, with its cash, back to the office to count it. Sure enough, $150. I brought the drawer back to the register and slammed it in like the other Partners did, with a sense of confidence. I had got better at this crazy cash business. There was already a line waiting at the other two registers.

Before I had a chance to take the first customer, Tawana called to me, 'I'm joining the Marine Corps.'

'Good,' I called back. 'You'll like that life.' And I wasn't kidding. Having worked with the Marines, I knew they were passionate, just like Tawana.

'I'm going in as an officer,' she called to me. 'After I do Quantico.'

'Good,' I replied again. Tawana liked bossing people around and would have a chance in the Marine Corps to release her rage in a positive way.

'Can I help the next Guest?' I asked.

First in line was Dr Paul. Like clockwork, he came in every morning for a tall cappuccino with a bagel. In the afternoon, he would ask for a grande skim latte.

'Grande Skim Latte?' I asked him.

'Right, Mike.' My memory for names had served me well at this job. And Dr Paul always called me by my first name. Not just me but all the Partners. This was a neighbourhood store and the Guests liked the feeling of connection. 'Your last day?' Dr Paul asked.

'Right,' I said, surprised that he remembered. Over the last week or so, I had been telling my favourite customers that I would be leaving.

'I'll miss you, buddy,' he said.

'Me, too,' I said.

I remembered back to my first few days, meeting him and all the other Guests. Several of them had asked, 'How are they treating you?'

'The best job of my life,' I would reply. 'How bad can it be to serve great coffee and pastries?' And I wasn't kidding.

I called out Dr Paul's drink to Tawana at the bar.

'Grande Skim Latte,' Tawana shouted back, slamming a cup under the espresso outlet. She did her job extremely well, and yet everything seemed to be done with a kind of focused fury. Let the bad guys watch out—warrior Tawana was on the way. Better them than me.

'Good afternoon, Ella,' I said, as Robert and his daughter, Ella, came in the door. Every day at this time, father and daughter would show up. Robert had become a househusband once Ella was born. His wife worked for Goldman Sachs.

'You're having a Latte and a Warm Kid's Chocolate?'

'Right, Mike. Is it true you're going?'

I nodded. 'Yes, to a store where I live.'

'Ella, Mike is going to go to another store,' Robert told his daughter.

''Bye, Mike,' Ella said with the bright upbeat attitude of a three-year-old.

''Bye, Ella. Take care of your father.'

'She sure will,' Robert laughed, picking her up and heading down the bar.

I was sure there would be other neighbourhood families I would get to know at my new store, but I would miss these two. I willed myself to take Ella's positive attitude. 'Hi' and ''Bye' were equally exciting to her. And should be to me.

An hour later, when Tawana's shift ended, I can't say I was torn up to see her go. As she headed to the back, she bellowed, 'Take over, Yvette!' She was not nice to anybody, I thought. Tawana pulled off her apron and cap, shook out her hair, and seemed to shake off me and everyone in the store as she headed out of the door without saying goodbye.

Yvette took over the bar. I immediately felt better. 'Hey, Mike.' She gave me a quick hug. 'How're you doing?'

'Good. It's my last day.'

'Oh? I forgot. That's too bad.' She looked sad.

'Moving to a store nearer where I live,' I told her. 'I'll save money on the commute.'

'Cool,' Yvette said, 'but I'll miss you. You're funny.' She gave me a tight, long hug.

Funny. Again. Crystal's favourite way of describing me. This time I laughed out loud.

'Hi, Rachel,' I said to the next Guest. 'Decaf Grande Latte?'

'Skip the Decaf,' Rachel said. 'Give me the good stuff. I'm not pregnant any more, Mike.'

Rachel held up her tiny baby, who was beautiful.

'Grande Latte for Rachel,' I called to Yvette, and heard her powerful echo.

I realised these Guests, the Rachels, Dr Pauls, and little Ellas, all had become good parts of my life over the last year.

I worked hard the rest of the afternoon. The store was busy. Teachers. Students. Business people on the run. People having meetings. Mothers with babies in strollers. The store was a good place—somewhere between home and work—to have a break. The line of waiting Guests never stopped, and I was too busy to dwell on it being my last day. One of the important gifts from my job at Starbucks was that it was always so hectic you couldn't think about anything but serving the customers. When I was working, there was no time for ruminations. It had been like therapy for me.

Around five o'clock I was surprised to see Charlie the Music Man show up.

'Hey, Charlie,' I called to him, 'this is my last day. I want to say goodbye.'

Charlie danced up to me, gave me a high five, and said, 'See you later.'

Then he headed to the back of the store.

I felt better. At least I had a chance to say goodbye to Charlie. I had put him in touch with a guy I had known from years ago who was in the music business. Charlie said the guy was helping him do a 'real professional CD'.

Then, at about quarter to six, just before I was going to pull my register and clock out, Kester walked in with a big smile on his face.

'Kester, this is great. I wanted to say goodbye.'

'OK,' he said, and also headed for the back.

On the dot of six, Crystal showed up. Something started growing in my heart, a warm feeling of gratitude. I was beginning to understand. My best friends were coming in to be with me at the end of my last shift. Even Anthony showed up. Anthony lived way out in the Bronx, almost as long a commute as mine.

I pulled my register and went to the back. There they all were. Crystal was at her chair. Charlie was moving to the sound coming from his ear-phones. Anthony leaned against the wall with a gentle smile on his face. As I entered the room, they gave a little cheer. They watched as I weighed the money. I was only a few cents off.

'Finishing strong,' Kester said, and everyone laughed. 'Hey, Mike,' Kester continued, clearly the ringleader, 'what are you doing tonight?'

'Just going home.'

'How about coming out to dinner . . . on us?'

I was deeply touched by the offer. 'Sure,' I said.

When we left our Starbucks, Kester pulled out a little camera and asked a passerby to take our picture. Everyone was feeling good as we went to a bar round the corner. I had never eaten there before, but Kester and the others were well known. They ordered the drinks and the food and wouldn't let me pay for a thing.

Crystal threw herself into the party, laughing and shooting pool. I shot pool, too, for the first time in forty years, and did not make a complete fool of myself.

Time seemed to dissolve, and when I looked at my watch, it was almost one o'clock in the morning. Everyone else was still going strong, but I was not young like them. When they saw I was getting ready to go, Crystal stopped me. 'I got something to say,' she said, standing up. 'You are a funny guy, Mike.'

Everyone laughed and cheered.

'You brought a lot of legendary service to us. . . . I'm serious . . . but more important, you brought yourself. We've got a prayer I wrote for you.'

'We all wrote,' Charlie interjected.

'Yeah, but I did more,' Crystal said.

'And I did nothin',' Kester said, 'but I'll miss you, Mike. We had some great closings together.'

Crystal read the prayer, crying a little at the end. I had them all sign it. This was better than any diploma or award to me.

'Now *I* want to talk,' I said.

'You always want to talk!' Kester said, and everyone laughed.

'Yes, and you saved my life. Kester saved my life one night.'

Kester had told me not to mention what he did to the out-of-control customer with a knife; he had said that Crystal would kill him if she heard. So I shut up about that and just went on to tell them what I felt.

'Crystal, you and Kester and Charlie the Music Man and Anthony—all my Partners, you have all saved my life.'

I couldn't say any more. I went around shaking hands, and promising to come by often to see them. Kester and Charlie pounded me on the back— hard. Anthony shook my hand and said, 'You've made a big difference in my life, man.'

Crystal did not say anything more, just gave me a strong hug that almost took my breath away.

Then I went out into the winter night, warmed by their love.

MICHAEL GATES GILL

Born: April 17, 1940, Hartford, Connecticut
Home: New York City
First career: advertising

RD: Would you say that you had a charmed childhood, living as you did in a mansion in Bronxville?

MGG: In a material sense, and from an external point of view, I had a very charmed childhood. I grew up in a twenty-five-room mansion, which included a gymnasium with rings, ropes and a basketball court, and we had several servants. But I missed my father, who spent more and more of his time in New York City, becoming a celebrated literary 'man about town'. I'd have traded a few rooms in our mansion for more days with him, more time one on one.

RD: What particular memories do you have of that era, beyond those that you share in the book?

MGG: My father loved everything about England and in the 1950s he took the whole family over there for several summers. We used to stay at a wonderful place called Park House near Cowdray Park in Sussex. Major Mike O'Brien, who had spent his army service in India, and his wife welcomed us. With the exception of the Gill family, the guests were there to play polo. It was like an Agatha Christie novel. I remember Rao Raja Hanut Singh and his many men servants and horses; several young Argentinian men (whom my sisters found devastating), and a whole collection of colonels who had spent a 'good time' in India. Every afternoon there would be a delicious tea of cucumber sandwiches and cakes, and the Gill children would descend like locusts. The current Lord Cowdray had a hook with which he used to hold his polo mallet—reminding us of Captain Hook from *Peter Pan*. The Duke of Edinburgh would come occasionally, as well as a few Rothschilds.

RD: Was advertising something you really wanted to do, or a career you just fell into?

MGG: I just fell into it—a friend got me my first job. I got paid to talk, write slogans, and to invent crazy ideas. Looking back, I stayed too long at a rather silly party.

RD: Did you enjoy the early days of your time with J. Walter Thompson?

MGG: I remember visiting JWT in London. I was met by a Daimler limousine at the airport. I was taken to have a drink at a bar reserved for senior management at the top of the JWT office building in Berkeley Square. The next day we entertained a client and I was impressed that the meal was served on bone china. The secretaries all seemed to be former 'debs' related to some of the great families of England. It was very jolly. I believe half the directors of our London office were in parliament, and the chairman at that time was a member of the House of Lords.

We did not live quite so well in New York, although we did have a bar in our office that we called 'the meeting' (if clients called they could be told truthfully that we were in a meeting), where waiters in dinner jackets served us as though we were members of a very exclusive club. The work was enjoyable because it was just the beginning of the television era and our clients were eager for 'creativity'. That I could provide!

RD: Did you feel bitter when you had to leave JWT?

MGG: I was shocked that after what I regarded as a lifetime of loyal service, and never a bad review, I was fired without warning. On the other hand, advertising is not known for being a kind career.

RD: Looking back on the corporate world, can you sum it up in a few words?

MGG: I think many corporations use fear as a motivator: fear of losing your job, fear of your competition, both inside and out. That fearful environment brings out the worst in many people. The corporate culture of win/lose is a loser for most of us.

RD: Losing everything—love, good health, a good job—would have brought many people to their knees. How did you keep going, before Starbucks?

MGG: My children were very helpful. My daughter Annie encouraged me to keep a journal which I wrote in every night—just a few sentences—and found helpful. All my children kept in touch and kept my spirits up. In addition, I had recently lost, through death, several very close friends. I would tell myself how much they would love to trade places with me—despite all my problems!

RD: You've written a lot about it in your book, of course, but, in a nutshell, why do you love working at Starbucks so much?

MGG: From my very first day I realised that Starbucks was driven by a very different corporate culture: in place of fear, they emphasised respect, and what I can only call a culture of loving kindness to everyone, on both sides of the espresso bar. My boss Crystal greeted me that first day by serving me a delicious cup of Sumatra coffee and a brownie. I felt I was in a world turned upside down: my boss serving me? I had never even thought of bringing a cup of coffee for anyone who worked for me in my twenty-six years of JWT! This initial impression of a whole new way of doing business has been confirmed in the four years I have now worked there. Tomorrow morning, when I go to open my Starbucks store, I am looking forward to a positive interaction with my Partners. We are not in competition, we are all working together to serve others.

RD: Do you think companies will eventually become more 'human', more like Starbucks?

MGG: I have worked with many Fortune 500 companies. Starbucks is the only one that actually lives the idea that each individual—irrespective of gender, age, class or race—should be treated with respect. That idea is still revolutionary.

RD: Do you feel you have always been entrepreneurial by nature, and that's why you feel happier now you're out of the corporate world?

MGG: After I was fired by JWT I tried to start my own 'consulting' business and be an entrepreneur, but I failed. I am much happier today as just one of many working in a large international family at Starbucks. I am not good at handling money or pushing myself forward. I am better at leaving money to accountants, and I love being in a position to encourage others.

RD: Are you still living in your small, attic flat in Bronxville, NY?

MGG: Yes. I am writing the answers to your questions there, and have no plans to move. I am much happier in my 'small life' than I ever was when I was earning so much more and living a big house with a 'big life' and a lot of status. I have been told that is why Tom Hanks decided he wanted to play me in a movie: the idea of discovering, relatively late in life, a whole new life that brings you such happiness.

RD: And are you still in touch with Crystal, who hired you at Starbucks?

MGG: Yes, I am. I think I will always want to keep in touch with her.

RD: Why do you think it is that you feel happier these days, with less luxury, less comfort and less security in your life?

MGG: Somehow, giving up the idea of being a 'master of the universe' and the need to live up to high expectations has been such a relief. I also feel so happy with my new, part-time job. It's great to be able to spend a few hours a day just going for a walk, reading or writing. In America we define ourselves too much through being busy. In my previous life I was so 'busy' I had almost no time for simply enjoying and savouring the moments we are all given. The gift of time— just precious time to be and to see—is one for which I am so grateful.

RD: What life lessons would you pass on to young people setting out in life?

MGG: I think there are three key lessons others could learn from my life:

1. Leap with faith rather than huddle in fear. I was stuck in a box and did not know how to get out. By leaping to a new job and a new life I couldn't have imagined, I found completely unexpected happiness. I could not 'think' my way out of my box, yet when Crystal—a kind of angelic intervention—asked me if I wanted a job, I leapt at the offer. Leaping without thinking is the way to get out of a rut. If I'd asked myself: 'Do I want to trade a Brooks Brothers suit for a green apron?' I might have continued to huddle in fear. I believe we all have moments when we know we have to change, we just don't know how.

2. Look with respect at every individual. All of us have so much to learn from those around us. Crystal, for example—someone from such a different background from my own—has taught me a great deal. Yet I used to see people not as individuals but as representatives of a certain class, or race, or background. It is so much better, and more fun, to greet everyone you meet without preconceptions.

3. Listen to your heart. You can't trust your head. It's is too full of noisy expectations, many of them put there by other people. Your heart will tell you what to do.

RD: And do you have any new ambitions that you'd still like to achieve?

MGG: I would like to spend more time with all my kids. Aside from that, I am filled with gratitude for having lived so long and, finally, having learned a little.

THE STORY BEHIND STARBUCKS

• The first Starbucks was opened in Seattle's Pike Place Market in 1971 (see right) by three friends, Jerry Baldwin, Zev Siegl and Gordon Bowker. Their small shop sold freshly roasted gourmet coffee beans and brewing accessories.

• The name Starbucks is derived from Herman Melville's *Moby Dick*. In the novel, the first mate on board Captain Ahab's boat was a coffee afficionado called Starbuck.

• Today, Starbucks has as many as 8,000 global locations. Amazingly, London now has more outlets than coffee-loving Manhattan.